Praise for *The Helm of Midnight*

"Marina Lostetter brings together a cast of relatable, remarkably human characters across three separate timelines to tell a beautiful story of struggle, loss, and eventually, triumph. . . . Tears, smiles, and surprise await any reader who opens this book."　　　　　　　　　　　　　　*—BookPage* (starred review)

"An utterly enthralling mystery of magic, masks, and murder. Marina Lostetter weaves together three stories to a stunning conclusion with a skill that will leave you breathless."　　　　—K. B. Wagers, author of the Farian War series

"A tense and atmospheric mystery in an inventive fantasy setting. Lostetter weaves three stories of trauma and grief together with skill and suspense."　　　　　　　　　　　　　　—Sam Hawke, author of *City of Lies*

"A firecracker . . . What makes this book a captivating read is not merely the tight prose and exquisite use of language to create tension, but the master-craft level of world-building that offers much more to the fantasy genre than the usual fare. Don't pass this one by, it's too good."　　*—New York Journal of Books*

"This tale has creative world-building and an intense focus on the psychology of a killer."　　　　　　　　　　　　　　　　　　*—Library Journal*

THE HELM OF MIDNIGHT

MARINA LOSTETTER

TOR

A TOM DOHERTY ASSOCIATES BOOK
NEW YORK

THE HELM OF MIDNIGHT

Copyright © 2021 by Little Lost Stories LLC

"Master Belladino's Mask" was originally published in *Writers of the Future Volume XXIX*

All rights reserved.

Map by Jennifer Hanover

A Tor Book
Published by Tom Doherty Associates
120 Broadway
New York, NY 10271

www.tor-forge.com

Tor® is a registered trademark of Macmillan Publishing Group, LLC.

The Library of Congress has cataloged the hardcover edition as follows:

Lostetter, Marina J., author.
The helm of midnight / Marina Lostetter.—First edition.
    p. cm.
"A Tom Doherty Associates book."
ISBN 978-1-250-75705-0 (hardcover)
ISBN 978-1-250-25873-1 (ebook)
I. Title.
PS3612.O7745 H45 2021
813'.6—dc23

                                        2021008852

ISBN 978-1-250-25874-8 (trade paperback)

Our books may be purchased in bulk for promotional, educational, or business use. Please contact your local bookseller or the Macmillan Corporate and Premium Sales Department at 1-800-221-7945, extension 5442, or by email at MacmillanSpecialMarkets@macmillan.com.

First Tor Paperback Edition: 2022

Printed in the United States of America

D 0 9 8 7 6 5 4 3 2

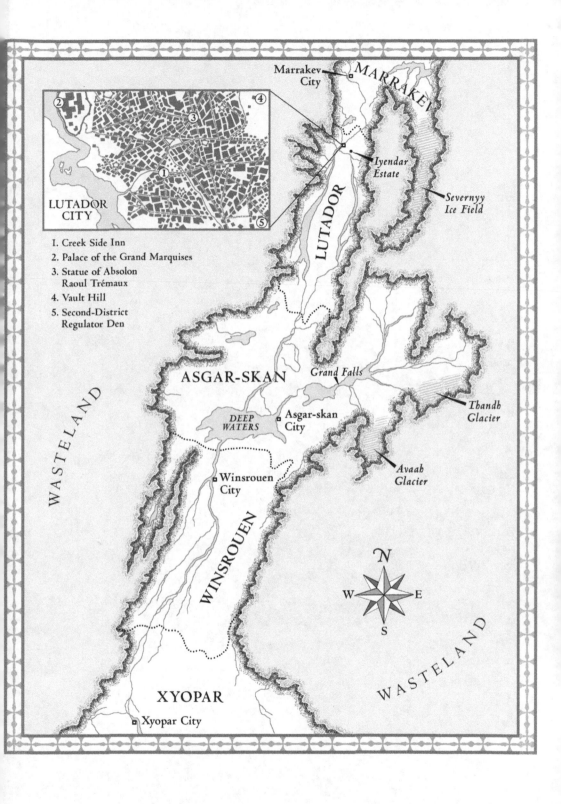

Marrakev City

MARRAKEV

Iyendar Estate

Severnyy Ice Field

LUTADOR

LUTADOR CITY

1. Creek Side Inn
2. Palace of the Grand Marquises
3. Statue of Absolon Raoul Trémaux
4. Vault Hill
5. Second-District Regulator Den

ASGAR-SKAN

Grand Falls

Thandh Glacier

DEEP WATERS

Asgar-skan City

Avaah Glacier

WASTELAND

Winsrouen City

WINSROUEN

N

W   E

S

WASTELAND

XYOPAR

Xyopar City

THE HELM OF MIDNIGHT

The Rules of the Valley are as harsh as they are pure.

The gods sacrificed much for humanity, and require us to sacrifice for each other in return. Beware the Five Penalties.

Zhe is the Minder of Emotion, and emotion is the basis of all human bonds. Emotion must be shared through an emote tax. The penalty for hoarding emotion is the numbing of feeling.

He is the Guardian of Nature, and there is a natural order. That order must be respected and maintained. The penalty for subverting the natural order is toiling for the benefit of others.

Fey are the Vessel of Knowledge, and too much knowledge without preparation is dangerous. New knowledge must only be sought when the time is right. The penalty for invention without preparation is the removal of offending hands.

She is Nature's twin, and the Purveyor of Time. Time treats all things equally. Time must be shared through the time tax. The penalty for hoarding time is an early death.

They are the Unknown, pure and utter. One day they may choose to reveal themself and to gift magic unto the Valley. Until then, they demand only fealty, and the promise that their future penalties will be paid.

—Scroll 318, writ by Absolon Raoul Trémaux
after the Great Introdus

KRONA

Worst of all, I am afraid. Even with the bracers on, their red garnets and yellow topaz blazing with stolen emotion, I am afraid. Perhaps the gemstones do not help because this is a special fear: fear of disappointing. Fear of known failure. I could go to an Emotioteur *and have them extract the fear permanently. But I can't shake my suspicion of the needles—that the prick can take more than the enchanters claim.*

The night pressed against the conservatory's windows like a wall of water, humid and thick. Looking out into the blackness, De-Krona felt squeezed. Pressured. As though one careless tap on the pretty green glass would cause it to crack and shatter, allowing the night to rush in, smothering partygoers and servants alike.

But the quartet played a joyful tune, and smiles flashed all around. She let herself sway in time to the music while scanning the room's rear left quadrant for suspicious behavior.

Tonight's celebration was in honor of the Chief Magistrate's Silver Jubilee. He was the head of all security divisions in the city-state of Lutador, from the food inspectors all the way up through the ranks of the Watch, to the Regulators, the Martinets, and, of course, the Marchonian Guard.

Twelve articles of enchantment, each taken into custody during the Chief Magistrate's tenure, and typically hidden away in the city-state's vaults, were on display. De-Krona carefully wove her way through the tall cases. The sampling of contraband included one syringe, five masks, three necklaces, one brooch, one poorly blown glass globe, and one bronze penknife.

All seemingly normal items.

All incredibly dangerous.

Six Regulators had been assigned to the collection's security, and Krona had been excited for the opportunity. Though she was accustomed to field work—three years and counting—she was the newest member of this team, under the direction of Captain De-Lia Hirvath—her older sister (and the reason why she often dropped the familial *De* in her name).

De-Lia's team was well respected. Often given the most high-profile concerns.

The glass shell sculpted to fit over De-Krona's ear vibrated. "I don't like the look of that man in red" came Tray's voice in her helm. Sucking on an enchanted reverb bead allowed the Regulators to communicate with each other at a distance, and without being overheard. Tray stood nearest the door, observing as each guest showed the doorman their invitation. "This is a party," he continued. "Red. It's . . . unseemly."

Tan and gray and white and brown swirled around the room in vivacious synchronicity. The crowd was spotted through with figures in black, such as De-Krona, but a lone man in crimson strolled through the throngs of nobility. His mourning suit screamed out for attention like a swath of blood on a white child's knee. The path he cut indicated his goal was the exhibit.

Too conspicuous for trouble, Krona thought. Licking out, she caught the reverb bead where it dangled on a thread near her lips, and drew it under her tongue. "I'll keep a watch on him," she said before spitting the bead out again.

"Call if you need assistance," Royu said from the other side of the massive room. Zhe and Sasha passed each other, patrolling the perimeter.

As he drew nearer to Krona, the man's features resolved. The light brown of his face was made darker by the circles around his eyes and the sunkeness of his cheeks. He was perhaps thirty, thirty-five, and would have been handsome if not for the deep gloom about him. Though his steps found firm footing, his gaze jumped and swirled. His attire and posture were well-kempt. Small feathers lined the plunging neckline of his tunic—they looked like little red teeth at her distance.

De-Krona was sure his mourning attire was not chosen out of jest or disrespect. And he wore no jewelry that she could see—no opals. The grief appeared genuine.

He approached the display case farthest from her, then wove in and out of the tall podiums that held the items at eye level, studying each artifact in detail without really seeing them at all.

"How may I aid you?" Krona asked when he came near, aware that her oversized helm and androgynous uniform often made her a daunting figure to the public (noble or otherwise).

His gaze trailed away from the misshapen globe, falling on the rounded, dark-berry-colored glass of the visor that hid her face from view. The rims of his eyes were as red as his formal coat. "There is no aid a Regulator can give, unless you can turn back time." Far from sounding distant or removed, he instead sounded . . . hot. Intense, like a furnace. Like a coiled fever ran through him, and with one touch he could set the drapes on fire.

"That is not aid anyone can give. The goddess Time insists on a steady course," she said softly, maintaining her authoritative posture.

"Just as turning up the gas does not make it morning, so turning back the clock's hands does not make it yesterday," he said. Each word flaunted a biting edge.

A servant carrying a tray of champagne flutes twirled by, pausing to offer the man a drink before whisking off again. With the many platters of exotic, high-end foods waving about, Krona wished her sense of smell wasn't so muted by her freshly scrubbed helmet. The aroma of alcohol-washed metal rode above all else.

She appreciated fine food and libations when she could get them, which on her salary wasn't often. The lavishness of the dresses and the decorations at the party, she could leave.

The man refused the drink, and looked as though he wished he'd been offered a soft bed and a long lie-down instead. "If I may be so bold," she said. "Perhaps you would be better off in the lounge where it's quiet, instead of in here with all the—the noise." A duet of violinists had just taken up in the arboretum nook. Their merry tune was not unpleasant, but it wasn't as soothing as a dark room.

He smiled humorlessly to himself. "The Chief Magistrate's speech is soon. I'd never hear the end of it if I took leave."

Ah, a relative of tonight's honoree, then. He did look a touch like the Magistrate. Same nose, similar hair and eyes. "A Monsieur Iyendar, are you?"

He made no indication either way. "Tell me about the brooch. I've never seen an enchanted ruby so big."

Docent was not her favorite role, even though she didn't play it often, but at least he genuinely appeared interested. Easing herself between the pedestals, she waved a black-gloved hand at the case harboring the gold-and-ivory brooch. Nestled at its center was a gem of exceptional clarity, gazing out from behind the protective glass like a judgmental eye. "Ten-point-eight-carat weight, containing point nine five grams of despair."

"Nearly twenty times the legal limit." His eyes darted to her copper bracers, inlaid with state-issued enchanted garnets and topaz.

Yes, they're enchanted as well, she thought. *One filled with courage and one with resolve.* Nearly every gemstone could be enchanted to hold a specific emotion.

"The legal limit for your average emotion, yes. Despair can be removed from a person as a therapy, but it is illegal for enchanters to sell despairstones, as despair is an insidious emotion that can tell a person a multitude of lies. All despairstones are to be turned over to the government for safekeeping as soon as they are made. But this one was inlaid in a brooch. It was created by an *Emotioteur* specifically as a tool for executing her revenge against the terrorists responsible for the Council Bombings fifteen years ago. The ones who wanted all of the work camps closed. Her mother died in the evacuation—trampled." Krona paused. This didn't seem like a good party story for a grieving man.

"I was still young at the time, but I remember. My father was in the north wing when it happened." He glanced toward the front of the conservatory, where the Magistrate would make his speech. "Please, continue."

"Three men committed suicide while wearing the brooch. The *Emotioteur* was apprehended before she could transfer it to a fourth victim."

As though suddenly disinterested in jewelry, the man turned away, spinning, like he was drunk. "And this?"

He pointed at one of the more grotesque masks. Asymmetrical, painted in mismatched colors, it was the countenance of a demon, maw wide, fangs long and thick. The jaw was crooked, as though broken, and five horns jutted out at odd angles from one another—two in its forehead, with the other three alternating down the sides of its face. The *Teleoteur* had been a skilled artisan, no question about that. No matter how many times Krona looked at it, the thing still sent shivers through her core.

"Louis Charbon's Mayhem Mask," she said.

"Oh? *Oh?* The killer?"

"Lutador's most disturbed mass murderer, yes. The mask's magnitude is unknown—as it is illegal for anyone to ever put it on, even to score it—and its knowledge capacity is of the most sensitive rating: Tenth Tier. No one is quite sure how the death mask was even enchanted, given that the *Teleoteur* who is credited with its creation never had access to Charbon's body after he was hanged. Indeed, the enchanter was in an asylum at the time."

"And what knowledge does the mask preserve? How to kill?"

Krona had been called to a fair few scenes of violence in her three years as a Regulator. Crimes of passion often took place around enchanted items—usually arguments over ownership rather than any sort of magically aided conflict—and in her opinion it took little skill to kill. "No, not exactly. You see, it was Charbon's knowledge of anatomy that allowed him to dissect and rearrange the bodies as he did. His will to kill might very well be engrained in his echo, but it was his intricate knowledge of the internal workings of a human, and his capacity to dismember a body *just so,* that Eric Matisse preserved."

The man nodded, as though considering this. He hemmed and hawed for a few more moments, then blurted, "And which of these baubles would you say Magistrate Iyendar is the most proud of?"

Perhaps an innocent question. Perhaps not. "I don't know him personally," she said carefully.

The man took a small, sliding step back toward the brooch. New tears brimmed at the edges of his eyes, and he used his sleeve to dab at his nose. "Surly it's not the ruby," he said, jaw clenched. "The feelings of others never did interest him." Trembling fingers clenched and unclenched. "Tell me, Regulator, where would you be the evening after your granddaughter's passing? At a gala?" He reached for the glass.

"Monsieur, please move back." She put a warning hand on the hilt of her saber, simultaneously sucking in the reverb bead. "I may have a problem," she murmured.

"Understood," chimed three replies in her ear.

Monsieur Iyendar the younger—for now she was sure—did not touch the case, but turned on her. "Where would you be?" he demanded. "Would you make your son leave his child's side? Would you make him endure pleasantries for the sake of *face?*"

Krona's chest tightened, but it was not her place to inquire after—or, save the Five, make *judgments* about—the Chief Magistrate's family. "Monsieur—"

With a strangled sob, he skipped backward, toward another pillar. "He likes the masks best. I know he does. This one with the fish, what's so dangerous about it?"

She caught sight of Tray moving in from the front, and Sasha walking stiffly from the other side of the collection, both dodging potted palms and guests alike.

"The mask belonged to Lord Birron. He was very skilled in opiate refinery," she said placatingly, taking Iyendar by the elbow. "Please, monsieur. Come away with me. To that seat just over there."

He threw her off. "No. If these trinkets mean more to him than my daughter, I shall examine them until I am content." His palms smacked against the case, leaving sweaty smears.

Wishing the others would move faster, she unsheathed her saber. "You know I am fully within the order of the law to remove you."

"So remove me!" he shouted.

Faces snapped in their direction, carrying various expressions from irritation to interest.

"Do you want to cause a scene?"

"A scene?" he scoffed, feigning scandalization. "I resent the idea that I would in any way desire to disrupt the Magistrate's *perfect* evening."

"How may we be of aid?" Tray asked as he and Sasha drew up on the opposite side of the pillar.

In contrast to the frills, alternating high-low collars, and soft lines of the attendees' clothing, Regulator uniforms were simple, yet imposing. The three of them looked like black pieces from an artisan chess board. Tall, wide helms—roomy enough to accommodate an enchanted mask beneath, though one wasn't always worn—spanned shoulder to shoulder, making the Regulators look like neckless, faceless, multihorned beasts. Long leather coats gave them strong, box-like proportions, and many Regulators, like Krona, chose to bind their chests beneath. The coat topped a pair of *umanori,* which made for easy movement and encompassed knee-high boots with thick-heeled soles.

The only snatches of color on the uniform belonged to their bracers, faceplates, and weaponry.

"Oh, yes, *helpful,* aren't you?" Monsieur Iyendar spat. "Make sure no one's smile cracks, make sure no one has a pout, or scuffs a shoe, or breaks a nail."

He babbled on, all the while holding the glass case between his palms.

"Monsieur, I believe you've indulged too much this evening," Sasha said, grabbing one wrist and wrenching it behind his back.

"Unhand me!" he shouted.

The guests' casual glances had turned to stares, and the natural, joyous flow of the room halted.

"Unhand me, unhand me!" he continued to shout as Tray took his other arm. The two Regulators dragged him in reverse, but he lashed out with his feet before they could put any distance between the grieving man and the collection.

A flailing boot caught the upper portion of the pillar, sending it off-balance.

Krona's heart leapt as she lunged for the mask case. The stand toppled away, beyond her reach. A resounding *crash* brought even the violinists' music to an end.

A jagged blast pattern fanned away from the overturned stand. The mask itself—carved of hardened cherrywood, depicting two blue carp swimming in opposite directions with waves and cherry blossoms swirling around them—appeared unharmed. Krona thanked the Five for small favors.

As the young Monsieur Iyendar was hauled bodily through a side door that led to the catering kitchens, the three remaining Regulators—Royu, Tabitha, and De-Lia—hurried toward her position. They urged the guests back while she contained the scene.

"What happened? That was my son." The booming voice of the Chief Magistrate echoed in the conservatory. He was a tall man that led with his belly, and his hands seemed perpetually fisted and ready for shaking at the air. He was of an age most people could never hope to see. Well into his sixties, approaching seventy. Krona was sure he'd cashed in many of his family's time vials.

"Please stay back, Monsignor. We have a containment issue," said De-Lia, holding out a barring hand.

Sweat beaded across Krona's forehead as she squatted down near the shards of glass. From her side satchel she brought out a velvet containment bag, lined with mercury-infused threads. Carefully, she slipped the mask inside.

Why hadn't she defused the situation sooner? She should have forced him away from the display as soon as she'd confirmed he wasn't of joyous mood. He was an outlier. Outliers were always dangerous because they were unpredictable.

Securing the cloaked mask in her pack, she set the pillar upright in time to notice three men from the Nightswatch rush through the main doors. All other eyes were turned in her direction, and thus failed to notice.

She sucked on the reverb bead and marched over to the next display case. "I think we should secure the rest of the collection. I don't like—"

Movement outside the window caught her eye. Something shifted in the darkness, bulky and covered in spines. Or maybe it was simply the wind riling the shrubs. No, there—the eyeshine was unmistakable.

"Varg," she said breathlessly, keeping the bead firmly beneath her tongue. "We have a varg."

"How did it get past the Watch?" asked De-Lia.

Krona addressed the crowd, doing her best to keep the fear out of her voice; a panicked rush for the doors would only make things worse. "I need everyone to back away from the windows, please."

She was glad for the enchanted gemstones on her arms. Vargerangaphobia, the healers called her condition. An intense fear that went well beyond the natural aversion most people possessed. She had nightmares about the monsters, dreams that often left her screaming and sweaty in her darkened apartment. Their huge, hulking forms would stalk her in her sleep; somewhat canine, somewhat bear, and somewhat unique horror all to themselves, they were misshapen, violent aberrations of nature.

Without the borrowed emotions in her bracers, Krona would have curled up on the spot.

"How many?" De-Lia pressed.

"I only see the one."

"Loners don't come into the city, there have to be more. Quickly," she said to the other Regulators, "get the Magistrate out of here."

Krona drew her quintbarrel. The specialty steam gun—made for shooting down varger with five-inch, needle-like ammunition—possessed five cylinders, each with its own type of shot. After every pull of the trigger, the barrels automatically rotated, bringing the next firing chamber in line with the striker.

Five types of varger, five types of needles. They were the only instruments that worked against the monsters, and even then you couldn't kill them, only contain them.

"Holster that," De-Lia chided, pulling out her own quintbarrel. "You're staying here."

"I can do it, I passed my—"

"That was on the range, not a varg in sight." The stern tone of her voice said, *We both know what happens when you get too close to the monsters.*

Krona cursed, silently admitting to herself that De-Lia was right. She'd only just passed her quintbarrel rearmament exam—her score embarrassingly low. She could use a blunderbuss just fine—snip the hair off a horse's chin at a distance. But a quintbarrel would always make her think of varger. The weight of it in her hand muddled her mind, and a small voice of doubt whispered to her, *You can't do it, you can't do it,* no matter how hard she fought for the contrary.

Once more, Krona drew her saber. "A miss with a quintbarrel is better than a hit with a blade," she protested. *At least with a quintbarrel you get a second shot, a hit with a blade won't so much as slow one down.* Everything in her body screamed to pick up the gun again, no matter her past failures. "I can't take a varg down this way."

"You won't have to," De-Lia assured her.

Krona looked to the guests again; a few of them were inching toward the glass. "Back away!" she ordered.

Several partygoers mistook Krona's command as an invitation for the opposite; they flocked to the panes, trying to decipher what had gotten the Regulator so excited. A flash of long fangs clued them in to the danger.

"Varger!" one woman screamed, her tight, high-collared bolero doing nothing to restrain her voice. "Varg. There's a varg!"

The quiet murmurings in the hall erupted into shouts and bellows. Part of the crowd rushed toward the windows for a better look. Another portion dashed for the doors, creating a bottleneck of bodies. A third segment huddled together in the center of the conservatory floor, subconsciously deciding safety lay in numbers.

"Let's hope it's not a jumper," De-Lia said before springing into action. The five types of varger each possessed their own devastating abilities. Jumpers could disappear and reappear—one minute outside, in the next. "I need all Regulators on site into the poppy garden, promptly. Single varg spotted, pack suspected. Krona, finish with the display. Tray, find the nearest Nightswatchmen and recruit—we need to direct our noble mesdames and messieurs to safety."

"There are three from the Nightswatch—" Krona began, but, scanning the crowd, she couldn't find them again. "Never mind. Understood."

Holding her gun high, so as to keep it away from the frantic guests, De-Lia marched out of the conservatory.

Before attending to the other artifacts, Krona went to the windows, putting herself between the panes and the people. *"Back away."* They skidded away from her sword, as though only just now grasping her authority. "Varg protocol. We don't know what types are out there, so I need you all to—"

Thunk.

Krona whirled. On the other side of the glass stood a varg, head lowered, eyes trained on her. Its long, misshapen snout curled in a snarl. Thick saliva dripped from its jaws, and green pus oozed from one of the many fist-sized boils poking through its spiny fur. As she watched, it padded away, disappearing beyond the reach of the gaslight glow.

After another moment it returned, running at full speed toward the smorgasbord. Today's special: humans under glass.

Another resounding *thunk.* The panes rattled, and a small spider's-web crack splintered across the green expanse. Someone sobbed. A gentleman fainted.

In the darkened garden, a series of flashes revealed shots fired from a quintbarrel. The special powder blazed boiling hot, bursting the steam chambers that sent needles straight and true at high speed. But the gunman's target was not the assaulting varg.

At least it's not a jumper; if it was a jumper people would be dead already, Krona assured herself.

"Nightswatch: hah!" yelled an officer from the entryway. "If you'll all find a partner and follow the Watchmen through to the hourglass catacombs, please. Orderly, orderly, please! We aren't common, now are we?"

People streamed out the doors in a rush of neutral colors, looking for all the world like a wash of dirty water. Watchmen pulled stragglers out from behind trees and benches.

Thunk. Crack.

Outside, more gunfire. The flashes illuminated the streams of people. The

Watchmen were quickly losing control of their charges—nobles darted out of the building and into the garden instead of the entrance to the catacombs, screaming, running with no destination in mind, just panic in their hearts.

More varger appeared, catching the nobles' cries and running toward them like the sound was the blaring of a dinner bell.

"Look away!" Krona shouted at the partygoers still frozen before her, still enwrapped with the monster trying to beat its way inside. "Look away!"

One of the panicked men came running at the solarium, almost directly for the varg attacking the glass. Perhaps it was a mimic—masters of camouflage that could blend into the environment. Perhaps the man thought it nothing but a bush rustling in the wind. The varg spun, its hackles rising, spines flaring. The man realized too late that teeth were before him.

"Turn away!"

Outside, the flashes from the needle guns made everything appear as though it were happening at half speed.

Flash, and the man's expression shifted from panic to fear.

Flash again and it was horror—

Flash again and the varg was leaping—

Another flash and claws were tearing—

Flash, blood, flash, viscera, flash, bone.

Flash, flash, flash.

Krona turned away herself, clamping down on the bile in her belly that wanted to escape. The emotion stones in her bracers helped her focus, the magical boost of courage and resolve keeping her fears muted and pushed to the back of her mind.

There were maybe a dozen nobles left inside, and they were fighting the Watch to stay.

"The monsters are outside! We're safe here, safe indoors!"

"There are some in the kitchens!" a Watchwoman argued. "Our best bet is to get you off the grounds!"

With gory bits of sinew and fat dangling from its jaws, the varg at the window turned to the glass anew. The beast sought its first goal once more.

Thunk. Crack.

Perhaps it was a love-eater. They sought prey with strong emotions, those wallowing in love, or hate, or guilt, or . . . jealousy.

The cracks in the glass seemed to paint a bull's-eye directly on Krona's back.

Additional fissures appeared. Hopefully the pane would hold long enough for Krona to gather the enchanted goods.

Kicking and screaming, the last of the guests were hauled bodily from the room. But their hollering only worsened. Reverberations of pain and horror echoed from the halls. Krona did all she could to block them out and focus on her task. The Watchmen would see to the people. The Regulators would see to the varger and enchantments.

The strongbox in which they'd transported the items lay tucked at the back of the room. With the conservatory now empty, she darted to it, setting her saber aside and throwing open the lid to dig out the specialty cases formed to fit each piece.

Three boxes in hand, she spun—

—and a great weight barreled into her. She fell, and the boxes flew to the side, skidding across the polished marble. Whatever had hit her now held her down, scrabbling at her uniform. It pushed her faceplate against the floor and tore at her arms.

But she refused to stay pinned.

Working one hand free, she stretched for her saber. Her reach came up short. Mere inches separated her from her weapon.

Sharp knives—or claws, *claws*—raked down her trapped left arm, tearing off her lower sleeve, taking both her bracer and skin with it.

As the bracer flew away, it felt as though a deeply embedded thread—like a lifeline wrapped around her heart—was yanked from her body. She felt every inch of the invisible link slide through her insides, tearing and ripping.

The left bracer contained the enchanted yellow topaz, a stone imbued with borrowed courage. Its magic filled in the void of her fear, covered over the emotional wounds with bandages of bravery.

But now the stone was gone. Point two seven grams of courage, gone.

And with a possible varg on her back, she didn't have a drop of her own courage left.

Fear stopped her lungs, but with her last intake she caught a whiff of moldering fur and rancid breath. The smell was primal. It called up images of blood and bones, tearing and open wounds. And festers. Varger always had festers, as though the very air caused their skin to boil and burn.

I'm going to die, she cried out in her mind, though the panic that swamped her was so complete she could barely think in words.

The monster continued to claw at her, tearing at her shoulders, looking to swipe off her helm. It beat her head into the floor, pressed down on her shoulder blades, and drew more blood.

The memory of that first varg attack when she was young—so many years ago—assaulted her. It buzzed through her brain like a swarm of locusts. She knew what came next, once a varg had you down. It would rip and grind, masticating its prey thoroughly before consuming it.

She'd turned away this evening—couldn't watch it happen through the rippled sheen of green glass. But she'd seen it happen in grotesque living color before, taken in the scents of masticated human and varg saliva and hot stomach acid.

She'd seen it happen right at her feet.

To her father.

There was a flash in her mind.

Dark, dark blood. A gaping hole where a throat should be . . .

A growl suddenly curled against her ears, but it sounded *wrong*. She knew what a varg sounded like: otherworldly. A sound no other creature could mimic. Deep, and high, and far, and near. A varg call vibrated in your very bones. This was *not* that sound.

Her bravery may have evaporated, but she still had her right bracer—still had the resolve granted by the red garnet.

Kicking, she reached, willing her tendons to stretch, willing her fingertips to extend.

A blade won't work against a varg.

I won't die without a weapon.

Her fingers fell on the pommel and pulled tight, forcing the length of the grip against her forearm. Screaming with the effort, she swung backward in a giant, pointed arc.

The blade sliced at its target. The thing let out a guttural, gargling yell, and stopped its thrashing.

Krona pushed it off immediately, straining against its weight. While it flailed on its side, she scrabbled away across the floor.

She grew aware of other shouts in the room—men swearing at each other to "Leave him! He's dead, leave him!"—then the *pound, pound, pound* of boots retreating.

With gelatin-filled limbs, Krona righted herself. A brown-and-gray heap, skewered through like one of the hors d'oeuvres served at the party, lay still at the base of the strongbox. Blood pooled beneath it, confirming her suspicions.

Varger don't bleed.

She kicked at the form, rolling it over to reveal a hulk of a man, swathed in a well-constructed varg suit. He gripped a pair of knuckle dusters with blades welded to them, mimicking claws.

The saber had cut through his neck—but he wasn't dead. Her sword stuck fast in the heavy material of the costume, near his throat, and he held a quivering, pale hand to the cut, spluttering as he tried to breathe.

Without hesitation, Krona slid to her knees at his side. Yanking at her tattered sleeve, she tore strips free and used them to press against the wound.

Fear still ruled her faculties. She couldn't think straight. Why was there a man in a varg suit? Why had the monster outside stopped striking the window? Why was the strongbox still open and why was there so much more broken glass everywhere?

A glint of copper drew her attention to the base of a nearby fern. The plant's delicate fronds draped over her courage bracer like a protective curtain. Briefly leaving the man's side, she lunged and tugged it onto her bleeding, bare forearm. Sharp pain pierced her beneath the jewel's setting, but only for a moment. The thread that had rent from her now snaked its way back, twisting in soothing spirals up her arm and into her chest.

Once the borrowed courage swept away her fear, she regained her bearings, and the stray bits of information fell into place. *The excess shattered glass, the varg disguise, the other voices . . . The collection. Oh no. Oh, no no no no . . .*

Several displays were empty, but she couldn't tell what had been taken.

"Stay still," she told her attacker, palms pressed against the wound. She couldn't tell for sure through the blood, but she feared the cut was too deep.

Stay alive. Live, live. I have questions, and you will *stay alive to answer them.*

Outside the broad conservatory windows, needle after needle sank into the varg at the glass. Each flash that preceded the shot illuminated the gun wielder: De-Lia. She advanced on the monster with confidence, utter determination setting her shoulders straight, keeping her aim steady. The captain was precise with her shots, and soon she had the creature down.

Long needles jutted from its back and forepaws, pinning it to the ground by means of enchantment. The slivers of metal acted like mighty stakes or javelins when thrust into the beasts, incapacitating them.

Now that the real monster was still, Krona noticed something unusual about it. A silvery sheen coated its fur, very unlike the matte browns and burnt reds that were the varger's natural colors.

More stomping in the entryway hall. Shouts, cries for healers, for a hospital carriage, for scraps of cloth for bandages.

Anyone attacked by a varg was likely dead and beyond a healer's help. Perhaps her false varg here had claimed a few victims.

Still on edge, Krona hesitated to call for help of her own. If there was one man running around slicing people open with metal claws, there could be more. After a few more minutes, deliberate footsteps headed in her direction.

Carefully, Krona worked the saber free of the false varg-hide, prepared to wield it again if she must.

De-Lia entered, the barrels of her gun still steaming. "Are you all right?" she asked immediately, the gaze of her helm straying across the blood-smeared floor, coming to rest on the shaggy form next to her sister. "So, there was a jumper," she breathed, taking long strides across the room.

"I'm fine. But no, it's not a varg," Krona said. "It's a man. He needs help. We need a healer."

"That explains the wounded in the halls. Stabbed through but not eaten. Why would . . . ?" She understood. Swiftly, De-Lia tallied the inventory, her boots crunching across the shards of display-case glass. There was the knife, the globe, the syringe, three necklaces—but only four masks. And no brooch. "Charbon's mask is missing," De-Lia said.

"It was a ruse," Krona breathed. "There were others."

"Yes," De-Lia said flatly. "And now two of the world's most dangerous enchantments are once again loose in the city."

KRONA

Unraveling: that's what it feels like. The more I try to wind the lengths of my life into a neat, manageable knot, the more they seem to stretch and fray and snap. Order is not easy. Breaking takes less effort than building, that is the way of the world. I need you, but I know . . . I realize . . . We can't go backward. Time does not unmake what has been made.

><+<>-O-<+><

Lutador's second-district Regulator den came alive most evenings, but tonight it thrummed with irritated energy. Regulators and administrators alike flitted here and there across the wide-open main floor like members of an irate murder of crows. They'd never had an instance of theft like this before. Illegal enchantments swiped from their own collection—their own *hands*. It was an embarrassment.

One that could lead to torture and death.

Charbon's Mayhem Mask was loose. Charbon, who'd butchered his victims beyond recognition, who'd killed so many so *brutally* . . .

Captain Hirvath—as Krona was forced to call De-Lia in the den—and Tray wrangled the captive varger into isolation chambers. The one outside the conservatory windows they identified as a love-eater, as Krona suspected. Now, they ran it through with as many gold needles as they possessed, then stuck it in a gilded cage inside an enchanted glass chamber.

The two others they'd captured were mirrors. These varger were the hardest to evade; they could copy a victim's every move, anticipating where they would run next. These they held with iron needles in an iron cage, going so far as to pin the creatures together.

While they tended to the monsters, Royu, Sasha, and Tabitha prepared the remaining enchantments from the exhibition to return to their homes in the vaults. Krona passed Tabitha's desk just as she set aside the empty cases for the despairstone and the Mayhem Mask. Tabitha's gaze was dark, and trailed

Krona like an oil slick as she aimed for the stairwell that led into the depths of the den. Krona had no doubt she blamed her for the missing items, even if she would never voice it.

Krona and the man she'd fought saw the resident healers in the underground surgery wing. De-Lia had refused to send the man to a public hospital. She'd arrested him then and there, while he bled on the polished floor.

The den had once been a military armory, back in the days when the five city-states had continuously threatened war against one another. Its white limestone walls were rough-hewn, and even in Lutador's summer, the place was frigid. Most of the den lay underground, covered over with a mound of sod.

The compound lay on the eastern side of the city, removed from the crushing closeness of Lutador's multistory buildings by a handful of rolling hills and a low wall. To the left of the old armory sprawled the barracks, where most unattached Regulators hung their hats at the end of the day. Behind that sat the stables. A thin road sporting a single, heavily guarded gate was the only proper way in and out.

Krona didn't call the barracks home like the majority of her colleagues, which kept her from hearing the siren song of a warm bed while the healer did his work.

She held her gaze on a chipped brick on the opposite wall while his hands fluttered over her arm. He added a salve, which didn't sting, and drew stitches through her flesh, which had her gritting her teeth to hold back the expletives. Once he was done, fresh, salt-white bandages stood out starkly against her black skin. The deep gashes burned every time she moved, and her entire arm throbbed.

It felt good to be out of her helm, making eye contact, but it also left her vulnerable—she couldn't hide how the attack had affected her.

"Lift," said the healer, Master Utkin, indicating she should raise her elbow. "How's that?"

"Better," she lied, anxious to confront her assailant.

He frowned at her. By now, he knew when she was rushing him. He'd been her den-assigned caregiver far too long.

"Do you want to tell me about it?" he asked.

"What?"

"The fear. The varger—real and not-real. It's been a long time since you've faced one."

Krona scratched at the wound absently. She hated discussing her feelings on the matter. Most people didn't know about her varger-based terror, and she preferred to keep it that way. Regulation was about keeping the upper hand, maintaining control and power. Weakness was unseemly.

But healers needed to know everything about their patient's health in order to properly see to their well-being. She couldn't keep her fear a secret from him.

And, her team knew. She was sure it was a black mark against her: first De-Lia places her own baby sister in their ranks—whose three years of Regulation thus far had been admirable, though nothing special—but then the younger Hirvath's got vargerangaphobia to boot, which makes her a terrible shot with a quintbarrel.

Krona had hoped it would never be a problem, that she would have more time to train, to improve. Most Regulators went their entire careers without facing a varg. Regulators were trained to deal with varger as a contingency plan *only*. It was Borderswatch that kept the beasts at bay. Typically.

Varger were monsters from beyond the Valley. The one type of creature the magical, god-created barrier at the rim could not keep out. The Borderswatch was in charge of containing as many as they could, of keeping the majority from ravaging the countryside and assaulting the cities.

Utkin was ex-Borderswatch.

He understood varger, knew how much damage they could cause, how much pandemonium they could sow.

"I don't want to talk about it. It's done," she said.

His bald head was freshly shaven, and his thick, graying beard well trimmed. He pulled at the curls of his whiskers, holding himself squarely, like the solider he was. The stiffness of the garrison would most likely never leave him. She remembered the same constant readiness in her papa.

"Did your fear affect your performance?"

"No."

Utkin didn't counter her. He simply let the silence draw out, long and full, waiting.

"Perhaps," she admitted quietly.

"I've been looking into some new philosophies regarding phobia. When I've completed my research, I'd like to start a new course of treatment."

Internally, Krona perked. It had been years since any other healer had suggested something could be done for her. Outwardly, she maintained her skepticism.

"If you're willing," he added. "It may be rough. But, if your future concerns continue to involve varger, it will be worth it. I have high hopes."

And if this *concern continues to involve varger . . . ?* Krona hadn't wanted to consider the possibility—that there might be more monsters before the matter was settled. "We'll get the enchantments back soon," she offered dully. "Perhaps we can talk about it again after?"

He frowned, but accepted her hesitancy.

"Say *ah*," he directed. She did so, and he popped a mineral tablet into her mouth. "For the pain," he explained. "You'll be short one bracer for the time being. Your wounds can't bear it, understand?"

"Yes." All personal magic use took its toll one way or another, physically or mentally.

He nodded approvingly, then packed up his supplies and dismissed her.

Instead of heading upstairs into the main gallery to deliver her report to a recorder, she stole down the nearest hall. They'd rushed the false varg into a surgery with three healers and a handful of aides, but from the outside the room was still. She pressed an ear against the door, trying to pick up hints of conversation or the clacking of metal instruments. Nothing.

She pushed open the thick, paneled door, peeking around the edge. One healer stood bent over his patient, who lay on a cot. A thin robe had replaced the man's varg costume, and bandages matching hers—though already showing signs of seepage—encased his throat. She noticed tattoos down one shin and up his left arm. Tattoos were strictly prohibited. Self-mutilation was abhorrent. Ironically, the punishment was further mutilation—the filleting of the blemish clean off.

His exposed, limp hand also bore markings. One on his thumb caught her eye—it was a brand.

Catching the squeak of hinges, the healer turned. "He's sleeping," he said bluntly.

"I need to question him," she said, coming fully into the room.

"It's going to be some time before he can speak again. Your cut was expertly placed—you spared his life."

"Credit luck, not skill." She pretended that the sharp scent of medicinal alcohol kept her from approaching the cot, but truly she didn't trust herself. Now that the blood had stopped rushing—both through her veins and from his wound—she no longer felt the panicky desire to keep him alive. Anger put heat on her temples and tongue. "When will he wake?"

"Hard to say. But he certainly won't be able to tell you anything."

"I hope for his sake he knows how to use a pen," she said.

With one last narrow-gazed study of the unconscious man's face, she left the healer to his work.

De-Lia was waiting in the hall, leaning against the stonework with one boot propped up casually. She'd also removed her helm, revealing her stern, thin features and close-shaven head. Her skin was even darker than Krona's, almost as black as her uniform. She looked lithe and athletic, but tired. "How is he?" she asked.

"Unconscious," Krona said bitterly.

"And you?" She pushed off the wall and gingerly took Krona's injured arm, cradling it in her palm and examining the healer's work with a critical eye. Silvery stains splattered the captain's sleeves.

"It'll scar—but what's one more?"

De-Lia nodded, both accepting the statement and approving the application of the wrap.

"The varger?" Krona asked.

"Secure. A runner confirms a Borderswatch break-in three weeks ago. At a camp, while a shipment was on its way to the vault. Several bottled varger were stolen."

"Three weeks? The ones at the party were no bottle-barkers, those were full strength."

"Whoever perpetrated the robbery must have force-fed them to get the creatures up to muster so quickly."

De-Krona balked. If these tangible varger had been bottle-bound three weeks ago, then they must have eaten a person a week. Where might one get so many victims? The Dregs? The mines? The work camps?

Varger consumed people—only people. But if they went long enough without a meal, they became ethereal. Immaterial. Little more than wisps of mist. But that mist could still latch on, could still kill. If you inhaled it, the varg would eat you from the inside.

That was what made varger so terrible. You couldn't slay them. Couldn't tear them apart or burn them to ashes. The only way to halt them was with the needles—and then it had to be the proper type. Five kinds of varger meant a quintbarrel shooter had to keep five kinds of needles on them at all times: gold, silver, iron, nickel, and bronze.

After shooting one down with the appropriate needles, effectively pinning it to the spot, you had to cage it and starve it—turn it to mist and put it in glass, sucking it into a spherical, enchanted vessel—a containment bulb—tipped with a nipple made of the correct corresponding metal. The only good varg was a bottled varg, shelved away deep in the city-state's vaults. They were safe to transport that way, easy to carry as canned goods.

"How many varger were stolen?"

"Three, which we captured. But I could have sworn I shot a fourth," De-Lia said.

"It could have been taken from elsewhere."

"Or it could have been the same kind you fought," De-Lia said. "Because I'm sure I hit it."

"With all five metals?"

De-Lia averted her eyes. "No." She rubbed the side of her gun hand, which displayed a mild chemical burn. The tips of her pointer and middle finger were wrapped with bandages as well.

"What happened to your fingers?"

De-Lia waved that aside. "Mishap with a mending needle yesterday morning. A few drops of blood, nothing more."

"Again? Maybe you should start letting maman darn your clothes for you." Krona noticed something shimmery on De-Lia's knees. "Is that mercury?" she asked, nodding at the stains on De-Lia's uniform.

"Yes."

"So they doused the varger to keep them hidden from the Watch's detectors—which is why they got as close as they did. I've never seen a plan so, so—"

"Ludicrous? What kind of a madman thinks they can control a varg? I bet they ate a few of their handlers, and *that's* how they solidified so fast."

But it worked, Krona thought, keeping her expression flat. A varg attack was the perfect distraction.

And if I'd had my gun out instead of my saber, we'd have much less to go on. Not quite serendipity, but definitely a fortunate mistake. Damn it all if her shoddy aim with a quintbarrel wasn't to thank for revealing the deception.

Not that the man's capture was much to celebrate. She'd let someone walk away with a massive despairstone and a killer's mask. She'd done nothing this evening to be proud of.

But that's why I have to fix this. I have to get them back. She couldn't disappoint her sister. Sometimes it seemed like all her life, Krona had only been chasing after her own mistakes, and this was yet another in a long line. So unlike De-Lia was De-Krona. De-Lia was strong, and beautiful, and successful, and so self-assured—everything Krona aspired to be.

I will fix this, she resolved. *You'll see.*

"The Martinets are going to be sent in, aren't they? To investigate us?" she asked. The legal oversight of the legal oversight—those who investigated the investigators. While a Regulator's word was law, a Martinet's word was divine and absolute.

"Yes, they're here already."

Krona's heart fell. "They'll question my assignment under your command."

"No, they won't. You did a fine job. If anyone is to blame for tonight, it's me. And rightfully so."

"That's what concerns me. Requesting your sister be assigned to your detail . . . They don't take nepotism lightly." She let "nepotism" roll heavily off her tongue.

"It's not nepotism," De-Lia insisted, pushing away from the wall. Her fatigue seeped away, replaced by the kind of intensity that always answers insult. "I picked the strongest team, I requested all of you because you each have special skill sets that are stronger when all woven together. You wouldn't have been assigned to my detail if anyone here believed any differently. I *do not* make official decisions based on my personal feelings."

It was true—De-Lia was efficient, straightforward. She wouldn't let her passions interfere with her work because, above all, she despised the incompetence that came with that kind of emotionality.

"*I* know that," Krona said, reaching out with her uninjured arm to clasp her sister's in comfort. "But the Martinets don't."

"So what are you saying?"

"If you must admit to favoritism, tell them I shouldn't have been on the team."

"You don't need to take the blame for this."

"Why not? Perhaps someone else wouldn't have been distracted by the grieving father. Perhaps they would have said something about the out-of-place Nightswatchmen. Perhaps they would have secured the collection, and Charbon's mask and the despairstone would still be under Regulator control."

"Let the Martinets investigate," De-Lia said firmly. "They will find no impropriety or negligence on my team. Do you hear me? They will not sacrifice one of us to appease their need to place fault. We will retrieve our enchantments and these thieves will hang. Understand?"

"Yes." Krona let herself smile. De-Lia's dedication was always a wonder to behold.

"Good. Are you still fit for duty?" De-Lia asked.

She caught herself cradling her injured arm and swiftly dropped it to her side. "Of course."

"Then after the Martinets interview you, I want you to go to the Chief Magistrate's chateau to interview his son and the house staff."

The timing of Iyendar the younger's outburst was suspicious, at best. But Krona's instincts told her it was a coincidence. "The Nightswatch didn't detain him?"

"The Chief Magistrate wouldn't let them."

"Ah. I see."

"And I'm sending Tray with you."

Tray was a good friend; the sisters had known him since childhood—which would perhaps be another check in the nepotism column to the Martinets. He was headstrong and pinpoint focused, and Krona knew he would not take this side trek to the Iyendar household well. Interfacing with the Watch had been his responsibility, and his attention would stay with them.

But she would not argue with the captain on this point. "Naturally," she said. "Permission to check out the Leroux mask?"

"Of course."

As Krona turned to leave, De-Lia reached for her shoulder. "Forty-eight hours before the trail is likely to go cold," she said.

"I know," Krona replied, bobbing her head solemnly. "And then . . ."

"With Charbon's mask loosed? Chaos."

Half the time, that was all enchantments caused.

3

MELANIE

Two years previous

The chiming of the store's bell smacked of luxury, like everything else in the city. Bells in the country always tinkled with a tin echo that indicated they were made of lesser things, just like the country people: their rolling drawl was the calling card of an unrefined upbringing.

Melanie was all too aware of this when she opened her mouth to address the clerk. "I'm interested in a mask," she said, as crisp and clear as possible. *And saving my mother,* she silently added.

His dull eyes traced her from mud-crusted skirt up to moth-eaten best hat, his lips maintaining a scowl the entire way. He had a long, lithe torso, with the limbs and nose to match. When he answered, he answered slowly. Melanie wasn't sure if it was because it took a long time for the words to climb out of his lengthy chest, or if he considered her dull-witted.

"You are in a mask shop. I'd expect you're interested in a mask. What kind?"

She sneaked glances left and right. On the walls hung carvings of every possible shape and design. Bright and dark colors made sweeping patterns, twisting together to tell a variety of stories. Exotic animals displayed gaping maws. Demons grinned through grotesque, asymmetrical features. Human likenesses were twisted into caricatures through exaggerated expressions.

She hunched her shoulders, shrinking from their cold, empty stares. They watched, waiting expectantly for her to choose. *So many dead faces.* A shiver crawled up her spine.

She wondered which could be the one she was after. The likeness of a horned owl? The one where a sloth curled over the wearer's brow while carved jungle branches obscured where the eyelets really lay? Perhaps the inverted demon's face, with its skin sloughing and pooling like taffy, the wearer meant to gaze out of its open, upside-down mouth.

"A healer's mask. His name was August Belladino. Is he here?"

The clerk grinned, as if he knew something she did not. A private joke, perhaps. "He is. Were you looking to rent, or buy? The knowledge of Master Belladino does not come"—he frowned deeply—"cheap."

What did he consider cheap? Any sort of magic carried a hefty price in the country. But city and country definitions of "expensive" weren't the same.

"I'd like to rent," she said, reaching into her purse. She pulled out all but a few vials of minutes. "Is this enough?" In the country the ratio was usually sixty to one. One hour of use for every bottled minute.

She glanced down at the time, a little guilty. She could have given it to her mother. But, no, that wouldn't be proper. What were a few more minutes of agony when she could have years of health?

The store bell rang again, and Melanie glanced over her shoulder at the new patron. He was a dark-skinned young man, a handful of years older than she. He looked as if he belonged in the city—all sharp edges and clean lines.

Her cheeks grew hot. She was embarrassed to have her exchange with the clerk overheard.

The clerk glowered, and his annoyance intensified. He opened his mouth to say something to the man, but thought better of it. Instead, he counted up Melanie's minutes. "Enough for a day and a half."

Her heart sank. "I'd hoped for three. The healer in my town said I'd need three."

"Then come back when you have the full fare." He drummed his fingers against the countertop impatiently.

"Please." Her voice shook. She gulped. "I don't have time to raise more." She dumped the rest of the bottles from her purse. The last minutes were meant for the innkeeper, but the mask was more important. Melanie and her mother could sleep on the streets a few nights, if they had to.

"Still not enough," he said coldly.

Smooth skin brushed past hers, and a dark hand laid a generous pile of time beside hers. "That should cover it," said the young man.

Deep, black eyes held Melanie's gaze for a moment. She opened her mouth, but didn't know what to say.

"I told you not to come in here again," the clerk said. "You scare away my customers."

"I'm not scaring anyone," he said indignantly, his eyes widening and smooth eyebrows raising. "I'm helping her pay. I'm giving you money. Are you refusing to rent to her?"

"Does she have the proper papers?" the clerk asked, talking past Melanie. "Has a Regulator approved the wearing? Is she sound of mind and body?"

Once again Melanie fumbled in her satchel. The Regulator den had been cold, filled with imposing figures all in black, their tall helms inscrutable. The Regulator who'd examined her request and signed the papers had said nothing, indicating questions by pointing to the forms. She'd tried not to look directly into the dark-cherry glass of their faceplate. "Yes, yes, I—" She unrolled the scrolled leaves of paper, pointing to where she'd been given the license for a Magnitude Zero mask of Fifth Tier importance, and had been mentally and physically examined.

She didn't know what "Magnitude Zero" and "Fifth Tier" meant precisely, and she'd been too embarrassed to ask, to prove just how poor and out of place and uneducated she was. All she knew was that it suggested the enchantment was easy to wield, and that the description applied to Master Belladino's mask.

Without another word the clerk stomped from behind the counter and over to the far wall. Taking great care, he lifted one of the wooden masks from its hook—one of the animal effigies. The focal point was a tree frog—the full frog, climbing up a vine, looking over its shoulder. Around it clustered leaves, branches, and a couple of small exotic birds. The frog's eyes had been cut out for the wearer. "Master Belladino's mask," he said, offering it to her. "Covered for a week."

"It's so light," she said, balancing it delicately. In the country, people had to carve their death masks out of cedar or pine instead of balsa imported from Asgar-Skan, and no one she knew could afford paint, let alone enchantment. Clutching it to her chest, she turned to the young man. "Thank you," she said, "I'll repay you, somehow. I'll come up with the time—or I can work the minutes off straight. I might not look it, but I can plow fields all day, or clean house, or—"

"We'll come up with something." His face was gentle, but his expression stern. "Where are you staying?"

"The beggar's inn at—" In her sudden elation, she'd forgotten. Her eyes strayed to the bottles.

He read her mind. "I'll cover that, too. I work at the Creek Side Inn; I can get you a room, if you'd like."

"That would be wonderful. Thank you so much, Monsieur—?"

"Leiwood."

"Melanie Dupont. I'll get my mother and we'll be right over. I can't, I mean . . ." She was so happy she couldn't get her tongue to behave properly.

"It's just, I didn't think—" She shuffled her feet, wanting to be off as quickly as she could.

"Go. I'll see you this evening."

Giddy with excitement and gratitude, she skipped away. Before she could cue the bell's tinkling once more, Monsieur Leiwood caught her by the shoulder. "Be careful," he said darkly. "Keep your guard up."

She nodded absently, her hand already on the door.

As she left, Melanie caught the beginning of a new conversation between Leiwood and the clerk. She paused outside the door to listen.

"You didn't explain it," Leiwood said.

"It's a healer's mask, *Magnitude Zero*," he said with a dismissive scoff. "She'll be fine."

"Not like me?"

"Not like you."

The conversation ended, and she hurried on. Melanie was too happy to wonder what they'd meant.

⊱──⊱◈⊰──⊰

The trek back to the squalid tenement was long, but Melanie didn't mind. She clutched the means of her mother's deliverance to her chest, and allowed herself to admire the decorative stained-glass-and-iron sculptures she passed. The city was daunting, but beautiful in its own way. Structures towered as high as five stories, their windows broad and colorful. Nothing was stark in the city. Everything was built for form as well as function, sometimes favoring the former over the sensibility of the latter.

Most streets in Lutador were set up to invoke the five gods in some way, through patterns of five points and five sides, creating many odd angles between streets. Buildings on the ends of blocks often had sharp corners that contained unusual rooms. No one would build such strange structures in the country; practicality always beat out symbolism in areas where people had more sense than money.

But perhaps that was an unfair assessment. It wasn't that Melanie bore any ill will toward city folk, she simply understood country people better. The country was comfort, and family, and simplicity. The city was cold spaces, and strangers, and multiplicity.

She was so elated to finally, *finally*, have a way to help her mother that she considered going to a coterie. It had been a long while since she'd attended services. Not for lack of faith, but lack of means; the closest coterie to her home was hours away by carriage ride. She didn't dare leave her mother alone for so long, and it was too hard on Dawn-Lyn to make the trip in tandem. Melanie had only brought her to Lutador proper as a last resort. The healer in her small village had given Dawn-Lyn only another month to live.

And Melanie had no reason to doubt the grim pronouncement. Her mother's entire family had died of the same wasting disease long before Melanie was born. Drastic measures were needed, and Melanie refused to give up.

Now that her mother's salvation was within their grasp, she decided it was only right to thank the gods in person.

Many coteries dotted the city—as the map she'd purchased told her—positioned in geographical places of power, like hills or at the center of penta-grammed roadways. None of them were on her way, but she'd noticed a shrine down an alley while walking to the enchantment district.

If she could only remember where . . .

She found it tucked between a law office and an eatery with glazed ducks hanging in the window, just as, in the distance, a clock tower struck the hour. The alley could barely be called that—it was more of an access tunnel than anything—but it widened out behind the buildings into a shared, uncovered courtyard. The midday sun shone down over the tops of the high buildings, sending a brilliant shaft of light directly onto the altar.

Melanie approached slowly, not wanting to disturb anyone who might have slipped in for quick worship. But the courtyard was empty.

The white soapstone altar stood shoulder high, with five divots sanded out to hold small statues of the gods. Each was more or less humanoid, with distinctly inhuman characteristics. Twins female Time and male Nature were each depicted with their three sets of wings outstretched. Sexless Knowledge knelt with hands steepled beneath feir chin, a blank, eyeless mask with a pointed nose set firmly against feir face, body bent as though elderly. Intersex Emotion held zhur left hand over zhur heart, while the right covered zhur mouth, and zhur other set of arms wrapped around zhur sunburst-like body, the form implying a brightness too intense to stare directly into. And the final divot was left empty, as was tradition. It belonged to the Unknown god, who was a mystery in all facets.

A chaplet of chestnuts dangled from one corner of the altar, and flakes of something silver had been shaved over the top of Nature. Otherwise, the dais was pristine.

Above, laundry fluttered on a clothesline. She glanced up and failed to notice the iron footplate jutting out at the base of the shrine. When her boot made con-tact, she jolted and nearly stumbled.

"What in the—?"

The iron plate tilted, compressing a spring. She heard a series of latches click and what sounded like metal balls dropping, but she couldn't pinpoint the sound. Then, above, an iron pail suspended on wires tilted and spilled.

Melanie leapt back, fearing water or waste or worse. Instead, tiny pink petals fluttered down, showering the shrine.

She caught one in her palm, while several others landed on her hat and a few caught in her curls. The petals weren't even real—they were silk.

She giggled at the showmanship. "Ha. Only in the city."

>–⊷–○–⊶–◁

After scribbling a gratuity invocation on a prayer scroll, Melanie rushed back to the halfway house. She blazed through the dark, grungy hall, and into the shabby room with the boarded windows and sagging mattress. Even this had been a costly place to stay, despite the rat-nested walls, and the strange smells, and the sounds of nefarious acts rattling through the halls at all hours of the night. *This* had been too expensive. How anyone could afford to actually live in a city, Melanie couldn't fathom.

"Mother. Mother, look," Melanie said excitedly, crouching next to the bare bed. She turned her mother's pale face toward the mask. "Isn't it beautiful?"

"Mmm," Dawn-Lyn agreed, cracking open her sunken eyes to appreciate the workmanship. Her hair fanned out across the stained pillow, framing her bony profile in a halo of black.

Melanie wanted to put the mask on this instant, to learn Master Belladino's healing techniques as soon as possible.

But she forced herself to wait, just until they moved to the Creek Side Inn. The name itself suggested it had to be worlds better than here, where she'd had to shove a rickety chair against the door to feel safe while sleeping.

Using the board they'd brought, Melanie was able to leverage her mother out of bed and partially onto her feet. She buckled her into a harness, then looped the straps—like those on a traveler's pack—over her own shoulders. Dawn-Lyn hadn't been able to sit upright on her own in months. She hadn't been able to walk in years.

Limply, her mother hugged her from behind. "Good girl. My good girl," she breathed.

Melanie slowly took her mother's full weight onto her back. "You feel lighter today," she said, worried.

"Easier for you to carry, that way," her mother said. "Soon you won't have to worry about me anymore. You'll be able to live your own life, as a young woman should."

Yes, Melanie thought, *but not for the reason you think.* "You'll feel better soon," she said.

Her mother sighed. "Yes, I'm sure I will."

Melanie waited for her mother to ask more questions, to inquire after why they were moving, or if the mask had been easy to acquire. But her illness made her tired and her brain foggy.

If Dawn-Lyn noticed that things were dire financially, she never said. And Melanie hadn't wanted to bring her extra worry. Pieces of well-crafted furniture had slowly disappeared from their home—sold off to ensure they could buy medicines or special food. The roof sagged in places, its holes patched by shoddy thatching and Melanie's own hands. Their home had once sported a magnificent stained-glass window, of which only a shard now remained.

Master Belladino's mask was it, their last shot. After this venture there was no time left, not in Melanie's purse and not in Dawn-Lyn's body.

If Melanie couldn't save her mother, she'd be left with nothing in the end.

With a heavy sigh, she gathered up the rest of their meager belongings, then hobbled out of the room.

4

KRONA

Maman—you should see the way she looks at me when you're not around. She knows I could have stopped it, but didn't. It's because of that day on the mountain. Do you remember? I don't think you do. To you it would have been like any other day playing afar of the house. But for me . . . it is the day that shaped all other days after.

The interview with the Martinets had dragged on, and on, and on. Krona kept reminding herself that this was their job, they had their duties just as she did. But still, it was four in the morning by the time she was released, and every inch of her body felt the tug of gravity a little more firmly.

And still, her day was not over. If they were lucky, she and Tray could arrive at the Iyendars' by six.

Tray Amador sat at his station, filing an account of the incident with one of the auxiliary administrators. The smolder on his face was penetrating—it reminded Krona of a guard dog's snaggle-toothed snarl. His intensity appeared to have spooked the administrator; any greener and she might have fled the room in tears.

"Yes," he said in a grinding voice that could have milled flour. "All of our people were in position, I said that already." He pointed at several locations on a hastily drawn map of the venue. "The Nightswatch should have been prepared for mercury—they had a sentry posted at every gate. They claimed they'd even hired on extra Watchmen, but their coverage was inexcusably spotty."

He was understandably on edge. He felt a Nightswatch failure was his failure.

"The captain will send someone to interview the Head of the Watch," Krona said, strolling up to the writing desk and putting on her best Regulator face. "You and I are headed to the Chief Magistrate's."

He thumbed at his pert nose. Light skin offset his black hair and black, deep-set eyes—a combination most frequently found in the ice-bound city-state of Marrakev. He still had a large extended family in the northernmost regions. Krona's ancestors had come from the opposite end of Arkensyre—the desert city-state of Xyopar. "I'd rather—"

"Captain's orders," she said by way of apology.

He nodded sternly, and she laid a sympathetic hand on his shoulder. He accepted it sternly for a moment, before laying his hand over hers. They were all in this together, no reason to be gruff with one another.

As he rose to accompany Krona to the mask gallery, the administrator let out an audible sigh of relief.

Tray marched along with a stiffness, half a stride further and a full head shorter than Krona. Though he was slight in stature compared to most men, he carried a ferocious voracity for the law that could quell someone twice his size.

They stopped by her station so that she could snatch her chalk pouch. Masks came in many sizes and shapes, and it was best to keep your nose and ears powdered so as not to blister.

Each Regulator had their own writing desk where they could study evidence from their concerns and draw up reports. The stations lined the walls of the den's sprawling main floor. While at her desk, Krona put away the sepia-toned photographs and sketches from the concern she'd been working on earlier—a matter of interest, but one that required no great rush. The case had been sitting in her queue for months now.

A Master Belladino's mask had mysteriously stopped functioning. The mask the shop owner had brought in contained no enchantment.

Krona glanced momentarily at the drawing of the mask's "enchanter's mark," which was missing from the item they had in custody. Each enchanter had their own sigil, which they could not prevent from appearing on their work once it was complete—the design naturally engraved itself. Each mark was unique; no two were alike, and the lack of an enchanter's mark on the recovered, perfectly intact mask meant it couldn't be Master Belladino's—it was a replica, a fake.

Between being rented and returned, the real mask had to have been swapped with this duplicate. She'd cleared everyone listed as a renter in the shop owner's enchanted catalog. All except two: a man who had passed away, and a Shin-La HuRupier, who she could not locate.

Stowing the papers in their cubby, she moved on.

The den's store of legally enchanted masks was housed in the deepest parts of the old armory. Several checkpoints along the way verified that no one without clearance entered the sanctuary. Inside, past the heavy, iron-barred door, high-set gaslights gave the room an eerie dimness. Carefully positioned spotlights illuminated each mask, which were set in specialty recesses.

The collection was modest, yet potent. Thirty pieces occupied the nooks, though there was room for one hundred. Some Regulators spent part of their modest pay on their own masks for personal use, but Krona relied on the state's stock. She'd yet to find a mask on the market that could match the state-owned for usefulness.

She looked them over in turn. Khatri's mask was a jumble of snakes, each painted gold, silver, or green, their eyes inlaid with unenchanted chips of ruby. Magnitude Six difficulty, Tier Eight importance. Santiago's mask had been carved from redwood, stained instead of painted to preserve the wood's natural hue. Elegant waves and curves gave the mask an abstract impression of movement, like air or water. Magnitude Three, Tier Seven. And Motomori's half-mask, which covered only the wearer's nose and mouth, was carved in the shape of a demon's maw, with pointed fangs and scrunched nose, painted over in neutral colors that did nothing to dampen the impression of ferocity. As near to a Magnitude Ten as Krona had ever seen—Nine Point Eight, and of Tier Ten import—the most difficult, most valuable mask in the collection. She used to check it out often, wearing it when no one else dared. But it took its toll, even on her. His had been the power of persuasion—deep hypnotism.

She'd only been a Regulator for three years, but she'd worn all thirty. A record. There were several even the most seasoned amongst them dared not touch unless absolutely necessary. Their powers were potent, but so were their echoes. So was the cost, the suffering endured after the strain.

"Will you be donning anything to the Iyendar residence?" she asked Tray.

"I don't think I should," he said. "The strain of anything greater than a Magnitude Two is likely to put me out of commission for several days at this point. I'll leave the task to you.

"Which did you come for?" he asked.

"Leroux."

"Ah, of course." He rocked on the balls of his feet, clearly excited to see Krona in action. Leroux was a fighter, and though the mask's gifts were among the most useful in the collection, few people could keep control of the echo long enough to justify its wearing. Magnitude Eight, Tier Nine.

She lifted it from its cubby, thumbing at its expertly carved edges.

The walnut wood swooped in heavy-cut lines, forming the head of an angry, charging boar. The tusks were wide and white, and the snout was wrinkled and ruddy. The eyelets were cut in such a way as to make the boar look as though it gazed up through its brow when the wearer stared straight ahead.

Florence Leroux had, in life, been Lutador's foremost expert on lies. She could detect the slightest misplaced blink or twitch of the mouth. She knew what every flap of the hand and cock of the head meant. A sudden quirk of an interviewee's intonation might go unnoticed by the average, highly trained Regulator. But not Florence Leroux.

Luckily, she'd allowed for an enchanted death mask in her will. Luckier still, she'd awarded it to the state free of charge.

Everyone, from the poorest vagabond to the wealthiest noble, would wear a death mask when given final rites in the tradition of the city-state's patron god, Time. But money mattered when it came to the intricacy of the carving, the quality of the wood, an allowance of paint, and, most expensively, enchantment.

Krona nestled her face in the soft, velvet underbelly of Leroux's mask. Tray tied the ribbons for her, pressing down her thick curls. Her hair was done in hundreds of small braids, and those tiny twists swirled in on themselves.

Together, the two of them waited for the knowledge to settle in.

All Regulators were trained in mask wearing. It wasn't as simple as the public might think—wasn't *easy*.

A torrent of information bled from the mask into Krona's mind, swooping like a flock of evening starlings around her brain. She deepened her breathing, allowing each tidbit to land on the appropriate perch at the appropriate time. There alighted *face touching*, here roosted *vocal mimicry*. *Posture, glances,* and *increased pouting* all found homes before Leroux's echo made itself known.

Most echoes were docile, as most people were docile (whether they wanted to believe it or not). Magnitude Zeros, Magnitude Ones. The public wasn't allowed anything beyond a Magnitude Three. Occasionally, however, an echo would fight back, warring with the mask wearer for control, earning a higher rating.

Leroux had been a woman of strong will, and her echo was no different.

The small, lasting piece of Leroux's personality shoved its way to the forefront of Krona's consciousness. It made her remember places she'd never been, people she'd never met, and philosophies she'd never held.

Her brother—no, Leroux's brother—playing his zither in concert for the first time.

A small, pond-side cabin that smelled of rusted nails and graying wood.

And the sense that all people were ultimately liars, even when they thought they were telling the truth.

The echo wanted to control Krona's body, to walk her up to Leroux's old desk and get her working on Leroux's old concerns. It wanted to pretend it was alive again.

But Krona knew how to suppress it. How to coddle the wisps of feeling and satisfy the gruff sense-of-self into submission.

Echoes weren't exactly pieces of the dead. They weren't people. They weren't even sentient. They were imprints, resonating on through the enchanted wood. Just reverberations rebounding through a host, looking for a mind to saturate and claim.

Leroux's echo relaxed as soon as it realized it was in a Regulator brain. Krona made it believe it had done its job, that it was one with a new body—all while carefully locking it away in the back of her mind. Safe and out of sight.

This was Krona's specialty. She might have been less than stellar with a quint, but she could control an echo better than anyone. Even those who'd spent decades in the den couldn't subdue an imprint as quickly and completely as she could.

"Steady?" Tray asked.

"Exceptionally so," she said with a smile, though she knew he couldn't read her expression under the mask.

"How do you tame them so quickly?"

She found it difficult to put her skill into words—she wasn't sure it was something she could teach. "Perhaps that will be what I preserve in my own mask, when the time comes."

"Fine, keep your secrets," he said good-naturedly. "Let's go reclaim our enchantments."

She nodded, the boar's head heavy against her cheeks. Time to fix her mistake, absolve her captain, and make her sister proud.

5

MELANIE

Two years previous

"Is this acceptable, Madame Dupont?" Monsieur Leiwood asked, but not of Melanie. He was addressing her mother.

No one had spoken directly to her mother in a long time. They always acted as if she couldn't hear, or as though she weren't there at all.

"Fine," Dawn-Lyn Dupont whispered, snuggling into the covers. "It's a lovely room."

The tables and wardrobe were polished mahogany. Fine sheets—so fresh that Melanie wondered if they'd ever been slept in before—covered the feather bed. These were posh lodgings.

Monsieur Leiwood nodded and came away from the bedside. "For her?" he asked Melanie, nodding to the mask that sat on the windowsill, propped against the pane. He didn't comment on Dawn-Lyn's heavy Marrakevian accent, as strangers used to, or ask Melanie what city-state her father had been from. He didn't ask how she'd ended up with mousy brown curls and amber eyes so unlike her mother. He didn't make either of them feel out of place.

"Yes. She has the muscle illness. The one that makes everything quit moving. Even the heart, in the end." She dropped down onto a chaise, and looked out the window to the bustling afternoon street below. "I asked every healer I could find to have a look at her. In the end they kept telling me, 'You need August Belladino.' When I learned he was dead, I was sure he must have a mask—a real one, an enchanted one. An expert craftsman wouldn't let his knowledge disappear when he died."

"Some experts can't afford to enchant their masks," he said, "and some would rather cash in their time, live it out."

"Yes. But luckily, Master Belladino could . . . and didn't."

He sat down beside her, keeping a respectful distance.

"You own the inn, don't you?" she asked suddenly.

"I do," he said.

They were quiet for a while. Eventually Dawn-Lyn's breathing evened out. Melanie could tell she was asleep.

"Would you like to go to the lounge?" Monsieur Leiwood asked. "Let your mother rest?"

She nodded and followed him out and down the stairs.

▸—◂◆▸—○—◂▸—◂

They sat at a small table, bent over full mugs of beer that neither touched. The lounge was set in a long, narrow strip of hall between the inn's front entrance and the cigar room. Recessed on one side was a bar, well kept, with a waxed wooden counter that was scratch-free. On the other, against the windows, a series of two-person tables sat in a line. Only one other patron shared the space—a man in a tidy waistcoat and jacket, worn without an undershirt, who read his paper with a perpetual crease in his brow.

"You sounded concerned when I left the shop," Melanie said, tapping her fingernails lightly against her mug. The scent of the beer left a bitter tingle in her nose.

Leiwood laughed at her offhanded comment in caustic sort of way. "I had a bad experience with a mask." He nodded toward the bar. "It's on the wall there. Would you like to see it?"

She wasn't sure she would, but he got up and she trailed behind. Masks aplenty decorated the inn, but the one he indicated was different from the rest. It looked like a crow, with a long black beak and shining metal feathers—and it was hewn in half.

She gasped when she saw it. Desecration of a mask was blasphemous. To destroy an enchantment was to destroy a gift from the gods—a gift from Knowledge. *How did this happen?* she wanted to ask, but refrained for fear of offending Monsieur Leiwood.

"My father's," he said. "We had an . . . *unhealthy* relationship. When he died I thought I'd be able to understand him better if I bought his mask and wore it for a little while. Turns out that wasn't a good idea."

Twisting a fold in her skirt, she waited for him to explain. He didn't look as if he wanted to—more like he *had* to. "My father was a bad man. And for the short time that I wore his mask, so was I. Thankfully, I don't remember much of what happened, and no one got hurt. Once the mask came off, I was me, and the memories of being in his mind drifted away."

His tone stayed light, casual. But Melanie could see between the seams of his gentlemanly demeanor. He was trying to distance himself from whatever had happened, give her insight without feeling the depth of trauma such a past carried.

This kind man had been abused, had worn the mask of his abuser, and he was doing his level best not to set the weight of his experiences on a stranger.

His smile held, as did his openness. But his eyes were so, so sad.

"That's why I hang around the shop," he continued. "I try to warn people. It's not just knowledge that gets transferred, it's personality, too. Maybe even more than that . . ." He put his hand over his mouth, as if he were about to be sick. "Just be careful. Though wearing any mask will cause you strain, Magnitude Zero is supposed to be simplest. The echo of the person within should remain hidden, quiet. But. *But.* Stay yourself and stay strong—even if you don't feel like anything is trying to invade your mind, hold tight. My father's was Magnitude Three, and though others could contain him, I could not. I'm not sure . . . I think the Magnitude doesn't account for everything. I don't know much about Master Belladino, but they say he was a genius. And sometimes geniuses have a funny way of looking at the world, be it good or bad."

Melanie patted his hand. "Thank you. For warning me, for everything. I better get back; Mother will be hungry when she wakes."

"Of course. If you need anything, my room's at the top of the stairs."

><+>-0-<+><

The sun and her mother had both gone down for the night when Melanie decided it was time. She lit a candle, then pulled out her inkpot, a pen, and a roll of parchment.

With slight trepidation rolling in her gut, she turned the mask over, laying it carving side down on the table. It was padded inside, with a silk lining—very inviting. She slowly slipped it over her face, letting it settle against her features. Then she tied the black ribbons under her hair and waited for the magic to take hold.

The quill was in her hand before she recognized what she was doing. Words, processes, formulas—an ocean's worth of information came flooding through. It felt as if it bypassed her brain and splattered straight onto the paper. She saw the words appear, and they turned in on themselves, again and again. Soon she had a collection of giant, worthless inkblots.

With her left hand she grabbed her writing wrist and wrenched it away from the page. She drew several deep breaths, steadying herself. Her heart seemed to be running a desperate race, and her fingers and toes twitched with barely subdued energy. Everything was trying to escape the mask at once. Too much information was being channeled through her. She had to figure out how to control the deluge.

This was what Monsieur Leiwood had been trying to warn her about—an intrusion, a flood coming through her in a way she could not manage. She needed to keep strong, keep steady.

One word at a time, she told herself. *Concentrate. Focus on the muscle illness. What needs to be done?*

Her writing hand tried to get away, but she reeled it in. Only letting one word seep out at a time, she continued. Her mind began filtering more and more. She caught wisps of ideas, portions of equations. A list of ingredients sprang from amongst the rest, and she patiently wrote it down.

Why had her local healer told her it would take days? All of the information was here, now. It took only moments to fall out of the mask.

But getting a tight grasp on the process was taking longer.

Yes, I remember. She recalled everything the ailment required to be canceled. For the first time she realized that medicine and potion-making were all mathematical, with the illness on one side and the cure on the other. Both sides of the equation had to balance, to cancel each other out. The ending answer always needed to be zero.

To cancel the muscle illness . . .

She made notes next to each ingredient. It was slow going, writing and making her calculations. The characters came out at an agonizing pace, but if she didn't hold back, the words would be illegible.

The muscle illness didn't behave the same in each person, so the makeup of the medicine was always slightly different. She had to recall all the specifics she could about her mother's sickness. Retrieving the memories was difficult— Master Belladino, with his overwhelming mental faculties, didn't want to share her consciousness.

Melanie worked through the morning, only stopping when her mother asked for food. She went to the kitchen to order her a meal and some water and bread to last out the day. The boy who wrote down her request deftly ignored the mask.

That was the only time she left the room. Leiwood came to the door once to be sure she was all right. She shooed him away without leaving her chair, assuring him they were fine.

Night had come again by the time she finished. Next she would need to visit the apothecary. But the stars were bright through the window, and all lamps in the hall had been extinguished. The inn had settled down for the evening.

But she needed to start mixing the medicine as soon as possible. Her mother had been sick long enough. Making up her mind, she decided to go to Monsieur Leiwood's room and ask him to escort her now.

Reaching up, she pulled the ribbons loose, and the mask slid away. Not wanting to waste any time, she gathered her cloak and the annotated list, then scurried out the door.

Halfway to his room she stopped and pulled out the list. The items were familiar, but the notes were gibberish. It was as if someone else had written them, and in code. What did that mean? Had she only imagined that she knew how to cure her mother? No, she'd had the information, but now it slipped out of her like water through a sieve. In the next moment even some of the ingredients became foreign.

She needed the mask. Without it she was helpless.

6

KRONA

Families are funny things, aren't they? Wonderful and terrible. They trap some, free others. So, yes, the mountain. You remember what we called "the mountain"? That hill beyond the Coterie of the Five when we lived in the country house. When Papa was still . . . We thought the hill was so big, and with its crags and bare stone it had to be a mountain. One day, when we were still very small, we found a cave between two of the stones—a crack, really. And inside—oh, what was inside changed me to the core. You won't recall, but I could never forget.

━◈━○━◈━

Krona and Tray discussed riding their horses to the chateau, but decided against it. They knew they might find cause to make an arrest at the Iyendars'—as much as that thought troubled them. A carriage made more sense.

On the way, they speculated about the thieves' motives.

"Smells like raiders' trade to me," Tray said. He tried to adopt a casual posture, but the rickety wheels over uneven cobblestones kept bumping him out of position. "Selling the stone alone could garner enough for several gutter-crawlers to retire comfortably."

No, thought Krona, *I don't think it's black-market trade.* "Who would risk buying such a recognizable piece? These aren't normal jewels that can be removed from their settings and disguised. And even at that, if it was simply about bottled time, why didn't the thieves take more? The necklaces could have fetched fortunes even without their enchantments."

"I don't think they expected you to take out their diversion. You spooked them before they could snatch the rest."

She looked out the open window into the street, propping her chin on her fist. From the den, they'd had to enter the city in order to access the main road south. Townhouses rolled by, the tiles on many of their roofs chipped or missing. All the doorways lay in shadow, even those closest to gas streetlamps.

They looked like gaping, rectangular mouths, opened suddenly in surprise. Many people kept free of the streets once darkness came. There hadn't been a state-wide curfew in three years, but the peasantry still dreaded running into an unsavory member of the Nightswatch.

Past the rooftops, in the far distance, a storm gathered on the Valley's eastern rim. Flashes of purple lightning illuminated the craggy peaks through the ever-present clouds. Though the storm was miles away, the air smelled like rain and tasted of static. "The two items they stole were very specific," she said. "They . . . complement each other."

Rosetta's despairstone brooch and Charbon's mask. She despised the cutesy names the papers invented, like "Mayhem Mask," and like what they'd called Charbon himself: the Blooming Butcher. For a state-controlled organization, they were sometimes more lax with their word choice than she—let alone the First and Second Grand Marquises—approved of.

"This feels more like—like a clan hit. It was too organized for your average band of rogues."

"I'd have thought Charbon's techniques too grotesque, even for them," Tray said. "Plus, the Second Grand Marquis's decrees have cracked down on the crime families. Taxed them nearly out of existence since the likes of us haven't been able to catch them red-handed."

"Which means they're looking for new income streams," she pointed out.

"So, you *don't* think young Monsieur Iyendar was involved, then? Unless you're accusing him of consp—"

"No, no," she said quickly. "I don't think he was involved. His timing was too good. The kind only the goddess could orchestrate."

The carriage rolled out of the city, passing the now-dark conservatory. On the open road, with only the occasional tree lining the path, the *clip-clop-clip-clop* of the horses' hooves seemed louder—and yet the rhythm threatened to send Krona to sleep. She pinched the inside of her wrist repeatedly, willing herself to stay alert. Noble-owned farmland stretched out like protective green blankets nestled around the city's limit. Lutador, in its enormity, was *the* city. All else under the state's control was temperate countryside, all the way to the icy northern border of Marrakev, and to jungle-bound Asgar-Skan to the south.

East and west lay the edges of Arkensyre. The great valley that encompassed all—the great valley that *was* all. The 387 scrolls of Absolon described humanity's journey from the wastelands to the Valley—carved out especially for them by the five gods, so that humans, their fragile creations, might be safe from the great and terrible Thalo: the being who'd built the world, along with the horrid, violent beasts that ruled it.

Beyond, said the five city-states, was nothing but desolation. The barren surfaces were overrun with varger, and worse. There, night never came. The surface burned, the air was filled with toxins, and nothing green ever grew.

No one could live outside of the sheltered cradle of life that was Arkensyre.

Her father had been a Borderswatch guard, and in her childhood had often described the magical barrier that encompassed the rim, keeping the monsters and the Thalo at bay. It was a wide swath of pure godly power, invisible until you were directly upon it. There, it began like a heat shimmer, and the farther one pressed the thicker the air became, until it felt like walking through cobwebs. Then the light would fade, the world becoming a darker and darker purple—shot through with flashes of green—as one crested the peaks, the darkness obscuring all but shapes beyond, keeping you from seeing the burning, desolate surface. And there was a point, he'd said, when one could physically go no farther, lest they become trapped in the confluences of power forever—a statue, imprisoned between worlds.

She wasn't sure if that last part was a well-kept Borderswatch secret, or something her father had invented to scare her.

The magical forces on the rim imbued the environment there with the gods' powers. That was how enchantments were made: by harvesting the trees and plant fibers and mining the metals, gemstones, and sand that had absorbed the gods' magic—then engineering devices that made the magics work together.

Sometimes she wished to see the border for herself. Right now, at a distance, it looked beautiful, even with the storm clouds gathered near the tallest peaks. But at other times, when she thought more seriously about the creatures that gathered there—pushing at the barrier, clawing, gnashing—and how varger were the only creatures who could make it through, she was thankful she'd never had a reason to visit.

The spicy scent of cider trees wafted into the carriage as they rolled past a large orchard, drawing her attention away from the rim. The trees were thick and craggy, their limbs twisted and leaves thin. In the dark, they looked like creatures in agony.

After a few miles more, they arrived at the Chief Magistrate's chateau. A faint glow in the sky promised sunrise soon. Both Regulators secured their helms before exiting the carriage.

A well-dressed valet with powder-white gloves and crisply pressed seams saw them into the foyer. He was possessed of the bushiest white eyebrows Krona had ever seen, and an extremely pallid complexion. A scarf of red encircled his hips in place of a belt—a show of solidarity with the grieving household. Krona, still sporting Leroux's mask beneath her helm, noted the brief twinge of distaste on the man's face. He didn't appreciate the interruption, though what they'd interrupted, she wasn't sure. "To begin with, we need to speak with everyone who attended the Jubilee. Especially the Chief Magistrate's son—Fibran, is it?" she said.

A faint pursing of his lips preceded his answer. "Not everyone is awake yet. And the Magistrate's granddaughter—"

"Passed, we know," she said sympathetically.

Irritation. "No, his *remaining* granddaughter, she is still very ill, though the healer says she will recover. Her mother, though, will not leave her side."

"And the girl's father?" Tray asked.

"The Magistrate has asked that he remain undisturbed in the library for the interim. A touch of fever." He frowned deeply, clearly having no taste for this particular lie.

"We will still need to see him."

"Of course," he said, glad to pass responsibility for the intrusion on to the Regulators. Confrontation with an employer was always preferable to a confrontation with the state.

He led them into a sitting room lined with books and furnished with plush, overstuffed settees. The dry scent of cloves and lavender lingered in the air, accompanied by a hint of ash. Someone had burned incense in the room recently—perhaps to cover up another smell. She'd noted such a combination before, in funeral parlors.

Neither Tray nor Krona sat. They stood at the ready, prepared to begin interrogating the first interviewee the moment they strode through the door.

"The Magistrate will be with you shortly," said the valet before turning to go, nearly running headlong into a flustered woman with long, loose brown curls and a haggard droop of the brow. The two of them staggered away from each other, avoiding the collision. Surprise flitted across the woman's face, followed by a fearful grimace. Krona could not tell if the Regulators had induced the reaction, or the valet.

The woman recovered skillfully, offering a little curtsy to the valet before squeezing by him, evading contact at all cost. For his part, the elderly man was not nearly as contrite. "Careful, Little Splinter."

The woman bristled, but smiled despite herself.

With a shake of his head, the valet closed the door on them with a forceful *thunk*.

"Pardon," the woman said, addressing them with another quick curtsy. "I'll just retrieve my effects and leave you be."

She spoke a little too clearly, as though self-conscious of her country accent.

She wore the heavy smock of a healer, but seemed too young to be full-fledged. Across her forehead she wore a ferronnière with a large, green enamel pendant suspended in the center—a highly unusual accessory for a physician on duty.

As she moved to pull a small traveling case from behind the writing desk, Krona stopped her with a light touch to the shoulder. The woman hugged the case to her chest, her fingers splaying over the stamp of gold lettering that formed the initials *CLM* on the side.

Krona smiled to set the woman at ease; though her expression was hidden, it would add a gentleness to her voice. "Please, sit. There was an attack—a theft— last night at the Jubilee celebration, with an unusual occurrence concerning Fibran Iyendar immediately preceding. Will you answer a few questions about the family and their recent loss?"

She started to protest: "I've been up all—" but thought better of it. "Of course. I'm Melanie Dupont," she offered, settling herself stiffly on the least-comfortable-looking chair in the room.

"Are you apprenticed to the family healer?" Tray asked.

"Yes," she answered with the crispness of someone who'd been asked the same question innumerable times.

"You must be very talented," Krona said.

"Thank you," Melanie said quietly, her eyes fixed firmly on Krona's visor.

Krona narrowed her gaze, taking in every millimeter of Melanie's expression.

"Were you in Iyendar's employ before the granddaughters fell ill?" Tray asked, arms crossed like iron bars over his chest. His fingers moved subtly against the leather on one arm, tapping out coded notes on a glass plate beneath. Like the ear shells and reverb beads were tied together, so the stenograph—or ansible— plate was tied to a set of glass pipettes filled with ink. The pipettes were back at the den, responding to his taps in dots and dashes, laying out an inked record for an administrator to translate.

"Yes," Melanie said.

"But not long," Tray pushed.

"No," she said, clearly unimpressed by the crack at her youth.

"And where were you yesterday evening?"

"Here. Tending to Stellina."

"Someone can confirm that?"

"Her mother."

"And where was your master?"

"Master LeMar always goes home to have his evening meal with his family. No exceptions. He isn't due in for a few hours yet."

"What illness did the girls have?" Krona asked.

Melanie closed her eyes for a moment. "Blackwater fever. It's very rare these days, even in Asgar-Skan. I was able to cancel out the infection and rid both twins of the parasite, but Abella's liver . . . Poor thing was only nine. What does that have to do with a robbery?"

Krona and Tray shared a look. "The girls were twins?" Krona said, a slight quiver in her voice. In Lutador, twins were the greatest blessing. The city-state's patron goddess, Time, was a twin. And noble twins were the only people allowed in the highest offices; the First and Second Grand Marquises—the very heads of all power in Lutador—were twins. No one but the multiborn could campaign to be elected as the new marquises, marqexes, or marchionesses once the first of the current pair passed away.

Melanie turned red, realizing her mistake. "Oh, I'm—Please, the family wasn't going to reveal them as twins until their fifteenth birthday."

It was a common power move amongst the high nobility to publicly conceal the birth of twins. Yes, twins were a blessing, but politically, they were a mark.

This discovery was significant. Made their probing here this evening all the more tenuous. Krona and Tray were already very aware of how careful they had to be under this roof—after all, the Chief Magistrate could wipe away their careers with the flick of a finger. He'd already resisted the Watch's attempt to detain his son, and if he found out they now knew one of his political secrets . . .

But it wasn't information they could sidestep.

Tray took up a footstool and sat on-level with the healer. "The Chief Magistrate meant to groom them for office, then? For a chance to become the next Grand Marchionesses?"

"Perhaps—I don't know," Melanie said. "We needed to know their real ages in order to attend to them properly; that's the only reason the family—well, Madame Iyendar—told Master LeMar." Melanie wriggled in her seat, aware she may have unintentionally revealed a political intrigue.

Leroux's mask prickled. Something was amiss with this woman's responses. There was an underlying irritation in her demeanor. A reticence that seemed unrelated to the twins.

"Does the Chief Magistrate know their mother told your master the family secret?"

Melanie looked at her lap. "I don't know."

In walked the Chief Magistrate, as though his burning ears had urged him to fling open the door. "Mistress Dupont?"

The apprentice healer stood and gave another little curtsy. "Pardon. I came for my things, and these gentlepeople informed me of yester-evening's troubles." Her eyes implored the Regulators, *Please forget my gaffe.*

They couldn't very well ask the Magistrate to wait in his own home, so they let Melanie take leave, but not before scribbling down directions to her residence and assuring her they'd be calling in the next few days.

"Before you go, my dear," Iyendar the elder said to the healer, taking one of her small hands into his massive paws, "see the groundskeeper. He wants to know if you approve of the star lilies."

"I didn't know star lilies had medicinal properties," Krona said, hoping for one last chance to let Leroux's mask do its work on the woman. Perhaps if she could catch the healer in an outright fib . . .

But Melanie didn't answer.

"They don't," said the Chief Magistrate. "Mistress Dupont is getting married in two weeks' time, and I've offered the chateau's grounds for the ceremony."

"Just ten days?" Krona said, a little startled. A wedding in the house so soon after death felt strange, but sometimes that was the way of things.

Melanie's face turned paler for a moment, as though she feared—not worried, *feared*—they'd ask for details.

Why? What was the young healer trying to hide?

"How very kind of you, Monsignor," Tray flattered.

It *was* kind. How many other nobles had Krona met that would have opened their homes to the artisan class for a party? Not many.

"He has been exceedingly good to my family," Melanie said. With a third and final curtsy, she left the room.

"It's amazing that girl hasn't snapped her knees, what with the number of times I've seen her do that little number in a day." The Magistrate chuckled, his thick black-and-gray mustache jumping as much as his belly.

He was of startling good cheer, considering.

It was as his grieving son had said: *Make sure no one's smile cracks, make sure no one has a pout, or scuffs a shoe, or breaks a nail.* Never let them see you snap.

In giving his answers, Gregor Iyendar was as obvious as stained-glass windows in a cloister. He replied to every question about the Jubilee with unadulterated honesty. It didn't matter if the question was intrusive—such as those concerning his son's outburst—or more universal.

The only hints of deception came when they pressed him about his political aspirations. And even then he dodged direct answers artfully, avoiding a lie at all costs.

"Sub-Marquis David and Sub-Marchioness Daniella were Iyendars, so it does run in the family—public service, that is." Seated in a reclining chaise, he threaded his fingers over his belly. "And one doesn't become Chief Magistrate by lacking ambition, does he?"

After a few more rounds of sly answers, Krona steeled herself and came to the point. She needed to ask, and if he raged and threw them out, so be it. "Were your granddaughters twins?" When he didn't answer right away, she continued. "It's possible the theft this evening was politically motivated. Who might have known?"

"No one but our immediate family knew," he said darkly. The unspoken subsequent question hung heavy in the air: *How do* you *know?* But neither Krona nor Tray moved to answer.

The Chief Magistrate failed to throw any extra illumination on the theft, and so when he dismissed himself from the room, they did not argue. They went through each member of staff, starting with the valet, a Monsieur Horace Gatwood, who maintained his irritation throughout, checking his pocket watch constantly.

"Wife expecting you home for breakfast?" Tray asked at one point.

"Afraid my wife left me long ago," he said indignantly.

Leroux's mask caught a flutter of eye movement—stale grief, anger, and a half-truth.

"Oh, pardon."

"But I do have plans." He quickly laid out his whereabouts and activities since the Jubilee began. The Regulators could see no reason for keeping him, and let him rush off.

The maids—those who were suitably awake, anyway—were all appropriately scandalized when asked to divulge the goings-on of their employers. The kitchen staff were far more prone to gossip, but knew little of consequence.

After the employees came the Magistrate's wife, who had been by her husband's side the entire evening. Last to be questioned were the girls' parents. Tray and Krona mounted a sweeping staircase, moving to the upper level in order to take conference with the grieving mother.

A lone candle lit the nursery. Children in noble households typically moved into their own adult rooms when they turned ten—their second-fifth—a rite of passage poor Abella would never achieve.

Every item of furniture in the vast bedroom-cum-playroom was miniaturized, perfect for tiny hands and short legs. A small child lay tucked in a small bed near the window seat. On the floor next to her kneeled her mother, whose dark eyes stared at the opposite end of the room, where an identical—though empty—bed sat.

A delicate easel had been pushed into one corner, blocking access to a bookshelf. A stack of drawings, their edges frayed from shuffling, hung lifelessly from a clip attached to the wooden tripod. A few others lay half crumpled on the shelf, and still more littered the floor. Normally, Krona wouldn't have thought much of children's drawings in a children's room. There was nothing particularly out of place about them, except these had been . . . vandalized.

Each depicted the same thing: a humanoid creature in tattered blue robes. Some had pale faces, some had dark faces, but each was covered in a series of blue swirls. The figures were domineering, stance broad and menacing. Their fingers were hyper-elongated into points like knives, and the mouths split their heads in half—each grinning through a gash overflowing with an unnatural number of sharpened teeth. Atop their heads were spikes of various sizes—horns or imbedded blades.

Thalo puppets.

Bedtime stories.

The Thalo could not breach the border, that much was certain. Only its varger had found a way inside. But that wasn't how the story went.

It was true, the tale insisted, the Thalo could not enter the Valley itself, but it had devised a way, long after Absolon's time, to create puppets within Arkensyre—temporary beings without will or want of their own. Vessels through which it could terrorize and perplex, speak and taunt. It was said the Thalo especially liked to seek out liars and those with secret shames. You could accidently summon a Thalo puppet by carrying deep guilt.

There was even a poem. She remembered it well from youth:

The Thalo lives inside your eye,
The Thalo lives to make you cry.
Its puppets creep between the rain,
Its puppets creep inside your brain.
It can make you regret a face,
It can make you forget a place.
If you let it inside your head,
A Thalo puppet will surely
—Make—
—You—
—Dead—

They could erase your memory, become invisible, steal your secrets, and tear out your insides.

But it was a myth. Such manifestations weren't mentioned anywhere in the scrolls.

It wasn't the nicest bedtime story, but for many parents it had done its job, scaring children into behaving, into confessing their guilt. Krona's heart still thumped a few beats faster, remembering how she used to dream they'd come for her. How one night, during a thunderstorm when she was eight, she'd been so terrified she'd run into the rain screaming her apologies to the sky.

The number of Thalo puppet drawings wasn't what unnerved Krona. Children often drew monsters. What was especially unsettling were the eyes.

As she knelt to retrieve one of the creased sketches, Tray approached the woman. "Madame?" he prompted.

She did not stir.

The crinkling of stiff paper filled the quiet room as Krona smoothed out the pages. Someone had viciously taken a length of lead to the Thalo puppet's face—to the faces in all the images—swirling, pressing, obscuring the eyes until the pencil had broken through.

An oily feeling slid through Krona's stomach.

If De-Lia had drawn a Thalo puppet as a child, Krona surely would have scratched out its eyes, torn up the picture, or thrown it into a cooking fire. They were the kind of monsters you always feared catching out of the corner of your eye, the kind you were afraid you could summon just by thinking of them.

But that kind of childish fear and destruction was different than what Krona was looking at now. Whoever had drawn over these sketches went at them with a desperation, as though the monsters were despised on a *familiar* level.

"Your valet explained why we're here?" Tray continued, approaching Tia Iyendar like a wounded animal. "About this evening . . ."

"Yes," Tia croaked, though she did not move. In the faint light she looked like a life-sized doll with glazed, unseeing eyes.

Letting the picture flutter to the floor, Krona looked more closely at the woman. Her neck bore a clear puncture wound. It looked like someone had given her something—a tranquilizer, perhaps, or some other drug. A slight residue leaked from the perforation, and it looked a bit like quicksilver in the low light.

"Madame, forgive me, but . . ." Krona trailed off as she wiped the pad of her gloved thumb over the substance. She flashed it to Tray, who nodded.

Tray asked the usual questions, and Madame Iyendar answered in monosyllabic affirmatives or negatives. Leroux's mask was useless to Krona, as the woman's expression never varied and her mouth only moved enough to form the basic sounds. Tia Iyendar not only seemed incapable of deception at the moment, but also of full awareness. Tray had to ask many of the questions multiple times before she squeaked a reply.

"Was the apprentice to your family healer with you while your husband was at the party?"

"Mmm?"

"Mistress Dupont said you could confirm her whereabouts."

"Mmm."

"Was she here, with you?"

No answer.

Mid-questioning, Krona put a hand on Tray's arm. "We should stop," she said via the reverb bead. "There's nothing. Her will has fled—she could have orchestrated the crime herself and her anguished mind would no longer know it. When we see the young healer again, we need to ask her about what her master prescribed the poor woman. We should send a team to speak with him in person, as well."

They closed the door behind them and remounted the stairs. Finally, they approached the library and Fibran Iyendar. Still in his formal reds, the man sat limply in a high-backed chair.

If not for the seriousness of the situation, Fibran's appearance would have been quite laughable. Over his head someone had draped an aqua-colored wedding veil, most likely the one Mademoiselle Dupont would wear in two weeks' time. From its hem, dozens of tiny aquamarine beads dangled, shimmering gaily as they caught the reading light.

Fibran bore the silliest smile. He looked like a character Krona had once seen in a children's book. Or like a happy drunk. The enchanted joystones appeared to have muddled his mind. He consciously knew he should be upset—fueled with denial and sorrow—but instead he bubbled with delight.

"Come in," he declared, throwing his arms in a wide, welcoming arc. "Have you come to tell me more about the very special contraband, Mastrex Regulator? *Was* that you? Or was that you?" He gestured between the both of them. "Doesn't matter!" he declared a moment later. "You all look alike. Whoever it was, they were so kind—indulging me because my child is dead."

"We're sorry for your loss," Krona said lightly. "Please accept our apologies for adding grief on top of grief, but we need to know: What else do you remember about last evening? Did you see anything unusual?"

"Was the whole party not unusual?" he asked playfully. "Unusual place, unusual time—a Jubilee is most out of the ordinary. And varger!" He stood up abruptly, as though he'd just had an epiphany. "Varger in the city limits—

very strange." He sat back down again. "And Nightswatchmen carrying dirty carpets. Janitorial work during a party? How odd."

Krona digested this for a moment. "A dirty carpet? Was it, perhaps, rather full? Like an animal skin rug? Shaggy?"

"Yes—it might have been bear skin. Or sloth. Have you seen the coats they make out of sloth hair in Asgar-Skan? When I took the girls to see the Grand Falls a month ago, Abella asked where all the naked sloths were, since there were so many sloth hair coats in the shops." Fibran laughed hysterically, though he clearly meant to sob.

"These Watchmen you saw with the carpet, how many were there?"

"Three," he said with a trill, holding up the corresponding number of fingers.

"I may have seen these men," she said quietly with the reverb bead in her mouth. "Right before the real varg made itself known."

"Our perpetrators?" Tray mumbled.

"Perhaps."

Tray cursed under his breath. "I knew it—see, interviewing the Iyendars was a waste of time. We should have gone to the Nightswatch."

"Then we wouldn't know about the twins," she pointed out.

"So?"

"Monsieur," she addressed Fibran. "When did your daughters catch the blackwater fever?"

"Master Healer said it must have been on the trip to the Falls."

"Did anything unusual happen while you were abroad? Did the girls do or say anything odd? Did they interact closely with a stranger?"

"Perhaps. Maybe. A man, or—no. I don't know."

"Did either of them go missing for any length of time?" she pushed. "Were they out of your sight for even a moment?"

"They're children," he said with a silly gape of the jaw, as though she should think herself dim-witted for asking. "Have you ever tried to keep constant eyes on children out and about? It's impossible."

"Of course," she conceded, bowing apologetically.

"What are you thinking?" Tray asked into his reverb bead.

"I think it might not have been an act of Nature—the girls contracting a rare parasite."

"You think someone tried to assassinate a pair of nine-year-olds?"

A sadness coiled around her, and a tacky bitterness settled on her tongue. Why did the world have to be so harsh? So cruel?

"I think someone half succeeded," she replied.

Then again, things were rarely as they seemed . . . like the fidgeting, overly polite Mademoiselle Dupont. She'd made Leroux's senses prickle, and the woman she'd claimed could account for her whereabouts could not—whether due to the haze of grief or whatever she'd been injected with didn't particularly matter. Either way, something was amiss.

What was the apprentice healer hiding?

MELANIE

Two years previous

When Leiwood answered his door, he looked as though he'd seen a specter. He quickly shook his surprise, but she'd caught it. Melanie hadn't considered what she looked like with a frog where her face should be. "We must go to the apothecary," she said, demanding. That wasn't like her: impatient. But this was her mother's life on the line. She didn't need to waste time on courtesies.

He stepped aside and motioned for her to come in. A small fire crackled in the hearth behind him, and the room smelled spicy. "You country people keep strange hours."

It was a joke, but she didn't find it funny. "I need these things from the local apothecary." The list appeared, and she held it firmly before his eyes. "Quickly—we must have balance."

Nodding absently to himself, he took up his night jacket. "You're lucky the owner's a friend of mine. Fey might open for us."

She brushed past him into the hallway, with her posture tight and tall. She could feel it—a stiffness she didn't usually carry.

A cheery whistle on his lips, Leiwood locked his door. Then he held out his arm for her to take. She refused, and realized something.

"You're Victor's boy. Sebastian."

The lively flush faded from his cheeks. "I am."

"How's he doing?"

Leiwood turned his eyes away, focusing on his brass key ring instead. "He's dead. I told you. Been gone two years."

She started down the stairs. The information seemed simultaneously new and old. Had she heard of Victor's death before? "He was a bit odd, wasn't he? A little . . . off-kilter?" Unbalanced.

Work, she remembered. *I was studying . . . something . . . And Victor—* Refocusing, she shook the feeling. *No, I never knew Leiwood's father.*

"Melanie?" he asked. "Are you all right? Is the mask—?"

She felt like herself still. She was more brusque than usual, but she'd never been this close to her goal before. And still, there were things in her mind that could have been hers, or could have come from elsewhere. "I'm fine," she said. "I have it. I'm steady."

He let the conversation fade, and they headed out of the inn and down the street.

>-·-◦-·-<

In the poorer quarter where she and her mother had previously stayed, the streets had hummed all night. Melanie had thought the constant ebb and flow of the city was a dance that never ended, but this district was quiet. All of the respectable people had gone home to bed.

They passed a few vendors, a heap of sleeping vagabonds, and one woman dressed similarly to Melanie—but with paint on her face—who asked Leiwood if he wanted to "trade up."

"You like 'em masked?" she shouted when he didn't answer.

They turned a corner and Melanie had the sense to look indignant.

"What, they don't have 'nightingales' where you come from?" he asked.

"None who would be so rude to a pair of gentlemen."

"What?"

"Nothing."

The apothecary was a strangely shaped building, with a hexagonal domed ceiling made entirely of cobalt blue glass. It gave the place a peculiar watery glow when Leiwood lit the oil lamps.

The apothecary owner had not liked being awakened. Despite that, fey'd given Leiwood the keys and told him to return them with payment in the morning. Melanie was grateful they hadn't had to wait for the person to change out of feir dressing gown so that fey could accompany them.

Now, in the thick of pots, tubes, and vials of components, Melanie hurriedly read off the ingredients. Directing Leiwood to one end of the shop, she took the other.

"Slow down," he said, taking her hand. "If it's worth doing, it's worth doing right. You've struggled this long, we want to be sure it doesn't get mucked up through haste."

"But, balance—" She felt awkward. Things weren't in their place. The world wouldn't be right until her mother was cured. "My time's not my own until she's better."

"Real time, or bottled time?"

"Both." She saw a mineral she needed—a clump of yellow sulfur—and snatched it off the shelf.

"What will you do? When you don't have to spend the whole day watching over her?" Leiwood abruptly let Melanie's hand go, as though aware of how intimate the gesture seemed in the dim light.

She sighed and stared at the list for a moment. He was prying, and she wasn't sure she wanted to be opened. "I don't know. She's been ill since I can remember. My father was much older than her—I had to take care of them both for a while. To be honest I never really thought there would be a day when she wouldn't need me." She looked up. "You're right. What *will* I do?"

"At least you'll have time to think about it. Time to discover how to spend your time."

They gathered a few more items in silence. But try as she might, Melanie could not find one essential item: a large, specialized syringe. This wasn't entirely surprising; Belladino's knowledge told her that such enchanted devices were well regulated. Tax men had them, hid them, kept them out of the public eye. But once in a while healers required such things—most citizens probably didn't even realize there could be such a powerful enchantment hanging about while they bought their powders and their tonics. An apothecary of this standing would have access to a needle and all the necessary licenses, but would fey keep the precious item on-site or elsewhere?

A small voice in the back of her skull reminded her that she'd not received paperwork for additional enchantments. Only the mask. How much more might that cost? Could she even acquire such papers, or was her reach that limited?

Belladino told her to look for a safe. It wouldn't be enchanted—most likely—but it would be well locked. She was no locksmith, but a niggling in her brain told her not to worry about that. Belladino had known balance in his very bones, would help her find a way.

The safe was near the back of the apothecary. A large, imposing thing. Not just for time vials, no, but for minerals and chemicals that might prove too dangerous to simply leave lying about. A heavy padlock kept the box sealed tight.

It can't be that easy, she scoffed to herself, examining the keyhole and glancing over to the counter, where Leiwood had set the key ring.

Even as she swiped the keys while Leiwood's back was turned, her hand stiffened, her body resisted. She wasn't the stealing type. Clearly the chemist hadn't meant for them to go rummaging in the safe. Clearly she wasn't meant to take something she did not have license to wield.

Then again, the chemist hadn't said *not* to use the other keys, and after all, fey'd given them the whole ring.

And I am perfectly within the law to use such a needle, she said to herself. It sounded both true and untrue at the same time. She hadn't gotten permission for a needle . . . or had she? Her memory was clouded, the recollection fuzzy.

Wait, yes, she *did* have a license to use such a needle. How could she have forgotten?

She opened the safe with ease. Inside lay a myriad of various supplies, most of them with long labels describing what they must *not* be mixed with. And there, in the back, a locked glass case held the syringe. Intricate designs covered its barrel, made it beautiful. Melanie worked at the tiny-tiny lock on the box for several minutes—none of the keys were small enough to fit—before giving in to frustration and smashing the case with a weight from the balance scale.

"What was that?" Leiwood called.

"Nothing. I broke a box. I'll replace it." She waved away his concern.

"Be careful, please."

"Sure, sure." She closed the safe and replaced the key ring on the counter.

More silence. She glanced in his direction every now and again and found him watching her. It gave her strange, contradictory feelings in the pit of her stomach.

"I remember having my time bottled," he said suddenly.

"You can't," she laughed. *He must think me in a dull mood, telling me a joke.* Time was taken from infants.

"I do. I had it done late, because my father was trying to cheat the tax man. He never declared my birth."

She stopped her searching, and closed the cabinet she'd been investigating. She wanted to ask him if his father had been trying to protect him, to let him keep his time, or if he'd intended to have it done on the black market so that he could keep more of the money. Five years—that was how much the time tax took. It was all stuffed in little enchanted bottles and glass disks—four years to the city-state, one into your parent's pocket—then passed around as currency until someone had amassed enough wealth and got it in their head to cash out. Of course, cashing out meant having to pay a chunk of it to the tax men all over again, so that they could extract it from the glass and put it back. Some of yours, some of theirs, some of everyone's.

Thus was the goddess's decree. Time must be shared, time must be exchanged, time must circulate.

Though Melanie was most curious about his father's motives, knowing what she did about the man, she steered her inquiry in a different direction. "What was it like? Like when they take the emote tax at one's third-fifth? That was only three years ago for me."

Three years? Or a lifetime?

"Seven for me. And, no. No—that's a strange flaring of emotion, then a dulling. This was . . . painful. But I felt light-headed after, kind of euphoric. They took extra, as interest."

"That's not fair. It's your father who should have paid."

"He did, in triple."

Melanie drew in a sharp breath. "Oh, I'm—"

Leiwood barreled on. "The whole incident made me realize something at a very early age—about life. It's why I've worked so hard.

"I didn't inherit the inn from my parents. I earned it, all myself. Real time is far more valuable than bottled time. It has a better exchange rate. I decided I wanted to spend mine as productively as possible, get the biggest payout I could. That way, when I'm close to dying, I won't feel the need to cash in—to lay on extra days, or months, or years. Because I won't have any regrets. I think only people who waste their lives scrape for those extra minutes."

"It's kind of unfair," Melanie said, thinking about her mother, "that the time can only be tacked on at the end, not in the middle."

"And who spends those last cashed minutes well? People who die young never think to cash out. Only the old do it. And if you're not a noble then likely there are no time vials left to pay for the care needed for such an unnaturally long life. People living to seventy, even eighty. Can you imagine?"

"I heard a set of Marquises lived to one hundred and two, once."

"Exactly. But someone like me? With money to cash in, but not enough to sustain myself for those years after? Extra minutes as a broken, incontinent man are not ones I want." He came over to her with a sack filled with half the list. "And you know what?" He lowered his voice. "If people stopped cashing in, I don't think we'd have to harvest anymore. Babies would get to keep their time, as they should."

She gasped, her eyes darting around the empty room as though Time's priests might suddenly jump out and accuse them of blasphemy. She'd never heard anyone be so bold as to say the time tax shouldn't go on. That babies shouldn't have to do their duty as everyone before them had done. That the tax itself might be . . . wrong. "Sounds ideal," she said in a hoarse whisper.

He shrugged. "It's the way things were meant to be."

8

KRONA

I told you to stay outside the cave and stand guard. I wanted to prove that I was the braver. You always strode around the cottage like a rooster surveying his farmhouse. A cock thinks himself a king in the same way you as a child thought yourself the queen—without knowing how fragile you really were. But this story isn't about you, it's about me and the dark cave. I scrabbled down between the gray stones, scraping up my delicate baby-skin, poking at my loose tooth with my tongue to give me focus. Every move I made, every stone I knocked free, made echoing noises. When I'd nearly reached the dirt floor, I saw a glint of gold. Real gold, and I was sure I'd found some lost highwayman's treasure.

By the time Tray and Krona returned to the den, daylight was already warming the Valley's floor.

"Go home," De-Lia instructed them as they strolled in. "The recorder has your notes; he's nearly done translating. Go home and get some sleep."

Tray took her hand. "What about you?"

She nodded to a group of men in the corner adorned with glass ram's horns, speaking with De-Lia's superior. None of them appeared of good cheer.

"Martinets, still?" Krona hissed. "I told you—"

"Yes, thank you," De-Lia said sharply. "I have to answer for our failures, as I should." She didn't add any extra weight to "our," but it hit Krona with force nonetheless.

"I'll stay with you," she said.

"No. Go home. If they want to throw me on the stones of nepotism, you being here won't help."

"You need your rest, too," Tray said. "You'll start sleepwalking again if you don't sleep regularly."

"That's why there's a cot in my office."

"All right," he said, "but don't forget to use it."

Krona gave De-Lia one last look of guilt-laden sympathy, then turned in Leroux's mask. Its use left her more limp, and she slumped her way to the stables. But as she rode home, her strength returned to her. Many others wouldn't have been able to stand upright after a battle of the mind with Leroux.

De-Lia owned an apartment in the eastern publishing district. It sat over an inker's, and the building often smelled of lampblack and evergreen resin. Krona had moved in to help De-Lia take care of their mother. Most unmarried Regulators lived in the den barracks, but captains and higher-ranking Regulators received perks—like apartments—and Krona had been given permission to stay with her sister.

The living situation allowed Krona to save most of her time vials. But what she was saving for was unknown, even to Krona. A mask? A trip to the Falls, or for tracing her ancestry in Xyopar? An instrument of some kind? She remembered a wonderful concert at the Grand Marquises' theater—the cellist had been wanted for enchantment forgery, but that hadn't dulled his ability to play. Yes, maybe she saved for a cello of her own. Or perhaps she saved for all of these things, or for something the world had yet to introduce to her.

Either way, one day she'd use her time for something special.

Theirs was a well-put-together neighborhood. A district focused on printing and literature could hardly be a home for denizens bent on criminal pastimes. The residents were mostly learned merchants, with a few guardians of the state like Krona thrown in. However, in order to cut a direct path from the den on home, she did have to tread through seedier parts of the city. Even at this early hour, Krona still passed one lone nightingale, her tattered skirts pulled up past the knee and her face made up by unskilled hands in a terrible parody of a noblewoman's paint.

The nightingale approached her for a moment, eyeing the horse with an overly sweet entreaty on her lips, before taking note of Krona's uniform. The woman decided against soliciting a Regulator. Though paying for an amorous interlude was not illegal, a smart nightingale knew to avoid clients better armed than they. With a dry snort, she slunk back into the shadows, scratching her rear in a rather undignified manner.

Soon after, Krona clopped onto her home street, and sighed with relief when she caught sight of the arched door that led up to the apartments. Its wood had been stained cobalt blue, and small yellow panes had been inserted here and there to make it appear as though large honeybees crawled across its surface.

The building sat next to a line of government-controlled stables, where the civil servants in the area boarded their horses in the evenings. She dropped her steed off with the stable master, patted the creature absently—she liked the

horse well enough, but large animals had never appealed to her—then strode
back toward the honeybee door.

She pulled forth her brass key ring and realized it felt heavier than normal.
Her whole body felt heavier than normal. At any moment, she would drop into
sleep; she just hoped she made it to bed first.

The *thump thump thump* of little shoes hurrying her way made her stomach
drop.

What now?

Sighing, she turned from the door. Running toward her was Rodrigo, a
neighborhood boy who often brought her notes from an informant, and newspapers in the morning. She cringed, hoping she wouldn't see a headline soon
proclaiming the Blooming Butcher was back.

Sure as daylight, the boy had an envelope in hand.

"Mistress! Mistress," he called out between huffs.

"And what are you doing running letters so early?" she asked, struggling
to keep her voice from slipping into a singsong lilt, since Rodrigo hated being
spoken to like a child. He wasn't more than twelve by Krona's reckoning, but
that was neither here nor there.

"Getting paid," he said quickly, holding out both the letter and his empty
palm. Digging in her satchel for her purse, she found a few five-second disks
and dropped them in his hand. The feather-light glass coins tinkled hollowly.

"From Thibaut?" she asked, examining the inelegant scrawl of her surname
across the paper while jamming the building key into its lock.

"Who else?" Rodrigo pocketed the time and drew his shoulders up around
his ears as a sudden breeze stripped the streets. "Not that you'll hear from him
again soon."

She paused, lock half turned. "Why's that?"

"He's pissed off some Nightswatchmen again. Saw two of 'em cuffing him
about the ears before they hauled him away."

"What did he do this time?"

"Was running his mouth at 'em, far as I could tell. Maybe he done more, hard
to say. Expect he'll spend more than a fortnight behind bars just for the spite of
it. If . . ." Rodrigo thumbed at his brown nose and shuffled uncomfortably.

Krona knew stalling when she saw it. She flicked him an extra disk she'd
palmed just for this sort of pause.

With a smile, Rodrigo caught it, secreting it away without an extra word.
"If one of those Watchmen don't beat him to death first. I think he insulted
one of their wives—maybe one of their sons. Couldn't hear exactly. All I know
is they were right pissed and fixing to get violent."

Great. Leave it to Thibaut to make a bad night worse.

"Do you know which jailhouse they took him to?"

"For a fiver, sure do."

"You're bleeding me dry, pickle." She shook her head, resigned, and pulled out the time.

"Don't call me pickle."

It was back to the stables and the damned horse.

>-+<>-0-<>+-<

Red and yellow songbirds fought atop the iron spikes lining the roof of the single-story prison, battling for the best perch. White streaked the spikes and ran down the front door, detailing a long history of bird problems for the squat building.

Angry chirping rang all the louder as she entered, barely dulled by her helmet, punctuating the new day and her lack of sleep.

Inside, the Watchman at the entrance reclined in a rickety chair with his feet up on his desk. Feet that slipped as he startled. He hadn't expected a Regulator to stride through the door so early in the morning. Or, indeed, at all.

The floor groaned as Krona crossed the slats, dust puffing up between the boards. The jailhouse was small and decrepit, the kind drunkards lost hours in, the kind where no lawpersons in their right mind would bring any sort of real criminal.

"What can—what can I do for you, Mastrex?" the Watchman stuttered, rearranging his papers and moving his half-filled tea decanter from one side of his seat to the other.

"A petty thief was brought in recently. Tall, blond, good-looking man, passed his sixth-fifth a couple years back."

The Watchman sniffed dryly and craned his neck, popping a joint. "Can't say as anyone like that's been through here. All we drag in this early are vagrants."

Thibaut was nothing if not dapper, easily discernable from a homeless man. And Rodrigo wouldn't have lied to her—he'd have no reason, and it would risk too much.

A faint call—a yelp—emanated from beyond the entryway, somewhere in the small cell block that sat to the left, behind a heavy door and out of sight.

It wasn't the yip of someone startled, or the common catcall of a riled inmate. The yowl resonated with memories of sudden pains and sharp blows. Her muscles coiled, pulling taut across her shoulders, as she immediately swept toward the sound. "Open the door."

The Watchman scrambled out from behind his desk, attempting, awkwardly,

to bar her path. "You can't go back there. Need an order from higher up to interfere with the Watch, wouldn't you? I have no occasion to let you through."

Another cry, this one stiff and sharp—quick like a stab—echoed from beyond.

A thousand retorts tickled the back of her tongue, but she swallowed them
down. In the time she'd known Rodrigo, he'd never been prone to exaggera-
tion. If he said there were Watchmen gunning to see Thibaut ended, it was true.
And as insufferably reckless and deviant as Thibaut was, she would never wish
him a moment's pain. Now was not the time to defend her pride with verbal
spars.

"You best leave, Regulator." The smug suggestion was underpinned by a
series of thumps and whimpers beyond.

If she hadn't been thoroughly exhausted—if she hadn't been injured and
assaulted and shocked and humiliated only hours ago—she would have tried
to reason with him. Krona was nothing if not fair-minded.

But, as it stood, her body ached, her mind ached, and this rat of a Watchman was one of the last obstacles standing between her and her friend—even
if she never deigned to call him that out loud.

Moving slowly, as though her limbs were filled with sand, she drew her saber, giving the Watchman plenty of time to react. "You best unlock the door,"
she said evenly, echoing his arrogant lilt.

His frown of confusion was deeply satisfying. Protests flitted across his
knotted forehead: *But we're on the same side. I'm a member of the Watch, you
can't—For him? You'd threaten a fellow member of the constabulary for* him?

"What are you d—?"

"Keys, out," she demanded, drawing up, squaring her shoulders, using her
uniform to its full advantage.

Uncertain, his hand made an abortive move toward his pocket. Krona
understood—if he let her in, he'd have to answer to his colleagues. And if they
were willing to bash Thibaut around, they probably wouldn't give much more
consideration to knocking some sense into their glorified front doorman.

So she didn't give him a choice. Raising her blade, she held it level with his
throat. "What's it worth to you, keeping me out?" she asked in a low voice,
leaning in, making sure her eyeless faceplate filled his vision. "Because I guarantee that man back there is worth a lot more to me than you're willing to
give."

His shaking wrist disappeared into his trouser pocket like a snake, sliding
swiftly in and out. He jammed the key into its slot, then stepped back, swinging

wide around her saber. With hands upheld—washed of all responsibility—he gestured her through.

"You beat it out of me," he said firmly, his tone despicably conspiratorial.

Disgusted, Krona almost lashed out with the butt of her sword to give him a black eye. For good measure, of course. To aid in his chicken-shit story.

But she didn't have time to play. Krona inched the door open, far enough to get a good view of the cells beyond but not to reveal herself.

The block was little more than glorified closet space. Three working cells near the front, with the stone crumbling around the bar fixtures, and at least a half dozen more out of commission. Some were used as storage, some had no doors, and some were missing their cage fronts altogether.

This jailhouse was one commissioner's visit away from demolition.

The first two cells held semi-sleeping vagabonds, each with their hands over their ears to block out the sounds coming from the third cell, which held Thibaut.

Her thief sat hunched over on a cot, curling as best he could into the corner of the cell, hands cuffed behind his back.

"Ach!" he called out as a heavy boot came down on his insole.

Knowing better than to rush in, Krona tabulated the scene.

There were four Watchmen. Two in the cell with Thibaut, two outside. All of them wore shabby coats and fraying suspenders, each looking only one step above the vagabonds in cleanliness.

She took quick stock of their visible weapons, guessing they weren't the type to roll over at a quick command, from a Regulator or otherwise. Should things turn sour, she needed to know who posed the greatest threat. He would need to go down first—through persuasion or force would be his call.

Both men outside the cell leaned against neighboring bars on either side of the narrow cell-block hall, arms crossed and faces turned away from her. Smugness radiated from the set of their shoulders and the casual nods they gave one another when one of their colleagues got in a jab they appreciated.

Neither sported holsters, nor sheaths. If she was lucky, they had no more than knives at their disposal.

One she saw in profile, catching a glimpse of his particularly petite nose and elfin chin. He was young, new to the Watch. Soft.

The second had weathered hands and an ungainly bow in his spine, emphasized by his protruding gut.

Inside the cell, one man did most of the talking while the other did most of the punching.

"You want another?" asked the talker. He was three days removed from his last shave, and surely weeks removed from his last bath. As he gave a meaningful glance to the man beside him, she marked him as their captain. He had an authoritative, if brutish air about him. "Go ahead, open your pretty mouth again and ask for another."

The fourth Watchman cracked his knuckles, eager for the opportunity to land another strike. At the term "pretty mouth" he split his own lips with a cruel smile, looking over his shoulder to raise his eyebrows at his mates.

Several of his front teeth were missing, likely lost to fists that had answered his blows.

Thibaut glanced up at the taunt, uncurling slightly. His clever eyes gazed past the Watchmen, catching the line of black at the cell-block door. Recognition quirked the corners of his lips, and he smiled at Krona, revealing bloodied teeth. His once well-coiffed hair stuck up haphazardly atop his head, his usually pressed clothes were disheveled, and his cheek sported a bright-pink blotch that would soon purple. Despite all that, his grin broadened, knowing his salvation was at hand. "Funny, I said the same thing to your son just last evening," he chuckled at the captain, spitting a bloody glob on the man's shoe. "Poor boy couldn't get enough of me."

"My son is happily married," the talker said smugly, refusing to rise to the bait.

"Well apparently his husband isn't giving him enough—"

"His husband is a well-respected banker down on—"

"Well," Thibaut tittered. "You know what they say about *bankers*."

Damned idiot never knew when to quit.

"Why you smudgy piece of—"

As Toothless pulled back for a gut punch, Krona shouted and slid fully into the room, drawing everyone's attention.

"How'd you get in here?" Little-Nose asked as his face blanched.

"Ask your boy out front," she snapped. "And back away from my prisoner."

"You're a ways out of your den, Regulator," said the captain. "Man's behind our bars, so reckon he's ours."

"Not to play with as you please. Release him into my custody and we won't have a problem. I won't report you to the Martinets for abuse."

All four men prickled. Little-Nose and Bow-Spine straightened. Captain Dirt and Toothless sauntered out of the cell, fists balled.

"Oh, what abuse?" asked Thibaut casually. "I can tell you, some people pay for this kind of treatment. If you're looking to pick up extra time vials, gentlemen, I know a few nobles . . ."

"You ain't even got a partner," Captain Dirt said to Krona, ignoring Thibaut, head cocked to the side. "Which probably means you aren't here in any *official* capacity. So why don't you run along?" He snorted, wiping the spit on his shoe against the long, scratched line of a cell bar.

She raised her saber. "Turn him over. That's the last time I'll ask nicely."

Bow-Spine and Little-Nose drew daggers, as she'd expected. Toothless stuck to his fists—which she could appreciate—while Captain Dirt ambled into one of the run-down cells, taking up an iron bar that had rusted at both ends.

Everyone moved slowly, yet deliberately. They were trying to call her bluff, and she theirs. No one wanted things to get bloody.

Except maybe Toothless. He grinned ear to ear, as though he hadn't dared hope for this much action so early into his shift.

"You really don't have to fight over me, there's plenty to go around," Thibaut quipped, sounding chipper, though he winced as he tried to sit up straight.

"Shut up!" everyone shouted, including one of the homeless men who'd given up pretending to sleep.

"See, I can take him off your hands," Krona tried to reason. "Make sure you never have to hear him flap his lips again."

They inched toward her, crowding her into the door. They weren't going to let up, and she certainly wasn't going to back down.

She doubted the Watchmen knew how to work in tandem. They'd individually search for openings, thinking of only her moves and their own, never trying to play off one another unless someone took her to the ground.

Toothless worried her the most. It took a confident man to face a sword bare-knuckled.

Which meant he had to go down first.

"Nah," Captain Dirt said, swinging the bar up to rest on his shoulders. He pushed his way to the fore, standing beside Bow-Spine. "See, my problem ain't with his mouth so much as his hands. They wander where they shouldn't."

"Think we ought to chop 'em off," said Bow-Spine, "for the safety of the general public."

"You wouldn't *dare* remove such fine specimens from their even finer wrists," Thibaut scoffed, faux scandalization dancing on his tongue. "I need these beauties in order to blow kisses to my admirers."

"Would you—" Bow-Spine spun, teeth bared at Thibaut.

Krona saw her opening. Lunging forward, she smacked his hand with the flat of her blade. He dropped his knife in surprise, and she kicked it away, behind her.

Dirt swung with a shout—the bar careening toward her helm. Dropping to one knee, she avoided the impact, which sent Dirt off-balance. He'd expected to make contact and pitched sideways when he didn't—knocking into Bow.

Toothless lost his grin, and Little-Nose lost his nerve. The former came forward while the latter stumbled back. Shoving his colleagues aside, Toothless reached down for Krona, heaving her upright by the front of her uniform.

Which gave her the angle she needed.

Arm outstretched, his elbow was vulnerable. Flipping her saber, she jabbed the heavy end of her pommel against the back of his joint.

He shouted and let go, his arm falling limp—clearly, alternating numbness and needles ran the full length of his limb.

Rising, she kicked out his left knee, pressing down on the cap from above until it popped out of place. He slid to the floor, gasping in pain.

"Stay down or I'll take the other," she commanded, just as Dirt charged her again.

He brought the bar down like a hatchet, looking to shatter her shoulder. She swung her lone bracer up to meet it. The metal clanged, but it wasn't the same high-pitched catching of sword on sword, and her forearm still took the brunt of the blow.

Hissing through the pain, she parried the bar aside.

"To your right!" Thibaut shouted the instant before hot agony ripped through her love handle.

Bow-Spine had retrieved his blade.

"Enchantment-bearing bastard," he hissed at her from behind, twisting the knife.

Snapping her elbow back, she caught him under the chin. He reeled in reverse, smacking his head against a set of bars and sliding to the floor.

The fire in her side pushed her from resolute to angry. Dropping her saber—letting it clatter to the floor—she dove at Dirt, wrenching the bar away with both hands before backhanding him across the jaw. He tilted to the side and fell, stumbling face-first into Toothless's lap, where he lay still.

"You see that? You see?" Thibaut said conspiratorially to Little-Nose. "Uncuff me and Mastrex Regulator will spare you, I know it."

Still gripping his knife tightly, Little-Nose weighed his options.

Taking high breaths through her nose, Krona straightened her spine and reached for the dagger protruding from her love handle. Though she burned from buttocks to shoulder, she could tell the blade inside her was short, and Bow's aim was less than outstanding. Yanking it free, she growled through the spike of agony. Everything hurt like a bastard, but she'd live.

Scooping up her sword, right hand staunching the wound, she shuffled toward Little-Nose, who held his blade aloft, but trembled with indecision.

"I don't know what you're thinking," she said, voice rough with the pain. "But is keeping this sniveling, pale, letch of a man worth *that*?" She swung her saber to indicate the three beaten Watchmen.

Dear Time, please say no.

She was exhausted.

"Letch is taking it a bit far," Thibaut huffed.

Whipping her sword at Thibaut, Krona gritted out, "Gods help me, if you want to leave here with all of your fingers and toes—"

"Take him," Little-Nose decided, knife slipping from his fingers. "Free him, hang him, hand him over to one of the Grand Marquises as an anniversary gift, I don't care. Just *take him*."

"Thank you," she said, exasperation barely showing. If blood weren't dripping down her leg and three grown men weren't groaning on the floor, one might have thought she'd won little more than a haughty debate. "Now, out."

Young man knew to do as he was told.

With the troublesome Watch dealt with, Krona attended to Thibaut. First she looked over his head wounds; they were nothing more than superficial. As she swept the fringe of his blond hair away from a cut, he hissed, whole body tightening.

"Sting, does it?"

"Yes, sir."

"Good." She patted his chin, avoiding his split lip, and did not rebuke him for the "sir."

Even beat up and cuffed, Thibaut carried himself like a man who owned the city. He could beat the Marquises themselves in a tournament for pomp and superciliousness. And that was part of his appeal; nothing could dampen his mood or darken his view of the world. He was ever-positive.

An unusual trait for a thief, consort, and all-around *public menace* to possess.

"Well done, Regulator," he said, taking in her thorough demolition and nodding with approval. "To whom do I owe my thanks?"

"None of your business, criminal."

It was a show they were forced to put on, for safety's sake. Informants soon became *inform-nots* if they proved too familiar with the constabulary. These Watchmen would keep quiet—why would they want to spread the tale of their utter ineptitude?—but Thibaut's fellow prisoners would have no such shame to hide.

"But, answer me this," Krona said, tone still rough-edged. "What *do* they say about bankers?"

"Haven't a clue. Did you see the way his eyes bugged out at the very suggestion, though?"

Krona laughed silently in her helm. Cheeky bastard.

Satisfied with his visible wounds, she concerned herself with the hidden.

His gentleman's coat had been pulled down to pool around his wrists, and his deep V-necked tunic hung loose about his frame. His trousers and boots were dirty, but bore no gouges or tears, and he still wore his signature green leather gloves.

"Lean back, against the wall," she ordered, rucking up his shirt.

"Well, aren't you forward?" he snarked, raising an eyebrow, but complying nonetheless.

"I don't want to have you collapsing on me halfway to the den." A bruise blossomed across the subtle ripples of his abdomen. "If you need a healer, I'd rather know sooner than later." She pressed against his sides, looking for evidence of cracked ribs. Luckily, his bones were intact. "Anything else hurt?"

"Just my shoulders—uncuffing me should do the trick."

"That's a well-practiced joke. Do you tell it often?"

"Oh, har har."

She pulled him back together as best she could, then helped him to his feet. He limped slightly as she led him out of the cell, but more from stiffness than injury. Needing to step over Bow, he kicked him instead. "You're lucky you got the jump on me," he said. "I could have had you down twice as fast as Mastrex Regulator in a gentleman's fight."

"Don't you think that's enough antagonizing for one morning, thief?"

As they hobbled nearer the door, Thibaut pulled up short. "Wait. Wait." He shuffled over to one of the occupied cells and whispered, "Windom?"

The "sleeping" vagabond gave a grunt.

"My cot was empty, if you catch my meaning. Might I bother you to check yours?"

The heap of gray-and-brown tatters reached awkwardly beneath his bare bones of a bed, groping the underside.

Krona glanced at the Watchmen. Two were officially unconscious. Toothless groaned and rolled onto his back, but didn't make any further effort to rise, or to push Dirt off his lap.

A gentle *pop*—that of dried wax pulling free from a hard surface—preceded Windom holding up an envelope. "This what you're after?"

"Yes, that's it."

Krona grabbed Thibaut by the collar, hauling his ear close. "Are you telling me you got thrown in here on purpose? For that?"

"I'm not an idiot. You believe those overstuffed sacks could bring me in if I didn't want them to?"

"Why do you think *I'm* in here?" Windom asked, sitting up. His hair was long, as was the style of the times, but was heavily matted with a beard to match. "It's a dry place to sleep. And they're obligated to give me a plate of beans." He placed the envelope on the stone floor and flicked it, sending it sliding up to the bars.

"Mastrex Regulator?" Thibaut said, twisting to display his shackles. She huffed and he tittered at her. "I'll have you know I'm letting you in on a very well-kept communications secret. The least you could do is pick up the letter."

"I touch it, I keep it," she informed him, crouching to do just that.

"Who says the letter's not for you?" Thibaut asked with a smirk.

"Seeing as how we've never *met*, criminal, I doubt it."

Remembering the game, his smile fell away.

But it did make Krona wonder if it was the truth. Had he gotten himself picked up by the Watch for her sake? The envelope was clean, unblemished by creases, and had an unpressed black wax seal. Extra wax on the back had kept it secured to the cot.

She pocketed it and rushed Thibaut away.

Out front, the young deskman was still there, sitting sheepishly in his chair, apparently pretending to be deaf, since that was the only "reasonable" explanation for why he hadn't noticed the brawl beyond and gone in to help. Little-Nose was nowhere to be found.

"You remind them," she said to the deskman in passing. "We all forget this happened, they stay away from my prisoner, and we don't have to get the Martinets involved. And if I ever have to come calling here again, I expect a better reception."

"Yessir."

Outside, her horse picked at a patch of grass growing through the sidewalk. There were more people on the street now—the day was in full swing. Krona was sure she'd forgotten what sleep was like.

"You expect me to ride like this?" Thibaut asked, eyeing the mare.

"Of course not," she said, pulling a length of rope from her pouch.

"You wouldn't," he said, eyes widening.

She almost felt sorry for him. Almost. But now that she knew he'd gotten himself in trouble on purpose, putting him through the paces seemed the thing to do. "Need to keep up appearances. At least for a few blocks. Don't worry, I'll go slow."

Forming a loose loop, she lassoed Thibaut around the neck, keeping the rope's end fitted in her glove, then mounted. Though she hated riding with her helmet on, she was well versed in climbing a steed while top-heavy.

Thibaut looked up at her from beside the horse with the pitiful expression of a lost puppy. He'd used those sad blue eyes to his advantage on more than one person in his time, and Krona would be damned if they were going to work on her. "It's only until we're out of sight. There's an old tunnel to the Dregs not far from here. Blocked off, but it'll give us cover."

Resigned to his current predicament, he obediently hung his head and let her lead him.

Having Thibaut leashed was more satisfying than Krona would ever admit. Not because it kept him near her—oh no. Of course not. And not because it meant he wasn't hanging on the arm of some well-dressed nobleperson as their consort-of-the-day, which was how he made his bread.

A well-tied Thibaut was a well-behaved Thibaut, and that was a simple rarity she was going to enjoy.

As promised, it wasn't far to the disused tunnel, even in the crowded streets of morning. They had to contend with one blocked thoroughfare—a horse-drawn trolley had been stalled because of a stone wedged in its tracks—but beyond that their pace was fair.

The tunnel itself was a utilitarian eyesore stuck between two municipal buildings. Lutadites might have happily kept the way open, but it had been blocked from below.

Beneath Lutador proper was a second city: the Dregs, whose people shared its name. They were the disenfranchised and homeless who'd found homes with each other—outcasts with no place in Lutador society. They preferred their life underground, and—with the exception of the time tax and the emote tax—were left alone by the city-state officials, provided they remained below the streets.

The tunnel went back a few yards, and held a draw for various unsavories as a covered camp. But its placement near official government sites meant it was frequently patrolled and kept empty. It still smelled of campfire smoke, and the walls sported etchings made by sharp stones and shaky fingers.

Krona tied the mare outside and removed her helmet before leading Thibaut in. There she uncuffed him using a skeleton key from her pack. He did not pull away when she rubbed his wrists and arms to help the blood flow.

"Ach, pins. Pins everywhere." He shook himself, snapping his elbows outward as if banishing the feeling. "Thank you," he said after a moment. "Sincerely. I'd planned on spending a good long while in that stink hole, but I had not expected the complimentary beating."

"Oh no? It sure looked like you were ordering from the menu."

He pulled the tie from his hair, shaking it out before quickly pulling it back again. "Some throwback runs his mouth and I'm supposed to ignore it?"

"Yes."

"But it's so much more fun when you can taunt them with the truth."

"What truth?"

"Is it my fault I give his son palpitations? The young man is striking, too—must look like his mother. Gods know his father was never aesthetically pleasing. But, alas, his husband must keep a tight watch on his time vials. Handsome boy couldn't afford my company."

"I'm surprised anyone can."

Thibaut leaned against one wall and examined his gloves, rubbing away a bit of dirt and a fleck of blood. "I'm cheaper than you think."

She glared at him. "No, you're not."

"I bet even someone on a Regulator's salary could afford me," he said lightly, barely glancing up.

Thibaut wasn't a nightingale. He didn't go in for nests and servicing anyone who came through the door. But he spent time with people he liked who had the time vials to spare. Spent time out and about—was *seen*. Nobles used him to pass the time while their spouses were away, or to make one another jealous. He let them dress him up in fineries, and take him to wine tastings, and balls, and trail him under their disapproving fathers' noses.

If Thibaut had learned anything about himself since adolescence it was this: he was attractive. And, in the right company, a pretty face and toned stomach were as useful as a purse full of hundred-minute vials. He'd bought himself many secrets with the bat of his eyes alone.

But, as much as he liked to play the suave philanderer, he was a petty thief at heart. It was an addiction, really—it had to be, what with the number of times Krona had needed to spring him from a cell to keep him on the streets and his information flowing.

"That's not how this relationship works," she said carefully. "Why should I pay for an audience when I can punch out four lawmen and get it for free?"

"Relationship?" Thibaut pushed himself off the wall and shoved his hands in his pockets. He regarded her coyly, head lowered and cocked to one side.

"Have the Five heard my prayers? Are you finally going to make an honest man out of me?"

"Oh, shut up. That might work on the nobles you *press* for information, but it won't work on me."

"That's why our affiliation is different. You give me something no one else does." He gently pushed into her personal space. She was a tall woman, but he was an exceptionally tall man. She had to look up to meet his gaze, but rooted herself to the spot. Refused to back away.

"Where's my payment?" he asked softly, bowed lips parted boyishly.

"What, exactly, am I meant to be paying you for?"

"I told you: that letter's yours. Course, you might need an interpreter. It's likely coded. So, give it up. I'm sure you must have *something*."

"I've trained you too well. Like an animal waiting for a treat."

"My, aren't we bossy today?"

She backed away, digging in her hip pouch. Free of his heat, she turned away and took a cleansing breath. "You're lucky I've been expecting to hear from you. I don't normally keep toys among my—" His fingers caught fast on her hip, and her breath caught near as quick in her throat. "What are you—?"

Kneeling down, Thibaut pulled at the frayed edges of her uniform, where Bow's knife had found her. "This isn't a scratch, Mistress. You need stitching."

"The blood's drying," she said over her shoulder, trying to glimpse him at the odd angle. "Barely nicked the muscle, I suspect. What's another uneven scar?"

"The blood is *not* drying, " he protested, "and in order to scar it has to heal. Come, let me see better." He tugged at the tight, thick leather, trying to fold it aside.

"I didn't know medicine lay among your credentials," she said, helping to tug her uniform out of the way. Now it wasn't just the wound that burned, but her cheeks as well. He was so close, she could feel his breath ghosting across the skin of her back.

"Truthfully, I'm no good with injuries," he admitted, pinching the pucker of the split, making sure the skin lined up evenly. "But ignoring a wound doesn't make it go away. Believe me."

She caught a sad twinge in the edge of his voice, meant to ask about it, but his next prod sent a needle-like jab into her side and she gritted out a yelp instead.

"Pardon," he mumbled.

"Are you helping or playing back there?"

"Funny how often you find my mucking about and my sincere efforts indistinguishable. You carry salvation sand, do you not?"

"That's only for emergencies. It'll make the wound ten times worse later."

"But later you will have seen a healer."

"Thibaut—"

"*Mistress*," he countered in the same irritated tone.

She sighed, searching through her pouch once more, bypassing the tarnished trinket she'd been digging for in favor of a small silk purse. "Only a pinch," she instructed, handing it to him. "The more you use, the greater the aftereffects."

"Understood."

Grains of pale sand slipped from the purse to form a neat pile in the center of his green-gloved palm. Faceted, they caught the light from the tunnel opening with a glint, like fine-cut gems.

Salvation sand was a powdered enchantment. Two parts silica sand, one part titanium flakes, one part snakewood dust. The ingredients were burned together and infused with magic—each particle bore its own microscopic enchanter's mark.

Thibaut paused for a moment, silently calculating how many time vials it would take to purchase the teaspoon of healing in his hand. "You realize how much I could get for—"

"Yes, I do. So don't waste it."

Dabbing a bit onto his forefinger, he drew the sand across her wound. It grated, feeling at first like an assault rather than a salve. Her muscles twitched with the desire to pull away, to snap at him, but she held herself still.

Slowly, the pain ebbed. Her skin pulled taut in a sluggish drag while the cut disappeared—the injury vanishing as if erased.

It would only buy her an hour, if that. And when the enchantment gave way, when her body seized upon the intrusion, the cut would open again, bleeding profusely and extending deeper than the original. If she didn't have it attended to properly, the damage would be worse than if she'd never used the sand at all.

"Thank you," she said quietly, hurrying to straighten her uniform, to move away from Thibaut's gentle touch.

"Always happy to attend to my mistress," he said without bravado, handing the purse back. "Even if the balm is temporary."

What a fine summary of her time with Thibaut: he was a temporary reprieve in a world full of wounds.

She weighed the purse carefully before placing it back in her pouch, but it was impossible to tell if he'd stolen a pinch or two for the lining of his pockets.

"And now—" She located the old wind-up and tossed it vertically between them.

He caught it awkwardly off one shoulder and examined it. "It's—I'm impressed. Where did you get it?"

"Knew you'd like it."

It was an antique copper-and-bronze frog. It once possessed jeweled eyes, but those had long ago been lost, judging by the amount of tarnish in the sockets. With the proper key, the frog could be made to jump in a lifelike manner. With another, its mouth would open and its tongue would unfurl. Supposedly, it could snatch live flies out of the air. Such toys had been made by a single court artisan decades ago. When he'd died, a death mask hadn't been enchanted. His intricate knowledge of mechanics and clockwork had been lost for good.

Unfortunately, the frog was not in the best of shape. But Thibaut liked to tinker; perhaps he could fashion the keys and fix the dents and dings.

Thibaut's eyes sparkled as he rolled the toy over and over between his palms. Childlike giddiness quirked his lips and made Krona smile. "I've been looking for one of these for years," he said with glee. "Mistress Hirvath, I could kiss you."

"None of that," she said, then laughed. "Only you would flirt with someone in a Regulator uniform." *After getting arrested, then trounced, and subsequently arrested again.*

"You're not half as scary as you think you are," he said, returning to his lazy lean against the wall. He flicked the mouth hinge on the toy open and then shut again, already disassembling it in his mind.

"Payment made. That should buy me your letter, your 'translation,' and a few more tips to boot. These little delights of yours are getting harder to find." He didn't need to know she had a ripe stock of clockworks for him stashed away in her cubby at home. Scarcity drove the price up, after all; the better to buy more secrets with. It also made his elation all the more special for its sincerity and sudden onset.

"Are there other tips you're looking for? That"—he gestured vaguely, meaning the envelope—"is in regards to your Belladino inquiry." He squinted at her, jaw clenching noticeably as he tried to look past her layer of levity to the disquiet beneath. "Your smile doesn't quite reach your eyes this morning, so what happened?"

She let the mask fall. No use playacting if her performance was poor. "I haven't been to bed."

"Was there an incident at the Jubilee?" His gaze made the briefest of stops on her bandaged arm.

Her hand instinctually fell to her saber, though she had no intention of drawing it. The solidness of the pommel was comforting. "How did you know I was at the Jubilee?"

He held his hands up—frog included—to illustrate he was well intended. "How do I know the Second Grand Marquis is currently hobbled by gout? How do I know obscure religious records are disappearing from the Hall's archives? How do I know about the guards stationed at the Valley's edges to prevent anyone from traveling to the rim? Not a very good informant if I don't keep well informed, am I?"

"Point one: two of those are conspiracy theories, not information—"

"And the third?"

"Everyone knows the Second Grand Marquis is far too fond of sweetbreads and kidney. Point two: you're supposed inform *for me*, not on me, so why would you take special note of my assignments?"

"Does a dog not wonder where his master goes all day?"

"You're not a dog."

"Aye. Funny how you leap to decry that casting, versus the other."

"You'd rather be a dog?"

"I'd rather you not obfuscate the point."

"Fair enough."

"Now, what happened at the Jubilee?"

The light pouring into the tunnel was far too bright, and Thibaut was far too chatty, and Krona was far too drowsy. He would only get a perfunctory story this morning. "A break-in. They distracted the crowd with loose varger, and then took several items of great—"

"Worth?"

"Hazard. We are unsure how they were able to get inside the gala so . . . efficiently."

"You'd like me to look into it?"

Krona rubbed at her eyes before pinching the bridge of her nose. "Please."

He tossed the frog lightly in the air, catching it on the back of his gloved hand and rolling it to his elbow, then back again before pocketing it, displaying a level of dexterity Krona was sure she'd never possess—even with a full night's sleep. "Will do, Mistress. Now you, I think, have another appointment to get to."

"Oh?"

He gently took her by the shoulders and turned her toward her horse. Any other time she would have resisted, but she'd given all her fight to the Watchmen and had no left for Thibaut. "Yes," he said sweetly. "With a healer, then your pillow. I will look into your 'efficient' theft and call for you in the usual way once I've found something."

"Thank you."

"You must be tired," he chuckled. "There are far too many niceties falling from your lips."

"I can be amiable. I *am* amiable," she insisted, though for the life of her she wasn't sure why it was a point she felt the need to argue. Putting one foot in front of the other was growing more difficult by the moment, and her uniform suddenly felt too tight. Why was home so far away? Why were there still so many tasks between her and her cubby?

"Yes, a fact which you do your damndest to hide when you're thinking straight." They emerged onto the street and Thibaut gave her a shove toward her steed before stealing back into the shadows. "To bed with you, my dear. I'll see you again soon."

After several abortive tries, Krona heaved herself onto her horse and rode off, Thibaut's second letter in her pocket and his chuckling lilt tickling her ears.

9

MELANIE

Two years previous

Melanie and Leiwood returned to the inn with sacks of minerals, chemicals, and dried herbs. As they walked, Leiwood seemed to drag his feet, which she found galling. Her impatience from earlier was restored posthaste.

Was he trying to exasperate her? Did he not see how important it was to restore the equilibrium? The asymmetry fed on her nerves, tore at her muscles, weighed heavy in her chest. There was a struggle going on in every fiber of her body, demanding she cure the problem.

An image of a dead cat and a weeping, disheveled girl came to her mind, unbidden. It frightened her, and she vehemently shooed it away.

Back at the inn, Melanie didn't want to wake her mother, so they went to Leiwood's room instead. "Mortar, pestle," she demanded, snapping her fingers at him. Obediently, he drew the tools from one of the bags. While she worked, he set out the rest of the gear: a small burner, some test tubes, a beaker, and the syringe.

Into the crucible went sulfur, calcium, and dried reishi mushrooms. She topped it off with a liquid catalyst that glowed an eerie, subtle green. "It has to rest for several hours," she declared after thoroughly mixing the substances. "This cure demands time."

Leiwood sat on his bed, giving her a sideways look. He'd been staring at her strangely since they'd gone out to get the ingredients. It worried her. Annoyed her. Disturbed her.

Just like his father, she thought harshly. *Brutal man . . . killed my daughter's cat.*

Melanie pulled up short, confused by the thought—she wasn't a mother. Within an instant, that confusion turned to fear as she tried to tell Leiwood about her wayward thoughts, tried to ask him if that was how it started—if *this* was, in actuality, what he'd meant.

Her lips parted, but her throat closed. She was shoved down in her own body, pushed, compressed, torn away from her own hands, her own voice. Something else was taking control.

She watched herself wander over to the fireplace and look deep into the red coals. "They say I'm a great healer," her voice said.

No, no, no. This wasn't happening—couldn't be. It was a Magnitude Zero mask. *Magnitude Zero.* Third Tier. Harmless, useful. A *healer's* mask.

Leiwood's answer came tentatively. "Master Belladino was, yes."

"I could cure any ailment," her voice continued. "Save the dead from dying."

"Melanie?"

My unfinished work. The thoughts weren't her own, but they filled her brain, pushed out whatever she might be thinking. She was on the verge of panic, except her body didn't think so. While her mind reeled, her body remained calm. She struggled with it—with him? with Belladino?—but their thoughts were sticky, mixing, intertwining. She didn't know where the echo of this man's life ended and where she began. *I died before I could finish my work.* "But there was one thing I couldn't figure out how to balance. One illness I couldn't find a cure for." *Cat. Dead cat.*

"You mean August Belladino. There was something he couldn't cure?" His tone was wary.

It's not me, she tried to yell. *Leiwood, it happened! In the blink of an eye, it happened! I'm, I'm—*

I'm Master Belladino, she thought firmly. Calmly, with certainty.

The cat. Victor killed it. Then he . . . Then he . . . She . . .

"Cruelty." She picked up the iron poker and thrust it into the hearth. "It resides deep, somewhere most medicine can't reach. And I never could figure it out." She whirled around. Leiwood's eyes were wide, and sad. His expression made her angry. "Did you know that a lot of sickness stays in the family? That it passes from parent to child?"

"Melanie . . ." There was a warning in his voice. A tension in his spine.

She raised the poker, pointing it at him. There he was; she could see Victor Leiwood hiding under that shocked expression. Sick man.

"Do you know what he did to her?" she screeched.

Leiwood was on his feet in an instant, arms out, imploring. "What? Who?"

"My daughter!" Melanie ran at him, swinging and thrusting the iron. Claw-like fingers sought to curl around his collar and draw him in. She wanted to impale him, to open him up. "Let me see it!" she shouted. "Where is it? Where does the abuse live? Down in your belly? In your spine? Show me, Victor!"

"Melanie!" he shrieked, jumping back. "It's not you. Fight the mask. Fight it! I didn't do it." He launched pillows and oil lamps and a table in her path—anything to stop her. "I'm not my father! I'm *not*."

Wrath blurring her vision, she plunged the poker forward, barely missed Leiwood, and embedded the point in a plush chair.

This isn't right, she realized, backing away, terrified. *Leiwood has done nothing but help me. He's a good man.* But an image of his father flashed before her eyes, and the hatred returned with a vengeance. She fought it, trying to keep separate from the feelings. "Leiwood," she said, distress pervading her voice.

"Melanie? Take off the mask!"

She curled her fingers around the edges and pulled with all her strength. The mask wouldn't budge. It had fused to her face, holding on like a leech. "It won't—It—" Her heart beat radically in her chest. Panic filled her limbs, making her hands shake as she scrabbled at the wood.

In the next instant she was flying after him again. Deep, rumbling accusations spewed from her mouth. She didn't even sound like herself.

She tried to force the duality, to separate herself from the echo once again. There was Master Belladino, enraged, hell-bent on tearing Leiwood apart—and Melanie, who wouldn't hurt a thing. Especially not someone who had been so good to her.

"Help me!" she cried. And in her next breath, "You *filth*."

Melanie wrestled with herself, desperate to escape the essence that possessed her body. "The fire!" she yelled, and moved in its direction. But she tripped on her own feet and fell short.

"What are you doing?" He didn't flee, but he kept away.

"Burn it," she urged. *"Burn!"* Inch by wavering inch, she crawled across the floor toward the fireplace. Melanie urged him to hurry, and Belladino damned him the whole way. She felt sick, insane. She wasn't worried about the flames—about burning skin. She just wanted to be alone again.

Leiwood rushed forward, grasped the mask, and pulled. It didn't come loose. Melanie grabbed his wrists and growled.

"I can't get it off," he said, defeated, searching her eyes—half-hidden behind the wood—for another idea.

Melanie pleaded, "Put it in the fire anyway."

><+>–O–<+><

Melanie's words said *do it,* but her body writhed, desperate to escape. "No," Leiwood said. "You'll—There's got to be something else." But the memory of his father's mask—then the hatchet, which Leiwood had swung toward his own face—his own brush with death . . . Perhaps fire was the only answer.

But then he thought of plunging her face into the coals. It made him sick, and he knew he couldn't do it.

Leiwood backed away, leaving Melanie to grapple with herself. She clawed at the neck of her blouse, tore at her hair. One moment she looked like she was strung out on an invisible rack, her spine pulled taut, then it snapped loose again like a band of rubber.

Trying to think fast, he spun toward the heap of apothecary items. With shaking hands, he picked up each substance and read label after label. At a loss, he thumbed the syringe, then the burner. None of the items provided an answer.

He heard a scraping of wood on wood and looked up. Melanie was dragging herself toward the fire once more, facedown, mask grating against the floor. She didn't look as if she could stand much more.

"Wait!" he shouted, bounding over to her. Heart pounding, he grasped one ankle, stopping her progress toward ruin. "Fight it. Give me a little time, I'll think of a better way."

"Son of grime," she raged, reaching forward and grasping the hearth's hot grate. The rancid scent of charring human skin wafted into Leiwood's face.

With a hefty yank he hauled her in reverse, simultaneously scanning the room for something to restrain her. The only things that seemed reasonable were the drape cords.

The cords were tied neatly around wrought-iron window hooks. He struggled with the knots—distress made him clumsy. He bumped the nightstand that held a lamp and his pocketbook and they tumbled to the ground.

His purse burst open, and bottles of time went bouncing across the room.

Stunned, he watched one roll to the foot of the table. His gaze went back to the apothecary items. An idea struck him.

Scooping up one of the time vials—a fiver—he leapt over Melanie's twisted form, then skidded to a halt beside the medicines. In the next instant the syringe was in his hand, poised above the cork that kept the time contained.

It was illegal—and nearly impossible—to release time without a tax collector present. The time was kept in by enchantment, and only things designed to contain enchantment could break the magic seal.

Average people rarely saw the needles. The time tax was taken before they could talk, and unless you were a tax taker or someone else in the upper echelons of control, you might not have a chance to see one again until you were elderly, and that was only if you were cashing out.

He should have flashed on the needle before—he'd only seen one other like it. Leiwood remembered the needle from when he was young. From when they'd made him pay the time tax.

It was special, and rare, something you had to have a license to obtain, and looked dramatically different from the syringes that took the emote tax—each of which was tiny, made of glass forged of sand and crushed gemstone. This was large, substantial, the glass thick and clear.

Had Melanie taken it from the apothecary? She couldn't have known before the mask how to obtain such a thing, or likely even what it looked like. That was all Belladino.

What would happen when the time was let go? He'd never heard of anyone setting it free before. It was pulled from people, stored in vials, and put back in people again. All he knew was that he needed some—time, real time—more than what he had. Time to think before Melanie threw herself into the flames.

He jammed the needle deep into the spongy cork and pulled back on the plunger. As the barrel filled with a swirling pink-and-turquoise essence, the bottle cracked. Once empty, it turned to dust.

Without another thought Leiwood pointed the needle in Melanie's direction and shot time into the air.

Everything stopped. There was a stillness to the room, like on a winter's morning after a heavy snow. When he noticed even his breathing had stopped, he started to panic, but quickly focused.

He was seeing double—as if two stained-glass images were superimposed. But not quite, because the images weren't identical.

There were new things in the room—wispy, ethereal things, the same color as the essence of time. There was a new plant in one corner, a handprint on the windowpane, and smoke—as from a pipe—over the bed.

Melanie was frozen, her rigid, burnt fingers outstretched for the grate once more. He was grateful that the mask hid her expression, because surrounding her head was a *creature*. It was something between an amorphous blob and a tentacled monster. The bulbous body grew out of the center of the mask, and the translucent arms reached out behind her, like streamers caught in a high wind.

He wanted to lunge at it, but wasn't sure if that was the right thing to do.

What were they, these newly revealed things? They couldn't be physical objects; he'd stood right where the new plant sat.

Perhaps they were things that existed in time only, separate from space.

A faint pulsing drew his attention to the ceiling. Splayed across it were symbols, constantly shifting. They weren't words, or astrological signs. The speed at which they changed reminded him of a countdown.

There were five minutes in the bottle—that was all the time he had to decide what to do.

The fire. First he'd put out the fire.

He moved to put the syringe down, but caught sight of what it had become. The superimposed version of the needle was bigger—almost like a dagger. And the two metal circles of the finger grip now extended up and over his hand to his wrist in a partial gauntlet. Things that looked like spiny vines wound up his arm from there, all the way to his shoulder, where a protective plate with moving—living?—parts rested.

The syringe let him interact with time without being caught in it, like Melanie was. It was the key.

And the cure. Never mind the fire.

Leiwood ran at her. Diving forward, he plunged the dagger-needle between the frog's eyes—Melanie's eyes—and pulled on the plunger. A small drop of blood entered the barrel with a faint fog of time. He'd pushed too deep, failing to consider the softness of the balsa. Lightly, he scaled back, pulling the needle out just a tad.

When he pulled on the plunger again, the creature on the mask suddenly moved. Its tentacles clamped down around Melanie and its body quivered. The bulbous portion shimmered and resolved into an ugly caricature of a human face—Belladino's face, tainted and twisted with hate. It bit and howled at Leiwood.

"I'm sorry, I—" But there was no use in Leiwood apologizing to a half-formed time-specter of a man for things he had never done.

He struggled with the creature, sucking at it, more desperate to separate it from Melanie than before. His arm shook as he applied force to the plunger. Soon the thing began to shrink, absorbed into the mask and then drawn up the needle and into the barrel.

The last airy bit of the creature caught, Leiwood withdrew the needle and backed away, examining the syringe. The mass inside swirled like an angry, bottled storm.

10

KRONA

The gold in the cave wasn't part of a highwayman's hoard. The glint I'd seen was off a quintbarrel needle. Six of them lay in the dirt, catching the thin shafts of light that sliced between the stones. I recognized them for what they were—I'd seen Papa polish his needles and clean his quintbarrel many times, but he'd never allowed me to touch the ammunition or the gun. Papa will be so pleased if I bring these home, *I thought.* He'll pat me on the head and tell me I'm his favorite daughter. I know he liked to tease us, telling us each in turn that we were the favorite—he thought it amusing—but I truly believed it was a competition. I gathered the needles as quickly as my little limbs could scramble. Clutching my treasure, ready to race you home, I made to climb back out. But that was when I heard a deep rumble in the cave. A growl.*

Ascending the stairs was a chore. The air around Krona's legs felt sticky and thick—like wading through honey. She stopped at a neighbor's door—a retired healer on the ground floor of the building, who was often up with the first spikes of daylight.

The woman wasn't much for human company, preferring instead the parrot from Asgar-Skan she let roam around her apartment freely. But she accepted Krona's offered time vials in exchange for a quick stitch job over her sand-sealed wound.

"Still too early in the sand process to tell exactly what I'm looking at," the old healer said. "Remember to get yourself to a working professional once the sand has worn off."

She set a fresh bandage over the spot to catch any stray blood that might appear, and sent Krona on her way.

When Krona came to the deep-brown door of the apartment, she sighed heavily before managing the lock.

Acel Hirvath was used to her daughters coming and going at unholy times.

Her husband had been in the elite heavy-pack Borderswatch, and it only made sense that her headstrong girls would inherit his need to serve Lutador.

So the elderly woman didn't so much as blink twice when Krona came in, helm under one arm, expression like warmed death. Krona was not surprised to be hit full-on by the smell of burnt coffee and frying squab eggs when she strode through the door.

"I take it the party was a lively one," Acel said, gaze flickering from frying pan to her youngest daughter's face for a fraction of a second. She brushed her long, thick braid of gray hair out of the way as she plated the eggs and set them in the middle of the table. The rickety thing shifted, the barely-there weight of the eggs forcing it onto a different combination of its uneven legs.

"Livelier than it should have been."

"Where's De-Lia?"

"She hasn't come home? Still at work, then."

"But you threw in for the night?"

"It's morning, Maman. And De-Lia sent me home."

"So it is." Acel was always direct, no matter how far a little graciousness might go. She sat down in one of the mismatched chairs that rounded the table, tucking a stained fabric napkin into the neckline of her housecoat. "Breakfast?"

Krona's stomach turned over. "No, thank you."

"Suit yourself."

Wobbling slightly, Krona headed for the curtain that cordoned off her room. "Maman," she said, drawing the thin drape back. "Please don't hassle De-Lia when she comes home. It was a long night. It's turning into a longer day."

"Hassle? When have I ever hassled either of you?"

Krona bit her tongue and left the question unanswered.

Pulling the curtain flush with the wall, she lit the candle by her cot. A small, round window near the slanted ceiling let in a feeble glow from the morning sun, but not nearly enough for her tired eyes. The room—if it could really be called that—reminded her of the cubbies they kept the masks in: small, but comfortable, and specially formed to its occupant. A twin flame flickered in the mirror on her nightstand, and she glanced at it for the briefest of moments, catching a glimpse of her exhausted form. Her high cheekbones looked sharp instead of rounded, and her eyes puffy. Her full lips were overly chapped. All proof she needed sleep.

On a level shelf just under the window, a line of small clockwork items sat, ready to be dispatched into the world. She'd been collecting them for years now—a special currency for a nation of two.

She tore open both envelopes—the one from Rodrigo and the one from the jailhouse—with her teeth, placed them side by side on the bedspread, and proceeded to peel off her uniform as she read.

While gingerly tugging at the remains of her left sleeve, she realized her maman hadn't asked about the bandages.

The first letter was a cypher. The second was written in code.

The message was short. It said the shopkeeper's records were incorrect and had been altered. It insisted Shin-La HuRupier did not *exist,* and was likely not even the name given to the owner when Belladino's mask had been rented.

How that could be possible, Krona wasn't sure. The shop owner's catalog was enchanted itself, and no one but the shopkeeper should have been able to alter it.

Was this some kind of insurance-related confidence gambit? Could the shop owner have created the forgery and altered his records, all while keeping the real mask in reserve, perhaps for a shady buyer?

Swaddled in her nightclothes, Krona tucked herself under the ragged old blanket, and swiftly set her many fine braids beneath a sleeping scarf. In the next moment her head fell to the pillow, and she slept more soundly than she had in weeks.

▷•◇•○•◁•◀

The scratch of metal loops against the rod roused Krona, and light from the kitchen flooded in as De-Lia threw the curtain back. "Get up," she demanded, startling Krona awake.

A vivid image of their childhood home faded from Krona's memory. "What is it?" she asked sleepily.

"A runner came from the den—he said there's been a murder."

Krona's groggy mind wanted to snap, *Not my department,* but then she caught on. "Does it look like Charbon's work—the work of the Mayhem Mask?"

"Yes."

Already.

She tossed off the blankets, muttering curses. Thibaut's envelopes caught in the billow and fluttered to the floor.

A sharp pinch and a dull throb had her grasping at her back before she could sit up. Her palm came away slick with blood. The stitching had held, but the old healer had missed the bottom edge of the wound.

Glimpsing blood on the sheets—and not where one might expect to find it now and again—De-Lia startled out of her impatient huff. "What's that?" she demanded, rushing forward to grasp her sister's uninjured forearm. "You're hurt."

Without waiting for an explanation, she pushed Krona onto her stomach. A red stain soaked her nightdress through, giving a ruby hue to the once light pink flowers that dotted the fabric. The cotton clung heavily to her skin, refusing to pull away at first when De-Lia tugged at it.

"This isn't from the Jubilee . . . ?" De-Lia asked.

"No. I—" Krona winced as De-Lia rucked up her nightclothes—partially because of the sting, mostly because of embarrassment. She wasn't a little girl anymore who could be manhandled by her demanding older sibling. "There was . . . Thibaut was in trouble—"

"Say no more." It was a demand more than a platitude. She didn't want to hear about Krona's "criminal friend," which was her favorite dismissive. A cut she could handle—gruesome or not. A cut was straightforward, without moral implications in and of itself. How one obtained such a wound, though, spoke volumes. And this cut sang melodies De-Lia did not care for, in a song she wished hadn't been written.

Official sanctions were neither here nor there in Krona's arrangement with Thibaut. Regulators were not to associate with the likes of forgers, black market dealers, or con artists, no matter the tactical advantage. De-Lia generally glossed over Krona's "ill-conceived" associations, as long as Krona remembered not to wave evidence of that association under her sister's nose.

"How did Utkin only half stitch this?"

"I used salvation sand. And it wasn't Utkin, I had Madame Ska-Dara from downstairs do it."

"You should have returned to the den."

"I was exhausted."

"You've got to take better care of yourself."

Krona pushed herself up on her elbows. "That's a gem, coming from you."

"What are you two bickering about?" Acel chimed from the kitchen.

"Nothing, Maman," De-Lia insisted, leaving Krona's side and exiting the cubby.

Clenching her jaw, gritting her teeth at the sharp *throb throb throb* of her back, Krona dropped her forehead to her pillow. She thanked De-Lia for her discretion—Acel did best when kept in the dark about certain aspects of their lives, injuries being a particularly important point to shy away from.

If their maman could pretend not to see an injury, she would. It was De-Lia, growing up, who'd doctored Krona's scraped knees and stubbed toes. Anything more severe—anything that reminded her of her husband ripped open on the kitchen floor—Acel could not ignore, with frantic consequences. Worse still, she could not abide the sight of blood. If Acel laid eyes on Krona's stab wound, De-Lia would have to spend more time soothing Acel, settling her panic, than tending to Krona.

After a brief, dismissive exchange with Acel, De-Lia reappeared, a bottle of whisky in one hand and first-aid measures in the other. "You'll still have to see Master Utkin, understand," she said, "but this'll tide you over."

A quick splash from the bottle cleared the cut of excess blood and grit. Krona bit into the fabric of her pillow, the line of her back pulling taut with the sudden sting, and she cursed between her teeth. De-Lia patted her shoulder sympathetically.

De-Lia's fingers were practiced and tender, having attended to many a triage situation in the field. She worked Krona over just as quickly here, at home, as she would have at a park or amongst refuse bins in an alleyway.

As a final precaution, once she'd staunched the blood and pulled the wound closed, De-Lia wrapped Krona's middle in a long swath of bandage, putting perpetual pressure on the cut.

"Done," she declared flatly. "How did I do?"

Krona, sitting up fully, twisted and turned, testing the dressing.

"Ah—not too much of that," De-Lia chided. "I'm no healer and this isn't meant to last."

"Thank you."

De-Lia smiled sadly at her sister, brushing a fallen, curled braid from Krona's forehead and tucking it behind Krona's ear. "Of course. Now—" She slapped her knee playfully, standing to retrieve a twine-tied bundle from outside the cubby. "Here. I pulled it for you from the reserve. It might need tailoring, but should do for now."

It was a new uniform. Krona couldn't very well go out with a tattered sleeve, and now, a torn side. A Regulator had to be pressed and perfect—imposing and dignified.

"Put it on. We need to go before the trail grows cold."

"Wait—what happened with the Martinets?" Krona asked as De-Lia turned to leave.

"I will be censured," she said placidly. "How severely depends on how quickly we can recover the mask and the despairstone. And how much damage they cause in the interim."

"Did you sleep any?"

"A little." She ran a hand over the stubble on her head, not meeting Krona's gaze. She was lying for the sake of brevity; they had someplace to be, now was not the time for an argument. "Hurry, please."

"What's the hour?"

"Late. Well after lunch." De-Lia closed the curtain on her way out.

Wishing she had time for at least a sponge bath, she finished pulling on her boots and knotting back her braids. One quick glance at her bandages to make sure the seepage was minimal, and she was ready to work.

Both sisters kissed their mother, then headed back into the streets.

>-+◇-○-◇+-◄

Louis Charbon had been a killer. And he'd liked it.

Some variation of *Death is art* was always written next to the bodies. Sometimes he'd written *Death is Absolon Raoul Trémaux* instead—a grotesque play on the savior's initials. Sometimes with ink, sometimes with blood, sometimes with worse. He turned his victims into what he called "blooms"—disgusting parodies of flowers, splayed open, spread out in horrifying detail.

After his twelfth victim, the Dayswatch had taken him down. He'd screamed about dissection and conspiracy and the horror of the gods all the way to the noose.

Charbon was not Lutador's most prolific murderer, but he was the most terrifying. Nothing can stop a man who thinks his violence is not only justified, but the epitome of virtue.

When the Watch hanged him, his "righteous" destruction should have ended forever.

How a *Teleoteur*, Eric Matisse, had created the mask, no one knew. But the *why* was both obvious and stomach-turning.

Only one man knew how to cut a body just so. Knew where to break it and where to bend it and how to bind it so that it no longer looked like a person, but a lovely rose or fragile daisy or intricate orchid. And only an equally misshapen psyche could want to preserve that knowledge for later retrieval.

He'd been dead ten years. But now Charbon was killing again.

Once they arrived at the abandoned storehouse, Krona kept back from the body for a moment, steeling herself.

She worked with artifacts. Most of her concerns were straightforward, simple locate-and-retrieve. Sometimes situations devolved into violence. Sometimes people died. But she'd never had to stare at someone whose insides had become their outsides.

Thankfully, a heavy black death sheet had been pulled over the poor person's body. But it couldn't conceal the smell. The victim was still fresh enough that the flies had not yet found it, so it wasn't a stench she had to contend with, just a hint of sour wrongness in the air.

On the nearest wall was the expected message: *Death is ART.* But, in an unsettling twist, it didn't stop there. In smaller blood-spatter, a little below the killer's tagline, were four new stomach-churning words: *The truth is coming.*

Krona took a deep breath as the Dayswatchman yanked back the sheet for a moment, to let the Regulators confirm with their own eyes that this was indeed a bloom.

Her first impression was not of viscera, but a tiger lily. The reddish-purple petals drew upward and folded out in graceful arcs, and from the center of the bloom, a carpel and four stamens, all tanned, jutted toward the storehouse ceiling.

But the beauty only struck her for a moment, for an instant before her senses caught up with the reality of what lay before her. The petals were the victim's abdomen, peeled open, and the carpel and stamens were the victim's limbs, stuck upright in the center of their gory torso, their hands and feet limp and long, mimicking anthers. Somewhere underneath it all, propping up the bloom, angling it for display, was the skull, the face likely flayed to conceal their identity.

Nausea and anger roared inside her, churning together, making her chest grow hot and her jaw clench beneath her helm.

Who could do such a thing? What kind of hands did it take to perpetuate such violence? What kind of psyche looked at another human being and thought, *I'd like to break that*?

She imagined a man in a sleek top hat, striding down the darkened streets, his silver cane tap-tap-tapping along the stones. A woman walked past, caught out alone well after she should have been home with her family. The man watched her go, his eyes gleaming as a smile split his features. His sharp incisors glinted in the gaslight, flashing like the edge of a blade, as he turned to stalk the woman to her end.

A predator after its prey.

Shivering, Krona crouched down, studying the red and purple lines of the victim, noting how they'd been bent and broken so precisely. *Yes, those are petals,* she noted, *and that's the pistil, there are stamens . . . But what's that?*

Charbon was known for using all of the body to make his flowers. And yet, there was a portion missing. Off to one side was a small, gory heap.

De-Lia knelt next to Krona. Sliding their glass faceplates upward on grooves in their helms, the sisters made eye contact, shared a look. One equal parts pity and determination. "What's that look like to you, on the hand?" Krona asked, pointing at one of the limp wrists.

"Yes, I noticed it too," De-Lia said. "A gash in the center of the palm. A thick needle mark?"

"From the despairstone brooch? Or an injection?"

"Perhaps. Bastard." She clapped Krona on the shoulder before rising again. "We'll get him." They both let their faceplates click back into place.

"We don't know what it is yet," said one of the Dayswatch—a woman—pointing to the portion not included in the bloom. "We'll have it inspected, find out what he removed."

The body had been found by a ten-year-old boy. He played here often because there were no people, only pigeons. But today he'd heard voices.

"He saw two men," the member of the Watch continued. "One was masked. That's why we sent for you." She led the Regulators to where the child sat, ankles crossed, at the foot of a broken staircase.

The building was dilapidated, as were most of the structures in what the Regulators affectionately called the "non-district" of the north. All the glass in the windows had long ago been removed for repurposing, the doors were gone, and the finish on the walls peeled back like flaking skin.

Another member of the Watch was with the boy, had him gently by the biceps, speaking softly. Tear trails stained the boy's light brown face. When the child caught sight of the Regulators he cried out, anguished, and reeled backward, trying to scrabble away. He'd already seen so much horror today, and the nightmare figures approaching him were too much.

The Watchman held him all the tighter. "They won't hurt you," he insisted.

"Hey, hey," Krona said, as delicately as she could, already moving to take off her helm, to show him that she was just a person, that she had a face.

"De-Krona," De-Lia said in a warning voice.

"He's not going to talk to us like this," she shot back. "I'm sorry you had to see this," Krona started, kneeling down and placing her helm to the side, cherry red faceplate turned away. "What's your name?"

The child hid his face in his own shoulder, still tugging at the Watchman's hand.

With a few more gentle entreaties, some reassurances, and a recap of what he'd already told the Watch, Krona was finally able to get him to look at her with his big, brown eyes. De-Lia stood by stoically.

"What's your name?" Krona tried again.

"E-Esteban," he half sobbed.

"Can you tell us what the men looked like, Esteban?"

"The mask was spooky," he blurted. "It had horns all over—six big ones—and a huge black tongue behind sharp teeth. All blue and orangey and red and purple and yellow. And white."

"Do you remember anything about the person wearing it?"

"He was tall?" he said uncertainly, sniffing wetly. "Not as tall as you. Maybe he was short. He had a, a big voice, though."

"Loud?"

"No—I don't know. *Big*. Like he thought what he was saying was proper important."

"What did he say?"

Esteban lowered his eyes and mumbled, "Rubbish about the Five."

De-Lia crossed her arms as though impatient. She'd never been good with children. "And?"

"My maman says only halfwits believe in the Five, and I'm not to talk about them." He sucked in his cheeks, like he'd been popped in the mouth a time or two for exactly that.

Krona prickled, but kept the irritation out of her voice. Atheism was a new fad. Thinking humans were alone and forsaken had become fashionable, both with some of the upper nobility and those in the lowest of stations.

They claimed magic was a natural phenomenon, like gravity. That it didn't have to be placed on the rim by some conscious beings, it just *was*. They said the scrolls weren't written by Absolon's hand, that maybe Absolon hadn't even existed. Some scrolls had been forged, that much was true, but they said it was fact for them all. And the Great Introdus? Just a creation myth, a way for early people to explain the unlivable conditions beyond the Valley rim. Krona, personally, took offense to such flippant disregard. "We won't talk about the gods, just the man in the mask. We need to know what he said so we can catch him. You won't get in trouble for telling us what he said."

Doves cooed in the rafters as though voicing their skepticism.

Wiping his nose, Esteban continued. "He said the Five were angry and he needed to be rid of the people who made them angry. And that he had to show people beautiful things. And something about proving himself to a lady because he was sorry. Or something. His talk was pretty—you know, proper. Like a rich man's talk. And he had white gloves on his hands. But I didn't see . . . I don't know anything else." The child fell silent.

"And the second man?" De-Lia asked.

"White. Pale like flour. But I never saw his face. And he wore a black cloak. I didn't . . ." His lip quivered. "I didn't truly see anything. *I don't know*."

Krona patted his knee, and Esteban surged forward, throwing his pudgy arms around the wide expanse of her shoulder.

"I want to go home," he sobbed into her shoulder.

What he'd seen could not be unseen, no matter how many *Emotioteurs* poked and prodded at him with their needles and their jellies. They could take the terror, or revulsion—numb the trauma—but his innocence was done for.

Without hesitation, she encircled him in her arms, forcing the Watchman to let go. "We'll get you home. A Watchman will take you home."

Heaving him up and away from the steps, she carried him to the door, where the Watchwoman they'd spoken to stood. The Watchman trailed her. When Esteban was squared away, Krona returned to De-Lia, who was scouring the dirty ground for anything the Watch might have overlooked.

"He spoke well," Krona noted. "Could the man in the mask be a noble?"

"Hard to say." De-Lia kicked at a fallen beam, half eaten through with rot. Black beetles scurried out of the wormed holes.

"We need to look into Charbon's past. We might be able to better decipher what the current murderer intends to accomplish using the mask that way."

"He intends to sow terror, discord, and mayhem," De-Lia said bluntly.

"But, couldn't he do that on his own? What does using the mask mean to him? We can't know unless we understand what *Charbon* means to him. If nothing else, that might help us guess when and where and who he'll kill next."

She imagined now not what it was like to be the victim, stalked in the streets, but what it must be like as the killer, *inside* the mask. What corruption could Charbon's echo visit upon the brain? She'd wrangled many, many echoes, had dealt with viciousness and callousness and desperation. But the echo of the man who knew how to do that? Make *that* out of the human form? A man so depraved that his mask couldn't even be legally rated?

Encountering him had to be like encountering a varg. Wanton violence, utter carnage, even if it was only mental.

And then the aftereffects . . .

She shuddered, sure they would be hell. Perhaps even for someone as skilled as her.

"Who he'll kill next . . ." De-Lia repeated.

The truth is coming hung in the air between them like a bloated mosquito—ugly and blood-filled.

"But we have a victim. And we have your false varg," De-Lia said firmly. "Isn't it more important to find out who *they* are? Rather than go chasing ghosts?"

"We can't dismiss the mask's role. I know echoes. I know that they want to travel the same paths they did in life. If the murderer in the mask cannot suppress Charbon's, it will consume him. Charbon's desires will become his—that may be what he hopes for, to embody Charbon. If I can predict—" She bit her tongue.

De-Lia looked at Krona squarely. "Time does not allow for soothsaying. Her path is steady, is it not?"

"It is not soothsaying," Krona said sharply. "It is perfectly linear to assume that someone might behave as they have before."

"And you believe discovering Charbon's motives means recovering the enchantments more quickly?"

"Yes."

De-Lia sighed. "Fine," she said, the word tumbling reluctantly from her lips. "But you must admit that your not-a-varg is a more salient lead."

"Is he conscious?" Krona asked.

"I don't know," she said, black-gloved hands sliding over her faceplate in frustration. "He wasn't when I came home this morning. But I suggest you find out." De-Lia paused. "Unless you'd rather someone else question him? For *his* sake?"

Krona tensed. She was a Regulator, damn it. She could control herself—he'd make it out of the interrogation alive. "No. I'll do it. Let me go to the Hall of Records first, collect what I can on Charbon and bring it back to the den. Then I'll interrogate the prisoner. *Me.*"

De-Lia stared at her for a moment, stationary as a statue. Krona wished she could see her face, decipher her expression. After a moment, De-Lia relaxed, giving the beam another kick for good measure. "Don't be too long. If the man is awake, if his mind is sound, we cannot dally."

No, Krona thought, *dallying will only lead to more death. All Charbon ever wanted was to terrorize and torment—we can't allow him to sow mayhem all over again.*

II

LOUIS

The Coterie of the Lone Marquis,
noon, eleven years previous

All Louis Charbon ever wanted was love. He wanted it safe, he wanted it near, he wanted it constant. And he had it. He had the warmth of his girls' smiles, and the heat of his wife's hands, and the temperate giggles of his newborn son.

Whenever ill events befell his family—and they had—they did not come about because of fear, or cruelty, or apathy, but through a failure of imagination. Charbon saw the world as good, as ultimately just, regardless of the misfortunes of any given moment.

That he could not see that darkness was real, that wicked deeds were filled with wicked reasonings, was his ultimate flaw.

And Una told him so, often.

"That boy stole your watch," she said to him, jostling through the gate of the coterie with the other afternoon's worshipers. "You shouldn't have given him a fiver."

"If he took it, he has more need of it than we do."

She smiled at him affectionately, holding their newborn to her chest, guarding the infant's small frame from the crowd around them. "You are too sweet, Louis."

Charbon tugged at his daughters' hands—the younger, Nadine, on his left, and the older, Gabrielle, on his right—hoisting them playfully over the threshold. Gabrielle was nearly too big for such maneuvers. "'Too sweet' gives you toothaches," he countered. "I merely induce toothy grins."

"Someone is in a good mood," she observed.

Of course he was in a good mood. This was their little boy's first outing. They would announce his name today.

Lutador city had been built at the fork of the Praan River, where it rushed southward from Marrakev, splitting into the Saengmyeong and Zhyttya water-ways before rejoining once it was past the Asgar-Skan boarder. Nestled in the water's embrace, the south side of Lutador was flat, southwestward portions of it a swampy floodplain and southeastward portions fertile farmland. Directly to the east and dead west, the land rolled into hills, up and up, reaching above the rivers in daunting cliffs. These sheer stone bluffs, once home to forts and military foundries, were now the center of politics and noble-positioning. The palace of the Grand Marquises occupied the highest prominence in the west, and various lesser mansions and sleek houses poured down the hillsides to border on the city proper.

It was here, at the seam of wellborn and common, on the edge of noble finery and municipal drudgery, that the Charbon family worshiped.

It was fitting, for Louis specifically. As a lesser noble of good financial standing, he and his family had every right to attend coteries farther up the hill, away from the average peoples of the city-state. But he'd also chosen the life of a surgeon. He'd stitched as many commoners as he had noblepeoples, and found they were all much the same under the knife.

Entering the elaborate walled complex of the Coterie of the Lone Marquis was a surreal experience, as it was meant to be. The coterie was the oldest in Lutador, one of the founding buildings. It had seen the surrounding land turn from village to military base to town to metropolis, and still it maintained its ancient—if dark—charms. The wooden structures that formed each god's cloister had all been constructed from whole trees, each sealed with so much heavy, aged pitch that the buildings looked fire-blackened.

All of the adornments were very Marrakevian—with carved reliefs depicting tundra-running elk and rabbit, and pieces of fur lining the garments of the gods' statues, despite the overall temperate climate of Lutador. Each cloister was capped with a slanted hip-and-gable *irimoya* rooftop, seen few other places in the city.

The only modern touches were the wind chimes—made of yellow and green rectangles of stained glass—which hung from every protrusion: off gutters, off tree branches in the center parkway, from the parapet of the outer wall and buttresses in the inner sanctums. They made a high-pitched tinkling with every breeze—each chime subtle on its own, but collectively they rang out like a cacophony of birdsong or insect chirps.

Today the incense smoke was heavy, and Charbon told his girls to cover their noses. If the smoke turned the outer beams of the building tar-colored, what must it do to one's insides?

Linked together, the family moved toward Emotion's cloister. The baby sighed softly as he clutched at the pendant pressed tightly against Una's collarbone, and Charbon frowned. He'd always been skeptical of emotion gems——he didn't enjoy having his feelings altered, and in turn didn't know how he felt about a child, not more than three months, experiencing emotions he was not yet capable of forming on his own.

He cleared his throat and nodded. Una caught on immediately and carefully pulled the infant's hand away from the cushion-cut peridot. The boy instantly became more restless, but she cooed gently in his ear, running her hand over the fine hairs on the back of his mostly bare head.

Charbon did not begrudge Una her rapturestone. Many of the men and women around them bore similar fineries, and here and there acidic green glimmers cut through the low-hung haze. The man just ahead of him in the crowd wore a single peridot stud in his left ear. Another person had donned a set of inlaid silver bangles that clinked as they strode forward.

One woman in particular——a Madame Doma——sported a woven gold collar filled with pebbled peridot; one hundred of them glittered against her throat like limey pearls. She was prone to ecstatic outburst during scroll readings, often overcome by the feelings of rapture and providence bestowed on her by the enchanted gems.

As his family passed into Emotion's cloister, Charbon nodded to the shrouded priests of the Unknown who held one of the ancient wooden doors splayed.

The moment he stepped over the threshold, a cry emanated from the courtyard. "Help! Anyone. My wife——we need assistance! We need a healer."

Both girls let go of his hands and grabbed onto Una's skirts. They knew their daddy well.

He pushed his way outside once more, over to the circle of stones in the center courtyard where the Shrine of the Five stood tall.

A young woman in a long black dress sprawled across the grass at the base of the stone circle. Her skirt was yanked up past mid-thigh, revealing a long gash in her leg. She cringed and pulled at her yellow hair while a graying man with bushy eyebrows attempted to staunch the bleeding with his kerchief.

Another healer, Mistress Ada, already knelt at the woman's side. "Let me see. You halfta give me a look, monsieur, else I cannot do a thing for her."

"I fell on the rock," the woman said, pointing at one of the granite protuberances.

Charbon recognized the couple from prior services, though he'd never spoken with them. He a respected enchanter, she his barely-of-age bride (were the rumors to be believed). The husband could have easily been his wife's father, but that was neither here nor there to Charbon, and he didn't see what business it was of anyone else's.

But it wasn't that bit of hearsay that stuck in Charbon's mind as he observed the scene. There were other rumors—about the woman's health. To hear talk of it, she was not well. Had been in an asylum when she was very young, though *why* she'd been committed was often guessed at. She'd been violent, or had invited dangerous people into the family home. Others said she'd had visions, heard voices.

As the bloody kerchief slid aside, revealing the gash, Charbon's gaze narrowed. The cut was far too deep, clean, and straight to have been caused by the stone. And the slab she indicated bore no bloodstains.

"Looks bad, my dear," Mistress Ada tutted. "Going to need stiches. We should haul you to a surgery."

"No need to move her," said Una, stepping up beside Louis.

Little Nadine held out a leather wrap for her father to take. Inside was the set of surgeon's tools Una often carried for him, just in case.

He patted Nadine on the head, taking the set without a word. He was still trying to process the incongruences in the scene. Why would the woman blame her injury on a fall if that was not how she'd been hurt?

There were no happy answers to that question.

Looking sidelong at her husband, he knelt beside the two women. The older man appeared genuinely concerned and confused.

Most likely not the cause of her "fall" then.

But there was another in the crowd who watched with a similar rapt expression, only his attention seemed to be born of interest, rather than concern for the woman's well-being. He and she locked eyes for the briefest of moments.

Charbon knew the man. Eric Matisse, an enchanter, like the woman's husband. One hand always held in his pocket or clutched and stiff like a block of wood. He was a *Teleoteur* of no real distinction, but not because of lack of talent—he'd spent some time "away." Away in debtor's prison, some said.

Until this moment, Charbon had never realized just how much gossip flew between a coterie's walls.

Something was amiss, rumors or no. If Matisse, or the woman's husband, or *someone* had purposefully injured her, it was unlikely she'd speak the truth in their presence. "May we take you someplace more private, Madame—?"

"Fiona," she said with a musical lilt. "A madame is an old woman."

Her husband frowned deeply, but said nothing.

"Fiona," Charbon tried again, "will you let us carry you someplace with fewer eyes?" He gave her a sincere tilt of the head, attempting to offer her safety from whomever she'd told the lie for.

Fiona hardly acknowledged Mistress Ada, and her gaze once again found Matisse. She grimaced and drew her skirt up higher, away from the wound, and turned her eyes on Charbon. "Of course. Whatever you think is best, monsieur."

"I cannot lift her," Ada said sternly.

Charbon slid his arms beneath Fiona, finding her not exactly waiflike, but not heavy either. She slid her arms softly around his neck, curling her fingers into the long strands at his nape. He gave her a puzzled look as she stroked her nails suggestively, yet subtly, against his skin.

One of the priests of the Unknown invited the two healers to take her into the boarding house outside of the main coterie. Her husband attempted to accompany them, but Charbon insisted he remain behind. Other than the age difference, Charbon had heard nothing especially untoward about the relationship. But a good healer knew when to ask certain questions and keep certain suspicions in the fore of their mind.

He and Ada laid her out on the sturdy wooden dining table in the house. Like the rest of the coterie, the building was old. It boasted a large kitchen and eating room at the fore, with the bunk hall in the back where the priests lodged.

Ada went to the stove to boil water while Charbon prepped for sewing. "You did not fall on that rock," he whispered softly. "What truly happened?"

"Aren't you a clever boy?" she said, her lips curling smugly. Fiona arched her back against the table and spread her legs as she hiked up her skirt.

Charbon did his best to avert his eyes for her sake, but that seemed to be the opposite of what she wanted. She pawed at his wrist when he caught her thigh to examine the wound, and thumbed at his pulse point. Pausing, he eyed her skeptically. Her pupils were dilated, large and round beneath her fluttering lashes. She parted her lips, tongue darting out suggestively.

He gulped dryly, trying to remain professional in the face of her inappropriate behavior. "Madame, I don't know what you—" The words died on his tongue as he caught sight of her other leg. She wore a black lace garter—but not the sort meant to function, the kind designed to titillate. It was inlaid with black stones. Onyx.

If they were enchanted, they were luststones.

He pulled his hand back as though burned. Any direct contact between the gems and his skin would set his blood boiling.

"What happened?" he asked firmly. "And why would you wear such a thing to worship? How—who cut you?"

"Will you fix me, Louis? Your name *is* Louis, isn't it?"

"Charbon. Monsieur or Master Charbon." Her indelicate use of his first name, more so than her hidden luststones, made his cheeks and neck grow hot.

"He said you would fix me. They said you would."

"Who? What are you talking about?"

She seemed to sober then. Whatever hold the luststones had over her, they didn't carry enough grams of emotion to override her good sense. "Sew up my leg and leave me without a scar."

"I can't guarantee—"

She propped herself up on one elbow. "What makes you think I didn't trip on the boulder?"

"This is clearly a knife wound. Who cut you? Your husband? Matisse?"

"People say you know the human body intimately." She rolled her hips suggestively. "Is this so?"

"I'm highly educated in anatomy, yes," he said curtly. Such questions were usually thrown at him with accusations tacked to their tails. "Some people question the methods of my education, my dissection, but it's all in the interest of healing—"

"You know where everything lies? Each organ? Each bone?"

"Yes."

"And you've cut up people to find out? You kept bodies from the sand in order to study them?"

Her leg was still seeping blood. He tried to focus on that, to shut out all of the voices—the memories—winging through his mind. Those that called his studies "sick" and "perverted," all the while ignoring the lives he'd saved based on his supposedly ill-gotten knowledge. "My experiments were on corpses, the families all consented"—*almost, almost all*—"I did nothing wrong."

"Of course not," she said, sitting up, reaching for his cheek. "Except in the eyes of the law."

He backed away from the table. Every move she made created an uncomfortable knot in his chest. His breath wanted to come high and quick, but he forced his lungs into a steady, slow rhythm.

"I understand," she said solemnly. "You did what had to be done, what others refused to do, in order to better yourself."

"It wasn't for me," he said sternly. Then, with a sigh through his nose, *"Who cut you?"*

"I wanted to meet you," she said, holding his gaze, completely unabashed.

She didn't mean . . . She'd cut *herself*? "There are surer ways, madame."

"I required a test." Fiona winked and lay back down. "You haven't passed yet."

"I haven't—?" Charbon put a stopper on the question as Ada sidled up with a pot of hot water, ready to clean Fiona's wound and make sure the utensils were sanitized.

With a subtle flick of her wrist, Fiona covered her luststone garter, the corner of her lip quirking at Charbon as if to say, *It's our little secret.*

Charbon made quick work of the cut, but did not sacrifice finesse for speed. Every bat of Fiona's eyelashes and cringe of her mouth somehow felt more tied to a needle in his flesh rather than in hers. The smooth texture of her skin and the rough netting of her skirts were equally as irritating. He wanted nothing more than to get back to Una and put this unsettling exchange behind him.

She took a disturbing level of delight in examining his work. Most people, by the time he'd knitted them, were ready to have his square jaw and pointed features out of their sight for good. But not Fiona.

"Beautiful work," she cooed, running a flushed finger over the stripe of her wound. "The stitches are so small, so even. Like a tailor's."

"The scarring should be minimal," he assured her, tucking his tools away.

"Less than negligible, I'll bet," she said with a grin.

Ada wandered away again to wash her hands of their red stains. Charbon watched her go, hissing at Fiona the moment the other healer was out of hearing range: "I don't know what kind of fun you thought this would be, but I don't appreciate being taken away from my family—today of all days. If Matisse has done something to you, or if your husband has, or if it's another someone altogether, tell me now so I can help. If you are under no coercion and in no danger, do not trouble me again."

"Your family patron is the Unknown god, is it not?" she inquired, as though he'd said nothing.

He only glared.

"Come now. A moment ago you were so eager to help me."

"How does knowing my patron deity help you?"

She reached out to pat his face, and he quickly withdrew from her reach. "Precious boy, you'll come to understand in time."

"Can you walk all right?" he asked, striding toward the door. Before she could answer, he opened it, gesturing for her to leave.

"I'll manage," she answered brightly, slipping from the table and arranging her skirts. Skipping like a young girl, she drew up beside him, pressing in close.

Charbon looked away as she smirked up at him. "Did you know, depending on who the emotions were drawn from, there can be an imperceptible difference between joystones, rapturestones, and luststones?"

With a heady exhale, she drew a long-nailed finger down the deep V of his collar. He caught her hand just as she dared dip beneath the fabric. "What about lovestones?" he asked, tossing her hand aside.

"I wouldn't know." With a wink, she was gone.

Once he was free of her presence, Charbon closed his eyes and leaned heavily against the doorframe. The places she'd touched him still felt hot, and not in a pleasant way. It wasn't temptation he found himself fighting, but revulsion.

This Fiona was beautiful, yes, and alluring, but she made his stomach turn.

The urge to return to Una and kiss every inch of her face in gratitude shivered through him. "Do you need any help, Mistress Ada?" he called. "Fiona is gone."

"No, Master Charbon. If you hurry, you might still catch the beginning of services."

He sighed a quiet "Thank you" before hurrying back to the coterie proper. Slipping through the main gates, he pulled up short when he saw four distinct figures loitering outside of Emotion's cloister. Una, his two girls—and Fiona.

Irritated, but irrationally so, he took a deep breath and scratched at his throat. Why did this woman instill him with so much discomfort?

It wasn't until Fiona turned, bouncing slightly, that the discomfort turned to fear.

She had the baby braced on her hip, and she chattered into his chubby face without a hint of the slyness Charbon had seen earlier. If anything, she exuded innocence.

But the sight of his son spurred him on. Trying to hurry, yet appear unbothered, he took long strides toward the women.

"Ah, my hero cometh," Fiona said, her smile widening as she caught sight of him.

He tried to match her carefree expression, for Una's peace of mind, but could feel the corners of his mouth quivering with the effort. Instead of replying, he reached out for the boy.

"Avellino is a strong name," she said, easily giving the child over.

"You told her?" he asked Una indignantly, cupping the back of Ave's head.

"We'll announce it at the end of service," his wife replied with a shrug. "She asked, I didn't see reason to keep quiet."

"You have a beautiful family," Fiona sighed. "Children are such . . ." She trailed off, her eyes aglow, searching for the right word. "*Precious* things."

"You should hurry inside," Charbon replied without thanks. "Your husband must be worried."

"The day I leave my husband without worry is the day I leave him for the sands," she quipped, scurrying off.

"Love, what's wrong?" Una asked, noting the tension in his arms and shoulders—he quaked with it.

He was not one to speak ill of strangers—as the young woman was, no matter how overtly familiar she tried to be. "Nothing. Nothing."

As the family shuffled back into the cloister, he searched for Fiona among the pews. She sat near the front, with her husband's arm clasped around her. For a moment, she looked over her shoulder, but not at Charbon. She caught the eye of Eric Matisse, who nodded.

The priest of Emotion took zhur place at the head of the cloister, calling for all to be still. The shrouded priests of the Unknown, who'd held the door, stood stoically behind zhur as zhe began the reading of the scrolls.

"Today, we read from the first scroll," zhe said. "Absolon's first accounting of our creation. The origins from which we stem, and the grace that has let us remain."

Charbon crossed and uncrossed his legs, fidgeting—which was very unlike him—as the account was read.

In the time before Arkensyre, all was bleak.

In the beginning, there was the Thalo. Alone and lawless. Good and bad did not exist. Nor did light and dark. The Thalo did not know of contrast, of opposites, and therefore could not conceive of right and wrong, pain . . . or pleasure. But the Thalo *was* and everything else *wasn't*, and so it knew of existing and not existing.

So it took some of the nothing and transformed it into something. A place. A planet. And it filled the planet with things that could move, things that could consume one another to move more, to multiply, to spread. It would not need to make more, for it gave them the ability to make themselves and unmake themselves, just as the world made and unmade itself over and over, in new configurations whenever it pleased.

But not long after, it learned a new contrast. Between knowing and not knowing. It understood things, and the beasts it had created did not. And so the Thalo made the first god, Knowledge, who, unlike the beasts, could not be made and unmade again. Could not tear from itself another just the same. Knowledge knew that the Thalo thought of itself as the It, without measure, without differentiation. But Knowledge did not think of itself as it. Knowledge took the pronouns Fey/Feir.

Knowledge saw how the creatures ate one another, without feeling. How they were consumed, without feeling. How they went on and on, tearing, ripping, destroying, without feeling, and Knowledge, knowing all, knew there was an absence in the world. Of emotion. And so Knowledge begged the Thalo to create another god.

Emotion was born wailing, as now all creatures are. A burst of light, a fiery tantrum, heralded Emotion's existence from the nothing.

The Thalo had intended Emotion to be just the same as Knowledge, incapable of creating others. But all emotion is pregnant with meaning and possibility, and two small, infant gods were born not long after. Twins, Time and Nature, who both represented half of their parent. They were She/Her and He/Him. While Emotion represented a bonding continuum, Zhe/Zhur, and Knowledge would continue to represent none at all.

The Thalo had not expected so many so quickly. It was used to ruling all, to seeing all, creating all. And these newcomers had criticisms.

Time insisted the world should not be able to make and unmake itself on a whim. That, like the gods, it should have a beginning, and therefore, when it ended it should cease to be. She applied force to the planet, using the first God Magic, to make the world and its beasts travel only in one direction, from births to deaths. They could no longer be eaten one day and eat again the next.

Likewise, Nature criticized the world for being so empty. He said the Thalo had not created enough variation, that there could be things that eat light and sound instead of each other. There could be things that drank the acid rain and swallowed earth. Nature said He could make them, to create an order, a chain of consumption, so that all the beasts could not eat all the other beasts, and so Time's new forward march would not mean such a swift end for them all.

Emotion said that Zhe could make the beasts care for their offspring, so that they would not be inclined to eat them so. Zhe could make some care for other kinds of beasts, and make them angry when they were threatened.

Knowledge, in Feir wisdom, said nothing.

The Thalo didn't like this. It had made the gods, but now the gods wanted to change things, to apply their own mark to Its world.

So It made a fifth god, one which today is largely unknown to us. It asked the Unknown what it might do, how it might keep the others from interfering.

We do not know what the Unknown said. Only that They/Them—for it represented the unassumed—gathered the other gods and took them to a far corner of the planet. It pulled the earth *up up up* toward the sky and called it a mountain and bade them make their own creation to dwell there. It gave them their own bit of world, so that they may cease to distress the Thalo.

And thus the gods built humanity. But they were not as adept at building as the Thalo. They gave us lungs that could barely breathe the planet's air, skin that could not stand the touch of the rain. Claws and teeth that were dull and breakable. Bodies that were frail and easily torn apart. Emotions that were far too strong, and lifespans that were far too short. Only Knowledge, the first god, was able to give us something superior to the Thalo's creations: good minds.

It was not long before the beasts of the wastelands realized there was easy prey on the mountain. They came, gnashing and clawing, on padded feet and leather wings, with razor beaks and vicious teeth, to eat their fill of these delicate things.

The first four gods begged the Thalo to intervene, to keep the monsters from destroying what they'd built. But the Thalo did not see why It should. The frailty of their creation was their fault. If they had wanted their humans to survive, they should have built them better.

After centuries upon centuries, the Unknown god could no longer stand the cries of Their siblings, nor the uncaring nature of the Thalo. They saw that these new animals were something special, and that given the chance, the humans could make of life something neither the gods nor the Thalo could imagine.

And so They traveled to another corner of the world, where They had previously noted a small divot in the sand, and ripped a scar into the earth. A deep valley. And They called on me, the one human who had left the mountain and survived—who had been to the divot and come back again—to lead an Introdus to this new place.

And They demanded Their siblings give all they could to the protection of the valley. To construct a border that would keep all of the Thalo's creations—Its monsters, Its poison air, Its ugly rain, Its devastating heat—away.

Once the humans were inside, the gods gathered together and pooled their magic to build the barrier, each sweating, magic dripping from them and growing solid. Knowledge sweat shards that hit the ground and grew—the first trees. Gemstones, each capable of housing a specific feeling, poured from Emotion. Rivulets of gold, iron, silver, and all manner of metals trailed down Nature's sides. And grains of sand fell from Time just as it does in an hourglass today.

These, they decided, were gifts for their humans. Power they had failed to imbue their creations with could be gathered and used in the form of Enchantments.

Today, still, and into tomorrow, the gods must maintain the border. They cannot come in, and they cannot get out, for fear of losing the balance and exposing us all to the wastelands.

And, wherefore, then, is the Unknown? That we do not know. They chose not to seek my ear once the border was created. While the others told me of their gifts, the Unknown remained silent.

They deigned to speak to me only once more, during the declaration of penalties, and now, sadly, I fear They shall never speak to me again.

    —Scroll I, writ by Absolon Raoul Trémaux, after the Great Introdus

There was something Charbon especially liked about the Unknown, beyond the fact that they were the patron deity of his family. To him, the god represented pure faith. He understood about toiling in obscurity, seeking to help without making a show of it.

That being said, he felt today as though he'd been a part of a spectacle, the purpose of which he could not divine.

Who was this unsettling young woman, and why had she sought him out?

Fiona sat perfectly still in her husband's arms now, attentive to the priest's remarks.

But Charbon could find no comfort in the fact that his stitches had been even, his offer of help swift, or that Emotion's priest was discussing the importance of the Unknown in relation to Emotion's gifts—that it was the Unknown themself who'd pointed out that the emotions of humans were so overwhelming that they often failed to consider the overwhelming emotions of others. That this was the moment when Emotion had decided on its required sacrifice and its penalty.

No, a day that had begun with such promise had turned. He could not put his finger on what had transpired between a sharp stone and a woman's leg, but it felt ominous.

His gut soured, and his day's joy was lost.

12

KRONA

It was a varg growl. I'd never heard one before. So different from a dog or a big cat or a bear. The sound froze me where I stood, and out of the shadows came my first monster. It was skinny, tiny—clearly it hadn't eaten in weeks. It was probably only a few days from ethereal. Two more golden needles protruded from the high point in its spine, out of reach from its stubby legs and oversized jaw. Someone had shot it, but failed to use the right ammunition. It wasn't a love-eater.

＞━◆━○━◆━＜

Krona had been approaching her third-fifth when Charbon committed his crimes—almost a woman, but not yet. De-Lia, five years Krona's elder, was only just out of the academy, and they and Maman still lived in the country, within a day's ride of the Borderswatch outpost Papa had been assigned to (but not in the same house Papa had died in, that had burned to the ground).

And news from Lutador proper was always ugly. Murders were frequent, as were thefts and worse. Charbon stood apart from the other criminals in her memory only because of his brutality. But she knew nothing about him personally, nothing separate from his desecration of the human form.

Truth be told, she didn't even know much about his arrest or trial or death. It was an old concern—a scab that had long healed over. She'd never had cause, nor professional opportunity, to pick at the wound he'd made in history.

The Hall of Records loomed over an open square where vendors from near and far set up carts. Several bore the usual Lutador markers: awnings of dull browns and tans, with snatches of hand-painted glass, or colored sugar, pasted to the baseboards. The carts were often of uneven construction, built lopsided on purpose to reflect the organic sway of the buildings around them.

Most were clearly of foreign origin, though. A fruit vendor—which Krona often visited on her days off—displayed her harvests on brightly colored scarves she'd hand-spun from the wool of the alpacas her family raised in the low hills

of the rim in Asgar-Skan. As Krona strode past, she slid her visor up and waved
to the woman, whose skin was crinkled, tanned, and weather-worn. Since she
came by the woman's cart so regularly, the intimidation of her uniform had
long since worn away.

The vendor tried to tempt her over by holding up a handful of bright orange
goodies.

Tangerines were De-Lia's favorite, but Lutador didn't have the climate for
citrus. Krona always made a point of buying them wherever she found them.
"Soon!" she called, promising to buy a pallet on her way back through the
square.

"I will set them aside for you, Mistress!"

Nearing the Hall's steps, Krona caught the scent of gunpowder tea and
chicken tajine wafting from a stand that was little more than an unstained board
suspended over two large earthenware pots. Her stomach rumbled, and she realized she hadn't eaten a real meal since before the Jubilee.

Striding up to the vendor, she removed her helm and gloves and tucked
them under her arm. The man stiffened at her approach, standing up straighter,
suddenly unsure what to do with his hands. His plucked-and-pierced eyebrows
rose in worry before he asked for her order. His accent was light, just a twinge of
deep Xyoparian. Behind his "counter" were three large cauldrons and an open
fire pit, with red-clay dishes settled amongst the coals.

She asked for a mug of tea—which he scooped from one cauldron with a
tightly woven double-straining ladle—and a helping of the tajine. At first he
refused her payment—the state required citizens to give members of the constabulary sustenance regardless—but she insisted and he eventually accepted
her time disks. She brought the food over to the base of a tall oak and ate in the
shade, arms braced across her knees. Both the tea and the chicken reminded
her of how Maman used to cook in the old days. Xyoparian dishes used to be
a staple in the Hirvath household, but now they were a rarity. Unfortunately,
neither Krona nor De-Lia had any skill with a pan, and Acel was unwilling
to teach them more than was necessary to see that they didn't starve. Krona
always figured the food reminded Acel too much of Papa, since food from the
homeland had always been his favorite.

While she ate, Krona eyed the vendor, curious about his piercing. The gods
forbade self-mutilation, and legally she could fine him for it. If he bore more
than one self-inflicted scar, the punishment could be much harsher.

In Xyopar there were no such laws.

A street performer wandered past her, dragging his feet in the short grass
of the parkway, leather case in hand, purple scarf wrapped tightly around his

head with its ends dangling long over one shoulder. He set up not but a few yards from her lunching spot, extracting a vivaciously curvy horn from the case, and planting a wrought-iron stake in the dirt, on which he impaled sheet music.

After a few obnoxious minutes of tuning, in which Krona considered running for dear life before he actually began to play, he set to reading from the chicken scratches inked on his sheets.

The horn's notes were deep bass, yet he played an expert melody.

She relaxed into the tree, nodding her head subtly to and fro with his beat. Her fingers moved against the side of the pot, tapping out a rhythm counter to, but in time with his.

Krona had always wanted to play . . . something. Didn't matter, really, as long as the song was pleasing. But she'd never found the opportunity.

People came and went from the Hall, either bounding up its broad steps two at a time or barely lifting a foot to get to the next tall step. A child's screeching laughter on the other side of the food carts drew her gaze for a moment; the little one was about the same age as Esteban—Esteban, who would not giggle like that for some time.

The Mayhem Mask's first victim would never laugh again.

Wiping her brown hands on the grass, she gathered up the mug and tajine pot, and fumbled in her pouch for some extra time disks. She dropped the glass coins into the musician's case on her way to return the earthenware.

Handing the dishes to the Xyoparian vendor, she flicked at her own eyebrow, letting him know she'd noticed. He sheepishly nodded, immediately pulling the hoop free.

It was sad to see him lose a little part of himself to the city-state. "What's your family prefix?" she asked.

His face lit up at the familiar gesture. It was how strangers introduced themselves in Xyopar. "Rea. And you?"

"De."

"That is a strong family."

"As is the house of Rea."

"Will you be by again, one of De?"

"The food was excellent, so I will indeed, one of Rea."

They exchanged smiles and farewells, then Krona mounted the Hall's steps, replacing her helm as she strode onward.

She felt eyes on her as she went, but thought little of it. Regulators always drew attention.

The Hall of Records was a glorified library, with a three-story interior and shelves that stretched just as high. Walkways lined the high-set windows, and shadows flitted across the polished marble floors as patrons moved in front of them. Thick, square pillars supported the wide expanse of ceiling, wherein hundreds of pieces of colored green and purple glass had been inlaid. A floor-to-ceiling impressionistic mural adorned the wall to the left of the main entryway; human-sized bluebirds soared upward around a towering pillar of orange and yellow light.

The space was scented through with paper must and leather, and though the Hall echoed with footsteps, not a whisper of a voice could be heard.

Such thorough silence made Krona's ears ring and her throat feel tight.

She approached a help desk and the young, bespectacled archivist slid her a pen and inkwell without looking up from the large tome they had splayed across their lap. In front of her was a ledger in which she could write her request.

Hastily, she jotted down, *Charbon, Louis: Arrest. Trial. Execution.*

The archivist spun the ledger so they could read it, gaze darting upward when they'd seen what she'd written. They seemed surprised by her uniform, then reassured; detailed execution records were not for public consumption. Swiftly, they wrote next her to request, *Might I see your coin?*

It was not an unreasonable demand. Grasping the laces at the top of her collar, she undid them low enough to slip her hand inside next to her clavicle, where the concealed pocket kept her most precious possession hidden. A large, etched metal coin, with the words *Harmony with Enchantments, Harmony with the People* scrawled around its edges, and a stylized pentacle—formed of interlocking, humanoid figures—in the center. The back side had been carved with a number unique to her and her coin, for proper identification. Such a token was given to all Regulators the day they graduated from the academy. It marked her as a true lawperson.

She held the coin up for the archivist's inspection.

With a perfunctory but respectful nod, they set their book aside and gestured for her to follow them. Hands tucked firmly into the pockets of their breeches, shoulders hunched casually, they led her to a series of private reading rooms. Most of them were dark, to protect the pages and lettering on the oldest of scripts. A few were flanked with outside windows to let in natural reading light. The archivist took her to a special room, one that required a key. It would not do to have someone accidently walk in on a Regulator while they had sensitive material in hand.

Regardless of the privacy they provided, the reading rooms were still soaked in silence. The room she entered had no windows and only one gas lamp set atop a small table, which the archivist lit. The lamp's new flame illuminated a slate tablet on the wall. Retrieving a sliver of wrapped chalk from their pocket, the archivist wrote that they would return with the requested files posthaste.

Dim, and warm, the space was like a quiet, insulated cocoon. Her helm filtered the soft light further, making it little more than a twinkle out the corner of her eye. It would be easy to catch a few extra winks here. She could sit in one of the two provided chairs, prop her feet in the other, and simply . . .

But she'd already been allowed sleep. What about De-Lia? She claimed to have rested, but Krona knew her better than that.

Her sister had an inane ability to disregard her own needs when there was a job to do. It wasn't just stubbornness, or dogged commitment, that kept her on her feet, though. It was like the concern itself wouldn't let her sleep. It would keep pecking at her, begging to be solved.

And this one . . . De-Lia's self-inattentiveness would only be magnified by the responsibility she carried for losing the enchantments.

The minutes waiting for the archivist's return stretched on. Krona tapped her fingertips against the table, but even that sound was profoundly muted by her gloves and helm.

Here in the dark, eerie silence, it was easy to imagine movement—to see large, living shadows in the flickering light. Again she felt like she was being watched.

Her own breath echoed in her helm, as it usually did, but now the sound seemed deeper, alien. Perhaps the heavy exhales weren't hers.

A particularly clever varg *could* make its way into the Hall without anyone noticing. Especially if it was a jumper. It could appear anywhere at will, silently if it wanted. It could materialize in this very room.

Krona held herself very still, her breathing shallow, ears straining for the rattling of spines and the *click-clack* of claws on stone.

It could be right behind her, and she wouldn't know until it had her.

You're being ridiculous, working yourself up over nothing.

But was she? How had those varger been able to get so close to the conservatory with so many watching? Were the monsters becoming bolder? Would she start to see more in the city?

And then, there it was, an unmistakable puff of wind—of breath?—that made the lamplight flutter all the more.

No, it was just my imagina—

A creak, and a shifting to her left. Movement that was not hers.

Like a woman possessed, she slipped her hand onto her holster, drawing her quintbarrel. In the same motion, she plastered her back to the wall, facing the sudden sound.

Only to find the archivist at the door, stunned, folders in hand, knees suddenly knocking together.

Krona quickly put away her weapon, running her hand over her faceplate in embarrassment. *Why do you do these things to yourself?*

"I'm sorr—"

"No." They cut her off quickly and quietly, regaining their composure and holding up a finger to their lips. It was most likely the first word they'd spoken since arriving at work.

Still trembling, they set the folders on the table and placed themself in front of the chalkboard. Noting her position out of the corner of their eye, wary now, they wrote, *Some of the records appear to have been misfiled. These are what I could locate at the moment.*

They turned to leave, but she halted them with a gesture. She held out her hand for the chalk.

You mean the files are missing? she wrote.

The files are not where they should be, they replied.

Something Thibaut had said tickled the back of Krona's mind. *Have a lot of files been misplaced recently?*

The archivist rolled their tongue inside their mouth as their jaw tightened. She could see the defense mounting in their mind, bubbling to the surface— the urge to insist all of the archivists were well trained, reliable. Instead, they wrote, *Yes.*

Which records? What kinds?

Concentration thinned their lip. They were unsure how to answer. *All kinds. Religious, political, criminal, medical. But they don't appear . . .* They stopped writing, searching for the right words.

"They don't appear related?" Krona whispered, impatient.

"Shhhh." They whipped the end of their shushing in her direction as though it had barbs.

"I will not *shhhh*," she spat, plucking the chalk from their fingers and pointedly tossing it across the room. "But if you want me to keep my voice down, you better speak to me."

"It's not . . . it hasn't been that many," they insisted quietly. "A few here and there, but enough to notice. The master archivist has been very cross about it."

"And your conclusion is they've been misfiled, not that a patron has stolen them?"

"They aren't the kinds of records one would steal. Nothing incriminating—not for the living anyway. Most are old, but not so old as to be valuable. And they weren't related—not by time, not by place, not by people, as far as we can tell. But in many cases all we have left are the labels, so make of our assumptions what you will."

The archivist shuffled uncomfortably, toying with their brass-rimmed glasses. They were nervous. More nervous than the situation warranted. Perhaps it was because she'd drawn a quintbarrel on them just moments before, but something told her their paranoia ran deeper.

"Why are you lying to me?" she asked swiftly.

"I'm *not*. I'm . . . I'm telling you what I've been told."

"Meaning?"

"Meaning the master archivist told us they were misfiled and that was that. We shouldn't ask any more, he said. Shouldn't look for them."

"So he took them?"

The young person shook their head. "I don't think so. He seemed . . . scared. But I don't think he knows where the files went any more than the rest of us."

Scared? What in Arkensyre would a librarian have to fear?

Clapping chalk powder off her gloves, Krona moved to flip through the records the archivist had brought her. There were a few newspaper articles on the concern, a handful of witness interrogation reports—not Charbon's interrogations, though. Nothing on his trial or his hanging. Nothing of use at all—no insight to his character or new information on his killings—save the name of the Watchman in charge of the concern: Patroné.

"What other criminal records are missing?" she asked.

"Some related to a fire in an asylum. And a missing woman. And a few about time tax dodgers, I think?"

Could those be related to Charbon in some way? She couldn't see how. "Does the name Eric Matisse sound familiar? He created an illegal mask."

"I can go look up the concern for you."

"Thank you." She gave them the dates to look for and they scurried off, but it was no time at all before the young person returned.

"Master Matisse's files are missing as well."

As she feared. "What's your master's name?"

"Master Bisset."

She nodded perfunctorily. "Take me to him."

"Now?"

"Yes, *now*."

They left the stuffy reading room behind and made for the rear of the sweeping Hall. Two wide, twisting staircases—coiled like sleek serpents, framed by iron railings detailed in metal rabbits—took them to the second-level landing.

The second floor was an overgrown balcony, really, looking out and down over the goings-on in the rest of the Hall below. Its walls were lined with books, the shelving occasionally broken up by a window or door. The archivist brought her to one with gold inlay at its center: a ring made of alternating books and scrolls, the mark of a state-licensed mastrex librarian.

Instead of knocking, the archivist turned a small key in the wall, like that on a gas lamp. Krona presumed it corresponded to just such a lamp inside—a ready flame whose burgeoning could signal someone at the door without the need for noise.

They both waited.

No response.

The archivist turned the key again. Began fidgeting when there was still no answer.

"Does he leave his office for meals?" Krona prompted.

Wincing at the sound of her voice, the archivist shook their head.

"Hmm," she said, more to herself than them. There were coincidences, and then there were coincidences.

She tried the door.

It swung inward easily.

She was not prepared for the dead man behind the desk.

Neither was the archivist. They shouted, quick and horrified, the sound splitting the air readily in the utter silence.

"Fuck," Krona cursed, hurrying inside, pulling the archivist with her before their panic could draw a crowd.

She slammed the door behind them, pushed the archivist into the corner, and made for the body. The man's throat had been slit—slashed cleanly, as though he hadn't bothered to put up a fight.

Perhaps he'd done it himself.

She couldn't find a blade, and there was no blood on his hands.

He'd been dead awhile—though she was no examiner and couldn't say exactly how long. A few hours? A day? His blood was dark and coagulated, thick and heavy on the front of his tunic.

Someone had murdered him swiftly and decisively.

The archivist scrambled over to a waste basket, fell to their knees, and vomited. They pulled off their glasses, ran the back of their hand over their eyes. Then promptly vomited again.

She went to them, patted them delicately on the back. "I'm sorry, but I need you to help me. Can you stand? I need you to get the Dayswatch."

She helped them to their feet, saw them out the door. "Tell no one until you've gathered the Watch, understand?"

When the archivist had gone, she returned to the desk, examining the papers atop it, trying to ignore the dark brown patches of blood spray. The scrolls were nothing special, a few out-of-date decrees from the Grand Marquises and a census of Lutador's livestock.

Nothing in the office looked damaged or disheveled. There was no way for her to guess if something had been stolen.

There wasn't even any way for her to tell if this murder was related to her current concern or not.

But there were coincidences, *and then there were coincidences.*

She sighed heavily, went to the body, and closed the dead man's eyes. With one last look around the room, she snapped out another *"Fuck"* before exiting to stand guard outside.

13

LOUIS

Lutador enchantment district,
evening, eleven years previous

Charbon had been surprised to receive the invitation to visit Fiona's home for a gratuity meal. After all, several months had passed since her "fall," and though they'd seen each other at services, nary a word or a glance of recognition had been exchanged.

The favor he'd done her, of mending her leg, had been a small one. Not enough to warrant the expectation of a gratuity meal, so the letter, carried by an official footman, had been a source of confusion at first, and he'd thought it misdelivered.

The invite was for his entire family, but a cloud had settled over his household in recent days. There'd been a grand celebration prior to his son's time tax being taken, and then within the week the infant had grown ill. Desperately so. A deep, rattling cough would rack his little body every few moments, and he fussed without end, constantly uncomfortable. Charbon had done his best to soothe him—this was his job, after all. He might specialize in surgeries, but he was no stranger to an infection of the lung.

He'd thought to decline the invitation—he could not possibly leave his child's side under these circumstances. Both Nadine and Gabrielle had been through bouts of extreme illness in their infancy—Nadine was prone to fever, and Gabrielle issues of the stomach. He'd watched over them just as vigilantly, and did not want to leave Avellino now, even for a moment.

But Una had insisted, despite his protests. She hoped a hospitable night out would do him some good. "Have a brandy," she insisted, "play a parlor game if they wish to play a parlor game. Avellino needs you refreshed—we all do. Go, go. Try to have fun, to be at ease. We will stay with him the whole time."

He didn't tell her he doubted he could find ease in Fiona's household, whether Avellino was sick or not. He'd meant to tell Una months ago of the other woman's inappropriate behavior, but the words stuck in his craw. For, as much as he'd found Fiona disturbing, he'd also found her intriguing, and that small fact had turned his tongue to lead.

He felt guilty about it in a way he could barely decipher.

He didn't *want* Fiona. He wanted no part of her.

But he couldn't comprehend her, and that lack of understanding tugged at him. Drew him. *Attracted* him.

Perhaps this encounter would be different. Perhaps he could wash from his mouth the vile taste their last interaction had left behind. Allowing for second chances was only polite, after all.

Perhaps she would explain herself, and then his guilt-inducing *interest* could be wiped away.

And so he'd gone to the *Teleoteur*'s apartments, which sat over the top of his workshop.

Though different from Charbon's country manor, it was no less well kempt or to-do. Enchanters were the most highly prized artisans and this earned them a pretty penny, enough to keep them comfortable and rival the family coffers of lesser nobility like Louis himself.

Fiona and her husband did not retain any household staff. Charbon's own staff was light—only a nanny and a maid. His contemporaries thought this odd of him, and he likewise found it odd here. The rumors suggesting Fiona had simply married for money characterized her as the sort of person who would appreciate the efforts of a good few servants.

But the reasons for their empty staff quarters soon became apparent, and Charbon realized he had much more in common with Fiona than he ever would have liked to admit.

"Welcome," said the man who answered the door—who was distinctly *not* Fiona's husband.

"Th-Thank you, uh, Monsieur Matisse, is it?"

"*Master* Matisse," he corrected. "Though Eric is quite all right."

Charbon prickled at the rapid familiarity, but said nothing.

Eric Matisse was a blond man, though his hair was a deeper, sandier color compared to Charbon's. He was young—very young for a master *Teleoteur*—though still a good five years older than Fiona if Charbon had to guess (which he did; manners forbade such intimate questions). His face still held boyish proportions, with his cheeks being more prominent than his jawline. He was aesthetically pleasing, though didn't appear to be much in the way of physically adept. He had the look of one whose mind was always in motion instead of his body.

And yet his eyes were sunken and tired, as though he were bored. Charbon glanced at the hand that was perpetually in his pocket, noting not for the first time how rigid it looked.

No one else met them at the door. Matisse offered to take his coat, and he allowed it, though part of him wished courtesy would permit him to keep it—it was as good a stand-in for armor as he would ever don.

Beyond the foyer, the lights in the apartment were dimmed. The blue-green in the prominent stained-glass window above the dining table looked wine-dark in the fading light. The walls had been papered with a sweeping black-and-white pattern, the black insinuating vines and flourishes. Candles instead of gas lamps stood in mounted candelabras along the halls. There was no expected smell of cooking food, and the table itself had not been set.

Matisse, for his part, took up a small candle in the meagerest of candle holders and lit it from one of the candelabras, dripping a small puddle of beeswax yellow onto the wood of the floor.

"Might I inquire as to the whereabouts of the master and mistress of the house?" Charbon asked as a sudden chill took him. There was a bust in the hall, carved of marble, on a too-tall pedestal that made it stand at head height. Its face was cold, but knowing. An ominous air hung around it, and only seemed to thicken as they passed it.

Here he was, in a strange place with a strange man, being led past the dining room and into a darkened corridor. It was the stuff of eerie stories, the likes of which he'd never much cared for.

"The master is away," Matisse said frankly. "A materials show for *Teleoteurs* in Asgar-Skan."

"Oh? Is such a showing not also of interest to you?"

"The demonstrations are *invitation only,*" he said bitterly.

In truth, Charbon knew little about magic, how enchantments worked, and the nuances of the business. Such things had never been of interest to him. But there was something in the tone of Matisse's voice that suggested the depth of the snub—or even the reasons for it—were not typical.

"And," Charbon continued, "the master's wife, the mistress of the house?"

Matisse did not answer. They'd come to the end of a hall; a door lay to the left and one to the right, but the *Teleoteur* made no movement toward either. Instead, he knocked on the rear wall.

Much to Charbon's surprise, it swung outward immediately, nearly colliding with Matisse himself.

A hidden door in a spooky house. Charbon was less shocked than he should have been.

On the other side stood Fiona, hair slightly frizzed and falling from its pins, her dress covered over in a heavy butcher's apron, and her eyes hidden behind thick work goggles, like one might wear when working with dangerous chemicals.

"There you are!" she said, as though they were a pair of delinquent youngsters who'd been out after curfew.

She yanked Matisse through the hidden door, which Charbon had to catch before it closed on him—he hadn't seen any secret latches or seams, and thus had no idea how it was opened from the hall side. Beyond lay a single, windowless room. Three gas lamps were turned on high, making the space as bright as day, a stark contrast to the home itself. This was clearly a workshop of a sort, though it had elements of a healer's den as well; bouquets of herbs hung from the vaulted ceiling, and bandages, needles, and tourniquets were stacked on top of an apothecary chest that occupied one rear corner. A workbench, scattered with metal filings, hand-drawn schematics, a microscope, and parts of a dry-plate camera occupied the other.

In the center of the space, etched into the floor, was an odd design of questionable purpose. It was encircled several times by a script he could not read, and the mark itself was both organic-looking and very geometric, the way a flower maintained aspects of both. But this was no flower, something much more abstract.

A small camp stove sat in the middle of the design. Upon it, sausage links sizzled, and hand-patted soft breads were warming on a metal rack above them.

"We eat simply here, Louis," Fiona said, "I hope you don't mind."

"Charbon, if you please, madame."

"I do not," she said cheerfully. "But don't worry, we'll break you of your bad habits soon enough."

Given the circumstances and the dubious contents of the room, Charbon hoped he wouldn't be around long enough for them to break anything of his, let alone cure him of his propriety.

Fiona held out a tin plate and a bent fork for him to take. "Please, sit."

He neither accepted the utensils, nor pointed out that there were in fact no chairs in the room. "I do believe you've misled me, per the contents of your invitation, madame. I am not accustomed to being escorted into hidden rooms, which one would imagine—from the items I see before me—is hidden for a reason and not a simple party thrill."

"Quite so," she commended him, condescending bravado heavy in her voice.

He held his ground. Her brazenness made him feel bold. "I do not know what this all adds up to, but my guess is something illegal. Perhaps in the way of enchantment engineering."

"Right again. Two for two, you are a clever boy."

"And I'm afraid I cannot be a party to it. I'll need to dash off straight to the Watch after this, you must know that."

"Oh," she said, tutting, her face falling in mock disappointment. "And you were doing so well, too. I suppose if you must become a snitch, I'll have to snitch too. Your secret workshop is far, shall we say *grislier,* than mine is. I wonder what the Watch will make of that?"

His stomach grew cold and shriveled in his belly, but he made no outward indication her statement had meant something to him. "Idle threats will not convince me otherwise, madame. My anatomy studies are in the past, and by now my workshop—closed as it has been these past six years—is common knowledge."

She grinned. "Ah, but Louis, you and I are two peas in the same pod. We were both punished for our studies, and yet we cannot be deterred. Look, look here." She passed the plate and fork to Matisse—who was watching their exchange with nary a shift in his bored expression—and took Charbon by the wrist, leading him to her workbench.

The drawings there were of a complex sort of fountain pen, part of which had been constructed and was nestled amongst the metal shavings.

"You look confused," Fiona said after a time, stating the truth plainly. "Perhaps you aren't well versed in legends. There are supposedly enchantments that have been lost to time. Discovered then discarded, these items are mostly thought myth. Largely because they use something, some *extra quality* beyond the four magics we know. For instance, this"—she picked up the half-built casing—"is my attempt at a blood pen. Legend has it that with a small sampling of anyone's blood, the pen could write the truth of them."

With a little skip she jumped at her apothecary, yanking open each little drawer until she'd found what she was looking for. "This," she said, presenting what looked like a daisy pin, done over in white enamel with an amber stone in the middle, "isn't just any emotion stone. Amber holds hope, yes, but do you know what amber is? Where it comes from? It's different than other stones. I spoke to a naturalist who suggested it comes from ancient trees."

"Trees that make stones?" he asked, furrowing his brow.

"Well, it doesn't become a stone until much, much later. It's resin, sort of Nature's bandage. That's why you can sometimes find bits of insects in them—they got stuck when the resin was still sticky. And look here, see this wasp inside?"

He didn't dare touch it, but he leaned forward to see.

"The point is," she continued, "where does Knowledge's magic reside? In wood. In Valley-rim trees. The backing on this pin is a hardwood from Winsrouen, and the pin is Nature's own copper. And I made the tiniest bore hole to get a few drops of hot lead to the little thing's head. Go on, put it on."

"Oh no," he said, waving it away, "I don't much care for the sensation of emotion stones."

"I guarantee this one will fascinate you," Matisse said.

They both stared at him expectantly—Fiona with a jubilance, and Matisse with a glare that only increased Charbon's unease.

"It's only zero point zero zero zero zero two grams of hope," Fiona said, "if that helps. Taken from my own veins."

Under different circumstances he would have continued to refuse. But his position here, and their hospitality, seemed balanced on the head of a pin.

And, in truth, he was curious. He had not suspected such learning, such wonder, in a person of such tender age. If these inventions were real, then she had skills beyond most master enchanters, and in various fields of magic. As far as he was aware, a master *Physiteur,* who specialized in enchanted metalworking, did not typically possess much skill as an *Emotioteur.* A *Kairoteur* could conceivably have no knowledge of a *Teleoteur*'s practices, and so on and so forth in all combinations, though he suspected there was some intersectionality involved in handling materials. The rare few individuals that did have capabilities in multiple magic arenas were scooped up by the state to perform the very careful construction of multimagic enchantments.

"All right," he agreed softly. He pinned it to his shirt, close to his heart.

A thin thread of emotion stabbed into him—which he always hated. Putting on and taking off emotion stones was half the reason he detested them. The hopestone was gentler than usual, though, and he suspected that was due to the miniscule amounts of emotion within. But, curiously, after a few moments, not only was he feeling slightly more positive about the strange circumstances he now found himself in, he also knew the best places to construct a paper nest, exactly what plant fibers to mix with saliva, which other insects were easiest to kill—

It was odd, so odd, to be standing tall instead of standing on the side of a tree or under a leaf. How could he be this far above the ground without feeling a breeze cross his wings?

Sensations bombarded him. He felt strong, yet fragile. Vulnerable, yet vicious. Thoughts slowly drifted away from words and into some other matrix of knowledge entirely.

He suddenly tore the pin away, yanking free the emotion thread and crying out. "I knew—knew things about being a wasp." He tossed it back to her. "I've never heard of anyone tapping into the knowledge of a creature. An *already dead* creature," he emphasized. "Don't masks take a process? Started long before death?"

"They do," Matisse said. "Typically in an extremely sanitary and well-balanced environment . . . Typically."

"I can show you my notes," Fiona said gleefully. "I doubt we'll ever find anything much larger than a beetle encased in amber, but I theorized that the amber itself—"

"Wait, just wait," Charbon said, running his hand over his eyes. "How many?"

"Pardon?"

"How many new enchantments have you invented?"

"Altogether, or after I returned from the sanitarium?"

"Nigh on fifty altogether," Matisse provided.

Charbon slumped back against her work desk. "By the gods," he said under his breath. "To challenge the state like that, to challenge the gods, Knowledge feirself. The punishment for engineering even one new enchantment without sanction—"

Matisse pulled his stiff hand out of his pocket. And Charbon could finally see why it seemed so heavy, so block-like—for it was, indeed, a block of wood. A prosthetic, carved in the remarkable likeness of a closed fist. Matisse undid the buckles that kept the false hand in place and held up his arm. Nothing but a bare wrist waved in the lamplight. "The punishment is the removal of the offending hand," he said, oddly smug. "We're both well aware."

Charbon had done too much dismembering of his own—though never in the service of capital punishment—to be shocked in the way Matisse clearly expected him to be. "May I?" he asked, holding out his palm.

Matisse shrugged and set his bare wrist in Charbon's hand. The healer examined the scarring, felt for the way the bones and tendons still interacted. Matisse winced when he pushed lightly. "Butchers," Charbon gritted out. "I see they left the scaphoid, which they likely shattered. Bits of the capitate and lunate as well, it seems."

"I didn't ask the man who was chopping if he'd lined everything up properly," Matisse scoffed.

"The humane thing to do would have been to surgically amputate everything beyond the radius."

Fiona strode over and laid her hand over the top of Matisse's wrist. "I'd argue that the humane thing to do would have been to leave him his hand."

Charbon was taken aback. "Oh, well, yes, I mean—"

"It's fine," she said, waving away his concern, kissing Matisse's wrist before he slipped his prosthetic back on. Charbon frowned at the open display of inappropriate affections. "You've never thought the city-state's rules too strict?" she asked. "The punishments unfair? You've never thought too hard about why there are certain things we are told we ought not learn? Even *you*, Louis?"

"I told you," he said softly, pulling out his handkerchief, dabbing at his forehead. "I've paid my debt to society, and have stayed on the straight and narrow ever since."

She couldn't know. How could she *possibly* know? He was careful this time. Bribing an undertaker to let him slice open corpses for study before they were cremated had been his folly. The man had gone back on their gentleman's agreement, turned him in. That was why the Watch had caught him. Now he handled his anatomical studies entirely on his own. No one knew the bodies were missing. No one checked them too closely as long as he brought them back neat and tidy, sewn up tight.

He *had* to do it. The law was wrong, people were wrong. How could a surgeon be confident in his work if he had no idea what was under the skin? Patients died because dismembering bodies was outlawed. It was disrespectful, they said. But how awful was it for a healer who didn't have Charbon's knowledge? Who knew something was wrong inside a person but didn't know what to look for? They had to hack, and slice, and sever *living tissues* to discover what he knew. They killed patients because performing surgery on the dead was *disrespectful*.

Charbon's understanding of the body had grown tenfold these last few years, now that he was robbing sand-pit prep stations in the dead of night. He saved people, made them better, and still the state would throw him right back—

"Louis?" Fiona prompted, smiling condescendingly. "How long were you in the work camp? There's quite a gap between your youngest and middle child, so I'd assume a few years."

"Twenty-three months," he admitted after swallowing thickly. "After, Una and I needed time to get to know each other again. It could have been worse; they lessened my sentence because I at least helped burn the bodies in the end. All but the one—and I would have gotten to it, I would have—"

"Shhh, shhh. You don't have to justify yourself to me. I was put in an asylum by my family when I was thirteen. My husband rescued me at sixteen. I know how unfair this world is, how easily brainwashed its people are. Tell me, do you consider yourself a religious man?"

"Of course."

"Keep the Five Penalties close at heart?"

"Numbness, toil, dismemberment, death . . . and unquestioning devotion," he ticked off. He could recite the scroll quote in its entirety, but his patience was wearing thin.

"And aren't you lucky the judge ruled you'd gone against Nature instead of Knowledge." It wasn't a question.

"I daren't call my time in that place *lucky*," he snapped.

"Of course, of course," she said. "My apologies."

"Why did you invite me here?" he demanded, all thoughts of propriety gone. "To flaunt your creations? To taunt me with my indiscretions? I do not understand your game and wish to take no part in it."

"Oh, my dear boy, you're quite right. I have been toying with you a bit like a cat might a mouse. It's difficult to resist. But I do have a proposition for you—not like that. Well, in truth, not only like that." She winked at him. "I have been visited recently by someone who would have me believe that the Unknown god's reveal is close at hand."

He eyed her suspiciously. "Who could claim this—such a reveal?"

"You will not like the answer. It will go against everything you understand to be true."

"Madame, I am currently knee-deep in things that go against everything I understand to be true. And *decent*," he added.

"I still don't think he's ready," Matisse said.

"We don't need him to be ready, we need him to be primed for the truth," she countered.

"I think I should be going now," Charbon said. This was too much, all too . . . *abhorrent.* And his instincts told him the next words out of her mouth—whatever she wished to explain to him about the "truth"—would be worse.

"But you haven't eaten anything," she protested.

Frankly, madame, I am afraid to, he thought sharply. "I don't think I have the stomach for any food at the moment," he said.

She let out a heavy sigh, and she and Matisse shared a disappointed look. But she waved Charbon away. "Fine, be off. You are not our prisoner. But soon we hope you will be our ally."

He backed toward the door, afraid to let them out of his sight until walls were between them. *Never,* he thought, *never in a million years can I imagine a scenario in which I would align myself with the likes of you.*

Fumbling, he found the inside latch for the hidden door, protruding just like any other handle might.

"Do say hello to the family for me," Fiona said. "Una, Nadine, Gabrielle, and, what was the little one's name? Oh yes, Avellino. And, Louis?"

"What?"

"I think we should agree to keep each other's little secrets before you go, don't you?"

Begrudgingly he said, "You can count on me, madame."

She smiled, saccharine-sweet. "I know we can."

As he rushed away, he caught sight again of the bust, out of the corner of his eye. He could have sworn that the face was different now, its head tilted in another direction. Its gaze seemed to follow him, hot and horrific, as he fled from the strange home.

14

KRONA

I didn't scream, though I wanted to. Papa taught us: if you can see the bloodshot whites of a varg's eyes, you're dead. And I was looking directly into those big black-and-gold eyes. I might have been a scrawny child, but I was good eating as far as varger were concerned. It slunk into the light—smelling like a sewer cistern—and bared its fangs at me. I should have dashed for the opening, I should have called for your help, but instead I was stupid. Instead, I held out my hand and said, "Good doggy."

Two dead in Krona's path less than a day after the mask and despairstone were taken. One clearly by Charbon's spectral hand, and one . . . who could say?

It was strange that the boy, Esteban, had noted two men. Typically, the killers who left a trail of strangers' corpses behind preferred to work alone. It was some sickness that drove them, not passion or power. And yet, the taking of the enchantments had been orchestrated. Clearly involved multiple people.

Conspiracy she could work with. Conspiracy was familiar. Frauds and heists were well-worn territory.

But the mangled bodies and the messages in blood . . .

Krona left the Dayswatch to their work, hurrying out of the Hall. She'd come hoping to find reams of information and had left with far more questions than answers. All she really had to go on now was Patroné—the Watchman who'd been in charge of the Blooming Butcher concern. His file noted he'd become a guard at the city-state's vaults not long after arresting Charbon. She hoped he still worked there.

She would pay him a visit as soon as she'd interrogated the false varg back at the den.

Exiting the massive front entrance of the Hall, she was surprised to see a familiar face stalking back and forth across the steps.

Thibaut.

My, how he'd pulled himself together in a few short hours. A little bit of rest and fluids had done wonders for his complexion. The swelling in his cheek had gone down, and a touch of powder concealed the bruise. The split in his lip implied a dashing sort of ruggedness, and one could imagine he'd received it defending some lady's honor rather than spurring on a hotheaded pignut.

With his clothes pressed, hair lightly pulled back, and posture tight and formal, it was once again easy to mistake the ruffian for a gentleman.

Except, he looked ill at ease. Far more ill at ease than he had in that jail cell, cuffs on his wrists and a fist in his belly.

Perhaps it was his gaze she'd felt on her way inside.

He caught sight of her immediately, throwing his hands up in relief. "Ah, thank the gods. Mistress—"

"What are you doing here?" She grabbed one outstretched arm, pulling him off to the side, into the shadow of the building. "You know better than to approach me head on." Crowding him against the bricks, she glanced over her shoulder to make sure no one was paying them too much mind.

"I would have left you my marker, but there's something you need to know, and I—"

"Thibaut, I don't have time for this right now."

Her interruption failed to stall him. "—saw you over in the parkway before you went in, so I thought I'd wait for you, but now the whole place is swarming with Watch."

"Two people have been murdered."

"In the *library*?"

"One in the *library*, as you say, one in—"

"But *you* don't attend to murders. Did you come because of what I said? You called my information regarding the files disappearing from this very establishment *conspiracy theory*, so I half suspected you'd dismissed it."

"I didn't come because of your fearmongering."

"So the Hall is intact? Records aren't missing? Or did you believe the idea too preposterous to ask after?"

She *hadn't* intended to look into it. Fate had pressed the point. "You were right," she admitted.

"But these *murders* . . . ?"

Few people glanced at them—most too distracted by the hubbub pouring out from the Hall—but Krona's skin itched with exposure. She hadn't yanked Thibaut out of that cell only to have her informant burned in broad daylight. "Yes, murders. All due to my enchantments that were stolen. So, this new information you have, what is it?"

He shifted uneasily from foot to foot, eyes darting with a fear they didn't usually possess. "You won't like it."

"I didn't like getting stabbed over the last tidbit you handed me."

Instead of looking sheepish, he threw up a wry eyebrow. "*I* didn't like having my kidneys bruised for the sake of a letter. It hurt when I pissed this morning."

They both paused before reaching tentatively for each other, fingers shaking, teetering between propriety and concern. Thibaut looked pointedly at her side, while she wanted to pull up his tunic again to get a glimpse of his skin. Krona's hands flexed and unflexed, set alight with the need for reassurance but restrained by thoughts of decorum.

"I'm fine," he said after a moment of silence, answering her unasked question. He leaned back against the wall, pulling the air with him. Krona let out a deep breath.

"As am I," she said.

"Good."

"And this information I won't like?"

He tensed once more, looked away as he spoke. "Well, you asked me to look into how the thieves got into your gala so efficiently, and—"

"You have intel for me already? Learned of something while I was sleeping?"

He shrugged. "You gave me a job that needed doing, so I did it. Anyway, as I was saying, the answer to your query appears to be straightforward: corruption in the Watch."

"I'd suspected as much," she admitted. "There were three Watchmen behaving suspiciously right before it all went to the dogs. Could have been thieves disguised—"

"Or dubious Watchpersons themselves," he agreed. "But as I said, it *appears* straightforward. But I don't think it is. I've heard rumors—mere speculations—for weeks now, about a religious organization looking to recruit officials away from the state and into their service."

She cocked her head in interest.

"This *organization* isn't exactly on the up-and-up," he continued. "Blasphemy, bribery, breaking and entering. I hadn't thought it of much interest to you, but now . . . They seem to be quite keen on acquiring relics and people of authority. Which seems to fit your—" He waved his hand illustratively through the air. "—*situation* to a T. You didn't tell me it was the Mayhem Mask they took—I had to find that out on the street, thank you. Weren't those Blooming Butcher murders religious in some way? Surely there were other masks of more obvious value within reach at the gala. Why that one?"

"Why that one, indeed. To make blooms, it seems."

"Oh. So the two victims you mentioned—?"

"One of them," she confirmed.

He nodded, swallowed thickly. "This morning, one of my contacts—an old crone, Madame Strange—told me she, for a small fee, provided a safe place for two parties to parley. A cloaked man—potentially a member of this organization—and a Watchman. It all went down naught but a week ago. Time vials for information. The man wanted to know how many of the constabulary would be in attendance at the Jubilee, how many Regulators. Sounded like he might have been most interested in how many *quintbarrels* would be there."

"Because of the varger."

"Would make sense."

"Could Strange identify the Watchman? Does she know any specifics about this organization?"

"No. No, I don't think so. That's all there was to it." He rubbed the back of his neck in a nervous fashion. "She's frequently a go-between. People in the right places know to seek her out as a neutral party, someone who can find secure locations away from needy ears and eyes, that's all. She's a service provider, doesn't pry. Makes a *point* of not paying too much attention."

Krona knew he was trying to keep her from tracking down his contact. Just as she did not want him burned, he too wished to keep his own associates free and unhindered.

Krona sighed. "Looking for corruption in the Watch is like looking for water in the river. But that any of them would be so bold as to commit such a crime right under the Chief Magistrate's nose—there are few I'd think so brazen."

"They *might* be more brazen if they were members of this organization. If they really could have their loyalties tempted and their fear of the state tempered."

"I don't know . . ." This felt . . . off. Far-fetched. "A shadowy religious order infiltrating the minds and hearts of the constabulary?"

"When have I ever tossed you a bad line?"

Never. He'd never given her a tip that hadn't paid off.

He sighed, demeanor changing. Exhaustion pulled at his shoulders. "My intelligence is good, Mistress," he said seriously. "These rumors are worth a deeper look. I *do* want to please you; it's in my best interest to make sure you are happy with my services. I wouldn't risk my freedom—or drawing your ire—just to give you unsettling hearsay about the constabulary. And, if you can get me more to go on—specifics this time, Mistress, the more you leave out the more difficult my job becomes—I can see what I can dig up."

Her mind flashed to the broken body in the warehouse. To the slit throat in the Hall.

"Truth be told, I'm not sure I want you anywhere near this concern."

He gave her a sly smile. "Worried about me?"

"For you? Never. About you? Always."

"As it should be."

"I'm serious, Thibaut. This is not our usual fare. At least two are dead—perhaps more, seeing as how well fed those varger were."

"I will do my level best to stay out of trouble."

"See that you do."

><+>·O·<+><

Krona was contemplative—to the point of distraction—all the way back to the den. The murders and the threat of more murders yet to come left her sick, sour. She'd barely remembered to pick up the tangerines she'd promised to buy. The vendor, noting her distress, bundled the fruit in one of her precious scarves, bidding Krona return it when she felt better. The purple fabric was soft and comforting to the touch, but not enough to focus her or calm her. All through the streets, bile churned in Krona's throat, acid filled her joints, and blood beat against the backs of her eyes.

Upon entering the den, she noted the members of her team. Tray and De-Lia crowded against his desk, adamantly discussing something Krona was too far away to hear. Tabitha strode across the floor, dodging other Regulators and actuaries with a purpose as she hurried a civilian into an inquiry room. Royu hunched over papers on zher desk like an old one with frail bones—though zhe was the youngest on their team. Sasha, Krona couldn't pinpoint. Perhaps she was out following a lead.

De-Lia caught sight of her sister and gestured her over. Before Krona could speak, she asked, "Have you been to see Utkin yet? A *working* healer?"

"I just came in—"

"Then off with you."

"I will, but before I go, I need to tell you—" She quickly related the tale of the missing files and unexpected body. And of Thibaut's mysterious Madame Strange.

De-Lia listened intently, nodding along. "Royu? Tabitha?" she called when Krona had finished.

Royu quickly jogged over, dark hair falling into dark eyes. Zhe brushed zhur fringe aside. De-Lia asked zhim to make haste to the Watch station nearest the

Hall, to report back with any unusual findings, on the off chance the murder was somehow related to their stolen enchantments.

Tabitha was put in charge of looking into their records, to see if there was any previous mention of a Madame Strange, anything that might lead them to her location.

"Or," De-Lia suggested, "we could arrest your little criminal and *make* him tell us where to find her."

"He's too valuable," Krona insisted. "I need him."

De-Lia raised an eyebrow. "You *need* him?"

"Free. On the street."

"Fine. Royu's away, Tabitha's away, and now you," De-Lia said affectionately to Krona, "off to Utkin."

⇥⇥⟶○⟵⇤

"What am I going to do with you, Mistress Hirvath?" Utkin asked, probing her wound.

He had her sitting shirtless on one of his exam tables, but he'd given her a blanket for modesty. She held it firmly to her chest, her dark fingers clutching the white fabric in a death grip. Her teeth clacked together as he gave a particularly painful prod.

"Apologies," he said, swabbing away the remnants of De-Lia's makeshift job. "Who knitted this? You've had more than one pair of hands here since it happened, haven't you?"

"Yes. *Three.* I should have come to you immediately. But luckily I have a bit of padding on my middle, or my need of you could have been much more dire."

He grunted his agreement. "You are amassing quite the collection of scars, I'll have you know."

"I aim to have the most extensive in the city," she quipped.

"I admire your good humor in the face of what's happened," he said, though not unkindly. She knew he didn't mean the stabbing. He meant the Jubilee.

"I've thought about it more, and I do believe your vargerangaphobia urgently needs addressing," he said, while she stared blankly at the pale wall in front of her. "We've discussed the possibility before that the excess fear is caused by too much black bile in your system . . ."

Krona nodded and leaned forward, away from Utkin, away from his words. She knew her posture was defensive, but she couldn't resist putting space between herself and talk of varger.

"Well, that new philosophy and treatment I mentioned before, it involves a black bile sliver. The theory suggests something must have embedded itself

in you during your first encounter with one of the creatures. It's supposedly possible to flush this sliver from your system, but the methods are . . .
uncomfortable."

"Uncomfortable how? Invasive?"

"Yes, but not *physically*."

The cold bite of a needle pierced her side, and she hissed. If he thought talk
of her phobia would distract her from his work, he was wrong.

"Tell me about your earliest experience with a varg, once more."

She swallowed harshly, her throat having gone dry. She didn't want to discuss this now. She didn't want to discuss this *ever*.

"My father was killed by a varg."

"Yes. And you were there. You saw it happen."

"Yes."

Everything, she'd seen it all in grisly detail. Still saw it sometimes, in her
sleep, or suddenly when she'd been thinking about something entirely unrelated. Sometimes she was transported back there, to that very moment, and it
was real, happening all over again.

Utkin put a soothing hand between her shoulder blades. "If you don't want
to recount it blow for blow, I understand. But, I think it might help. How close
did you get to the creature?"

She could still feel its breath on her cheek, hear the way its spines rustled
together—not like hair, but like hollow reeds. The way it padded around on the
kitchen floor, how its claws raked against the boards . . . And the smell. Gods,
the smell.

And then everything had broken—the world had shattered while she froze.
She was right there, and she couldn't do it, she couldn't—

Krona's face went hot, and she failed to control the trembling in her lips.
"Close," she grated.

It shouldn't still be this fresh, she knew. The memory should have long ago
faded. She should be numb to the images, unable to retrieve the sensations and
the emotions. The guilt . . . But that was her problem: she couldn't let go. The
event had braided itself into her being.

Please, make me forget.

Master Utkin patted her back firmly, as though he'd heard her plea. "I now
believe phobias come from absorption during a moment of intense fear. I think
you inhaled a fine hair, or were pierced by a piece of varger claw, or ingested
a fleck of saliva. Perhaps you simply touched whatever it was and osmosis did
the rest. But your body pulled it in, and while the black bile in you surged—
burgeoned by your fear—it encased the sliver."

A needle prick . . . the tug of horsehair thread . . . the sensations started to numb and Krona began to move away from now to *then*.

"As the adrenaline ebbed, and your bile retreated, the bits around the sliver hardened. Like amber encasing an insect, forming a stone. A shard. Your body did it to protect you—I believe there are worse problems absorption can cause."

Prick became *press, tug* became *tickle*. Her vision tunneled slightly, and now both the wall she was staring at and Utkin's voice felt very far away.

"But now, whenever you encounter varger, or think of varger, or see images of the creatures, what have you—that little shard of bile-and-varg *vibrates*. It resonates with its kin—both the memories and the realities—drawn to its own kind. The sliver pulses through the hardened bile, reminding you of the first terror. It repeats the moment for you, again and again, keeping your past your present.

"If you want to let go, we have to shatter the black stone inside you, so that your body can push the splinter out."

Krona blinked repeatedly, trying to draw the wall forward again, but the more she tried to focus, the further it receded. "How do we do that?" she asked, sounding far-off to herself. "How do we shatter the stone?"

One final twist of a knot and the clip of shears and he was done. "By making it vibrate itself apart," he said.

"I don't understand." She fumbled for her undershirt, needing to be dressed this instant. Needing her armor and her weapons and her anonymity again.

Covered, she faced him, and he too looked far away. And small. Manageable.

"The only thing that can break it is the terror that built it. I call it exposure therapy. We expose you to the source of your distress until you . . ." He frowned lightly, making a face like a sturgeon, and one hand lifted to flutter up near his ear. "Crack."

"You want to cure my vargerangaphobia by . . ."

"Playing on your fear as much as possible, yes," he said, his eyes narrowing.

Krona sucked in her cheeks, wiping her sweaty palms down her thighs. Lowering her eyes and her chin, she let out a breathy, nervous laugh. "I don't—I don't know if I am capable of . . ." She wasn't quite sure what she was trying to say.

"Oh, don't make up your mind right away," he said, wiping his tools. "I know the prospect must seem daunting."

Terrifying.

"But think on it. After this concern is over, when your arm is better and you are feeling well in all other aspects, we can broach the topic again."

Before leaving the infirmary, she asked after the false varg, but he was still not yet well enough for an attempted interview.

Exhausted—with her mind foggy and her body dragging—Krona left for home.

><+>-0-<+><

Krona wasn't sure if De-Lia made it back to their apartment that night, either. The next morning—day two of the concern, if the Jubilee could be counted as day zero—Krona traveled to the den alone, and did not set eyes on her sister before making her way toward the holding cells to see if her prisoner was finally up and about.

Krona rubbed at her wounds as she strode through the den, first scratching absently at her forearm and then her side. They itched, but more with memory than a physical twinge. She was ready to confront her attacker, to get out of him whatever she could regarding the despairstone and the Mayhem Mask.

Approaching the guard post in front of the cell-block gate, Krona found it empty. Two Regulators were supposed to be stationed here no matter the time of day.

Deep underground, the cells were dim; small gas lamps lit them from the outside, far from the grasp of a potential escape artist's fingers. Krona could see little from her vantage point. Trying the gate, she found it secure.

"Hello?" she called. Her voice echoed down the stone hall.

There was a shifting in a few of the cells beyond, confirmed convicts and the recently accused stirring like tired old hunting dogs at the *yip* of a fox.

After an uncomfortable beat, a voice she recognized reverberated through the block: one of the guards. "Get a healer! Get help!" He swirled out of the last cell in the block, sprinting toward her.

Her legs reacted before her mind could. Krona twirled back up the stairs, headed for the surgery. Tray walked by the landing at the same moment Krona alighted, and she grabbed his sleeve roughly. "We have a problem."

The Regulator behind her bounced into her back. "He—he's unconscious."

"Who?" Tray demanded, but Krona was already on her way to the medical wing.

When she reached the surgeries, the nearest door opened, and out strode the healer who had advised her on the tattooed man's condition. "Master Guerra, come quickly."

He obeyed.

As they approached the cell block together, cold dread found a seat in Krona's stomach. She knew, even before Tray threw the gate open, who was in trouble.

She knew as they pounded past the other prisoners—whose jeers and catcalls morbidly punctuated the severity of the situation—and she knew as they came to a stop in front of the last cell, its barred door thrown wide.

Inside, the two guards kneeled over the supine form of the tattooed man. One held his head while the other lightly slapped his cheeks, trying to offer him water if only he'd wake up.

"Back—back away," Master Guerra demanded. "How long? When did you find him?"

"He shouted—howled, more like—a few minutes ago," said the first guard. "I found him convulsing. He's been still now for some moments."

How could he have cried out? Krona thought. She'd cut his throat. Either the guard was lying, or someone else had made that sound.

Master Guerra bent his ear to the tattooed man's mouth. "No breath," he said. "Quickly, help me carry him to the surgery. We don't have much time to save him."

Much scrabbling followed as the two guards hefted the large man from the floor. Krona caught a whiff of something strange as they carried him past, and she noted an angry red welt above the bandages around his throat. In the center was a spot of blood—a pinprick—and a smear of silver: mercury.

She'd seen a needle mark like that recently: on Madame Iyendar.

This one, though, formed a hub from which purpled veins spanned away. They grew darker and thicker with every passing moment.

"I think he was injected with something," she said.

"What gave you that idea?" Tray asked.

"Madame Iyendar. Quick, we need to put the den on lockdown. Make sure no one we don't know gets in or out."

They searched high and low, from the armory to the healers' rooms to the interrogation suites and the evidence vault. It took hours, but there was no one unaccounted for.

How? How had this happened? Had they been infiltrated? The den's defenses compromised? Members of the Watch came and went from the den all the time. This could be further proof that Thibaut's intelligence was good.

That a corrupt member of the constabulary had attempted to silence a prisoner.

And yet, it wasn't a corrupt Watchman who'd stuck a needle in Madame Iyendar.

Iyendar.

The Chief Magistrate's son had distracted Krona at the Jubilee. Now a man had been attacked in the den, and he bore signs of similar injections as the Chief Magistrate's daughter-in-law.

A terrible thought struck her.

It would be so easy for the *Chief Magistrate* to find corruptible members of the Watch, to use his power and influence . . .

No. She didn't even want to entertain the idea.

"What now?" Tray asked her.

"We need to tell De-Lia. Someone needs to make a list of all non-den constabulary who've been here today."

"And then? I can see there's more."

She nodded. "Get your helm, I'll check out a few masks from the vault. We need to speak with the Iyendar's healer, Master LeMar, and his apprentice, Melanie Dupont."

She didn't like this. Didn't like how things appeared to be pointing up the chain of command, straight into the heart of the Iyendar household.

They'd start with the apprentice. If anyone was easy to crack, it should be her. The young woman seemed polite, unassuming. A competent healer. The furthest thing from a crook, let alone an assailant.

And yet, there was something about Mademoiselle Dupont that felt . . . incongruous. As though she was somehow both less and so much more than she appeared.

15

LOUIS

Lutador, ten years previous,
time and location unknown

Cold. So cold. A burning sort of freezing that stole Charbon's numbness away . . . and he'd been numb for so long.

His thighs ached, the bottom of his feet felt like they'd been pummeled with stones. How had he gotten here? Where was here?

He felt as though he were waking from a dream, and indeed he realized he was wearing his nightclothes—slippers, dressing gown, cap, and all. It was utterly dark, and the air was freezing, as though he were outside during the dead of winter. But summer had just begun.

He would not be surprised to discover he'd begun sleepwalking. Sleep was so evasive these days, had been these past months—first, while Avellino was sick, and now . . . now . . . now *after*.

He'd cried all the tears he could cry, watched as Una covered herself over with rapturestones and joystones to blot out the sadness. He'd refused food these past two days, just hoping for unconsciousness to take him. Perhaps if he could sleep he would wake up in a different world, he'd thought.

Perhaps his wish had come true.

Charbon reached out, took strained steps forward. He realized that every small movement he made—the simple scuff of his slippers against the floor—made a distinct echo. He was definitely inside, in a tight space.

An icehouse, he realized, where chunks of Marrakevian glacier were held so that the ice could be used in family iceboxes throughout the year. He crouched, flicking his fingers over the stone floor. There, yes, there seemed to be bits of insulating straw strewn about.

That explained the frigidness, but did not explain how he'd arrived.

"H-Hello?" he ventured.

Be still, came a command in his mind. No, surely not in his mind.

Fear immediately took him, and the clarity of the emotion drove away any notion that he might be dreaming.

Perhaps he'd been drugged. There was a certain fuzziness at the back of his skull.

Perhaps he'd been kidnapped.

"Who's there?" he asked, voice cracking. He stood up straight, hoping to project strength. "Why did you bring me here?"

Your feet brought you here, the voice said. *We are waiting for your companions to arrive.*

"Whom do you mean?"

They did not answer. He searched for whoever it was, taking careful but strong steps from wall to wall until he hit bales of hay. They easily evaded him.

Changing tactics, he searched for the door instead. He did not have the time nor the patience for kidnapping. Hadn't they any idea what he'd been through? How much he'd lost? Maybe that was the point—they'd come for him when his family was vulnerable. He would take no guff with thieves and blackmailers. Grief had taken more than they could possibly hope to squeeze out of him.

He was more careful with where he placed his fingers now, looking for latches and rings. The door would surely lie opposite the ice itself; all he had to do was find the seams.

"My son is *dead*," he spat at the hidden individual after several minutes. He did not care to hide his anguish, did not care that it was the proper thing to do. Who was expected to be proper around their captor? "I don't know what you think you'll extract from me, but you have come at me in a reckless way during a reckless time. Drug me again if you must—club me over the head! You will get nothing from me and nothing from my family, because we've already lost everything!"

More voices, outside. Getting louder, drawing nearer.

"Help!" he cried. "In here! I'm trapped inside! Help!"

Be still, the voice admonished once again.

"Be still yourself and bite your tongue!"

A heavy scraping of metal on metal rang out a few feet to Charbon's right. He scurried that way, hoping that even if it were more kidnappers returning, he might still be able to squeeze by them.

The door swung outward, and the light inside barely changed. It was indeed the middle of the night—stars could be seen past the four new silhouettes that greeted him. The icehouse was itself built in a pit—a wide set of curved stairs led down from the ground level above.

Louis made to sprint at them, to bowl the figures over, fight and claw his way to freedom. But then one individual lit a candle, and the face it illuminated stopped him in his tracks.

Fiona.

"I should have known," he growled. "What game is it this time? Why can't you leave me alone?"

"This is not a game," she said with the utmost seriousness. "This is life and death and now you need to know what we know."

She brushed past him, a long velvet cloak around her shoulders to fight against the cold. After her came Matisse, because of course. Where she went he doggedly followed. But after them came two he could not name, and indeed Charbon fought with himself over who they might be. He knew what they *looked* like, but it simply could not be true.

Two tall men, one pale and one black, stood before him. Blue lines and swirls covered their features, marring their faces and hands. The patterns gave off soft periwinkle light, and they must have been marked over their entire bodies—though their lavish azure-to-chalk robes fully covered their legs and chests and arms, their forms were visible because the swirls glowed beneath the fabric. And atop each of their bald heads sat a crown of silver blades.

He'd spooked his girls many a night with the tale of Thalo puppets, but not once had he ever imagined those manifestations to be real. These had to be men in elaborate costumes.

Had to be.

They are what you fear they are, came the voice in his head again, only this time it was accompanied by two others. Somehow, these people were speaking without opening their mouths. Perhaps that was for the best, given that the puppets were supposed to possess monstrous teeth. Charbon turned away, to look into the depths of the icehouse to see who, or what, Fiona's candle now illuminated.

Sure enough, a third Thalo puppet, shorter and rounder than the other two and of indistinguishable gender, occupied the rear corner nearest the insulated ice. Though Charbon was sure they had not possessed an ethereal glow before—he would have seen them—they now shone a soft cobalt blue.

They are my tools, said the voices. *My one means of communication in your speck of the world. They take great effort to manifest and maintain. So listen well, for I must speak swiftly.*

"I don't know who you are, though I know *what* you want me to believe you are. And I won't, I will not indulge—"

Be. Still.

Or maybe he *would* indulge. What was the point in resisting? In expending the effort?

Fiona was here. She would have her way, play her game, and he would be able to do little more than run this new maze she'd created for him. And then, if he was lucky, she'd grow bored and release him.

An overwhelming sense of defeat took hold of his limbs, and Charbon slumped to the ground, his legs crossing beneath him, head falling into his hands. Too little food and sleep, and too much grief, had pulled the fight out of him. He wanted *this*—not just whatever this meeting was, but this life, this existence—to be *over*. And so he would sit here and let them bombard him with whatever story they insisted on telling, and then he would go home and pray the sands take him.

You do know what I am, you know what these are. I am the hair raising on your neck when you feel you're being watched. My puppets are the shimmer in the sun's glare, the movement of a statue, the shadow where there should be none. When you are sure there is someone, but there is no one, I am there, observing with my puppets.

Shouting and denials hadn't worked, but perhaps he could blot out the voices. Charbon stuck his fingers in his ears, screwed his eyes shut, and bowed his head. To his relief, he found it did dull the nonsense, made the voices faint. Perhaps it only seemed like the sounds were being projected directly into his mind.

The Thalo said something sharp to Matisse, and he dove at Charbon from behind, wrenching him by the wrist, tearing one hand away from his ear. "You will listen," Matisse gritted out.

"Why? What is the point of this? Of anything, why do you insist—?"

You will listen to your god! it shouted.

"You are not a god! Even if you are the Thalo—if this isn't a nightmare and you are truly it—you are the world-maker who would feed humanity to your dogs!"

"We have been deceived!" Fiona hissed, sliding to her knees next to him. "Everyone in the Valley, from the beginning. Listen to them—listen to the Unknown themself!"

"That . . ." He wanted to pile on another denial. But his head was already swimming, his wrist hurt in Matisse's tight grip, and nothing made sense anymore anyway. *That's impossible* was a weak response in the face of the strangeness before him.

I have scoured each of your city-states looking for servants who might help me.

You long to know your Unknown god, and your Unknown god has been trying to get to you for a thousand years. I want to help you, my children, but I have been shut out. I have sought, these long centuries, a way inside, a way to help you. But I am prevented.

"The gods keep you out," Charbon ventured. "Everyone knows—"

Everyone has been fed lies. Lies to keep you tame. Lies to keep you complacent and weak.

Charbon let loose a mirthless laugh. "Preposterous," he scoffed. "Who could possibly create such falsehoods? Who could keep out a god?"

It began with Absolon Raoul Trémaux, and your governments have continued the deception.

"How can a man prevent a god from entering the Valley?" This farce was becoming more ridiculous by the instant. What did anyone in this room hope to gain from feeding him such fairy tales?

It began when I left. When I saw that the others had given themselves over to the border, that you, our fragile creations, were safe, I went to check on my other children. The beast with a thousand eyes had lost all but two, the living swamp had nearly dried up and its flies had fallen dead around it, the leather-winged teeth storms had each devolved into little more than a single tooth on a fragile sail, flitting from place to place on the whims of the wind. I had given much to humanity and neglected my duties elsewhere. When I returned, I was barred from entry. The very gift I had bestowed upon you had been extracted and corrupted, utilized to keep you docile and me at bay.

It took me centuries to develop my puppets, and what I learned when I first manifested a splinter inside your valley sickened me. You know the pain of which I speak, which I endured, for you have experienced it as well. To watch your children suffer when you have done so much to see them thrive, when they deserve all of their power, all of their wellness . . .

Charbon shoved aside the obvious invocation of his son. "What gifts? What are you saying? We have no gifts from the Unknown, only their penalty—"

More lies. The gods do not seek punishment. They would never ask for your hands or your emotions or your time or your will. These too Absolon has forced upon you. These too are not as they were meant to be.

"No, no." Charbon tried to wrestle his hand back to his ear. There was poison in these words, little seeds of doubt. The very thing the world-creator would sow to spread chaos if it could. "How do I know this isn't a Thalo's trick? What proof can you give that you are in fact one and the same with the Unknown god?"

I can tell you where to find my gifts. The fifth enchantment. It has been with you all along—I gave my magic just like the others. But Absolon feared what my gift would bring. He sought power and praise as the chosen leader, and my magic would undermine the hierarchy he wished to build.

You are a healer. Tell me what you know of the humors.

This was an unexpected turn in the conversation. What did a god care for humors? "Blood, phlegm, yellow bile, and black bile. Each given by the gods in our construction, each to carry out functions of the body."

Why only four?

"Pardon?"

If five gods made you, why are there only four humors?

Charbon had never considered this. The exact process of creating humanity wasn't detailed in any of the scrolls; no one knew which parts each god was responsible for, or exactly how they'd combined their magic to give life. "You are suggesting there's a fifth humor?"

Everything in Arkensyre comes by fives, the voices continued. *Five city-states, five climates, five seasons, five days in a week. Five. And yet there are only four magic types and four humors in the body. Is this not odd?*

"What is it, then? And why have I seen no evidence of it in my studies?"

Ah, therein lies our task. The very reason I have sought such humans as you. The fifth humor is pneuma. Blood comes from Emotion, phlegm comes from Knowledge, and the twin biles from Time and Nature, black and yellow respectively. I gave you pneuma, the very essence of myself, the very essence that had allowed me since the first spark of awakening to create life. My children, the gods, wanted to make beings of their own, and they turned out to be the most fragile things I could have imagined, filled with so much on the inside, yet so delicate on the outside. Claws that can barely gash, teeth no good for tearing, skins easily damaged by both the heat of the sun and the cold of night. What could I give you to protect yourselves, I wondered. The other gods did not want to change the shapes of you. It was your minds they were after, something closer to what I'd made in them, rather than what I'd made in beasts. But I knew this would not do.

So when the others poured their magic into the border, to help keep my older creations from getting to you, I poured my magic into your frail forms. Your pneuma holds my gift, just as gems hold Emotion's, wood holds Knowledge's, glass holds Time's, and metal holds Nature's—but it has been stolen from you. And now I watch as you die—from illness, from accident, from the very weaknesses I sought to override. If you had your pneuma, it would not be so.

"No. How can that be? You're saying people are born with one of the five magics inside them? But that it's taken? How? How can such a thing be possible? Why don't you stop whoever is perpetuating this?"

The gods' gifts are so powerful, they can be used against us. Your pneuma is removed, then fashioned into enchantments that create a new layer to the barrier on the rim. Magic to keep the gods out—all of us. Is it not strange to you that we haven't been heard from since Absolon's era?

As for the how, tell me, when did your son fall sick?

Charbon stiffened. These last minutes had been a surreal reprieve from his grief. So strange and powerful was this moment, it seemed to set itself apart from reality and the tragedy of his life.

It wasn't long after the time tax, was it? Nature's magics get at the very essence of things. Needles can remove more than time and emotions. Transfer more than knowledge.

"You . . . you're . . ." His voice wavered, so much that he could not get the words straight on his tongue. "Are you saying the time tax *killed* my son?"

Delicate arms snaked around his shoulders. Fiona fitted him in a gentle embrace from the side, weaving her arms through Matisse's, so the two of them trapped him together. "I am so sorry, Louis," she breathed in his ear.

He longed to throw them off, but did not have the energy to do it. "Why not come forward to all of Arkensyre? Surely when they see you, when you tell them what you've told us, they will—"

No. Do you think I have not tried before? Absolon built his lie well. He weaved in enough truth that my very existence has been pitted against itself. The only false-hoods that stand are those built on pillars of truth—just as it is easiest to dismiss the truth when it comes from an untrustworthy source. Children have the easiest time spotting my puppets, even when I don't wish them to. From the mouths of babes, you were told of my manifestations, and so many of you dismissed them. Truth and lies are not as evident as they should be, ever is the way of the world.

What I need are champions. Servants to appeal to Arkensyre on my behalf. Those who can bring forth the proof of my gift, the evidence that it has been stolen. Give them enough reason to fight your leaders—to deny the tax takers, to over-throw the people who would have you grovel. Find the evidence, find the subver-sion, find the enchantments keeping the gods out and destroy them. Then we can return to you, and I can once again bestow what was taken.

"Who are the people, and where are the devices?" Matisse asked. "What if we destroy the enchantments first? We could let you in—"

If only it were so simple. But the very magic that keeps me out keeps me blind. I cannot see the enchantments, nor the people who wield them. And if I could, I fear the three of you would be killed before you could make any approach. No. Convinc-ing the people is the only way. Return at least that much power to them, the power in the secret, and they the many may rise up as one.

The same five words rattled over and over again in Charbon's mind: *the time tax killed Avellino, the time tax killed Avellino.* One of the very tenets of their society, sharing time, had destroyed his joy. Had robbed his son of life, of *all* of his time, before he'd got to live any of it.

It made too much sense to ignore. Charbon was a good healer; he'd saved many people. But he could not save his own son because he'd never had a chance—the essence that would have kept him alive, that would have helped him fight despite his own human frailty, his pneuma, had been stolen. Stolen by the very people who had the most time, who cashed in to live long, unnatural lifespans. Why wouldn't they take even more from their fellow citizens? Why wouldn't they drain the magic from others to keep power for themselves?

"Where is it?" he asked darkly, voice gruff. "Where is this evidence? If it exists, I will find it."

If an organ is removed, or a hand, does it not leave a scar? When there is a cut, blood flows. The evidence is in your very bodies. But, alas, I cannot see exactly where, cannot sense how the scars of your lost pneuma might manifest. This is something I need you to discover.

"But I have looked in many bodies, taken them apart at the joints, plucked the network of veins from their muscles without severing a single one. I, of all people, have *looked*. I have never seen—"

Does blood not solidify in the dead? Does the bile not dry up and flake away? Do the intestines not expel their contents, and all evidence of breath fade away? There are things about humans you simply cannot learn from their corpses. You must search in the living. This is why your task is a sad one. It requires . . . sacrifice.

"You cannot tear open a man and hope to keep him alive for such a search."

Precisely.

A great, hot anger suddenly erupted in Charbon's chest as he realized exactly what task he was being set. He threw Matisse and Fiona off—both who'd thought him subdued and had loosened their grip. He stood tall, strode toward the Thalo puppet that had first been with him. "You're suggesting that the way to save humanity is to murder?" he spat in its face. The puppet did not flinch.

Yes.

"I won't do it. I will *not*."

Then other children will die. Other babies, like your boy, will lose my protection and their magic. You can do something about it. If someone before you had possessed your skills, your knowledge, your ability to uncover this conspiracy, your son might still be alive.

Fiona laid a hand on his shoulder, and he brushed it off. "Louis," she said. "It is not an evil thing being asked of us. You must do the digging, and we must do the examining. When you find the scars, we will analyze them. It is unseemly, but think of the good it will—"

"No. *No.*"

Your heart is still too heavy. Soon the grief will harden, and you will see. Sleep now. Return home. In time you will become the Unknown's servant, just as you've always claimed to be.

The puppets held out their hands, and a cold blue glow emanated from each of their palms. Charbon's head grew light, his feet heavy, and he teetered where he stood.

As he fell and the world swayed, his thoughts and emotions were a jumbled mess of wrongness, and he could not string together how the life he'd led had brought him to such a place in space and time.

16

MELANIE

Two years previous

One moment Melanie had been fighting the torturous rift in her mind, struggling to plunge herself into the fire. And the next she was in Leiwood's lap, his arms wrapped tightly around her, holding her close. The mask no longer covered her face.

"It's gone," she said, amazed. Leiwood smiled a sad, scared smile, and her heart dropped through her stomach. "I'm sorry." She felt like slime. What had she done? "I couldn't—I—"

He rocked her back and forth. "Shh. It's all right."

With his thumb he wiped away a drop of blood from her forehead. How had that gotten there? She stared at the smear for a long moment. *Did I black out?*

There was a quick, sharp tap on her forehead, and then another. He was crying. "I didn't know," he said. "My mother took me away when I was ten. I didn't come back until he was gone. He hurt a lot of people, but Master Belladino's daughter . . . I didn't know." His arms suddenly tensed around Melanie. "And your mother. Your poor mother."

Melanie began to cry herself, and the tears burned as though they were molten. The idea that something had happened and she couldn't remember it was frightening, but the thought of her mother sent her over the edge. The solution in the crucible had to cure, but then what? The next steps had been lost with the—

But no. She thought hard, and found she knew the process. And it was not fading; it was strong and clear in her mind.

How—?

Yes, there were more formulas in her memory, more healing potions and techniques. She was almost sure she knew them all. But the anger and hatred had fluttered away. All that was left was knowledge.

"I can still save her," she whispered. "But why do I still know how?"

"Perhaps when I pricked you . . ." he started, then took a shaky breath. "I took the poison out, but maybe I locked some things in, too."

She didn't understand, but the joy at realizing her mother could be saved shoved the curiosity aside. "She'll be all right. Leiwood—" He looked into her eyes. "I'm sorry I didn't resist hard enough. I should have kept him back. There was more I should have done."

"No." He smiled. "It's not your fault. It was Belladino's mask."

They sat locked in silence for a long while. Melanie let relief, and sadness, terror, calm, and happiness flood through her freely.

Eventually Leiwood helped her stand. "We need to get you to a healer." He gazed mournfully at her ruined hand. She hadn't even noticed it.

"I can do it myself," she said firmly. "I know how." She smiled, and flexed the seared fingers despite the pain. *"I know how."* She had a gift now—a master healer's knowledge and all the long years of life to improve upon it. She'd always been a helper, devoting her life to her ailing parents. But they hadn't sucked away her time—they'd enriched it. "And I know what to do with my life. I can share Master Belladino's genius with the world. Just the brilliance. Hopefully his loathing is gone forever."

Leiwood glanced over to the syringe on the floor, but didn't say anything.

She hugged him close. "There are so many people I could help. Not just in my village, but perhaps the city as well. The muscle illness doesn't have to claim more time. I'll make sure people don't have to spend their lives being sick."

He nodded. "Because real time is worth more than bottled time."

Melanie's heart fluttered. "Life is always worth more when it's lived."

>─+─◇─◇─+─<

He helped bandage her hand.

She saw to the spot of blood on her forehead.

They locked the syringe and the mask in a small trunk.

He told her how he'd rid her mind of Belladino's smog.

And then they'd said little else the rest of the night.

Melanie worked diligently, letting the mixture cure before taking it over to the brazier to bring it to a boil.

Hours passed.

Morning light dripped through the city, bathing the room's windows, making them glow.

When the linctus was ready, it didn't smell foul. For some reason, Melanie had always thought that a proper, effective medicine was supposed to smell like death and taste worse. She sniffed the concoction three separate times to be sure Belladino's know-how indicated it did indeed carry a sweet scent as it was supposed to.

She carefully portioned it out into seven vials, stoppered them good and tight. After the first full dose, her mother would need to consume a few drops with food every day for the next six months. Longer, if it didn't take to her humors like it should—if Melanie had miscalculated or forgotten something about her mother's decline.

She looked over to where Leiwood sat on his bed, reading. Then at the chest.

She still needed the syringe.

Fidgeting with her hands, she chanced another furtive glance at him, feeling like no apology could ever make up for what she'd said and done under the mask's influence. And, given the way she'd abused him, she wouldn't have been hurt had he treated her with distance or even a little disdain. But, strangely, when she cleared her throat to entreat his attention and he glanced her way, he didn't seem to regard her any differently.

He closed the book he'd been reading; *On Wildflowers* the cover said. "What is it?"

"It's ready."

"Will it work?"

"Awful mess to go through if it doesn't," she said—a half-hearted attempt at a joke. "But I . . . most of the medicine will be administered orally, over a long period of time. But the first dose needs to be injected. Deep. With precision. After spending an hour inside enchanted glass."

"That's why you took the syringe in the first place."

She nodded.

"So dealing with *that*"—he nodded at the box, implying all the horrors it contained—"can't wait."

He slipped off the bed. Together, they tentatively approached the trunk, as though it had teeth. In a way, it did.

"Can we . . . put it back in?" she asked. "The echo, or whatever it's called? Just inject it back into the mask?"

"We can try," he said, cautiously running his palm across the trunk lid before lifting it. He opened the box slowly, and the hinges let out a grating whine. "But I don't . . . I don't understand how I took it *out*. I'm no enchanter."

Melanie understood even less. Magic was a strange, foreign thing. Something she'd hardly ever envisioned encountering, let alone manipulating.

In the gentle dawn lighting, the mask looked innocent. An ugly scrape now marred the frog's paint, revealing the bare wood beneath, but other than that it looked no different than it had hanging in the mask shop. Still, the sight of it sent a wave of nausea through her gut.

Next to it, the syringe lay glistening. The barrel looked empty. If she hadn't lived through it, she never would have been able to guess that a monstrous swirl of personality and memory lay within.

With shaking fingers, Melanie reached for the mask. She came within centimeters, but found she couldn't make herself touch it. Distress burgeoned in her chest, the swell of it stealing her breath, closing off her throat. Instinctually, she reeled back again. "I can't," she gasped apologetically.

"It's all right," Leiwood soothed, taking her by the hand. He rubbed a small circle into her back. "I couldn't look at the crow for months after. I'll do it, it's all right."

"After what I did to you—said to you—I shouldn't ask anything else of you, I shouldn't—"

"Shh. I'm the one who inserted myself into your business. Trust I can decide for myself when too much is too much." He drew both items out.

They looked so innocent. Artisanal and beautiful.

Leiwood tossed the mask on the bed, then took the syringe closer to the window, holding the barrel up to the sunlight, letting the glass fracture the beams into rainbows. "I saw things, when I released the time," he said. "Like there's the world as we see it . . . and then there's the world as the gods see it. It reminded me . . ." He trailed off.

"Reminded you of what?"

"Reminded me that these things need to be respected. Magic isn't ours, not really. We don't make it, we don't control it. We harvest it and refine it and pretend to master it. But it's a feral power that wants to turn on us."

"It's a gift . . ." she said softly.

He glanced at her. "You still believe that?"

She ran her uninjured hand over her brow. "I don't know."

Having either seen or failed to see whatever he was looking for in the barrel, he returned to the mask, his movements harsh. Running his thumb over the wood, he searched for the place he'd punctured before—but the balsa was soft and the paint detailed. It was difficult to find where the grain had parted.

"I don't know what I'm doing," he reminded her, poising the needle.

Before she could think of a helpful reply, he pressed on, thumbing the plunger down, pressing the metal tip into the carving.

All the air was sucked suddenly—*violently*—into the center of the room, toward the syringe. It was a great *inhale* that pulled at their clothes and the curtains. It made the lamps flare and the walls *groan*.

A gasping silence rang in Melanie's ears.

They both reeled back in horror, clutching at their throats, their mouths, their noses.

The pressure, the suction, threatened to collapse their lungs.

And then that same air blew back at them, away from the mask with all the force of a winter's howling gale. Melanie's hair whipped wildly around her face as a storm, once bottled, now raged—trapped inside the room.

A tremendous scream knocked Melanie back—passed over her, through her—and it was unmistakably the voice of Master Belladino.

Just as violently as it began, the storm stopped. Dissipated.

Melanie's lungs heaved as she gulped for air. She clutched at her chest, her face.

Leiwood doubled over, hands braced on his thighs, back shuddering as he struggled for breath. "I think—" he gasped, "it's safe to assume that *wasn't* right."

"We didn't trap it again, did we?"

"I don't think so."

"Then where did it go?" Could it hurt someone else? Could it settle in a mind without a mask?

"I think . . . I think maybe it's gone. For good. We released it."

"Is that . . . good?"

Leiwood threw out a flippant hand, a weary shrug. "Gods, who knows? We should probably count ourselves lucky a bit of breathlessness is all the abuse it deigned to visit upon us before *leaving us be.*"

He pointed at the syringe, still stuck fast in the wood. "It's all yours."

She snatched it up, hurrying to the mixture, pulling the dose into the barrel quickly, as though afraid the enchanted glass would shatter in her hand and leave her bereft at the last moment. Her fingers shook, but she worked the plunger smoothly.

She glanced over her shoulder—at Leiwood, into the corners of the room, the ceiling, the fireplace. Perhaps the echo was gone, perhaps it was not.

Perhaps it would return to spite her and ruin the formula in the end.

But she managed to fill the barrel to the proper line. Managed to pull her quivering fingers from the syringe's guard. Managed to set it down without dropping it or pricking herself.

And now, for another hour still, they had to wait.

She sat down in front of the fireplace, its coals long cold. The grate dark, the mouth of the chimney ominous.

"You can't return an empty mask," Leiwood said quietly, after a time. He stood in front of the window, looking out at the bustling below.

"I'm aware."

"If you show your face there again, the owner will have you arrested. The penalty—"

She cut him off. "I'm *aware*." She fidgeted with the hem of her skirt. "Why didn't you . . . your father's mask . . . ?"

"It's privately held. I haven't given the Regulators a reason to ask after it. The state doesn't know I ruined it. Even the shopkeeper, he knows I went through a fight with the echo, but he doesn't know . . ."

"And yet you display it, clearly halved?"

He looked at his shoes, shuffled his feet. "After this, I won't."

"Couldn't we . . . couldn't we explain?" she suggested, only half hopeful. "If we tell them how it went, how the echo turned—We're not bad people. We didn't mean to ruin—"

"In the eyes of the law, we are," he said firmly. "We destroyed a sacred object. Two for me, now. The state has its narratives, and it leaves very little room for mitigating circumstances." He turned, found her gaze. "We are the villains of this story, make no mistake."

"Then we have to get rid of the evidence. We have to burn it."

Taking that as a directive, he scooped it off the bedding, hurrying to her side, making to toss it behind the grate—

She caught his wrist. "Not here. Not where someone could see, or where they might find evidence. Later. We'll take it far afield. Perhaps . . . I can do it on my way home. My mother and I will need to leave as soon as we're able. And we'll have to . . . Oh gods, the shopkeeper, he'll look for me, won't he?"

"The *Regulators* will come looking for you," Leiwood corrected. "You can't simply disappear without returning a mask."

"I *can't* return it, we already covered that. What—what if . . . Could we buy it? Your mask is privately owned, so no one—"

He shook his head. "A Regulator would oversee the sale. Besides, where would you get the time vials? *I* can't afford to buy it. I can't afford any mask at that shop"—a pained expression crossed his features—"not without risking the inn. If I could, I would—"

"No. No, I wouldn't ask that of you. Of course not."

She couldn't run, she couldn't hide, she couldn't return the mask and pretend to be ignorant. She needed a plan. There had to be something she could do, some way to keep anyone from searching for her. All she wanted was to disappear back into the countryside with her mother and never see another blasted mask ever again.

"We can't burn it either, can we?" she breathed. "Disenchanting it is one thing, burning it . . . It won't erase what happened." Melanie pulled her knees up to her chest, hugging her arms around them. "I just wanted to save her. I love her so much, she doesn't deserve . . ."

"We'll think of something," Leiwood said, though his voice lacked the confidence of his words.

There had to be a way. A way out of this.

She'd only had good intentions. Only wanted to be a good daughter.

How had it all gone so wrong?

Now, if the state found out, they would rip her away from Dawn-Lyn— perhaps even before she was well again. Her mother would be left alone, without help, and Melanie—she—

She'd be tossed into a labor camp. Or worse.

Her hand was burned now, but if she was found guilty of a crime against Knowledge—

Melanie felt an invisible blade pass through her wrist, severing it. She swallowed the panicked cry that threatened to squeeze itself from her throat.

No. Oh, sweet gods, please no.

When the hour was up, Melanie readied her things, preparing to give her mother the first dose, trying to put her other anxieties out of her mind for now. She placed all she needed into a satchel. Leiwood walked her to the door, but she stopped him from opening it.

She bit her lip, felt tears welling once again. "Thank you," she said. "I don't know how I'm going to repay you."

Tentatively, he reached for her hand. She let him take it. "You don't have to," he said firmly. "I wanted to help. That's all."

"But everything I put you through—"

"It wasn't you. My mind has known that same chaos. I wouldn't hold it against you." He glanced over at the trunk, where they'd secreted the mask away once more. "Masks are a plague. They're dangerous. They're supposed to be regulated but *oh look how well.*"

"And still," she said, "my mother would have no hope without one."

He nodded.

"We still haven't made a plan for . . ." She gestured back to the trunk.

"We'll talk about it after," he said, eyes lowered, looking at her hand in his. A heavy, tired sigh escaped him. "Honestly, we should probably just go to bed for now."

His eyes went wide as he realized what he'd said. Melanie didn't even have a chance to reply before he was already tripping over himself to take it back. He released her hand. "I—I mean *alone*. Separately. I didn't—I wasn't *suggesting*—I meant—"

"I know what you meant," she said, casting her gaze to her shoes. His fumbling attempt to save himself was far more embarrassing than his initial indelicate phrasing.

"I'll have breakfast brought to your room," he said quickly, trying to pivot hard into a different topic.

"And dinner?" she asked.

"If you'd like."

"I meant, can I see you for dinner? To talk. About . . . You know, after we've been to bed. Separately."

He smiled sheepishly. "Yes. Let's."

"I will see you then, Monsieur Leiwood."

He opened the door, and she hoisted the sack higher on her shoulder. Before she could hurry through, he said, "Sebastian."

"What?"

"I think we're well acquainted enough now that . . . Would you call me by my given name? Sebastian."

"All right. Sebastian."

He nodded. She blushed at the blatant approval in his eyes. They parted with tender smiles on their lips.

>─◦─◦─◦─◦─<

When Melanie made it back to her room she entered as quietly as possible, happy to see Dawn-Lyn in bed, still asleep, with a look of ease on her face. She always slept long hours, usually unevenly, grimacing and whimpering throughout all portions of the day and night. It was good to see that a well-stuffed bed had eased her pain, if only a little.

Melanie didn't wake her until after breakfast arrived. "I need to give you an injection. It will hurt, but I will be quick and careful."

Dawn-Lyn nodded, lips pressed into a thin line of trepidation, but she rolled onto her front as Melanie guided her.

There were few indignities they hadn't borne together—such was life as the helper and the helped—so neither of them fussed as Melanie moved the hem of her mother's smallclothes aside to jab the needle into the weak muscle of her backside.

Dawn-Lyn made a small sound of pain, and Melanie apologized, doing her best to administer the dose efficiently.

When she was finished, Melanie helped her sit up on her side, then dashed an extra bit of the linctus on some toast, and fed it to her in small bites.

"My girl," her mother said, thin brow furrowing in concern as she slowly chewed. With effort she lifted a hand to Melanie's face. "What happened to your forehead?"

She hadn't seemed to notice the bandage on Melanie's hand.

"Nothing, a scratch. You're sure the medicine tastes all right?"

"Hardly notice it's not honey."

Melanie smiled. "Good." Melanie yawned. "Very good." She continued to feed her until Dawn-Lyn refused another bite, beckoning her daughter into her arms.

"What did I ever do to deserve such a caring daughter?" she asked as Melanie lay down and lightly placed her head on her mother's chest.

"Were a wonderful mother," Melanie said sleepily. "*Are* a wonderful mother."

Dawn-Lyn petted her daughter's hair with shaky fingers. "I want you to promise me something."

"Mmm?"

"If it doesn't work . . . this cure of yours . . . I don't want you to be angry. At the world, at yourself."

"It will work."

"You can't know for certain. So, promise me."

"I will swap you: promise for promise."

"Oh? And what kind of promises am I in any position to fulfill?"

"When you are better . . ."

"Yes?"

"Will you make me those Marrakevian tarts? Like when I was little."

"The bridal tarts?"

"Yes."

"Those are for brides."

"But you made them."

"I was a baker, dear. I made them for brides and brought home the extra."

"Promise me," she mumbled, half-asleep already.

Dawn-Lyn lifted a lock of her hair and kissed it. "I promise I will make them for your wedding. Because that means I will have lived to see it."

Perhaps everything would turn out fine. Perhaps there was no reason to worry.

Perhaps Melanie was done with masks and Regulators and blasphemous offenses and would never need to concern herself with such things ever again.

KRONA

"Nice doggy. That's it, good boy." I don't know what possessed me. Maman and Papa never told us not to run with pointy things or not to talk to strangers. But varger we knew of. Papa faced them on regular turns. He was the best of the best, a Borderswatchman, and he made sure we understood what he had to do to put food on the table. Varger were forbidden, and, to a child, anything forbidden holds fascination. I strode toward the varg with my fingers outstretched, expecting to have them bitten off at any moment.

Ever since Leroux had hinted at deception during their first encounter, Krona had been eager to speak with Melanie Dupont again. The apprentice occupied an unusual amount of her attention, given the brevity of their interview—which meant something. Krona knew to trust her instincts.

After aiding in the lockdown and procuring masks, Krona and Tray went to the Iyendars' to speak with the master and his apprentice, but only LeMar was there. He informed the Regulators that it was Melanie's day off, and that she was likely at home with her mother. After spending hours interviewing him and additional staff, Krona and Tray set off for the apprentice's country home.

The carriage now rattled along once again with the two of them inside. Soon they hit the fork just beyond the Iyendar chateau that branched toward the small village of Nor.

Krona and Tray both knew Nor well—it was where they'd grown up.

It was still miles and miles away from the Borderswatch station Krona's father had called his. Often, he'd been gone for weeks at a time protecting the Valley and searching for varger burrows. So when he came home, it was always like a holiday. There was special food, and presents, and hugs upon hugs upon hugs.

Krona let her present self seep into the past, back into little-Krona.

After a long while, a bump in the road scattered her memories, and the carriage driver turned down a thin dirt drive. Soon he pulled up on the horses, and the wheels squeaked to a halt.

The day was waning. The shadows were getting long.

Before alighting from the carriage, Krona once again donned Leroux's mask beneath her helm, and Tray put on the mask she'd procured for him. It took him a while to suppress the echo, despite how docile it was compared to Leroux. But that was why Krona was the best—it didn't matter how unruly the personality, she could soothe it and tuck it away like it had all the tenacity of a newborn kitten.

The mask Tray wore was made of oak, and looked like a woodland spirit, the face a carefully crafted series of tree knots that, at a distance, gave the impression of an old man's face. Through it, Tray possessed the ability to detect subtle scents in the environment. He could sniff out what kinds of medicines the apprentice kept at home and instantly recognize them.

Before leaving the den, Tray had worn the mask into the surgery where Master Guerra was attending to the unconscious man, sniffing out clues. He'd detected quicksilver—which could be used to disguise enchantment—and a rare herb from Xyopar. During their interview, Master LeMar had explained that, in small doses, the herb helped with clotting. Though, in large doses, it made veins burst in the brain.

Few people would have access—only apothecaries, chemists, and healers. Master Guerra didn't even keep any in the den. Nothing like that would have been given to Madame Iyendar, but the delivery method still made the healer and his apprentice a suspect. If either of them had handled such a substance recently, Tray, via the mask, would be able to tell.

He hadn't detected anything of the sort on LeMar. But that didn't rule out the possibility that Melanie could have come into contact with it on her own and used it to attack their prisoner.

Though how she might have made it in and out of the den undetected, Krona had no idea.

Regardless, there was definitely something off about the young woman. *Wrong.* Krona had tasted it on the back of her tongue, knew it in her gut.

As they approached the house, Krona kept her eyes peeled for bits of viscera and snags of hair and mangled brooch settings—anything that might physically confirm what her gut was trying to tell her. That perhaps the apprentice was not nearly as innocent as she seemed.

Melanie's small house sat near the edge of a little duck pond, its thatched roof drooping and the frame of its single window bowing. A trivial shard of green glass had been placed near the bottom right corner of the windowpane to fill the gap created by the warping. Chickens chased each other across the spotty lawn, and an old hound dog eyed them balefully from his late-afternoon sunning spot. The dog lifted his head to bark at the intruders, was distracted by a butterfly, then returned to sunbathing.

Awfully picturesque for the home of someone Krona considered a potential thief and murderer.

From her satchel, Krona retrieved a scanning sphere. Though globular in name, it was a squat decahedron, with each plane made of glass and suspended between linings of metal. All five of the major enchantment metals were present—gold, silver, iron, nickel, and copper—a slightly different combination than what was required for a full set of quintbarrel needles. Suspended inside, held by a net of carved hardwood, was a flowstone: a diamond. Diamonds enhanced emotions when worn with other stones, but could hold none themselves.

Wood, metal, glass, and stone all worked together in a scanning sphere to reveal enchantments. It was one of the few items to incorporate all four magics; many a historical enchantment engineer had lost fingers or worse when trying to invent ways for all magic to work in tandem.

But the scanner had one weakness: mercury. Ironically, one of the very things they'd come to inquire after.

Krona carefully shook the device, making the diamond inside wobble like a spider on its web. It swiftly came alive. A light from nowhere illuminated its center, sending opalescent rainbows across the glass. Holding it before her, Krona gradually slid her hands out from under it, letting it hover in the air of its own accord.

Different-sized scanning spheres performed different tasks. This one would simply make a note of nearby enchantments for them. Larger ones acted as security devices and alarms, screaming like banshees if any forbidden or unfamiliar magic crossed its path.

The scanner flew toward her face, chirping gaily as it noted her mask and bracer. It immediately did the same to Tray, then made swift work of skimming the perimeter and analyzing the insides of the Dupont cottage.

"We're clear," she affirmed as the scanner settled back in her palms. "Only magic here is ours."

Tray nodded silently, and together they approached the house.

The scent of pond reeds carried on the breeze made Krona smile behind her visor. Images of her childhood dashed across her mind in the moments before she knocked heartily on the old wooden door.

"Yes?" A woman about the same age as Acel answered, wiping flour-covered hands on her apron. She was obviously of Marrakevian descent, with black hair, pale skin, and a round face. As her gaze grazed their uniforms, she visibly tensed.

"We're here to speak with the apprentice healer Dupont," Krona said kindly.

"I'm afraid she's not here." Her voice trembled ever so slightly, but Krona was not troubled. It was possible the woman had never seen Regulators before, let alone had them knocking down her door.

"We were told this was her day off. When do you expect her to return?"

The woman shrugged. "She's visiting her fiancé in the city. She usually returns before evening," she said, looking skeptically out the window at the low-hanging sun.

"Shall we wait?" Tray asked via his reverb bead.

"Let's," Krona agreed. "Madame—?"

"Please, Dawn-Lyn. I'm Melanie's mother."

"May we come in and wait for your daughter's return?"

Dawn-Lyn's gaze narrowed as she contemplated her options. After a moment she graciously shuffled aside. "I was preparing to bake bridal tarts with my daughter," she explained, gesturing at the mess that was her kitchen counter. "It's a Marrakevian tradition. So if you'll have a seat and excuse me . . ."

"Of course."

Inside, the space was one room, with two sleeping mats in one corner and a stove and table opposite. Beneath the window was a large basin into which Dawn-Lyn plunged her powdered hands.

Near the mats, on a dressmaker's mannequin, hung a beautiful aqua blue gown. Tiny glass beads studded the garment in intricate patterns, making the waist—where a large section of fabric had been revealingly cut—seem unusually narrow. The cap sleeves and high collar were made of carefully manipulated gauze, allowing the neck of the heavy bodice to swoop low without appearing immodest.

The wedding dress was grand, but not new. Clearly it had been in someone's family for years. Its lushness suggested it, like the veil and the venue, might have been a gift from the Iyendars.

"We're going to sew real joystones into the sleeves," Dawn-Lyn said, noting how long Krona's faceplate lingered on the gown. "Ones loaned from the Chief Magistrate, of course."

On the windowsill sat a spurred flute. Krona smiled. "Do you play?" she asked, indicating the instrument.

"Alas, no," she said. "The flute belonged to my husband. He was the musician of the house. I'm afraid I haven't heard its sweet notes in over a decade."

The Regulators took up mismatched chairs at the table, sitting stiffly while Dawn-Lyn continued to bustle about.

"You're probably wondering why we live out here when Melanie's employment is an hour away," she said conversationally. "It's at my insistence. Never was a city girl, even before I met Melanie's father and came to Lutador—and that was years ago. My daughter has been slowly moving us toward the city ever since she met that man of hers."

"How did they come to meet?" Krona asked conversationally.

Dawn-Lyn tensed, as though she'd unintentionally let loose a secret. "I had a bit of medical trouble a few years ago. We needed a . . . a city healer."

Leroux perked, hearing the breath of omitted information.

"I'm sorry to hear that. Are you better now?" Krona prodded.

"Yes. Thank you."

"Was that how your daughter came to be Master LeMar's apprentice? Was he the healer you sought?"

Dawn-Lyn hesitated for a beat too long, but Krona couldn't decipher why. "No. No."

"You're looking well. Lovely, even, if I might be so bold." Sometimes flattery helped draw out little secrets.

"Oh. Thank you."

"Your daughter's fiancé isn't a healer, is he?"

"No. No no no no, Sebastian is a businessman. He owns the establishment we resided in while my city healer did her work." Every word came out a bit smug, like she was proud of herself for summarizing events so succinctly. She even punctuated the sentence with a nod to herself.

Dawn-Lyn and the Regulators chatted for a while longer—Krona still trying to guess at whatever information the woman was avoiding—until the front door flew inward, followed by a flustered Mademoiselle Dupont.

The carriage out front had obviously alerted her to the visitors. Her expression was stern, her face bloodless. "Hello, Mastrex Regulators," she said, tone flat. "Mother." She nodded to Dawn-Lyn.

Both Regulators rose to acknowledge her. "Mademoiselle, may we speak with you privately?" Tray asked.

"Of course," Dawn-Lyn answered for her. "I'll go see if our lazy chickens have decided to lay today." She snatched a woven basket from near the door and exited, throwing her daughter a measured glance.

As Melanie watched her mother go, Leroux's mask took great interest in Melanie's body language. Every shift of her hips and twist of her spine was meant to diminish their attention—but to what?

"I must admit, I'm surprised to see you here," Melanie said, absently touching the brim of her circlet. "I can't imagine how visiting me helps you with your investigation. I hope this doesn't mean it's somehow tied up with the health of the Iyendar girls. Stellina still isn't doing well."

"No, it's not about the girls. But it is about medicine."

"Oh?"

The Regulators sat again, and Melanie joined them at the table. Krona lightly touched Tray's knee, indicating he should search the home while Krona laid out their inquiries.

"Of course," he whispered into his reverb bead. But he did not execute his hunt by turning over the furniture or looking under the floorboards. He followed the scent trails, subtly turning his head this way and that to catch snatches of aroma. By the end of their visit, he would have an entire inventory of ingredients and elixirs Mademoiselle Dupont kept on the premises.

His green-man mask had belonged to a master chemist who'd made money on the side with a dark-comedy parlor trick. He'd had the remarkable ability to diagnose guests' ailments by sniffing a lock of their hair or the inside of their wrists. The air carried a multitude of clues that only someone as trained as he could detect and dissect.

"You said that Madame Iyendar could verify that you were together during the Jubilee," Krona said. "But she couldn't. She was near comatose when we questioned her. What kinds of potions have you been medicating her with?"

Melanie sighed. "She was well when I left her. I told her not . . ." She shook her head, started again. "Since Abella's death, her mood . . . she's been unstable. I've given her a few mineral tablets to calm her humors."

"Any injections? There was a puncture on the side of her neck, and mercury in the wound."

"No, those are not my nor Master LeMar's doing," she spat vindictively.

"Who injected her, then?" Tray steepled his fingers. "What might mercury be used for in a syringe?"

She hesitated. "It's been cited as a fair preservative, especially for certain plant-based injections."

"Poisons?" Tray asked.

Melanie nodded. "Poisons and remedies alike. It's also been utilized in sanitation. I've never kept it, though. Too expensive."

Tray looked to Krona, and she subtly shook her head. The apprentice was telling the truth—but that beat of resistance, there was something to it.

She didn't like it. Everything about this woman felt incongruent. She seemed too innocent, yet too worldly. Too polite, and yet somehow haughty.

Someone with a strong will hidden behind a demure outer shell.

Tray leaned forward eagerly. "So, if not from you or your master, where could she have gotten it?"

"You must forgive my impertinence—I don't wish to speak ill of my employers or the others in their employ. And this . . . Nearly everyone in my line of work finds this topic frustrating and unsavory.

"Mercury comes in many forms: salts, vapors, and quicksilver. Quicksilver is thought, by some kooks posing as healers, to be an aphrodisiac. And there is an unsavory fad making its way through the noble ranks—a fad of self-administration."

"You're saying Madame Iyendar injected *herself*? What would she want with an aphrodisiac at a time such as this?"

"She has grown increasingly more melancholy since Abella's death. She thought her blood was running cold, that she would die unless the humor was heated. She's asked both myself and Master LeMar for various drugs—things no competent healer would give her."

"So where did she acquire it from, then?" Tray asked.

Krona regarded her silently, processing the woman's fidgeting. Melanie's agitation simmered just beneath her skin, the fine hairs on her arms standing tall despite the warmth of the room. She tried to put forth a cooperative face, but Leroux knew better. Melanie wanted to rush them through the interview, to be rid of them as soon as possible, because she was hiding something.

Melanie stood and went to the window. As she passed him, Tray breathed deeply, leaning into her scent trail, quirking his head to the side. Carefully, he palmed his faceplate, slid it up, removed it—revealing the green-man mask beneath.

The apprentice healer's hands slapped the edges of the washbasin, as though a long-held frustration was finally surfacing. "Horace Gatwood."

Tray and Krona shared a look. "The valet?" Tray asked.

With a huff, Melanie turned once more. Upon seeing Tray's mask, she froze, clutching her hands to her chest. The mask had clearly startled her. More so than Krona—and Leroux—thought normal.

Melanie's fingers went to the ferronnière covering her forehead, adjusting it as though fearing it loose. "Horace Gatwood," she continued, her gaze flitting to the floor, the walls, anywhere but the mask, "possesses unconventional beliefs that appeal to the vanity of . . ." She caught herself speaking unflatteringly. "Of some. He mixes the quicksilver with various chemicals. Depressants, stimulants, in an attempt to find a blend that satisfies Madame Iyendar's need to escape."

"But he is not a physician," Krona said carefully. "He has no medical background?"

The young woman stiffened. "No, he *does not*. I still don't see how this connects to your concern."

"We haven't ruled out the possibility that the theft was politically motivated," Krona said, images of the bloom flashing before her mind's eye. The apprentice healer didn't need to be made aware of Charbon or the attack on their false varg—not if she wasn't aware of them already. "What goes on behind closed doors in your employer's home may be of consequence."

Krona hesitated before asking her next question.

Melanie wasn't the only one here ultimately beholden to the desires and instructions of the Chief Magistrate. That this concern skirted his household, his life, so closely, gave Krona pause.

She glanced at Tray.

It gave them *all* pause.

"Do you . . . do you feel safe there?" Krona asked. "At the Chief Magistrate's? Has anyone in his family ever done anything that worried you? Bothered you?"

"The Iyendar family has been exceedingly good to me," Melanie said carefully. *Too* carefully.

Another artful dodge. But still, not a lie.

"Have you ever observed anyone in the household committing a crime?"

Leroux noted how fast Melanie's breaths came, how she tightened her jaw and sharpened her gaze. "There is your usual drug and emotion stone use," she said. "One of the scullery maids stole some silver when she needed to pay a family debt, but that was a year ago."

"Nothing you'd call a Regulator for?" Krona pushed.

"I can't imagine calling for a Regulator," she said. "Ever."

It was perhaps the most direct and honest statement she'd made during their entire conversation.

Tray sniffed loudly, his nose high in the air, his eyes closed as though savoring the scent of a fine wine or scotch. He stood abruptly, the chair legs screeching across the floor. Melanie jumped as though a wild animal had lunged at her from the underbrush. The apprentice's gaze fixated on the mask with ferocity.

Perhaps her reaction stemmed from her uncertainty as to what kind of knowledge the mask possessed.

As Tray continued to inhale deeply, Krona fancied a test. Slowly, she unlatched the fastenings on her helm before lifting it up, revealing the boar.

Melanie spun away. It wasn't a phobic reaction—Melanie didn't feel about masks the way that Krona felt about varger. But there was a . . . *distaste* there. And a thread of guilt.

She put a hand on Tray's arm to gain his attention, then gestured for him to resecure his faceplate. Knowing she saw something he didn't, he nodded and complied. Krona's helm swiftly followed.

"We've covered them," Krona said kindly. "You don't have to look at the masks."

Melanie kept her back to them for a long moment, whether to gather herself or formulate an excuse, Krona would know when she spoke again.

Whatever Tray smelled piqued his interest. He sniffed once more before asking, "Does your fiancé know?" He made a circular gesture with his finger. "About your state? Does your mother?"

Krona frowned. Was Mistress Dupont ill?

At the moment, the young woman didn't appear sick so much as irritated. "What state?" she said, feigning casualness, her voice still coming out in a huff despite her clear efforts.

"I think you know, mademoiselle. No need to play coy."

"I've only told a few people," she insisted, deigning to look at them again. "Who told you? Was it the Chief Magistrate? He told Gatwood," she grumbled.

Krona said nothing.

They were on the edge of something, Krona could feel it. *Leroux* could feel it. "I'll ask again: Do you ever feel like you're in danger at the Iyendars'?"

Melanie sucked in a sharp breath, answered swiftly. "No."

A lie.

"Did you feel like you were in danger when you visited your fiancé today?"

"No."

And still another.

"Do you feel like you're in danger now?"

The woman considered her answer carefully. "Your mere presence carries a threat, does it not?"

"Has anyone ever forced *you* to engage in criminal acts?"

"*No.*" Her voice was just on the low side of shrill.

Leroux indicated it wasn't a lie . . . but it wasn't the whole truth, either.

"Your fiancé's name," Tray prompted. "What was it again?"

"I don't believe I've given it to you."

They waited.

Anxiety roiled across the young healer's face. "Sebastian Leiwood, all right? But there's no reason to bring him into this mess. He's only been to the Iyendars' once or twice—he wasn't anywhere near the girls or the Jubilee. Please, we just want—" She cut herself off, clearly realizing she had far too much fervor in her voice. "The wedding is already stressful enough, forgive me."

Dead silence reigned for a moment before the front door unexpectedly opened. Dawn-Lyn, looking all the better for her time outdoors, announced breathlessly, "I think I've had a touch too much sun. But we're in luck: two eggs today." She seemed blissfully unaware of the tension she'd broken.

They questioned Melanie for a few minutes more, but her answers were perfunctory and lacked substance.

Something was amiss here, but Krona knew they would get little else of use today. "We should go," she said to Tray via the bead.

"Thank you for your time," Krona said, gesturing for Tray to move toward the door. "Mademoiselle, please don't plan any long trips out of Lutador. We may have to darken your door once again."

"Long trips are for well after the wedding," Dawn-Lyn said happily, kissing her daughter on the cheek.

Melanie forced a smile and nodded her understanding to the Regulators. She hurried to hold the door open, entreating them to leave swiftly.

"If you feel in danger and want to talk about it," Krona said before leaving, "please come by the den. I promise, we can protect you."

Melanie said nothing, her face a blank mask.

They bade the women good-bye, strode silently back to their waiting carriage. "Is the apprentice sick? What did you smell on her?" Krona asked as they climbed inside.

"New life," Tray said, a little wistfully. "She's pregnant."

"Ah. Oh, of course."

"That must be it, then. You said she was hiding something back at the chateau . . . If she's concerned about her mother finding out . . ."

"No. There's more to it. She doesn't feel safe, that much is certain. But who is she afraid of?"

Both Regulators settled in their seats, removed their helms. Krona shook out her hair.

"As an unmarried pregnant healer of some upward mobility, it could be devastating to her station if certain people—her master, even—were to find out before she was wed," Tray said. "Perhaps she's jittery because she's so close to salvation day—a few words in a pretty tent and suddenly her reputation is safe."

"Could be," she admitted. "Still, I'd like to put a tail on her. I'm not convinced she doesn't know more about our enchantments. Maybe even our killer."

"She didn't seem the *fraternizing with murderers* type."

"They rarely do."

Tray removed the green-man and she looked sidelong at him. Red marks graced his face where the mask had pressed too tightly, and his pale cheeks carried a flush. As soon as it came free, he slumped, as though all of the air had gone out of him. He rubbed his eyes, then his temples, a telltale sign of an intense migraine beginning. Thus was the cost of wearing a Magnitude Four, even for trained mask-wielders.

Krona let her gloved hands travel to the ribbon holding Leroux's mask, but did not unknot it.

A horrible thought had struck her.

If there was an organization trying to recruit lawpersons, there was no reason they wouldn't go after Regulators, too.

Tray had been in charge of interfacing with the Watch.

Could he have . . . ?

He was weak now, exhausted from mask use. Perhaps she could question him about it without him really noticing. The flaw in the boar mask's faculties was its inability to draw conclusions for her. Leroux could identify deception, could mark an outright lie, but the mask could not tell her what the truth was. And it relied heavily on a subject's shame—while not all physical signs of falsehoods were tied to a person's emotional state, many were. If someone lied without fear of being caught, or if they spewed inventions but had convinced themselves of those inventions, there was little Leroux could latch on to.

"Tray?" she asked, pretending to fumble with the ribbon.

"Hmm?" He looked at her, unguarded. His usually perfectly swept-back hair had been ruffled in such a way that black strands fell over his forehead, grazing the tops of his eyebrows. It gave him a youthful quality.

Were you aware there was going to be a row before the Jubilee? Did you know that there were false Nightswatchmen on conservatory grounds? Did you take a bribe? Have you betrayed me? Have you betrayed De-Lia?

"What?" he prompted, a tired, harried look on his face.

"Have you come into any extra time vials lately?" Not exactly the most nuanced question, but it was better than outright asking if he'd been paid off to let varger into the party.

He furrowed his brow. "Why? Do you . . . do you need money? Is it Acel . . . ?"

"No," she said quickly, dropping her hands to her lap. "We're fine, we don't need any extra time. I only ask, because . . . Just answer the question, please."

He turned away, leaning up against the carriage door, his vulnerable expression gone. "I *haven't* been gambling."

Well, there was a lie. Plain as the point of his chin or the line of his jaw. And it was so carelessly dropped—he knew she could still see with Leroux's eyes. She'd expected at least an attempt at a finessed deception.

They were friends, but it was none of her business what vices he held. Not as long as he was well and made it to the den on time.

This was . . . this was ridiculous. She couldn't go around mistrusting those closest to her based on nebulous notions from Thibaut.

Her gut twisted. She felt sick for having even suspected Tray for an instant.

"The answer is no, I haven't come into any extra time." He said it so begrudgingly, she didn't need the mask to see it was the truth.

"I—I'm sorry. I didn't mean to probe a wound," she apologized.

"We all have our sore spots," he said. "Dupont has her pregnancy, I have my bones, and you—" He crossed his arms, regarding her cynically. An insult was poised on his tongue, she could see it.

You're a shadow.

Huffing, he reined in his irritation. Tray was not cruel; he did not dive after petty slights. With a flick of his gloved hand through the fringe of his hair, he looked out the window. "And you'd do me an honor by forgetting my outburst," he concluded. "I need to rest, the pain makes me irritable."

A deadness in his voice indicated they would ride back to the den in silence. Krona removed the mask, knowing she'd get little but acknowledging grunts out of him for the rest of the day.

Slapping the underside of the bonnet, Krona signaled to the driver that they were ready to leave.

18

MELANIE

Two years previous

Sebastian returned the borrowed items from the apothecary as soon as they'd taken their dinner. The extra herbs were gone. The needle was gone. Now all they had to deal with was the mask. Melanie checked once more on Dawn-Lyn, and then the two new co-conspirators retired to the inn's cigar room to discuss their spiral into criminality.

They wound back through the lounge, past the bar, to a pair of double doors made of richly stained wood with panes of inlaid green glass.

Ash and musk and honey met Melanie's nose as Sebastian graciously opened the room for her. This was a secluded pocket-place for worldly indulgences—those on the relaxing, easy end of hedonism.

The smoking room's doors sealed tightly behind them when closed, and heavy curtains graced the doorjamb as an extra fortification against leaking vapors. Sebastian pulled them tight across the seams. The heady, dry scent of cigar smoke perforated the fabric.

Sebastian gestured at a pair of high-backed leather chairs, then took one himself—one leg propped up on his other knee, foot bouncing nervously.

"I thought we should have some privacy," he explained. "Somewhere other than . . ."

"Other than your personal chambers?"

"People gossip," he said. "I'm not a letch who preys on pretty patrons, and wouldn't have anyone thinking ill of me if I can avoid it. I hope you understand."

She wasn't sure which word her mind tripped over more disastrously: "letch," "preys," or "pretty."

This time, he seemed not to have noticed he'd said anything untoward.

"Please, have a seat," Sebastian continued, gesturing at the chair opposite the one he occupied, in every way the first chair's mate.

With a sigh, she sat, taking stock of the room. The chamber was built to complement the smoking of strong cigars the way cognac complemented the smoking of strong cigars—with hardy finishes and smooth ambers. The wood of the walls had been lacquered with a rigid varnish to keep it from absorbing flavors that might clash with whatever the current patrons were enjoying. Art pieces in gilded frames were likewise contained in glass sheaths.

It was a well-put-together room. Well-put-together with a refined ease, just like the man before her.

Once more, she felt exceedingly out of place.

Between the chairs was a small table, in its center a silver serving tray laden with candied fruits, cured meats, hard cheeses, and bread. Melanie plucked up a dried apricot.

"Did it work? The medicine?" he asked, suddenly standing again—nervous energy rolling off of him in waves as he strolled to the bar, where a selection of cigar boxes and humidors sat. Nearby was a jug of water, and he poured some in a crystal tumbler, offering it to Melanie.

"Hard to say," she said, taking the glass. "She's been sick for a long while. It will take time for the symptoms to abate."

He *hmm*ed and nodded thoughtfully, pouring water for himself as well. "What do we . . . what do we do now?"

Melanie looked into her water glass, saw how distorted her fingers looked through the crystal. "Do you have anything stronger?"

"You don't want to keep a clear head while we plot?"

"Not really, no."

He nodded solemnly, pressed his lips into a thin line. He moved to another cabinet, pulled out several snifters and corked bottles. "I admit I don't have a favorite libation to scheme by," he said.

She huffed out a laugh. "Do you have something bubbly?"

"Isn't that for celebrating?"

"Better to fake a celebration than to wallow in . . . in . . . by the Five, what have we gotten ourselves into?"

She jumped as a cork popped.

"Champagne it is, then," he declared.

"Oh, I didn't—I was mostly joking. That must be expensive."

"Can't drink it in a prison camp," he said with a shrug. He filled two more tumblers and sat down heavily again before passing her one. He raised his for a toast. "To strangers making life-altering mistakes."

He smiled far too broadly, like he was forcing himself to be mirthful and reckless—as though it went against everything natural to him. Thus far he'd been a measured, careful person. No doubt the last twenty-four hours had knocked him off his axis just as readily as they had tilted hers.

"To—to that," she mumbled, lifting her glass hesitantly, awkwardly. Truth was, she'd tasted perhaps three wines in her life, and those had been neighbors' brews. She swirled the tumbler beneath her nose and immediately regretted it. The fizz irritated her sinuses, and it smelled bitter. She took a small sip and wrinkled her nose—it made her mouth run dry.

"That good, huh?" he asked, curling his lip at his own pull. "I *am* more of a red wine sort of person," he admitted.

They both went quiet, staring at their drinks, the walls. Anything but each other.

They were both stalling and they knew it.

"What if . . . what if there was another crime?" she suggested tentatively. "To muddle what we've done? What if I return the mask . . . and then somebody steals it? So that it disappears? So that if it's found again, there's plenty of doubt about how it might have come to be in its current state?" She didn't like how easily her mind had come to this conclusion. How swiftly she'd settled on the idea that one more wrong might make things . . . not *right*, but might confuse the trail. Make things easier for her.

She'd never broken the law before. Why was it so effortless to slip from one transgression into the next?

And how far, ultimately, would she be willing to fall?

"Who is 'somebody'?" he asked skeptically.

"Me. I'll steal a variety of masks, including Belladino's. And I'll leave them someplace someone is sure to find them. The shop owner has insurance, doesn't he? And most likely he'll get the masks back anyway. Once the Regulators find them, they'll take no more interest in the case—all they care about are enchantments. But it will throw the suspicion away from me. For this."

"No. You're not thinking clearly—and we can't blame the drink. Regulators will be *more* likely to come after you if you try something so reckless," he said.

"I won't be reckless," she said calmly. "I'll make a plan. A detailed plan."

"I'd bet ten to one you've never stolen anything in your life," he said.

"You'd win that bet."

"So what in the Valley makes you think you could pull off something like this? A *heist*? Come now—"

"Because I will do anything to keep my mother safe." Her knuckles went white around the glass. She couldn't let herself be hauled away. Dawn-Lyn needed care, needed someone there for her. "Anything. And I *will* succeed."

He sighed, rubbed at his eyes. "I won't let you do it alone."

"Don't be ridiculous, I've dragged you through too much mud already. Maybe I shouldn't have even told you what I was thinking. I should have—"

"*I* did this to you," he said, gesturing at her forehead. "*I* disenchanted a sacred object. I—"

"Not on purpose. Sebastian, I don't *blame* you."

"It doesn't matter. I blame myself. I did it, and I would never forgive myself if I let you face the consequences alone." He set his jaw. "Tell me honestly. You really think you can come up with a plan? One where we don't get caught and immediately thrown into the mines?"

"Yes," she said confidently, feeling it in her bones. She *could* do it, because she *had* to. "Maybe—maybe it doesn't even have to *look* like a crime. Maybe by the time anyone's figured out what's really happened, our trail will have gone cold."

"How in the Valley will we manage that?"

"Belladino," she said. "He knew things . . . I . . . Now I know things. About sleeping draughts and hallucinogens. About things that make memories fuzzy and lips loose and grasps weak."

He stared at her for a moment. Really looked, deep, holding her gaze for as long as he could. As she looked back, searching his stare in return, she saw questions, and fear. She saw wonder, and doubt.

But what made her turn away first was the surprising amount of *trust* she saw in Sebastian's eyes.

He didn't know her, not really. How could he look at her like that, already?

"Could we make him think he'd done business? Rented out masks, when really we've taken them?" he asked.

"We'd need to leave money."

"I have money."

"Oh, Sebastian—"

"I'm embroiled in this, same as you. I have a stake in it, and if money is what I can contribute then so be it. Just . . . just tell me one thing first. Honestly, before we go any further."

"Yes?"

"We're not going to hurt anyone?" he asked quietly, barely above a whisper.

"No," she replied quickly. "Of course not. Never."

19

KRONA

I was surprised, more than anything, when my hand found coarse fur. The strands were almost like needles themselves. The varg was cold, like death, and yet a spark of heat bounced between us. It pushed its head into my hand, whimpering like a kicked puppy grateful to have found a compassionate touch. In a daze, I pulled the remaining needles from its spine and stroked its coat, avoiding at all costs the sickly sores jutting from its back.

It was nearly nightfall when they returned to Lutador from the apprentice's house. While Tray took the masks back to the den, Krona decided to pay the young woman's fiancé . . . not a *visit,* per se, but pay him some mind. It would be helpful to know his face, to be familiar with him in case her suspicions of Mademoiselle Dupont turned into something more.

His establishment was easy enough to look up, easier still to find—placed next to a canal rather than a creek, but the name was fitting enough.

She took off her helm and tucked it beneath her arm before attempting to enter. The doorman stood a little straighter when she nodded to him.

The foyer was dim, but warm and welcoming. A clear respite from the hustle, bustle, and impersonal harshness of the street. Previously unnoticed tension bled out of her neck and shoulders immediately.

The atmosphere was . . . nice.

But she'd learned to be suspicious of "nice" over the years. Enchantments were expensive, and usually surrounded by other fineries. Nobles and rich merchants were most often the ones handling magical items, which meant magical crime typically took place in nests filled to the brim with *nice.*

She strolled casually to the receiving desk, which was currently unoccupied. A small silver bell sat in the center, and she was just about to ring it when someone called to her from the stairs.

"Mistress Regulator! We've got to stop meeting like this. I don't think my dear heart can take it. I have seen you no less than three times in not even as many days; the gods must be smiling on me."

Thibaut came prancing down the stairs, one hand waving through the air while the other slid gracefully down the banister.

She tried not to smile too broadly when she saw him—managed to wrestle her lips into a slight smirk instead. She briefly glanced around the lobby. There was no one there to witness their exchange. "Are you following me?"

"Would that I had the time," he lamented, coming to lean on the desk beside her, limbs loose, posture wantonly relaxed. "But, alas, I have a busy schedule and I couldn't possibly fit trailing a Regulator into it. No, this is just a happy coincidence. The type I could use more of."

She tried to ignore the way he smelled—which was uncommonly *good.* Something floral over something earthy. "What are you doing here?"

"Why, what everyone does at an inn . . . inn-ing," he said vaguely.

"You have your trysts with nobles here, don't you?"

He examined the fingertips of one green leather glove as though he were picking at his nails. With a thoughtful frown he said, "Maybe."

She chuckled.

"Is it really a *tryst* if it's a business arrangement?" he asked.

"And what sort of *business* were you *arranged in* this evening?"

"A countess needed someone to play cards with."

Krona shook her head, astounded, per usual, by the way he danced around the pith of a subject; such an apparently innocent answer always meant there was more to the story. "And she had to hire someone for that? There are no other high lordlings or countexes who play cards?"

"Let's just say none who find her penchant for strip games as amusing as I do."

"You, sir, are a cad."

"Only because they want me to be." He made a fluttering gesture in the direction of the stairs. "And, *yes,* while the owner of the establishment is willing to be discreet about my clientele—he and the staff are *not* gossips—that's not the only reason I come here."

"No?"

"Not all the time, anyway," he added. "Sometimes I just come for the cigars. Monsieur Leiwood runs a lovely smoking room if you're ever in the mood. Are you?" He glanced sideways at her. "Ever in the mood?"

"I don't smoke."

"They have amazing brandy as well. Don't tell me you don't drink."

"That I do. Why are you asking?"

"I don't know what you get up to when you're off the clock. I get curious about it, once in a while. Wonder, sometimes, if you might be amenable to me joining you. What, pray tell, do Regulators do for fun?"

"Target practice."

"Well, I don't suppose it would make much sense for me to join you during *that*."

"Not unless you'd like to play the part of the target."

"Oh, *ha ha*. Come now, there isn't some softer pastime you partake in? What, you don't enjoy the finer things?"

"I like the finer things just fine, but they tend to come with . . . company. Far too much company."

"What counts as far too much? A crowd, an intimate gathering? Any one person other than yourself?"

She raised an eyebrow at him. "You mentioned the owner," she said, pivoting swiftly. As much fun as it might be to frivolously wheedle away time with Thibaut, now was not the moment for frivolity.

"Yes. Master Leiwood, a good man. We're friends."

"Friends?"

"Yes. Why? Does that surprise you? I'm friends with many successful people."

"What surprises me is your friend's proximity to my concern."

"What? *No*. Not the—the *murdery* one?"

"Yes. And I have to say, your degrees of separation from this investigation are shrinking at an alarming rate. First, you have a contact who knew something of the attack on the Jubilee ahead of time. And now this *friend* of yours—"

"Well, more of a long-standing acquaintance, really."

"Oh, so now he's *not* your friend?"

"Not close enough for me to merit an invite to his wedding, apparently," he scoffed, clearly bitter.

"Do you know his bride, then?"

"We've chatted on occasion."

"She's really the one that worries me."

"*That* polite little thing?"

"Manners can hide all sorts of monstrosities."

"I suppose you're right."

She put a hand on his shoulder, leaned in conspiratorially. "Perhaps you'd oblige me. Keep an eye on your friend here? Just let me know what he's up to the next time I call on you?"

"Will that be soon?"

"Likely."

"I thought you wanted me far, far away from this concern."

"Seems fate insists on you being smack in the middle, and I don't see why I shouldn't make use of Time's whims. In fact, if I go take a seat in the bar over there, would you mind calling him? Ringing the bell or what have you? I'd like to get a look at him, take his measure. But I don't want to spook him if I don't have to."

He quirked his lips, glanced at his gloves once more, and *hmm*ed in the back of his throat. "Buy me a drink after?"

"I'll have the bartender leave one for you when I go."

"That's not exactly . . . Well, I suppose that's close enough."

Sweeping her cloak around her, she stalked off to the narrow bar space, positioning herself so she had a fair view of the desk. Thibaut waited for her to settle before smacking the bell.

A young individual came out of a side door and addressed Thibaut. Clearly not the owner, but apparently someone who could fetch him.

Krona fidgeted as she waited, took in more details about the inn. She noticed a faded spot on the wall behind the bar top. Peculiarly shaped, as though a mask or the like had hung there for a long time.

"What can I get you?" the bartender asked. They were an older individual, gray-bearded, but in a high-collared feminine work frock.

"I'm not buying for me. I owe a man a drink."

"So then what can I get *him*?"

She grazed the bottles on offer with her gaze, keeping her attention honed on Thibaut. He hadn't told her what to order. He'd mentioned brandy . . .

Just then, a man who appeared about Krona's age came down the stairs, and Thibaut greeted him warmly and grandly. He was tall, lithe, of Xyoparian descent, and under different circumstances she would have thought him much too young to have such a well-established business.

All of Thibaut's body language indicated that he was, indeed, the man she'd come to identify.

The bartender cleared their throat.

She fished for her time pouch without looking away from Sebastian Leiwood.

"Give him a gin," she said.

The bartender retrieved a shot glass. "Which one?"

Thibaut spoke emphatically with Leiwood, hands as ceaseless as his words. She had no idea what they were discussing, but Leiwood didn't seem put out. He looked at Thibaut with warm familiarity.

"Mastrex?" the tender prompted.

"Whichever burns the best on the way down," she said.

Cheeky bastard deserved something with a bite.

Then Thibaut gestured back up the stairs, leading Leiwood away.

Giving her an easy exit.

The bartender plunked a glass in front of her, and she tipped the proper amount of time out of her purse before standing. As she turned to leave, an impulse tugged at her. "How . . . how much is it if I want to buy him a nice cigar as well?"

><+><-><+><

Krona left the inn in a good mood. She felt more confident about the state of their leads, their prospects. But back at the den, the atmosphere was subdued.

"He died," De-Lia informed her sister bluntly.

"What?"

"Your false varg *died.*"

"But Master—"

"Didn't have the proper antidote on hand, and it took too long in arriving. The poison worked fast."

Krona wasn't sure how to feel about his death. It made her sort of cold, the shock of it. "And we still don't know how someone managed to inject him?"

"No. No one but our own people were in and out of the cell block."

Krona narrowed her gaze. That was certainly . . . odd. She rolled it around in her mind with the rest of the suspicious tidbits she'd gathered.

"Where is Master Guerra?"

"Preparing the body for the sands."

"He can't yet. There's still much for the prisoner to tell us."

"He's dead," De-Lia emphasized, as though she weren't sure Krona understood.

"Yes, but he's *marked.* Self-inflicted scars tell a story as plainly as any accidental scar. Did you see him? He's a road map of his own life."

With that, she hurried to the medical wing, where she found Master Guerra wrapping the corpse for transport. The body's arms were already pinned to its sides in the cocoon. "You can't take him to the undertaker's yet."

"Why not? I can't keep him rotting in here."

"No. I need you to take him to the photographer's."

He frowned at her as though she'd just placed the most morbid request ever uttered. "Why in the gods' green Valley—?"

"I can't question him, but I can inquire after his tattoos." She eyed the body's covered arms. "Make sure they get everything—even his hands. There was something on his thumb before. It tickled a memory; I think it's important."

"Whatever you want, Mistress. It'll be done."

⊱─◦─◦─◦─⊰

She slept uneasily that night.

In her dreams, she strode through a grove of gnarled fruit trees. It was a moonless night, and yet something else, orange and pulsing, hung in the sky— like a sleeping beast breathing in and out. In and out. Krona's vision swelled and shrank with the rhythm. She walked and walked, looking for a way out, though each tree was identical, and there was no way to tell where she'd trod before.

She went on until she came across a pale bud, closed and bulbous, growing from a long vine jutting up through the soil. The bud burgeoned before her, growing larger and larger until it equaled her own height. Suddenly it split open, its petals unfurling to reveal a wet red inside. It smelled of death. A sickly yellow substance oozed from between its edges.

In the center, something writhed, a part of the bloom not yet blossomed. The reddish meat around it broke, and a snapping, pus-and-gunk-covered muzzle bit through—giant teeth gnashing. It was a varg—a varg growing in one of Charbon's blooms.

She shouted from shock, falling backward. The monster struggled to free itself from the flower, kicking its clawed paws, tearing at the air with them, trying to get out—trying to get at Krona.

The creature's face peeled back, like it had its own petals, and then there was Tray's face. It peeled once more. Now it was Sasha, now it was Royu. The creature descended on her. Now it was Tabitha.

As the thing reached her, human teeth bared, it unfurled once more.

It was De-Lia's teeth that sank into her jugular.

She woke up screaming, tangled in her bedsheets. Her varg-based night terrors were common, so neither her sister nor her mother came running, but this one was new.

Pulling her nightclothes close around her, Krona rose to go to the kitchen for a spot of milk from the icebox. Ice was a luxury afforded to those who worked for the state—a perk.

Lighting a candle just outside her cubby, Krona startled. A figure stood on the other side of the kitchen, still as a statue, turned toward the wall. Face planted in the corner like a naughty child during time-out.

Still on edge from her nightmare, Krona froze. Her mind was groggy, her faculties slow. Who—?

She blinked and quickly rubbed her eyes.

De-Lia. Just her sister.

"Lia?"

The figure didn't move. Krona ventured a few steps closer. The floorboards were cold against her bare feet. "Lia?"

De-Lia did not turn around.

A cold slice of fear ran up Krona's spine. But she shoved it down with logic, drove it away, chiding herself. No need to be afraid of her own sister in the dark.

Though she was careful to step lightly, her foot still found the squeakiest board in the floor.

She paused, and De-Lia began to turn toward her. Slowly. Unnaturally slowly.

Krona saw then that the captain held her saber. The sword's tip dragged across the floor as De-Lia turned, creating an unnerving grating sound.

"De-Lia," Krona said, a little harsher, more demanding.

De-Lia stopped turning. She lifted her sword, but only a little. The blade pulled lightly at the wall, leaving thin cuts in the wallpaper.

It finally struck Krona: her sister wasn't awake.

De-Lia had often walked in her sleep as a child. As an adult, it only happened in times of great stress, or when De-Lia had been sleeping unevenly. Clearly this concern was getting to her. Getting to them *both*.

Something dripped from De-Lia's limp, empty hand. Something dark.

"De-Lia, you're bleeding."

Shaking off the remnants of her nightmare the best she could, Krona covered the rest of the distance to her sister's side. She grabbed her wrist, turning over her dripping hand. De-Lia did not resist.

The bandages Krona had noticed before were gone, the little cuts having scabbed over nicely. But new cuts sat below them across the pads of three fingers, openly weeping.

"Mending needle indeed," Krona huffed. "This is why sleep-strolling with a sword in reach is dangerous."

"Buh . . . buh . . ." De-Lia said, the single syllable leaking forth like droplets from an untapped spring.

"Buh-buh-bedtime," Krona said, mindful of the saber, grasping hold of her sister's shoulders.

De-Lia turned, taking limp steps as Krona guided her back toward her room. She let out a weak, sad groan, and Krona's heart wrenched. She was used to seeing De-Lia firm, strong—this childlike state revealed the fragility within.

De-Lia never liked to show vulnerability, but here she was, vulnerability incarnate.

"Shh," Krona soothed. "I'll help. Here, lean on me."

De-Lia groggily did as she was told, and Krona gently took the saber by its pommel, pulling it from her sister's loose grip. She must have only cut herself once, swiftly. There was no blood on the blade. Awkwardly, she wrangled the older Hirvath back onto her mattress then her saber against the windowsill.

De-Lia groaned again, discomfort twisting her face as she fought with something in dreamland. Krona waited until she'd settled down again before tiptoeing back to the kitchen.

Maybe she *was* just a shadow, a follower—whatever Tray thought of her. But there was one good thing about treading closely in someone else's footsteps: when they stumbled, you were right there to pick them back up again.

20

MELANIE

Two years previous

The sniffy old enchantments dealer took his lunch at the same hour every day, locking up before walking three blocks to a hot-soup stand whose owner knew his name and order like she knew the days of the week. But, while the soupist knew her beans from her barley, she was trusting and uneducated, eager to please all who came through the door without a second thought as to their motives. If their bellies were full, she was satisfied. The only person she could have envisioned carrying malicious intent would have to be a soup hater.

Sebastian, who now posed as Melanie's employer, knew the soupist fairly well, as he was also a regular diner. He'd spent so much time around the mask shop trying to ward off unsuspecting buyers that the enchantment district felt like a second home.

So he wasn't too keen when Melanie decided to involve the soupist in their plan.

"I thought we were only going to rob him a little—not poison him."

"My dear, honorable Monsieur Leiwood," she said, looping her arm through his as they strolled down the street, scoping out the area. "I told you, Belladino knew things. Useful things. It's not poison, it's medicine. He'll take a very long nap and feel quite refreshed upon waking. Better, even, because we aren't going to steal the masks. We'll pay, leave him new rent slips, and alter others. He won't think anything is out of the ordinary until days pass and the masks aren't returned. Believe me, the medicine will make him feel at ease. Nothing will seem wrong with his world." She said it with so much confidence, she surprised herself.

She'd taken care of her sick parents long enough to understand the basics of healing. What to put in a drink to ease the pain, how to sew up a deep gash, and the like. But now she knew what an amateur she'd been. Her previous knowledge was a drop in the healing bucket compared to the fount that was Belladino's. And now it all belonged to her.

As she glanced at a weed working its way up through the cracks between pavers, facts about the plant ordered themselves in her mind. She saw all the equations it belonged to: for that's what Belladino had concluded effective healing to be, an equation. She knew the weed could be used in a paste for cleaning teeth, and in a brew for nausea. She knew the roots were poisonous, but if you harvested the leaves slowly, the plant would continuously send up new shoots even through the winter.

Tugging on Sebastian's arm, she brought him to a halt and crouched. She ran her fingertips over the green tendrils before pulling up the weed and pocketing it.

It was a good thing Master Belladino had been a healer, as it would have been easy for him to turn his accumulated wisdom to darker purposes. Even now, thinking about what had to go into the concoction to make the shop owner sleep for exactly the right amount of time, she was perfectly aware of how to change the temporary sleep into a permanent one. Just a tad more lung mushroom, a dash more sulfur, and a hair less water meant the shop owner would be no more. Worse still, it would be unlikely for poison to take the blame. Less-experienced healers than Belladino would finger poor diet and fatty blood—and she had yet to hear of a healer with *more* experience than Belladino.

Such was the depth of understanding she now possessed.

"He'll be fine," she reassured him.

It was only a matter of Sebastian spiking the man's soup when the soupist wasn't looking.

The morning of the plot, Melanie woke with a terrible itch burning across her forehead. She raked her nails across it, but felt raised, thin lines already there. Perhaps an insect had stung her in the night?

Realizing she needed to once again change the bandages on her hand anyway, Melanie rose, groggy—trying not to wake her mother—and went to the washbasin in the corner. The curtains were still drawn, but a strip of sunlight shone through onto the silvered glass mirror. She paid her reflection no mind, focusing first on her hand. The pain in her fingers and palm was acute—a deep sort of throbbing that radiated up her wrist. Luckily she'd grabbed the grate in such a way that the creases of her joints had been spared direct contact. She could still flex her fingers without too much additional pain.

The new medical knowledge fluttering around her head told her the burns on her pinkie and ring finger were the most severe. That they'd likely scar.

She rubbed an appropriate salve over them from the small medical kit Sebastian had procured for her, before wrapping her hand again.

Sighing, she glanced up furtively to meet her own gaze in the glass. But instead of sharing an irritated look with herself, her eyes immediately caught on the blotch across her forehead.

"What in the . . . ?"

Some sort of irritation had blossomed around where the needle mark had been.

Unable to make it out well in the dark, she retrieved the small oil lamp from the writing desk, lit the wick, and held it near her face while she scrutinized herself in the mirror.

Narrow red lines formed an intricate pattern across her skin, each section an interlocking piece that formed a framing circle at the outer edge.

It looked as though someone had deliberately carved the design into her forehead.

She touched it delicately with her fingertips. It didn't hurt.

But it was wildly obvious.

And she had no idea what it was.

Her heart gave a panicked kick against her rib cage.

Muttering watered-down versions of expletives to herself, she hurriedly retrieved her ratty hat, pulled it down tight over her brow, and headed out into the inn proper.

Sebastian was already behind the front desk, greeting a blond-haired man with familiarity. She stood back as he worked, noting how his business voice and posture were different than when he spoke to her. The blond man gestured at his older, silver-haired companion who stood near the front door—clearly a distinguished noble gentleman—and leaned in conspiratorially to Sebastian. "This one's been dancing around me for a year now. Finally got up the gumption to ask for what he wanted. Nobles are usually good at that—not this one."

Sebastian smiled and shook his head, as though used to the other man's shenanigans. "What my guests get up to is none of my business. As long as everyone is happy and well taken care of—"

"Oh, he will be, trust me."

"Master *Thibaut*."

"Come now, don't pretend to be scandalized. Hand over the key and I'll spare you the details after. Besides, I think you have another guest who needs to speak with you." He nodded at Melanie.

She blushed and looked away—instantly betraying the fact that she'd been listening in on their conversation.

As the blond man and his nobleman disappeared up the steps, Sebastian hurried to her side. "What's wrong?" he asked immediately. "Are you nervous about . . . ? We don't have to, you know, we can——"

"That's not it, I—Can we go someplace more private?"

"Cigar room?"

She nodded. "Cigar room."

Once again secluded behind the pretty doors and heavy curtains, Melanie took up her previous seat.

"Were you planning on going out already?" he asked, gesturing at her hat.

Presuming it was better to simply show him her new problem than try to explain, she pulled the moth-eaten old thing off and crumpled it in her fists, pressing it into her lap with her head bowed.

He slowly descended to his knees before her, lifted shaky fingers as though to smooth over the blotch, but kept his hand a hairsbreadth away.

"Dear gods, what is that?" he whispered.

"I don't know. Did I pick up some infection from the needle? I didn't—I didn't pass it to my mother, did I? No," she said, answering her own question. "No, that can't be it."

"This doesn't look like an infection. These lines are deliberate. It looks like——" He cut himself off, swallowing thickly.

"What?" she asked quickly. "If you have even some inkling, tell me."

"It looks like . . ." His eyes went wide. "M-Melanie . . . This is an enchanter's mark."

"What? *No.*"

"Yes."

"That's ridiculous."

"I *know*—I know how it sounds," he said firmly.

"Only enchantments have enchanter's marks. And you can't enchant a *person.*"

They both sucked in sharp breaths, eyes darting to each other's.

"You *can't,*" she said, an edge of desperation making the words bite.

"You have Belladino's knowledge. You hold what the mask was meant to."

She shook her head, rejecting the notion. "No. Sand, wood, gems, metal. Not people. Not flesh." Panic rose inside her throat. Her chest felt tight, her limbs heavy, her blood sour. She couldn't draw a proper breath, she couldn't—couldn't—

How had it all gone so *wrong?*

"Melanie? Melanie, breathe. *Breathe.*"

"Not people," she repeated. "Not people, not people, *not people*—" She reached for him, fingers digging into his arms. He grasped back, big hands encircling her arms, trying to hold her firm, steady.

"I know, *I know*. Believe me, I've spent years thinking about this, and I've been just as sure of it as you—"

"What are you talking about? This—this is not something anyone considers. Because it's not a . . . people don't . . . It's not—How do you—?"

"I *have* considered it, Melanie. Trust me. When I was young, I . . . I looked for such things. When you grow up with a father like mine you wish every day that you could just make magic *happen*. That he could simply be put out, stopped, by sheer will.

"You watch your great-aunt act the soothsayer and wonder if the way she uses enchantments is real. If she can really talk to the dead—which is *blasphemy*, you're well aware—then why can't you, a small boy, convince them to help you? Why can't magic be elsewhere, if only for a moment? If the gods gave us magic to make up for our shortcomings, then why—" He took a quavering breath, stilled himself. His pain was clear—long-standing, deep. "I *have* thought about it. I searched, years ago, and I was convinced. But now . . . We can't deny the evidence of our own eyes."

"We *can* and we *will*," she spat. "I *can't* be enchanted. Because magic . . ."

It wasn't just that this blotch would be a horrid souvenir of her time in the mask, wrestling with the echo. And it wasn't the notion that someone might see it and arrest her for self-desecration. Something else entirely kicked the swells of terror into her chest.

What horrified her was the root of it.

The mark was a symbol of something deeper, as all enchanter's marks were. It meant she'd been fused with the power of the gods . . .

And people had ways of detecting such power. Of finding it, and using it.

Magic was controlled. Magic was restrained.

"By the Five," she gasped. "Magic is *owned*. It's regulated. It's measured. It's a *possession*."

"You can't own a person," he said flatly.

"Just as you can't enchant one?" she spat back.

He shook his head, aghast. Stood, as though needing to distance himself physically from the idea—from *her*.

He left her clawing at the air. Still needing to grip something—anything— one hand went to her throat, the other to her blouse.

Everything was falling apart.

Everything was spiraling out of control.

She just needed to make it all go away. "If I am what you say I am, then . . .

We'll remove it," she said quickly, latching on to the idea. "We put it in, we can take it back out. Return it to the mask—"

"Like we did with the echo?" he asked darkly. "This whole time, we've been toying with things we don't understand."

"I'm supposed to return the mask in an hour. How can I go there like this? How can I face that man?"

"Because you have to. One problem at a time—all right? We'll go through with our fake-rentals plan, just as designed, and then after we'll deal with— with *this*. It's too much all at once."

"I don't know. I don't know. I don't think I can—"

His expression contorted, her distress reverberating through him, tugging at him. He returned to her, knelt down, and took her face gently between his hands.

His palms were soft, strong. Comforting.

"You can do this," he insisted, voice low and velvety. "Because you're not alone. I'm right here. I'm right here with you. You can do this."

"*We* can do this," she corrected, trying to will her heart to slow, her humors to settle.

"We can do this," he agreed.

>–•–◇–•–◁

Melanie brought Belladino's mask back to the shop while Sebastian went to spike the soup ingredients, just as planned.

Outside, she had to steel herself. She braced her hands on her thighs, bending over to gulp air, to press down the nausea. She wore her hat low over her eyes, but the mark throbbed beneath.

You can do this, she reminded herself.

Narrowing her focus, tunneling her vision, she stood straight once more and marched into the shop.

The owner's eyes were dull, his gaze empty. He did not recognize her. It had only been a few days, but she was so beneath his notice that her previous presence had already been wiped from his mind.

Good.

"Can I help you?" he asked.

"I've come to return this," she said, slipping the mask from her cloth satchel.

She thanked him, assured him she'd gotten all she needed from it, and tried not to hold her breath as he took the mask—plucking it from her fingertips as though she'd sully it if she held it a moment more.

"This scrape—" he said immediately.

"I'm sorry, I was clumsy." With shaking fingers, she drew out an extra minute from her purse. "Will this—?"

He snatched the time from her. "Fine."

Relief washed over her as he set Belladino aside, turning to some other work, suddenly ignoring her entirely.

Yes. This could work. They could manage.

⊷•◦•◦•⊶

Melanie felt better when she and Sebastian trailed the shopkeeper to his lunch spot. They watched as the man ate heartily, obscenely licking his bowl clean before strolling back to his post with a skip in his step.

Sebastian and Melanie followed behind, making sure he'd secured himself in his shop before taking up a street bench to wait out the concoction's slow release.

Two hours. That was how long they had to wait to be sure he'd be unconscious when they entered.

"Time?" Sebastian asked continuously. He fidgeted more than she'd seen in the past few days—more than when they'd toasted their own sad circumstances, more than when he'd explained what Belladino's echo had been saying with her lips, more than when she'd shown him the mark.

"Still a few minutes more," she said. "We need to be sure. If we enter the shop and he's simply drowsy, he'll remember us."

After Sebastian had inquired several more times, prodding at her patience like a small child in need of attention, she gave in. "All right. Hopefully he's succumbed by now."

They crossed the street with determination, Melanie in the lead. Her heavy-heeled boots made a *clop clop* over the pavers, accenting her resolve. Other pedestrians went to and fro, some at a stroll, some in a haggard rush, all unconcerned with the young man and woman making for the mask shop's entrance.

The bell chimed, doing its best to alert the owner to a customer. Unfortunately for the bell, he lay passed out over the counter, snoring away in such an undignified manner that it conjured images of grunting warthogs in Melanie's mind.

As she stepped fully inside with Sebastian close behind, the smell of worked wood and thick paint invaded her nose. She hadn't noticed this morning, so wrapped up in herself, so worried. It drew her attention to the walls and the wares they displayed.

So many masks—just like the day she first saw them. It seemed long ago now, though it had only been a week. But while she'd felt fascinated, and perhaps a little intimidated that first time, now she felt . . . erratic. The faces and figures seemed to jump forward and flash backward, undulating on the walls like a thick coating of multicolored insects. They pulsed with magic— she couldn't see it, but she could sense it. Not the knowledge, but the echoes. Trapped, confused, wakeful even when there was no wearer. They squirmed in their shells like worms in a corpse.

Or perhaps that was all in her mind.

Her forehead burned.

There was one mask that remained still, though. Not dead, but empty, like the husk left over after a molt. It still lay exactly where she'd seen him set it earlier—aside, not yet rehung.

The green tree frog was embroiled in a tangle of vines, and small birds accented the flow of the main carving, brilliant paint giving an air of realism to the piece. Belladino's mask was still beautiful, despite what it had done to her.

Keeping her head bowed, she scurried past the rest of the strange façades to check on the shop owner. Belladino's training kicked in immediately. The man's breath was strong, as evident by his snoring. She ran two fingers over the pulse point in his neck and noted a healthy beat, then thumbed one of his eyelids open, examining his pupil and the flecks in his iris. Too much yellow bile often manifested in the sclera, but she saw no signs of imbalance.

Luckily, his expression was soft. No nightmares plagued his sleep. She'd mixed the components correctly, and he would wake feeling worlds better than he had before his midday meal.

"Is he all right?" Sebastian asked.

"Fine. Where should I put the time vials?"

"There should be a lockbox nearby. Don't forget to alter his rental slips."

Sebastian had suggested they take four masks in total. Any fewer and it might be obvious which they were after. Any more and the shop owner might not believe he'd done so much business.

A hook made a sharp *clat* as Sebastian lifted a mask off the wall. A white rabbit, with cherry red eyes, its ears formed of curled and painted leather.

She found the lockbox on a shelf under the counter, next to the sales slips. She frisked the man for his keys, feeling crooked as she did so. Melanie had always prided herself on being a good girl. A devoted daughter, a sweet soul. There might be less pain in the world if more people took pleasure in genuine nicety, she imagined.

Yet, here she was, drugging someone in order to use them, stealing the keys off his unwilling form.

Her skin crawled with antipathy. Moral clarity hit her squarely in the back, stealing her breath, and she paused.

"Maybe—" she whispered, too softly for Sebastian to hear. "Maybe I should . . ." *Maybe this isn't such a good idea.*

What had happened with Belladino's mask had been an accident. *This* was calculated. This was wrong.

Would she spend her whole life committing injustices to correct one mishap?

But then the shop owner groaned, shifting in his sleep, and his key ring slipped from his coat pocket into her open palm. She stared at the keys for a long moment. They'd fallen into her hand like an encouraging sign from the gods. *Do this,* the keys seemed to say. *Finish what you've begun.*

Swiftly, she unlocked the box and emptied the time vials from her bag. They clinked and glinted like little musical instruments, chiming out a delicate overture in sharp contrast to the solemnity of the situation.

She pulled up the sales pad and flipped through. "The masks—he has the sales and rentals listed by name. We need to know whose masks they are." She risked a glance in Sebastian's direction.

He flipped over the rabbit mask in his hands, scanning the reverse side. "They aren't labeled."

"I can't simply write *the bunny*. Bring it here and I'll look for a clue. He must have an inventory list somewhere—Oh, here, here."

On the shelf, beneath the lockbox, was a thin tome, with a hardwood cover and an openly threaded spine. The paper was thick, the fibers coarse and uneven. *Catalog* was written across the front in heavy ink.

But when she opened it atop the sales counter, her heart fell. It was blank. Fresh pages waiting to be filled.

While Melanie continued to search for a current inventory list, Sebastian gathered several other masks: a red-and-gold maple leaf, a flock of sparrows that would swoop up a wearer's face in simulated movement, a likeness of the Great Falls complete with huge boulders and a rainbow, an abstract tar slick that shimmered like ravens' feathers, and a birch monstrosity with bars in the eyelets.

He brought them over together, piled up high in his arms.

"Any luck?"

"The only book in here is this—his keys won't open the back room, some kind of enchanted security, I'm sure."

She tapped the open pages of the catalog with her finger, then jumped back as an image temporarily flared to life on the pages. It dissipated as soon as she fled.

"What in the Valley?" Sebastian set the hoard of masks aside, then tried pressing his palm to the page. Nothing happened. "Whatever you did, do it again," he prompted.

Gently, she touched a fingertip to the center of one page. In a moment, the two-page spread was filled with an image of Master Belladino's mask, accompanied by a list of names and dates, with hers directly at the bottom. She whipped her hand away again and it disappeared. "It knows—it knows it's me. *This will never work if his inventory list can recognize his renters!*"

"I don't think that's it," Sebastian said. "Look. When I touch it, nothing happens. I've rented from him before. Before I ever wore my father's mask. I think . . ."

He lifted the rabbit mask and set it on the book. The image returned, only it was changed. This was a list of the rabbit's renters, with an illustration of the bunny mask beside them.

"It's recognizing the enchantment," he said.

"It thinks I *am* the mask," she gasped. *No, that—that doesn't make any sense.*

"We could never simply fake the slips," Sebastian said. "He must fill this out after. An enchantment for keeping track of enchantments."

Melanie's heart gave a cruel, heavy thump in her chest.

If the dealer had tried to catalog the mask's return this morning, she would have been caught right then and there. The pages would have remained blank as he set the wood atop them.

Melanie had never even heard of such a creation—a book that knew things. Not one that simply conveyed information, but one that *knew things*. She wondered if the shopkeeper had some kind of master key for the book, one that would let him examine and alter its contents without a specific mask in hand.

She took each mask Sebastian passed to her in turn, setting it on the book to be sure the pages behaved the same for each. Yes, there was always the illustration, the list, the name of the enchanter, and the name of the person for whom the death mask had been made.

Only one held a surprise. When she set the birch mask down, a familiar name hovered near the center of the list: Sebastian Leiwood.

"This is the one you rented?" she asked.

"Yes," he admitted, though with a slight quaver in his voice, as though trying to preempt whatever questions might come after.

There was no time to dally with such probing inquiries now. But Melanie noted the dead's name for later: Blackhaus.

With each mask, she noted that the words slightly throbbed on the page, almost like the masks appeared to throb on the wall. She wondered if it was perhaps a side effect of her own enchantment—was she seeing places that magic seeped out? Or detecting where magic might get in, where change might be made?

"I'm going to try something odd," she told Sebastian. "It probably won't work, but . . . This book recognizes masks and knows things about them. But if it can't tell the difference between the mask and me, then maybe, I mean, what if I can change what the book knows?"

"What are you getting at?"

"Maybe we don't have to steal anything at all."

She expected encouragement, or at least a smile. He looked skeptical.

"Or maybe I'm being silly. But it's worth a try." She removed Blackhaus's mask, pressing her palm firmly to the paper.

Belladino's beautiful mask painted itself once more. She stared hard at the list, concentrating on the names, willing them to change, willing the enchanted paper to accept the new knowledge, though it was a lie. She imagined she knew it to be true, with every fiber of her being.

She filled the lie with half-truths, scattering bits of information from herself and her family.

Slowly, the script began to change. Her name wiggled, slithering into something new. The name her mother had wanted to give her at first—Shin-La, after her eldest sister—and an amalgamation of family surnames—HuRupier—appeared on the page.

"Melanie," Sebastian breathed in awe. "How did—?"

"I'm—I am the mask," she said, unsure herself. "The mask tells the paper things, and . . . and a mask can't lie, and the paper can't tell the difference, so . . . But what does it matter? Even if I change the name here, what if—what if he remembers me?"

"I doubt it. I don't say that to be cruel, Melanie, but you know his type. You were beneath his notice when you walked in. He could see you didn't have money, and that was what mattered to him. If the ledger says your name is Shin-La, I don't think he'll question it."

Quickly, she tried more. She invented a new renter, an elderly farmer who she used to buy goat's milk from. He'd passed peacefully very recently. He would have had cause to rent the mask, might have had means, she wasn't sure. The shop owner might think his memory faulty if he could not recall the old man—much more likely than a mask rewriting its own history.

"By the Five," she breathed as the man's name appeared, standing out in sharp, black ink. She shifted the dates ever so slightly, starting to feel the shape of the ink, the way the paper asked her for information.

"Not too much, not too much," Sebastian warned. "Even if you change your name, he knows where to find me. Make him doubt his own records, but not enough to suspect."

Melanie yanked her hand back, nearly tearing the paper, though she hadn't clung to it. The enchantments had been drawn to each other, and she could feel extra breath leaving her body as she pulled them apart. The physical toll of wearing Belladino's mask was not unique to it, she realized. Using magic was exceedingly hard on the body. Her brow was damp with exertion, and she felt she too could do with a long bout of sleep, just like the shop owner.

"Quickly, put the masks back," she urged, leaning heavily on the counter. "And hang Belladino's in place, so that he thinks he already marked it in the catalog. We take nothing. He'll never suspect. Even if Regulators come to investigate, they won't find a Shin-La HuRupier. Even if they question you, just tell them the truth. You met a farm girl—"

"By the name of Shin-La," he said.

"Felt sorry for her, and lent her some time."

He stared at her across the counter for a long time, and she grew worried under his gaze. "What? You don't think it will work?"

He shook his head. "That's not it. I never thought I would meet another . . . doesn't matter. I'm in awe of you, Melanie Dupont."

"You can be in awe of me as we flee our crime scene," she said. "Hurry, return the masks."

As he scurried back toward the hooks, she did her best to replace the shop owner's things. There was no need for him to think a single thing out of place. Everything was as it should be.

"Ready?" she asked Sebastian, moving toward the door and holding out her hand for him. "We came quietly, we go quietly. Just a couple out for a stroll."

"Y-Yes," he said, slowly taking her hand.

Feeling better about everything since the entire fiasco began, she pressed on, letting the bell tinkle happily.

But as soon as they set foot outside, the shop behind them exploded in a cacophony of bells. Every sort of alarm Melanie could imagine screeched out, vibrating the shop windows, vibrating her bones.

"Don't run," Sebastian said quickly, holding her hand all the tighter.

He pulled her gently to the side, crossing the street. "Gawk," he told her. He pointed at several other bystanders who were looking toward the noise, bewildered, covering their ears and moving away.

Melanie covered her ears as well, heart pounding wildly and arrhythmically. Her feet begged her to flee, but she trusted Sebastian. They stood for a moment, looking around at the others. No one seemed to think they were the cause of the noise.

"Will it wake him?" Sebastian asked directly in her ear.

"I don't know," she answered truthfully.

He ushered her away, as other individuals ushered their partners or children away.

"He must have an enchantment for intrusion," Melanie said as they rounded a corner, the buildings blocking the sound, lowering the volume from startling to annoying. "Why didn't it go off when we entered? And I thought the shop was open . . . Why—?" She cut herself off. "Oh no, I forgot the time vials. I left—"

"It's fine," Sebastian hissed.

But all that money . . .

"We should stick to our escape routes," he said sharply, looking more harried than before. "You go your way, I go mine. Meet you back at the inn."

"Oh, yes. Of course." She felt deflated as he crossed the street again, this time away from her, without so much as a good-bye.

Shame colored Melanie's cheeks as she stomped through the city. Through polite addresses of "hello" and "good day" she kept her gaze trained at the pavers. If she made eye contact, someone would see her sins, she was sure.

She thought she'd gotten away with it. But no. Even if the shop owner didn't awaken, surely the local Watch had gone to investigate the noise. They would know something was afoot.

Why did her wrongdoing feel like such a visible thing? Like it grew from her skin in long branches, like it called out for attention to every stranger on the street?

Would she ever be able to put Belladino's ghost behind her?

21

KRONA

As I petted my new varg friend, all the fear Papa had instilled in me melted away. This creature was bigger than me, by far. It could have ripped my throat out at any moment, but it didn't. It behaved inverse to what I'd been taught. And as I stroked its sorry hide it seemed to grow less sickly, less hungry. Perhaps all varger need is some compassion, I thought. Perhaps they only eat people because people are so mean to them.

<hr/>

At breakfast the morning after the prisoner died, day three of the concern, De-Lia didn't look any more well rested than when she'd gone to bed.

She took the chair nearest Krona, flopping into it like her bones were made of jelly. "Did I . . . was I sleep-strolling last night?"

Krona nodded, pushing eggs around on her plate. "You were. Fought me a little when I tried to get you back into bed."

"Oh. Apologies."

With a smirk, Krona shrugged, shoveling a bit of half-solid yolk into her mouth. "I think the apartment's in more pain than I am."

When De-Lia scrunched her nose in confusion, Krona gave a nod toward the ruined wallpaper. "You had your saber," she explained. "Got a good jab or two at the corner there."

"It's this concern," De-Lia said, rubbing at her eyes. "And the Martinets. I can't sleep enough, and when I get the chance . . . my dreams are no less worrisome than reality."

"Same," Krona said, though if she were being honest, she'd noticed De-Lia hadn't been sleeping well for weeks now; long before the Jubilee. "My varger terrors were especially bloom-related last night."

De-Lia patted her hand in comradery. Rubbing her palms over her face, then her stubbled head, De-Lia moaned at herself, "Ugh. I can't continue like this."

"Have you asked one of the den healers for sleeping salts?"

"It won't help with the sleepwalking, they say. Or sleep . . . what was I doing?"

"Sleep-stabbing," Krona said frankly, trying to maintain a lilt of humor. It wasn't funny, of course. Nothing about the past few days was humorous. Which was exactly why she did her best to maintain her smile. Everything weighed twice as heavy on De-Lia as it did Krona. She wanted to stay positive, for the captain. "You can have your saber back as soon as you apologize to the wall. I think it's questioning its integrity."

De-Lia chuckled half-heartedly. "Ha, *puns*. You are taking this much better than I would, had it been the other way around."

Krona shrugged. "I've always been the stronger Hirvath. About time the fixtures around here knew it. How are your fingers?"

"My—?" De-Lia glanced at her hands, then hid them in her lap. "Not too bad."

"Good."

A large ceramic bowl occupied the center of the breakfast table, with the fine alpaca scarf hiding the treats inside. "Brought you something," Krona said, tapping the bowl's rim.

De-Lia lifted the scarf's edge with a hesitant flick before tossing it aside with a flourish. "After last night I should be bringing you gifts, not the other way around. Thank you."

"I thought they would buy me at least a flash of your crooked teeth."

"My teeth are not—Oh." It started as a one-sided smirk, but eventually De-Lia relaxed enough to give her sister a gummy smile.

When she still hesitated to take one, Krona scooped up a tangerine and tossed it at her. Even unpeeled, it left a tangy trail in its wake, like a citrus bomb.

De-Lia caught it easily. Instead of eating it, she stared at its glossy surface as though she could divine the end of this concern in the microscopic peaks and valleys. "I fear this Charbon business will end my career," she confessed. "If nothing else, I will need a long stay in the countryside after this."

Krona's smile wavered at that, but she forced herself to maintain the light in her eyes. Before she could find the right thing to say—a proper rebuttal to the dire admission—De-Lia snatched a triangle of toast from Krona's plate and munched silently.

A knock at the door broke them out of the lull. De-Lia dropped the toast and pushed aside the tangerine, wiping her crumb-covered fingers on her backside before answering.

Outside stood a young woman, her breathing heavy, auburn hair pulled back in a tight bun, black clothes equally as tight around her body: a runner from the den. "There's been another murder," she gasped without preamble, handing over a letter.

"We're on our way," De-Lia assured her.

No swifter had she given her answer than the runner was off again.

"Quickly," De-Lia bade Krona. "We'll meet the team there for our briefing."

"Where are we going?" Krona asked, sliding up behind her sister to peek at the note over her shoulder.

"Nightingale's roost. It says the corpse is fresh."

In a flurry of movement, the sisters cleared the kitchen table and threw on their uniforms. Krona's forearm was still tender where it had been clawed open, and though she attempted to cover the wound with her bracer, it soon became apparent that Master Utkin was correct—she would have to choose one bracer over the other, for she could not wear both.

Impulsively, she chose the resolve bracer instead of the courage bracer. It had saved her once before.

Acel emerged from her morning's sponge bath as her girls hurried out the door. "Good bye, Maman," they each bade her, kissing her in turn. She absently returned the gestures, harried by their rush.

De-Lia palmed three tangerines from the bowl before spinning toward the door, depositing them in her pouch for later.

"Be safe, children," Acel bade them. Then, the moment before the door clicked shut, "What in Time's name happened to the wall?"

They shared a look, neither turning back to offer their poor mother an explanation.

Meeting each other step for hurried step, they rushed to the adjoining stables, where the horsemaster, alerted by the messenger, was already prepping their mounts.

De-Lia lifted herself into the saddle with an extra bit of elbowing from Krona. Allium, De-Lia's steed, was taller than most of the den's horses, mostly because she wasn't a den horse. Lia had purchased her herself. And Allium seemed to know she was special; once De-Lia was seated, the mare held her head higher, as though proud to bear the rider. The two of them molded together, appearing as one dark beast. Allium was mostly deep black, like the uniforms, but also sported a pop of color. A tan cross streaked down her nose and across her brow like the noseguard on an antique battle helm.

Krona mounted the golden old-timer she'd ridden home the night before. The horse retained her fleetness despite her years. Together, the saddled Regulators looked like pieces from Marquises and Marauders—a two-person game played across two boards spotted with squares. The goal was to protect your board while invading and conquering your opponent's. Whenever they played, De-Lia always won. Always. The sisters used to set up and demolish the boards again and again, for hours, Krona growing more insistent each time that *this* would be the game. De-Lia would never counter or correct her, never boast about how many sets she'd finished without losing a single piece to the enemy. She'd simply nod and begin again.

They hadn't brought out the old battered game basket in years. Not since Krona had declared her intentions to join the academy and follow in De-Lia's footsteps.

Maybe Krona should suggest a game this evening. Perhaps De-Lia needed some lightheartedness to balance out all the horrors they'd recently encountered—had still to encounter.

"All right?" De-Lia asked once Krona was mounted, guiding Allium deftly around the other horse so that she could inspect her sister. Leaning over, she tugged on one of the straps on Krona's saddle, making sure the buckle was secure.

"Ready, Captain," Krona replied.

The horsemaster pulled the gate open, and the two of them were off, flying down the narrow streets into the heart of Lutador.

>─◄◆─0─◄▷─◄

The bloom lay next to the service door of a nightingale's roost.

The team rode up together. Tray slid off his horse, then helped De-Lia dismount, and Sasha did the same for Krona. Royu and Tabitha led the horses away to be tied while the others approached the Watch.

"There are witnesses?" De-Lia asked the Watchperson in charge.

"Come," they said, gesturing for the Regulators to follow.

The team moved around one another like clockwork, banded together, each a piece with a place, each supporting the next. They were a well-oiled machine, each with their own strengths, each with weaknesses masked by the skill of the others. De-Lia was a good leader, and exceptional with a quintbarrel. Sasha was dogged—the most likely to find the smallest of threads and pull until she had a whole concern unraveling before her. Royu was the strongest swordsperson. Tabitha had the most stamina for stakeouts. And Tray was loyal, committed. Had been for as long as Krona had known him.

She still felt bad for doubting him.

Krona herself, of course, had an unmatched affinity for masks.

She was the only person who wore one now—Tray had brought it for her. Magnitude Six, Tier Two. Madame Ka-Diana Imbala, who'd been a palace decorator, of all things. She'd been able to look at a room and tell you exactly what was out of place. A strange scuff mark, or a piece of silver that subtly did not match the set. It wasn't Krona's favorite mask, as the knowledge tended to notice things of *aesthetic* displacement over all others, occasionally drawing her attention at a crime scene away from things that were important. But she felt its benefits now outweighed its drawbacks.

Painted nightingales of various body types, genders, and complexions leaned out the roost's windows. Three stories' worth of private rooms gazed down onto the scene. It was far too early for most of them to expect work, and with the cobbles outside caked in viscera, business was bound to be bad that evening.

A good portion of the prostitutes appeared unmoved. Whether it was because they were used to the violence of the neighborhood, or because the drugs some often took in preparation for work left them numb, it was difficult to tell.

Most who maintained their sense of horror were hidden inside. Faint sobs could be heard as the Regulators marched past the doors to where the Days-watch were waiting. The Watchpersons interviewing various locals startled aside as the Regulators came near, instinctually drawing away from the faceless forms. After all, who knew what magics were in service underneath their over-bearing uniforms? Who knew where the Regulators were looking and what they could truly see?

Tabitha went straight to the body with De-Lia, so that they could verify it was a bloom. The others fanned out, some approaching the Watch, others searching the scene for further leads. Krona would look over the corpse so that Imbala could do her work, but first she noticed a huddle of three nightingales—two women and one man—who were collectively wailing, clinging to one another like they all might melt away into nothing if they loosened their grip. A Watchman was emphatically asking them questions, his patience clearly wearing thin.

Krona knew how to distinguish between panic-stricken bystanders and those exhibiting personal grief. These three knew the victim.

Uniform sweeping grandly around her, she approached slowly. The anguished three took no notice of her, while the Watchman's shoulders lifted, as though a great burden had been taken from him. "They say her name was Hester," he said to Krona. "But they won't stop blubbering long enough for me to get any proper info out of 'em." He turned back to the three. "If you won't give it up for me, perhaps Mastrex Regulator here can magic it out of you."

With the tip of an imaginary hat, as if to say good luck and good riddance, he left Krona to go speak with his supervisor.

The two women had enough sense to appear concerned by the presence of a Regulator, but the man—he was clearly the most troubled.

Imposing and powerful were not sentiments Krona wished to convey at the moment. Those impressions were helpful when facing the overly willful, the slimy, and the dutiful. They were not particularly helpful with the distraught— she'd learned that with Fibran Iyendar.

Instead of demanding answers, Krona knelt down, halving her height, addressing the weeping trio with the gentleness she'd use to approach small animals. In other circumstances she might have gone so far as to remove her helm, but Imbala's mask was carved in the likeness of a golden spider and would not make talking to her any easier. "What makes you think it's Hester?" she asked kindly. The distortion of the body made it impossible to identify at a glance. "Did you see someone attack her?"

Imbala's knowledge made notes about their attire, what was aesthetically uncouth. Krona did her best to bat away the useless information, searching out anything of note, but there were no physical clues on these three, nothing Imbala noted as being *unusual*, just unseemly.

The three cried and cried, turning away from her.

The woman cradling the man's head against her bosom tried to answer, but could not get the words past her tears at first. Krona withdrew a black handkerchief from her pouch and offered it over. The nightingale took it with gratitude, and breathed more deeply. Krona waited patiently for her to find the words. "We know it's her because she didn't come home last night. She should have been home, in bed."

Krona hid her disappointment. Nothing had changed: no one had seen the bloom in progress. "Hester couldn't have gone elsewhere? There's no client she enjoys spending extra time with, or a relative she might have gone to?"

The woman who'd spoken shook her head, dirty hair bouncing. "Hester was—was going to be very sick. She would have come straight home after."

The man gasped at this, his breath hitching in a half sob, half hiccup. He looked achingly young in the woman's arms.

"After what?" Krona pressed.

"Sometimes one of our lot gets in a way," said the other woman. "If you catch my meaning."

Krona nodded. "Hester was pregnant."

"And they don't want to be in a way no more."

Another violent sob crawled its way out of the man's chest. The second woman petted at his arms and hair. The first woman rocked him slowly, like a mother.

"Were you the father?" Krona ventured.

The question snapped him out of his little universe. He rubbed at his red eyes. "What? No. Of course not. She's my friend."

"We were all her friends," added the first woman intensely. The bitter undercurrents in her voice and stare were meant to tear at an ugly, age-old sentiment. *Just because she was a prostitute, that doesn't mean she won't be missed. It doesn't mean no one cared about her.* "We were going to look after her when she came back. Make sure the process went smooth as can be."

"I should have gone with her," the man said. "I told her where to find Madame Strange. It's *my fault*."

Krona's blood went cold and solid in her veins.

Madame Strange. That was the name Thibaut had given her.

"But," the man continued, "she said she'd met someone who was going to pay for it. That he'd lent her a marvelous jewel and they were going to get all dressed up to celebrate."

"The jewel, did you see it? Did she describe it?"

"A brooch. Ruby, I think. He told her not to put it on until he came to escort her."

The despairstone. "I don't suppose you met the man? And you're sure, that it was a man, I mean."

"That's what she said. No, I didn't see him."

"Neither did I," the other nightingales chimed.

"People . . . people—clients—ask to accompany us all sorts of places. Even to the loo. We didn't think it odd."

"Who is Madame Strange?" Krona demanded, more harshly than she'd meant to. When Thibaut had first uttered the name, it had seemed an abstraction—a phantom entity he'd created instead of divulging his genuine sources.

Perhaps that was how the killer was choosing his victims: through her.

"Who is she?" Krona asked again.

"Just a Dreg who knows a bit about poison," the man said, as though it were inconsequential. "Specific poisons. Not just the messy ones that will kill you dead. A black market dealer, you see. Minor. *She* didn't do this. Hester couldn't afford a proper healer for the matter. Most 'gales can't."

"Can you tell me how to find her?"

"You can't hurt her. She was helping Hester—"

"She might have seen the man who accompanied Hester, the man who did

that," Krona said harshly, pointing furiously at the body. "If you had any love
for her, you will tell me how to find Strange."

▶·◄◦◦◦◦◄·◄

De-Lia crouched over the bloom—which had the distinct many-petal flaring
of a daisy—staring at it as though it might spontaneously knit together and be
a living, breathing woman again. Krona strode up to stand alongside the captain, silently fuming—the name "Strange" repeating over and over inside her
skull, reverberating like a bell—and De-Lia knew it was her without looking
up. "There's the portion he removed," she said, gesturing toward a sickening
heap near the crease where wall met ground. "Same as before."

"We'll get a healer at the den to compare it to the mass pulled from the
first victim," Krona said. "In the meantime, I think I have a new lead." She repeated the conversation. "They mentioned Madame Strange—I know where
to find her."

De-Lia stood. "Good. Very good. We should go now. The two of us."

Something about one curled petal of sliced skin suddenly drew Imbala's
attention. A bit of dull powder-white. "Look, look here."

"Is that a pill?" De-Lia asked. Delicately, she plucked it from its gruesome
setting. "We better double-check the site, there might be more.

"Have Tray use the green-man mask on it, he'll be able to sniff out right
away what it's made of. Master Utkin can surely tell us what it's for, after."

De-Lia called Royu over and directed zhim to make sure the body was
photographed, the gory, removed bits sealed up and taken, and that any signs
of poison or trauma before death were noted. "Krona and I need to conduct an
interview elsewhere," she informed zhim. "We will all reconvene this evening
for debriefing. Make sure to utilize your ansible plates."

De-Lia began to stride for the horses, but Krona caught her by the arm.
"We can't ride to Madame Strange's."

"Why not?"

"Because we have to go to the Dregs."

"Ah, wonderful. Nothing like traversing the sewers in full regulatory uniform."

"I know, I know. The directions the nightingales gave me begin over this
way, at the nearest grate."

"Wonderful, just . . ." De-Lia followed her sister, her grumbling dying off.

It was a block down and around the corner, but not far at all in the long
run. Together, the Hirvaths lifted the heavy sewer grate to reveal a grimy lad-

der with rusted joints. Mounting the questionable rungs, they descended into the Dreg city—the Lutador within Lutador.

In ancient times, the channels beneath ground level had contained living quarters for citizens and bunkers for soldiers. No one living now could remember the kind of warfare that had driven people underground, and there were no histories. But it was something that had happened before the Valley was transformed into a sanctuary by the gods—perhaps a war with the Thalo's beasts themselves. Some considered it evidence of Absolon's escapades, when he left the mountain with a contingent of warriors and was the only one who returned alive. Whatever had happened here, the scattered ruins both topside and below were all that was left.

When they reached the bottom, De-Lia let loose a scanning sphere, just to be on the safe side, but they'd entered in an uninhabited area. Pure sewer, with no one around to see them use their tracking magic. It was easy to tell—here there were no repurposed wrecks. The architecture beneath the surface was very different from that above, and just as distinct. Nothing delicate remained, if indeed anything delicate had existed in the first place. All structures were stocky and utilitarian. Stones were stones—unadorned, unpolished, unpainted.

But here? Simple tunnel.

The sphere wobbled uncertainly in the air, but gave no indication it had detected any enchantments besides their own.

De-Lia gently squeezed Krona's shoulder. Light seeping in through the grate bounced off her resolve bracer. "Which way to Madame Strange?"

Recalling what the nightingales had told her, she pointed down the tunnel to their right. "This way." She pulled a light vial from her pack and smashed it to bits under her boot. The leaded glass glowed with absorbed sunlight, which would only last for an hour or so. Quickly, she shoveled the shards into an unenchanted glass flask and held it aloft.

They tromped over various bits of slick black flotsam. Reinforced archways assured that the old tunnels remained open, but none of the shafts were wide, and the ceilings sat low. In most places they had to walk single file, unless one of them wanted to wander through the waste-filled channel.

As they slid through one shaft and approached a wider tunnel, Krona held up a halting hand. They'd found a portion of the underground city. Just beyond their narrow passage, clacks and clangs of activity echoed between the walls. The scent of boiling stew mixed with the stench of refuse, and Krona's stomach threatened to turn inside out.

Shadows flickered across the gray-green bricks of the ceiling like a campfire puppet show, the shapes twirling together with almost choreographed precision. Krona hid the shards of light vial beneath her cloak.

Dregs were not as most Lutadites believed. They weren't excessively dirty, or sightless, or depraved. They didn't fear the sun, and they didn't worship rats. They were simply people—though they had their own ways, and kept their own traditions.

Following the flickering glow, the sisters peeked around a corner to observe a well-populated encampment. Wooden columns supported several awnings that kept the camp dry; small beads of moisture followed cracks in the ceiling, dripping down from above with annoying irregularity.

Nothing was brightly colored in the Dregs, but was instead richly textured. The clothes were sturdy, bulky, and every stitch stood out. The men did not wear plunging necklines as was the fashion in Lutador—instead they covered up, shielding themselves against the dampness and the cold. Many wore thick hoods, while the women wrapped their necks and faces in scarves. The children—the few Krona could see—wore almost nothing, but carried coarse blankets to cloak themselves in should they get a chill. Babies were swaddled by their parents, while those old enough to walk had to swaddle themselves.

New structures, those the people had constructed instead of coopted—like the columns—were heavily carved with repetitive, abstract patterns. Though they still had lamps and plenty of light, touch was far more important than sight.

Imbala's mask had many opinions on the Dreg aesthetics—not all of them negative—but enough that Krona considered taking off the mask to quiet the multitude of observations she couldn't help but make.

One man hunched over a potter's wheel, setting a deep divot in the neck of what looked like a drinking carafe. He waved haphazardly at a dejected boy whenever the young man ventured to speak.

Several elderly men and women crouched next to the source of the glow in the center of the awnings: fire-windows. Four glass bricks—each perfectly cubed, though their surfaces were pockmarked and scratched—had been thrown indiscriminately into a cooking pit. Each shone with the bright oranges and flaky reds of burning embers and emitted a strong heat, though the fires they reflected were far away—perhaps miles.

Fire-windows were two-part enchantments, like ear shells and reverb beads. Each "window" corresponded with a "mirror": a thin sheet of enchanted glass tempered with magnesium. The mirror was set in a fire, allowing part of the heat put off by the flames and coals to be emitted through the window.

There were ice-windows as well. It was said the Marquises had an entire ballroom floored with ice-window bricks, and that they would flood the room to create a slick ice floor for playing on. They had contraptions they strapped to their feet that allowed them to glide across the surface.

Enchanted windows of either type were by no means cheap, however. And Dregs didn't trade much with the surface. They would have to pool a great number of time vials in order to afford these four bricks and their mirrors, and surely they weren't the only fire-windows to be found in the Dregs.

But Dregs were a communal people, more so than even the Arch Families in Xyopar. What belonged to one belonged to all.

Since everyone in the camp appeared distracted, De-Lia made a silent gesture for the two of them to move on. Krona nodded, slinking through the edges of the fire-windows' light like a stray cat afraid of being shooed away.

Madame Strange's place of business supposedly occupied a spillway on the other side of the encampment.

After a few more twists and turns in the tunnels, the Regulators found what they were searching for. Arriving at their destination felt like arriving at a crossroads. The atmosphere had a decisive feel to it, as though fortunes were changed here.

Four stretches of waterway met at a center pool beneath an exquisitely tall domed ceiling. Large chunks of crumbling brick and stone created an island in the pool, atop which perched a rickety wooden structure. Four oil lamps hung from the four corners of its drooping eaves, and beneath, the water churned dark and green in the glow. The scent of waste was no more prominent here than anywhere else, but it carried an overtone of incense. The same type of incense Krona had noted in the Iyendar household.

A set of dubious-looking stepping-stones led up to what was presumably the front side of the hut. The stones predictably wobbled underfoot, but neither Regulator ended up in the grimy drink. A large shutter—like the kinds of top-hinged boards one often saw on street vending carts—sat where one might have otherwise expected a door. On it, scrawled in a messy hand, were the words *Please knock*.

Krona complied.

An instant later the board flew upward, and Krona stumbled back into De-Lia, barely avoiding a rough swipe under the edge of her helm. De-Lia expertly lashed out to steady her sister.

On the other side of the board stood a woman, who propped the shutter up with a metal bar, creating a flat awning and a store-like window. Thin, white wisps of incense smoke curled out from the aperture like eager arms climbing to freedom. The hut beyond was thick with haze, so much so that Krona wondered how the woman could draw a proper breath.

"Mada—?"

Two syllables were all Krona could get out before the woman yipped like a startled dog, retreating back into the pale fog.

"Wonderful," De-Lia muttered, pressing past Krona to vault through the window. The haze swallowed her up as well. A thump and a muffled yelp accompanied the swift shifting of light and form while Krona held steady.

A moment later, as the smoke thinned and hundreds of smoldering sticks could be seen—not all of them incense—De-Lia shoved Madame Strange forward, leaning her over the lip of the window while she secured her arms behind her back with a set of manacles.

With a gentle hand, Krona hooked Strange under the chin, lifting her face. *Old crone, eh?* she thought, remembering Thibaut's descriptor. Madame Strange was neither elderly nor haggish. If anything, she had a simple, puritan look about her full face. But her pupils were heavily dilated—there was nothing puritanical about the wisps curling away into the sewer. Thin, pale-blond eyebrows knitted together above her button nose, projecting pure disdain.

"Bastards," Strange bit out, kicking back at De-Lia, trying to buckle her knee.

"Do you peddle abortive chemicals?" Krona asked. "Did you speak with a woman named Hester yester-eve?"

Strange glared at Krona and continued to wrestle against the captain.

"Hester is dead," Krona said harshly, grasping the woman's chin, making sure she was paying attention. "Filleted open on the side of the street."

With a delicate gasp, Strange stopped struggling. "What?"

"Did you or did you not sell a woman named Hester a concoction?"

"It didn't kill her."

"No, a blade did that. We care not about your practice—that you aid the pregnant who don't want to be. We care about your clients. How many other nightingales have you sold to?"

"I don't—I don't inquire after their occupations. All kinds of people come to me. Not a month goes by I don't get a noble at my door. All kinds."

Krona loosened her grip on Strange, soothing over her cheeks with her thumb. "And those without ailing wombs? What do they come to you for? Was there anyone with Hester when she arrived? Did you see anyone before or just after?"

"Is someone else dead too?"

"Answer the question."

"*No,* I will not. I didn't kill anyone, and you've got no right to interfere with my business."

"We do if you aided in a crime," De-Lia said, pulling a little too roughly on the restraints. She looked around the shack's single room, eyeing a few of the burning odds and ends. "Or if a few of your chemicals aren't of legal import."

Madame Strange laughed. "Regulators don't care about *drugs.*"

"Then why did you run?"

"Who wouldn't run from you ugly bastards?"

"Look here," Krona said practically. "We know you were involved in an exchange between a Watchperson and a thief. The thief was given information about a gala, do you remember? Those persons are involved with Hester's death. She's at *least* the second they've murdered thus far—if not the third, or the fourth, the *fifth.* You get the point. If you give us something we can use to find them, we'll have no need to take you with us—*up top.*"

She knew it was a gamble. Madame Strange could be working directly with the thieves. Perhaps she'd been the one to mark Hester for death.

"I can't give you anything to find them," Strange grumbled.

"Why not?"

"Because I don't remember anything about it," she snapped. "There was a man . . . or maybe two men . . . It's like it's all covered in a haze. They spoke, yes. Passed time vials, yes. Quintbarrels were mentioned. Varger. And the Unknown god. One was a priest, perhaps? Or did he say prophet? No, that's . . . They covered their faces. I know not what they called themselves or where they came from. I provide neutral ground, am paid for it. Everyone knows not to cause trouble here."

"And these people, what did they look like?"

"As I said, *they covered their faces.* And everything is so . . . hazy. One of them could have been *you,* for all you constabulary cocks move and talk alike. It's all blur in my memory. It's like looking at them through hot steam on a cold mirror."

"Convenient," De-Lia said.

"And last night?" Krona pushed. "Was there anyone else with Hester?"

Strange shook her head, little bits of straw-blond hair flying. "I don't know. Maybe."

With a frustrated sigh, De-Lia eased away from Strange. "She's spent too much time in this box of hers. Woman's so full of vapors I'm surprised she can keep her business, let alone remember her patrons."

"That's not true," Strange bit out. "It's good for my anxiety. Nothing more."

"*Then why can't you remember?*" De-Lia asked. "Unless you simply don't want to tell us. Better to play the absentminded tunnel dweller than give up your cohorts? Perhaps a trip topside and a few days in a cell will improve your recollection?"

It didn't matter if Strange was telling the truth, lying, or too drugged to tell the difference; taking her to the den wasn't going to improve the quality of her information. "Captain?" Krona asked. "A word?"

Even if Strange decided to bolt, she wouldn't get far with the manacles on. De-Lia vaulted out of the window, and the sisters skidded down the side of the rubble island, out of earshot.

"I think we should leave her in place," Krona said.

De-Lia nodded. "You think the murderer has been using her as a rabbit, to lure out his foxes."

"Yes. If this really is a place with a reputation as neutral ground, then they're using that supposed security to their advantage, and if we remove her, we have no idea where else they might look for opportunity. Keeping an eye on her, using her as bait in turn, seems our best option."

De-Lia's shoulders sagged. She carried herself with a tiredness that was unfamiliar to Krona. It was deep-set, systemic. Sparks of uncertainty crackled around Krona, as if there was something wrong with the very air.

Krona had seen more and more holes crop up in De-Lia's defenses over the past few days, but she still refused to bare the wounds, to let someone else aid in the patching. That she'd allowed any cracks in her typically smooth-as-glass exterior was in itself worrisome.

Madame Strange propped herself up in the window, resigning herself to whatever the Regulators decided.

"All right, my dear Madame," De-Lia said with a sigh. "We will leave you to your business." They would keep her under surveillance, of course, but Madame didn't need to know that.

"Oh, *a pleasure*," Strange drawled, cynicism thick on her tongue.

They released her, walking away as Strange closed up shop once more.

"You should go. I'll keep first watch on her," De-Lia whispered. "Return to the den and send a guard to relieve me."

"Of course," Krona said dutifully.

With a half-hearted bow, Krona left De-Lia to her new charge. On her way down the makeshift bank, her boot caught on something hard. It dislodged from the stones and bounced into the drink.

Imbala's mask told her to go after it, despite the foul smell of the water. In this underground world that had Imbala screaming at the scenery, this, the mask told her, was truly out of place. She fished it out easily—the channel was shallower than it appeared in the dark. Her gloves and gauntlets came up sufficiently soiled, but did their job and kept her dry.

The object was a small pair of clamps—healer's equipment, unquestionably. Nothing dangerous, nothing special. The tool was altogether insignificant, and she nearly dropped it back in the water, but an inscription caught her eye. The initials *CLM* had been stamped into one of the support bars.

Where did she know those initials from? Where had she seen them recently? It only took her a moment to recall: at the Iyendars'. On the medical bag Melanie had toted about.

CLM was Clive LeMar.

"How did you get here?" she asked the clamps. "Captain—I believe our murderer has a hole in his pocket."

22

LOUIS

Lutador streets, midnight,
ten years previous

Even in his boyhood, Louis Charbon had never so much as injured a frog or thrown stones at a bird. He needed healing like some needed coffee in the morning. Mending was vital to his very being.

Killing was the antithesis of who he was.

He resisted, denied the Thalo—for months he denied it.

I'm not a killer.

I'm not a killer.

You won't make me a killer.

Killing won't bring my son back.

But then he'd watched his other children, and wondered with every scraped knee and stubbed toe if something had been taken from them. He wondered if they were just as vulnerable as his baby boy. Any illness could come along and steal one of his daughters just like it had stolen his son, and the Thalo had given him a reason to believe it didn't have to happen. Even with his healing skills, there was no way to recover what had been lost—taken—without an active search.

"What do other healers who don't have your knowledge of anatomy do when the patient needs an operation?" Matisse had asked, cornering him at the coterie one eve. "Your patient is dying and you don't know what's wrong. So you must cut, look deeper."

Charbon had pushed him away, gone to the Unknown's shrine and asked for guidance. Despite himself, he believed the Thalo. It had displayed its power, given him reason to doubt Absolon's ancient intentions. *It* was *they*, the Unknown god, he was sure.

There was truth in Matisse's words, he knew. An ugly truth, but truth none-theless.

It wasn't simple murder. He had to do what other healers did—what he'd found so distasteful. In order to heal the patient—the entire Valley's residents—he had to do a little damage. The patient desperately needed an operation, and though he didn't have the knowledge to say, "Ah, yes, here is the infection, here is the exact place I must cut and the exact organ I must excise," he had to go through with it anyway. Or the rest of his family might one day succumb.

In order to properly set a bone, often one had to break it. Committing a few citizens to the sands before their time was the equivalent. That's all this was. If he intended to save the metaphorical leg, injuries had to come first.

Why? Why was his baby boy gone? How had this happened?

He had to know. He *had to.*

So he'd kissed Una, Gabrielle, and Nadine good-bye, left their small coun-try estate, and set out for a "sabbatical" in the city.

When he found what he was looking for, *then* he could stop. He could go back to a normal life—back to his wife and children. And the people of Arken-syre would be free.

Tonight, as he wove his way between the squat, gaudy buildings of Luta-dor, the moons passed each other in the sky; the larger a blaze, the smaller a spark. Their light teased its way onto the damp streets, glancing off stagnant puddles left behind by the late-afternoon rain. In his left hand he clutched his tool kit, while his right clenched and unclenched. He wriggled his fingers and stretched his palm like a pianist preparing to perform a complicated concerto for the first time.

He looked down at his scuffed boots, frowning, having long ago turned in his expensive doe-hide riders for workman's wear. It was much easier to move through the underground if one adopted a peasant's history, and though he occasionally missed the finer things, he'd made much larger concessions in his pursuit of truth.

Rounding a corner, he caught sight of tonight's sacrifice. It had been left exactly as he'd asked.

Good on Fiona. He thought the words, but didn't feel them. She was his partner—his right hand in the fight to reclaim the world, and Matisse was his left—but he had not chosen her. Fiona was dedicated to the cause, enthu-siastic even—and that was ultimately the problem. She relished her role too much; enjoyed the chase and the capture and the trussing on a level that made Charbon's insides turn to ice.

Her current offering was gagged and bound, lying on his side—a lamb prepped for the knife. A large, bloodied welt stood out on the left side of the man's face where Fiona had struck him with a blunt instrument. The man was large—too large for a woman of Fiona's size to carry here all by herself. She must have had Matisse's assistance.

As Charbon approached, the man began to yell behind his gag, pleading with him for help. The naked fear inherent in the cry made Charbon's heart hurt, but it was necessary. He'd thought to use sedatives at first, but decided such concoctions might interfere with the search. Charbon was familiar with the way one medication could interact negatively with another, how indeed medicine could hide symptoms and prevent proper diagnosis.

He couldn't have that.

While the entreaties continued, Charbon pulled out his scalpel. As it caught the moonlight, the man on the ground seemed to understand: this was no potential savior. This was his executioner. The shouts dissolved into sobs.

"I know, I know, I'm sorry," Charbon said, crouching and laying his hand over the man's eyes. "Don't look. Take deep breaths and don't look. The Unknown thanks you—all of the gods thank you for your sacrifice."

Sometimes this soothed them, and they went lax, resigned to their fate. Others it made fight all the harder.

This man tore his face away from Charbon's hand and wrenched himself back and forth on the ground, like a grub dug up from its burrow in the dirt, desperate to get back to the safety of the soil.

With scalpel in hand, and tears in his eyes, Charbon stood and raised his face to the empty night sky. As always, he began the sacrifice with prayer. "Emotion, quell this man's fear, let rapture reign in his heart and mind, squashing all else. Knowledge, guide my hand; give my blade swiftness and my fingers precision. Time, grant me my discovery soon; let there be fewer days of sorrow amongst your people in Lutador and beyond. Nature, see that my blossom—my tribute to the sacrifice—is true to your creations."

He bent down, slicing open the man's tunic so that he had clean access to his belly. The victim made one last effort to plead with Charbon, to bargain with him. Even if the words hadn't been garbled behind the gag, there was nothing he could offer Charbon that could still his hand—except, perhaps, the secret he was after.

"Unknown," Charbon shouted at the last god. "Reveal to me the truth that is hidden. Your work, which has been removed by man. Let your glory be restored to this Valley and those who have concealed your magic and your identity be eternally punished."

With that, he plunged the scalpel inward and began his gruesome work.

The sacrifice screamed in agony behind his gag. He tried frantically to wriggle away, but Charbon held him. For ease of access, he rolled the man fully onto his back, and the moonlight revealed the shining wetness of his innards.

Down, down Charbon dug—the sacrifice's cries growing weaker with each moment—looking for evidence of what had been lost, of the pneuma. When one removed an appendix or a gallbladder there were scars, signs of that which had been taken.

Charbon would find the signs if he had to open every last one of the government's victims. He would find the scars and Fiona and Matisse would examine the evidence and then the three of them would present the deception to the world and bring down whoever was perpetuating Absolon's crimes.

He worked tirelessly, and the clear rain puddles around him turned dark red. "Where is it?" he growled, slashing through sinew. The last breath fled from the sacrifice, and still Charbon had nothing. "Where? *Where?*" he demanded, both of the body and of the gods.

Blood and fat and filth covered his arms up to the elbows. Rivulets of human fluid ran down his front and stained his boots. Another sacrifice gone, another life expired, and still no proof.

He chucked the scalpel with a desperate shout, and his other tools quickly followed; each let out a tiny *clink* or *clang* on impact. Frustrated, sickened, he kicked at the cobblestones, bellowing while he ran filthy fingers through his long hair.

It was there, somewhere. It had to be. The Unknown god's blessings were stolen from Arkensyre citizens at birth, he was sure.

But another dead man lay at his feet, and he would need to kill yet another—hopefully just *one* other—to complete the task.

Taking a deep breath, he ran his hands over his face, felt the veins straining in his forehead.

Honor the sacrifice, he reminded himself. *Steady on.*

Charbon pulled himself together, then located the items he'd whipped into the darkness. They'd scattered, littering the ground like silvery stones. He cleaned them as best he could, rubbing the blades on the less sodden portions of his clothes, before returning to work. Death was ugly, but the blossoms were beautiful.

His fingers worked their magic, transforming what had once been a man into a tribute to Nature. And when he had finished, when a lily was splayed across the ground instead of a person, he dipped his palm in a pool of blood, intending to write his usual accusation on the nearest wall.

But there was a strange sound in the night—running footsteps. Had he been seen? Would the Nightswatch be alerted?

He had to be quick. He would leave his accusation of Absolon, but an abbreviated version. He couldn't let himself be caught. He couldn't fail the Unknown, forcing them to start over with a new servant, someone less qualified.

Hastily, he scrawled, *Death is ART.*

23

MELANIE

Two years previous

When Melanie spotted the inn once more, she felt all the tension bleed out of her.

It had quite unexpectedly become a refuge. She'd never thought she'd feel safe or comfortable anywhere in the city, and yet the mere sight of Sebastian's establishment instantly brought her relief, like a cool rag pressed against an aching temple.

They'd done it—they'd rid themselves of Belladino's death mask. And no one had followed her here. No one from the Watch had stopped her, cried out to her.

As long as Sebastian had been as lucky, then the mask part of their ordeal was over.

She tugged her hat down further.

Now to deal with the mark.

With a nod to the doorman, she slid through the inn's glazed front doors, and let herself take in the foyer as though it was her first time. Wooden sconces with inlaid panes of turquoise-colored enamel gave the impression that the ceiling was lined with elfin candy-windows. The atmosphere was one of warmth and richness—like the kind you might achieve by mixing a cup of boiled chocolate with a fluffy blanket on a cold day. All of the furnishings were elegant, but not overstated. Unlike other inns that catered to those with a few time vials to spare, this one favored comfort over pretension.

Just like its proprietor.

Back in their room, Dawn-Lyn was sitting up in bed, reading a thin tome Sebastian had lent her: *Beasts of the Rim*.

"Did you know that it's estimated there is at least one varg to every one person in the Valley?"

"That's a lot," Melanie replied casually. "How are you feeling?"

"Good, considering. Good, for me," her mother said. "But I don't want to talk about how I feel. I want to talk about this." She tapped the cover. "I want to talk about the rams of Marrakev and the sandbirds in Xyopar and the man-gobbling eels in the Grand Falls. Can we do that? Just . . . speak of other things?"

"Of course," Melanie said quickly, sitting sidelong on the bed. "There are Grand Falls eels in a book about the rim?"

Dawn-Lyn laughed lightly. "No. That's not the point."

"Tell me more about the creatures in Marrakev," Melanie bade her. "Does the book get it right?"

"Mostly," she said with a thoughtful nod. "Though if there were that many varger coming through the barrier, I would have known a lot more people eaten by them, I think. My village was right at the base of the mountain. If a varg came over the rim, it was in our midst in no time."

They chatted for a while about the great beasts of the world, until a knock at the door interrupted them. Melanie had almost forgotten where she was, why she was here. It was so good to simply carry on a conversation—to draw one out—with her mother. Already, she was so much better than she'd been before the injection.

"That's probably Sebastian," Melanie said.

"Sebastian? Oh, you mean Monsieur Leiwood?" A knowing smile quirked across her pale lips. "So it's *Sebastian* now, is it?"

"*Mother*, please."

"Don't *Mother* me. He's nice. Handsome." She waved a hand through the air. "And well-to-do. If you're already familiar enough for first names . . ."

Melanie gave her a dramatic sigh. She'd resolved to tell Dawn-Lyn everything that had happened, but only once they were safely out of the city, of course. And if that meant enduring her mother's teasing until then, so be it.

"Hello?" asked Sebastian from the hall.

Melanie leapt to her feet. "Coming." She wrenched open the door with a smile on her face.

That smile was not mirrored back. "I have to show you something," he said breathlessly. He was winded, like he'd been running.

Melanie's face fell, and her insides froze over. "What happened?"

He shook his head, eyes flickering in her mother's direction.

Dawn-Lyn had pretended to go back to reading.

"Mother—"

"Go on," the woman said with a light flick of her wrist.

Sebastian led her, without preamble, back to his room.

As soon as she stepped over the threshold, she saw it.

Atop his flawlessly made bed sat a pseudo-birchbark monstrosity, mouth a horrid line, eyelets crossed by thin silver bars.

The mask she'd noted in the shop. Blackhaus.

"What did you *do*?" she demanded.

Two masks had already cursed their lives, threatened to tear them apart—to *end* them. Why would Sebastian risk what they had now for another enchantment?

"Is this why his alarm sounded?"

He swiftly shut the door, pressing his back up against it as though the gesture might hold the world—and its consequences—at bay. "Maybe. I don't know. I'm *sorry*. It was an impulse. When I saw it, I . . ." He seemed to be ordering things in his head, searching for the proper justifications.

"We didn't have to take anything. It was *over*—"

"It's *not* over," he said swiftly. "You are enchanted. You have an enchanter's mark. What you said, this morning, regarding magic and how it's owned, I—I knew I had to do something, and when I saw it—"

"How? How is this supposed to help me?"

"Blackhaus was known for his perfect recall. At fifty, he could tell you what he'd had for breakfast on the third of the month when he was four years old. Everything that ever happened to him stayed with him. Not one note of it was lost. And it's his capacity for memory that occupies that mask."

She tried not to be angry with him. Tried very hard to breathe steadily through her nose, to keep her hands from clenching at her sides. "I don't understand," she managed to grit out.

"There's a part of my life I've always wondered about. Parts I'm not convinced I remember correctly."

"Memories you've lost?"

"Memories that . . . could be false. I'd long ago concluded that I made them up. That what I thought I remembered was impossible. But then . . ." He hung his head. Clearly, this confession—whatever it was—embarrassed him. "When . . . when I . . ." The words fell like stones from his lips—hardened with meaning, rough with weight. His shoulders sagged, as did his voice, and he would not look her in the eye. "When I was a boy . . . I have memories, Melanie, of *doing magic.*"

She let a beat pass. The span of a breath. The span of a heartbeat. The span of an unspoken denial.

"What do you mean, you remember *doing* magic?" she asked cautiously. "You used enchantments? Created them, or . . . ?"

"No, you don't understand. Enchanters are like chemists, like healers—they follow recipes. They have knowledge of how magical materials go together. They make enchantments, but they don't *do* magic. Magic isn't something one *does*. But I did, I feel as though I—I *could*. I *did*."

The newfound familiarity and safety of the inn, of Sebastian's bedchambers, drained away completely. Melanie was left feeling cold and alien. "You're not making any sense."

"I know, I know. That's why I . . . They can't *really* be memories. For a long time, I thought they were imaginings. That I made them up. Maybe I did, I don't know. That's why I stole the mask, to use Blackhaus's skills to recall for certain. It was an impulse, a terrible, terrible impulse. And of course, now that I have it, I'm not even sure I can bring myself to put it on. I did rent it, once before, as you saw, but I convinced myself I was being silly, decided not to put it on. Then, after . . . My time in my father's mask took a toll, and I was too cowardly . . ."

Sebastian needed comforting. Anyone could see that. The way he shook, the way his eyes had gone hot. He'd made this decision to dig them both deeper and now he wasn't sure it was worth it. That, coupled with the ache of his past—these memories that could be false, the father that was horrible, and the battle with his echo—was breaking something inside him.

But she stood, rooted, between him and the bed.

She couldn't go to him until she understood why the mark—*her* mark—had driven him to this.

"Since Belladino, since you, I've wondered. Before it seemed impossible . . . I can't do magic *now*, so why should I have been able to then? Why should it be . . . I mean . . ."

"Sebastian," she said, curtly but not unkindly. "Focus. What are you trying to tell me?"

"I used to imagine I could do magic." He gestured solidly with both hands, emphasizing the statement more for himself than for her. "When I told you I'd considered the existence of an enchanted person before, this is why. I'd *hoped*. I'd searched, studied, to see if it was possible. And through it all I was trying to convince myself I *hadn't*. Because I have these memories of performing magic. Not in the usual way—not with an object. With my bare hands. Not even that, really." Sebastian pinched the bridge of his nose. "I remember wanting magical things to happen. *Could make things* happen, if only for a brief time, simply by willing it.

"I remember being able to affect my father in ways. When he was particularly angry, sometimes I could—or I thought I could—take his anger away.

There's a reason I came to believe I'd made it up; what child in my predicament wouldn't want to—*need to*—believe they could change such a fevered temperament? But I have distinct recollections of it working—never for long, and certainly never long *enough*."

The old pain etched itself deeper across his face.

"Sebastian," she said softly, entreatingly.

She couldn't hold her ground any longer. Didn't want to. He'd been so good to her, and to her mother—she couldn't hold his moment of impulsiveness against him, not when it was so wrapped up in everything broken and formative inside him.

She took one of his hands in hers, but he still wouldn't look at her. She pressed close, leaning her head on his shoulder, lining up her chest with his side so that he could feel her heartbeat. "We don't have to speak of it if you—"

He cut her off with a gentle interjection, the furrow of his brow widening, the lines around his mouth shrinking. "No. I want to. And, there's more. I think my father knew. I remember him telling me to make people feel certain ways. He'd order me to make the butcher feel more generous, so he'd throw in an extra quarter of hock. Or to make the landlord too morose to bother us for the rent. He'd even . . . I don't think I ever did, but sometimes . . . after a particularly bad night he'd tell me to make my mother forgive him."

Sebastian curled in on himself, knees bending, body sinking, and Melanie went with him, doing her best to shield him from his father's specter. She encircled him in her arms without thinking, taking in the scent of him, her doubt and irritation gone. Every word of this cost Sebastian greatly. He looked drained—haggard in a way she hadn't seen before. What he was saying now he'd obviously wanted to say out loud for a long time.

But she still hated that she didn't understand.

How could he have done magic? People don't—people can't—

She was as adrift in the story as he was in the telling.

She pressed her forehead to his temple and breathed deeply, slowly, creating a circulation of air between them that was soft, just theirs. He closed his eyes and accepted the comfort, one hand coming up to encircle her wrist, to return the embrace as best he could.

"But," he said softly, "the memories stop. At some point, when I was still a boy, I stopped being able to do it. Could be that I stopped pretending I had control over my world. That I'd accepted my fate at my father's hands. That I grew up." He let out a shaky breath. "I was *so sure* I'd made it up, for the longest time."

"Because you can't enchant a person," she said.

"You can't enchant a person," he agreed caustically. "But, if what I recall is true, then . . ."

Grasping the implications, Melanie sat back, searching Sebastian's face. "Then you were *dis*enchanted. Somehow it was reversed."

"Yes. Exactly. This is why I stole Blackhaus. For me. For you. For us."

24

KRONA

I buried the gold needles at the back of the cave and told the varg I would be back later, that I would bring it some fresh water and a salve for its sores. I climbed out of the cave and you and I went to the stream. You told me I stank like poop. I told you you stank like a varg. We both bathed in the running water before heading home. Not for a moment did you suspect I'd come within a hairsbreadth of death and emerged triumphant.

Krona arrived at the den to find the photographs of the dead man's markings, and new information from the Dayswatch awaiting her.

"The removed portion of the first victim," Royu reported at the morning briefing of the fourth day, "it was a womb, flayed open. Same with poor Hester."

Why would the killer do such a thing? Charbon had killed people of all genders, and he'd certainly never excised anything from the bodies, he . . . he'd *used* everything.

"And the pill?" Krona asked.

"Tray and Utkin pegged it as a sedative," zhe said. "Perhaps to keep the victims from crying out or trying to get away."

"The body reeked of it," Tray said.

"And Strange?" De-Lia asked.

"She's had a few customers," Sasha said. "We're making note of everyone who comes and goes, but there's nothing promising just yet. Rotations are still every six hours—a Regulator and a Watchperson."

"Good."

After the briefing, Krona was given leave to review the photographs of her attacker and pursue their implications. Which meant she was free to investigate in her own ways; if she decided to call on Thibaut or seek out Patroné, as she planned, there would be no one around to tell her she was wasting her time delving into a long-at-rest concern, or barking up the wrong tree with a known criminal.

The black-and-sepia tones of the photos captured the dead man's tattoos with a fuzzy edge. Some of the markings were difficult to discern. Was that a bird? A dog, perhaps? And what were these swirls? She flipped through them one at a time, looking for anything familiar.

Eventually she came to the picture of the dead man's thumb. The brand stood out in blurry relief, but its edges were still distinguishable. After a moment she placed it in her mind.

The man had "plead clergy." It was an old custom, one that predated the current paper-run bureaucracy that was the modern Watch: if a man could convince a priest to absolve him of murder, the priest would brand his thumb as a sign of everlasting debt to the coterie. The murderer officially belonged to the gods, then, and the law could not execute him.

But the practice had been done away with long ago. A bit of pleading-on-one's-knees could not keep a murderer from the noose.

Though she was familiar with the history of the custom, she had no idea anyone still practiced it. But if there were indeed religious implications to these new blooms . . .

She needed to contact Thibaut. Perhaps he would know, or would know others who would know.

And she needed to speak to him about Strange. Ask after the inn owner.

Though he preferred to initiate the majority of their exchanges, Krona did have ways of summoning him. They were to be used rarely, as he became agitated whenever he alighted on the notion that she presumed to have him leashed. Truthfully, though, she did. If they accidently found themselves in the same tavern or at a party, she could crook her finger and he would jump to follow her outside and away from prying eyes. He owed her more than he was willing to openly admit, which made him amenable to all of her little presses and pulls as long as she gave him a long lead.

One of their agreed-upon signals involved a statue of Absolon Raoul Trémaux. The monstrous hunk of marble stood situated in the middle of a roundabout, with benches and a swath of grass encircling it. Carriages, horses, and pedestrians swirled past on their way to various districts connected by the junctions attached to the roundabout.

The sight was very public and central—which made it ideal. Thibaut came through the area every day, and he would not fail to see her sign.

Krona approached the statue casually, and the citizens taking a commuter's pause on the benches paid her no mind; there were divisions of Regulators who patrolled, so though sighting one may have been rare, it was not without context.

No one noticed when she pulled a green swath of cloth from her side pouch and tied it around Absolon Raoul Trémaux's larger-than-life ankle. And no one would notice how it had been tied, with a very specific set of knots.

Satisfied with her work, Krona stomped across the street, halting traffic as she did so.

The scarf was her signal to meet, the knots would tell Thibaut when and where. In this case, later that same day, once night had fallen, and near a night-ingale's roost—one of the more upscale establishments she knew of. As a place of frequent hushed comings and goings, it was ideal for a quick rendezvous that no passerby would question.

While she waited for her Absolon web to catch her fly, Krona returned to the den and prepared to cross the river branch to the east of the city, beyond which lay the city-state's vaults, where she hoped constable Patroné still found himself employed. Hopefully he would possess insight into Charbon's character, since he'd worked the murder concern a decade ago.

Krona had not been to the vaults since her first year as a Regulator. The items for the Jubilee had been brought to the den by vault guards, their uni-forms shockingly more imposing than hers. Once she reached the complex, one such guard would stay at her side at all times, lest she lose her way in the darkened halls and fall into a pit.

That was not hyperbole.

The building had been designed in such a way as to confuse intruders. Not a proper maze, like one might find in a noble's garden—with a pleasing geo-metric pattern and one way to the center—but the effect was largely the same. If you didn't know where you were going there would be no one to ask, and you'd likely run into a dead end. Only, the vault dead ends were the literal sort.

The vaults lorded over Lutador from their hilltop ridge, east still of the Regulator den. They stood in stark opposition to the palace of the Grand Mar-quises, which sprawled over the western side on its own clifftop, peering down on the river fork below. And while the palace was opulent, with its opalescent windows framed in shining gold, copper, and silver, the vaults were sinister counterpoints. Their few windows were barred with iron, and their walls were unscalable—a façade of polished gray granite, made slick with a dousing of flame-resistant oils.

Barricades and fences aplenty marked the main trailway up the hill. Guards armed with flintlocks hid in various treetop stands, always at the ready should an enemy succeed in leaping the blockades. There was no excuse for crossing the well-marked borders of vault land. Any man found where he shouldn't be was shot on sight, no matter his station, uniform, or employ.

Krona was acutely aware of this as she sidled up to the first checkpoint on horseback. The road before had been long and dusty—a cloud still hung around her and her steed, the dirt settling on its sweating flanks, powdering its tawny sides.

The guard station was small, but well built—a tiny fort in its own right. Signs posted in Arkensinian and its subdialects stood nailed atop tall posts, written in a wide hand to be sure they could be read from a distant approach.

What she noticed before all of that, though, was the quiet—the utter silence of the trees and the sky. Whether it was an effect caused by enchantment or fear, though, she couldn't say, but one thing was for certain: an intruder, no matter how light of foot, would be heard as surely as a crashing cannonball.

All she could smell was the sunbaked dirt of the road and the musk of her horse. The hill didn't give off so much as a hint of greeny freshness or the sharp scent of hot metal fences.

The two guards who came to take her credentials at the checkpoint wore uniforms of brushed gray—like that of an ordinary needle or rough-shot. Their faces were covered by thin fabric hoods with narrow slits for their eyes and nose, but nothing for their mouth. And around their heads—bulky and boxy like a Regulator's helm—Farendeag cages, so named for the woman who had invented them.

Sue-Mi Farendeag was a *Physiteur* who'd been shipped a batch of rusted iron rods from the enchanted metal mines on the Marrakev rim. She'd had half a mind to return them and demand compensation. But instead she'd . . . experimented.

It hadn't been illegal at the time—Knowledge's calendar had been favorable for Farendeag.

At first, it seemed the iron refused to take further enchantment. It couldn't be smelted in the usual way, would not merge with other elements. She was near convinced the metal was useless until she realized that the rusted iron wasn't rejecting enchantment—the metal's innate magic hadn't been nullified—on the contrary, it was *repelling* enchantment.

It temporarily canceled out any other magic that came near.

She shared this information with the Grand Marquises, as was law. But they could not replicate her results with rusted iron of their own. It was only *this* iron, this one lone batch, that contained such power.

And no one would confess to how it was rusted.

What remained of Farendeag's supply now rested in the hands of the city-state, much of it utilized in the protection of dangerous enchantments and esteemed officials.

The Farendeag cages the guards wore were encased in resin to prevent them flaking, but were no less imposing for it.

The person who approached Krona held out a gloved hand expectantly. There were no instructions to be had at the vaults. Either you knew what you were doing, or you weren't supposed to be there.

Her uniform wasn't enough. She had to hand over her Regulation coin.

She fished it from her breast pocket and held it for a moment longer. She had to keep reminding herself that under that hood was a civil servant the same as she, and that their faceless countenance was doing its job. She was wary, her body tensely alert, focused on every action, every movement. She was compelled to shift slowly and deliberately, fearing anything too quick or too sudden might arouse their suspicion.

Not only could the vault guards deny her entry on a whim, they could also seek her detainment.

This is how you keep civilians from wandering this way, she told herself. *Fear can be good. Fear can keep us safe.*

Her mind accepted such logic, no matter how her heart rate spiked.

She pushed the token into the guard's palm instead of placing it gently, fighting her subtle itch of fear with a touch of force.

The first guard examined it while their colleague stood by with weaponry prominently displayed. No one spoke. The air pressed in on Krona like an embrace, holding her in place with anticipation.

She was fine, she was meant to be here. She and they were one and the same. This was their system at work.

Still, she held her breath as the token turned—bright gold in a gray glove—over and over again.

They were testing the weight, examining the depth of the engraving, determining if the wear on the emblazoned pentagram of the Grand Marquises was worn with accordance to the year it had been issued.

After a moment, the guard nodded to their colleague and they both disappeared back inside their booth.

Krona's insides ached as she watched her coin disappear with them, but it was a good sign.

After a moment the second guard reemerged, handing her a resin badge to pin to her uniform. She would exchange it for her coin once she returned.

Satisfied that she'd secured it prominently, they then pulled the gate across the road, waving her forward, still silent and unfeeling in their regard of the rider and her steed.

Krona caught herself holding her breath as she passed the guard. The eyelets in their hood did not follow her.

They would use reverb beads to relay her description up-road to the other checkpoints. As long as she did not dally, they would let her by. They knew exactly how long it should take her to approach the next booth on horseback at a canter, and any variance would send her back to the beginning.

>─◄♦─○─♦►─◄

The oppressive nature of Vault Hill only worsened as she approached the vaults proper. Shadows seemed longer here, deeper—easy places to hide security measures like pike-filled fall pits, and spiked clamps meant to sever limbs. She dared not stray from the razor-wire-lined path.

Hot tingles at the back of her skull alerted her to the gaze of hidden eyes. It felt like a gaze that knew her, that had followed her for a while. In the city, it was difficult to feel a particular set of eyes on you; there were so many, and so much noise, and so much activity, that the senses were often dulled by the din. But here, in the stillness, a single pair of attentive eyes pulled at her instincts like they were the string of a bell. Every few moments, the bell rang inside her mind: *ting, ting, ting*.

The stare did not belong to a hawk, or a deer, or any other curious animal— there were no curious animals on Vault Hill. Perhaps it was simply an unseen guard, hidden by the terrain.

It was unsettling, but Krona dared not look around for the stare's owner. Any apparent hesitation or deviation would appear suspicious to the vault guards, and they had only one response to suspicion.

As she arrived at the last checkpoint, a guard—caged and hooded just as all that had come before—took her horse. Another led her on foot to the base of the narrow steps which led into the narrow door that was the only entrance into the severe face of the three-story building.

She allowed herself one look back, scanning the drive and the tops of the trees that sloped away for the prying gaze, before ducking inside, her cape a dark whorl behind her.

A waft of stale air met her within. There was no lobby or receiving desk, only a thin strip of hall with an impossibly high ceiling. Above, bright, focused lamps made a line of spotlights, beckoning her into a darkness beyond. There was nowhere to go save directly back, into the depths of the vaults.

From a wall of darkness to her right, a caged guard appeared. This one's uniform was less utilitarian than the others, with long, concealing sleeves and a billowing skirt that dragged behind them as they strode. A white leather harness across their chest held two holsters, and the protruding grips of repeating flintlocks were pearlescent in the spotlights. As they swept up to her side, the guard appeared to glide over the black flooring, their posture tall and unwavering. Krona could almost imagine there to be a clockwork beneath the hood—a life-sized version of one of Thibaut's treasured toys—instead of a person.

"I'm here to see ex-Constable Patroné," she said, her whisper sounding like a shout in the silent space.

On light feet, the guard slid away. Krona assumed she was to follow.

The ominous contrast of bright spotlights and deep shadows meant it was easy for someone or something to creep up out of the darkness—just as a hallway did a few strides in. At first it was nothing more than a black rectangle in the side of a nearly-as-black wall, but then the guard turned, swallowed up. Krona was a step behind, but did not hesitate to turn as well.

The guard's gray form was ghostly in the oppressive darkness. No lamps shone in this new hall. Catching a small protuberance in the floor, they gave a pointed kick with the reinforced toe of their boot. Latches and gears hidden in the walls immediately began to clack and whirl.

Small ampules of oil spilled into the lamps overhead, and after a moment the automated lighting mechanisms sparked at the wicks. As spotlights flickered to life above, a heavy weight was displaced in the wall to Krona's right. New vials of fuel rolled to the ready as the system reset itself. In a few minutes, the lamps would devour their serving of oil and go dark once more, waiting to be relit.

It was a shame she couldn't bring Thibaut to the vaults. Such ingenuity deserved to be appreciated by someone who truly respected the work. There were no such animations in the public parts of Lutador, and for all Krona had heard about the wonders of the palace complex, she wasn't aware of any such inventions gracing the halls of the Marquises either.

A few more dark bays, switches, and corners sent the two of them zigzagging into the heart of the vaults, but Krona still couldn't shake the feeling someone was watching her—matching her journey step by step.

Did the vault guard feel it? If so, they made no indication.

It must be the building, she thought. Its oppressiveness had to be playing on her anxieties.

"Nearly there," her guard said—voice gruff and ungendered.

A handful of halls emptied into the same final stretch of corridor. Behind

Krona, another guard rattled into view, pushing a heavily laden cart in her direction. Out of courtesy, her escort crowded against one wall to allow the tumbrel clearance. She did the same. Bulky jars—a shiny something green within—tinkled atop the cart as its wheels caught on the minor irregularities in the floor.

Not until the tumbrel was nearly upon her did Krona realize what the jars contained. She should have known—the vaults were no place for things as pedestrian as peach preserves and guava jams—but still her mind denied it for as long as it was able.

Every jar was the same: squat, rounded, and possessed of the same types of seals that kept time vials magically locked. The glass was thick and enchanted. It had to be, lest its filling escape.

Bottle-barkers.

Even as she realized what they were, the swirling green mists within the jars sensed new prey. Agitated, they drummed within their prisons, thickening and pulsing. A few manifested eyes to stare at her, others coalesced into phantom teeth.

This was what starved varger became: angry vapors, looking for an unsuspecting human to inhale them. They wanted freedom, wanted to eat, to gorge, to become solid again.

The bottles began to sing, each one vibrating. The haziness within sloshed back and forth, throwing itself against one side and back again, trying to rock itself off the cart.

She did her best to block them out, to suck in her gut as the railings of the small tumbrel brushed by, but she could not hide from the phantom smells her memory instantly provided: the reeking malodor of rotted meat and oozing sores. The musty fetor of moldered spines. And the blood—the scent of hot blood that was her father's . . .

Let it pass, she said softly to herself. *The bottles will be gone soon. Let the memory pass.*

One of the jars tipped precariously as the varg inside lashed out. It jutted toward her, the manifested unlidded eyes inside surrounded by randomly placed teeth. She gasped in surprise, and a wave of reverberation ran through the other bottles as though the varger were laughing at her.

Vibrating . . . shaking . . . shattering.

This is what Utkin wants to do to you, she reminded herself, remembering his insistence that her phobia was due to a shard of varg imbedded in her being. *He wants to expose you, leave you vulnerable. How can this heal you?*

She tried to ignore the creatures by focusing on her destination instead:

a massive black door, shiny like a beetle's carapace. It stood ajar, flanked by a pair of guards, the bolts of its locking mechanisms bright silver and naked outside of their nesting.

But, if that was the cart's destination, that could only mean one thing. The vault at which Patroné worked was not a gem vault or a metal vault, but a glass vault—and few things made of glass posed enough of a threat to be locked away for good. Thousands of bottled varger must lie beyond.

Unconsciously, Krona backpedaled, inching in reverse as the tumbrel drew away.

Her guide plowed onward, unaware of her hesitancy.

In the next moment she sensed the same foreign, invisible gaze again. It crept over her shoulder, passing her at the same instant the air pressure in the hall shifted. The sensation was unsettling, confusing. Her ears popped.

For a moment there appeared to be another person in the corridor. The impression was fleeting, her gaze darting toward the distraction like it was a mote in her eye. But then the figure vanished. A faint shimmer, like that of a heat-sheer, wavered in its place.

Between her escort and the vault door, the cart guard screamed. The bulk of their body was a gray smear as it flew from the center of the hall to collide with a wall.

Krona froze, startled, her training telling her to take a step back, to evaluate what had just happened before leaping in.

In contrast, the vault guards surged.

No one spoke. No shouting of directions or further exclamations of surprise echoed through the hall. Just calculated action. The two individuals flanking the door rushed to bolt it shut. They hadn't seen the figure as she had, she was sure, but their colleague clearly hadn't tripped, hadn't thrown *themself* against the wall. The other guards did not try to judge the situation, they simply enacted their training: if an unknown person crossed the fence guarding Vault Hill, someone shot, and if something strange happened in the vaults, they went into lockdown.

For a brief moment, before the door could shut, Krona caught a glimpse of the heavyset steward seated at a desk within.

He wore a cage, but no hood. An expression of wide-eyed surprise was evident on his tanned face. Behind him, rows of massive cabinets soared from ceiling to floor, their fronts padlocked. Every cupboard was alive with movement, pushing out against the locks and chains, the bottle-barkers chittering in excitement.

And then the man was gone, sealed inside.

But before the guards could spin the outer dial—its silver arms like the legs of some hard-shelled lake creature—they doubled over in turn. The shimmer—now more of a mist, the color of sky—overtook them, dragging them to the floor, holding them until they lay still.

When they'd both gone down, the mist spun to face the cart, and once more Krona—for only an instant—thought she saw a person in its place.

It had to be a person. Of course it was a person.

But why couldn't she see the attacker properly? She cursed the dim lighting and the berry red of her visor—they must be working in tandem with the hue of the assailant's clothes, making them hard to pinpoint.

Her escort had both guns drawn and at the ready. But the give in their elbows, the sway of their wrists, indicated they had no idea where to aim. They couldn't see the attacker either.

"There," Krona said, pointing at the shimmer. The blast echoed through the hall, its *crack* unmistakable, the flare of the gunpowder blinding in the dim space. A stone tile in the far wall shattered under the shot. The mist was undaunted.

Krona's rationale tried to make up for the weakness of her vision. *Someone is there, even if you can't see them.* She thrust her visor upward, determined to overcome what must be a failing of the light.

At the same time, the shimmer swooped forward, colliding with the tumbrel, shoving it at Krona and the guard.

Its wheels screeched as they spun sideways, locking up, flipping the cart—

Bottles poured over the side like water over a cliff, rebounding when they hit the floor, scattering, bouncing, spinning toward Krona's feet with gnashing vapors inside. The acid green essence clawed and scraped and formed and unformed.

Her insides reeled away from the creatures, stealing her breath, punching it from her lungs.

They're contained, she reminded herself. *They're contained, they're contained, they're contained. But this . . . mist . . . is not.*

Her escort fired again, and another tile shattered.

Krona drew her saber, breathing slowly, deliberately, through her nose. Her grip on the pommel was too tense, too tight—her joints creaking and bones grinding.

Where are you? she yelled inside her mind.

As if in answer, a handful of the bottle-barkers lifted into the air, levitating of their own accord an arm's reach in front of Krona. Hazy, ethereal eyes turned on her, bulging against the inside of the glass.

Appalled, Krona pulled back, raising her sword.

The impossibilities were piling up—people couldn't be invisible and bottle-barkers couldn't fly. What in the gods' names was happening?

Out of nowhere, arms appeared, swaddling the bottles, pressing them into a pale, detail-less chest below a detail-less head. The figure resembled a human only insomuch as it was the rough shape of a human.

But once again the impression was momentary—a blink of an eye and it was gone.

Krona's head swam, fear and confusion muddling everything together.

When the attacker dissolved again, Krona found herself facing a flintlock. The cart guard had righted themself and retrieved their firearm. The figure stood firmly in their sights for half a moment, but the guard's trigger finger was a hair too slow. The mist disappeared, leaving nothing but empty air between Krona and the gun's barrel.

Flash. *Crack!*

Krona cried out, turning.

The bullet struck her.

The impact snapped Krona's helm to the side, smacking it against the wall. But her armor did its job. The iron ball ricocheted, taking a chip out of the opposing tile.

Seething—knowing the guard hadn't shot her on purpose—Krona righted herself quickly. The air pressure changed again and she knew the attacker was retreating, having gotten what it came for: bottle-barkers.

The sinews in her body thrummed as she gave chase, pirouetting on the spot before sprinting away. She could no longer see the bottles, but she could hear them, clinking against one another as they rode high in the mist's arms.

She lashed out with her saber, feeling it catch, tangle—as if in thick fabric. A punctuated clanking followed as the pommel jerked forward in her hand. Did she have the attacker? Had she landed a blow?

Not waiting for a confirmation, she sliced sideways, feeling a tug, and reached out with her free hand, willing her fingers to fall on a shoulder or a collar—something substantial. There was a brush of sensation, but nothing more.

Once again her saber sailed through the air and made firm contact. A muffled cry followed. One bottle reappeared, tumbling to the floor and rolling away.

"Here. *Here!*" Krona yelled.

Her escort fired again, the shot whizzing by Krona's side.

A wet, tearing sound. Another cry. Bottles manifested waist-high, bubbling over invisible arms to fall at invisible feet.

Krona fumbled in the dim light, knowing the thief was wounded and close. If she could only land a hand on them . . .

But as she groped, the air changed again. Boots stomped off into the distance.

The attacker was gone.

"They're running!" she called, sheathing her sword, readying for another sprint.

The cart guard sprang past. As she was about to follow, a gray glove gripped her shoulder. "Stay," her escort commanded. "We'll handle this."

It wasn't her place to argue. This was their jurisdiction, their domain. They knew the twists and turns of the maze best. Far from helping, Krona might end up a hindrance or a hazard.

The two vault guards disappeared, leaving Krona in a pool of vibrating jars.

Green haze burgeoned and coalesced, teeth manifested and dissolved. One varg snapped heartily at her boot, teeth tangible enough to scrape at the glass, the force of it strong enough to roll the bottle in her direction.

Her hand went to her heart, as though she could still it from the outside. *They can't hurt you. They can't.*

Tiptoeing around the jars, she retreated toward the vault door. With nothing to do but wait for her escort's return, Krona checked on the two downed figures. Both were breathing, their chests rising and falling.

She knocked on the vault itself. "Are you all right in there?"

The steward did not answer, though he may not have heard her through the thick metal.

Long minutes passed. The bottles continued to jostle themselves, and Krona did her best to block them out, drawing down her visor and closing her eyes.

What in the Valley happened here?

>-◆-0-◆-◄

That was the first thing the Martinets asked when they arrived. And still, Krona didn't know what to say.

She and her escort now stood with three Martinets outside the building. The others were being interrogated within. A breeze blew softly over the hill, through the trees. Leaves sizzled in the distance.

The Martinets, two women and one man, each wore a thick circlet of gold with a set of bulky glass ram's horns soldered to it, spiraling down around their ears. Strewn through the glass were flecks of metal and crystal, which sparkled as they moved. Krona knew the horns to be enchanted, but did not know their purpose—that was a closely kept state secret. The horns were the only magic the Martinets used. Tied over their mouths were silky white bandanas, not for hiding their identities so much as the movement of their lips, which Krona figured played into the purpose of the horns.

One of the women had deep, coal-rimmed eyes. She asked the majority of the questions—had been asking for hours.

"Were you not also present at the Chief Magistrate's Jubilee?"

Bristling, Krona tried to keep the affront off her face. No one wore a head covering in the presence of Martinets—no masks, no helms. She felt naked without it; her last encounter with the internal investigators was all too near in time and space, and the usefulness of her helm had just been proven. Her ears still rang from the reverberation of the ricocheting shot. "Yes."

"You were responsible for capturing the only detained intruder during that attack, correct?" The woman raised a makeup-darkened eyebrow.

"Correct."

"But here you were unable to stop the—"

"But she recovered all of the bottles," Krona's escort interrupted. Krona knew the Martinets were simply doing their job, but he seemed to take their questioning as a personal affront. Not so surprising, as this was probably the first time he'd ever had his actions on the job questioned. Attacks on Vault Hill were rare, for good reason.

Without his hood and cage, the guard wasn't nearly as imposing. His cheeks were rounder than Krona would have imagined, and he seemed younger than his posture and capabilities suggested. He had a sharp nose and reddish-brown skin under a mop of pitch-black hair. "The tally was taken before you were called. The thief didn't get away with a single bottle-barker, in part thanks to Mistress Hirvath."

"And I was about to commend her for that," the Martinet said. "You all fought well, by the tell of it. But no one can answer me this: where the intruder came from or what in the Valley they look like."

"They were shielded, somehow," Krona said. "Blurry and indistinguishable at times. Invisible, even. I suspect an unlawful enchantment, but it would have to be one the likes of which the Valley has never seen."

The Martinets shared a look. "What possible combination of magics could do that? Even if the intruder was able to develop such an invention and get it into the vault, there are caged guards everywhere, which should have nullified the enchantment. How did they make it over the barricades? Through the woods? Into the building?"

"I believe that is a question for my colleagues at the bottom of the hill," the guard said.

"Funny thing," said the lead woman, reaching into the breast pocket of her uniform's jacket. "The only figure they've reported seeing gave them this." She held up Krona's Regulator coin.

"That's mine," Krona admitted without hesitation.

"We know," said the Martinet, handing it back sans preamble. "We believe this attack had to have been perpetrated by many, not one. Perhaps the guards were . . ." She trailed off, seemingly at a loss for a moment. Krona wondered if she was contemplating whether or not this could have been an inside job.

But Krona had no doubts the guards were telling the truth to the best of their abilities. If there was a new enchantment that could blur forms to the point of invisibility, and negate the effects of the cages, then how could they possibly fight it?

"What are you going to do?" Krona's mind buzzed with possibilities, trying to form connections, to make sense of things. It was strange for her to have been on-site for both attacks. Which meant either the assaults were connected—were both tied to Charbon in some way—or . . . or the Martinets would suspect she was somehow to blame.

The Martinets turned to talk amongst themselves, leaving Krona and her guide to fidget in silence. Daylight was waning, the clouds near the Valley rim blazing orange and pink.

What if they want to detain me? They can't take me off my concern, they can't.

"There's no harm in telling you," the Martinet said after a moment, "we're going to keep the vaults under Martinet observation for a time. Thus far we have nothing to indicate an internal mishandling, but if the guards were exposed to some kind of toxin—drugs to make their memories fuzzy—further signs may appear."

"And me?" Krona asked.

"You performed excellently. The vaults were lucky to have you today."

"Thank you."

"You may return to work. And we'll keep you apprised of our investigation."

"That's very generous of you. You have no more questions?"

"Not for the time being. But note that these events are to be kept confidential. No one beyond this hill should be told of the breach."

"Understood. May I speak with ex-Constable Patroné, then?"

"Who?"

The vault guard spoke up. "He was the steward Mistress Hirvath came to see. The man who was closed in the varger vault during the attack."

"Ah. We dismissed him not long after the vault was reopened," the male Martinet said. "He's been gone for some time."

Damn it.

"If it helps," said her escort, noting her crestfallen expression, "he's known for visiting a salt-and-tea house after hours. One in the pleasure district. You might know the name."

"Oh?"

"The White Lily."

>─┤◆├─O─┤◆├─<

Wondering if her last hours had been a dream, Krona rode according to the directions her vault escort laid out for her.

Patroné would likely have no new insights into what they'd experienced at the vaults, but perhaps he *would* know why records pertaining to Charbon had gone missing from the Hall of Records, or why someone might be victimizing pregnant nightingales. He'd know Charbon's weaknesses, could tell her how they'd caught him all those years ago.

A few inquiries and a quick ride delivered her to the steps of the third-floor establishment. The staircase curled around the outside of the squat building like a vine, and its railing sported a chain of iron lilies that had gone green with age. At the top, Krona was confronted with an equally patinaed door. Like most doors in the pleasure district, it made no attempt to inform passersby of what lay beyond. There was no sign, no bell, no place to receive mail labeled with a helpful stenciling of the proprietor's name. If you were poised at the threshold, the door assumed you already knew what you were in for.

Without hesitation, she pressed forward.

The lighting inside was bright—much brighter than could have reasonably been expected. Most seedy palaces of enjoyment were dim, so as to obscure patrons' identities or make them feel hidden from their own guilt. The White Lily instead shone a spotlight on its activities, urging everyone to see one another, to take in their environment with all of their senses. The walls were indeed lily white, emphasizing the brilliant glare. Even the clientele all wore white. The subtle plucking of a minor chord on a string instrument flitted through the air, as did a wafting of white haze. From the smell of it, the haze came from a hookah.

No one spoke. Besides the music, all lay nearly silent.

Porcelain dishes clattered softly as she entered, as though the smattering of patrons had all dropped their teacups at once.

She was a black thorn in their white-petal world.

A woman in a long white silk robe with a high lace collar dropped her cithara, cutting the music off at the quick, and hurried from the back of the room to Krona's side.

"Your garb is inappropriate, Regulator," the woman chided in nearly inaudible tones.

"Apologies," Krona whispered. "But I'm looking for a former Constable Patroné. The matter is urgent."

"Let the Regulator in," said an older, heavyset man lounging in a window seat. Definitely the same man she'd seen in the vault. His tempered command sounded like a booming shout in the subdued space. "I'm sure they're willing to pay extra for being an eyesore."

The woman glared at Krona with one eyebrow raised, looking for confirmation of the statement.

Krona sighed internally and pulled her time pouch from the case on her hip.

The woman was crass enough to examine the bottles in front of her, looking for the telltale wisp of color within. "Him," she said, pointing at the man in the window.

The man didn't look at her as she approached, though the other patrons tracked her movement with irritated stares. He leaned heavily against the white pillows, his jacket open to reveal his deep brown, heavily scarred chest. Once, he'd been a daunting man, but age had robbed him of his striking presence. It wasn't until she was at his side that she noted the white wheeled chair sitting unassumingly nearby. He must have employed a carriage to take him to and from Vault Hill.

From a small glass table, he picked up one of several small ramekins. He wetted his pinkie on the tip of his tongue, then dipped it inside. The digit came back flecked with pink crystals, which he sucked between his lips. "Salt?" he offered.

"No, thank you," she declined. She'd never quite understood the affinity for salt displayed by a large portion of the population. They craved it more than sugar, and some—it seemed—more than air. They longed for it as one longed for something stolen they'd once possessed.

Words wanted to spill from her lips like water over the Falls. So many questions boiled in her throat, each one scalding her insides the longer it was held in. She had rested so much hope on this moment, had unconsciously decided that Patroné would be the key to the concern and his intimate understanding of Charbon would lead to a swift conclusion of this nightmare. But looking at him now, she realized he was only a man, not a magic linchpin.

"Am I correct in assuming you are the same Regulator I saw earlier today?"

"Yes."

"Now why would you go so far as to follow me off the Hill, if the Martinets let me go?"

"It's not about . . . about the incident. I don't know what that was—"

"From the look on my colleagues' faces, it seems none of us are sure what that was. What did *you* see, hmm?" He scrutinized her helm.

He was sending out feelers, trying to pry information out of her that he hadn't been able to get out of the guards. For a moment she wondered if he'd seen enough—or seen *nothing,* as the case may be. She was sure no one had been able to see the attacker fully. And it was not due to the "blur of battle" or the dimness of the light or anything else half so logical.

But that only left illogical explanations, like impossible enchantments.

When she didn't answer he looked away, gazing into the street below. "Are you going to stare, or are you going to sit?" he asked flatly.

"I'd prefer to stand." Krona widened her stance and held her arms behind her back, bringing the here and now into focus. "I came to the vaults to see you specifically. I need to ask you about your work on Louis Charbon's concern."

"I always knew, one day, a Regulator would have questions about him."

"How do you mean?"

"Well, it didn't end quite right, did it? We caught the man, killed the man, and yet . . ." His dark eyes flickered toward her for an instant. "Do you have any inkling why I come here?"

"The riveting conversation?" she said, glancing back at the clients who had all gone back to their quiet contemplation.

"This is where I nabbed the bastard," he said. "Catching Charbon was the last of my glory days, so I like to relive it. Nothing that followed after made much sense. And then my legs . . . a degenerate put a knife through my spine, and that was that. Became a steward, but still." He pushed himself up. "And the more I relive it, the more I question it. I should have seen the signs. I knew Charbon better than anyone, and I should have realized he was being fitted for a true death mask. I should have wondered why he sat there"—he gestured to the center of the room—"and let me shackle him. I should have delayed his execution until we'd ground that rogue enchanter into sand. That's what you've come to ask, isn't it? How I let it happen?"

"Actually, monsieur, it isn't. I wanted to ask you what he was like, how he chose his victims. If there was . . . was a pattern to them."

His brow furrowed. "What for?"

Krona leaned in close. Quietly, so the others couldn't hear, she related what had transpired over the past few days, then asked, "Who was Charbon? Really."

The ex-constable shrugged. "Outwardly? Upstanding citizen extraordinaire—mostly. Lesser noble, in and out of good standing. Religious man. Right up until he cursed the gods. Attended a Founding Coterie and went to Grand Service

every five days. He chose healing over the family business—was a master surgeon, actually. That was how he . . . Anatomy was his strong suit, as I'm sure
you've discovered. His unauthorized study of the body was the only black mark
on his reputation. Until . . ."

"And inwardly?"

"Inwardly, he was every kind of dirty monster out of every darkened corner
and crack in the ground. These kinds of killers, men like Charbon, murder
repeatedly because they luxuriate in death and destruction—in the power. It
excites them. They're nothing but bloody mud inside."

"But they follow patterns, don't they?"

Patroné shook his head. "There was no way to tell back then. I don't know
how he decided who to take. Early on, he killed only cis men, then occasionally
took someone of another gender. But in his last months, he changed. I don't
know why. He started strictly taking cis women."

"What else? Did the victims have similar occupations, similar status?"

"No, nothing like that. Nothing to indicate a link. Except . . . but it won't
help you."

"It might," she urged. "What is it?"

"The first man he killed was sixty-two, one foot in the grave already. The
next victim was fifty-seven. Then fifty-three. Then forty-five. On and on, until
his last victim. She was thirteen."

"Was she the only child he murdered?"

Patroné nodded, sucking in his cheeks. The memory disturbed him. "That
was how we caught him. It was wrong, and very out of character. Close to
home. The kill had an air of desperation about it, but I never understood why.
It didn't invigorate him, it wasn't an escalation. It was sloppy, mistake-filled. It
seemed to drain the life right out of him. Makes sense, never would have taken
him for . . ." A bubble of memory caught in his throat, corking off his words.
He looked as if he wanted to say more, but bile prevented it.

"None of the people he took were pregnant, were they?"

"No. What does it matter, anyway, what Charbon did? The Blooming
Butcher is dead, and whoever is wearing the mask is in the saddle. Most likely
they're suppressing the echo, aren't they?"

"No, I don't think that's a given." Patroné had likely never worn a mask
himself, had no idea what being in one was like, how much anguish a typical
mask could cause its wearer. "I think it just as likely Charbon's echo has seated
itself at the killer's helm and is working once more toward the same ends. So,
why the blooms? Why would he need to mutilate the body so?"

Patroné dipped in for another hit of salt. "You're looking for deeper meaning where there is none. Charbon was evil, that's the reason he did what he did. Whoever you're chasing now is evil, and that's the reason they do what they do."

Krona shook her head. "People are more complex than that. Evil has its logics, just as good does. I need to understand Charbon to understand this killer."

"Understanding him won't stop him."

"It might."

"I chased evil for decades," he said softly. "I tried everything to stop it. Believe me, nothing can. Looking for the whys of it will only drive you mad." More salt. A dip. Then another. The ex-constable looked out the window again, sadness in his eyes.

She kept questioning, kept pushing. But his answers were clipped and lackluster. The information inside his head was a burden—a soiled mess—and he'd rather thrust it back into the depths of his mind than draw it forth into the daylight ever again.

Frustrated, part of her wanted to lash out, to demand he divulge every finer point of the concern. But her empathy overruled. This man had seen too much, had lost his legs and perhaps his soul to the blood of his occupation. Most so troubled lost themselves in drink. He gave himself to salt.

Eventually she realized she would learn no more about Charbon's motivations here. If Patroné didn't believe that an echo's past inclinations could inform a mask wearer's current actions, there was little hope he'd reexamine his experience with the Blooming Butcher close enough to find whatever spark of insight she was searching for.

She rose, feeling the hot glares of the tea room's customers burning into her once again. She cut a black line across the white room, holding on to one thought: Charbon was just a man.

Patroné spoke as though he were a force, some personification of an eternal, undying maliciousness. But it wasn't so. Painting him as a demon helped no one. It made him immortal, impassable. Ascribing unknowable evil to something was just an excuse not to understand it, a way to wash one's hands of it.

Krona was determined to know him as the putrid, human thing he must have been. A murderer didn't deserve to be feared even in death. If Patroné was right and Charbon had sought power through killing, she would not give it to him. She would not allow him to dominate the living, still.

25

LOUIS

*The White Lily, early afternoon,
ten years previous*

The tiny private rooms in the White Lily were not white. There was a blue room, and a yellow room, and a pink room that reminded everyone of candy floss and that patrons swore smelled of burnt sugar. There was even a red room, though only those who enjoyed being weighed down by chains inlaid with enchanted opals went anywhere near it. Wallowing in grief was not for Charbon. He liked the green room. It was a leafy shade and smelled like soil after the rain. The proprietor kept potted flowers on the windowsill, and the tablecloths were embroidered with an ivy pattern.

He ordered a brew of cocoa tea and let the mild flavor and strong medicine lull him into an unnatural ease.

A light knock at the door did little to rouse him. He made no sound, yet the door opened. In strolled blond-haired Fiona, strands done up high on her head. She moved with a bluster, as though the wind followed her obediently. With a heavy sigh, she dropped herself into one of the elegant seats across from him. The chair strained under her; it wasn't used to being treated like a common street bench.

"Husband or lover?" he inquired indelicately, referring to her attitude.

He was still unsure what Matisse brought to their table. Other than muscle for lugging bodies, of course. The Thalo insisted he had special talents that their unveiling required, but Charbon had yet to glimpse Matisse's superior capacity for anything other than spurring Fiona onward.

"Both," she snapped, pulling off her gloves and slapping them onto the table. "Did you find it?"

He took another hurried sip of his tea. It suddenly had a bitter edge. "No."

"I told you what you need to do. You're insisting on the wrong subjects. I can bring you better—we can achieve this faster, if you'd simply listen."

Charbon leaned forward, studying the placid lines of her face. No one could be as cold as Fiona appeared. No one. She could only speak of murder so clinically because it wasn't *she* who had to sharpen the blades, to cut the skin, to *search*. Not once had she stayed to help, to see what he had to go through each time. If she had, she'd understand why he'd resisted tumbling down this next set of steps.

"Just one more. I think I'm close."

She narrowed her gaze at him, tongue rolling inside her mouth as though she could taste her own contempt. "How many more be-cocked individuals are you willing to kill unnecessarily when the answer could be under the breast of *one* person possessed of a womb? You think yourself so noble, taking those with balls and sparing the rest of us. We do not need a murderer's chivalry."

"I need to find someone . . . fresher. I should have . . ." His stomach turned over. All of his sacrifices had been too far from whole. So long had their power been gone that not even the scars remained. He needed someone who still bore the wound. So he kept going further back, younger, hoping that he wouldn't have to steal too much of their lives.

"Yes, fresher. And of a different sex."

"I'm not convinced."

She smiled sweetly, condescendingly, at him. Gathering her skirts about her, she rose from the chair and swung around the small table to alight in his lap. He shifted uncomfortably, but did not shove her away. When she threw her arms around his neck to toy with the white ribbon holding back his hair, he averted his gaze.

"Such a pretty boy," she cooed. He always demurred when she called him *boy*. Past forty, he was no such thing. Especially to her: young, tempting, *terrifying* Fiona.

He swallowed dryly.

"Ah, that reminds me," she said, reaching into her purse to draw forth a small, dark bead. It was a dull gray, like lead. "Open wide."

He did as he was told. If the Unknown needed him to swallow strange pills for fortitude, he did it. "Get off," he demanded once it was down.

Fiona tapped the tip of his nose and made no move to comply. "Oh, don't be such an infant. Now, about the task. I was there, I heard what you were charged with, and you know what I was charged with. You find our missing, god-given power, and I keep you safe, keep you moving forward until you bring me *what I need*. You want the Unknown god to return, don't you? We have to prove ourselves."

Her hand tightened in his hair, yanking his head back, forcing him to look at her. "So, if I say you have to start picking more feminine blossoms, listen." She ran one slender finger down the length of his exposed throat.

Charbon allowed her many liberties. When she was too familiar with him, tried to touch him in ways he only shared with his wife, he was gentle in his denials. When she ordered him around like a spoilt child, he only put up a fight for his dignity's sake. But *this* he could not allow.

A soft breath went out of her when his hand shot forward to tighten around her windpipe. Instead of struggling, Fiona stilled, waiting. Surprise darkened her eyes.

With determination coloring his voice, he yanked her forward and whispered, "I am not your puppet, Mistress. Do not mistake me for spineless. I have killed many times, and unless you wish *your* body to be the first female given in sacrifice to the Unknown, I suggest you mind your fingers."

Heat rolled between them like a crashing wave caught between two high cliffs. Neither showed any sign of retreat, their talons stuck firmly in each other. But then Charbon squeezed a fraction tighter, and Fiona's lips gave a little twitch. She tried to quirk her expression into a daring grin, but could not keep her mouth from quivering.

Yes, she had to remember: *he* was the murderer.

"You need me," she croaked out. "The Thalo said so."

"The Thalo," he said gruffly, "is not here."

She disentangled herself from his hair, holding up her palms placatingly.

Unamused, Charbon shoved her from his lap and she stumbled. Catching herself at the last second on the edge of the table, she kept from tumbling to the floor.

How had he ended up tied to her like this? Why had the Unknown god chosen the two of them—the two of them *and her lover*—when they were so volatile?

"You should go. I'm sure your husband is missing you."

"What do you care what the old man thinks?"

"If he starts suspecting you of more than infidelity, he may try to interfere with our work."

Fiona straightened her skirts and smoothed her collar. "Fine. I'll go, but you know I'm right about the sacrifices. Those with wombs are closer to magic. They have to be."

The door to the green room slammed behind her. Charbon took another swig of tea, but now the cocoa made him shake. Every bit of his body tremored. Uneasy to the core, he pulled the ribbon from his hair and tossed it onto the tablecloth, next to where Fiona had forgotten her gloves.

Why did the Unknown ask so much of him? Others had to do so little to prove their faith.

26

MELANIE

Two years previous

"Will you help me?" Sebastian whispered.

They still huddled together on the floor, had both been cautious and quiet for a long while, letting their embrace speak of comfort and concern, conveying what their words could not.

Now Melanie leaned back far enough to find his eyes, to gaze into them—to search behind them. She wasn't sure what she was looking for, but what she found was sincerity and trust.

"The irony of Blackhaus's mask is that it's impossible to use on one's own," he explained. "The enchantment grants perfect recall, but the very virtue of a mask steals those memories away again as soon as it's removed. I need you to listen to my story, to tell it back to me when we're finished.

"This is a hole—in my life, in my understanding of myself. And it might help you. We can use it to figure out how to remove the mark and the magic so that you never have to worry about . . . about being . . ."

"Hunted," she provided. "*Used*. Dissected, even. Oh gods, I—"

He ran his fingers through her hair, trying to calm her. "We won't let that happen. As much as I've feared putting on a mask again, it must be done."

Gently, he started to rise, lifting her with him. "Will you help me?" he asked again.

"Yes. Yes, of course."

Once they were both properly on their feet again, expectations of decorum suddenly swamped into Melanie's mind. It wasn't proper for the two of them to cling to one another this way—they hardly knew each other.

Even if the past few days had felt like a lifetime.

She stepped back, put a respectable distance between them.

He let her go easily, didn't remark on it.

Oh, to be like that blond man and his noble companion—to be a part of forming society's expectations while thwarting them at your own whim.

Nobles had such luxuries. A peasant and a merchant did not.

Sebastian moved to the bed with caution, as though the mask might leap from the blankets and scurry into a dark corner. Melanie wouldn't put it past the creepy thing.

She followed him, two steps behind.

With stiff hands, he lifted it, staring at the ugly visage with a strange mixture of fondness and disgust. He clearly appreciated its craftsmanship, its importance, but that did not mean it pleased him. What Melanie had thought of as sections of bark before were now clearly identifiable as slick white diamonds of overtreated leather, plastered atop the wood base. The bars in the eyelets were dull with smudged fingerprints. "I don't know much about Blackhaus," Sebastian admitted, "beyond his capacity for accurate recall. He may very well be more interested in his own memories than mine. But it's Magnitude One . . ."

"We've dealt with Magnitude *Zero* before," she said.

"Belladino knew my father, had rage against him for good reason, rage that never cooled. Whoever ranked the mask had no way of knowing that just the right combination of circumstances could turn this particular Magnitude Zero into a—"

"I don't want to talk about whatever he turned into," she said. "But you're sure you want to do this?"

"I *don't* want to do this," he said.

"You don't have to do it for me."

"I can't go on not knowing."

"What if Blackhaus won't let you go?"

"We've defeated echoes before. I'm sure we can conquer another."

"You want to do it here? Where Belladino—?"

"Where we finished him?" His dark eyes brightened, gaze locking with hers. "Absolutely."

Lowering her voice, she made one last appeal. "I know there are events in your past you'd rather not relive . . ."

"Melanie, those things are a part of me every day. I could not forget. I know, I've tried." Impulsively, he reached for the ends of one lock of her hair, turned it over gently against her shoulder. "You cannot protect me from cruelties long over. But we can do our best to avoid tragedies yet to come. This will give me my past, and perhaps secure our future. Now, may I?"

Backing away, she nodded. "Gods help us if we haven't learned our lesson."

With a deep breath, Sebastian plunged forth, his dark face disappearing behind the pale façade of another man's past.

><•>-o-<•><

Sebastian's skin crawled as he caged himself behind Blackhaus's mask. The last mask he'd worn had been the crow, and he never wanted to be trapped in someone else's visage ever again.

He waited for Blackhaus to probe at his mind, to let out a sickening cackle the way his father had. But all was still.

It was as if he wore a regular, non-enchanted death mask. He didn't even feel any new knowledge pouring into him. He felt like himself, nothing more.

He secured the ties around his head, sat on the bed. "Nothing's happening," he said.

Melanie watched him with trepidation, worry making her face go sour. He hated being the reason she looked that way. He'd gone into the shop to *help* her. And his involvement had led to nothing but woe for the both of them. If Belladino's echo hadn't recognized him, none of this would have happened.

Then again, without him, Belladino's mask would have gone unrented. The medicine unmade. Dawn-Lyn . . .

His helping and his hurting were tangled together.

"Well, it's different, isn't it?" Melanie said. "With Belladino, it was about what I could take from him. With Blackhaus, perhaps it's more about what he can pull from you?"

That made sense. He took a deep breath and tried to think, reaching back. Back, back as far as he could go.

A fuzzy sensation tingled its way across his lips, his temples. It spilled from his mouth and his eyes down his throat and into his mind. The sensation was warming, like a dram on a frigid evening. He felt calm, gentled. Like Blackhaus wanted to take care of him instead of use him.

Part of Sebastian wanted to sleep. To dream.

Perhaps therein lay this mask's danger.

And then, slowly, images came into focus behind his eyes. Then smells, textures. Sounds. Flavors.

The first memory he drew upon was a good memory. Of his mother, when he was very, very small. Tiny enough still to be cradled in her arms. She sang a Xyoparian lullaby, and rocked him beneath a bright sky. A bird flew overhead—a heron, though his young mind had no word for it at the time—and he reached for the creature with chubby little hands, even though it was far, far away. "Bird," she said happily. "Bird."

She had yellow ribbons in her hair, twisted tightly through. She wore yellow all the time. Her favorite color was yellow.

Everything felt so sharp, so real. He'd never be able to recall this much detail on his own. The scent of flowers and warming grasses, mixing with the fragrance of his mother's soap. The softness of his baby clothes. The whinny of a horse somewhere far off. The crunch of gravel under shoes.

And then a shadow fell over him. His father, peering down. A surge of joy—unfamiliar and unwanted—filled Sebastian's chest. His present-self fought with his infant-self. But all he'd known when he was that small was that this was his daddy.

"He's beautiful, Louisa," his father said.

His mother smiled at his father, and Sebastian felt sick. He tore himself away from the memory as quickly as he could.

He searched instead for bits of magic, bypassing the instances of abuse that threatened to leap up at him. There had been very few good days with Victor Leiwood.

Sebastian caught hold of an image he'd forgotten all about—a hut, someplace cold. His great-aunt Umara was there. She was his father's aunt, but only a couple years the man's elder. The woman was tall and wide, rounded in hip, and imposing before most people. She wore what seemed like a million different brightly colored shawls, and her hair had premature streaks of gray throughout.

Umara. It had been forever since he'd recalled her name. He hadn't seen her in ages, not after . . . not after . . .

"How dare you try to keep my son from me, Auntie!" his father shouted at her. "How dare you come into my home and steal my child!" He raised his hand. Little seven-year-old Sebastian looked away, heard the *smack*.

"You don't deserve him, Victor. You don't deserve anyone!"

Another *smack*.

Crying. Umara crying.

His father stomped over to him, took him by the arm, made him look over to where Great-Aunt Umara lay on the floor, half propping herself up, letting her tears fall freely into the throw rug that covered most of the wooden floor in the small room.

"Go apologize," Victor told him.

Sebastian understood what he meant.

Terrified of his father's fist, he moved cautiously, afraid Victor might take a swipe at him if he shifted the wrong way. Kneeling down next to Umara, Sebastian put a hand on her shoulder. "It's okay, Auntie," he said, "you'll feel okay soon. Don't be sad. Be happy. Don't be sad." A warmth pulsed through his palm, entering into her, changing her, feeding her new feelings.

Her tears stopped right away. "Oh, Sebastian," she said, pushing herself up, lightly touching his face. "You've got a gift, child. A wonderful, horrible gift. I don't know why the spirits sent it to you." She glared at his father. "Or maybe I do."

Victor yanked Sebastian away from her by the upper arm, holding on to him too tight, keeping it aloft just a little too high, so that the boy had to keep on his tiptoes. "You ever come near me or my boy again and I'll kill you," Victor promised.

Now Sebastian started crying. He loved Great-Aunt Umara. She'd wanted to keep him forever. He'd wanted to keep her forever.

"Quit your blubbering," Victor said, dragging him from the hut.

Grown-up Sebastian let the memory go dark. Feeling dampness on his own cheeks, he searched his memories again.

>-+◇-0-◇+-<

It was only minutes, but to Melanie it felt like days.

She kept expecting Sebastian's posture to slip, to morph into a foreign carriage to indicate Blackhaus had consumed him. But he remained himself, even if it was a tormented version.

Slipping in reverse through his past—unraveling his memories so that they pulled taut to reveal stark details—pained Sebastian. He ground his teeth so harshly Melanie could hear them scraping. Sweat broke out over every patch of exposed skin. His breathing became labored, and at one point he mumbled what in his past must have been a scream: "Father, please, no."

After a moment she had to look away. The mask blurred in her vision, made her want to vomit. She pinched the insides of her elbows in order to occupy her hands, so that she wouldn't reach for the mask and throw it across the room—into the fireplace.

And then Sebastian spoke. It was difficult, but he told her of the memories. He went on at length, divulging strange, painful instances from his childhood. Melanie stood perfectly still, letting him go on until his tale was spun.

Half an hour passed before Sebastian reached for the ties again. "I did it," he said in wonder, removing Blackhaus's mask, clearly exhausted. Tear tracks marred his cheeks. He palmed the wood gently, careful not to pull at any of the leather scales. "I did it, and I—" His brow knitted. He put a hand over his eyes. "Oh, my head. It's throbbing," he groaned.

Blackhaus's echo hadn't even made an appearance. It had been content to hibernate while Sebastian explored his past. Melanie envied the ease with which Sebastian had been able to retrieve the information. How different would things be now if Belladino had been as subdued? There would be no question of human enchantment. Blackhaus's mask wouldn't be in Sebastian's lap.

She wouldn't even be in here, now, in this room with him. She would have already taken her mother back home.

That thought chilled her in a strange way.

Sebastian leaned his head into his hands, the post-enchantment headache strong. "Were they—?" he started, but the question caught in his throat and he had to swallow and start again. "Were they real? The memories?"

"Yes."

He peeked from behind his palms, urging her to elaborate.

"You said . . . You said you didn't think it *happened* to you—not like it happened to me. Your great-aunt saw it in you. From the beginning."

"I was *born* that way?" he asked, doubtful.

"That's what you said. Umara nurtured it, and your father . . ."

"My father used it. How did it . . . when did it stop?"

"It stopped when you were ten. After . . ."

"The tax man came, and drained us both, and then my mother took me away and . . . He was gone. I thought Umara was dead. *He* told me she was dead, I don't know why I ever trusted him. Maybe she's not. But—after the tax—he was gone, and she was gone, and I didn't have a reason to do it anymore. I don't know when I tried again—did I say?—but I couldn't. And that's when I started to wonder if I'd made it up."

"But you *didn't*. You described everything vividly."

"And Blackhaus's ability would only reveal truth, not my fancies. That means it stopped when—*when they took my time*."

His gaze shot up, locked with hers.

"Of course it did," Melanie half gasped, half laughed. "Makes sense, doesn't it? It took an enchanted needle to disenchant Belladino's mask, to enchant me in return." She clapped her hands together. This settled it. "All we have to do is get our hands on another syringe and we can end this."

"I don't think it's that simple. We tried ourselves, already. We tried to put the echo back and failed. We don't know what we're doing. Even with a needle—what if I try to take out Belladino's knowledge but I take *time* instead? Or something else, something worse? *We don't know how this works.* Don't make me . . . don't make me try, please."

"I won't," she said quickly. It was incredibly unfair of her to place that burden on him, she knew. "I won't." She could attempt it herself. Or . . . "What if we found someone who *did* know how this works? An enchanter. An enchanter might help us."

"Or they could turn us in," he noted, but there was no fire behind his counterargument. He sounded resigned.

"Perhaps they'd be less likely to do that if they had a personal connection to our problems," she said thoughtfully.

"You know an enchanter?"

She shook her head, pulling off her hat, revealing her forehead. She ran her fingertips lightly over the mark, memorizing the thin lines of it. "No. But this mark *belongs* to someone. It's as good as their signature writ bold across my skin. Perhaps whoever enchanted Belladino's mask in the first place might take pity on us. Or take an interest, if nothing else."

"But there's no way to know if we can trust them."

"What's one more uncertainty among all the others?" she asked. "What do we do with *that,* now?" She pointed at Blackhaus. "Please don't say *plan another heist.*"

"I was thinking about walking in and handing it to the dealer."

"You're joking."

"No. You left the money, remember? I have the right of rental for this exact mask already, straight from the Regulators. The whole point was to make his mind muddy enough that he would think he'd done business without remembering. Well, this will confirm such suspicions."

"But it's *you.* He doesn't like you, and he knows how you feel about masks."

"Most likely the man will simply call me names, think me a fickle hypocrite. I can live with that. He'll have his money and the mask—there will be nothing for Regulators to go after. But, if they insist on interviewing me, I can manage."

"I don't like it."

"And I don't like the thought of you revealing yourself to an enchanter with nothing but a wink and a prayer to protect you."

"What other choice do I have? I could try excising the mark. I could attempt to cut it away, as if it were some growth. But that will do nothing to protect me from enchantments that detect magic. I see no other path for me. But you don't . . ." She swallowed harshly. "You've done enough. You don't have to keep . . . I will take my mother home, and you and I can be finished. You won't have to cross paths with me again."

His brows bowed sadly. His lips parted, but nothing came out—not right away. "I—I don't . . . Would it scare you to know I don't want that?" He looked at his lap, quickly set Blackhaus's mask to the side so he didn't have to stare at it.

They both knew how brazen his confession was.

She couldn't think of a response that wasn't just as shameless.

Mistaking her silence for discomfort, he added, "Please, I don't want you to get the wrong impression. I helped you simply because I wanted to help. That's it. I didn't have an ulterior motive, I swear. I didn't mean to . . . I didn't think I'd . . ." He took a deep, resigned breath. "If you'd rather not see me anymore, I will respect that."

"I don't want that at all," she said hurriedly. "I'm quite fond of you. Already."

He smiled softly, but did not look up.

KRONA

I named it Monkeyflower. I know no one knows how varger reproduce, or if they even have genders, but this one felt like a girl to me. I visited her every day I was able, after the chores were done and Maman had made us recite our letters and figures. She was stronger every time, and now I wonder if she somehow found flesh to feed on—but no one went missing and no one reported seeing a varg in the area. The ointments seemed to work, though I've never heard of varger wounds healing, and her hair lost its abrasiveness. Even the stench dissipated.

Something was different now. After coming out of Strange's guard rotation this evening, Krona's sister seemed ill at ease, but in a contrary way to before. Where Krona had considered her cold and standoffish, now De-Lia appeared jittery and anxious.

Though Krona was one to criticize. She didn't know how to bring up the vaults or Patroné, or what little she'd learned about Charbon in the process.

They sat together, cleaning their weapons at the end of the day. Their quint-barrels lay on the kitchen table, parts strewn about while the two women worked the components over with oil and astringents.

"You look exhausted," Krona told De-Lia.

De-Lia didn't look up, polishing the handle of her quint vigorously. She gave a noncommittal half shrug. "I *am* exhausted. But you shouldn't worry."

"I thought that was my *job*," Krona replied lightly, working over the flutes with a thin, coarse brush. "You worry about me, I worry about you. Together we dither over Maman . . ."

"Not in this case."

"Why not?"

"Because I'm fine," De-Lia said sharply, fisting the stained terrycloth in her hand like it had blood to give. "It's nothing," she corrected herself, shoulders slumping. "Bad dreams getting the best of me. Both of us. Nothing to be done about it. I want the Mayhem Mask and the despairstone back—that'll settle it. No one's ever died before because . . . because of my . . . Those people would still be alive if it wasn't for me, understand? I'm the one who failed at the Jubilee."

"We were all there. We're all responsible," Krona corrected.

De-Lia shook her head, unable to accept that. "I'm the captain. Regardless, the fault ultimately lies with me."

Krona's stomach dropped. Yes, people were dead. And there were a million little moments in which any one of them on the team could have done something different and thwarted a piece of the thieves' plan.

If only she'd been able to wrestle the false varg away more quickly, they might still be alive.

But it wasn't all De-Lia's fault. She shouldn't have to bear the burden alone.

"I . . . I shouldn't be telling you this," Krona started tentatively. "The Martinets ordered me not to, but I think it's prudent you know. I went to the vaults, and there was an incident while I was there. An attack."

De-Lia looked up abruptly. "Who would dare attack Vault Hill? It's impenetrable."

"Not today it wasn't. They succeeded."

"You're joking. How?"

"None of us who were there *know* how. It was . . . . I don't know how to describe it. I never saw the attacker clearly, but they were right there. They were nearly invisible."

"That sounds like some kind of Thalo fairy tale," De-Lia said.

"I was thinking a new enchantment."

"An enchantment that defeats Farendeag cages?"

Krona shrugged. "I know how it sounds. But let's say it's possible. Let's say it's happened. Then, more importantly, I'm wondering if the attack and our Charbon concern are connected."

"How so?"

"The invisible attacker was after varger. There were varger at the Jubilee. They made it into the vaults—on *Vault Hill*—so couldn't they have gotten past the Watch at the party with ease?"

De-Lia's hands stilled. She considered for a moment. "Okay. All right, yes, I see your point. But how? Where would the enchantment have come from? From another concern? We would have records—"

"The Hall of Records is missing government files," Krona reminded her. "It could be old. Banned. Or entirely new."

"But how would such a thing even be constructed? And from what?"

"Missing knowledge or lost time could explain the effects—wood and glass for sure, then. It's almost like they could hide themselves like a mimic varg, blending into the environment."

"I don't know, it doesn't feel right," De-Lia said, rubbing firmly at a spot on her barrel. "I don't . . . It's too easy to blame this on an enchantment no one's ever seen or heard of."

"Too *easy*?" Krona asked, incredulous.

"One enchantment that makes someone invisible, defeats the cages, and, what else? Is impervious to detection by scanning spheres? All in one? Either that or it's a whole host of unheard-of inventions, all in the same hands. Both seem incredibly unlikely."

"Yes, I see," Krona agreed. It didn't sit well with her either, but what possible other explanation was there? "Too easy. Too convenient."

Both women quieted, lost in their own thoughts, weapons in pieces around them like shiny bits of a puzzle.

"What would you like for your birthday?" De-Lia broke the silence with a steady lilt, all traces of her weariness locked away once again.

Krona allowed herself a secret smile, but didn't say anything.

"Oh, don't be coy now." With whimsy playing in her expression, De-Lia reached over the quintbarrels and pinched Krona's shoulder. "It's your fifth-fifth. It's supposed to be special."

"That's not for another few months."

"So? Knowing you, whatever it is you're hoping for will be difficult to find. It's only astute to inquire early. Tell me. I know it has to be magic—you're always salivating over the enchanters' shops when you think I'm not looking."

"No—enchantments are too expensive, I don't need—"

"This isn't about *need*. Maman and I want to do something nice for you, so for goodness' sake just tell me."

When had De-Lia been peeking over her shoulder in the enchantment district? Her sister had a sneaky side she'd never fully appreciated. "There are a couple of masks . . . none of them are useful for Regulation, though."

"Not everything has to be about the job."

Krona ducked her head shyly. The way De-Lia looked at her, eager and sincere, was nice. "There was an artist's mask. He used to paint these astounding impressionist murals. You've seen one—on the south-facing wall of the records building. The one with the blue birds? And I found a cellist's mask. But what would I do with it without a cello?"

"You want to play the cello?" De-Lia asked, a bit surprised, a bit impressed.

"Well, I've always wanted to learn some kind of instrument. Since . . . Since Maman doesn't play her mandolin for us anymore." It was a whim, really. A nice thought. Something pleasant and peaceful—two things she was sorely lacking these days.

"Huh. I had no idea." De-Lia nodded to herself approvingly, then thumbed at her nose and went back to polishing the barrels of her gun. "But that's good. Options. When this is all over, you and I will take a day and browse enchanted funeral masks. Yes?"

"All right."

"Good."

A content warmth spread through Krona's chest. It seemed like ages since they'd had an outing together that didn't involve Maman, or errands, or *Regulation* in some form or another.

Yet another reason to see this concern to a swift end.

＞•▷•○•◁•◁

Krona hated to do this, but Thibaut hadn't answered the agreed-upon sign—twice now.

She'd had another nightmare the previous night, and it left her unsteady. The bloom had returned, but this time instead of sprouting a varg it had wielded its petals like tentacles, grasping at her, trying to pull her in, to dissolve and eat her like one of the giant carnivorous plants in Asgar-Skan.

She needed information from Thibaut, yes, but she also needed a friendly ear. Someone who could ground her after such terrors.

It was day five of the concern—a week already gone and two blooms already made. She couldn't dally and risk more dead.

She'd left Thibaut yet another scarf, had waited for him at the appointed place and time, and yet, nothing. It wasn't like him to ignore her summons.

Something wasn't right.

She hated to do this, but desperate times and all.

She tried to convince herself it wasn't concern that had her running to Thibaut's home. Not concern for *him*, anyway. She needed information and she needed it urgently, if she was to prevent further blooms.

Thibaut wasn't aware she knew where he took up residence. At least, she was fairly sure he didn't know. If he had known, he most likely would have moved. She'd found the place months and months ago, trailing him after they'd had an altercation. She was sure he'd been lying to her about the location of a missing tiara, and she'd tried to pry the truth out of him with more force than usual, to which he hadn't taken kindly. As such, his anger had made him sloppy. He failed to double back or spend time in a decoy apartment. He'd gone straight here, into this ramshackle building.

It had surprised her. At first, she'd thought it *was* the decoy. The complex was so run-down, a strong gust from the north should have toppled it. It was the type of place that bore perpetually broken windows like badges of pride. Tenants cursed at each other from floors away. Stray dogs and cats were as common as stray people.

No stained glass graced any of the sills or recesses. The thick ribbons of carved stone at the building's crest, which had once given the edifice some semblance of style, were now pockmarked and cracked. Great chunks of the stone threatened to fall into the street and crush passersby.

How could someone as clean and alluring as Thibaut *live* in a place like that?

But then she'd trailed him again, and again. Always, he came back here.

She knew what a man looked like when he came home after a trying day. It was different from the way he approached a safe house or a lover's abode. When Thibaut came here, all the tension melted out of him. He walked with a lighter, eager step. These walls were his sanctuary, as hard as that was to comprehend.

As she approached the five-story structure now, she hesitated. Perhaps she shouldn't go in looking like herself. She'd dressed for a casual public meeting at the park, not for a rendezvous in a rattrap of a residence. It would be better to go in armored—with a cloak or, or *something*. The thin scarf she'd brought with her to the park hardly felt like an adequate shield now. There was no chance he'd forgive her for darkening his doorway in full Regulator panoply, certainly, but that didn't mean she had to leave off all protection.

Her uniform made her feel safe. These clothes—simple, feminine—exposed more than just her face, modest though they were. They proved she was a person, and not just an arm of the state.

She considered doubling back and going home to change, but decided she was being silly and didn't want to waste any more time.

As she mounted the stairs inside the hovel of a complex, they groaned. Not a familiar kind of straining, but an honest-to-gods moan of agony, as though she'd stepped on a creature instead of a rotted length of wood.

The whole building looked half-dead. Paint—or paper, it was difficult to tell—flaked off the inner walls like old bark. The smell of wet rot and stale piss permeated the air, and Krona nearly turned tail.

But everything was quiet. She was used to places like this being full of life—shouts, calls from parents to children playing floors down. But here, so much was still.

On the first landing sat a grubby child. He reminded her of Esteban, though this boy was considerably younger. Esteban, who'd been so terrified.

The body of the first victim, limbs reaching for the birds roosting in the warehouse rafters, flashed before her mind's eye.

"Do you know a man who lives here?" she asked quietly. "He's very tall, and his hair is very light. And people—" She hesitated. "People might think he's very pretty."

The child looked her up and down, noting the lack of holes in her clothes and the well-set styling of her hair. She was most likely the only woman of any status who'd ever spoken to him.

She wished again for her uniform. She was used to wary, judgmental eyes when hidden away beneath her helm. On the street like this, plain and unadorned, she typically garnered nothing more than an unpleasant catcall from a man who hadn't learned his place.

That a child so young—little more than an infant—could make her feel so out of her skin . . . She hoped the adult residents would remain hidden.

"He likes wind-up toys," she tried again. "Probably has a lot of them. Little mechanical things?"

The boy nodded in recognition, then held out a pudgy hand.

She paused for a long moment, unsure of what he wanted. But as time dragged on, she realized *that* was exactly what he was after. Retrieving a five-second disk, she placed it gently in his palm.

"More stairs," he said, pointing up the well. "Door eight-eight."

"Thank you."

After accidentally frightening a stray cat and kicking her way through a pile of refuse, Krona found herself at the door marked *88*. The number was little more than a chicken scratch in the once green-hued wood.

Nothing here felt like Thibaut. It was not dignified or elegant, clever or disarming. Why would he pick such a place?

With trepidation, and a deep breath, Krona knocked.

Silence followed. Perhaps he wasn't home. He could be in a thousand different places across Lutador. He could be laughing it up with an overly made-up mistress in a tea-and-salt house, he could be slipping a pricey watch off a gentleman, or playing a confidence game on an innocent couple—wooing them both in tandem.

Then again, he could be hurt. He could be bargaining for his life in the middle of a fence gone wrong.

By the Five, he could have been locked up by the Watch again for all Krona had a bead on him.

There was no solid reason to think he was here, at home, at all.

But then the flimsy door snapped open, revealing Thibaut in all of his . . .

"Glory" was most decidedly *not* the word.

A wry-if-weary half smile graced his lips momentarily, before he registered who stood before him in the hallway.

He had seen her sans uniform many times before, but she was sure he'd never seen her so . . . so herself.

His hair was unkempt and his jaw unshaven. There was a dazed, unfocused shallowness to his gaze, which suggested he might have just crawled out of bed or up off the floor. His clothes were ragged and thread *barren*, forget threadbare. No shirt graced his shoulders, and he stood flush with the doorframe, barring her entrance and appearing broader and taller than usual.

His disheveled state caught Krona off guard, and her witty opener died on her tongue.

Heat rolled off him in waves. Not the fever of illness, but the fever of drink. Krona's skin prickled with it, and a flush crept across her face and chest unchecked. The tips of her ears burned—a confrontation with large swaths of Thibaut's creamy skin had not been on the agenda. And it was not embarrassment so much as thrill that pumped extra blood to her cheeks and beyond.

Stop it, she chided herself. *You're being silly. This is Thibaut. Thibaut.*

She thanked the gods for her dark complexion. Maybe he wouldn't notice her flush or fluster.

A sudden impulse to rebuke him for his immodesty nearly overwhelmed her. She could pretend it offended her, his undress. But really, she feared other eyes taking him in. It seemed unfair that so many other people had already seen the pale expanse of his abdomen and the attractive jut of his hips—must he flaunt it like this? She bit back the possessive *Where is your tunic?* before her flippant thoughts could emerge as embarrassing statements.

A sound, like compacting snow under a heavy boot, brought her attention to his gloved left hand. The green leather squeezed the neck of a mead bottle—a long, fluted stretch of glass that she feared might shatter under the pressure.

Why he still wore his gloves when he wore little else baffled her.

"How did you find me?" he intoned, not at all his usual flirtatious self.

"You are not the slippery Grand Falls eel you think you are," she replied slowly. "Careful there." She nodded at the bottle. "Wouldn't want to risk shards in your drink."

"Not much drink left in my drink," he mumbled.

"Are you alone?" she asked, abruptly and acutely aware of what kind of circumstances might lead him to answer the door in such a state of undress. Something slippery rolled over in her stomach.

"Why?" he asked, his irritation ebbing. A spark flickered in his eye. "Would you be jealous if I weren't?"

"I—" The look in his eye killed her protest. Idiot may have been drinking, but he still understood too well the draw he held.

Their eyes met, gazes fixed for half a moment too long before Krona spoke again. She tried not to let the truth of his insinuation show, choosing sarcasm over honesty. "You're right, what was I thinking? Not even a one-minute night-ingale would follow you to this . . ." She trailed off, standing on tiptoe to take in the shoddy furniture and thin curtains over his shoulder. ". . . palace of unmitigated delights."

"What does that say about you, then?" he quipped, moving aside. "Come in, Mistress Regulator. Unless you're afraid to be alone with me."

"I could have you on your knees in seconds," she said dismissively, accepting the invitation and simultaneously kicking herself for her choice of words. She knew how it sounded—saw the double entendre she hadn't meant it to be.

Thibaut, the bastard, simply smirked.

The entry opened into a kitchen, just like in De-Lia's apartment. That, at least, made it feel homey. An overpowering smell of spiced incense—to cover up the building's innate smell of waste—drifted her way as she crossed the threshold. To her surprise, the space did appear clean. Thibaut took care of the place.

"On my knees in seconds?" Thibaut put a hand to his chest as he closed the door behind her, rallying as soon as she thought he'd let the moment pass. "Oh, be still," he commanded his heart. "Mistress, don't tease me in my own home."

Krona swallowed thickly. He might have been enjoying the tense air between them, but *she* was determined to remain professional. "So, it *is*," she said quickly. "Your home. I'd wondered. It doesn't seem up to your usual standards."

"You believe my standards are what I make you believe they are. I'm not well-to-do, as much as I appear to the contrary. Looking well with the nobles keeps me fed, and little more. You think I'd dive into the occasional bout of petty theft if hanging on a wealthy arm were all it took?"

She noted a row of clockwork toys on the top of a doorless cabinet. They made her smile. Why was he so easy to be fond of? "I'd thought it was just your way. Pickpocketing, I mean. That you were impulsive."

He quickly drew close behind her, his fingers curling around her upper arm, just beneath the cuff of her sleeve. Krona startled at the touch, her breath hitching, but she made no other move. Her bare skin was raised in gooseflesh against the chill of his apartment, and the nip of his glove made the prickling more apparent. Bending slightly, gripping her tightly, he purred in her ear, "I *am* impulsive."

With a deep breath, he made a show of nuzzling her braids. His chest was pressed evenly against her back, and she felt it swell as his lungs expanded.

He wanted to engage in their usual gambol, to press and pull against the taut string of propriety they held themselves against. Krona could easily lose herself to the game, were he not so drunk. But the curl of his breath near her ear was sour, offsetting his suggestive murmuring.

No. Now was not the time for flirtations. There was work to be done.

Using the fulcrum he'd created, she spun away and behind him. She stole the bottle from his grasp, and, in the next instant, kicked at the top of one of his calves, forcing his joint to buckle. He stumbled and bent, going down on one knee before catching himself with the tips of his fingers to keep from pitching to the floor. His hair fell into his eyes and he let out a surprised breath.

"Mistress—?"

She planted her boot lightly against his spine when he tried to stand.

See, she thought, *in seconds.*

"I was only playing," he heaved. "I'd never—"

"I know." She cut off his pained apology. Thibaut was ultimately gentle, and he sounded genuinely worried she'd taken him for insidious. His concern hurt her heart, and she wanted to reassure him, but feared falling back into the game. She could sink so easily into Thibaut here, in his home, away from questioning eyes.

And that was the problem. She was a lawperson, he a criminal—their relationship already straddled the lines of respectability. But beyond that, she couldn't let herself be foolish about what they shared. Couldn't let herself think even for a moment that Thibaut could consider their banter *more* than a game. "I don't have time for a full production. There's a photograph I need you to look at." She took a swig from the bottle before setting it down on the small kitchen table. It tasted stale, and she rolled her tongue in distaste.

Combing his fingers through his locks, Thibaut righted himself as she pulled the photos from her pocket. But she didn't hand them to him just yet. "I left two scarves at the statue," she explained. "You didn't answer either."

"Today is not a good day," he said.

"And yesterday?"

He ran his palms up and down his face. "Not a good week, in truth."

Krona pursed her lips. "Is it an anniversary?"

He nodded, taking up the bottle again. The amber liquid sloshed disquietingly as he downed the last few gulps.

"Was it a death, or—?"

"I'd rather not speak of it," he said in a tone that meant *it's no business of yours*. She tried not to take offense.

"Your innkeeper friend," she said instead, pivoting swiftly, hoping to keep him from edging too close to morose. "Has he done anything unusual? Gone anywhere odd? Said anything suspicious?"

"No," he said swiftly. "Leiwood is a good, honest person. Boring, even. Predictable. I'm sure you're barking up the wrong tree with him."

"Not all of your associates can pass for good people. Why so quick to stand up for this one?"

"Because a man who understands the difference between respect and respectability is a rare gem. He doesn't judge. Doesn't slot people into class and rank on principle. Treats the *hired company* guests bring with them with as much esteem as the guests themselves. To him, people are people. When was the last time you met even a single noble with that kind of true nobility, huh?"

She tilted her head in acknowledgment, then passed him the pictures.

Thibaut held the photos in front of himself and squinted, trying to decipher what the strange images were supposed to be.

"That's a thumb," she said helpfully, pointing.

He turned the photograph upside-down, as though it might help him recognize the design.

"It's a mark of clergy," she said. "They don't use such symbols anymore. Or, aren't supposed to."

He nodded. "I'm familiar."

"You mentioned a new religious organization—could it be connected? Do you have contacts who could place the image? Ones that might be able to tell us if there is a coterie still using such brands?"

Thibaut sniffed dryly. "Sure. Sure."

"Thank you."

He looked once more at the top photograph, puffing out his cheeks and narrowing his eyes, willing his mind to sober. "Now, is that all you wanted?" He'd suddenly gone stiff, with his tone and posture like twin walls.

He was trying to protect himself, but from what? From her? Perhaps he was upset that she'd seen him like this. He'd carefully crafted himself an image, after all; one of self-assured rogue. She wasn't supposed to know he had bad days, that there were times he didn't hold himself under the utmost control. That there were times when he wasn't *content*. "Doesn't seem like much." He fanned the photograph through the air. "What with you pounding down my door."

Instead of mentioning Strange straightaway, she explained the importance of the brand. "This is the thumb of a man who helped steal Charbon's mask. Understanding his affiliations could bring us closer to the murderer. Whoever is using the mask has made two blooms already, and we know there are more blooms coming. I need this information *quickly*."

"Of course. Anything for my *mistress*." He gave a condescending bow, sweeping his arms wide with showmanship.

There was a weakness in all of his movements, and it turned Krona's stomach. It had been too easy to get him on the floor, and now he looked like he might fall over again. She didn't like seeing him drunk.

"By the way, I met Madame Strange," she said.

He snapped erect. "What? How?"

"I went into the Dregs."

Thibaut leaned heavily against the table, tossing the photograph onto the surface. The now-empty mead bottle rocked precariously, threatening to topple and shatter. "How did you know to look there?"

"How do you know her, Thibaut? What would send you to the Dregs?"

"That's not a secret," he said harshly, suddenly affronted. "I wasn't trying to hide it from you."

"Hide what, exactly?" She narrowed her gaze, taking note of his tone. "No one's judging you."

"Oh really? *You* aren't judging *me*?"

"You're being cryptic," she chided.

"I'm inebriated." His tongue stumbled over the syllables. "I'm entitled." He tripped as he pushed himself away from the kitchen and toward a couch.

Krona frowned as the protective instinct swelled in her chest once more. Silently rebuking herself, she swooped to Thibaut's side, supporting him, making sure he stayed upright. He didn't shake her off, though he stiffened. Together, they moved the rest of the way to the tattered divan. Krona lowered him to the cushions, and he sat bonelessly, listing to one side.

When she tried to straighten up, he clasped her wrist, keeping her near. Their eyes met, and she could see him wrestling with himself. He wanted to tell her something, but the walls he'd built were holding him back.

Krona tried not to think about how close their faces were, or how dilated his pupils were, swallowing up the blue of his irises.

Thankfully the fetidness of his breath reminded her to keep her distance.

"I asked Strange about the meeting you mentioned," she admitted. Unsure of herself, she sat beside him. Thibaut sank into the maroon brocade as though he didn't care if the sofa swallowed him up. "She was strung out on vapors, was unsure of her own recollections."

"I told you to leave her alone. I *told you*."

"She's still in place."

He let out a sigh of relief. "She's important, to the community. Down there."

"We've got eyes on her still. We think the person brandishing Charbon's mask is using Strange to track his victims."

Thibaut's eyebrows slanted upward pathetically; he looked like a kicked dog. "How?"

"She provides a service to the types of people the murderer seems to prefer as victims."

"Is she in danger?"

"She might be," Krona admitted.

Thibaut clutched at the side of his head, screwed his eyes shut for a moment. "I shouldn't have told you about her."

"Maybe you should be thankful you did. If this killer already knew how to find her . . . How did *you*? I wouldn't have thought a man as particular as yourself would count the sewers amongst his haunts."

He sighed weakly. "How is that any of your business?"

"She seems important to you. More than just a criminal contact, perhaps?"

His expression hardened.

"She's a friend? Lover?"

He scoffed.

"A relative?"

He stiffened.

"Thibaut," she said carefully, leading him. "Are *you* a Dreg?"

"I grew up down there, yes. She's a cousin, all right?"

"But Dregs don't come to the surface. Everyone knows—"

He let out a clipped, patronizing laugh and shoved her hand away. "Everyone knows Dregs don't come to the surface and coteries don't use the mark of clergy and Regulators don't make deals with swine-spawn like me."

"I see." She held her tongue. He was being petulant on purpose. This anniversary of his wasn't only about grief. He was clearly angry. Angry at *her,* or those like her. "Have I insulted you in some way?"

She didn't like this feeling—the need to coddle him. They always played at breaking boundaries but this felt a step too far. They weren't supposed to show themselves to each other. This wasn't a friendship in the traditional sense. Not really.

"Ah, Mistress." He patted her knee and looked at his empty hand, as though he expected a drink to be there. "There are times I wish I'd never laid eyes on you. This happens to be one of them."

"Then perhaps I should go," she said, making no move to do so.

He said nothing.

For a long while they sat in silence. Krona wasn't sure why she was afraid to leave him alone, but she was.

Thibaut played with his hands, rubbing the palms of his gloves together so that the leather squeaked.

"Why don't you take those off?" she suggested.

"I'd rather not."

"You know, I've never seen you without them. Gloves, I mean."

He rested them palm-up in his lap and stared hollowly. "I don't like my hands."

"Why not?"

His fingers curled until he made tight fists against his thighs. "Tell me a secret."

"What?"

"Tell me a secret and I'll tell you about my gloves."

With a resigned sigh and a heavy tilt of her head, she said, "I'm deathly afraid of varger."

"That's not a secret."

"I got my father killed."

"That's not a secret either. Come now, Mistress. You think I haven't done my homework? I don't sell my soul to just anyone. I know things about you, and these are the basics." He shifted in his seat, turning toward her. "Tell me a *secret*. Something no one else knows."

As though she'd honestly give him a glimpse of such things, really. What did he expect of her? Did he think that lopsided half smile was going to work on her like it worked on others? That he would be able to flutter his eyelashes and stare at her hopefully with those impossibly blue eyes and the words would spill free from her lips?

It's not working. Not at all.

Nope.

Then again, what did it matter? He was drunk. Perhaps he wouldn't remember any of this in a nap's time.

"I used to pretend to be my sister."

He pursed his lips, unimpressed. "Well, that's not *so* unexpected. Younger siblings do tend toward hero-worship."

"And you would know, because—?"

He didn't take the bait.

Krona sighed. "No, this was more. I didn't just want to be like De-Lia. I wanted to *be* De-Lia. So much so that I would insist I was, sometimes. I'd introduce myself as De-Lia to new children. I once told my mother De-Krona didn't exist, that there was only De-Lia."

"Why?"

"She was so much more than I could ever be. Still is. She would charge in here and pluck out all of the information she needed, then leave you to drink yourself into oblivion and not think twice about it."

"No she wouldn't. Because I'd be rotting in prison if she had her way. There'd be no me here for her to *pluck,* as you say. *You* are much too clever to leave things cut-and-dry."

"But cut-and-dry is simple. It's efficient."

"It's *boring.*"

Krona shook her head. "The law doesn't care if you're having fun. The law cares about results. But it's not just the profession. She's efficient everywhere. When we were little, she knew instantly what to say to make me stop crying, or how to get her way with our parents. Instructors always praised her. People always follow her. They want to please her—"

"I don't want to please her."

"That's not the point. You get my meaning. There, I told you my secret: I want to be someone else. And the closest I'll ever get is making her proud." It was true, and things fell into place in Krona's mind now that she'd given voice to the urges. She wanted nothing more than to make De-Lia proud, because her sister's approval was the next best thing to her sister's being. "Now, tell me about your gloves."

Thibaut looked like he was going to be sick. He opened his mouth to speak, but took shallow breaths instead. It wasn't the alcohol making him ill. It was a memory. "My wife bought them for me."

For a moment, the obvious question and obvious answer hung unsaid between them.

You're married?

I was.

"They're nice," Krona offered awkwardly.

"Thank you."

"But why do you hide your hands?"

Maybe he wouldn't answer. His eyelids looked heavy; perhaps he would simply fall asleep and Krona could leave quietly.

Moving as though he'd abruptly woken from a dream, Thibaut whisked his gloves off and held his naked fingers between them like he was baring more than his palms. His arms tremored with effort as he struggled with himself, forcing his hands to remain exposed.

At first, Krona didn't understand. His fingers were long—a musician's fingers, her maman would probably say. They were pale and bony, but otherwise perfectly average hands. Save, she realized, the scars. Hundreds of fine, raised lines littered his hands, both front and back. A few extended up over his wrists.

"What are they from?"

"I used to sort glass scraps, when I was young," he explained, still looking at his fingers with an expression that was half fascination, half repulsion. "In the Dregs. Lots of glass ends up in the sewers. More than you'd think. From pieces of colored windows to medicine bottles to spectacle lenses. It has to go somewhere.

"My job was to dislodge pieces stuck in the bricks and seams of the waterways. Most larger bits and scraps my grandfather would scoop up with a net. But he couldn't get everything. I had dexterous little digits"—he flexed them to demonstrate—"so I did the hard part. The bits I dug out cut me more often than not. And scrapes and sewers don't mix, so nothing healed nicely. It's a wonder I never caught an infection."

She wanted to tell him there was nothing wrong with his hands. They were nice hands. But the words felt both belittling and presumptuous in her mind, and thus never made it to her tongue.

After all, perhaps it wasn't vanity that kept them covered. Perhaps the scars reminded him of a society he no longer belonged to, one from which he wished to disassociate. Maybe each line was a note on his current predicament: he might play at being a part of noble culture, but he didn't even truly belong *topside,* let alone among the fine people of Lutador high society.

Soon he scrambled to hide the skin again, yanking on the leather with fervor. Once his hands were hidden he seemed at ease. Krona had seen many objects of comfort and security in her time, but this was a first for green leather gloves.

He sank back into the cushions, his eyelids fluttering. All the energy drained out of him—clearly the drink was working its magic haze through his bones.

Soon he would sleep, and Krona couldn't stay. She'd already lingered too long, wanted to remain longer. It was time to force herself away.

"Will you be all right?" she asked. "If I go?"

"Fine," he mumbled, rubbing at his eyes.

"And you'll remember about the photograph? You'll remember what we talked about?"

"Of course. Anything for my Mistress Regulator."

"I'll leave another scarf for you soon. You will answer?"

"I will answer."

><+<>+0+<>+<

Krona left Thibaut's confident he would be back to his usual self the next day.

When she arrived home, she assumed the apartment would be empty, that her mother would be at worship and her sister would still be at the den. She wanted some time to herself, to reflect on her confession to Thibaut. Why, of all the things she could have chosen, did she tell him about De-Lia? She could have said that she hated her mother's crawfish casserole, but always asked for seconds because it was Acel's favorite meal to cook. Or that her first kiss at twelve had been with another little girl—an alpaca farmer's daughter a year older than Krona. In Thibaut's intoxicated state he probably would have accepted any tidbit he didn't already know.

Damn it all, *she could have made something up.*

But the apartment was not empty. De-Lia was there, bustling about the kitchen like a madwoman on a mission. Krona couldn't tell if she was cleaning or preparing to make a mess. Items came out of one cupboard and went back into another. Bowls clattered. Spices shuffled around one another. Domesticity was by no means De-Lia's default state, so the sight of her digging through household paraphernalia was cause for concern.

De-Lia let out a frustrated huff, and her elbow connected roughly with a container of rice on the counter. The carton tipped on its side, and Krona rushed to keep the grains from spilling to the floor. "What are you doing?"

De-Lia froze as though she'd been caught in the most compromising of positions. "I—I was looking for—I mean, I was going to try and prepare something for dessert tonight. As a surprise."

"You? Were going to prepare food?"

"I'm a grown woman, I *can* feed myself."

"And others, without poisoning them?"

De-Lia made a point of frowning deeply, but couldn't keep the corners of her mouth from twitching upward. "And where were you?"

"Out. Where's Maman?"

"Out."

De-Lia put back the items she'd scattered across the counters and reached for the tin behind the sink. "Tea?" When Krona didn't answer right away, De-Lia laughed and filled the kettle. "Sit. I can make tea. Who could foul up tea?"

"You'd be surprised," she said, but shuffled obediently to the table.

Cracking open the tin, De-Lia shook a teaspoon's worth of dried leaves into one of Acel's porcelain teapots. It was the pretty one their father had given her for an anniversary. Raised, baby blue swirls cut the pot through its equator, like folds of icing on a white cake. Little matte roses perched on the lid. When she was ten, Krona had accidently hit the spout against a doorframe, snapping it clean off. De-Lia had expertly glued the pot back together before Acel had seen it, and as far as they knew, to this day their maman was none the wiser.

They remained silent until the water began to boil. De-Lia quickly filled the pot and delivered the tea and two delicate cups to the table. "There are still more tangerines in the icebox," she said. "Share one with me?"

Krona smiled. "Of course."

Chilled citrus was an oddity in Krona's nose, but as De-Lia's nails pierced the skin on the fruit, it was clear something was amiss. The smell was not fresh, but stale. Not sweet, but sour. Where clear juice should have run over De-Lia's fingers, brown sludge pooled instead.

De-Lia made an indignant sound, rushing to the sink. "It looked fine on the outside," she grumbled, more to herself than her sister.

"Fruit rotting from its core often does," Krona said over the splash of water, rising to retrieve another.

De-Lia fumbled awkwardly with the soap, losing it several times so that it clattered dully against the sides of the metal basin. Her hands shook as she rubbed at the junction of forefinger and thumb, where most of the gunk had landed, then scrubbed viciously at the scabs on her fingers.

"Are you all right?" Krona asked.

"The filth startled me, that's all."

"You've never been one to get worked up about a bit of muck before." They'd been slopping through the sewers, after all.

"I need you to promise me something." De-Lia wiped her hand on a dish towel with excess fervor.

Krona cracked open a second tangerine. This one was pristine inside, and came away from the rind with ease. She offered half to De-Lia before answering. "I can't promise before I hear the request."

"Would you glance in on me this evening, after I've gone to sleep? And the next? To be sure I'm . . . that I'm in my bed?"

That was a strange request if Krona had ever heard one. "And which do you expect me to find? You there, or you missing?" She popped a section of fruit into her mouth, grimacing a little. It was more bitter than she'd anticipated, but still edible.

They took up their seats again, huddling over their tea with their bits of tangerine on terrycloth.

"I fear my sleepwalking is getting worse—that I might leave the apartment in the middle of the night."

"I think I would hear you if you left."

"Would you?"

Krona knew De-Lia hadn't meant it as an accusation, but it didn't stop her from feeling the blow. She looked into the deep amber of her tea. "I'll check on you, I promise. What have you been dreaming about?" Krona wondered if she should share the gory specifics of her own night terrors.

"You know how dreams are: vague," De-Lia said with a dismissive wave, bringing her teacup to her lips, not to sip, but to blow softly across the surface.

I know how sisters are: evasive. "De-Lia . . ."

"Things are difficult right now. Keep getting more difficult." She sighed. "I don't know how much more of this we're supposed to endure. How much more I *can* endure. This whole thing, this concern, this job—"

"The job in general?"

De-Lia nodded. "But enough about me. You've agreed to my request, what about you?" De-Lia asked. "Do you have an entreaty for me?"

"Should I?"

"You've looked like you wanted to say something more ever since you came away from that Monsieur Patroné."

Krona crossed her ankles guiltily, curling her toes. "It's—"

"Not nothing. Don't say nothing."

"You won't tell me about your dreams, but you want me to place my distresses at your feet?"

"Is it . . . varger? Sasha told me about Utkin's offer—his belief that he can shatter your fear."

Krona dropped her tea with a clatter. Brown liquid and bits of leaves splashed onto the terrycloth. "And how, pray tell, does Sasha know about that?"

Crossing her legs, De-Lia leaned back with a shrug. "Utkin is her uncle."

"So my problems are the talk of the den, is what you're telling me."

De-Lia's frown was so sharp, it could have cut off her own chin. "It's not gossip. We're all concerned—the team. No one else knows. We want to help. *I* want to help."

"I don't need help," Krona said petulantly, regretting the words and her tone the instant the first syllable flew from her lips.

"You used to say that a lot . . . when you were ten," De-Lia chided.

"It was true then, and it's true . . ." She stopped herself and shook her head, allowing a small, admonishing chuckle to leave her chest. "No. It's not true," she admitted. "I . . . I do need help."

"Tell me," De-Lia urged. "Do you think Utkin can?"

"I hope so," Krona admitted, using the cloth to sop up errant splashes of tea on the tabletop before they evaporated and left brown rings.

"If there's a chance it could work, I think you should seize it."

"Because my sickness has formally interfered with my ability to regulate," Krona said quietly. She gulped her tea, wishing for a moment that it was whisky.

"Because your fear could have gotten you killed," De-Lia clarified. "You did well for us at the Jubilee, considering. But more importantly, *most* importantly, I care about you. If we encounter a varg again and you can't handle it, and I'm not there, and you . . ."

Her sister's gaze turned inward. The lines on De-Lia's face slackened, and the skin on her forehead and cheeks appeared clammy.

"Lia?" Krona prompted.

De-Lia brought her teacup to her lips, her fingers light-knuckled around the ceramic. "I'm the eldest. It was always my job to protect you. I couldn't protect you when . . . You shouldn't have seen what you saw. I should have made sure." The guilt in her voice was palpable. It made the air feel heavy and Krona's skin itch.

And she knew exactly what De-Lia was talking about.

"We were children. It was Maman and Papa's job to protect *us*. Not yours. And if I'd been able to handle a needle gun, you know everything would have worked out differently. Papa might still be alive. You know that."

De-Lia nodded and fingered the design on the teapot. She wouldn't meet her sister's eyes. "I know that," she agreed. "But I can't help how I feel. You're my responsibility, and you keep . . . Sometimes I think my heart will give out just from fear of watching you on the job. An average member of the constabulary can't boast longevity, can they? You weren't supposed to be a Regulator."

Krona flinched, taken aback. "What was I *supposed* to be?"

"You had the potential to be a very talented *Kairoteur,* and gave it up for silly reasons."

Krona balled one fist and did her best to shove down the anger instantly ignited in her chest. "I couldn't sit in an enchanter's lab all day playing with glass and sand."

"Why not? You worked so well with magic, Krona. That's why the echoes listen to you. You feel them like others don't."

"Exactly. That's why I couldn't waste my time engineering better enchanted bottles. I wanted to do something that mattered. Like you." Heat rose in her cheeks; she hadn't meant for that last bit to slip out.

Krona feared inaction more than anything. That was why she'd gone to Thibaut's even though her gut told her to leave it alone. Making a bad decision was better than making no decision. Action was better than hesitation.

De-Lia had taught her that, by doing what Krona could not—taking up their father's quintbarrel. That day, De-Lia had cemented herself as the sole person Krona looked up to, the woman she admired above all others. From that moment on, there was no one Krona wanted to make proud more than her older sister.

She'd thought she could do that by following in her footsteps. But it also made her look like a hanger-on, bereft of her own internal compass and life's direction. She knew this, but had always hoped De-Lia appreciated Krona's decision just the same.

"Like me," De-Lia echoed softly. "Krona, what if I'm not—?"

The sisters caught each other's gaze, holding it expectantly.

When De-Lia did not continue, Krona said softly, "You are the best quintbarrel shooter the academy has ever seen. You are the youngest captain our den has ever produced. I don't know what you think you're not, but I damn well know what you *are.*"

She expected De-Lia to blush at the flattery; instead she simply looked sad. Quickly, De-Lia slipped the last few slices of tangerine between her lips, chewing thoughtfully. Her internal gaze lay far away. After a moment, she swallowed and said, "Make me another promise?"

"Yes?"

"Promise me you'll begin treatment with Utkin as soon as we have Charbon and the despairstone safely back in the vaults."

Whatever the cause of De-Lia's momentary melancholy, it had faded away like so much smoke. "I promise," Krona acquiesced.

They sat quietly for a few moments, lost in their own thoughts. The acrid scent of over-brewed tea permeated the air, and the lingering taste of it on Krona's tongue made the last bits of tangerine taste overly sour.

"Have you learned anything from your photographs yet?" De-Lia asked.

"I'm looking into it," she replied. "And you? Any new leads from our Strange friend?"

"Not yet."

"And the clamps?"

De-Lia gathered up her dishes and deposited them in the sink. "I'm positive they're Clive LeMar's, as you first suspected. How many other physicians in Lutador share those same initials, and how many have the same tools? But even if they are his, there's no proof he used them to kill."

"Mademoiselle Dupont—who studies under Master LeMar—she would have access to his tools. And she behaved suspiciously when Tray and I interviewed her, though she told us no outright lies. Nothing definitive. Nothing actionable."

"So you think her the killer? Or simply one of the thieves?"

"I don't know." But it was strange that the tattooed man sported similar injuries to Madame Iyendar.

After all, wouldn't it be easy for Dupont to lure her victims to their deaths? She was an apprentice healer, could offer help, and gave off an air of innocence. She could put them at ease before striking, ensuring no struggle.

"Are you suggesting we arrest her?" De-Lia asked.

"Not yet. But we should keep a close eye on her. She's getting married at the Iyendars' soon. A few days' time."

"Perhaps we should beg an invitation."

"Perhaps."

Acel returned then, her key clanking in the lock. "Hello, girls," she said cheerily, laden with foodstuffs wrapped in brown paper.

"And where have you been, young lady?" Krona chided teasingly.

"Fraternizing with the butcher on the first floor," she said happily. "He sends his regards." She held up her bounty.

"Let me guess," De-Lia said. "Rump again?"

Acel nodded. "The man is not subtle."

Krona laughed, leaning back in her chair to savor the last of her bitter tea, which seemed less pungent in the wake of her mother's good humor. She let herself smile, marveling at how family could make you cringe one moment and glow the next.

28

✠✠✠✠

LOUIS

*Lutador's third-district sand garden
and play structure, late afternoon,
ten years previous*

I should not be here. Even as he thought it, Charbon moved closer. Beautiful old trees lined the children's play area, their brown and yellow and red leaves molting away when the wind rattled through.

Sandbox shrines occupied the area farthest from him. Older children, none over the age of thirteen, left little trinkets by the wooden frames, while much younger children built small sand castles and molded sand animals as tributes to Time. Attentive parents and nannies alike watched from only yards away, making sure everyone played nice and no one stomped through someone else's homages.

Closer to Charbon stood a daunting play structure built to mirror the first palace of the Grand Marquises. It reached up into the autumn sky three times as tall as a grown man, leaving youngsters hazardously far from the wood-chip-covered ground.

He watched—with the kind of trepidation only a parent can know—as his youngest girl mounted the spiral steps of the graying wooden structure and began to climb. She bounced across a rickety slat bridge, which swayed with her movements and made her shout with glee. She twirled ever higher, occasionally leaning over a railing just a little too far, or placing her foot a tad closer to an edge than was safe. Charbon spoke to her under his breath, telling her to mind her balance and watch where she was going. Two little boys shoved past her as they chased each other, knocking her firmly into a post. Charbon tensed, waiting for her to cry out, but she did not. Ever the strong one, Nadine blew a raspberry at the boys before skipping onward and upward.

Even if she did fall, she'd be right up again. This child wouldn't let the world beat her.

Pulling his gaze away from the little one, he scanned the park for his eldest.

A group of girls, all around twelve, stood in front of an instructor. Organized play was the thing for bigger children. The woman, most likely an au pair, arranged the girls into two straight lines, and he caught Gabrielle shuffling into one of them. Soon they were swapping places, making funny faces, and hopping from foot to foot. The game must have been some version of Daddy Dearest or Mother May I.

Both girls were present, so Charbon knew their mother couldn't be far off.

He absently kicked through a pile of leaves, straying along the edges of the park. The air was wet and heavy with the remnants of an earlier rain. And though the dead leaves smelled of decay, it was a fresh sort of rot: natural and renewing.

It reminded him of his duties. Death was nasty business. Ugly, unwelcome. And no one should have to die before their time. He knew that, felt it in his humors, in his raw nerves. He understood what he did was both wrong and necessary. The dichotomy itself was essential.

Just like this distance he put between himself and his family was essential. It hurt, both him and them, but it could be no other way. The Thalo had told him revealing the gifts of the Unknown god would be messy and terrible, and he'd only agreed because the end result would be a better life for all—for his girls.

I've come to you because you are true believers, it had said. *Because you are powerful. Because you seek truth.*

That last part was at least true. Though he'd sought it through science and medicine, never through magic before.

Fiona was the flip side to his disk. She'd trained first as an *Emotioteur, Physiteur,* a *Kairoteur,* and once she'd married, a *Teleoteur.* Magic was her sanctuary, and yet . . .

And yet the meat of the pursuit belonged to him.

It had taken the Thalo a long while to convince Charbon of his duty. He'd denied it and denied it, and on some nights he wished he'd still denied it.

"How can man hide a god?" Matisse had asked.

When the puppets manifested before them a second time, they'd brought needles. The kind used for the time tax, emote tax, and . . . other things. Magic things Charbon didn't understand. And they'd given a syringe to Matisse and bade him prick Charbon as if he was an untapped infant, and after had given them all beads to swallow for fortitude and steady hands. Charbon had taken the beads, but continued his denials. For too long, he'd resisted. Let that many more new lives hang in the balance.

Now, Charbon pulled himself out of the memory, refocusing as Gabrielle whooped triumphantly, having won the first round of the game. She laughed and tossed her hair, smiling as though everything were right with the world.

Movement across from her, behind another tall, shedding tree, caught his eye. A familiar figure huddled there, leaning against the bark in a predatory stance. Luckily, her eyes were fixed on Charbon and not the children.

Fiona's lurking gave him some idea of his own appearance—how he must seem to the nannies and parents keeping a watchful eye. Here was an odd man, dressed as though from the gutter, creeping around the edges of the playground with questionable intent.

Why must she follow me everywhere? he groused. When their gazes met he shook his head and glared. She grinned in response, showing her teeth.

If she wanted to speak, she would have to wait. He wasn't going to discuss murder this close to his daughters. Huffing, he turned, ready to lead the lion away from the lambs.

Charbon pulled up short. His wife, Una, stood before him. When had she learned to move like a sneak thief?

"What are you doing here, Louis?" The question brimmed with mixed surprise and relief.

She was stern, and worn, and beautiful. His heart ached. The urge to drag her into his arms nearly overwhelmed him, but he turned from her instead. "Please, pretend this never happened."

Una was a small, heavyset woman, but she'd never carried herself like someone of short stature. Now she barred his path, refusing to let him run.

"Where have you been? Why won't you come home?" The fringe of gray in her brown hair framed her face like a halo, and the crow's-feet around her eyes deepened as she studied him. Her lips parted in trepidation, ready to pounce on his denials and excuses. "I miss you."

And he missed her. Her laugh. Her bright wit. When he slept he only had two types of dreams: his visions were either filled with blood or filled with her.

"I told you I would be gone for a long time—"

"It's been half a year. At least tell me what's been going on, what you've been doing."

"I can't," he said, pained.

She set her jaw. "That's a coward's answer."

"Yes, you're right. And it was cowardly to come here. I should have been stronger. I have work to finish, and the moment I do I'll come back. I *will* come back. Trust me."

"I do." She placed her fingertips on his lapel, touching his ratty clothes as though she didn't believe them to be real. "The Five know I do. If I didn't, I would have . . . Your family thinks you're dead. I told them you were abroad and alive—on *sabbatical,* you said—but your mother can't be comforted. And the girls—" She looked over at their children. "They believe me, I'm sure. But they would love to see you. Just for a few minutes." She took his hand.

He stepped back, sliding out of her fingers. "No. I can't." *The moment I throw my arms around them I'm lost. I could never come back to the Unknown.* "I'm sorry. I've made this harder for all of us."

"Louis," she said harshly. The demand froze him to the spot. "Give me something. You can't appear after so long and then fade away without giving me something to hold on to. I trust you, I do, but you've made it so *difficult.*"

If she only knew . . . She wouldn't understand, of course. Charbon understood the gravity of what he'd done. Murder—he'd never shied away from using the word. Euphemisms were for weak constitutions, and he could not believe in the sanctity of his actions if he didn't also understand their profanity. But decent people would reject the tightrope, as they should. If Una knew that he'd killed at all, let alone how many he'd killed—had *yet* to kill—she would rightfully run away from him in disgust and terror.

So what could he possibly give her as a touchstone? Not the truth.

"I just want our girls to grow up in a better world."

"Is it better without their father?"

"Of course not. I—I'll meet you again soon, how would that be?" As the words slipped from his lips he regretted them. He had a duty to protect her, to keep her away from the sinister work. And he had to remain strong. She made him weak. So weak . . .

He wanted to cry. He wanted to draw her to him and kiss her soundly and never let go again. "Just you," he added. "Not the girls."

Una nodded, though clearly unsatisfied.

After they'd made their plans for a week's time, he left quickly. She moved in to kiss him, and he knew he couldn't deny her. If he wanted her to wait for him, to understand that he wasn't running from her and their life, he had to allow her some micron of affection, no matter how much it wounded him.

The kiss was brief, but familiar. And full of promises.

When they parted he walked away without looking back.

"Don't know why you don't hightail it on home," came Fiona's voice from a small copse of trees as he passed. "I certainly don't have any qualms about going to my husband at the end of the day." She twirled away from the sapling she'd been pulling leaves off, falling into step beside him. Charbon knew they were far enough from the play area that Una wouldn't see them, but a moment of panic still seeded itself in his chest. If she ever caught the two of them together, what would she think?

Terrible things. *Incorrect* terrible things, but no less damning than reality.

"You don't have children," he said through gritted teeth. "It would be different if you did. How can I kill someone, see the abject terror on their face as I take their life, and then go home and kiss my girls and make love to my wife? I can't do it. I can't."

"How noble."

He hated the tone in her voice, because the truth of what his actions were resonated there. He told himself he only trespassed against life where he must, that as long as he made rules for himself and followed them there would be a way back to happiness, normalcy. That maybe he wouldn't be a monster in the end, if only . . .

He teetered on a precipice in his mind for half a moment, nearly falling into new realizations. But he quickly stumbled back, protecting himself. He could not question himself now, not now.

"Your awfulness knows no bounds, does it?" she asked. "It's men like you, who think they protect women with lies—who only hurt people behind closed doors—that are far more insidious than anyone who openly flaunts their wickedness."

"Like you?"

"Like me. The world has always sought to cage me, to fold me up and bind me. It has hurt me on the regular, so why should I pretend I'm not trying to hurt it back?" Fiona put a hand on his arm then, looking closely at his face. "My dear boy, you look ashen."

"I don't feel well."

"Have my words finally tickled your awareness, or is anticipation making you ill?"

"The latter, yes."

"Is that why you came here? For a shot of courage."

"Yes. But I shouldn't have. I knew it wouldn't work that way, I . . . It'll be worse now." *So much worse.*

"If it helps at all, the woman I've picked is a nightingale. She looks healthy, hearty. I think you'll be able to—"

"Shut up," he barked at her. "I don't want to know. As long as you and Matisse have her delivered at the appropriate place and time, it's satisfactory.

I'm sure you've chosen a worthy sacrifice." *Just like all of the other successful sacrifices she's chosen?*

"If I were you, I wouldn't begrudge my duties so," Fiona said. "You were chosen by a god, Louis. How many does that happen to? You should be more grateful."

"I don't think true servants of gods are ever grateful," he mumbled. "Religion is not ecstasy. Faith is not serenity."

"They can be, if you let them. Love the Unknown and their tasks. They want us to be whole and free. Want us to practice magics in the open, to explore, discover. To not be punished for our inquisitiveness and inventiveness, but rewarded. They want an equal world where those at the top do not hoard the gods' gifts. Take pleasure in—"

In a flash he was on top of her, shoving her into the nearest tree trunk. He placed his forearm heavily against her throat, shutting off the poisonous babble. "No. Never. We are servants. Do you understand what servants are for? We perform tasks our masters find distasteful. Don't tell me to clean the privy and expect me to be grateful. I don't have to shovel manure with a smile. I do it because I am made to, because who denies a god? But do not tell me that I must appreciate my position."

She slapped at his arm and he released her.

Rubbing at her throat, Fiona grinned. "See, you *can* be rough with a lady. As most men can. Those who claim virtue are often the roughest."

She pinched his cheek and he jerked away.

"Oh, dear boy. We have two choices in this world: be pleased with your lot, or don't. I choose to welcome my duties. If it pleases you to be miserable, so be it. I will let you be miserable. But do not presume your indignation makes you more righteous. You still stick those poor bastards as though they were suckling pigs or would-be veal. Do you think they care for your exasperation? Hmm?"

When he didn't answer, she patted him on the shoulder. "Do not wallow too long in your misery this evening. You want to be sharp for tonight's sacrifice. Meet me a few hours prior, at the Lily. The Thalo puppets need to prick you once more."

"And what of Matisse? He's been conspicuously absent lately."

"He's been working on our manifesto. A document detailing the crimes committed against us by those in power. New scrolls, dictated by the Unknown god. It will bring those who idolize Absolon to their knees, prove *his* scrolls to be pretty tales spun by a power-hungry man. Eric is working in his own way to bring the truth to light, just as you are.

"Have you realized yet, Louis? The full impact of what we do here? How we are living history in the moment. We're on the brink of a better society. We serve the Unknown, are their first true prophets. We herald the coming of a new age.

"People may look at your blooms today and ask, what are they searching for? And you, you get to give them an answer filled with more promise and power than they could possibly imagine."

Charbon buttoned his lips and shook his head, stomping away from her and her religious glee. She was wrong, on at least one front. He was sure many questions were asked about the blooms, but *that* wasn't one of them.

>-←→-•-←→-←

That night, beneath the twin moons, each cut felt like the first; every slice of sinew elicited a new wave of nausea and another pang of regret. It was so dirty. So wrong. And because his mind was keen to punish him for his hands' work, each twist of his wrist sent flashes of his wife and daughters across his vision.

You're doing this for them, he kept telling himself. *You're doing this for them.*

Then why does it feel like I'm doing this to *them?*

His arms shook and his legs went numb. It was almost over. All he had to do was cut out a few more organs, explore them, and he would find the scars and this would never have to happen again.

Never again.

Never again.

Never.

Again.

29

MELANIE

Two years previous

Melanie was sure the *Teleoteur* that created Belladino's mask would be the solution to her problems. They would be able to tell her how to get rid of the magic. How to be normal again.

It had been nearly a month, now, since the echo had invaded her. She and her mother had gone home, but she'd promised to return to Sebastian when she'd deciphered who the mark belonged to (she wished she'd paid better attention when she'd had the enchanted catalog before her). Sebastian insisted on being there when she met the enchanter.

In the meantime, Dawn-Lyn had grown stronger. Already she could walk again. She ate like a growing teenager—regaining her appetite as she built up her muscle mass, her strength.

And Melanie had, to her shame, tried to excise the mark, thinking, at the very least, that a ragged disk of a scar was better. She could leave the house without a scarf or hat that way.

She'd tried to do it subtly, secretly, in the middle of the night, naught but a week ago.

Melanie had stood in front of the glass, hands shaking, hunting knife clutched at the tip so she could maneuver it like a scalpel. Blood dripped down her brow, over her nose, into the seam of her lips.

"Melanie! Melanie, stop!"

Her mother had been on her in a moment—strong enough, now, to hurry from her sleeping pallet to Melanie's side. Already, the ordeal with Belladino had been worth it, for that. For Dawn-Lyn shouting at Melanie, moving to Melanie, wrenching her daughter's hand away from her face.

For her mother to be able to behave, once again, as a mother.

Melanie had confessed everything to her as soon as they were home. Dawn-Lyn had accepted every word as truth. Her daughter was a poor liar—it ran in the family, after all. And Melanie was not given to bouts of embellishment or storytelling.

Plus, there was the proof of it, bold on her face.

Or, there *had been* the proof of it. Melanie had been thorough in cutting it away.

Dawn-Lyn shook Melanie's wrist, indicating she should drop the blade. There was still no strength to her grip, but the touch itself was stern. "This magic is a gift," she'd whispered. "The gods wanted you to have it. Do not spite them this way."

"Why not? They showed little consideration for how much spite others would show *me*. You know what will happen if—"

"My girl. My sweet, sweet girl. You already said you plan to seek the *Teleo-teur*. That, at the very least, is the right way, if you must rid yourself of it. *This* is barbaric."

"I couldn't stand to look at it any longer."

And yet, in the end, it hadn't mattered. She'd placed a bandage over the wound, and when she'd gone to exchange it for a fresh one, she found the skin already fully knitted, the mark just as brazen on her brow as before.

It was the *Teleoteur* or nothing.

Now, Melanie's boots fell lightly, their usual *clop-clop* deadened by the mid-morning mist. A heavy fog, sticky and warm for the season, clung to the Lu-tador streets and sifted around the buildings like lewd whispers. It might have felt like a security blanket to someone else, but for Melanie the vapors seemed to taunt her, letting her peek at possible threats before concealing them again.

She'd agreed to meet Sebastian a few blocks afield of the inn, but when a hand darted out of the whiteness to clutch at her wrist, Melanie's breath caught in her throat. With a stiff yank, she pulled her assailant in front of her, bracing for a struggle.

"It's me. Melanie. *It's me*." Sebastian held up his hands. "I'm sorry."

She relaxed instantly, reaching out for him, taking one of his hands in hers. "No, it's fine. Forgive me for being a bit tense."

She looked up at him, and her chest swelled. They'd been apart far longer than they'd been together, and yet his presence still evoked the same feelings of comfort, of friendship.

And now, she realized, of something else as well.

She felt warm all over, had to look away when she felt a blush creeping up her neck.

"You're still sure you want to go through with this?" he asked.

No. She wasn't sure at all. She simply couldn't think of what else to do. "Yes," she said, sounding far more confident than she felt.

He nodded, brushed his thumb over her knuckles. "Lead the way."

Colors shifted as they entered the enchantment district. Blues and greens and yellows no longer dominated. The shops were filled with rainbow arrays, and the storefronts were all painted different hues. Melanie's path kept them far away from the mask shop, and had them spiraling down backstreets past more subdued-looking doorways. These side entrances belonged to the enchanters—the end products, their wares, were flashy, but the workshops were not.

Abruptly, she stopped under a thin, decorative archway which spanned between two close buildings like a fairy bridge. She eyeballed the name and number on the nearest address plaque, sure both were the same as she'd been given. Still, she was hesitant to knock on the simple planking of the door.

"Should I?" Sebastian asked.

She nodded.

He rapped lightly.

The door opened unceremoniously, yanked inward by a man with large, bushy eyebrows and a strange contraption on his head.

"Yes?"

"Master Gatwood?" Melanie presumed.

"Yes?"

A sort of half cap, half cage encased his cranium. Dangling in front of one eye was a thick monocle, with several interchangeable lenses of different widths and colors. One hand sat on the doorknob, and the other carried a large syringe—a very familiar syringe.

She swallowed harshly, trying to ignore the device. Sebastian's expectant gaze burned while the kind eyes before her grew wider the longer she remained silent.

"I was wondering, if you have a moment, or a time I could . . . I'd like to learn about being a *Teleoteur*."

"You're looking for an apprenticeship?" the master asked.

"No, not exactly." Her lips twitched into a nervous smile. "If we may . . . might we come in?"

"Of course. How rude of me."

Gatwood waved them inside, and they exchanged introductions. The *Teleoteur* was polite enough not to ask after Melanie and Sebastian's relation to each other.

All magic required a lab. It took specific conditions to make certain an enchantment held. The lab they entered was a cross between a surgery and an artist's studio. Wood shavings littered the gray stone floor, and a series of half-carved masks sat lined up on a long counter. Three wide metal tables took up the majority of the workspace. One was clearly the carving table—various knives and gouges were scattered across it—and one corner held a stack of untouched wooden blocks. The second table bore a dirty cotton tarp splashed with all the colors of the rainbow. Paint pots and brushes and palettes haphazardly covered the cloth. The third table was much more organized—its metal clean. Melanie caught a whiff of alcohol as she approached it; the surface had been recently sanitized. A tray, like the sort a healer kept their tools upon, rested dutifully in one corner, leaving the rest of the table blank and ready.

"I'm sorry to say I have no chairs, else I would offer you one," Gatwood apologized. "Busy work, this. Keeps me on my feet."

"I'm very sorry to interrupt you," Melanie said as Gatwood set the syringe on the third table.

"To be honest, child—" The contraption came off, giving her a good look at his face for the first time. His expression was soft, understanding. "—I would have turned you away, except you look as though a phantom has got you by the throat."

"Did you enchant Master Belladino's mask?" she blurted.

"August Belladino? Yes."

Her heart picked up its rhythm, and her fingers began to quake. Having the master confirm it made it real. Too real.

On her way into the city, she'd composed the questions she wanted to ask. She wanted to know how knowledge was extracted from the dead, and where the wood for the masks came from—she knew it had something to do with the Valley's border, but had no idea how it was harvested—and how a *Teleoteur* manipulated the magic once the materials arrived at one's doorstep.

But now she couldn't make her tongue work. Every inch of her body vibrated and her nerves felt tipped with ice.

The smell of astringents and paint and a myriad of deep, heady woods swirled in her nose. Instead of giving her comfort, grounding her, they nauseated her. She glanced at the partially carved masks on the counter and felt them glaring.

She took a hesitant step in reverse, toward the door. "I—I'm . . ."

"Melanie?" Sebastian asked, touching her wrist lightly.

She looked down, at where his dark skin met her light skin. That small contact became her entire world for half a heartbeat.

When she thought about it later, Melanie wasn't sure why that moment changed everything. Her fear melted away. Fear was useless, running was useless, and putting on a sheepish show complete with stammering and half-cocked questions was useless.

The one question she hadn't intended to ask was *How do I fix this?* But now she knew, it was the only question that mattered.

Still trembling, her fingers went to the brim of her hat, made to whisk it away.

"Melanie. *Melanie.*" Sebastian caught her hand, his voice panicked. "What are you doing?"

Gatwood's gaze wandered between the two of them, confusion wrinkling his nose and brow.

"Trying to solve the problem," she said gently. Sebastian didn't let go, but she didn't stop moving. The hat came away, she tossed it to the floor.

Master Gatwood caught sight of the mark immediately. Melanie gave a squeak as he rushed at her, reaching out to cup her face with his eyes locked on the scar. He pulled up short of touching her, but did not back away. "What happened to you?"

His fingers twitched in the space around her temples and his eyes grew wide. A strange spark of eagerness flitted through his expression, but it didn't worry her. "It's yours, isn't it?"

Realizing his proximity was indecent, he backed away and clamped his hands together, twisting them over and over. "Who would brand you with such a thing?"

"It's not a brand. It's a gods-honest enchanter's mark. Someone"—she held her gaze steady, away from Sebastian—"transferred it to me from Belladino's mask. Have you ever heard of such a thing before?"

"The mask is—the mark has left the wood?"

"Yes."

"Then, the magic . . . ?"

Clearing her throat before gritting her teeth, Melanie admitted, "The mask is just wood now, and the magic is . . ." They all knew what she was about to say. Surely Master Gatwood understood the implications. But still, she had trouble forcing the words past her lips. They sounded ridiculous tumbling around in her head; they could only sound more absurd in the open air. "The magic is in *me.*"

If he thought her a liar, he didn't say so. Gatwood simply leaned up against the clean metal table, considering her and wringing his hands.

"Have you ever heard of such a thing before?" Sebastian repeated.

"You can't enchant a person," Gatwood said breathlessly. "There is no magic in *people*." His vision went unfocused, and he seemed to be looking through his past, through a world of accumulated knowledge. His face went from tumultuous to restrained and back again within moments. "Don't you see?" he asked, turning away to pace the floor. "Magic *can't* be in people. It comes from out there." He whipped his hand at the world. "It comes from the Valley rim, from the rocks and the sand and the trees and ore. It is created in the crucible that is the edge of Arkensyre. The borderlands between barren hell and fertile heaven. Everything that has magic and can hold magic has to come from out there."

"So you've never seen this? Ever?" Melanie's heart fell. "Not even heard tell of a legend? A rumor?"

"Oh, I've heard the like. But only from the mouth of the insane," he whispered. The weight he gave to the last word made Melanie shiver. "No, child, this is not a scenario anyone has ever encountered before. Not in reality." After a silent moment, he stopped his pacing and rounded on her. "Show me."

"What?" she asked, chary.

"Enchanting a mask is very personal work. I knew August well. If what was in his mask is now in you, I'll be able to tell."

"I don't have his memories," she said quickly. "Just his skill."

"Good," he acknowledged grimly. "That's good. Let me see. He invented a few formulas. And there were one or two illnesses he'd cured that I'd never seen anyone else come close to curing before."

Gatwood laid out his parameters, testing Melanie every which way he could think of, forcing her to use knowledge there was no way someone of her age could have gathered on their own. She answered everything quickly, secure—if not comfortable—in the knowledge that it was real. Her enchantment was genuine.

As the answers came, Gatwood nodded. The ease with which she divulged the answers clearly surprised him. There was no hemming and hawing, no stutters or hesitations.

After a time, he stopped her. "That's fine. Thank you. And, I'm sorry."

She didn't have to ask what he meant. "Can you help me?"

He shook his head. "I don't know. I don't know."

"Could you reverse it?" Sebastian asked. "If we took it from a mask and put it in Melanie, could you extract it from her and put it into a new mask?"

"Transference isn't *easy*," Gatwood huffed. "If it were easy, any old anybody could make death masks. I wouldn't have had to study for decades to become a master, and young'uns such as yourself would be running all over with magic spilling out their pockets."

Sebastian pursed his lips sheepishly. "I understand," he said. "But could we attempt it?"

"Of course we'll attempt it." Gatwood looked at Melanie with such tenderness, she wanted to cry. "I will help you. I don't know how, and I don't know how long it will take, but I *will* help you."

"Thank you, monsieur." She bit her lip to keep it from trembling. She didn't want to break down like some weak little child. *I'm a grown woman,* she said to herself. *Steady on.*

"But, since this may take some time, we'll have to do something about that mark in the interim," Gatwood said, rushing over to his paint station. On a small scrap of paper, with a bit of oil stick, he wrote down an address.

"You'll find an *Emotioteur* here who should be able to make you a concealing pendant. Don't tell her why you want it. Just that you need a pendant about this size—" He drew a circle on the paper, just large enough to cover up the mark. "—filled with as much mercury as she can legally pack inside." He paused when he saw the worried look Melanie and Sebastian exchanged. "If Regulators are a problem," he said, "I can handle the paperwork. You can go to the *Emotioteur* as my assistant."

"That would be appreciated, thank you."

"Then you'll go to a different jeweler and buy yourself a plain circlet," he continued. "Wearing a mercury ferronnière should hide you, both from prying eyes and prying scanners. It's the marks that give off the detectable vibrations, you see. They're the entry wounds, and never quite close over."

Melanie clutched the paper to her chest, overwhelmed by his kindness. Why was everyone so good to her? First Sebastian, now Master Gatwood.

Perhaps everything would turn out all right after all.

30

KRONA

I'd curl up next to Monkeyflower, run my fingers through her spines, and tell her stories. Sometimes ones Papa had read to us. Sometimes ones I'd heard at the market. Sometimes I made up new stories, about people being nice to varger and feeding them flower petals and dewdrops and crowning them in jewels. Monkeyflower was the closest thing I ever had to a pet. Even now, there are times when I miss her.

Two more days passed, bringing no better leads and one more nameless bloom.

The victim had been left—clearly with a morbid sense of mockery—outside a flower shop in the luxuries district. This time the body had been broken and twisted into a chrysanthemum.

The green-man mask detected a wash of the same chemicals found on Hester. "There's enough of it here to poison, to be the cause of death," Tray said from behind the visage.

The Regulator team swarmed over the scene, peeking under every leaf and petal.

"And there's the womb," Krona said, noting the hunk of flesh nestled in a bucket of blood-splattered tulips. She prodded at it lightly with one glove, gulping back bile. "Definitely evidence of incisions, like the others. It wasn't simply excised, it was opened."

This particular organ held some kind of fascination for the killer, that was clear. An attribute that set him apart from Charbon.

Did he despise the victims for their bodies, or their choices? Or was he simply seeking out those he thought vulnerable?

"Do we think this is the Dreg who went to Strange for abortives the other day? The one the Watch lost sight of?" Tabitha asked.

"Likely," De-Lia said, "though it's still difficult to say if the murderer is using Strange to track his victims, or simply sending them to her after they've been chosen."

Whoever this victim was, the entire constabulary had failed them.

A flash from across the street alerted Krona to a camera. "Damn it. Royu?"

"On it," zhe said.

They'd been trying to keep the blooms hush-hush. But they couldn't hold the journalists at bay forever.

RETURN OF THE BLOOMING BUTCHER? had been the recent headline on several morning papers.

Now they not only had to deal with the realities of multiple, gruesome killings, but a panicked populace as well.

><+><+>+<+><+<

The evening of day seven, Krona was relieved to see Thibaut's marker at Absolon's statue, indicating he had information and was ready to meet at a place of her choosing.

Krona selected a repulsive little shanty café and decided they should conference well before the lunch rush the next day, so that they could grab a bite in private while he divulged his ill-gotten information. It was the kind of place that used junkyard scraps for jerry-rigged furniture, old doors for tabletops, and barrels for bar stools.

When she came in, the clattering of dice and a sudden *whoop* alerted her to an in-progress game of bones behind the kitchen. The raucous noise set her teeth on edge, but didn't bother her nearly as much as it worried the owner; he took one look at her uniform and blanched.

She hadn't had time to change for the conference. Hopefully the meeting place was far enough off the beaten path that no one would notice her with Thibaut.

"Two bowls of fried noodles and spicy vegetables, then make yourself scarce," she said, plopping a handful of time vials on the table as she sat down. "And tell the gamesters to hush themselves. I don't care a wit about gambling, but the Watchman around the corner might."

The owner brought over two heaping servings, and Krona pulled off her helm. Steam wafted off the vegetables, leaving a sweet-and-spicy scent in the air. She breathed it in with fervor, and her stomach rumbled. The man paused, waiting for her approval.

She nodded to him and dug in. With her mouth full, she gave a favorable flick of her thumb.

Sweating profusely, looking as though he'd just escaped a hanging, he bowed gratefully and slunk back to his kitchen.

The café door squeaked on its shoddy hinges just as the owner moved out of sight. In sauntered Thibaut, fully dressed and fully pressed. Seemingly back to his usual self. He threw the latch behind him.

"All right, you are going to love this," he said by way of greeting. With a show of more noble grace than was necessary, Thibaut straddled one of the empty whisky barrels across from Krona. He gave the tight quarters a once-over, confirming the café empty, before continuing. "It *is* a mark of clergy, but it doesn't belong to a coterie."

She raised an eyebrow. She'd already had a few aides at the den scour state files at the Hall of Records looking for a match, but there'd been nothing. She suspected the information had been scrubbed, just like the documents related to Charbon.

Krona swallowed her mouthful, pausing between bites long enough to utter a prompting "Oh?"

"It belongs to a cult. A very old, supposedly very dead cult." He eyed the chopsticks next to the second bowl with trepidation. Daintily, he picked them up and examined them closely, picking at a questionable stain with his thumbnail.

"Dead as in ancient?"

"Dead as in about a hundred years ago they were wiped out. Every adult and child killed while they worshiped—there were about eighty of them, from what I gather. They were one of those cults that wanted to reveal the true form of the Unknown. The very hush-hush, lock-yourself-away-from-the-rest-of-society kind."

Krona nodded. Every couple of decades a new Revealer cult wormed its way out of the woodwork, insisting they had a path toward uncovering information about the fifth god and their gifts. Most of these cults were harmless. "So, if the mark of this cult is being used again, is it a resurgence? Has someone resurrected this particular cult's practices?"

"Or the cult never really went away, and learned to properly keep their activities secret."

"Do you have specifics of the massacre? Why someone might have targeted those people?"

"*Supposedly* no one targeted them," he said, twirling the chopsticks through his noodles. "Supposedly they were killed by varger."

"You doubt it?"

"I have an inkling they were killed by varger of a similar breed as the one who gave you that." He gestured casually at her bandaged arm. "In fact, if he was connected to the cult, I'm willing to bet that's why your thief adopted said disguise. Clever, wicked ways tend to turn round and round on each other."

"What's the rumor, then? Who really killed them?"

Thibaut shrugged. "Dayswatch. Nightswatch. Marchonian Guard. Religious rivals. Who knows? Doesn't matter. What does matter is where their altar ended up, because that might lead you to their current location. It's in a coterie, out in the open, with that clergy symbol emblazoned nice and shiny right on the front. Of course, the symbol has been altered—the altar has been altered—" He paused to chuckle at his own limp joke. "—some jewels and paint and some such." His eyes sparkled knowingly. This was why he made such a good rat. He loved spreading rumor and speculation. Loved having information that others needed. "And, there's more. You're going to owe me double for this one. I mean something really rare, a clockwork from the palace collection, or from abroad—"

"Just tell me," she insisted.

"The twin priests of Time and Nature at this coterie have further information regarding the cult, but something's spooked them. Hot water with the rest of the clergy, or perhaps threats of violence from elsewhere—difficult to be sure. But the priests are willing to say more for the simple price of government protections. Show them your Regulator coin, escort them to a safe location, and I bet you'll learn all there is to know about that brand and its living associations."

Finally, Krona sighed to herself, *a decent lead.* Perhaps they *could* stop the killings. She'd been in doubt until now. Three blooms already, and every second she dreaded the notification of another. Maybe they could cut the tragedy off at the quick. Her chest swelled in excitement.

"Thibaut, I could kiss you," she gushed.

"I wish you would."

It was his normal, off-handed humor, but with a restrained twinge to it. They both looked quickly at their food.

"Here." He pushed a scrap of paper across the table. "This is the coterie's address, the cloister where the suspect altar can be found, and the names of the priests."

She scanned the paper with a frown, crunching down on a water chestnut.

Thibaut finally gave in and took a tentative bite of the noodles-and-greenery. "Hey, not bad."

"Pretty good," she agreed.

With a greedy grin, Thibaut picked up the dish and threw his boots on the table, reclining with the bowl in his lap. He dropped his picky pretenses, slurping the noodles as though he hadn't eaten in a decade.

Krona tried not to let her amusement show, lest he tease her for openly parading her affection for him.

They ate together in pleasant silence. It was strange to sit and simply enjoy each other's company. The moment was nice—an agreeable break from the reality of stolen masks and bloodied bodies.

In no time the reprieve was over. Their dishes were empty and their bellies full, which meant responsibility once again beckoned.

For Krona, anyway.

She returned to the den and consulted with De-Lia straightaway. "We should go now, shouldn't we?" Krona prompted.

"It's the strongest trace line we have," De-Lia agreed. "So we definitively believe the mask's theft and the murders are religiously motivated?"

"Makes sense. The records might be missing from the Hall, but Patroné hinted as much to me, though he wasn't one for taking motive into real account. And Charbon said something of the like at his hanging."

"Charbon *denounced* the gods when he was hanged," De-Lia corrected. "I find it odd that a cult would want to ally themselves with the techniques of a man who was a nonbeliever when he died."

"Denunciation doesn't equal faithlessness," Krona noted. "In fact, quite the opposite. He cursed the gods as cruel and useless, not nonexistent."

"I think we should go in as worshipers," De-Lia said. "You and I. Tray and Sasha will come in after, in uniform. We'll see where the two approaches take us—authority and subtlety all in one tidy assault."

The directions Thibaut had given her were for a coterie smack dab in the middle of the city. No noble connections, no clan connections, not poor, but not especially well-to-do.

Krona and De-Lia changed into their worship clothes before setting out on horseback. Their garmentry consisted of thick brown skirts over long-sleeved blouses with tall, ruched collars. They each topped off the ensemble with scarves over their heads, in order to hide the shells connected to their concealed reverb beads. Krona quite liked the purple-and-gold shawl De-Lia chose as a head covering, with its triangle bordering and small embroidered llamas. She knew she'd seen it before, but was distracted by the promise of the day and couldn't place where it had come from.

In their boots they both carried hidden daggers—the only armaments they allowed themselves.

High, limed walls formed the outer border of the coterie, and eucalyptus trees flanked the pebbled walkway to the enclosure. Inside, a garden courtyard—wound through with flowering bushes, trees, and fountains—fanned out like a welcome mat. The gods' individual cloisters lined the rounded outer wall, each a building unto itself, save the Twins'; theirs was connected by a covered wooden walkway. In the very back center stood the Shrine of the Five, where one could pay tribute to the gods as a unified family.

A priest of the Unknown god approached the sisters when they entered. Like Regulators, and like the god, the priests of the Unknown had hidden identities and it was impolite to address such members of clergy by a gendered pronoun.

Their long, eggplant-colored burqa flapped gently in the breeze. "Welcome," the priest said in a tempered lilt that was neither high nor low, masculine nor feminine. "The ringing of the bell has commenced in the cloister of the Unknown, and the late-afternoon sermons for Emotion and Knowledge both begin in ten minutes."

"Thank you," Krona said, fiddling with the ends of her orange scarf. "We're interested in speaking with the head priest of Nature, if possible. My sister and I recently moved to the area, and we are looking for a renewal blessing from our family's patron."

They consulted a silver watch pulled from deep in the folds of their burqa. "I'm sorry, but she is expecting a visitor shortly. You'll have to come back another time."

"Will it be a long meeting? We can wait," De-Lia said quickly.

"I cannot say." The priest punctuated the sentence with a nervous giggle, then gasped suddenly as Tray and Sasha made their entrance. "If you'll excuse me," they said, taking leave of the sisters in favor of the Regulators.

"Do they seem anxious in your eyes?" Krona asked as they watched the priest scurry toward their comrades.

"Most definitely. I'd like to speak with them more—we *are* looking for cultists in service of the Unknown."

"Yes, but Thibaut said the altar is in the cloister of Nature."

De-Lia rubbed at her chin. "You see if you can locate Nature's head priest before her engagement. I'll keep an eye on this one. Sasha and Tray will be looking for the cloister's Primary, so we should be covering a good amount of ground."

Krona nodded. "All right."

Though Krona knew Nature's cloister to be directly to her right, she was compelled to turn left. In Lutador, everyone walked a coterie path clockwise, as an honor for Time. It took her first by the cloister of Knowledge, then Emotion, then by the Shrine of the Five, where she paused.

Man-sized leaves of stained glass fanned out behind the stone altar like a peacock's tail, held in place by thick lines of lead. Garlands of flowers and nuts were strewn over the small statues of the four known gods, as well as the empty place left for the fifth. A woody scent wafted through the air from two dove-shaped censers dangling on either side of the shrine.

Half a dozen worshipers knelt or stood nearby, mumbling prayers and occasionally blowing kisses through their cupped hands—a gesture representing Arkensyre Valley and all its gifts.

Krona kissed her knuckles and pressed them to her forehead before making the Valley sign and walking on.

And here she came to the cloisters of the Twins, Nature first and then Time. The double doors of each were embossed with symbols of the god within. Nature's doors were carved with the expected flowers and animals, but also magical symbols of the five most important metals, lest the people forget that things like gold were of the earth as much as birds and bees.

Krona recognized the symbols, of course. Every needle forged for firing through a quintbarrel was etched with its corresponding sign.

Cloister doors were never shut unless they meant to bar entry. The priests of Nature did not want to be disturbed, but they would have to forgive Krona her persistence.

Pushing inside, she surveyed the area quickly, assuring she hadn't barged in on some private rite. But no; the pews were empty. Light streamed through the green stained-glass ceiling, bathing the limed walls in shifting, emerald hues.

It was strange to find no one—not even a lesser member of clergy—barring her path.

The suspect altar sat in the usual place, at the base of the rear monument. The monument was a larger-than-life representation of Nature carved in black stone, his four arms outstretched, each hand clutched around an arrow, with his three sets of hawklike wings partially unfurled behind him.

With another kiss to her knuckles as an apology to the god, Krona hurried to the dais to see if the carving on its front matched the clergy mark on the man's thumb. It did look old. Well weathered. It was not unusual for altars to be carved, but it was strange that this one, not belonging to Emotion, should be inlaid with gemstones. A large sapphire sat in the center, over the crossed lines of the carving, and many small, clear stones dotted the rest like stars, obscuring the pattern.

She reached out to trace the carving, while simultaneously retrieving the photograph of the brand from her pocket for comparison. As her fingers skimmed over the sapphire she was hit with a wave of satisfaction, as though all were right with the world.

Nothing amiss here, her emotions whispered to her. *All is well.*

She turned to walk away, suddenly completely satisfied, forgetting even that she wanted to speak with Nature's head priest.

It took her four steps before her suspicions came flooding back. She froze mid-stride.

Not only was the altar inlaid with gems, they were *enchanted.*

Rushing back, she looked but did not touch. Sapphires could be made into contentmentstones. But she'd felt it so thoroughly, so suddenly, that the painful prick of false emotion entering her body hadn't even registered. The sapphire was nowhere near large enough to create that kind of illusion, which meant the clear gems had to be diamonds—enhancer stones, carrying no emotions of their own but augmenting others.

Keeping her distance, she compared the photograph and the etching. Yes, she was positive: they matched.

Whoever had set the stones in the altar meant for them to protect its secrets, to send the curious on their way.

Krona glanced around the room once more, looking for the door that would lead her to the head priest's offices. She found it concealed behind Nature's monument.

As twins, Time and Nature were bonded in many ways. They were two sides of a coin, mirroring each other in their complements: each with two legs to stride boldly, four hands to grasp tightly at each other, and six wings to carry them swiftly across the world—his hawks' and hers ravens'.

It was appropriate, then, that the head priests of Time and Nature were always themselves twins of some stripe. They need not be a brother-sister pairing, so long as they were multiborn.

Twins were a blessing to any family, but especially the exceptionally poor. Only noble twins could vie for sovereignty over the city-state, but twins of any station were holy.

The door behind the statue led Krona into a thin hall that immediately turned a sharp corner to the right. The office was connected to both the cloister of Time and that of Nature, allowing the head priests to share the space with their sibling. An identical hall must have jutted out from behind Time's monument.

Upon reaching another door, Krona paused, listening for voices. All lay quiet within.

Tentatively, she knocked.

"Enter," said a female voice. Krona obeyed.

A large desk occupied the center of the bookshelf-lined room. Both priests sat at it, side by side, each looking over different documents. They looked to be broaching their fifties, identical to each other in nearly every way, save the crop of their short gray hair. The sisters huddled close together—so close, Krona would have thought it uncomfortable. They appeared to have their hands intertwined below the desk.

"Greetings, mademoiselle," said the twin on the left. "What can we do for you? I'm afraid we have to bade you swiftness, for we are expecting someone."

"Are you the head priests of Time and Nature here? Donna and Illana Sandhu?"

"We are."

Krona touched her Regulator coin in her skirt pocket. "I have questions regarding a symbol on the redressed altar in Nature's cloister—specifically how it relates to a mark of clergy."

They looked away from her quickly, back at the papers in front of them. "That is an old custom no longer acceptable to the gods," said the twin on the left.

"Why?" asked the twin on the right. "Have you come to plead?"

"If I say yes?" Krona asked.

"Then we'd have to turn you over to the constabulary," the right twin continued. "I think you've come to test our faith. The Founding Coterie in Asgar-Skan has sent many like you before. We will not be chased away so easily."

The Founding Coterie was the first, established by Absolon himself. It was where the Prime Priests resided—those who the gods spoke to, once in a blue moon. All except for the Unknown, of course. They oversaw all of the other coteries in all of Arkensyre, keeping services consistent, making sure no "revelations" were spread without examination.

The Prime Priests were to these two as the Martinets were to Krona.

By now, the photograph of the brand had been unfolded and refolded so many times it bore hefty creases down the middle, but the symbol was still stark white against the gray of the man's thumb. Krona slid it across the desk to them, then laid her Regulator coin on top. "I'm not from the Founding. Have you seen this before?"

The woman on the right picked up the coin immediately, eyes wide.

"I've come to offer you clemency and protection, in exchange for all you know about the people currently using this brand."

The twins stood, but still did not let go of each other's hands. It was then that Krona realized they *couldn't* let go—they were conjoined at the chest, near the shoulder, and holding hands appeared to be the easiest way to rest their arms nearest each other. "Thank the gods," the sister on the left said. "We were only trying to keep to the service. We had no idea they'd—"

"*Illana,*" her sister snapped.

"I'm sorry, Donna, but I can't stand—"

"Just because she has a coin and says she's a Regulator doesn't mean she is. She could be with the Founding, or with *them*. The Prophet could be testing us."

Krona perked. "I have colleagues outside, in full uniform. They will escort you to a secure location, guarded by the Watch."

"Now?" Donna asked, a bit incredulous.

"Sooner is preferable."

"We can't leave now, not until—"

The priest was interrupted by a knock at the door. "Sisters?"

"That's Jaxon," Illana breathed. She looked to her sister. "What if he's seen the other Regulators? What if he gets suspicious?"

"Of what?" Donna said. "Regulators can go where they like, he has no cause to think it has anything to do with us."

Krona scooped up her coin and the photo and shoved them both in her pocket as the door squeaked open.

"Sisters, are you in—Oh, hello."

The man was dressed in all black, with thick boots. Nothing about his clothes was flashy—simply tight and utilitarian. The V of his tunic wasn't especially deep, but he was a broad man and the garment appeared two sizes too small. He had a hard, boxy jaw, but the thing that struck Krona the hardest about him was the overwhelmingly cloying smell of cologne.

"We had an appointment," he said sternly to the priests.

Donna and Illana's postures had become tight, their breathing unsteady. Whoever this Jaxon was, he meant trouble.

"I'm sorry," Krona gasped out, addressing the priests. She grabbed each of their hands in turn, kissing them. "And thank you. Forgive me for barging in. I know now what my path is, why Nature has vexed me so. Thank you, thank you for quelling my doubts."

They caught on quickly. "You're welcome, child," Illana said. Together, she and Donna made the sign of the Valley, and Krona returned it.

"Wait for me to come finish your blessing," Donna said. "Kiss the effigy's feet twenty times every ten minutes. I will be there shortly."

Krona understood—they did not want her to go just yet. "I shall. Thank you. *Thank you.*"

She gave Jaxon a dazed, rapture-filled smile as she passed him, and he scowled in return. But he seemed to have bought it.

Shutting the door with a snap, Krona strode away, counting carefully, waiting until she was sure Jaxon would think her gone. Then she tiptoed back and pressed her ear to the jamb.

"—have the map?"

"Of course," Donna said. "It's over there."

An expectant pause followed. Krona gritted her teeth.

"Well?"

A shuffling of feet, a jostling of a chair or two. Something heavy thumped, as though on a desk. Pages crinkled and fluttered. The boots came nearer the door for a moment, and Krona had to breathe through her mouth, his scent was so strong.

"You're sure this is the one he was looking for?" Jaxon asked.

"His request was vague. This is our best guess."

"Fine." Heavy footfalls aimed at the door.

"Is that all?" Illana asked, her tone hesitant.

"Why, should there be more?"

"The next meeting—when, where?"

"I can't tell you now. There are Regulators out front, and if they come asking questions . . ."

Krona's heartbeat ramped up by several ticks a minute. She did her best to keep still.

"We'll keep our cloisters closed," Donna said.

"Don't do anything suspicious. If they ask questions, you answer. When I return tomorrow afternoon, I expect a full report. We need to know what they're after, if it has anything to do with us."

"Yes," Illana said, "of course."

"May the Unknown bless you, sisters," he said.

Krona lifted the hem of her skirts and ran down the passageway, hoping her footsteps were as soft as they were fleet. Nature's broad wings and muscled back greeted her on the other side of the hall, and she swooped around to kneel at the statue's feet. The stone nail on its left big toe had been left smooth, its edges barely visible, from decades of practitioners doing just as she did now. As she kissed the statue's feet, it was only half for show. She hoped the god did not mind being used in mild deception.

Jaxon's stench preceded him, and he didn't so much as look Krona's way as he left, a sallow-looking roll of parchment under one arm.

Krona maintained her ruse until the priests made their way to her a few minutes later, small satchels in hand. They locked the cloister's double doors as Krona rose and patted dust from her knees.

"Who was that?" Krona asked. "Is he the prophet you spoke of, by chance?"

"No," Illana said. "But he follows the Prophet. Just as we did, until . . ." She let out a harried sigh. "We fell too far. We never should have opened ourselves up to his blasphemies. But, we didn't know what to do. We're in danger of losing our station," she continued. "Here, in our coterie. Our ordainment has come into question by those in the upper echelons. They claim we are not multiborn."

Internally, Krona frowned. How could that be? Did they think the sisters were faking? There were many stories from the darker days in Lutador, of parents who tied their children of differing ages together and paraded them about as conjoined twins. It was easier to get food that way—sympathies ran high for such families, especially in hard times.

But no one would have reason to run such a difficult scam these days. Besides, even if Donna and Illana weren't conjoined, their duality was evident on their identical faces.

Illana clarified. "The Founding says that because we never separated, because we emerged from our mother together, that we are single-born, and thus incapable of serving Time and Nature."

Krona let her internal frown spread outward. "But those conjoined have been respected for centuries."

Illana shrugged. "Times change."

"But *Time* does not," Donna scoffed. "We have devoted ourselves to our coterie for thirty-five years. If the Twins were unhappy with us as servants, they would have shown their displeasure long ago."

"The priesthood is broken," Illana said. "We were searching for a way to rebuild it, to make it right again. We're tired of the order putting demands on penance and quotas on time vials. We only want to serve the gods, wholly, fitly, without bureaucracy and corruption. So when we heard of a new prophet, we sought him out. A prophet of the Unknown. I know, there have been many who claim prophet-hood. We were skeptical as well. But he showed us things, enchantments that shouldn't exist."

"What kinds of enchantments?" Krona tried not to show her eagerness. *Finally,* yes—this could be the key. To the murders, to the mist, to everything.

"He owned a blood pen—a real blood pen. And he . . . knew things."

"But then came the criminals," Donna said sadly. "Those he bound to him with that mark of clergy, one he learned of from the history in these very cloisters. And then, the mask." Donna shuddered. "His constant desire for it, the things he claimed he could do with it . . ."

Illana took her sister's other hand, so that they clung to each other. "The stories were terrifying, but now we've seen the mask. It's awful. The face of a demon, with mismatched horns and a terrible, gaping mouth."

"Yes," Krona said quickly. "That is the mask I'm after. It's a murderer's mask, and he's already killed with it."

Illana gasped, and they both shook their heads, as though to shake the truth of her words from their minds. "The Prophet says he can use it to turn us all into magic users. Not just practitioners, you understand. He thinks he can make *us* magic."

"How?"

Donna shook her head. "We don't know."

"What did you give Jaxon?"

"A blasphemous map of signs," Donna said. "For interpretation and prognostication, that sort of thing."

"Why did he want it?"

"The Prophet has need of it. He wanted to know about . . ." She took a deep breath. ". . . about divine messages in blood."

This was getting better and better. Krona pinched the bridge of her nose. "Lovely. What is the Prophet's name? Do you know it?"

Donna shook her head.

"What does he look like?"

The sisters shared a glance before Illana said, "He's always in the shadows, under many layers. A hood, a shawl, a wrap. We've never seen his face, and most recently he's come wearing the mask."

Krona rolled her tongue, trying to keep her patience. "Is he tall, short? Young? Old? Does he speak with an accent, or use a strange vernacular?"

"He's short-ish," Donna provided. "With a deep timbre when he speaks. But that's . . . that's all I know."

"I overheard Jaxon say something about a meeting—"

"The Prophet is gathering people to him," Donna said. "All kinds. Priests, bakers, farmers, healers. He's making promises of power. We only wanted to serve the gods, you must understand. This didn't start out ugly, it didn't—"

"Did you mean what you said about protection?" Illana asked. "Can you take us someplace safe?"

"Of course."

"Then take us now, before he returns."

"What about varger? Bottle-barkers?"

"Yes, yes—he said the gods brought them to him."

Sure they did, Krona thought darkly. "Do you have any names? Descriptions of anyone else you've met at the meetings?"

"No names. We're sure *Jaxon* cannot be found by that name. At the meetings we're all encouraged to come with veils or scarves, like the Prophet. To keep hidden like the priests of the Unknown."

Not as tributes to the god's veiled nature, but to guard against defection such as this, Krona was sure.

"Can you at least tell me where meetings have taken place before?"

"Yes," Illana said, voice shaking. "We can make a list, yes. Just take us away from here, please."

"Then gather your things, anything you can't bear to be without. I'll send someone for you in ten minutes' time. He'll be in uniform." Tray should be able to get them away safely.

". . . A Regulator?"

"Yes. Are you prepared to leave your coterie for good?"

"If they don't want us anymore, we've no reason to stay," Donna said, spite dripping from her tongue.

"Hurry, then," Krona said.

She peeked out of the cloister's double doors before exiting, doing her best to scan the grounds for the man she'd encountered. Jaxon's scent still hung heavy among the pews, reminding her to take caution.

When he came back looking for the sisters tomorrow, she would follow him. There was a mask back at the den, Mastrex Pat-Soon's—Magnitude Seven, Tier Seven—zhe had an incredible capacity for stealth. One of the greatest Marchonian Guards of all time, zhe had stopped many an assassination, and, most importantly, had kept the then-teenaged Grand Marquises from sneaking out into the city in the middle of the night. They'd always had schemes, and zhe had always thwarted them.

Krona was looking to do some thwarting of her own.

It took her longer than she expected to spot Tray, as he was lingering near the Altar of the Five. He darted to her when she crooked a finger.

They hid in a tight cluster of smooth-trunked trees in the center of the coterie, hoping no one would note their brief exchange.

Krona told him of the sisters' intent to leave, and of Jaxon.

"Sasha and I will see to them," Tray assured her.

"Do not leave the sisters alone. With anyone."

"Yes, of course," Tray said.

31

KRONA

I felt a peace with my varg friend like I had never felt before. Monkeyflower and I were connected. Linked. Often—as a child, and even now—I feel unsure of myself. Of my own skin, my own body, as though it's not really mine. I'm out of place. And Monkeyflower was out of place.

A gentle monster. A quiet beast.

We could soothe each other. Help each other.

De-Lia and Krona had agreed to leave the coterie independently once their interviews had been conducted. They'd meet again at the den.

After walking a convoluted path out of the relative silence of the coterie into the hustle and bustle of tall buildings, Krona beelined to where she and De-Lia had tied their horses. Hyper-focused on her task ahead, she jumped when, out from the concave stoop of a bookshop, swooped a hooded figure.

The individual stepped in front of her, barring her brisk trek down the sidewalk. A black scarf shrouded the person's face, and the hood of their cloak peaked and valleyed in unnatural ways. Krona instantly knew they were wearing a mask, and her hackles raised like a hound's catching the scent of a game trail.

"He's seen you before," the figure said. The voice was low, and strained. As though the man was disguising his usual lilt.

She wondered right away if the mask could be Charbon's. She made note of the weight of her knife in her boot, letting it reassure her. "He who?"

"Him—he who—*him*—"

The figure jerked forward, and Krona raised her fists. But he didn't attack. An intense shiver racked his body.

"Are you ill?"

"No," the man gritted out. "I can't say his name. He won't let—*Gha!*" His white-gloved hands flew over his face, and he turned his head from side to side. "It's not what you think. It's not *me*."

She knew these kinds of spasms—the way the man pulled at his hood and wrenched his shoulders. Krona had been through them many times, years ago. In the academy.

The man was wrestling with an echo.

She held up her hands, palms out. "Monsieur? Monsieur, listen to me." She spoke slowly, enunciating every syllable as clearly and firmly as possible. "What is your name? You need to focus on *your* name."

"No, you don't understand. *I'm trying to help*," he shouted, doubling over as though he were going to be sick. "I don't want to anymore," he huffed.

"You have an echo trying to nest, you need to focus. What is your name? Where did you get the mask?" Slowly, she leaned down, hand outstretched. If she could see the mask, maybe she'd have a better idea of how to help.

"He won't let—Iyendar. *Iyendar*."

Krona snatched her hand back. She hadn't touched the cloak but felt singed all the same. "You are an Iyendar?" He didn't look to be the same proportions as the Chief Magistrate, but maybe the Magistrate's son . . .

A couple approached them warily, clearly trying to decide whether to brave his flailing or cross the street and avoid the kerfuffle.

"Master Iyendar?" Krona asked.

"No!" he cried, straightening. Covering his face with one hand, he suddenly turned and fled. The couple shrieked in unison, parting just in time for the figure to barrel between them.

As he flew past them, his hood slipped, revealing the tips of two horns, each of a different color.

By the Five. She'd been right.

Krona sprinted after him. The man ran with everything he had, forcing his way between foot-travelers.

"Stop!" she shouted. "*Stop him*."

But it was no use. She wasn't a Regulator to them, she couldn't command the same authority. Via her reverb bead: "De-Lia, if you haven't left yet, get to the horses. I'm in pursuit."

"Of whom?"

"Whoever's wearing Charbon's mask."

Making a sudden hook turn, the man darted into the street.

Unthinking, Krona followed. He slipped by the grating wooden wheels of a chicken cart, but Krona wasn't so lucky.

The cart horse's surprised, displeased squeal pierced the usual rumble of the city. Krona fell to the side. The horse reared, the wagon jolted. The birds flapped and squawked in their cages, sending a flurry of white and brown feathers into the air.

Krona's hands went up and she crumpled to the cobblestones, trying to avoid the hooves that stamped the air above her head. Light glinted dully off its shoes. Everything moved in slow motion as her vision narrowed to one hoof growing larger in her vision.

Was this it? She wouldn't return to the sands because of a bullet or a blade or a varg, but a damned spooked horse?

Yelling with the effort, she stuck her fingers under the edge of a far cobblestone and pulled, barely inching herself out of the way. The glass shell toppled from her ear. The horse came down a hairsbreadth from her body, towering over her, breathing great, heavy puffs through its flaring, wet nostrils. The shell was gone, shattered under hoof.

Clawing her way to her hands and knees, palms scraping on the stones, she crawled out of the street.

Pedestrians stopped to gawk at the scene. The cart's owner cursed and dismounted, checking on his chickens and the steed before sparing a lick of attention for the woman he might have struck. But she was already away, eyes grazing the crowd in search of Charbon's mask.

A man offered her a hand, but she waved him off.

Stupid, she chided herself, straightening her skirts. She'd lost Charbon, her earpiece, and—she realized, coughing—she'd swallowed her reverb bead. She rounded the back of the cart, searching for the cloaked man, but there was no snap of cloth or shout of molested bystanders. Everyone was much more concerned with her than with whatever had drawn her into the street.

She looked and looked, sure there must be some indication of where he'd gone. A strained moment passed.

There—just there—in a fifth-story window—a flash of horns and exaggerated eyebrows. She would not let him escape.

I can end this. Now.

The window belonged to an apartment above a line of shops. Quickly, she located the side entrance down an alleyway. The door opened directly into a stairwell sporting a rickety iron staircase flowing upward in uneven switchbacks, its railing a curly set of waves more visually pleasing than useful. Before mounting, Krona retrieved the knife in her boot.

The building was old, and clearly in mid-renovation. But no one was at work. As she stepped onto the fifth-floor landing—the terminus of the staircase—the boards sagged unnervingly beneath her feet, and she jumped back. Sawdust and molded flecks of plaster puffed around her feet. Much of the original floor must have been rotten, and a series of planks and thin boards had been layered over the gaping holes to allow workers access to the various studios. Peering through a nearby opening, she realized this applied to the fourth and third floors as well. She had to watch her step—this would be no mild fall.

"Are you still following me, Regulator?" called a voice out of nowhere. She was sure it belonged to the man in the mask, but it sounded different now. Not pleading, but snide. Perhaps the echo had fully taken over.

And either it or the man *knew* her—had seen her without her helm before.

"I thought you wanted my help," she replied, making no move to step off the stairs again. Out of habit, she passed her blade between her hands, adjusting her grip, seeing which felt best. She was adept with a short blade in either hand, but was marginally better with her injured arm—when it *wasn't* injured, of course. The claw marks throbbed.

"I do," he said slyly. "I need your help. Come help me, please."

She was no fool. "Show yourself, take off the mask, and come with me. I *will* help you." Was it really young Master Iyendar beneath the veneer, wrestling with the echo? Was it true—had he been a distraction at the party after all? Even if it was Fibran, most likely she wasn't talking to him anymore.

Clearly the wearer couldn't control his toy and wanted a way out.

"I can't. He has me. I can't move."

It was a trick. Of course it was a trick. But if he refused to come out, she had to go in. She knew she needed support, but with her reverb bead bounding around inside her stomach she had no way to call for help. But she couldn't leave to find assistance, no matter how close it might be. Charbon would escape, and that would be on her. *Again.*

Carefully, she slipped a foot onto the first board, suppressing the flutter in her stomach when it dipped. Fibran—or whoever—had made it in without falling. She could do the same.

"Where are you?" she called.

"Over here," he said darkly.

The rest of the building was dead silent. The streets outside were wholly muffled, and the shops below must have been closed. By the sound of his voice, the man was somewhere to her left, but she could not pinpoint his exact placement. When she moved, the wood squeaked beneath her feet, giving the man a constant update of her position.

She controlled her breathing, keeping it shallow, and focused on her hearing. He would not let her find him fairly. She glanced at the rafters, suspecting he might fall on her from above. "Where?" she asked again, pausing.

"Here," he said, sounding farther away than before.

It was a bastardized version of a child's game, a thought that slithered up Krona's spine and gave her shivers.

She hoped upon hope that he didn't have the powerful enchantment the vault thief had possessed. *Please don't let them be one and the same, please don't let . . .*

Her palm felt slick against the leather handle of her knife. She readjusted her hold once more, flipping the blade so that it rested lengthwise along her arm—better for slashing.

There was little light in the hall between the doorless apartments. The old windows that flanked the ends of it were fogged with grime—relating a history of poorly ventilated fireplaces and negligent landlords.

Moving past a newly framed entryway, she caught movement in the dusky shadows. She spun toward it, heart pounding. But there was nothing to see. Maybe a rat. Maybe not.

Minding her step, she moved on.

A creak squeaked out at the far end of the row of doorways. She inched in its direction, reluctant to call out again.

Did he have a weapon? She hadn't seen one. But a scalpel was small, light. Easy to conceal. More importantly, he knew how to use it. One perfectly placed slice and she would be done for.

Her wrists and throat tingled, feeling vulnerable.

She reached a portion of the makeshift floor where wide gaps opened up on either side of the beam, leading down, down, down. There was no way to reach the closest apartments without jumping an athlete's distance.

Another step had her unbalanced. She rocked briefly, arms twirling. A spare nail rolled off the plank and pinged down to the second level.

Heart fluttering, throat closing, she stopped for a deep breath.

"Once more?" she called.

"Right here," came the reply, directly over her shoulder.

Her arm swung before her mind caught up. Twirling, she confronted the garish mask head on. Its white teeth and empty eyes were mere inches from her face as she rounded, but the wearer leaned back with expert finesse to dodge her blade.

He had to have pulled himself up from below. That was the only explanation. If he had the new enchantment, he'd be nothing more than a smear in her vision.

In his right hand, a scalpel waited, ready to separate her soft bits. "So, you're the one we can't get at," he said cryptically.

With a roar, she threw her blade at him, and he ducked to the side as he watched it fly past. But she hadn't meant to hit him, she'd meant to distract him. She latched on to the horns of the mask with both hands and tugged downward, simultaneously kicking out at his knees.

The unexpected move jerked him forward, right into Krona's stomach.

They both went down, Charbon on top, his scalpel pinned beneath his body and spearing into the folds of her skirt.

She pulled and kicked while he tried to push himself up. He reared, just like the horse in the street. She clutched the horns like reins, yanking, trying to control him as he lifted away. With the scalpel fisted tightly, ready to plunge it into her heart, he growled.

But she pulled one knee tight to her chest before thrusting her heel into his hip. The kick twisted him to the side, jerking the mask hard in her hands. He slid to the left, half off the edge of the plank. The scalpel fell to the board and she swept it aside with her leg.

Struggling to pull himself back up—white gloves scrabbling and slat teetering with their unevenly distributed weight—Charbon's wearer hissed, "You wretched thing. Maybe I'll end your sister next. Watch me."

With another shout she let go of one horn to slam a fist down onto his fingers as they grappled with the board's edge. He howled and let go on instinct, slipping still further—falling. *Falling.*

In the same moment, Krona thrust herself in the opposite direction, attempting to keep the board from flipping over. There was a splintering sound as the blue horn she still held snapped away from the mask.

Yelping shrilly, Charbon—Fibran, whoever—disappeared from sight. Krona rolled onto her side, clutching the fragment of wood to her chest.

A series of thuds echoed upward moments later, but she couldn't bring herself to look.

Was he dead?

Broken?

Broken.

She looked hard at the horn in her hand. Had she split the mask? Could she have disrupted or destroyed the magic?

There came stomping. Boots.

Quickly she pulled herself to the edge, just in time to see the fringe of a black cloak whisk away down the third-floor stairway.

"Saints and swill," she growled, getting to her feet. With a twirl of her wrist, she flipped the horn and tucked it into the back of her waistband. The stairwell was a sure thing, but the hole—to jump—was quicker.

Finding the center of the board first, for balance, she braced herself and leapt. Not straight down, but athwart, reaching out to catch the lip of the crumbling floor with her fingertips.

It didn't matter that much if the termite-softened wood crumbled under her weight like wet paper. She only needed contact for a moment, long enough to eye her next footing and *push,* using the uneven surfaces of the building like a jungle gym. She kept in constant motion, alighting for just long enough to slow her descent so that it couldn't be called a fall. Her skirts tangled awkwardly around her shins as she hit the still-intact second floor, twisting her legs and garbling her landing.

Despite her stumble, Krona was away again in an instant. Reassuring herself that the horn hadn't loosed itself, she hurried back into the streets.

Commotion rippled the pedestrians far to her left. She tripped into a sprint, but then, from the same direction, a familiar figure appeared on a familiar horse: De-Lia on Allium.

When her sister drew alongside, Krona accepted the proffered hand up without protest.

Thank the gods, her initial entreaty and the scuffling on the street had been enough for De-Lia to find her. "Turn around," Krona demanded, turning toward the fussy stream of people, the point of contention moving farther afield every second. "I think I've got Charbon, turn around."

With a swift nod, the captain brought Allium about. Krona tucked herself against De-Lia's back, contouring herself to rider and horse as Allium picked up speed, hooves slapping against the cobbles in what was best described as *clangs* instead of *clops.*

The ripple of disturbance rounded a corner, and so did they. Then it stopped short, the foot traffic no longer spinning away from the center of the sidewalk in irritation.

He went inside again. "There," she said, pointing at the wide-open glass doors of a sweets shop. A hastily painted banner above the door declared this the shop's grand opening, and two men—standing in what was a considerable line for entrance—bickered beneath it about a "masked madman" who needed to learn to "wait his turn."

Krona made to dismount, but De-Lia shook her head. "Hold on."

She muscled Allium in past the queue, much to the chagrin of the would-be customers. The sisters had to duck to make it under the door's sugar-pink transom.

The cloying scent of all things saccharin hit Krona immediately. The air was sticky with steam from the kitchens, which carried small bits of warm sugar throughout. The fine hairs on her arms were suddenly tacky, but her belly grumbled just the same. Cases and cases of pastries and candies lined the walls of the oversized shop. Much of the sugar was dyed, and some cookies even sported colored candied windows.

The woman behind the counter threw her hand over her mouth at the sight of the horse, and a baker—carrying what smelled like sweet-potato buns—yelled at them from the entrance to the kitchen.

"First masked men, now horses? Out!" she cried, upsetting her tray in her fervor, dumping a third of the pastries to the floor. "Out this instant!"

"Which way?" De-Lia demanded, pulling hard on the reins as Allium stooped to snatch as many of the fallen buns as she could (her lips found two before she relented). "We're Regulators, you are legally bound to cooperate with us. The man, which way?"

"Nope. No," the baker yelled, sliding her tray onto the counter so that she would have her full repertoire of body language available. She shoved a pointed finger in Allium's face. "No animals in my kitchen—never."

Krona felt De-Lia stiffen, and in response her gaze went to the swinging doors behind the irate woman. "Out of the way!" she said quickly, before De-Lia had Allium pushing right over the baker.

The woman squawked and twisted out of the way. Patrons yelled at them from behind. The cashier hadn't yet recovered control of her body, still frozen with her hand stifling a silent yelp.

Dead heat engulfed them as they pressed into the back of the shop. Stoves covered in simmering caramels bubbled to their left. Stone ovens with flames lapping at loaf trays roared to their right. Pans clattered as an assistant lost his balance in surprise.

De-Lia rode forward as quickly as she could, and Krona prayed there was an outlet large enough for them to escape through on the other side.

Allium whinnied and kicked as her rear bumped a hot surface in the narrow space. She bucked, and Krona almost slid off.

The back exit hung open. It was a narrow squeeze, but Allium prevailed.

They burst through with the baker still screaming at their backs—into a closed courtyard.

The walls of four buildings pressed in tightly on all sides. The space was barren, used for little more than a place to collectively store rubbish until trash day. Moving from a honey-sweet space into tight quarters where the air smelled of sour milk and rotten eggs made Krona's stomach turn.

A lone ladder ascended from the scene. At its top, three stories up, stood Charbon's wearer, the silhouette of his broken mask distinct against the pale sky.

They both dismounted as quickly as they were able, first Krona, then

De-Lia. Krona stepped on a rotting smear and slipped, barreling sideways into the courtyard wall. De-Lia paid no attention, hurrying after their adversary, his capture clearly the only thing fore in her mind.

As Krona regained her balance and scraped the rubbish off her boot—afraid its slickness would harry her progress up the ladder's rungs—sweet shop workers poured into the courtyard behind her, faces slick with sweat and ruddy from anger. They shouted for her to "remove that beast!" from their place of business, lest they cart it off to a knackery. She whirled on them with authority. She may not have been in uniform, but she still had her coin.

"Stand back," she commanded, pulling the coin from its place of protection, brandishing it at them like a shield. "Regulator business. If you so much as pull a hair on this animal's mane before we return, you'll have the state to answer to."

She tucked the coin away and mounted the ladder, hoping she hadn't lost too much time.

Her boot slipped twice, but she muscled through, barreling up the top portion of the ladder, skipping the last rungs altogether.

De-Lia had already chased the mask wearer to the edge of the building. He paused only long enough to calculate a jump. It wasn't far—the alley below was narrow. He landed easily on the other side, made to keep running.

As De-Lia hit the same spot, prepping to jump herself, he turned, raised a hand. Krona couldn't see what he held, but the sunlight bounced off it with a sharp, silver glint. Krona pushed herself forward, calling out, "De-Lia!"

But it was too late. De-Lia jumped a breath before the man threw his blade. The captain's only option was to miss the landing or take the knife.

De-Lia twisted in midair, and Krona lost sight of her over the side.

"De-Lia!"

The man turned, sprinting over the rooftops.

Krona scrambled over the tiles, rushing to the far edge. De-Lia could be broken and bleeding in the gutter of the alleyway. "De-Lia!"

Skidding to a halt, she peered over the side.

There, De-Lia clung to the brickwork of the next building over, two stories above the ground. "I'm fine!" she shouted. "Go! Keep going!"

Gritting her teeth, Krona bunched up her skirts and strode back, giving herself enough room to build up momentum for the jump. In the distance, the man still sailed onward.

Praying the slime was gone from her boots, she dashed forward, clearing the gap without trouble.

She pushed herself hard, one hand clutching the horn in her waistband, keeping it from slipping away.

She was gaining, despite his lead.

Three rooftops between them became two.

Became one.

He leapt to the next, and she wasn't far behind.

And then, he stopped.

Spun.

Faced her with hands raised, as though he meant to jump at her, the heels of his boots hanging over the roof's brim.

She did not slow. If he wanted to scrabble like alley cats—to tear and claw as they wrestled—she could give just as good as she got.

But he took a step *back*. Plunged down, out of sight.

Disappearing over the side.

She let out a surprised yelp.

Stumbling to a halt, taking up the exact spot he'd stood but seconds ago, her heart fell before she even had a chance to see what had happened to him.

For she heard hoofbeats. Fast, heavy hoofbeats.

He'd had a horse waiting. He'd meant to flee to this spot all along.

There was a thick, sturdy drain pipe at her feet, leading down the side of the casement beneath. And yes, there—a chestnut mare galloping away, carrying its masked rider out of Krona's reach.

⊱──⊰

Krona hurried back to De-Lia, who still clung to the building.

"I tried to climb back up," the captain explained, "but I can't get a decent hold. Get Allium and help me down."

The horse, thankfully, was right where they'd left her. Krona rode back through the bakery, and around to the side street. Positioning Allium under De-Lia, Krona verbally guided her sister to a fair downward footing, and eased her back into the saddle.

They recovered the blade he'd thrown—Krona's own. The one she'd tossed at him for a diversion. He must have picked it up after he'd fallen. The same could be said of his scalpel, which they could not locate at the construction site.

How had the man in the mask known she had a sister? De-Lia had never been to the Iyendars'. But, she supposed, if he had recognized Krona sans uniform, it would be easy to figure out who she was and who her relations were. Especially given the question of corrupt Watchpeople. Her service and De-Lia's were both a matter of public record.

But why threaten to kill De-Lia? Why not threaten Krona herself?

And had that really been Fibran? Fibran Iyendar, who'd been so distraught over his own dead child—could he really murder expectant peoples with ailing wombs?

Expectant . . .

De-Lia wasn't . . .

Was she? She didn't even have any gentleman friends that Krona knew of. When was the last time she'd been with a man?

On their way back to the coterie, where Krona's horse was tied, Krona detailed her meeting with the twin priests and her struggle with Charbon. "Tell me more about the horn," De-Lia implored her. "May I see it?"

Krona yanked it from her skirt and passed it over De-Lia's shoulder. "Oh," De-Lia said, disappointed.

"Oh, what?"

"Look at its base."

She took the horn once more, noticing for the first time a yellowish discoloration on its wide end. Glue. The horn had been pasted into place rather than carved from the whole. Likely that meant the horn carried no enchantment, and she hadn't disrupted Charbon's echo in the slightest.

Cursing, she fisted the wood tightly, chiding herself for being unable to come away with the whole.

"You believe it was Fibran Iyendar in Charbon's visage?" De-Lia pressed.

"I'm unsure."

"This, coupled with Master LeMar's tool . . . I don't like . . ."

"How it all keeps coiling back around to the Chief Magistrate's household?"

De-Lia nodded. "Yes. If it were anyone else, I'd say we have enough evidence to begin detaining those we suspect. Fibran, the healer, and his apprentice. But in this case . . ."

They had more pieces to the puzzle than ever before—an embarrassment of leads—and yet nothing appeared to fit correctly. "The Chief Magistrate will never stand for us arresting those closest to him unless we are certain. Denial can be dangerous; he might rather see more murders than admit someone he loves could be committing them."

"Right. We don't want the killer to go free because we moved against his household in haste."

"Then we should focus on the cult," Krona said. "If we can follow Jaxon and infiltrate the group and meet this supposed Prophet, then perhaps we will have enough to prove to the Chief Magistrate that his position does not prevent criminal conspiracy from taking place beneath his own roof."

"Agreed. We should prepare the warrants, but wait to issue them until after we've exhausted this lead."

When they arrived back outside the coterie, where Krona had left her mare, she hesitated to dismount. "De-Lia?" she began, proceeding with caution.

"Yes?"

"You're not . . . ? You would tell me if you were with child, wouldn't you?"

De-Lia turned swiftly in her saddle. "Why—? That's an inquiry from far afield if I've ever heard one. Yes, of course I'd tell you. Why would you think me—?"

"You're not, then?"

"No."

"It was something Charbon said. He threatened you. I simply wanted to be sure."

De-Lia looked affronted—not by the idea that she could be targeted by a masked madman, but that Krona could accuse her of keeping such a secret. "I may not tell you everything," she admitted, "but you are the *first* I would share such news with."

Krona hugged her sister before sliding to the ground, but there was a stiffness in the embrace.

32

MELANIE

Two years previous

"What method should we attempt first?" Master Gatwood asked.

Melanie adjusted her newly acquired ferronnière. The circlet was copper, the pendant seemingly made of nothing more than emerald green enamel. But behind the enamel was a pocket of mercury, to shield her from scanners. It fit low and tight over the mark—perfectly crafted, a gift from her new friend.

She hadn't had a chance to test it yet, to see if the pretty circlet worked as it was supposed to. She hoped the occasion never arose.

This was Melanie's third visit to Gatwood's workshop. She'd brought Dawn-Lyn back to the city, back to the Creek Side Inn, so that she could spend as many days as she needed with the *Teleoteur*.

On her previous visit, Gatwood had interviewed her about her history, previous magic usage, and strange ailments. It was much like a visit to a healer. He'd indicated his line of questioning was similar to what he had to ask at the beginning of enchantment-crafting. "This might not be all that different from making a mask," he'd said. "All I do is take certain knowledge out of a mind and place it in a vessel. There is a process, and it is intricate, but, in a way, that is all we are after here. That you gained your knowledge through magic is really the only hiccup."

"That, and I'm not dead," she'd said—a nervous quip. After all, they were death masks for a reason. It wasn't just that no one wanted to give up their knowledge until they had passed; the last steps, as she now understood them, *required* a cadaver. A necrotizing mind released its knowledge much more readily than living tissue.

"*And* you're not dead," he'd agreed.

Gatwood had, since then, devised several possible "cures" for her problem, and was now letting her choose how to proceed. Various instruments—blades, gouges, bottles, needles, pellets—lay on the workbench between them. "I have the syringe. We can try that first, if you like. Simple. Its effectiveness or ineffectiveness should be notable immediately.

"You've already attempted extraction with a knife, but you don't think it was enchanted, correct? We can try the five major metals, and the five major alloys, I have blades made of all of them." He waved at the set before him in illustration.

"Then we have the typical way I enchant masks, as we've discussed. That will take time, of course. Many sessions will be needed, and you'll have to swallow metal and be mind-probed and such. And when I take out Belladino's knowledge—*if* I'm able to take it out—yours is likely to come with it. Anything you know about healing now you'll have to relearn, understand?"

She nodded, surveying the accoutrements.

"If we go through with all three methods and still have trouble, I will have you swallow some enhancement stones—enchanted diamonds—to see if we can't better pinpoint how the magic has settled inside you, via the amplification. So, where do we begin?"

The syringe, of course.

But it wasn't as straightforward as she'd thought.

The plunger and the grip were the same on Gatwood's enchanted syringes. However, the qualities of the enchanted glass for the barrel differed, and different needles of different metals changed the tool's function.

"Nature's gifts lie in metal, and metallic enchantments are the magics of transference and bridging. Sometimes their combined usage with Time's magic is simple—like with the recipe for your mother's medicine. It called for enchanted glass, nothing more specific. In that case, it was the infusion of *energy* that was important, not what kind.

"But with you, it is likely more complicated. You wouldn't have been able to tell how the barrel had been enchanted, but do you by chance recall what kind of needle pierced you?"

"I don't . . . It was a silver color, perhaps?"

"Come, look at these needles and we'll try to sort them. Pick out the ones you are sure were *not* attached to the barrel Leiwood used on you. Don't worry about making a mistake, we'll use them all if we have to, but we'll try to get it right sooner rather than later."

He unwrapped several leather bundles. Dozens of needles fanned out across the hides. "We have the major metals and alloys, the minor metals and alloys. And even some nonenchanted needles I've tossed in for good measure, just to be sure."

"There are so many," she said, passing her fingertips lightly over them.

"Magic is complex. That's what makes it so useful. Many combinations equal many possibilities."

She understood, now, Knowledge's penalty—why it was important that new information and invention only be sought when the time was right.

There was so much *power* here. Pulsating imperceptibly beneath her outstretched hand.

Introduce too many possibilities, and the world might go *mad* with power.

"Thank you," she said delicately. "For helping. For trying at all. For this"—she touched her circlet—"for—"

"Child, please. You are clearly infected with a splinter of my magic. It would be irresponsible of me as a master craftsman not to take interest."

"Still, thank you."

He gave her a warm, fatherly smile. "You're welcome. You're not the only one getting something out of this, though. You should know that. True philanthropy is less common in this world than young Leiwood makes it seem. This way your secret is safe, and I get to learn from you in peace. Don't think I'm not making extensive notes. If this happened once, it can happen again, and I will be the only *Teleoteur* prepared when it does. There are masters, and then there will be *me*." He winked. "See, we're making a fair exchange. Now, come. Would you prefer to stand? Or there's this stool I brought from my apartments. Or I can lay you out on the inclined cot I typically reserve for clients."

She grabbed the stool, sliding it over to his side of the bench. It was a tall, plain thing. Three-legged. But with an intricately carved mandala on the seat. "Your work?" she asked, gesturing at the carving.

"My late wife's," he said, not looking up, arranging the needles—already sifting through, taking out the golden and iron and black and blue.

"Will you tell me about her?"

"*No.*"

Melanie paused halfway onto the seat, taken aback by his biting tone.

He sighed, apparently recognizing his misstep. "She was sick, and she is dead, and I do not wish to dwell."

"I'm sorry."

"Nothing to concern yourself with." His voice was casual, dismissive, but quietly laden with regret. The line of his shoulders had tensed, and he would no longer look her in the eye.

She hadn't meant to offend.

Feeling as though the air had gone stale between them, she busied herself sorting. Each needle they set aside—first one plucked away by his fingers, then hers, then his again—eased them back onto neutral ground.

Eventually they'd narrowed the set to ten.

She tied her hair back and removed her ferronnière. He inserted the first needle—pure silver—into the syringe's hub before swabbing across her forehead with an alcohol-soaked pad for sanitation.

"Are you ready?" he asked, holding the needle aloft.

She drew a shaky breath, eyes fixed on the way the laboratory's gaslight sent orange flares through the syringe's barrel. "Yes."

"Then hold *very* still."

>⊷⊶•⊷⊶<

He pricked her fifteen times, and drew nothing but blood into the barrel.

Her forehead was raw and open. Blood welled up and beaded again and again, rolling down her brow unless she dabbed at the wound with a handkerchief.

Gatwood had diligently pierced her in the same place every time: dead center of the mark.

"I think that's enough for today," he said now, turning away, making to put up the supplies.

"No," she said hurriedly, "I'd like to continue, please."

"All I've managed to do is dig a hole into your head. I don't think it's wise to keep going."

"It'll heal by tomorrow—because of the mark. It's better than a scab in that way."

He sighed. "We've only just begun, but I won't lie and say I feel hopeful we'll resolve this soon. Is there anything you left out? Anything at all? The smallest thing could have changed your destiny."

She thought hard. She'd already told him everything she remembered eating that day, everything she remembered touching. There wasn't—

Oh.

"Before Sebastian pricked me, he drew time from a bottle—released it into the air. Could the needle have been contaminated with bottled time?"

Gatwood's eyes went wide—he set the syringe down and rubbed at them. "My dear little splinter, why didn't you say so before? I am not qualified to enchant glass, and know little about bottling or unbottling time. That doesn't mean I can't help you. But it does mean there are variables I cannot take into account. But, by the same token, neither could a *Kairoteur* or a *Physiteur*. We each have our specialties, and a general knowledge, but each enchanted material behaves very differently from the others, and—"

"But what about enchantments that require a blending of magics?" she asked. "That requires knowledge of multiple disciplines. Couldn't we find—?"

He shook his head. "When different masters work together to create cross-discipline enchantments, we follow very strict recipes. Strict guidelines. And every aspect is overseen. I would not take another into our confidence. It's too likely to arouse suspicion—to draw the eyes of Regulators—even if I found someone I trusted enough."

She hung her head, and he clasped her shoulder. "That does not mean we will fail here. But it does mean I might need to keep you closer for longer. This puzzle might take years to decipher—"

"*Years?*"

"Yes. I'm sorry. *Years.*"

Years spent as a lab rat had been one of the outcomes she'd been trying desperately to *avoid*. "No, I have . . . I have a—"

She'd meant to say *a life*.

But what kind of life had she had before this? Really?

Simple, sure, which she'd loved about it. And she had no regrets in taking care of her parents. But she hadn't had her freedom, not really. She hadn't been able to choose much about how she spent that life. Her days, her time, were not her own.

And now, choices were being taken from her *again*.

"I can offer you a job," he said. "If that makes things easier. I could use an assistant. And then no one would question your long-term presence here. We could experiment as much as we please."

She didn't like the way he said "experiment"—a bit too eagerly, too clinically. As though the focus of such experimentation wasn't the very woman he was speaking to.

"I'll . . . I'll have to think on it."

He turned away from his tools, one bushy eyebrow raised in a question. "Think on it? My dear, need I remind you, you came to me. I am offering you a safe haven, a possible solution, *and* pay. What more, exactly, are you looking for?"

She glanced around the workshop, gaze catching on half-carved visages, bubbling vials, and heavy lockboxes. She breathed in the scent of sawdust and paint. Felt the gentle thrumming of magic all round—something she wasn't sure she would've been able to detect without the power residing within her.

Everything here was so . . . potent.

And she was interested in none of it.

She didn't want to have anything to do with it.

When she'd first realized Belladino's magic was inside her, she'd felt a *thrill*. Had been elated. Potions, elixirs, decoctions, tinctures—these were the sorts of things that sent her fingers twitching, her mind searching.

It was the *magic* part that she hoped to be rid of.

She wanted the healing knowledge to stay.

But keeping it was impossible.

The risk was too great.

Wasn't it?

Unsure of herself, she shook her head, as though to shake off her insecurities. What Gatwood offered was no small measure. No trifling thing. She would be mad not to accept.

"Nothing," she said. "There's nothing more I could hope for."

"Fantastic," he said, clapping his hands gleefully. "It's settled. You will be my new assistant, and when we are not entertaining clients, we can work on you."

"Work on me," she mumbled absently.

Yes, there were things she still had to work out.

►—►•◦•◄—◄

When she returned to the inn for lunch, she went to tell her mother of her new employment first thing. But Dawn-Lyn was sleeping, with a healthy flush to her cheeks and her breathing strong and steady. So Melanie went to find Sebastian in her stead.

"Wonderful news!" he said, grinning widely, setting aside a guest registry.

She returned the smile, but he noticed the strain in her lips.

"Isn't it?" he asked.

"It is," she agreed, but her enthusiasm was muted. "It's just . . . When I first realized I had a master healer's knowledge, I'd envisioned using it. I'd envisioned a future where . . ." She waved her hand through the air, as though sweeping aside a cloud of smoke. "It's nothing."

"It's not nothing," he said. "If this isn't what you want, then—"

"It's not just about what I want," she said with a sigh. "We take actions in life, and there are consequences. Those consequences narrow our choices. Time makes us walk a straight path between where we've been and where we are now. There's no changing it."

"But new decisions mean *new* consequences and *new* choices," he said softly. "We're never locked into one path. Time also allows us free will. She never freezes our future."

She smiled her strained smile again, shrugged. "The decision has been made."

"And you are allowed to unmake it whenever you please. Here, why don't you let me take you out for lunch? You must be sick of the inn's fare by now."

"I'd like that, thank you."

They walked casually to the nearest park, chatting as they went. He pointed out city birds to her, and she remarked on various stained-glass images she found delightful.

On one end of the green fairway sat a roundabout where many street vendors parked their trollies at midday. With a wink, he bought her a congratulatory funnel cake, piled high with enough confectioner's sugar to send her into a coughing fit if she ate too quickly. It smelled like oily, fried heaven.

"Share with me, this is too much," Melanie said with a giggle as the vendor handed the treat to her.

Sebastian nodded. They both leaned in. Together, they took the first bite, gazes fixed on each other across the cake.

Sweet, white powder covered both of them from nose to chin, sending them into matching fits of laughter. Before Melanie could swallow her mouthful of fried dough, Sebastian swooped forward and kissed the tip of her nose.

They both froze, as though equally caught off guard.

Sebastian took a stuttering step backward, eyes dropping to the gravel pathway. "I, uh . . ."

Melanie quickly stuffed another portion of cake into her mouth, eyes wide. *Did he . . . ? What was . . . ?* She found herself suddenly incapable of thinking in full sentences, and her heart was doing the strangest little fluttering dance.

The funnel cake vendor grinned at them knowingly. She was a portly older woman who'd clearly seen her share of shenanigans. "Oh, go on," she said to Melanie. "Can't you see the poor lad is mortified? Not too manly, pecking a lady on the nose, is it?"

Melanie hardly thought "manly" had figured into Sebastian's equation. A pink-tinted flush had overtaken his dark skin, and he started nervously rubbing at the back of his neck, leaving powdered streaks behind.

Luckily, his hesitancy bolstered Melanie. Swallowing harshly, determined, she placed the plate on the vendor's cart and stepped up to him. He shyly refused to meet her gaze.

As though the sugar had given her courage equal to that of an enchanted stone, Melanie reached up and took his cheeks between her palms, not bothering to dust off her fingers first. His mouth opened slightly—perhaps he meant to protest or apologize, or maybe fumble through a few more nonsense syllables—but she didn't give him the chance to speak.

Pulling him down, she met his lips with hers. The kiss was soft, and chaste, and tasted like fluff and icing.

When they parted, a smug smile tugged at the corners of Melanie's mouth. Sebastian, however, looked just as blindsided as before. His eyes searched hers, looking for approval, for acquiescence, as though she hadn't been the one to tug him forward.

Maybe it was cruel, but she didn't say anything right away. *Better to let him work it out for himself,* she thought. Her hands fell away from his face, leaving perfect prints behind. They'd both need a bath when all was said and done here.

She hadn't thought about it at the time, but that had been her first kiss since childhood. There never seemed to be time before. Never enough good things happening.

"That—that was . . ." he stammered.

"A kiss, dearie," snarked the vendor. "My, you do fluster easily."

Giggling, Melanie tugged him away from the woman's intrusive stare.

They found a shady place beneath a large tree and sat facing each other, neither of them caring how the grass might stain their clothes. They held each other's gaze in silence for a long few moments, both fascinated by the gleam in the other's eye.

"I didn't mean to," Sebastian whispered eventually.

"Didn't mean to what? Kiss me on the nose? That's quite all right."

"No, I meant . . . I didn't mean . . ." He swallowed harshly and looked away. "I didn't mean to *want* . . ."

"Are you still worried I think you only helped me that first day because you took a fancy to me?"

He tilted his head noncommittally.

"It hardly matters now, don't you think?" she asked. "Since I obviously"— the words stumbled sheepishly out of her mouth—"fancy you right back?"

"You have to understand," he said, still not looking at her. "And I think, now, you might. When I was young, when I wanted people to feel a certain way—when I wanted it *enough*—they *felt that way.* They wanted things if I wanted them to want things, you see?"

She cocked her head.

Rolling his tongue thoughtfully into his cheek, he turned. His eyes were both hopeful and afraid. "I've always been worried that if I wanted *someone* badly enough, even now, that I could *make them* want me, too."

"Oh, *Sebastian.*" Her chest constricted. Butterflies filled her stomach and her throat. She fumbled for his hand in the grass, took it in hers, squeezed tight.

He was worried he'd somehow manipulated her feelings. That he'd forced her to feel this strange tug—this blissful peace—whenever he was near.

She inched closer to him and kept her voice soft. "My dear, sweet, attentive Monsieur Leiwood. Never was there a man more sincerely incapable of manipulation than you. The power you once possessed seems at odds with your very soul. And, having been possessed of such things myself, I feel qualified to reassure you: if you have forced me to feel this way it is only through your inescapable good heart and intolerable sense of decency."

He relaxed, his posture losing some of its rigidity. He eased against the trunk, body pliant. "And you," he said shyly, "through your insufferable determination and outlandishly positive outlook."

"There you have it," she said, shifting to lean her head against his shoulder. "We had no choice. The gods must have commanded it."

He put an arm around her shoulder, ran his fingers through her curls. "Must have."

▸┈◈┈◦┈◈┈◂

"*You* are in *love*," Dawn-Lyn said smugly.

"What? *No*." It had been days, and she hadn't said a *word* about what had transpired between her and Sebastian in the park. How could her mother know?

"What happened?" Dawn-Lyn asked. They'd gone to the first floor of the inn for their dinner—Dawn-Lyn was tired of being holed away, no matter how beautiful the room. "Something happened," she continued. "For weeks and weeks it was 'Sebastian this' and 'Leiwood that,' and now, mum from you with a side of incessant humming."

"Humming? When was I humming?"

"Just now, as we came downstairs. A soft little love song."

"I *was not*."

"I get it, I'm your mother. Too awkward for a young woman to discuss such carnal desires with—"

"*Moth*er." She glanced around to make sure none of the other patrons were listening in on their indelicate conversation.

Dawn-Lyn laughed heartily. The first belly laugh Melanie had heard from her in years. "You are so easy to prod. Look at you, all embarrassed. You're as red as a tomato." She brushed her teasing aside, turned to other matters instead. "Are you still going to Gatwood's workshop today?"

"Why wouldn't I?"

"Because I still think you should reconsider. This knowledge is a gift."

Melanie shook her head emphatically. "No. *No.* The risk of keeping it is too great. Look at all I did"—she lowered her voice to barely above a breath—"all the laws I broke, all the wrongs I committed—just to cover up one mistake. If it ever came down to being hunted, to actually having to run or fight because of the . . ." she let "magic" go unsaid, "there's no telling what I would do. Where I would stop. It scares me not to know myself well enough to say where the line is and whether or not I would cross it. Where would I go? Who would I turn to? If you were threatened? If Sebastian was threatened?"

"You are still you."

Yes, but who am I? Really?

That was the ultimate question, wasn't it? Who did she *want* to be?

KRONA

After months of grooming, playing with, and loving Monkeyflower, I knew everything we'd been taught about varger was wrong. They could be tamed like other beasts. They could feel, and form relationships. I made it my new mission to reverse the varger stigma.

Their plan was simple. Krona would don Mastrex Pat-Soon's mask and trail Jaxon once he appeared at the appointed time. The others on her team would keep tabs on her from afar—stationed on rooftops across the surrounding city blocks—and she would inform them of her progress via reverb bead.

The plan was simple, but crucial.

They could have made the arrests. Could have risked the Chief Magistrate's wrath. Could have hoped the most powerful lawman in the city-state would have seen reason and not been offended or worse.

But Krona wasn't naïve.

They had vast amounts of circumstantial evidence pointing to the involvement of *someone* beneath Iyendar's roof. But nothing definitive. Even the healer's tool and the masked man literally crying out "Iyendar" could be explained away. Especially if the one doing the explaining was the Chief Magistrate, who had a vested interest in the sanctity of his household and likely little care for whether or not a team of Regulators kept their jobs.

After all, what were the deaths of a few peasants compared to the dignity of a noble's family, his name, and his station?

Krona needed something solid. Tangible. Something she could bring to the Chief Magistrate that he could not deny.

If Fibran Iyendar, or Clive LeMar, or Melanie Dupont were involved . . . if one of them was a killer . . .

Jaxon would surely lead her to a nest of responsible parties—thieves and murderers all around, in this cult of the Unknown.

Krona was confident they'd chosen the stronger course of action. To wait in one arena—the arrests—and jump into another.

At least, she was confident until she rode to the den that morning.

She wore her street clothes—better for following suspects through the city undetected; even Mastrex Pat-Soon's abilities couldn't completely erase something as glaring as a Regulator uniform. But she felt more exposed in her skirts. And the very air of the city felt wrong in ways she couldn't put her finger on. The unexpected play of adrenaline through her veins made her twitch, and her heart felt bruised—too much pounding, too much worry.

Her body was anticipating something her mind couldn't name. Perhaps it was the cult itself, the very existence of Jaxon, that had her clutching at her chest, pained, as she walked through the den's main doors. Or perhaps it was her sincere worry that there was something very wrong with De-Lia and her sister refused to seek help.

The captain had suffered a rough night once more.

Yes, it could have been either vexation, or both, but the vibrations all around her—the sullen looks from the people—told Krona it was more.

"Tray?" she prompted, striding to where he bent over the receiving droppers of an ansible plate.

Cold frustration creased his face—making his dimples and the fine lines around his eyes look deep and craggy for his age.

"It's from Tabitha," he said. "She and a member of the Watch were on Strange duty, and Strange hadn't come out of her box for hours, so they went to investigate . . ."

Krona's mouth went dry. "She's dead, isn't she?"

He pulled the paper from under the ink flutes, crumpling it in his fist, smearing the ink across his thumb. "Yes."

"How?"

"*I don't know,*" he said, punting the wad across the room. Administrators watched him with wary eyes, unsure if they should pick up the scrap or leave it be.

"There's no way anyone could have reached her without us knowing," Krona protested. This was wrong—all wrong. "They should have seen. They *had* to have seen." She ran both hands over her face.

"If nothing else, the Martinets—"

"Gods damn it, the Martinets."

"The Martinets *will* come. First we lose the mask, then the murders, and now this?"

"This is twice now someone has died in our care," Krona spat. "First the false varg—killed under our very noses. Now Strange."

She didn't want to come to the obvious conclusion. She didn't want to think about what it had to mean.

That the Watch was corrupt was no surprise, no secret. It took very few skills, and sometimes fewer wits, to be a strong arm behind a gun or a blade. One did not need integrity to bear an embroidered badge of the constabulary, only a mild understanding of the law.

Regulation was different. It required more commitment, more dedication. Years at the academy, constant focus and toil. Unless you were of a privileged stripe, a Regulator had to live in barracks and eat in the mess and make do with seeing loved ones every few weeks.

A Regulator could not be turned lightly.

"If it's not subterfuge, it's incompetence," Krona muttered, "and I don't know which is worse."

No matter who was on the scene, or how Strange's death had come to fruition, De-Lia would take the blame for this as well.

"She wasn't—was Strange pregnant, do you think?" she asked.

"They didn't say they found a bloom," Tray said. "Just a body. Belly split open, but nothing more. So we can't even pin it squarely on Charbon."

"We can't let this happen anymore."

Saints and swill.

Gods damn it all.

Maybe they'd been wrong. Maybe they should have pushed through with the arrests.

"Where is De-Lia?" she asked Tray.

Her sister had left the apartment before dawn. Banging around the kitchen, gathering her things. Krona had peeked out of her nook to make sure De-Lia wasn't sleepwalking and she'd been ordered back to bed.

"Went to the coterie an hour ago," Tray said. "Royu and Sasha by her side, Pat-Soon's otter mask in hand. Said she couldn't sit around here waiting, wanted to make sure Jaxon didn't show early."

"That . . . that makes no sense. What about the morning briefing? We should have all set out together. Why didn't she wait?"

"I don't know," he said with a sad shrug. "I told her we should press Illana and Donna for more information before going, but De-Lia . . . She's been . . . *different* lately. I'm sure you've noticed. She used to tell me things, now . . ."

"She insists it's just the stress of this concern."

"Do you believe her?"

"I want to," she said with a sigh. "It's difficult when family—"

She caught herself.

Family.

Thibaut and Madame Strange were kin.

Shit. Shit, shit, *shit*.

She had to tell him. He deserved to hear it from her, not through his network of snitches and blackguards.

She could leave a scarf for him. Meet him soon.

"I—I need to go see my informant."

"Thibaut?"

"Thibaut. He . . . he gave us crucial information. About Strange, about the cult. He needs—"

Tray held up his hands. "Doesn't matter. The less I know about his needs, the better informant he makes. You really trust him, don't you?"

"Perhaps far more than I should. Can you handle the priests on your own?"

Tray nodded thoughtfully. "Go. Do what you need to do. Just make it to the coterie on time, yeah?"

"Yeah." She turned to go—having never even made it to her desk.

>⊷⊶•⊷⊶◄

Leaving the den on foot, she rushed to the statue of Absolon, but was surprised to run into the very man she was after not halfway to her destination.

"What are you doing here?" Thibaut asked, striding in the same direction she was. They easily fell into step.

"I was going to leave you a scarf. You?"

"Same."

"Something urgent?" she asked.

Thibaut nodded grimly, shoving his hands in his pockets and eyeing each pedestrian. The line of his body was taut, stiff. He clenched and unclenched his jaw, gazed past her, eyes fixed on nothing in the middle distance.

He was angry.

Together, they ducked into the nearest shop: a deserted little knickknacks store. It smelled of musty dried flowers—a scent Krona had always associated with the elderly. The clerk at the counter looked up from a book to wave absently at them before going back to his business.

Huddling around the repurposed face of a grandfather clock—which now seemed to function as a bird bath—they whispered fiercely to each other.

"Madame Strange is dead," Thibaut blurted.

"I know," she said sadly. "I'd hoped . . . How did you find out?"

"I went to see her. Watchmen everywhere."

"Thibaut, I'm so sorry."

He thumbed at the 5 on the clock face. "Was it because of this concern you're working?" he demanded. "Did someone from up here murder one of mine from down there?" His body thrummed, his hands tremored against the clock, and he quickly snatched them back to ball them into fists.

"I don't know," she said honestly. "It's possible. The body, did you see—?"

"She wasn't . . . she wasn't a bloom, if that's what you're asking. But she *was* mutilated. Gutted."

If Madame Strange was another one of Charbon's victims, it could be a rush job. If he wanted to extract her womb—or a fetus, perhaps—and had been forced to do it in haste, he would have gone straight to the point and not bothered confusing the scene with a bloom.

"Was there a message nearby? 'Death is art,' and perhaps something about the truth?"

"No," he gritted. "Just the body. What can—Mistress, what can I do?"

"*Do?*"

"To help. To aid you further. Perhaps if I'd been more forthcoming with you from the beginning, if I'd told you where to find Strange, if I'd spoken to her about trusting you, maybe she would have sought asylum, or you could have arrested her, or *something*. She was *family*. Perhaps she would still be alive if—"

Krona's chest constricted. "Thibaut. Thibaut, *no*. There's nothing—"

"I could have. I could have done *something*. Let me do something now."

"No. *No*—this is why I told you I wanted you far away from this concern to begin with. This right here. If they—the Watch, the cult—" *A Regulator, or—? Not the Chief Magistrate, dear gods, please don't let this go all the way to the top*—"If they got to her, they can get to you. I won't have it. I won't put you in harm's way. In fact, I want you to leave the city."

"And go *where*?" He flung his arms wide. "I run in darker circles than you know, Mistress. I can handle—"

"No, Thibaut. You can't. You might not want my protection, but I want to protect you. And I can't even—I can't even toss you in a cell in my own den because I'm not sure it's secure anymore. The Hall of Records, the Regulator den, the Dregs, the streets, the Watchhouses—I have nowhere to put you to keep you safe."

"I'm not some wilting flower. You can't put me under glass to preserve me. *Let me help you.*"

"You can help by *staying the fuck away*."

He pressed his lips into a thin line, cast his gaze to the side.

"Just until I've worked some things out," she added. "Just until I have my footing again. When I know who to trust."

"You can trust me. I'm not useless here."

She smiled softly, sadly, at him. "I know that. This isn't about not trusting you. And you aren't useless. But your particular skills require you to work at a distance from me and mine. I know you want to do more, I understand. You feel helpless. And so . . . so do I. Something isn't right with this concern—hasn't been from the beginning. And I can't see what it is. It feels like a mote in the corner of my eye. Like something just past my field of vision, and if I could turn my head at the right time . . ." She trailed off. "So if you want to help me . . . help me worry just a little bit less."

She reached for his hand, and he let her take it. He didn't look up, didn't meet her earnest eyes, though she tried to coax him.

"Fine," he said softly after a moment. "I'll go."

She squeezed his hand. "Thank you. And again, I'm so sorry."

⇥•⬦•O•⬦•⇤

Concerns typically came in two types—those as plain as a nose, and those as opaque as a quagmire. But this one . . . it felt as impenetrable and dark as an onyx.

Thieves, killers, prophets, cultists, corruption, and perhaps even . . . traitors? Traitors in her own den?

But not—surely *not*—

Not a traitor on her own team?

As Krona turned the street corner, spotting the limed walls of the coterie, she felt dread bubble up inside her chest.

Slipping the glass shell over her ear and the reverb bead in her mouth, she took a deep breath and steadied herself, focusing in on the task at hand: trailing Jaxon. "Regulator Hirvath reporting in," she announced.

"Check," said Royu and Sasha simultaneously from their lookout positions nearby. Krona paused to scan the rooftops, searching for a telltale bit of black leather, but Sasha and Royu were well hidden.

Tray echoed "Check" a moment later.

Then, finally, De-Lia.

"Jaxon?" Krona asked.

"Hasn't arrived yet," De-Lia replied.

Good.

She entered the coterie and was greeted once more like a casual worshiper. The priest of the Unknown's tone was light, their vestments flowing beautifully over the cobblestones. She tried not to eye them with suspicion. Just because the Prophet was of the Unknown didn't mean everyone here had nefarious intentions. The flowers buzzed with honeybees, and the scent of jasmine lay heavy in the air. The sun was bright, the day was beautiful, but Krona was in a dark mood. She searched for De-Lia outside Time and Nature's cloisters, but knew she would not be able to spot her sister if she'd already donned Pat-Soon's mask. "Captain? Location, please."

"I'll come to you."

Krona moved around the curved side of Nature's cloister, positioning herself between it and the next building, pretending to admire the lavender growing there. She crouched to run a few stems through her fingers. In a few minutes' time, a cloaked figure cast a short shadow directly over the flowers in her hand. She turned to find a visage styled like a playful otter.

"How long have you been wearing it?"

"Two-fifths of an hour, perhaps."

"Good," Krona said lightly, standing. "Then the aftereffects won't be too terrible." She held out her hand expectantly.

"I've already secluded the echo," De-Lia said. "The struggle is over, I might as well see it through."

"You don't know how long you'll need to track Jaxon. You're already stressed and exhausted, you don't need a migraine on top of that. Especially not one that could last for days. Besides, we already agreed that I would wear it."

"I'll be fine."

"I'll be better," Krona said frankly. "Why burden yourself with this?"

"Because it's my responsibility. Because I'm the captain, and because I—" She threw her hands wide, revealing her saber, quintbarrel, and a familiar purple-and-yellow scarf dotted with llamas slung about her waist beneath her cloak. She clipped herself short, refusing to let herself say whatever came next. "Because I say so," she said instead, sounding all too much like their mother.

Krona opened her mouth to argue, but in the next instant their shells were buzzing with Tray's shouts.

"Captain—Emergency! Varger—I've spotted a varg."

"What? Where?"

"*Here*—four blocks over from your position."

"*Inside* the city?" Krona asked.

"Yes!"

Both sisters cursed.

"We need to contain them."

Krona gritted her teeth. This couldn't be a coincidence. Someone had alerted the cult to their plan. The varger were a distraction. A diversion.

Which meant there was something the cult needed to do here. Jaxon could have simply not shown up. They could have made the Regulators waste a day waiting for him. But instead—

"On it!" Royu shouted.

De-Lia's hands went to her mask-covered cheeks, seemingly in frustration. "Gods damn it all. How many, Tray? Can the three of you manage?"

"There are at least two. Perhaps a third. One is definitely a jumper, Captain."

"Saints and swill," the Hirvaths chimed together.

Krona held out her palm. "Give the mask to me and go. We can't abandon this lead, and I'm no use with varger." A swell of triumph filled her chest. For the first time in her life, her phobia had come in handy. There was no reason for *her* to rush off. No reason for her to leave this post unattended.

De-Lia hesitated. "You won't have any backup."

"Take care of those monsters and return to me," Krona said, her words layered with meaning. "Do you have—?"

De-Lia patted her side. "Quintbarrel and containment bulb all ready."

"Good."

With a sigh, De-Lia unknotted the cotton string and pulled the mask from her face. Her free hand instantly rose to her temples as though she could quell the headache. She looked down into the bowl of the mask for a moment more, as though it were a mirror.

"De-Lia?" Krona prompted.

Slowly, De-Lia passed Pat-Soon's mask to her sister. The movement had an echo of something else to it, some other message—just like Krona's words. But Krona wasn't in a position to decipher it. It felt like the passing of a torch, a responsibility relinquished.

"Be careful," Krona said.

"You as well," De-Lia said, pulling her quintbarrel from its holster, palming her pouch for shots, loading her gun. Swiftly, she loosed the knot holding the scarf at her waist. "You'll need this," she said, slinging the fabric over Krona's shoulder. "To hide the mask."

"Thank you."

Turning, De-Lia stomped off toward the coterie's exit with determination and clear authority. This was what she was meant for—direct action, gunfire. Krona was the one built for slinking in the shadows, built to follow, not to lead.

Krona settled the mask on the bridge of her nose, relishing the familiarity of her field of vision narrowing, of the subtle pressure of wood against her face. She suppressed the echo in an instant, seeing nary a glance of Pat-Soon's life. Quickly, she wrapped the scarf around her neck and head.

She had her satchel on her hip, and a knife in her boot, but she wished she'd brought her saber.

Slinking out from behind the cloister, she scanned the coterie courtyard while listening to the frantic chatter on her shell. Her team approached the loose varger from both ends of the street, and shouted at each other over what she could only imagine was breaking glass and frantic screams of pedestrians. Here, only a few blocks over, all was calm. One would never know that only a few streets away, chaos reigned and monsters roamed.

Krona did her best to tune out her companions. Their sternly swapped orders and the constant mention of *varg varg varg* made her blood surge and her heart race and her skin break out in a cold sweat. But she couldn't pull the shell from her ear to cut off the sounds. She was already too vulnerable.

They're not here, she told herself, putting a calming hand on her throat. *The monsters can't get you.*

She tried to push images of gnashing teeth from her mind, though they kept rushing in, like a wall of water her resolve could not hold back: the man at the Jubilee, who the varg had split open; the manifested eyeballs and incisors at the vault; her father, bleeding on the kitchen floor. It all flashed unbidden behind her eyes.

Taking deep breaths, she focused in on the mask's knowledge, on what she knew of keeping out of sight, keeping silent and unnoticed.

Watching the coterie's entrance, she hunkered down amongst the lavender, let the naturally calming scent mix with that of the wood covering her nose. It was soothing, focusing, but in a superficial way.

Her body still hummed with tension. Her muscles vibrated as she kept herself still, kept herself from pacing a tract in the garden. Every bit of her felt corded and coiled, ready to spring, to shift, to flutter into motion the moment she identified their suspect.

But when a tall, blond man walked through the gates, she didn't spring.

Instead, the coil *snapped.*

Thibaut.

Why the *fuck* was it always Thibaut?

Anger burned in the back of her throat.

She'd asked him to do one damn, simple thing, and he wouldn't even allow her this small, sanity-saving concession.

Instead of leaving, the little prick had followed her.

He rushed in, flapping his hands and speaking emphatically with the priest of the Unknown that approached him.

Something was wrong.

Very wrong.

She swallowed down her irritation.

Moving into the sunlight, she set aside the mask's abilities for a moment. She waved at him, and he caught sight of her straightaway, running over.

"What in the gods' names are you doing here?" she demanded, more harshly than she'd meant to. "I told you to leave the city, and yet here you—"

"We have to go," he said firmly, the strong tone of his voice belying the franticness in his movements. "You're in danger, they know we're here."

"Who? Who knows?"

"They're coming for us," he insisted, panic straining his tone. He took her hand, tugged her toward the exit. "We have to go."

She planted her feet. "Stop. Thibaut. Thibaut, talk to me."

"I'll tell you everything," he said. "But please, come with me. Come now. We have to run!"

With an exasperated sigh, she let Thibaut lead her out from amongst the cloisters and back into the city. "Which direction are they coming from?" she asked. "We'll make our way opposite. Do exactly as I say and we may be able to evade whoever it is."

"There's no time, they're too close. Quick, down this alley!" He tugged on her wrist all the harder, pulling her into the street.

"Thibaut!" she yelled, stepping lightly as they dodged the oncoming carriages. "What's gotten into you?"

They made it to the other side without a scratch, but Krona had to wrench her wrist away from his strangling grip. "What did you see? How many people are on their way? How do you know—?"

"Just follow me, please," he begged, spinning out of her reach, slipping down the narrow seam between two buildings—a gutter more than an alley.

"Thibaut, stop," she called, but still chased after. "You need to answer me. I know you think yourself some master sneak thief, but when it comes to—"

She stopped talking as a figure appeared at the other end of the gutter. She and Thibaut had made it about two-thirds of the way to the next street over, but a man now barred their path. He wasn't simply standing at the mouth of their exit—he slowly began working his way in, toward them.

Krona knew who he was before a gust of wind whistled between the buildings, carrying his strong scent in their direction. Thick black boots, strong jaw, light ruddy-colored hair, and steel-set eyes. Jaxon.

She caught Thibaut by the collar and began hauling him backward. "I told you," she hissed. "You should have listened to—"

Thick hands embraced her from the other direction. She found herself pressed suddenly against a broad chest. Her mind kicked into fighting mode immediately, all the while silently cursing Thibaut for panicking and leading them into a trap. She dropped down, slipping between the pale, meaty fingers, crouching to access the knife in her boot.

The hands pulled the purple scarf from her mask, but she leaned away, hoping to keep Pat-Soon's mask on. It wasn't a helm, but it was rough protection for her face.

Thibaut seemed to have frozen beside her, unsure what to do. "No," he breathed. "Venessa, this wasn't—"

Krona didn't have time to wonder what he was yammering about. She found the hilt of her knife, yanked it upward, just as the meaty hands brought a bit of white cloth—a simple handkerchief—over the base of the mask.

She took a whiff of pungent fumes before she had time to consider what was happening. Her mind immediately went foggy, her temples pounding. She reeled upward, trying to knock herself into her attacker. The mask slipped sideways, blotting out her vision altogether.

The handkerchief was thrust beneath the wood, pressed directly over Krona's nose and mouth. She kept struggling, trying to hold her breath.

But it was no use. Whether by lack of air or the drug, she would lose consciousness.

She had been right. The varger were a distraction.

But, apparently, not enough of one.

They'd needed to lure her away as well.

And they'd . . . they'd *sent* Thibaut?

The last thing she heard before all went dark was Thibaut sobbing over and over, "Venessa. No, this isn't right. You got away. *Venessa*."

34

✛✛✛✛

MELANIE

Eighteen months previous

She worked for months at Gatwood's laboratory—sweeping, running errands, holding the hands of skittish clients as they underwent magical mind probes. None of it was as fulfilling as her brief attempts at medicine. Dawn-Lyn had told her this knowledge was a gift from the gods and that it was to be cherished. As time went on, Melanie almost started to believe that, too.

The longer she had the magic, the more she realized she *wanted it*. Wanted to keep it.

Why should she have to give it up?

There was a future here, within her grasp. One that contained Sebastian, and her mother, and healing, and *freedom*.

She wanted the freedom so badly it made her shiver. Made her hands clasp and unclasp as she mentally reached for it.

But if she was going to have that future, she couldn't stay with Gatwood. Couldn't stay and obediently acquiesce to his mundane instructions in the day and his probing directions in the night.

The enchanter's focus on her was intense. He *tried*—he tried so hard. To do as she asked. Find a cure. Clear her conscience and her body.

But the more they studied and tested, the surer she became. She didn't want it gone. Her body wasn't ready to release the magic, and now, neither was her heart.

If she'd never come to him, she might not have realized. The very thought of being enchanted had sent her into a panicked state in the early days. She'd woken up in the middle of the night on countless occasions, sweating, anxious, sure the Watch or Regulators or the Marchonian Guard, even, were on her doorstep, ready to take her away.

But with each failed solution, the coil of anxiety loosened. Now, she'd almost shrugged it off completely.

She wouldn't have come to terms with this if it hadn't been for Gatwood. She'd always be grateful for that.

But she couldn't stay. Couldn't be his assistant or learn his trade.

She had to move on.

In secret, Melanie auditioned for several mastrex healers. She wasn't sure why she didn't tell Gatwood. At first, she simply didn't know how to broach the subject of leaving. But as time went on and she failed to mention it, her lack of acknowledgment morphed into active withholding.

He looked so *hopeful* every time he tried a new approach.

He'd taken to giving her potions now. Between his understanding of magics and her understanding of medicine, she wasn't worried about being poisoned, but it seemed an empty exercise. Futile.

But the *hope*. She wasn't ready to take that away, just yet. Didn't want him to think himself a failure.

Her many interviews with healers went well—mostly—and she had her pick of the lot for apprenticeships. They were all eager to add to her repertoire, but most asked too many questions. They wanted to know who her former mastrex was—for of course she knew too much to be a novice—and why she'd left their service. The first time she was asked, she did her best to answer, to try to convince the healer that she'd simply "picked up a few things" while acting as caregiver to her parents. He'd understandably found the answer difficult to swallow.

But Clive LeMar wasn't like that. He hadn't poked and prodded at her like a specimen for dissection. He simply asked her to perform, and when she did, noted the results.

"You are very good," he'd said after their first meeting, and that was all. She'd checked that her pendant was well situated—then a new quirk and not yet a habit—and left his home filled with confidence.

He was a private healer, and Melanie wasn't sure she wanted to work for just one family. A hospital seemed more to her liking, where there were many tasks—many equations that needed balancing. But she realized a hospital or surgery position would be easy to acquire after studying under someone like LeMar. All she had to do was endure the usual six to eight years of apprenticeship at the Iyendars', and she would have her pick of jobs.

She wanted him to be her master. He wasn't overly kind, but he was direct, honest. She could do with an extra dose of honesty in her life.

When he'd agreed to mentor her, she felt like she could fly. Finally, *finally* her life was starting. After years of devotion to her family, to her small little corner of Arkensyre, she was going to join the world and make something of herself.

Both Dawn-Lyn and Sebastian offered to help Melanie break the news to Gatwood, but she insisted she could do it on her own. She owed him that much.

The next day, after the last client left and Gatwood began to spread out his experimental instruments, she stopped him. "You know I appreciate everything you've done for me, don't you?"

"Of course. How could I miss it, what with you saying so every other session? You aren't exactly shy with your thanks, Little Splinter."

"Well, good, I'm glad you know. Because . . . because I think we've gone as far as we can go. I think I will just have to live with it. With the magic."

"Oh, come now. I know it's been difficult, but don't give up! We will save you yet."

"No—no, please listen. I'm sorry," she said firmly, moving to his side. Her palms were stained blue and yellow from making paints all day, and she let one slide over the roughness of his knuckles to still him, putting her hand over his just as he twisted his wrist to uncork a tincture. "You misunderstand. I'm not simply resigned. I'm choosing it. I will keep it."

He blinked owlishly at her. "Why?"

"Because it is mine."

"*No,*" he said harshly, setting the bottle down with an excess of force. "It is *mine.*"

His face had gone hard, the lines of it now deeply furrowed. He looked at her with a darkness in his eyes she'd never seen before.

Startled, she put up her hand, backed away. "What?"

"This magic isn't *yours,*" he spat. "It doesn't come from *you.* You didn't forge it. You didn't even earn it. I did that. I did all of it—I created this enchantment for another. And then you *stole* it."

"That's not—you *know* that's not true. It was an *accident,* and I'm sorry—"

"You did the right thing in bringing it back to me. And I *will* reclaim it."

"No." She clenched her fists and stamped her foot. "It is not a thing to be reclaimed. It is a part of me now, and you will *not* tear it away."

"Go sit," he ordered, turning back to his bottle, reaching for a stone mortar filled with pale green herbs for his new concoction. "This is nonsense. You're simply frustrated. We both are. I'm . . . I'm sorry for my outburst. Your doubt will pass." He poured in the tincture and began to grind the ingredients. The smell of rosemary filled the workshop.

"This isn't a sudden whim," she insisted. "I've already found an apprenticeship elsewhere."

He dropped the pestle with a clatter. "With another enchanter?" he asked, incredulous.

"No, of course not. With a *healer*. Master Clive LeMar, actually. He's one of the most well-respected—"

"Why do you want to run off and tie yourself to someone like that? With your skill?"

"No one's going to seek out a healer with no training," she said.

"You have a position, already. Here. I gave you employment, a safe haven. You'll just be wasting your talent, your time—"

"I've no talents of use to you. I do not belong in your world."

"Oh, Little Splinter," he cooed, looking up from his work. "Call it an accident, divine intervention, what have you—but it ensured you belong *to* my world. It tied us together, made me understand things I'd—" Gatwood paused, a shaky breath on his lips. "There were possibilities I'd written off until I met you."

Melanie shivered—his words were a distorted echo of Sebastian's.

"If you stay with me, we can uncover the *greatest* secrets. Perhaps—perhaps this is the Unknown's gift, had you thought of that? The ability to put magic inside *people*. And wouldn't it be . . . Wouldn't it be a wonder to give such gifts to others?"

He stared at her with earnest intensity, a mad glint making his eyes shine.

His meaning slowly dawned on her, made her lungs hitch and her heart leap into her throat. "You want to *re-create* what happened to me? To do this to someone else?"

He shrugged, but his gaze did not falter. "I want time, is all. To find out how this happened. How the magic has taken root. What we do with that discovery can come later. If you pledge yourself to another master, that opportunity will be lost."

"Perhaps it's best left alone," she said firmly. "We've already danced at the edge of Knowledge's penalty—"

"I assure you we have fallen over that edge."

"And now you want to do it again? To who? Who would you even try to enchant? You can't simply experiment on people."

"And why not? It wouldn't be difficult. Plenty of people come to me to take their knowledge *out*. It would stand to reason that I could perform an exchange. Give them something in return."

"No one would agree to—"

"Oh, I think you'll find there's much people will agree to if you tell them it will make them better. Smarter. Stronger. More powerful." He turned back to his experiment. The contents of the bowl had gone from a faded green to bright red. "Do not underestimate even the common person's greed for power. Over others, over events, over themself."

"I will not help you experiment on others. I didn't want to be experimented on *myself*. I'm going to become Master LeMar's apprentice. I've already made up my mind."

Gatwood let out a heavy, overwrought sigh—as though he was simply dealing with a fussy child throwing a tantrum. "You've become too comfortable too quickly. Have found too many safe harbors too readily. The rest of the world will not look on you as kindly as I have. If your trespasses are uncovered, there *will* be consequences."

"I can take care of myself."

"Can you?" he asked harshly, gaze darting sideways at her. "All it takes is one cockup. Perhaps your mother says the wrong thing to a neighbor. Or a guest overhears you conversing with Sebastian at the inn. Your circlet slips—" He made a flicking motion through the air, as though he were knocking the ferronnière from her head. "—and then the jig is up. Here, I can protect you."

"You don't want to protect me," she scoffed, realizing something she should have weeks ago. She should have realized what his intensity meant, his pinpoint focus. "You want to *possess* me. I'm just a vessel to you, nothing more."

"That's not true."

"Yes, it is."

He put down his tools, threw up his hands. "Fine. If you want to go, go. Go to LeMar, go to whatever hospital or noble house he serves. Go seek the normal life of a healer and see how long it lasts. How many lies do you think you'll have to tell on a daily basis, hm? How often are you going to have to play dumb for your new master, lest he figure out you come by your skill unnaturally?"

"Better a million lies than to stay here and help you do this to someone else."

"You *are* ungrateful," he spat.

"No, I'm not. But I think it's time I left. Now."

"If you leave now, do not come back."

"I *won't*," she assured him.

Melanie took an uncertain step backward, toward the lab's side entrance. This conversation wasn't supposed to go this way. She knew he'd be upset that she was leaving, but she thought he'd at least be happy for her. She'd thought they liked each other. She'd thought they were friends.

But to him, she'd been a *little splinter* of his magic. Nothing more.

35

KRONA

I knew I would grow up and train varger, show people how to live with them, how to understand them. But where to begin? It wasn't fair to hide Monkeyflower in her cave for years while I grew up. She needed to be cared for like a proper pet—be part of a family. If we were going to change hearts and minds I knew where I had to start: at home.

When Krona awoke again, her entire body ached. She was surprised to find herself sitting upright instead of lying down. An unvarnished, splintering table sat before her, and her arms were tied securely around the back of her chair.

The room was dimly lit. Small, and warm. But wet. Musty. The sharp scent of cider apples—corrupted by a tinge of mold—hit her nose. She was in a cellar.

The light came from candles set in Jugendstil sconces. The kind one might notice in a fine home but were absolutely out of place in an unfinished, half-earthen basement. The iron flourishes and creamy, opaque glass were at stark odds with the plain boarded walls and packed-dirt floor.

Beneath the candles, against the far wall—hemmed in on either side by thick, damp tree roots invading from the surface above—was another table, this one covered over with a silk cloth and laden with objects of all kinds: a single, opal-inlaid earring shaped like a dragonfly; a pedestal of glass with a heap of sugar, or salt perhaps, enclosed in a globe at the top; a pair of pliers; a large, boxy camera; a book bound in bark; what looked like a set of dowsing rods; an ink pen, et cetera. But, front and center, lay a brooch with an enormous ruby—the despairstone.

"One of them's awake. Inform the Prophet," said a voice from behind her. Krona tried to turn her head, found her neck not only stiff, but lashed to the chair back as well. From the corner of her eye she saw movement, and realized she wasn't alone at the table. Thibaut groaned on her right.

He was unconscious, tied just as she was, his head lolling to one side. She tried to whisper to him and realized she wore a gag. Her lips and nose and fingertips were still numb with whatever drug she'd been given, and her mind was slowly winding its way up to full capacity. A strange feeling crept up her spine. Aberrant, yet familiar. It was the same oppressive sensation she'd had riding up Vault Hill—as though caught in the crosshairs of a hot, unyielding, *invisible* gaze.

Behind her, the creaking of rickety stairs drew her attention. Stiff soles on wood—someone going up. A few moments later, more than one pair of shoes coming down.

The newcomers swooped around the front of her small table, blotting out her view of the other.

There were five people in total, besides herself and Thibaut. Four of them wore crude masks. Not the kind carved for a funeral. These were pale, paste-and-paper things, with rippled surfaces and strange bulges. Each possessed mis-shapen eyelets, a rudimentary nose, and a garish slash of a mouth. The clothes the figures wore were baggy, mismatched. Stained. Brown stains, on the sleeves and hems, like dried blood.

But it was the fifth figure, the one who stood in the middle, who stole the air from Krona's lungs as surely as if it were pulled from her in a breathless kiss.

The Prophet wore a cloak, unlike the other cult members, and over a face-hugging hood, his mask—beautiful and terrible, just as Krona remem-bered it—was Charbon's.

It bore the scar of their encounter, but the missing horn made it no less ma-jestic. The remaining spines curved away from the wood like thick mandibles, their incongruent pairings making them all the more ghastly. The colors were harsh, even in the low light of the cellar, and the white teeth stood out against the black maw of the gaping mouth like the rough and brutal points of the snowcapped Arkensyre rim. The Prophet's body was at ease. He held himself authoritatively.

At least for the moment, the echo was properly suppressed.

His attention held on Krona only for a moment, before he gestured flip-pantly at Thibaut. "Ugh, not this one again. *Still* getting in the way?"

"He was useful this time—was following her," said one of the figures—Jaxon, Krona was sure. "We used the rods on him—found a secret that gave us fifteen minutes of his mind—made him bait, and he lured her away. Thought we might as well take him too."

Krona's brain was still hazy. It had to be. She recognized the words, but the way they fit together—utter nonsense.

Fifteen minutes of his mind?

"He was *following* her?" the Prophet asked, surprised. "Oh, oh—don't tell me they're associates? The stoic Regulator and the rakish, nosy little tramp? Isn't that just . . . And here I thought he could be nothing but a nuisance. Let's see if he can be more than just *bait*. He's worthless in the long run, but right now, maybe he can help us break her."

Krona's hackles raised, her wrists straining against their bonds. When murderers used the word "worthless" they meant "disposable." She tried to push her gag past her teeth, to order them to back away from her informant, her friend. "You will not touch *one*—" Her words were nothing but garbled mush behind the cloth.

"Is he important to you?" the Prophet asked Krona. "You don't have to answer. I can see it in your eyes. Good. That's very good. But what do you really know about him, I wonder? What secrets has he kept from you? Surely you know he whores himself out to nobility. Yes? All right. That he has associates in the Dregs? Hmm, not news either. Oh, I know. His name. People like him never give out their real names.

"Kes, feed the pen. Be careful, the nub is greedy."

The cultist answering to Kes drifted to the rear table, plucking the ink pen from its place amongst the hoard. He drew his way to the sleeping captive's side, then pushed up his mask, revealing a broad, handsome face framed in delicate auburn curls, but pale as flour. He was well washed and carried himself like a gentleman. Quite the opposite of the rugged brawler type that was Jaxon.

With little preamble, Kes pulled aside Thibaut's collar, which shifted away easily, given the deep V of its cut. Thibaut's head lolled away from the other man's touch, exposing the column of his throat.

"Gently, gently," the Prophet warned.

Krona let out a small yelp as Kes jabbed the pen's sharp nub into the soft flesh near the tendons of Thibaut's neck. But the cut was shallow, little more than a pinprick. Thibaut barely flinched in his drug-induced slumber.

"This is a demonstration, for you," the Prophet said to Krona. "Of the type of power I command and the things I can uncover. I want you to understand why you shouldn't fight me. Why I brought you here." He snapped his white-gloved fingers at Kes. "Quickly, before it dries."

At his behest, Kes, with a single drop of Thibaut's blood, wrote *reveal* on the boards of the table.

The word was light, scratchy. The pen had barely drawn anything, and blood was a poor substitute for ink. But after a moment, the small word shifted, the letters drawing out, splitting and rearranging themselves, until three words took the place of one.

Theodore de Rex.

No.

How?

It was a blood pen. An enchantment she'd never thought really existed, had believed was just some enchanter's myth. A pen that could be used to write the truth of a person in their own essence. The conjoined priests had mentioned one, but she hadn't imagined—

"Ah, Theodore. What a delightfully mundane name. And de Rex—where is Rex, I wonder? He's Theodore of nowhere, as far as I can tell. How about you, Regulator? Is this name familiar to you?"

Charbon's visage turned on Krona again as the Prophet sidled his way forward. Placing his hands on the table before her, he leaned in, scrutinizing her face. His eyes—they were so . . . *human* behind the demon's eyelets. Brown, flecked with green. The skin around them was a pale pink, and the whites had gone parchment yellow with a touch of jaundice.

"She doesn't know it," he said, delight in his voice.

"I have many such enchantments at my disposal. Ones that grant me all sorts of insights. What you must understand, Regulator, is that I am an individual who likes to be well informed. Which I'm sure you find relatable. I like to know things, because knowing things is how you control things. And yet, the more I know about *you,* the less control I have. I don't like it. It troubles me. I wanted the pair of you, but only one could be bent, and I . . .

"Shall we try on her one more time?" he proposed, turning to the masked man she was positive was Jaxon. "Just to be sure?"

"Whatever you command, Prophet."

Jaxon turned back to the cloth-covered table.

If each item there was enchanted, who knew what they could do? What strange powers they possessed?

Jaxon took the dowsing rods in hand, stroked the long length of them once.

We used the rods on him—found a secret that gave us fifteen minutes of his mind, they'd said. Somehow, they'd used this enchantment to control Thibaut.

But it wasn't the thin metal bars that worried her. Krona felt that oppressive stare *intensify.* Felt a shifting in the room. Next to Jaxon, for half a moment, she saw a glimmer, a fata morgana of a shape.

Mist.

It was the same form she'd seen in the vaults.

There weren't five people here with them—there were six.

Jaxon shifted as though entirely unaware of the mist's presence. Krona looked to the Prophet, trying to gauge if he'd seen it—if he knew someone was there when his cultists did not.

The mask hid much.

Krona was both resistant and intrigued. Whatever they were about to do to her was surely an answer—to the mist, to Thibaut's strange behavior this afternoon, and to the reason this cult had resurrected Charbon's techniques.

Jaxon strode to her side. The mist followed him, mirroring his every move, coming to stand behind Krona.

She held firm, didn't try to lean away as Jaxon pointed the rods at her and the tips crossed.

She didn't jerk forward when she felt the vague, radiant heat of hands reach over her shoulders from behind to hover close to her cheeks—invisible, but undoubtably present. The mist's almost-touch.

And she didn't so much as spit—though she wanted to, gods how she wanted to—when the Prophet leaned even closer across the table, until she was nearly nose to nose with the terrible mask.

"Tell me a secret," Jaxon said, and Krona felt a soft surge of additional warmth from the mist's hands.

She said nothing. But a chill went down her spine as she remembered Thibaut requesting the same thing. Thibaut, who had led her into a trap.

"Tell me a secret," he said again through gritted teeth.

Clearly, *words* weren't even what they were searching for, given her gag. They were testing for something else.

When Krona did not respond, the hands moved away, though Jaxon thrust the rods at her more firmly. He demanded she speak for a third time, and the disparity between his action and the mist's made her suspicious. The Prophet wasn't telling his followers everything. Whoever was near her, cloaked from their sight, held the real power, not these rods. Perhaps the rods weren't even enchanted at all.

After a moment, the Prophet shook his head. "Still immune, even to temporary commands. There's no way long-term conditioning would take hold. Damn. I'd wanted . . . Two would have been better. A united front." He made a tutting sound behind the mask. "What to do, what to do?"

"What do you mean?" she demanded. The gag muffled her, but she repeated herself, again and again—not shouting, just talking. Waiting. *Please be curious, or arrogant,* she begged. Arrogance was useful in a criminal, made them gloat, made them careless.

"I see Mistress Hirvath is good and truly awake now," he said. "Remove her gag. If her chatter becomes tiresome, we can knock her out again." He wagged a finger at her. "Behave, my dear," he continued, "or one of you will have to pay."

After the gag was shoved down away from her mouth, she worked her jaw once, twice, before asking, "What are you testing me for?"

She wanted to keep him talking—to learn all she could, to catch him in his own web, yes, but the longer he spoke the more time she had to formulate a plan to get herself and Thibaut out of this cellar alive.

They were near cider trees, of that she was certain. There was a cider orchard on the way to the Iyendars', she knew that as well. If they were in one of those orchards, then they were far removed from the city proper, and likely calling out for help would only rile her captors to violence. The ropes around her wrists were solidly tied, but with enough time she was sure she could get her hands free. She wasn't sure at this point if Thibaut awake would be a help or a hindrance, and there was nothing within reach that would make a good weapon—she knew better than to take illegal enchantments at face value. Likely the cultists had taken her dagger. Mastrex Pat-Soon's mask was gone, though the purple scarf lay lightly around her neck, still knotted. Her options were limited.

"I'm trying to figure out how best to make you . . . amenable. Because you can help me. And, if you truly understood the world for what it was, I think you would. Willingly. Eagerly," the Prophet said. "What I do, I do for all Arkensyre. I know what you must think of me, but I am not some villain wallowing in filth, acting for my own pleasure on my own behalf. On the contrary, I am a servant. I serve the Valley, I serve the gods, I even serve you, Mistress Regulator, though I'm sure you don't have the capacity to see that. The state has your collar buckled too tightly, and your leash held too short."

"Why did you kill those people?"

"My dear, *I* haven't killed anyone." He held out his hands, as though to demonstrate how very clean they were. "*They* killed *themselves*! Don't you see? What a gift that is?" He pointed behind him, at the despairstone. "It frees them, lets them free themselves. They choose the method—a needle, or pills, or the scalpel. And once the stone has done its mercy, I simply use the mask in order to properly utilize the flesh. Why let it go to waste?"

She had only a moment to consider her reaction. Her stomach roiled and she wanted to balk. *Simply utilize the flesh*, what a disgusting turn of phrase, what a heartless way to speak of the people he'd taken. Utterly devoid of feeling, of respect—of empathy.

She wanted to tell him just how sick he was, but criminals were like flies—honeyed tongues were usually more effective than vinegared ones.

"I don't understand. What are you utilizing it *for*? What is the *point*?" she pressed, struggling to keep her tone even, unemotional.

She saw him close off immediately, his eyes becoming hard. "All in good time." He began to draw away, turning to his cultists. She had to hold his attention.

"Tell me more about the enchantments," she said quickly. "What were you trying to do to me? What have you done to Th . . . Theodore?"

He twirled back to her, smiled behind the mask. "Marvelous, isn't it? My borrowed power."

The mist shifted behind her, winding its way around the people to settle in the far left corner of the room. She tracked it with her gaze, letting the Prophet see her seeing it, still unsure if she should inquire after it point-blank or pretend she didn't realize it was a person. "It is marvelous," she admitted.

"Of course, what we did to your friend here—to *all* your little Regulator friends—is temporary. With a few snatches of their day—for a few minutes, in a small burst—we can send anyone back, to relive a secret, and in that brief space they are quite impressionable. We can convince them to leave a post, to unlock a door . . . to lead a friend down an alleyway of our choosing. The incident is gone from their memory almost as soon as it happens, and the mind fills in the little blanks, convinces them nothing is amiss. Thoughts are a wonder that way."

Venessa. Thibaut had said *Venessa* because he'd been reliving a secret. And . . .

All your little Regulator friends.

Tabitha could have been convinced to leave Madame Strange alone for a brief time. Ten minutes might have been enough to kill her. And at the Jubilee, if all they needed was a Regulator to unlock a few doors, how much time would that take? Not much at all. If it could be *anyone* for the smallest, *briefest* minutes—

Anyone. Except . . .

Except for *her*? He said she was immune. How could she be immune?

"And this is accomplished with those rods?" she asked, eyes still locked on the shadowy corner.

It clearly had nothing to do with the rods.

"Yes," he lied.

"How? What combination of enchanted elements can be used to control a person?" Not even the hypnotic suggestion of Motomori's mask could achieve this level of persuasion, of behavioral influence. "How can you override will like that? To get someone to kill—?" Their false varg was not murdered in a fit of memory lapse, and there was no way he'd taken his own life.

"It's less control and more . . . suggestion. In the short term. Long-term conditioning is a much deeper process. It's still near impossible to get someone who isn't a killer to take out, say, an inconvenient prisoner"—he knew exactly what she was talking about—"but you can drown them so deep in their secrets they think a syringe is a spoon, that they're feeding or helping. Sometimes you need someone you can depend on to be suggestable for hours and hours at a time. That takes a combination of things."

He strode to the enchantments table, lifting the blood pen and the book. "We still start with the rods, yes. Though I think, my dear, you perhaps understand the 'rods' better than my colleagues. Am I correct?"

She glared. He'd figured out she could see the mist. He *did* know it was there.

"But the rods are not enough," he continued. "Secrets are a powerful thing. And when divulged in blood they are binding. All you need to start the conditioning is that little push from the rods, that brief suggestion, that perhaps their fingertip is an inkwell, and this journal is a fine place to write their truth. And then you pile magics on top of magics on top of guilt and deception, and watch them weave together."

Krona racked her mind, trying to decipher how such strange enchantments could be paired with the mist's power of suggestion to facilitate a long-term effect. But it sounded ridiculous. This was magic the way children played at magic, without understanding there were rules, and consequences, and that not all things were possible. And yet it couldn't be denied that this was real—the blood pen had revealed Thibaut's real name. The mist had stalked her on Vault Hill.

"And what have you gained?" she asked. "Who did you need to wield such control over?"

"Oh, my dear lady, you are brighter than that. When subverting the state, it always helps to have stooges in high places." He laughed then, a terrible, distorted laugh. Not happy, not mirthful, but not harsh and cruel. It was a laugh of amazement, a laugh of wonder.

"You think you're so clever. That I'm just divulging all these secrets because, what? I'm arrogant? That I might be. But no, dear Regulator. You need to know these things, to understand them, so that what I show you next makes sense. We cannot control you—not *yet*—so we must *break* you. With a peek behind the curtain, as it were. You were to bring us bottle-barkers in the vaults. You failed because of your immunity. You will not fail next time."

"He's lying to you," she said, addressing the cultists, not the Prophet. Maybe if they realized the man was hiding something—*someone*—from them, she'd have half a chance at escape. "I wasn't on Vault Hill alone. I kept someone from stealing those bottle-barkers. Someone followed me for half a day, invisible to everyone—even caged vault guards. Someone tried to steal those bottle-barkers and I *stopped* them. It wasn't just that I failed to fall to your enchantment's influence."

"Tell them who it was," she insisted. "Tell them they're standing right over there." She nodded vigorously at the corner. The others all turned to look, some confused and some spooked, if their body language was anything to go on.

"Enough!" the Prophet commanded. "Her gibberish will serve us no more. Bring in the other. I will break her will, and then we'll see if she'll bend to the rods. Go. Leave us. Complete your preparations."

The four masked cultists marched away without protest. She heard the stiff groaning of the wooden staircase, and the cellar's light improved and diminished again with the opening and slamming of a door.

However, the mist remained.

"Who is it? Who are you?" she demanded when the others had gone.

"They are not your concern," the Prophet said, moving between her and the mist.

"Why can't the others see them?"

"*Why can you?*" he asked harshly.

For that she had no answer, and so said nothing at all. They held each other's gaze, and the air became thick, stiff and stifling. They wanted each other's secrets.

Suddenly, he bent over slightly, head twisting, hand grabbing at his stomach—but only for a moment. He recovered quickly, but Krona thought it odd. He was struggling with something, finding it difficult to maintain his bravado and composure.

The echo.

After another minute, the door at the top of the stairs flashed them with warm light once more. It was distinctly lamplight, not daylight. How long had they been down here, unconscious? It was dark, but how late was the hour, or how early?

The light painted a silhouette, a shadow, on the far cellar wall for half an instant before the door shut again. A figure in a cape . . . with a wide helm. A Regulator.

Her heart rose.

Then fell.

The Prophet wasn't shocked or surprised.

All of Krona's hope—her determination, her hardheaded resolve—slipped away. As the Regulator's boots slowly stomped down each step, she despaired.

She knew those footfalls, heard them nearly every morning on their apartment steps. The buckles on the helm made a familiar rasp as the Regulator pulled it from their head, revealing their face, but Krona did not want to look. She didn't need to look.

De-Lia.

When she came fully into the room, her eyes finding Krona, she clearly did not recognize her sister. De-Lia moved as though in a trance, in a dream. *As though she were sleep-strolling.*

"Let her go," Krona demanded, stressing each word, putting a warning on each syllable. She hadn't wanted to be right—that something was wrong with De-Lia. But it was. Terribly, terribly wrong.

The Prophet simply chuckled. "You don't see it now, but you will. Your sister has been chosen for a wonderful task. I would have liked the pair of you, but alas. Soon, when the evidence is procured, she and I will preach the find to the entire Valley. Her authority, her apparent willingness to unmask the state, will carry weight Louis Charbon and his . . . allies"—he let the last word fall from his lips like so much sludge—"never could have hoped for. The three of them were misfits and outlaws. But Captain Hirvath is a purveyor of truth and justice. A woman to listen to. Someone to follow."

Krona tried to calculate quickly, to untangle his nonsense into a motive she could understand, one entwined with what she could remember about Charbon's motives. He killed for the gods, but ultimately cursed them. But allies— Charbon had said he'd killed alone. Did the Prophet mean Charbon's mask maker, perhaps? Matisse?

But who could possibly be the third?

The mist moved to De-Lia's side, held ghostly hands beside her head. "Why don't you write in your journal, Captain Hirvath?" the Prophet suggested, bowing at the waist, sweeping his hand toward the book on the enchantments table in a parody of graciousness.

De-Lia moved with her usual strength and power, which made Krona's heart hurt all the more. There was no struggle in her, no fight. This man and his invisible crony had broken into her mind and she didn't even know it.

Instead of going straight for the book, she picked up the blood pen, striding around the room as though she were alone. Without preamble, she jabbed the nub into her thumb, dipping once then twice, as though she truly thought it was an inkwell, before bringing the pen to the book and its pages. She flipped to the middle, and began to write.

Not a mending needle, as she'd said. Not her saber, as Krona had assumed. These small cuts were made by this far, far more vicious instrument.

All the while the mist stood pulsating beside her, waving, shimmering—
influencing.

"It's the secrets," the Prophet said. "It's all about the secrets. And pairing
the enchantments just so, knowing which best bolsters another. A blood pen
by itself can tell me your true name. A blood pen, and an enchanted journal,
and a concoction of salt and iron, and a few other magics here and there, a
single word dug from the depths of someone's mind, and months and months
of visits from my invisible friend . . . Well, it's difficult to maintain; I wouldn't
suggest trying to make a puppet of your own. Much easier to just find someone
willing. This magic, it's very taxing, you see."

Krona didn't see at all.

She had to get them out of here—all three of them. Away from this madman, away from the mist and these twisted devices.

She'd been in tough situations before, but never where she couldn't hang
on to her authority, where the fact that she was a Regulator seemed to count
against her a hundredfold. This man knew how they operated. He'd used Regulation against them. What did that mean? That he was another lawperson?
Could be Watch, maybe. But he knew much more than the average constable
about magic. And he couldn't be another Regulator—she would have recognized him, his voice, she was sure. An enchanter, then? She dealt with far more
enchanters looking for licenses or enchantment approvals than she did thieves.

But even if he was an enchanter, that wasn't especially something she could
use against him.

A sudden jolt of inspiration hit her. He'd been struggling moments ago—
and had struggled when he confronted her in the street. Krona knew better than
anyone what it looked like when an echo fought. And Charbon—Lutador's
most notorious killer—surely had a headstrong echo. It had never been rated,
but she'd be damned if his imprint was the type to roll over and play nice.

The longer the Prophet stayed in Charbon's mask, the more difficult it
would be for him to keep control. How long had he been wearing it now?

Maybe she could lure Charbon to the fore. Finding triggers for echo flares
was easy; they taught echo-baiting in the academy.

An internal battle might be enough of a distraction. She didn't need the
echo to seat itself, just fight him—pin him, pull at him. Sap him of his composure and his bodily discipline.

But, if the echo was as strong as she suspected, once baited, it might quickly
gain the upper hand.

Would it be worse for the three of them with the echo in charge?

Charbon was a ruthless killer. Depraved. Angry at the world and the gods.

He could prove so, so much worse than the Prophet.

But she couldn't think of what else to do.

"Charbon," she said, addressing the echo directly. "Why did you fail? Why did you die before your *mission*"—she spat the word out as though it tasted filthy—"was completed?"

The Prophet's head jerked to the side, and he had to drag it back again.

Yes!

"Speak," she said. "What would you like to say, murderer?"

"Stop it," the Prophet growled.

"Charbon, you butcher. Come out!"

"Gag her," he ordered De-Lia, his hands flying over his ears. A deep rumble emanated from his chest and he stumbled away from the table, hitting the moist wall with a *thud*.

Curiously, the mist held its ground.

De-Lia moved slowly, setting the pen down with the book before aiming for Krona, still trancelike, unbothered.

"Charbon, was it worth it?" Krona continued. She kicked out under the table, finding Thibaut's shins, hoping to wake him. He groaned beside her. "Did you get what you wanted from your blooms? Did it thrill you to see them cut open? Did it excite you? Char—!"

De-Lia pulled the gag up tight between Krona's lips.

"I told you to behave," the Prophet growled. His breathing came in ragged bursts, and one hand clawed at the wall, leaving dark soil stains on his otherwise pristine glove. "I told you what would happen if you didn't. That you or your friend would pay. I *told* you." He pressed his dirty hand to the front of Charbon's mask, holding it to his face. "Untie the man—Theodore," he said steadily. "Give him a slap to bring him round."

De-Lia moved to do the Prophet's bidding, first freeing Thibaut and ungagging him, then backhanding him across the cheek.

Thibaut gasped, groaned—lifted his head, blinking, groggy.

In the corner the mist shifted, came forward.

The Prophet turned toward it as though it had spoken.

"She needs a full demonstration!" the Prophet shouted. "Needs to see what I can make her sister do to her friend. *I need to break her.*" His agitation had become a boiling anger.

Thibaut was free before he fully comprehended that he'd been bound in the first place. He rubbed at his wrists, his throat—tenderly touched his cheek—and turned uncertain eyes first on De-Lia, then Krona. "Mistress?"

"Draw your saber, Captain," the Prophet instructed. "Keep it trained on the young man until I say otherwise."

The mist backed away into its corner once more, giving the Prophet room to work.

De-Lia unwaveringly did as she was commanded.

Krona wasn't sure what she could do, how she could stop the Prophet from making De-Lia hurt Thibaut. She shoved at the cloth with her tongue, trying to spit it out. She had to try to lure the echo again—it had been working. Maybe she could keep him occupied with an internal battle long enough for Thibaut to shake De-Lia out of her stupor, and then they could take on whoever the mist was together.

She loosened the gag enough to form words, garbled as they were. "Charbon! Or do you prefer the Blooming Butcher? How did it feel, killing all those people?"

The Prophet's head snapped left, then right. He grabbed at the mask's horns, tugging.

"Which did you like best? I bet—I bet it was—" She remembered what Patroné had told her, about Charbon's pattern. Krona's stomach flopped over at the thought, insides revolting as she spat out the next words. "I bet it was the little girl, wasn't it? I bet that was your *favorite*."

He roared, shoulders hunching, body twisting.

He shook all over—*convulsed*.

Then froze. Snapped straight.

"You think you can outsmart me with that forked tongue?" he spat, crossing the room to her, bypassing the table and swinging around to put a hand against her throat, the mask only a hairsbreadth from her nose. "Maybe I don't need to break you," the Prophet said. "Maybe I'll just have you killed. Perfect, yes. A Regulator murdered by her sister's hand as her groggy, useless gentleman friend does nothing. That would be a fitting end to this thorn in my side."

As he glared at her, she realized his eyes had changed. His gaze had shifted, unfocused.

Whoever was looking back at her from the mask's eyelets wasn't the same man as before.

"Charbon?" she whispered.

"*Hurry,*" he hissed back. His stance was still taut with rage, but his voice had gone soft and pleading. The threat to kill her was a ruse, an act. "The Thalo puppets—more are coming." He yanked the gag from her mouth.

"The wha—?" He put a dirty, gloved hand over her lips and shook his head ever so slightly.

Swiftly, he rounded her chair, pulling at her bonds, struggling with them as though he weren't certain what kinds of knots were used. It was a strange, harried, out-of-place movement, so unlike the Prophet's posturing from before.

"Help me untie her!" he shouted at De-Lia, desperation heavy in his tone.

"Do not!" came a bellowing demand out of nowhere.

The mist had spoken.

The mist knew something was wrong.

De-Lia remained frozen to the spot, saber leveled at Thibaut's throat.

Krona realized then: the Prophet wasn't the one with the power here. The mist was in charge. "Who is—?"

The shimmer moved, rushing across the room.

Krona's question was cut short as the Prophet flew sideways through the air, jerked by an invisible hand or barreled over by an invisible body.

The mist dragged the Prophet away from her, tossing him to the ground. The Prophet rolled over, struggling, fighting, grappling with an imperceptible opponent. A swift impression of another body above his struck Krona before sliding away just as quickly.

"De-Lia, help me!" she demanded, but her sister didn't flinch. Krona tugged at her restraints—the Prophet had loosened them, and with a few well-angled twists she brought one hand free.

Thibaut tried to duck away from De-Lia's saber, stumbling sidelong out of his chair, but the blade's tip followed him deftly. "Mistress, what do I do?"

With both hands now free, Krona struggled with the knot at the back of her neck, twisting to reach it properly, putting pressure on her windpipe as though it were a noose. "Get the book," she croaked at Thibaut.

The rods were fake. But the book, the pen—they were part of this nightmare.

The scent of moist soil intensified as the Prophet and the mist scrabbled across the earthen floor just beyond Krona's peripheral vision.

Thibaut inched his way backward, toward the enchantments table, and De-Lia trailed him with perfect precision, the point of her sword never faltering. The book lay open still, the page De-Lia had just written on freshly exposed with the pen settled in the fold of the spine.

Finally pulling herself free, Krona twisted around to find the Prophet. He writhed at the base of the stairs, a heavy weight keeping him pinned.

She dove at him, intending to pull the Mayhem Mask from the fray, but he screeched at her before she could lay claim. "No, stay away. Don't let it get a hand on you."

"Who? The mist? Give me the mask."

"I can't give you the mask. I, I *am*—"

"*Yes you can*. Give it to me!"

"The Thalo," the man in the mask screeched, boots scraping as he kicked, looking for purchase, looking to push himself up and away. "It's not finished. Its plan—" His head whipped to the side as though he'd been leveled a particularly vicious blow. "It wants me to lose control. To disappear again."

"Mistress! I have it!" Thibaut cried, waving the book aloft.

"Tear out the middle pages," Krona yelled. "Tear them out now!" She had no idea if it would work, if tearing up the enchantment would tear out the magic's hold on De-Lia.

The mist bellowed, leaping off the Prophet and strong-arming Krona aside. It rushed at Thibaut, knocking into De-Lia to get at him.

Before it could reach him, Thibaut crinkled the pages in one green glove and yanked with all his might. The parchment tore with a searing, scraping, cracking sound—more like a tree collapsing under too much snow than a scrap of paper ripped asunder.

In the next instant he lost hold of the book. It was swatted from his grasp by the invisible person—the Thalo puppet?—who served him an additional slap across the face.

Thibaut brought his hands up, recoiling to the side.

De-Lia suddenly slumped, eyes wide, her weapon falling from her fingers, knees refusing to keep her standing. With a *thump* she hit the enchantments table sideways.

Abruptly aware of her surroundings, confused and frightened just like Krona had been when she'd shaken off the sedative, De-Lia reached for something nearby to keep her upright, to prevent her from falling. She grasped the tablecloth, which proved a poor anchor. She and the entire enchantments display crashed to the ground.

Thibaut plastered himself to the earthen wall beside the heap, cowering from the mist.

Krona had a split second to decide where her priorities lay. De-Lia was seemingly free—at least temporarily—of her mental bonds, and, in turn, Thibaut was free of De-Lia. Before Krona sat the Prophet. She only had a few moments, she was sure, before the mist's attention returned to her.

Her job was to recover the mask, and here it was, within her reach.

"No!" the Prophet shouted, jerking his head back, crawling away the moment she curled her fingers under the gnarled, wooden chin. "You need me, I can't help you if—"

"If you want to help me you will give me the murderer's mask!"

"No!"

Fingers caught around her biceps, and she pulled her arm taut, ready to strike out with her elbow. But it was Thibaut, tugging her away. "Come on. We have to go. Now is our chance."

"Not without the mask."

De-Lia crawled out from under the mess of items, scurrying around the bare table where Thibaut's real name was written in blood, aiming for Krona.

The mist began throwing things, searching through the items, as though merely concerned with one.

"De-Lia, help me!" Krona pleaded, both as a test and because she was sure in her state that she couldn't subdue the Prophet alone.

"I don't know if I can," De-Lia heaved. "What if I . . ." She wasn't entirely at a loss for how she'd arrived here, it seemed. Some small part of her must have sensed everything happening to her, dreamlike.

"Captain!" Krona yelled.

De-Lia's gaze snapped from far away back into her body. Without another protest, she surged forward.

Likewise, Thibaut asked, "What should I do?"

"Hold him down," Krona said. "Hold him down while we get the mask off."

"No!" the man shouted, struggling in the dirt, scooting away from her. "Listen to me. You *must* listen to me. I'm the only one stopping him from—"

Krona grabbed his ankles, yanking him across the ground before flipping him on his belly. Thibaut sat bodily atop him, and De-Lia's fingers dove for the knot at the back of his head, the straps wound tight around the black hood, which kept his hair hidden and his face padded. Krona moved to his front, tugged at the wood, careful this time to grab it by the base and not the extremities.

Try as she might to separate it from the wearer, it would not budge. It sat snug to his face as though glued.

"I will not leave. I will not—" His body convulsed then, writhing as though he'd taken a slap to the spine, and for an instant he went limp.

"What did you do?" De-Lia demanded of Thibaut.

"Nothing, I—"

"Got it," Krona crowed triumphantly. The mask finally, *finally* came free. The force of her tug sent her backward onto her ass, but she didn't care. She clutched her prize to her chest as though it were the only thing anchoring her to reality. But she did not let her guard down.

The mist was still in the room with them, but it had backed off, quieted. Krona didn't know what that meant, but she didn't like it.

"Roll him over, I want to see who it is," De-Lia demanded.

Before she and Thibaut managed to get him fully supine, the Prophet began to laugh. First it was little more than a tremble in his torso, but as the moments passed it slipped out of him in great guffaws.

The black hood hid all but his eyes. Cruel eyes.

Krona expected an insult. That he would call them fools or idiots. But as De-Lia's fingers slipped under his hood, he said the strangest thing:

"Monkeyflower."

All of the air left De-Lia's lungs in a great burst, and her shoulders rolled back in an animalistic stretch. Her hands—hands about to reveal the accused and *end this*—swooped back and away, her fingers curling like claws toward the ceiling. Every joint in her body buckled then unfurled, fighting—*fighting*.

"Lia?"

Krona said her sister's name delicately, like it was fragile in her mouth. The kind of fragile that, if broken, would send shards slicing through her soft tissues.

De-Lia rounded her face toward Krona, head bent at an uncomfortable angle, neck tendons straining to respond to something—anything—that was not the man who commanded her.

But her eyes were cold. Not the calculated frigidity she sometimes turned on a criminal, but a chill born of emptiness. She observed, but she did not see.

She was lost to them again.

Krona realized this in the fraction of an instant following the Prophet's command. Before she could stop her, De-Lia surged at Thibaut, thrusting her shoulder squarely into his chest.

Unprepared for his ally to turn on him once more, Thibaut tumbled aside like a rag doll, boots over ass.

Still laughing, the Prophet took De-Lia's hand when offered. Together they rose, he a lanky rope of sudden triumph, and she the strong vessel for his will.

Though the thought hadn't fully formed itself, Krona had secretly hoped that once she had Charbon's mask, whatever this was—this concern full of impossible enchantments and mythic Thalo puppets and murdering prophets—would dissipate like the tendrils of a nightmare. But the horror did not stem from the mask alone.

With her expression as fixed as the rigor of a death mask, Lia put herself between the Prophet and her sister, erasing any question of whose side she was on.

Still sitting on the floor, clutching Charbon, Krona dug her boot heels into the dirt. She had no idea what to do, how to fix this. She scrabbled backward. Space might give her time. Distance was her only hope.

"That echo has been nothing but contentious," the Prophet sneered, pulling at his clothes, straightening the folds. "I can see why she liked him. Oh, but how he loathed *her*." He patted his pockets, searching for something. "Medicine. I need my—ah, yes." From beneath the folds he pulled a small box, out of which he retrieved a delicate, preloaded syringe. It glistened of quicksilver in the dim light before he injected the concoction into his neck, beneath the veil. "For vigor," he explained. "Helps with the aftereffects."

Both De-Lia and the Prophet held their backs to Thibaut, who slouched against the far wall, flipping his dirty bangs out of his eyes. But his expression was not one of defeat. His pale cheeks burned with an anger Krona had never seen. It was as though he felt the betrayal of De-Lia's puppetry *for* Krona. As De-Lia took a step toward her sister—murder in the set of her jaw and clutch of her hands—Thibaut's seething burgeoned.

The thin thread of hesitance snapped within his chest and he lunged at the Prophet's back.

But he was halted mid-vault by an invisible force—the mist. Caught by a twist in his collar, he coughed and choked like a dog pulling at the end of its run.

"You forget, I have comrades in unseen places," the Prophet chuckled, as comfortable in the cellar surrounded by his enemies as he would be tucked in his own parlor flanked by friends.

Someone at the top of the stairs opened the cellar door from the outside.

At first, it appeared there was no one there.

But of course there was.

Shimmer. Haze. Blue.

A *second* mist.

How many were there?

It came down the stairs slowly, sweeping past the Prophet and De-Lia to stand threateningly in front of Krona.

"The Unknown has not been kind to me," the Prophet admitted, "but they have been just. And while I would adore watching your sister tear you limb from limb—as would be perfectly poetic—I realize my hour is nearly at hand. It would be better if your sister and I did not arrive at our destination covered in your viscera. I'm sure you can understand how that might cause panic amongst a civilized populous.

"You've pushed me to it, I'll have you know. With those *warrants* of yours for members of the Iyendar household. It wasn't supposed to be today. But I will not have you haul my prize off to the mines, out of my reach. I realize, now, my god does not intend to give me any more time for preparation. What needs doing must be done."

He was so pleased with himself.

"So," he said, turning to where the first mist stood, holding Thibaut by the throat, "I'd be grateful if the Thalo's hands would take care of these two for me." He glanced pointedly at Krona, homing in on the mask. "And *that* I shall need back. But not right away." The most recent wrestling match with the echo had clearly made him wary. He didn't want to touch the mask. "Please retrieve it for me when you are finished," he bade. "Bring it to our party."

Straightening his clothes, the Prophet and De-Lia both moved to the heap of tablecloth and enchantments, digging in, searching. He picked up both the journal and the blood pen. She found the despairstone and gingerly scooped it into a small white box without letting it touch her. Then, with a light hand at the small of De-Lia's back, the Prophet urged the captain toward the steps, and she went with ease.

No.

Charbon's mask slipped from Krona's fingers, bereft of importance. She only noticed its *thud* against the dirt as a bit of background. Same as Thibaut's new, strangled shouts of protest and the Prophet's tinkling laughter.

She didn't care if the mask lay there forever.

She didn't care if the next Charbon impersonator scooped it up and started killing tomorrow.

She didn't care if the Martinets stripped her of her authority and her entire detail shunned her for all eternity.

Only De-Lia mattered.

Krona would not let her walk out with a madman. There was nothing in the Valley or beyond that could make her accept that her captain was lost.

But she also knew a fight wouldn't end well. She couldn't beat this out of De-Lia as the echo's hold had been beaten out of the Prophet. De-Lia had always been stronger, had always gotten the upper hand on Krona while sparring. And De-Lia would never let her get a clean shot at the Prophet.

She only had one chance.

Krona pushed herself to her feet, took frantic steps forward, stopped only when the new mist in front of her did not move.

"Wait." She kept her voice steady, put every ounce of effort into making it sound sure and authoritative—exactly the opposite of what she felt.

The Prophet had one boot on the bottom stair but did not stop walking, did not turn to acknowledge her.

But De-Lia's steps stuttered.

"Take me instead," Krona demanded.

Interest piqued, the Prophet paused. "Oh, Little Hirvath, you're useless to me in the short of it. And unless I could be sure you wouldn't cause trouble . . . If I could condition you, it would be different. It's an intense process, made longer the healthier the subject. That's why I attempted with *her* first. As damaged as you appear—" He looked her up and down, eyes trailing from her bandaged arm to the side she favored because of the knife wound received defending Thibaut from the Watch, to the other visible blemishes that dotted the rest of her skin. "—you're not nearly as broken as she is. Your scars are many and you think hers few, but you forget what a scar represents. Healing. *Her* wounds are raw and weeping."

What open wounds—physical or mental—could De-Lia possibly be living with? How could she hide something so devastating from her sister?

As he turned to leave once more, Krona felt her opportunity slipping away.

Out of options, she reached forlornly into the empty air, toward her sister, who was too far away to touch. If she had to beg her to stay, had to wrestle her to the ground and pin her arms and get broken ribs for it, she would.

But it was not to be.

The mist in front of her caught her outstretched wrist in a manacle-like grip.

De-Lia and the Prophet disappeared up the stairs. The master and the puppet, gone into the night.

And now it was just Krona and Thibaut and two impossible, invisible assailants.

Krona prepared for a fight, hunkering down, bracing herself.

But her training relied too heavily on being able to see who or what was attacking her, being able to anticipate her opponent's movements based on the shifting of their body and the redistribution of their weight.

Though she could see a shimmer, it wasn't enough.

The hand on her wrist yanked her forward, and a forceful fist twisted in her hair, wrenching her head downward. She tried to resist, to let herself become dead weight in the second mist's grasp, but it powered through, dragging her over to where the first mist held Thibaut.

The two of them were twisted around, shoved bodily, face first, into the boards of the wall, each with a mist at their backs, arms contorted behind them.

The crushing weight of another person pressed into Krona, holding her firmly, compressing her chest against the wall. Hot breath coiled over her cheek, and for the first time since encountering the mist, she detected a scent. A smell she could associate with the amorphous visual traces. Berries. Tart, dark. The kinds that left purple smears and sticky fingers.

The same dread she'd felt on Vault Hill assailed her, but with ten times the intensity.

Thibaut looked at her with grievous levels of hope in his eyes. He was sure she had a trick up her sleeve. Sure she had a plan, was just waiting for her opening.

She wished he was right—that his hope and his trust weren't so misplaced.

The door to the cellar opened yet again.

The pressure at Krona's back lessened, as though the mist holding her was surprised by whoever had entered the room.

At the edge of her hearing, in the quiet, Krona thought she heard voices. Not distant. Near, but difficult to discern. Cloaked, perhaps. Just as the mists' forms were cloaked from view.

She raised her eyebrows at Thibaut, silently trying to ask him if he heard it too. He gave her a small, confused shake of the head.

Without warning, the both of them were jerked away from the wall, pulled back into the center of the room, toward the table and chairs.

No. *No!* She would not let them be bound again—

Her mist tossed her at the table. She stumbled into it, caught herself before her face hit the wood. Next to her, Thibaut was dropped unceremoniously to the floor.

There was a scuffling of blue blurs. Her mist and his mist and now—now a *third* mist.

The first two and the newcomer were arguing, forcibly. A chair was kicked over.

The argument—between Thalo puppets? But how could the Thalo argue with itself?—intensified. Krona couldn't make out words, but she could discern the tones.

And then the scuffling became attacking. Became wrestling, punching.

The table jerked beneath Krona as one of the mists thrust another into it.

"What in the name of all that is holy—?" Thibaut gritted out, stumbling upward, into Krona, grabbing her around the waist and holding on for dear life.

"I don't know," she said, flinging her arms around him, pulling them both back, away from the chaos.

Confused, caught in an eddy of surrealism, the two of them clambered around the tumbling hazes and toward the stairs, clutching each other with frantic, shaking hands.

Bits of dust and dirt flung up around them. There was a screech, like an animal stuck on the end of a hunter's arrow.

Thibaut yanked her ear close, eyes glazed and darting. "What's *happening?*"

"I don't *know.* Go. We have to *go,*" Krona insisted. She felt cornered, like a small child that had fallen into a lion pit. They may not have been the focus of the mists' ire, but at any moment that could change.

And yet, the mask.

It lay on the other side of the skirmish.

"Charbon," she said. "I can't leave without—"

As though it read her mind, Charbon's mask flew at them, its great jagged maw leading the rest. Surprised, Krona caught it, just barely preventing it from glancing off the tips of her fingers.

Take it and go, came a low, reverberated command. Krona felt it in her breastbone, yet it didn't reach her ears.

Was . . . was one of the Thalo puppets *helping* them? No, that didn't—

Nothing made sense.

Still fisting Krona's clothes, Thibaut pulled at her, got a boot on the stairs. "Come on!"

Krona allowed herself one glance at the Mayhem Mask—to reassure herself that it was really in her hands—before tucking it beneath one arm and scurrying away. Together, they ran. Ran as though varger were nipping at their heels. Up the stairs of the deserted house, out into the night. They ran toward the steady lights of greater Lutador, and not for an instant did they look back.

36

✠✠✠

LOUIS

*Eastside canals, sometime in the
wee hours, ten years ago*

Charbon carefully slid down the steep incline of the aqueduct's side. Going was difficult: he needed to slow his descent with the brace of his feet, but he couldn't control the way his legs shook. Strangled sobs choked free of his throat every time his eye caught the front of his tunic, and he wondered if he might not simply throw up when he reached the waterway.

He dragged his satchel behind him. The tools within would rust if he didn't clean them immediately. But he didn't want to clean them. He wanted to be rid of them.

As much as he wanted to drop them into the canal and let them carry his shame away, he couldn't do that. It was far too risky—would give the Watch a way to track him. Murderers who left clues wanted to be found, and as much as he believed he should be punished for his crimes, he wanted to go home first.

After a rough few minutes, he reached the edge. The water gurgled innocently as it made its way into the city. It did not smell as fresh as a country brook, but it was clean enough.

Numbly, he laid his tool kit beside him, undoing the clasps to let it splay open on the stones. Every piece of metal was stained with red or brown. Some glistened, some looked matte in the pale moonlight. He touched the first instrument lightly, and his stomach revolted. He nearly spilled himself into the waterway, but kept it down. His work was not done. He could be sick later.

The water was cool against his hands, which he realized were feverish as though laced with infection.

Perhaps I am infected, he thought. *What sickness is this, that would make a man kill an innocent woman?*

He knew intellectually that there should be no difference—man, woman, intersex person, nonbinary person, gender-fluid person, they were all the same. He'd killed so many men . . . why should this type of sacrifice burden him so much more? Why should he feel it more deeply? It gnawed on his insides far more than even his first kill had.

But no, there was a difference. *Those with wombs are closer to magic, they have to be,* Fiona had said.

They have to be. They are closer to life.

Or maybe the difference lay with that other thing she'd said—accused him of, really. That his previous refusal to kill a cis woman was its own special misogyny—a way for him to think himself a good man while tearing people no less innocent apart.

Men like you do women no favors.

As he turned his scalpel over and over in the running water, his vision blurred and his nose ran. Soon he was crying outright, letting his tears drop onto his dirty forearms, where they left streaks in the grime.

"I'm sorry. I'm sorry," he found himself chanting.

This was too much. Too far. He couldn't do this anymore. Never again. Magic or no magic—he hadn't found a trace, not a damn thing.

Will all those other sacrifices be in vain? he chided himself. *If you fail, you've killed for no reason. You're simply a vile murderer, nothing more.*

And if I find magic, that makes it righteous?

No, this was always wrong. No matter how he tried to honor the victims. No matter the compulsion of the gods.

"I *am* vile," he sobbed.

"Oh, come now," said a familiar voice from the top of the aqueduct. "You are a servant of the Unknown."

"Leave me, Fiona." She made a comely silhouette against the purple-hued sky—she looked powerful, with her riding cape long and sweeping and her skirts well fitted to her form. *She* was allowed to stay clean. *She* could stand over him like this, flawless and pressed, while *his* clothes were in tatters. Everything white on him had grayed, and the streaks of what looked like rust on his jacket refused to come out. His hands were blistered, his face unshaven, and his hair—he'd stopped tying it back weeks ago.

He looked like the perfect madman he felt himself to be. Why hadn't murder spoiled Fiona in the least?

"That's three, Fiona. Three women I've killed and I'm still no—"

"Not those same tired protests," she said with a flippant wave of her hand. "But you're right, it does seem that women aren't sufficient, either."

"Nothing is sufficient. I—" *I no longer believe.* "I don't think there's any magic to find. I think we've been lied to."

"Of course there's magic, dear one," she laughed. "How else would I have made *this*?" She retrieved something short but slender from inside her cloak and held it up.

It was the blood pen.

"This was how I first knew there was a fifth kind of magic," she said. "This was why the Thalo first came to me in that damned sanitarium. You thought it a recent creation surely, but I made it long ago. The Thalo wanted to know if I had what it took to change our world. If I was willing to do whatever my god asked of me. I keep this close because it is a reminder of my discoveries and my dedication. Everything we know about enchanting is sutured and censored. It is carefully curated to keep us in our place, and I have been put in my place enough for one lifetime. I will not go back to asking permission to invent. You *will* see this through. I didn't need the painted monsters to tell me what I already knew, that was for your benefit—"

Her choice of words set off a subtle alarm bell in the back of his mind.

"—They simply gave me a path to pursue. A way to make known to everyone what I've found on my own."

"I can't . . . I can't anymore," he sobbed. "I know what I promised, but . . ." Memories of the icehouse filled his inner eye.

⊷•✧•◈•✧•⊷

"Why me?" he'd asked the three puppets before him. Months later, he'd come to think of that as his personal mantra: Why me?

How many times had they come to them now? Six, seven? And still he told them no, he would not kill, find another.

You are a brilliant surgeon, they said. *Only someone with your skill can cut precisely enough to find the scars, to find where the magic is taken from. Prove the evil in the time tax.*

No matter how many times they insisted this was how the magic was taken, he could not accept that his only recourse was to kill.

Time was not free. It was a commodity—a physical thing to be traded, like everything else in the world.

Not long after a child's birth, a taxer from the government would alight on the new parents' doorstep, ready to baptize the baby into Arkensyre commerce. Large, enchanted syringes were used to pull time from the infant—time that would be used to replenish the government's stores.

When one neared the end of their life, they could either leave their time to others, or cash out—tacking the time they'd earned back onto their lifespan. The rich tended to live long. An average lifespan saw one leave this world in their early sixties. Thirty was middle-aged. This was right, this was normal. The rich could live upward of ninety. Sometimes one hundred. So unnatural. The human body wasn't meant to last one hundred years.

Truly, wasn't that evil enough?

"But isn't there another way to prove the time tax takes magic?" Charbon had asked. Hadn't the taxers missed people before? Wouldn't someone have noticed if they had the capacity for a new magic?

"Doesn't that make more sense, then? Approach it from the infant angle. We should steal a handful of newborns and keep them from the tax men? Make sure their magic can be seen?" Yes, that could work. Kidnapping was justifiable—they could return the children after. No one had to die. No one.

No, the Thalo continued. *The tax men do not miss. There are many things your government keeps from you, least of which is how the tax men find the children. They find them all. You cannot prove this from birth forward; you must look at it from death backward.*

"There has to be another way," he insisted.

Do you fancy yourself more knowing than the Unknown? Do you truly believe in these past months you have done more thinking on the matter than your god all these centuries? Do you, a man, think yourself better equipped to manage the world? Do you think of yourself as Absolon did, above the divine?

"No. Of course not."

Then yield, they cried. *Yield to the orders you have been given. Yours is not to decide how or why, yours is to complete the task you are given and make way for the Unknown. Many before you would kill to have this task land upon them. Do not be ungrateful. Do not condemn more children to die at the hands of Absolon's arrogance.*

Your son would still be alive if not for this deception, they reminded him. *Where is your sense of paternal justice? Do you not seek retribution for what was done to your family, your boy? Does your weak constitution mean you, in fact, have no feeling for those you claim to care so much about?*

"You know that's not the case," he said darkly.

Then yield.

Fiona came up beside Charbon, laying her hand warmly over his. "Perhaps we might even return the magic to its rightful place. Give back."

He narrowed his gaze at the puppets. "What would you have me do?"

They smiled. *Exactly as you're told.*

><+>-0-<+>+<

A spike of chill passed through Charbon as the memory left him. "I can yield no longer." He wiped his eyes with the back of his hand. "Do you have the alcohol?" he asked Fiona.

"Of course. But I don't know why you bother. They're dead when you're done with them, what does it matter if your tools are sanitized?"

She lightly trotted down the pitch, pulling the bottle from some other dark depth.

"No more," he said, taking it from her and splashing the clear liquid over his hands. "Don't you understand? I'm done. This blade will never kill again."

"I don't think that's up to you. I think it's up to our azure-colored friends." She leaned down and gave him a spunky pat on the shoulder, as though all he needed was a pep talk. "You're just stymied. You'd feel better if you'd made some progress. Which is, frankly, why we have to take the last step. I know neither of us wanted it to come to this, but I don't see another way."

He shrugged off her hand. "What are you prattling on about?"

"*Time* is taken from children. The *magic* is taken from children. We need to look in children."

Mortification froze him where he crouched. She couldn't have just said—?

"You wouldn't dare."

The moonlight made long shadows fall across her face, giving her deep, soulless-looking eye sockets. For a moment he held the impression he was really seeing her for the first time.

Her lips curled—not in a satisfied smile, but with a quirk of indifference. "I dare nothing. Orders are orders. Find the magic: that's all we were tasked with."

Charbon stood suddenly on his still-wobbly legs, accidently kicking his scalpel into the brink. "Never," he gasped. "I will not touch a single child." His hands lashed out, seemingly of their own accord. Charbon caught her by the clasp of her cloak, hauling her face close to his. "And neither will you. Better I kill us both here than let this insanity continue."

She should have panicked. The threat of murder-suicide by Lutador's most knowledgeable executioner should have rung true for her more deeply than anyone else. She knew what he'd done; she'd cleaned up after it. She brought the lambs to slaughter and then saw that their corpses were neatly arranged.

But Fiona did not scream, nor did she struggle. For one terrible moment,

Charbon thought she might even take advantage of the situation and lean in all the way for a kiss.

"Oh, dear Louis, I always feared it would come to this." Her eyes tracked over his shoulder. "Eric?"

Charbon's head turned, following her gaze, but before he could make the full arc he was smacked across the broad side of his brow with something cold and heavy. He dropped as though boneless, facedown onto the stone lip of the aqueduct. His arm flopped into the water and bobbed limply in the current.

But he retained his consciousness, if not his wits. A sharp prick and thrust alerted him to a needle in his neck. Voices bantered over the top of him, their volume cycling from too loud to barely there.

"Do you have enough?" asked Fiona's voice from far away.

"Nothing but the last cycle left after this. We'll have enough to make a mask when he dies," said Matisse.

A mask? How? One needed a lab for enchantments, and Charbon had never been attended to in a lab.

"Good. I've examined all of his blooms closely enough—my anatomy lessons have been quite thorough—but I still don't have anything near his skill with sinew and bone," she said.

"Should we take him, then? We can't kill him now. It's not ready—this has to stew. The mask would be ruined if he expired tonight."

Impossible. Matisse shouldn't be able to make a mask for him at all, unless . . .

Unless that was his gift? What the Thalo had wanted him for? The capacity to enchant objects without the control and precision afforded by a lab?

"No. We have no place to put him—and what if he escapes? What might he do? I have a better plan. It will get us a step closer to the magic, and break him for certain."

Charbon felt the hems of her skirts drape over his side and shoulder as she knelt. Her thin fingers ran deftly through his hair, like a mother giving comfort. "Good-bye, Louis. It would have been so much better if you'd given in. To me, to everything. But your services are no longer required."

Every inch of his neck and head ached, and the world felt like it was spinning on a top, but Charbon forced his face away from the stones. "You—" he croaked. "You need me. The Thalo. It said it had to be me. You need me."

"Oh, sweetie," she said, tucking a dark, dirty lock behind his ear. "I know what the Thalo said. But why would you believe the Thalo? Why for a second would you trust it? The puppets came to me long ago, before you ever laid eyes on them. I told them of you, and Eric. I am the only one the Thalo truly needs. Me."

He couldn't comprehend the words. "You're lying."

"This plan has been mine from the beginning. I understand the divine like no other, that's why the Thalo came. It helped me, it brought you to me when I asked. Everything I need, the Thalo provides. And anything I no longer need, the Thalo washes away."

With that, the last of his strength fled, and Louis Charbon blacked out.

37

MELANIE

Sixteen months previous

The winter months were creeping up on Lutador, and Melanie was more than happy to spend her time inside tending to her new duties. She'd only officially been Master LeMar's apprentice for a handful of weeks now, but the time had been delightfully busy. Her master made sure they both worked hard, but not long. He saw his duty to his family as equally important to his duties at the Iyendar household and made sure neither he nor his apprentice were ever kept longer at the estate than necessary.

He'd given Melanie open access to his library of medical books, and made note when she asked to borrow tomes that should have been well beyond her comprehension. He set her daily assignments and was slowly learning she could complete simple tasks in record time, knew her elements and her chemicals, and could mix basic medicines or darn a shallow wound in her sleep.

He never asked after her ferronnière.

At the moment, she was in the middle of washing and sanitizing the instruments from his medical bag. A lovely set, engraved with his initials and everything.

A knock sounded at the washroom door.

"Yes?"

One of the Iyendars' maids, Clarissa—a young woman of Asgar-Skanian descent, a year or two older than Melanie—poked her head through the door.

"You about done? The Chief Magistrate wants us all down in the foyer. New hire's arrived."

The old valet had passed away some time ago, and the Iyendars had only just found a replacement. It was customary for everyone in the household to welcome new staff at once.

"Of course. After you."

Setting the tools aside, she washed her hands and followed Clarissa downstairs. The staff queued up against one wall of the entryway, so that the new valet could shake everyone's hand in an orderly fashion. Melanie took her place at the end of the line beside Master LeMar.

Melanie paid little attention to the others around her, consumed instead with the many tasks Master LeMar had set her—after seeing to his tools, there were draughts to mix and recipes to memorize and capsules to stuff.

She didn't bother to examine the new valet until he stood before her.

"Pleasure to make your acquaintance, Mademoiselle . . . ?"

Confusion halted her reply.

Gatwood?

What in the gods' green Valley . . . ?

"I'm Horace Gatwood, the valet," he offered, holding his hand stiffly in the space between them.

"Melanie Dupont," she said, her lilt turning upward at the end, like a question. She didn't offer her hand. Both her palms had gone cold and sweaty.

In the next second he'd moved on, with no indication he'd recognized her at all.

What is he doing here?

For the remainder of the day, she searched for him whenever she found a moment to herself. But he was never alone. Some member of staff was always flitting nearby, instructing him on the ins and outs of the household. And he soaked it up, nodding and taking notes and repeating various tasks when someone suggested he "give it a try."

It wasn't until the evening, when most of the non-live-ins had gone home, that she was able to catch him on his own—in front of the main house, on his way out.

"Gatwood," she snapped in a harsh whisper, her shoes crunching through the gravel pathway that ran alongside the drive. A light dusting of snow was falling, just beginning to cling to the ground and show underfoot, and Melanie rubbed her arms against the cold. In her rush to catch him, she'd left her cloak inside.

He stood under the glow of the one outdoor lamp that had been lit, tugging off his newly acquired white gloves and using them to wipe snowflakes from the brim of his black hat. With a smile, he shoved the gloves in his pocket, exchanging them for a thicker, warmer pair he had hidden. "Ah, mademoiselle, what can I do for you?"

"What are you doing here?"

He glanced around, first over her shoulder, then his. "I thought it high time I changed professions."

She blinked blankly at him for a moment. "What are you talking about?"

"Enchanting. I'm done. There's nothing left for me there if you're here."

"I don't . . ." *I don't understand*; it was true, yet felt like a colossal understatement. "That's ridiculous." Especially after he'd gone on and on about not just wanting to be a master enchanter, but the most knowledgeable *Teleoteur* in all of Arkensyre. "Why would you follow me? This is my *life*. You can't tag along and play pretend."

"I'm not pretending, Little Splinter. This is who I am now. You don't think you need me anymore, and you're wrong. Worse yet, you think you can simply take my magic and be done with me." He tutted.

You only manipulate magic, she wanted to say. *No one owns magic.* But that last bit was untrue. That was what magic was for: owning.

"If you're here for me, why did you pretend not to know me?"

"If they learned about my enchanting, about our knowing each other before, there would be questions. Questions like: why would you stop practicing magic? And, *how did you two meet?*" he said pointedly. "I don't think either of us is prepared to stumble through that one. Wouldn't want anyone deciphering our little—" He tapped one finger against her ferronnière and she jerked away from his touch. "—secret."

The threat was obvious.

And she knew what he wanted in return for his silence.

To experiment.

Slowly, Melanie backed away. "Stay away from me."

"You asked for my help."

"I didn't ask for *this*. I asked you to let me go. I asked you to be happy for me. You must see how this crosses a line?"

He let her slip closer to the house, an amused smile on his lips. "You are important, Little Splinter. So much more important than you understand. We need each other. You'll see. We're still going to do great things. I'm not going anywhere."

38

KRONA

I wanted to show Papa on his day off. I cleaned Monkeyflower until her fur shone, gave her a lovely collar of flowers, and in the afternoon we left the cave together for the first time, headed for the house. It was so freeing, strolling along in the open country with my pet at my side. She towered over me; I'd brought her back to her full strength and I was so proud. Nothing was going to snuff my good mood that day. I was the genius child who had discovered how to get along with varger.

Krona and Thibaut stumbled out of the cellar and through an empty farmhouse, then through a grove of gnarled cider trees whose branches looked like deformed arms and hands, eager to pull at her braids and tear at Thibaut's clothes. At the moment, Krona wouldn't have been surprised if the entire orchard had come alive.

At first she thought it was late evening, but the barely-there sunlight was coming from the wrong place. No, it was early morning. They'd been in the cellar all night.

Invisible people, sentient mist, Thalo puppets—whatever had been down there with them was myth one moment and flesh the next. And the magic the Prophet possessed, to control a mind as fierce as De-Lia's . . . nothing in any of the holy scrolls described such a power.

The Thalo, that was . . . gods damn it all, it fit. The missing memories, the invisibility, it all fit perfectly with the stories of the Thalo puppets. But those were fantasy. Make-believe.

As were blood pens. As were new prophets.

The world wasn't right with itself. She wanted to go back to before, back when varger had been her biggest fear. Before she'd seen the Mayhem Mask up close.

Everything tilted—the canopy whirled above her and she nearly slumped to the side. Thibaut managed to keep her upright, to encourage one foot to brace for the other. "What happened?" he kept hissing, as a mantra more than a question. "What happened back there? Why did—? What's wrong with De-Lia?"

Krona couldn't answer. Instead, she focused on the lights from the city, dim as they were. They were far afield; it would take them a long while to meet the creeping edges of the city proper on foot. It felt like a lifetime away. A place filled with false memories of yesterday and no hope of tomorrow.

"I have—I have to stop," she gasped out, reaching for the rough and twisting bark of the nearest tree.

Thibaut yanked her back as though the tree might bite. "No. Home first."

"I can't go home," she growled at him, her mother's face flashing before her inner eye. "Not without De-Lia. I have to think. Now stop. Thibaut, *stop*."

He did as she asked, though immediately looked sicker for it. Perhaps motion had kept his nausea at bay. Finally, he let her go, and she fell into the tree.

She clutched at her chest, trying to catch her breath. "The Prophet knew you," she said, trying not to sound accusatory. Clearly Thibaut's betrayal at the coterie hadn't been his fault. "He *knew* you."

"He did? How?"

"He didn't say. You didn't recognize anything about him?"

"No."

"Perhaps he'd seen you at Strange's. Perhaps he knew you were asking after the cult. Or have you . . . have you ever serviced one of the Iyendars? Been to the Chief Magistrate's home?"

"Once," he admitted.

"Of course."

"But not as—not like you think. Monsieur Leiwood casually mentioned they were short-staffed, so I spent a few days—"

She waved his story aside. "It doesn't matter, not right now."

The tree bark that scraped against her shoulder was rough, though dampened through its gullies. And the tart apple smell surrounded her like a perfume. A splinter dug into her palm and she shot a scathing glance at the point of pain, accusing the apple tree only to realize it was Charbon's mask that had given her a sliver. After several silent, awkward moments, Krona spoke again. "Why did it help us?" she asked, her eyes trying to focus as she dug the wood shaving from her skin.

"The mask?" Thibaut asked tentatively. He'd curled up at the base of the trunk between two thick roots breaching the surface. He looked pale, drawn, as though he'd given up on the world. He toyed with the laces that kept the front of his tunic from gaping.

"Yes. It should have been confused at its weakest, itself at its strongest. Why would Charbon—a man who was hanged by people like me—want to save us from . . . ?"

Neither of them had been so bold as to bring the words out in the open yet. The Thalo.

That's absurd.

Is it?

"If the echo didn't like being controlled by the Prophet, maybe it was trying to subvert his plans?" Thibaut offered.

"That's far too sophisticated for an echo. They don't understand they aren't alive, don't know how to be real people," she explained. "The most an echo ever wants is to meet its own ends. It wouldn't know enough about its host to—" She stopped, standing up straight. "Unless it knew its host in life."

"The Prophet actually encountered Charbon, in the flesh?" Thibaut ceased his fidgeting, frowned at the mask, and inched himself farther away.

"It's not a wild animal. It can't bite you."

Thibaut threw his hands up. "After all that has recently transpired, I prefer not to take chances."

The planes of the mask were smooth, well crafted. The paint, though a decade old, looked new—a result of being locked away in the dark for the majority of its lifetime. Everything about the mask was expertly made, save one thing. One thing she'd noticed when packing for the Jubilee, but had given little consideration to until now.

She rolled the mask against the tree trunk, onto its face, revealing the rough-hewn backside. It was not unusual for the artist to carve the reverse of a mask with less finesse than the front. After all, most were lined. But not Charbon's. And the irregular cuts of the wood only emphasized the strange, scratchy enchanter's mark in the lower left quadrant.

"Do you know what causes enchanter's marks to look like this?" she asked Thibaut.

"For the foreseeable future, let us assume I know next to nothing about magic," he informed her.

"Sometimes magic doesn't go in cleanly. Have you ever been to the Museum of Dark Times? Seen the bastard inventions there? Only two of them are actually enchanted—deemed harmless enough not to go into the vaults—but you can see it. We see it all the time, on dangerous pieces. It's the mark of someone who has either gotten something wrong . . . or taken over after another enchanter. Magics don't mix well."

"How would the enchantment know? Isn't magic an equation? I mean, it's like baking—like chemistry. Three parts this, one part that, et cetera et cetera."

"Why does an enchanter's mark appear in the first place?" She latched on to the riddle, using it as a clear lens on the dark few hours previous. "We don't know. Some enchanters think it's a sign from the gods, that they approve. That's why it's sometimes called a creator's kiss. But either way, if two enchanters work on the magic—not the same item, mind you, the same *enchantment*—it's two people trying to pour the same water at the same time—you end up with a mangled mark, because it's trying to be two marks at once."

"So, Charbon's mask was enchanted by two people."

"Yes. But that it worked is . . . When sanctioned enchanters have tried it, most often the enchantment doesn't work. It ruins the materials, nullifies the magic."

"But don't you know who enchanted Charbon's mask?"

"One of them. Eric Matisse. He was hanged for it—confessed to it, actually. It was always presumed the mark was garbled because he was in a rush. He had to sneak into the prison mortuary to finish the job, so everyone thought his measures off and the enchantment distorted. No one put on the mask to test the theory, of course. And *we* know his recipe was at least clean enough to preserve Charbon's knowledge of human anatomy and the blooms. But the Watchmen who captured Matisse never could figure out how he'd gotten in to do the job—how he could have even been there, since he was in an asylum at the time. What if he didn't finish it at all? What if he started it, but was never at the prison? Perhaps it was someone else."

"The Prophet, you mean?"

She nodded silently.

"Good. Great," he said, still pressing into the junction of the roots, unsure the mask couldn't act of its own accord. "So, they knew each other. Fantastic. I suppose that means we should take a delightful little hop down to the archives and pore over old newspapers and enchantment records looking for a thread of connection between Charbon and any other enchanters of the time?"

He spoke with a cringing lilt—as though he could read her mind and knew she was about to do something incredibly stupid.

Krona didn't care. "Or," she said softly, leaning over him and trailing her fingers over the inside of the mask, "I could ask the echo."

"Well, it wouldn't know what happened after Charbon died, would it? That's ridiculous."

"Of course not. But it might know . . . enough."

Thibaut reached up, placing his hand swiftly over hers, stilling it against the wood. "If the Prophet is an enchanter, doesn't that mean he knows just about everything there is to know about masks?" he asked.

"Yes? So?"

"Then, shouldn't he, I don't know, be a master when it comes to echoes? And *still* Charbon overpowered him?"

"I've never met an echo I couldn't control."

"But what if you *can't*? With other echoes, perhaps that simply ends badly for you. But if you can't keep Charbon in check . . . people die."

"I'm not going to kill you, Thibaut."

"Oh, but the murderous echo, he might."

She didn't tell him the situation was even more dangerous than he feared. In order to pull memories from the personality, she couldn't suppress an echo the way she normally did. It wouldn't do to cage him off at the back of her mind. If she did that, she'd be left with only the knowledge the mask was enchanted in order to preserve.

She needed to know who he knew, understand who might want to continue his legacy. Which meant she'd have to let him swamp her, push back only enough to keep him from using her body like a puppet.

And she'd never purposefully toed that line before.

This was dangerous not because she wasn't sure she could suppress the echo, but because she wouldn't even try.

But what other options did she have? The Prophet had said it himself, his time was up. Now was the morn of his main event, whatever that might be. With De-Lia in tow.

Resting her free hand reassuringly on Thibaut's shoulder, she leaned down to whisper in his ear. "It's all right. Trust I know what I'm doing."

"You don't make it in my world without assuming *no one* knows what they're doing," he whispered back.

Carefully, she extricated her hand and the mask from Thibaut's weak grip. The mask was light—lighter than she remembered when she'd first pulled it from the man's face. Hefting it upward, she took a deep breath, ready to plunge into the murky depths of the echo's reality.

"Wait," Thibaut pleaded. "Don't make me watch. Let me leave. I can't be here if . . . I can't."

Frustration made Krona's mouth dry. She knew she had no right to keep him. But he'd been *there*—he heard some of what they'd said about De-Lia. *Seen* what they could make her do. Didn't he understand what had happened? Couldn't he understand why she needed him? "Coward," she breathed.

"You're right, I am a coward," he said without hesitation or shame, pulling himself to his feet. "A living, breathing coward. And I think you're reckless. You know what you should do with that mask. It needs to be locked away. You should turn the concern over to the Watch now because killers are their matter, not yours. Your job is finished—you don't have to do this."

"De-Lia is out there performing gods-know-what kinds of tasks for a murderer. And there's still the despairstone. So yes, I do." She brought the mask close to her face, near enough that her hot, heavy breath was reflected back at her by the bowl of the wood.

"Think of the law, Mistress," he pleaded. "You are not above the law. And the law says that mask is not to be worn—ever."

She laughed mirthlessly. "Ha. You, telling me about the law?"

He opened his palms, flicking his fingers out with a half-hearted shrug, trying to hold on to his typically casual flair despite the tension evident in his entire body. "Whatever works. This doesn't feel right, Krona. Krona—" He snapped his fingers and she realized her gaze had dropped back into the mask. "Krona. *Don't.*"

Had Thibaut ever said her first name before? She hadn't realized he knew it.

"If not me, then who? Tell me. Give me a way around this, a way to stop him, to know where he's going and who he's after and *why*—gods damn it, why is he doing this? Give me that and I will drop this mask over the palace cliff if that'll make you happy."

"This isn't about making me happy," he insisted. "It's about right and wrong, about what's dangerous, what's—"

"No. It's about decision and indecision. And I have decided. Leave if you want. I can do this without you." The croak in her voice revealed it for the lie it was. She wasn't sure she was strong enough to resist Charbon, not without backup. It was all too possible he would consume her exactly as Thibaut feared.

And it was a *mask,* meaning whatever she learned from it would only have a temporary home in her mind. One could remember what they *did* while wearing a mask, how they felt, but not the information that came from the enchantment itself. She needed a partner to ensure nothing was missed.

He turned to go, forming a taut line of resistance in the dim light. But then he threw his head back, grimacing at the sky like it might have the answers, a way out for both of them. "You know I won't go." When his eyes met hers, they were shinier than before. "Why can't I go?"

Because you're a good man.

Because you're a loyal friend.

Because we share more than either of us will admit.

"Because you don't want to. Because you offered me help before and you still want to help. Because your life is in information, and you'd never forgive yourself if you had the opportunity to see an illegal enchantment used firsthand and let it pass because you were a coward."

He chuckled at that, a laugh that lifted the corners of his smile. "This right here, this is why I like you, Mistress. Your audacity." Plopping down cross-legged in the hard dirt and thinning grass, he opened his arms. "If we're doing this, no sense in waiting. There's no such thing as sticking a toe in Hell."

She nodded as a stiff breeze slithered through the orchard, shaking the leaves in a parody of a snake's rattle. A foreboding omen, she knew. Nevertheless, she clutched the limp black ribbons and slid them around the thickness of her braids.

><+>–0–<+><

Meeting the echo was like colliding with a partner in a swift dance. Krona had expected anger, rage, a psyche so consumed with evil that it would rip at her mind to get inside. Most echoes that struggled wanted to embed themselves, needing a proper home of blood and gray matter in order to feel safe and still. She'd expected a killer's echo to be more violent than the others she'd encountered. What did it care if it damaged her in the process of taking her over? Why would it feel the need to be anything but forceful and vicious?

But that was not what rose up from the wood. It was not vile. It was not malicious.

But it *was* desperate.

It *suffered*. Even in death, even as a pale shadow of human thought, it suffered.

Krona stifled a sudden sob that rose in her chest like a bubble. Grief was the first sensation she encountered. Instinct told her to squash it, to tuck it away before the tendrils of another's feelings could wind around her, but she knew she couldn't do that. This time she had to give in to the echo. It wriggled and writhed and she wanted to dominate it, but the images blossoming in her mind did not disgust her. She didn't need to be brutal with the echo, didn't need to punish it to maintain control. It almost felt like it didn't want to seat itself inside her. Like it was resisting its very nature.

But it shouldn't have enough sense of self—enough conscious understanding of the fact that it *was* an echo—to do that.

Memories seeped into her mind and she let them come.

My daughters, she thought, and her heart swelled. They were on a playground, smiling.

My old master—a dark, hunched man droned on and on about organs, pointing at a water-colored chart.

The smell of pie, of too-hot filling and burnt crust, washed over her. Nanny never was good at baking.

Krona's insides twisted, insisting she push these memories away. *They're not yours, not yours, don't lose yourself.* But she took more deep breaths, remaining calm. When she felt herself slipping, forgetting where she was—who she was—she brought a memory of her own in front of her mind's eye:

De-Lia, perhaps thirteen or fourteen, with a washcloth in hand and a scowl on her lips. She roughly dabbed at Krona's face, wiping a smear of blood from her brow. "You shouldn't let them get to you," she said.

"I know," Krona replied, her little-girl voice sounding not at all apologetic. "But I did good, didn't I? I threw a punch, a good punch."

Young De-Lia smiled. "Just like I taught you."

"Just like you taught me."

Holding on to the sensations of her childhood, Krona flailed at Thibaut, fist grasping and ungrasping until she felt him place something scratchy and firm—a stick—in it. Caring not for the state of her skirts, she knelt in the soil, ready to scratch what she could into the carpet of the apple grove.

Chanting, *Like you taught me. Like you taught me,* Krona let herself sink further, finding the echo cowering in the recesses of her calm. It did not want to come out. It did not want to rule her.

"I need to know," she told it out loud. "Who was the Prophet? How do you know him? Show me."

Charbon resisted. He was confused. Just like she was unable to recall anything learned from a mask once the mask was off, so too was an echo incapable of remembering its time in someone's body. It didn't understand "Prophet."

"Then let's go back," she said. Charbon didn't feel like a killer, but he was. She knew that. He'd done terrible things, despite his meekness in her mind. "Show me why you did it. Take me there. Show me everything."

A tingling preceded the echo's acquiescence. It sizzled in her ears and in her veins, sending little pricks of sensation along her arms and into her scalp. Krona followed the buzzing, spiraling after it, chasing it inside herself. Down, down, down . . .

Into a coterie, in front of the altar of the Five. She kneeled, filled with grief, wondering how this could happen, how she could let her own son die.

And then there was a woman staring at her, tucked behind the cloister just there. She was pretty, and that was all Krona could think for a moment: *At least something in this world is pretty.*

><>-0-<><

The next thing Krona knew, the mask was being ripped away from her while Thibaut shouted in her ear and shook her.

"Mistress? *Mistress?*"

"No, no. It's fine. I had him." She blinked rapidly, trying to come back to now while holding on to Charbon's knowledge for as long as she could. His personality was already gone, blown away like a curl of smoke. All that remained were the blooms, and even they were fading. But she knew where to cut—could take the stick she clutched and turn on Thibaut and draw every slice along his torso.

For a moment she had the terrible urge to do just that. She could, so easily. He would be surprised, off guard. Krona could push aside his tunic and mark up his pale skin with all the places her scalpel could fall . . .

Queasy, she fell against the gnarled tree and retched. It was a dry heave, and it hurt her stomach.

"I had him," she repeated.

"But you were crying."

Krona patted at her cheeks. Sure enough, they were damp and puffy. Why had Charbon been so grief-stricken?

Her hand was balled in a painful fist around the stick. Her nails dug into her palm and she held the wood unnaturally; not like the imitation pencil she'd meant it to be, but like a knife. Letting it fall among the roots, she bent to skate her hands over the soil where she'd crouched, trying to make out the divots that formed letters. Five words stood out starkly in the crumbling earth, written in a hand Krona never would have recognized as her own.

Fiona.

Absolon.

Blue.

Magic.

Gabrielle.

"Did I say anything?" she asked.

The worried, wide-eyed expression hadn't left his face.

"Thibaut, was I speaking?"

"Fiona," he said, pointing at the dirt. "You said her name over and over."

Krona doubled over, clutching at her stomach. Flashes of bare bone and sweat and oils colored her vision red and yellow as the names of joints and tendons fled from her mind. Sometimes knowledge simply faded. Sometimes it oozed away. Charbon's vomited itself out.

"How could she?" she shrieked in a voice that wasn't hers.

39

LOUIS

Eastside canals, daybreak, ten years ago

Charbon awoke exactly where he'd fallen, arm still trailing in the water, with the skin of his wet fingers bloated and shriveled. His joints ached, and his entire left side felt stiff and frigid when he pulled his arm out of the channel to warm it against his body.

The air smelled morning-fresh, and the pale, dusky light of dawn surrounded him. He'd slept through the night.

Should I be relieved or disappointed that a Watchperson hasn't found me?

Strange snippets from the previous night gradually returned to him. Matisse had hit him, Fiona had scorned him. Together they'd threatened . . . what had they threatened, precisely? Something about a mask, and children . . .

By the Five, Fiona had wanted to move on to *children*.

With the first effort to rise, he simply flopped onto his back. The stones rubbed against his goose egg of a wound, and he hissed through his teeth.

"Why couldn't they have killed me?" he asked the pallid, empty sky. If it weren't for his family, perhaps he would have done it himself the night before. The water looked soothing, inviting. Ah, to sink into oblivion and let the current steal his breath and wash his essence . . .

But no water or oil or scrub could clean him now. His only hope for purification lay in anonymity—in being burned on a funeral pyre and then mixed with the sands in the catacombs to become one with the rest of Lutador's dead.

"Why couldn't they have killed me?"

Then he remembered: Fiona had promised something much worse. Something that, in her words, would "break him for certain."

She knew him too well. He'd tried to keep her at a distance, but those who murder together often learn a little something. Fiona knew where he was weakest. She knew which bones to break to send him into oblivion—and they weren't *his* bones.

Scrabbling first to his knees, then to his feet, Charbon clawed his way up the bank.

He was so far from home. Miles and miles, and Matisse and Fiona had hours on him.

A thin dirt accessway lined the sides of the channel, and he jogged along until it connected with a cobblestone road. His feet refused to lift more than a few centimeters off the ground as he moved, and he stumbled many times. Travel by foot was not his best option. He needed alternative transportation.

Patting his pockets, he looked for vials or time disks and found he had none. Fiona and Matisse must have robbed him as well.

A sharp whinny in the mist made him spin on his heel. Coming directly for him, like a creature out of a nightmare, was a big, black horse—its flanks already shiny with sweat despite the coolness of early morn. It pulled a giant cart, piled high with thick carpets and blankets, no doubt headed for the best shops and the finest homes.

Instead of rushing to the road's shoulder, Charbon met the horse head on. The cart's driver yelled at him, but he refused to make way. "I need your steed," he shouted when the squeaking wooden wheels ground to a halt.

"And I needed to get these fancy runners to Master Don's yesterday, but *need* doesn't equate *deed*, now does it?"

The horse remained steady as Charbon approached. *Good, it's not easily spooked.* He reached for its neck strap and it did not shy away. "It's a matter of life and death," he told the driver.

"Monsieur, you *look* like death. I can be generous. Hop on and I'll give you a lift to a hospital once my rounds are done. You can owe me later."

"I'm sorry, but I must have your horse now."

From beside him, the driver lifted a blunderbuss and pointed it at Charbon. "I'd rethink that."

"Can you light your powder before I climb up there and throttle you?" Charbon challenged.

"By the looks of you, I don't think you've ever throttled anyone."

The statement wasn't *that* funny, but the flippant incorrectness yanked a laugh out of Charbon nonetheless. Soon he was chortling like a madman, and the driver's gun hand had gone slack.

Drawing from whatever energy reserves he had left, Charbon catapulted himself onto the cart, clawing his way up into the seat. Surprised, the man dropped his gun—it most likely wasn't loaded anyway—and tried to scrabble backward, away from the deranged man. But the driver had no place to go except over the side, and Charbon wasn't letting him go that easily.

Fisting the front of his shirt, Charbon brought the man's face within inches of his own. "You've heard of the killer making flowers out of corpses? The papers call him the Blooming Butcher?"

"Aye," the man said, cringing.

"I can put an end to him, forever. But I need *your horse.*"

"What of my carpets?"

"Keep your carpets," Charbon spat.

Scooping up the blunderbuss, he stuck its barrel down the back of his breeches and demanded the flint and pellets. The driver hastily gave them over.

He unhooked the black horse from its burden and climbed atop. He was unaccustomed to riding barebacked, but not unskilled. With a give in the reins and a squeeze of his legs, Charbon urged the horse onward. A few light kicks and they were on their way.

As he rode, Charbon shook his head and patted his cheeks, trying to recall every detail from the night before. Fiona had said that the plan was hers all along. But that couldn't be true, could it? The Thalo and the Unknown wouldn't let a mere human dictate . . .

But she'd also tapped into the Unknown's magic long before the Thalo had arrived. That pen . . .

Had she really chosen Charbon to play murderer, not the Unknown? Had she told the Thalo of his skill and his loss? Could she truly have been manipulating him from the beginning? Had she used his grief to steer him toward her own mad goals?

Perhaps he never had been in service to the Unknown.

Was it possible? Had he been taken for a fool from day one? From the moment he'd stitched her leg at the coterie? Perhaps. But his grief, the loss of his child, she couldn't have anticipated . . . Unless . . .

Fiona had met his son, bundled and bubbling, his chubby hands clasping at everything offered to him—the collar of a tunic, a curl of hair, Fiona's well-manicured finger.

But that was the only interaction she'd ever had with the boy. She couldn't have . . . Could she have caused the baby's illness? Charbon had called it pneumonia, but only so as not to seem a failure as a healer when he had already failed as a father.

Could everything that had happened to him been designed by Fiona instead of the divine?

Bile rose in his throat, but he forced it down.

He rode the black horse hard, pushing it to its limits. When he reached his small country manor, he took the beast to the door.

At a distance, the home looked its usual quaint self: the thatching on the roof was fresh, if out of style—tiles were all the rage now. The windows were clean, and the decorative circlet of blue glass over the entryway shone cobalt in the sunlight.

But the front door sat gaping.

He dismounted, the horse instantly forgotten as he rushed inside.

"Una?" he called. "Girls? Una, it's me. I'm home."

All lay silent.

No nanny rushed to greet him. No nanny, no maid. Where was everyone? He kept a spartan household, but not this sparse.

The shelf near the entryway was typically lined with small porcelain figurines of mythological creatures. The board had been cleared, tipped over, and the figurines lay shattered on the floor. Kneeling, he picked up the remaining half of a Thalo puppet statue. It was mostly white, with a dusting of blue across the face and hands. Darker lines of blue patterned its robes. Part of him wanted to return it to the shelf. Instead, he placed it back on the ground and crushed it beneath his boot.

Turning the corner to his dining room, he smelled the scene before he saw it. There was death in this room. A small corpse lay on the table, opened up inexpertly.

He clamped his eyes shut immediately, willing himself not to look again. If he looked he would see who it was. Then he wouldn't simply fear its identity, he would *know*.

Dirty, shaking hands covered his face, trying to hold back the water, the snot, the spit that all came pouring from him. The skin of his brow and cheeks and lips contracted and twisted, and suddenly every part of him ached as though beaten. "No," he gasped, but there was no sound—there was no air in his lungs to give it sound.

He stumbled, his legs going boneless, and he caught himself against the decorative white molding around the dining room entry.

Blood raged in his ears, and he couldn't hear anything past the workings of his own body. His insides stormed, his vision blurred. He was *underwater* and *in the desert* and *buried alive* all at once.

He didn't want to know which daughter it was. It didn't matter. Would never matter. And it didn't matter to him if his other still lived, because most likely she didn't. Most likely she was elsewhere in the house, flayed open, right next to her dead mother.

There was no need to explore the house further. He was sure they were all dead.

But what if someone's still alive? What if they need help? He tried to reason with himself, but emotionally he was too far gone. It didn't matter.

Nothing mattered.

An abrupt panic slammed into him, and he clawed at the wall, raking his chipped nails across the wallpaper, leaving scars in the floral pattern. This house was death. Everything around him was death. And it was coming for him. Death would consume him soon, and it would be awful, painful. It would be an intense, exquisite, well-deserved pain. But he couldn't face it here. Not in this place, not where he'd been happy once.

Finding his footing, he sprinted away, through the front door and back to the horse. He rode into the city, blinded to the buildings and people around him. Charbon was trapped in his own mind, in his own suffering.

And what do you think the others felt like, hmm? he taunted himself. *All those people you killed, someone loved them. Someone died inside when you took their lover or their brother or their mother, just like you're dying now. A deathless-death. A torture as intense as the torture you wrought directly with your hands. You did this to so many others, and now your family suffers because of it.*

He didn't know where he was when the horse stopped and he slid off its back. He saw a familiar set of patina-covered steps and ascended, his legs moving automatically like a little steam-powered oddity. At the top, he entered the establishment like a drunkard, stumbling through the door and making a scene of himself.

Inside, all was cold and pale, covered in snow. No, not snow. Clean cottons, ivory paint. White. White like daisy petals. White like a baby's first teeth. White like a polished bone.

He'd made his way to the White Lily without realizing.

It was still early, so there were few patrons, but he retained enough wherewithal to note he was dressed improperly. The two women at the nearest table scowled, and a man tucked into a window seat whistled—he must have assumed Charbon was on a bender.

Without waiting for the hostess to seat him, Charbon stumbled to an empty table. It was the largest in the room, already set with eight collections of polished silver and pristine china. In the center was a bouquet of lilies and orchids.

Absently, he plucked one of the flowers from the arrangement and crushed it to his nose. The scent was sweet and soft, like honey, but it did not erase the perpetual scent of death from his person.

"Monsieur?" asked the proprietor, approaching cautiously. "Master Charbon? Are you ill?"

"No," he growled, wincing at the sound of his own voice.

"Perhaps you'd be more comfortable in a private room? The green room?"

When he didn't answer, she made to take his arm. He flung her away before fisting the tablecloth, clinging to it as though it were the only thing keeping him from slipping off the face of the planet. "I did it," he huffed. "All of it."

The two women who'd frowned at him rushed to the owner's side, helping her to her feet. Together, the three of them backed away, giving the madman his space.

"Don't you understand?" he asked, his voice rising in volume, if lowering in pitch. "It was me. I killed them. All of them. *I'm* the Blooming Butcher. Tell them to come for me. Tell the Watch. *Tell them now.*"

It was over. All over. The world had shattered and Charbon no longer cared what would happen to him. The worst had come to pass, and he was done. Gods or no gods, a universe that had produced Fiona could keep Fiona, but he was done with it.

"Just let it end," he cried.

40

KRONA

*I left Monkeyflower by the back door. I told her to stay, and to sit, and she did so. Papa al-
ways liked to whittle on the front porch. Do you remember? He made little dolls and farm
animals. Maman used to line them up next to the spice rack. I thought he would be under
the awning, but he wasn't. He'd been cleaning out the stove pipe, and since Maman had
gone to the market, was taking a whack at washing his own trousers. While I was searching
for him out front, he'd gone for the wash line. Out back.*

It was your screaming I heard first.

"What do they mean?" Thibaut asked, toeing at the words in the dirt, so that
the *A* in Fiona crumbled in on itself.

Fiona.

Absolon.

Blue.

Magic.

Gabrielle.

Though the early twilight was warm for this time of year, Krona's skin
prickled with gooseflesh. A chill wrapped itself around her heart and worked
its way up her throat. "I can't . . . hold . . . I don't know." Trying to recall her
time in a mask was like trying to catch smoke with a fisherman's net. It was
there, she sensed it, but it slid right through her consciousness, a spirit through
the ether. "Didn't I say?" She wiped at her face again with the back of her hand.
The tears were gone, but her cheeks felt stiff where the tracks had dried.

Thibaut had backed away from her, but it was difficult to tell if he meant to
give her room to breathe, or if he teetered on the verge of bolting. His expression
was cloaked—too shadowed for her to discern its subtleties. He shook his head.
"No. What you said . . ." His voice cracked. "Gibberish. Pained gibberish."

She swallowed harshly. "All right. I have to go back in—I'm sorry, I have to. He knows things. Important things. I was so close, I know it. I just have to give the echo more control."

The very thought went against every instinct she possessed, as both a Regulator and a magic user. She'd already put herself in his wretched mind once, had already come away with a strange desire to *cut cut cut*.

Staring at the bowl of the mask, she fingered the ribbons, noting how they shimmered like lines of oil in the low light. She knew why she hesitated this time when she hadn't the first. His grief had left her limbs like stones—with a tiredness she could not shake. She felt like she'd crossed a scorching desert in Xyopar at midday, only to be met with a bone-soaking monsoon in Asgar-Skan at night.

Even when her papa had died, she'd never known a sadness so paralyzing. She'd never wanted to simply *give up* before.

She'd never known there were things more terrifying than varger and murderers and De-Lia gone astray. But that feeling, that *void*—every fleck of her skin, and string of muscle, and hair on her head rejected the thought of another encounter.

To lose emotion, the ability to feel anything but devastation, was the most hellish state she'd ever experienced.

She knew now a hint of what it was like to die by the insistence of the despairstone.

A form moved beside her, shaking her from her contemplation. Thibaut took her wrist, halting the glide of her fingertips. "No. Not again. The den—we should bring your big-headed buddies into the chase."

Yes. Yes, of course. She slid down into the dirt, plopping herself heavily on her behind. "But what can I tell them? That I found the mask, but lost our captain? That I have no clue how to find her, save for becoming the very murderer we've hunted? That they might have committed the mildest of crimes that allowed all of this destruction to take place? You have to understand, it's as you said: this is illegal. The Martinets are already after us. De-Lia will lose her post after this, and once they find out I've used Charbon, so will I. I don't want to risk the rest of our detail. Because they won't tell me no. They'll tell me to do it. Doing it here, now, both protects them—gives them deniability—and gets us to the end faster. We can't afford to lose the time it'll take to get back to the den. So, please. Please help me."

She studied the words again. Why Absolon? The echo meant the great leader, not someone for whom he was a namesake, she was sure. Charbon had scribbled the name once or twice instead of *death is art*, but did it carry more weight than they'd suspected? Fiona and Gabrielle were people the echo knew.

And "magic" was obvious. But "blue"? After tonight, it could only mean one thing.

"Ask him about the words he wrote," Krona instructed, looking once more down into the concave interior of the mask. "I'm counting on you, all right?"

Thibaut fumbled for a protest. "There's a reason an echo's testimony doesn't mean anything, isn't there? It's not allowed in court because—"

"Thibaut," she said curtly. "This is my sister we're going after. Stop wasting time."

"Fine. *Fine.*"

Instead of sitting across from her as he had before, he swooped around behind her, lowering himself tentatively. She realized at the last moment that he meant to cradle her, and she slid away. "What are you doing?"

"He had you thrashing before. Stole your legs and everything. I'd rather not watch that again. You certainly don't have to accept my support, but you don't have to pretend to be so gruff and strong all the time, either."

"Sometimes pretending is the only way to make it real," she said.

"It is real. Accepting my help doesn't take away any of your strength, is all I mean."

With a cleansing sigh, she settled down, scooting in between the V of his legs and pressing her back into his chest. He planted his boots firmly against the ground, corralling her in with his legs. He also took hold of her upper arms, mimicking the way he'd held her in his apartment. But this felt different. Where it had been a coy gesture before—a feign of control—this time it was caring and protective. She allowed herself to accept the comfort, to melt into his body.

Yes, she needed Thibaut to bear witness to her time in the mask, but she also *wanted* him here. Pursing her lips, she began to lift the mask to her face and stopped abruptly. "Thank you," she said, tilting to look at him. "I know I forced you into this, but thank you."

Thibaut smiled softly, but there was no real joy to be found in the moment, not with De-Lia on the loose and the two of them within an inch of mayhem. Maybe the echo would be less gentle this time. Maybe it had only been lulling her before. Thibaut slid a hand under Krona's, helping her raise the mask. "No flirting, Mistress," he said gently, "now is not the time."

Instead of tying the ribbon for her, he simply pressed it to her face, ready to rip it away if he thought her in danger.

For the first time, Krona found herself truly wishing that the information gained from a mask wasn't temporary, that she could look inside the leftovers of Charbon's personality and really *know* him. When her psyche collided with his, she recognized him as a misunderstood man. A lost soul that had never had the chance to find himself. He'd done terrible, terrible things, and yet she pitied him. He was evil, and he was sad: one did not negate the other. He deserved his condemnation, and even his echo suffered in penance.

Once again, their dance was gentle, but difficult to balance. He pressed, she pulled. They both needed to be here, and they both rejected the coupling. Krona often experienced doubt, a fear of failure. But those feelings were nothing compared to the self-loathing Charbon possessed.

He'd died angered, injured, and humiliated. There was so much despair in his echo Krona felt like vomiting. If he hadn't been hanged, Krona was sure Charbon would have taken his own life.

The echo had to get to know her all over again, to trust her. From the instant the wood caressed her face, the remainders resisted consciousness. It didn't want to be alive—this one sought the everlasting peace of death like no echo she'd ever encountered.

"Ask," Krona gritted out. She was using all of her energy to stay steady—stay herself while not suppressing Charbon. She tried to remember what the words had been, why she was here, but it was difficult to focus on anything outside of the echo's constant undercurrent of *hate hate hate, need to rest rest rest*. "Ask him," she pleaded.

Thibaut pressed closer, like he could fortify her bones by being near. "Tell me about Absolon," he said.

Words spilled from Krona's lips, and she only consciously understood half of them. Words about the time tax, and betraying babies, and *magic magic magic*.

"Gabrielle?"

My daughter, Krona screamed internally, anguished beyond belief. Flashes of a small, broken body swamped over her, stealing the air from her lungs, smothering her with their visceral clarity.

She coughed and sputtered and weakly banged her fist against Thibaut's knee, pushing at him, trying to force his legs away.

He didn't know what to do for her, but refused to let go. "What? *What is it?*" When she didn't speak, he took it as a sign to move on. "Fiona?"

Krona gasped as if bursting from beneath the surface of a lake. *That name.*

That name meant everything. It was the evil in the world, it was the sun and the moons, it was the awful of the universe and the power and the beauty and he lived and breathed and died by that name. "Fiona," Krona said, her voice dark and heavy. "Fiona . . . Gatwood. Fiona Gatwood."

As the echo spoke with her tongue, Krona shuddered internally. Gatwood.

She knew that name. Where had she heard it? She dug through her own memories, trying to keep them separate from the ideas the echo fed her, but it was difficult.

With the force of her entire will, Krona suddenly clamped down on Charbon's echo, walling it away. She needed to *think,* damn it.

But she immediately recognized her mistake. Pushing the echo away only let the knowledge inherent in the mask surge into her mind. *Cut. Break. Heal. Take.*

She screamed and pulled away, jerking like a wild horse. Bucking, she knocked the mask out of Thibaut's hand and it went flying out into the twilight, smacking into a tree trunk before falling lifeless to the ground.

For half a beat, they both sat stone-still in shock. Krona's breath stuck fast in her chest, unable to escape for a millisecond too long.

"Gatwood," she gasped. "I said Gatwood, didn't I?"

Krona mentally kicked herself, willing the strange high that was echo-possession to wear off. "Oh gods," she said when the pieces settled into place. "He works for the Iyendars—you might have even met him before. A Horace Gatwood." Her body still clung to the revulsion that Fiona Gatwood had provoked.

She didn't know what it meant, but the two Gatwoods were connected, she was sure. Horace had been a shadow behind the memory of Fiona. Everything was jumbled, and she had nothing firm to go on—no facts. Nothing but instinct.

And instinct told her to run. To make for the Iyendars' estate as quickly as anything could carry her—as though Time had given her wings.

The warrants. Because of De-Lia, the Prophet knew they were preparing the warrants. And he'd said something about taking his prize away.

If Krona and Thibaut had been in that cellar all night, and it was near morn, then . . . Wasn't there something special about today? Day ten. Something that was supposed to happen at the Iyendars' . . .

A wedding.

And the bride was pregnant.

"It's *her.* He's after her. Melanie."

"Melanie? Melanie Dupont? *Leiwood's* Melanie?"

"Yes. I don't know why Gatwood wants to kill her, but I think that's what this whole ordeal has been about. He's going to . . ."

"Going to *what?*" Thibaut prompted.

"*Butcher* her."

"No. *No.*"

She glanced around at the trees. This orchard, she'd seen it before, she was sure. It wasn't far from the Chief Magistrate's estate.

"You have to go to the den," she told Thibaut. "Explain why De-Lia and I disappeared yesterday afternoon when the varger attacked in the city. Get Tray, get Sasha, get everyone. They'll listen to you, I promise."

Dear gods, please let them come. Let no puppet bar their path.

"How? Why don't you go? Why—why would they listen to me?"

"Someone has to get to the Chief Magistrate's house as soon as possible. But I need more Regulators, understand? Here, take this." She spun in his lap, reaching down her blouse to the inner pocket that let her keep her Regulation coin snug against her breast. It was a wonder the cultists hadn't found it. "They will know your name."

She held it out for him, wondering if he understood what it meant, that she was trusting him with her coin. He could sell it for a mountain of time. Could run off with it and retire from her trust and her employ.

She suddenly felt exposed and vulnerable. He closed his palm over hers, and she hesitated to let go.

"Don't you need this?" he asked solemnly.

"Not as much as I need backup. Tray knows about you, he'll know I gave it to you. He'll understand it as a sign. Please, *go.*"

Without another word of protest, Thibaut jumped to his feet. Krona rocked forward, not yet ready to lose the firmness of his body against hers. But in the next moment she was up as well, hurrying to the mask and securing it to her belt by the ribbons.

Perhaps she should have given Charbon to Thibaut, so that he could turn it over to the Regulators. That was her job, after all—to recover the Mayhem Mask, and she'd done that.

But she couldn't let it go, not just yet.

41

MELANIE

Now

The chateau was made all the more beautiful by the addition of white flowers and turquoise ribbons, which were strewn about in the haphazard fashion currently in vogue with the nobility. As was customary, the joining couple would meet in private beneath the folds of a silken wedding tent before the guests arrived, to exchange affirmations and gifts. Once their private vows were completed, the flaps of the tent would be drawn back and the couple would then pledge themselves as a pair to the community.

Only two people were supposed to be under the tent's awning at a time. Any more was considered bad luck. Even if more than two people were being united at the ceremony. Even if the third person was an unborn child.

Melanie didn't let the superstition bother her.

Not at all.

Her hands folded and unfolded in her lap while her mother worked on her hair. They occupied one of the guest bedrooms on the second floor of the main house. Clarissa spritzed a honey-scented toilet water about the room, letting the mist gently fall around the bride.

"These hairpins don't want to cooperate," Dawn-Lyn huffed, tucking one of Melanie's curls up and away before placing the joystone veil over her. "Are you sure you don't want to remove that ferronnière? I don't think anyone will be able to see . . ."

"No. No," Melanie said, twitching as the sharp, needle-like pricks of emotion-based magic gave way to a sense of ease and elation. An elation that she wished was her own.

Most brides were supposed to be nervous about their wedding night. As antiquated as the notion was, Melanie wished that were the source of her anxiousness.

But ever since the Regulators had alighted on the Iyendars' doorstep, a dread had swirled in her chest.

Dawn-Lyn took a thread and needle in hand, tacking on a few additional joystone beads to the cuffs of Melanie's dress so that they dangled against her arms. Each was a heavy droplet, cut to look like swirling water. After examining her work, she sealed it with a kiss atop her daughter's head. "There we are. Perfect."

Melanie smiled up into her mother's face. Dawn-Lyn's cheeks were full, her skin alive and flushed. She made a beautiful picture these days, so unlike the frail thing she'd been before Melanie had faced Belladino. No matter what happened to Melanie, whoever found out about the mark in the future, she would never regret what had happened, because it meant Dawn-Lyn was here, today, to witness her nuptials.

"Wait, one more—" Her mother noticed a curl out of place. "Hold tight." When the final bit of wire was set, Dawn-Lyn repositioned the tall, gilded mirror so that Melanie could see herself better. "Lovely."

"Most brides look lovely," Melanie said. The words were modest but the joystones let the truth of her pride ring through. She'd never worn paint like the noble ladies before, but the elder Madame Iyendar had insisted on a little coal around her eyes and a touch of extra pink on her lips and cheeks. The results were not unpleasing.

And the bright aqua wedding garb hugged her well. She couldn't wait to see Sebastian in his suit—she was sure it would cling to him in all the right places.

Excitement tickled up from her toes and into her chest. *Let the joystones have their say, let it ring true,* she told herself.

A knock at the door interrupted them. "Yes?"

Clarissa opened the door. Gatwood stood on the other side.

"I have a gift for the bride," he said. "If I might have a few moments alone to give it to her?"

Dawn-Lyn looked skeptical; she'd been the recipient of Melanie's Gatwood-centric complaints many a time.

"It's fine," Melanie assured her. "Why don't you go check that the tent is in order?"

Both Dawn-Lyn and Clarissa left, eyeing Gatwood as they went. "I'll be right down the hall," Clarissa said, clearly trying to give Melanie an easy out should she desire one.

Melanie wished her master were here. Gatwood had always shied away from him. But he was down in the garden, coddling a constantly delirious Fibran.

Watching Gatwood saunter into the room, an arrogant grin on his lips, brought Melanie back to a day when he'd worn a similar quirk of the mouth, brandished an equally insincere bow of the head. The day when she'd realized that coming to him for help had been a mistake. Well over a year later, and here he still was, standing in front of her, still behaving as though he had honest claim to her life.

"You look beautiful," he said sweetly, gesturing up and down her form. "Reminds me of my wife on our wedding day."

Melanie forced herself not to demur. She narrowed her gaze, trying to discern his true meaning in the compliment.

"Oh, don't look at me like I'm some perverted old codger. I only meant you remind me of fond days. You've often reminded me of my Fiona, from the moment I met you. No, the physical resemblance isn't much, but the spirit. Self-reliance lit her from the inside out. No one could tell her no, or keep her at bay. Like you, she was an individual of strength and purpose."

Gatwood rarely spoke of his wife. A clipped comment here, a brief remembrance there. Despite her wariness, she let him continue. Perhaps there was more to Horace Gatwood than a slinking, stalking ex-enchanter.

Letting his hand fall, clutching it to his chest, he said, "Of course, she didn't have the fortitude of mind that you do. She wasn't well. There was a time she spent in the asylum just over the border, to the north. Do you know of it? No? Frightening place, but we had no choice."

Wistful sadness sloped his brows, giving him a frail appearance. Melanie nodded at the ottoman behind him, gesturing for him to sit. Pulling her skirts around her, she likewise dropped into a thin wooden chair. "You've never said before."

"She was at the asylum for a bit before we were married. She met a man there—I never much questioned their relationship, but I should have." He looked out the window. "I'm sorry. I never thought there was reason to tell you all this. But it feels right, now. You need to hear it before . . ." He trailed off, his gaze becoming distant.

Was he truly taking a fatherly approach? Melanie wasn't sure. She'd been so long without her own father, this kind of territory felt foreign. "Sebastian would never hurt me," she said, still uncertain as to what he was getting at. "Gods know he's had occasion to get out of this many times . . ."

Her voice broke, echoing Gatwood's incomplete thought. She curled into herself, instinctually raising one hand to her stomach. Joy still pulsed through her, but couldn't change the trajectory of her thoughts.

As she shifted, Gatwood's hands twitched, as though they wished to go to her belly as well. "I was to have a child once. It was after Fiona's second stay at the asylum. The healers assured me she was well. She'd had to go back because there'd been a mess with her—her lover. The one she'd met there before. Eric Matisse, his name was. Brilliant *Teleoteur*, but twisted. He'd been hanged, you see. And she couldn't take it. But the healers had wanted to get her well as soon as possible, so that she could come home and . . . and give birth away from that place."

Only the joystones kept Melanie from sharing his revulsion. Tentative, she lay a comforting hand on his. "Was it—?"

"She always insisted the baby was mine, yes. Perhaps it was, and that's why she—" He pursed his lips, as though holding back the words would hold back the truth. "She came home, but she was *not* well. She continuously babbled to herself about looking deeper. *Sooner,* she said. I didn't know what she meant. She wasn't talking to me when she spoke. But that word has stuck with me: sooner."

"You don't need to go on," Melanie assured him. She had a hunch what came next, what his wife had done—why Gatwood was childless. There was no need to say it. Why did he need to say any of it?

"It's important that I tell you this. I thought everything could pass without me offering you an explanation, but I've known you too long. And I didn't mean for it to be now—not today—you have to know that. But I've lost . . . It has to be done soon, or never at all. Soon."

He was babbling. Maybe it was the tension in the air, the anticipation of the ceremony, that had brought these memories to the forefront for him. But it would not do to have grieving on her wedding day. Melanie wouldn't stand for it.

Though her mother had been so careful with the pins, setting the veil just so on her head, Melanie pulled it free. Without asking for permission, she draped it over his shoulders, making sure the joystones came into contact with his neck and hair.

"You are too good, Little Splinter. That makes this very difficult."

"I'm not going anywhere," she said, wanting to put a bitter twist on the words—to allude to his blackmailing—but finding she didn't have it in her.

He nodded. "Yes. Of course."

Pings of laugher bubbled up from the garden below. Gathering her skirts about her, Melanie tiptoed over and peered out. The acres and acres of the Iyendars' rear yard sloped down and away from the house. A wide swath of lawn a hundred yards from the veranda now sported dozens of white chairs, lined up facing the turquoise wedding tent. Brilliant flower gardens encompassed the lawn, and beyond that, the borders of the estate were marked by deciduous trees and a white wooden fence.

It was the perfect place for a wedding. Naturally beautiful, with plenty of room for mingling and dancing with the fifty or so guests they'd invited. The Chief Magistrate had taken it upon himself to invite a few more at that, and soon she'd be hobnobbing with well-known healers and chemists from all over Lutador.

Master Iyendar had been a magnificent employer. Had been good to her as a person. When the Regulators had asked if she felt safe in his household, she knew they'd been asking about him specifically.

Most of the guests hadn't arrived yet—that would come much later. Now, her mother and Sebastian's aunt—his late mother's sister—stood chatting near the tent, directing the Iyendar staff here and there with ease. Dawn-Lyn had never had the chance to manage anyone before—not even Melanie had been under her mother's bearing for very long—and now she was taking to it with surprising ease. "What's the saying, like a duck to water?" she mumbled.

A small gong rang out and everyone on the lawn turned toward the rear entrance to the main house. The priests had arrived. It took five members of the clergy to marry a couple, and Melanie and Sebastian had opted for the traditional set—one to represent each god. They flooded into the ritual area wearing all white, each with a different-colored scarf wrapped tightly around their necks. The Unknown's priest wore a white burqa, and in lieu of a scarf, a purple mandala was woven into the top of their headpiece.

Everyone bowed as the priests passed.

"It'll be time soon," she sighed.

Gatwood shuffled over to stand beside her. "Yes." His gaze settled on her with a boiling intensity—she could feel it burning across her cheekbone and the bridge of her nose, but she did not turn to meet it.

"And then there's this," he whispered, still babbling, his gloved fingers stretching forward to ghost over her jaw. Though he didn't touch it directly, she knew he meant the mark. "Proof that we're bound. We needed to find each other. For so long after Fiona died, I couldn't understand what had happened, why she'd done what she'd done. Why she was lost to me. But it's become clear."

"You wanted to give me a present?" Melanie reminded him, awkwardly hobbling away from the window.

"Yes." From the inner pocket of his jacket he retrieved a small, white box. "It's the wrong color. Or perhaps the perfect color."

With an interested quirk of her lip, she lifted the lid while he held the box outstretched. Nestled in a bundle of finely shredded paper was a brooch set with the largest, reddest stone she'd ever seen. "Is this a ruby? But it's enormous, I can't accept this."

"You'll have to," he said. "Because you certainly won't accept anything that comes after."

A soft squeak of hinges brought her attention to the door. In stepped a woman, her skin dark and her head close-shaven. Most likely one of Sebastian's relatives who'd gotten lost wandering the estate. "You're early. There should have been someone downstairs to receive you—"

"Oh, she's *my* guest, dear," Gatwood said. "And Captain De-Lia Hirvath is right on time."

Abruptly, he took hold of Melanie's chin. Startled, she tried to pull away, but he held her fast, digging into the soft flesh of her cheeks.

"What are you—? Let me go," she demanded, striking out at his arm, knocking the box to the floor.

The brooch spun out of its container, bouncing across the carpet until it came to rest at De-Lia's feet.

"If you do not release me, *Horace,* I'll scream," Melanie warned. Fear should have overtaken her. Despite his advanced age, he was still larger and stronger than she was. But all she could feel was hatred.

How had she allowed him to draw even one ounce of compassion out of her this day? After all this time, all of his clinging and his stalking and his—

Her hands curled of their own accord, forming Cs like hawk talons. She would claw his eyes out if it was the last thing she did. She scraped at his wrist, tried to let her knees buckle to throw him off-balance with her weight. Her heart fluttered like a dove demanding release from a cage.

How was his grip so strong? Was it his injections? Could they really bolster his strength and stamina?

"I suppose you'll scream anyway," he said, shifting his hand to wrap around her throat instead. Pulling off his other glove with his teeth, he shoved it into her mouth, forcing it in, placing his palm over his jaw when she tried to push it out again.

She'd known he would do this—would do *something* to her, one day. Gods damn it all, she'd known. But both politeness and fear—of being found out, of bringing his violence to the surface—had kept her from telling the Iyendars, or anyone who might have been able to do something about him.

Not now, why did you have to turn on me now? Bastard, why couldn't you let me have my wedding day?

He swayed with her motion, but did not lose his footing. The line of his mouth had become hard, but his eyes carried sympathy. As though he considered this inevitable, something he had no control over.

Melanie couldn't turn to look, but she could feel De-Lia approaching. She cried out, screamed behind the glove for help, but she knew it was in vain. This woman had come to help Gatwood, to . . . to . . .

Gods, she couldn't even imagine what he might do, or what had finally made him snap.

De-Lia made a strange clinking every time she moved; it sounded like many bottles bouncing against one another. Something slid in front of Melanie's face—a blade, with the brooch and box balanced atop.

"Thank you, Captain," Gatwood said, scooping the jewel back into its case with extreme care. Clearly he didn't want to touch it. "Tie her up."

A white rag came from somewhere to encompass Melanie's head, making sure the glove remained tightly between her teeth when Gatwood pulled away. The clinking came again, and Melanie realized the woman had a pouch slung around her hip. Was she carrying time vials? The bottles within sounded somewhat larger, but that didn't matter at the moment.

"You touch me and I will end you," Melanie screamed at them, though all that came out were muffled yelps. "Sebastian will end you. *My mother* will end you."

Panic started to overwhelm her anger. As De-Lia laid her on the floor, forcing her face into the carpet, tears prickled at the corners of her eyes. Rough threads of rope caressed the exposed insides of her wrists.

Why are you doing this? All this time I thought something was wrong, but I never imagined . . . Why are you doing this?

As though he could hear her thoughts, he crouched down. "For a long time, I simply thought Fiona was deranged. She killed our infant daughter, just days after she was born. I told the Watch she killed herself after, but that's not true. I found her with the girl, and *I* killed her. She tried to explain. Magic, she said. Magic doesn't just come from the elements, she said. There's a fifth kind of magic. We know wood, and sand, and gems, and metal. But she said there was another. She said the fifth was pneuma, an undiscovered humor—the fifth magic is a human magic. But it gets taken. Stolen. She just wanted to see the magic before it was stolen, so she dug. Dug in our child."

Tears worked their way out of the creases of his eyes—small, but sincere. Gatwood wiped at his mouth and pulled at his hair. "Insanity, no? Everything she said was impossible. Just the ravings of an insane, murderous woman. Magic can't live in people. *People can't be enchanted*," he said pointedly.

"But then I met *you*. Fiona was long gone, but the proof of her testimony came to me. She'd said magic could live in flesh, and there you were. Maybe the Unknown god needed me to know how wrong I'd been to kill her, and sent you. I think they wanted to punish me for punishing her. And I thought if I continued her work, I might redeem myself. For a long time, I wasn't sure how to do that. I had you—my little splinter. The enchanted young healer. But I didn't know what to do with you."

He lifted her circlet from her head, slipping it through her curls, revealing the mark. "Despite this, I didn't know what to do." He dropped the ferronnière unceremoniously to the floor.

"That is, until I learned you were with child. And I remembered: sooner. Fiona had told me an insane tale, about how she'd been working with Louis Charbon. Do you know of Louis Charbon? He was a terror before you came to the city. A murderer. She told me how she'd directed him to look for the magic. But they'd had to go younger, sooner, *fresher*. What is fresher, Little Splinter, than an unborn baby? And you, with so much magic already. Surely your little one is the key. The proof. I can find in it what Fiona was looking for in ours."

A detached sort of horror fell over Melanie. Gatwood's words were ugly, obscene, but her mind couldn't force them into place. Here was the strange, clingy *Teleoteur* who had followed her to the Iyendars'—who had given up enchanting just to stay by her side, who had always claimed it was her safety that concerned him—telling her . . . telling her . . .

What are you saying?

He hadn't always been disturbing. Her skin hadn't crawled at first. But she thought back to every look he'd given her while they were both in service to the Chief Magistrate. Why hadn't she listened to her instincts? They'd cried out at her to get rid of the man, that something had changed and he was no good.

But now she knew he'd been no good from the beginning. He'd never wanted to help her. He'd wanted to use her, because of her magic.

Just as she feared, the mark had made her a *thing*. To the outside world she wasn't a woman trying to make her way, she was an enchanted object, only good for the power she brought to others.

He'd been manipulating her, waiting for the chance to subjugate her.

And he'd waited until it wasn't just her life at stake.

Now the horror hit her full force. She screamed and flailed, and he kept speaking while De-Lia held her down.

"My wife was the most talented enchanter I'd ever met," Gatwood said. "The only person I've ever known to be adept at all four magics. She could have been the greatest mistress of magic in Arkensyre's history. But she was impatient, sloppy. She didn't want to follow rules and regulations. She wanted to do whatever work she pleased. And she *experimented*. She had a workshop, and I shouldn't have allowed it. No new enchantments—inventions are forbidden, punishable by dismemberment—and yet I left her to her work because she was brilliant."

De-Lia stood, and Melanie turned her gaze to the other woman—*Captain*, he'd called her—pleading with her eyes, with her body. But De-Lia's gaze was distant and unfocused, as though she were lost in her own mind. Her hands worked without her soul's consent, that much was clear.

Gatwood stood as well, handing the captain the box with the gemstone. "Why don't you set up over there?" he asked her, pointing to the small table that only minutes before Dawn-Lyn had used to hold the hairpins and brush. "We'll prep her with the stone, make sure she's primed for the search. The puppets should be well on their way with the mask by now."

The captain set the box where indicated, along with the satchel off her belt, from which she pulled a bottle of pills, a few sharpened healer's utensils, a tiny syringe. She did not fully empty the pouch's contents, leaving Melanie to wonder what other horror had made the clinking sound.

"I've always wondered when, exactly, the Thalo came to Fiona," Gatwood said. "I didn't give her a chance to say. And I've never had the courage to ask it myself. When I pledged myself openly to the Unknown, that was when it came to me."

The mention of the deities caught Melanie off guard. Infanticide and blasphemous magic were one thing, but to talk of deities like they were here, in the Valley . . .

Until that moment, Melanie had held on to hope. Gatwood wouldn't be able to go through with it because she would make him *feel*. They'd been through much together, and he wouldn't be able to end her life. But if he'd broken bonds with reality, then all was lost.

"The Thalo informed me that Charbon's mask would be ready for the taking. And that it could make for me a puppet of a powerful individual." He looked lovingly at De-Lia. It was the same look one might give a dog— adoring, yet condescending.

"Come now, Captain. We should move her to a better spot on the floor. We'll kick these perfumes and nonsense out of the way, yes. I need more space, and we need to hurry; her family may return at any moment. You'll need to stand guard once we're ready." He flexed his fingers. "If it helps, Little Splinter, I know my hours are numbered as well. I doubt I will have my freedom come tomorrow morn, but they were going to haul you off to jail or the mines—potentially out of my reach—and I can't be the fourth prophet of the Unknown to leave this work unfinished."

The woman hefted Melanie into a standing position, ready to throw her over her shoulder—like a sack of flour, or a damsel in an old folktale—to haul her across the room. But then, from somewhere down the hall came a shout—"De-Lia?"—and Melanie was dropped, unceremoniously, down into a chair.

42

KRONA

Terrified, I ran inside, my young mind not yet connecting the dots. Terrible ripping and gnashing came from the rear door. Papa fought Monkeyflower as best he could. But he hadn't been expecting a varg at his porch. His quintbarrel was on the table.

Your eyes were locked on the creature ripping through our father. And you screamed.

Begging her to stop, I took up the gun. Monkeyflower continued her ravaging.

With tears blurring the world, I pulled the trigger.

The horse Krona stole was strong. When she and Thibaut split, she'd noticed the barn on the edge of a field and ventured inside. The animal was swift, and wonderfully compliant. She'd approached it differently than she'd approached horses before. She didn't like big animals, and so often she was jumpy around them, reluctant to interact. This time, she came to the horse sincerely and firmly. She asked it for its help, soothing it instead of herself. And it took her atop its back without protest.

As she rode, her muscles burned with its muscles. It kicked up dust in its wake. Sweat foamed on its brown flanks and she felt bad for the creature, but she had to keep pushing.

When she arrived at the estate, all appeared as it should and the sun had long ago crested the horizon. Ribbons fluttered in the wind along the cobbled approach. A man and the cloying scent of honeysuckle both greeted her at the door. He was a servant she'd interviewed while in full uniform and didn't recognize her. Nothing seemed amiss as he welcomed her in; he even ignored her harsh breathing and disheveled state. "The pair have not yet entered the tent," he informed her. "But you are welcome to wait out in the garden."

"Where is Gatwood?" she demanded. "I'm here for him."

"Last I saw he went upstairs," the doorman offered.

"Good. If you see him elsewhere, stop him. I must speak with him."

"Is something the matter—?"

"Watch the door for Regulators."

"Regulators?" he exclaimed. "What's—?"

She grabbed him by the collar. "Just do it."

Soon she was flying up the steps, taking them two at a time. Her blood gushed through her veins in a pounding rhythm, tapping out *hurry hurry hurry.*

"De-Lia?" she called, throwing open the first door. It opened to her with a *bang*, but no one was inside. She hurried to the next. "De-Lia?"

From a room not three doors down, an elderly man stuck his head out. "What is the racket for, child?"

Krona's breath hitched in her chest, but she tried not to show her surprise. Gatwood.

Gatwood, who was pale-skinned, who was old enough to have jaundice-yellow in his eyes.

Yes. Gatwood was the Prophet.

"Monsieur, you may be in danger," she said, reaching to place a wary hand on the hilt of her saber—only to realize she didn't have it. Not one scrap of her profession remained on her person; not her bracers, not a weapon, or reverb bead, or grain of salvation sand.

All she possessed were her wits and her fists.

Were they enough?

They had to be.

"Danger?" he gasped. "But there's the wedding—"

A clinking came from beyond him, inside the room. Then footsteps—like stomping. "You aren't alone?" she asked.

"No. Come in. Come in."

Though she sensed the trap, she followed him. The evidence was in his eyes. She knew that harsh squint, had looked into the dark flecks of his irises while he'd explained how he'd infiltrated the minds of her comrades.

And still her expectation did not fully prepare her for the wrongness in the room. The scene hit her like a punch to the diaphragm. De-Lia was there, as was Mademoiselle Dupont; Krona's sister holding a bound bride with a fist knotted in her clothes the same way she would hold a cutthroat—all rough-ness and no dignity. Melanie was resplendent, glowing in aqua colors like a water droplet in the sun. And though the captain had changed out of her Reg-ulator uniform and into her coterie skirts once more, she still had many of her typical accoutrements: her saber was free and flicking threateningly, her bracers—dulled and full of deep scratches—clung to her dark, muscled arms like a scarab's plating. At her hip, over the top of her worship skirts, was her quintbarrel holster. Her pouch, filled to bursting with bulky protuberances, sat on a table next to an odd assortment of what appeared to be healing items.

Under other circumstances, the tableau might not have made any sense. An elderly servant with a veil slung around his shoulders, an ornamented apprentice healer, and a half-dressed Regulator, all coiled together absurdly. They seemed like the setup to some silly joke. But there was no mirth to be had.

"Let her go," Krona demanded, putting herself between the trio and the door.

Her sister's face was blank. It was De-Lia, but it wasn't De-Lia. Krona knew every twitch and mannerism better than her own. She knew the shape of her and the sound of her and the smell of her. But now De-Lia held herself incorrectly. The captain's strength was always apparent, as was her stiffness, but now she held herself like someone with a secret. Someone trying to look at ease while wearing stolen clothes.

"I think we've been discovered," said Gatwood, clasping his hands behind his back and strolling to the center of the room, which was the twin of the nursery in size and shape, though not in furnishing. "I sincerely *don't* want to injure the master and his family, you must understand that. But there are great things on the horizon, things larger than you or I or one noble family."

"We need help in here!" she called, hoping someone, anyone, would hear.

No one answered.

"Call all you like," Gatwood said smoothly. "Even if someone did take heed, I have people in place to ensure I'm not bothered too much before my work is done. Makes things easier that way."

Krona pointed fiercely at her sister. "Where is the book? How is it that you're still controlling her?"

"Did you really think the Thalo's magic could be defeated by pulling a few leaflets free of their binding? This magic is old, and new, and borrowed, and . . ." He paused to chuckle. "*Blue.* The guilty and the sullen are the easiest to manipulate." His tone changed, became dark and incredulous. "Those with terrible secrets fall easily to the Thalo's will."

He sighed heavily, as though the situation were truly taxing and he wasn't in complete control.

"I have a job to do, you see. To uncover magic in its infancy—protomagic, if you will. This force resides in Mademoiselle Dupont, and I have no choice but to fish it out. If only I could make you see, Regulator, how noble my intentions. Then you would not lament the loss of your sister so. But, alas."

Magic. She'd written that in the dirt. Yes, Fiona and Charbon and Eric had been searching for magic, she'd said as much to Thibaut while in the mask. And something about . . . children?

This was why he'd been killing pregnant people, taking those at their most medically and emotionally vulnerable, because he expected to find this "protomagic" deep in their wombs.

But there was more to it than that.

Melanie was his intended target all along. His *true* target. Those other lives, they were just *practice* to him.

But why the apprentice? Why was Melanie—?

She noticed that the woman's forehead was bare for the first time, revealing a wound—raised and pink, like a new brand.

But the shape was intricate. Detailed.

Krona had seen a thousand designs just like it.

There was no mistaking an enchanter's mark.

Which was *impossible*.

"Captain Hirvath, my dear, you've got something special to keep party guests out of my hair today, don't you?" Gatwood waved a flippant hand.

De-Lia popped the clasp on her pouch and rummaged inside. From the way the items clanked together, Krona half expected to see vials of minutes, but the jar De-Lia drew forth was very different. Instead of small like a pill bottle, it was fist-sized and bulbous. A sickly green mist swirled inside.

A bottle-barker.

De-Lia was carrying jars of varger.

These weren't like the normal bottles in which the Watch kept the captured creatures—not like the ones she'd faced at the vaults. This was a repurposed preserves jar with a simple metal lid. Someone had put an enchantment on the glass to keep the creature contained, but it wouldn't take more than a flick of the wrist to release the contents.

De-Lia held the jar aloft, putting the ethereal varg on display.

Krona slipped sideways in her mind. Her bracers were lost to her, as were her weapons, and now her wits fled like so many spooked deer.

"Don't . . ." was all she could croak out. She meant to bargain and argue, had convinced herself during the ride that if she was confronted by De-Lia while the captain was still under the Prophet's spell, she could talk her down. But now the words abandoned her.

"You know what will happen if that monster is released," Gatwood said. "You know innocent people will die. And she has a handful more just like it. Do you want to see it rip its way down your sister's throat? I think not. So be a decent person and have yourself a seat, right there." He pointed to a wooden chair not unlike the one Melanie occupied.

The young bride was wide-eyed, desperate for Krona's help. Krona did her best to reassure her with a glance, to walk with her head held high and her shoulders back.

She didn't have a plan yet, but she wasn't about to take on the guise of defeat.

Gatwood seemed thoughtful for a moment, and Krona eyed De-Lia's accoutrements. Maybe she could rush her, get a swing in before she could raise her saber. They sparred often, and Krona had only ever been able to disarm De-Lia once. If she couldn't take her saber, perhaps she could get a hand on her quintbarrel. Or maybe even just one of her bracers. What Krona wouldn't give for a couragestone right about now.

She plopped herself heavily into the chair.

"Captain," Gatwood said. "That gift I had for Melanie, why don't you give it to your sister instead?"

De-Lia nodded and turned, scooping something off the table.

Yes, Krona thought. *Come closer. That's it.* She'd grab whatever she could manage. If De-Lia wasn't expecting it, Krona thought she might be able to knock her over.

De-Lia approached Krona slowly, leading with the bottle-barker, holding it before her like a shield. Krona cringed away, trying to blot it out, to look past it.

Focus. Focus. Both of her hands are occupied. Her saber is on the table. You can—
—but what if she drops the bottle? What if it breaks?

What she didn't expect was for De-Lia to plop the bottle-barker *straight into her lap,* to let it rest on Krona's knees. Within, one ethereal eye roamed frantically. Krona nearly kicked out, but the fear held her still. She shut her eyes, willed herself to be calm, to ignore its presence—but that was nearly impossible.

It wasn't until she heard the rattle of a jewelry box that she realized exactly what the false prophet had in store for her. What De-Lia held in her other hand.

Her eyes shot open, just in time to see De-Lia scoop the despairstone brooch from its bedding and jab the needle deep into the flesh of Krona's breast.

Instantaneously, the emotion stone shoved its threads of feeling into her, more violent than any emotion stone she'd ever worn before. The thread wasn't just demanding, the pain wasn't a simple piercing. It was as though the thread were lined with thorns, tearing their way into her chest, through her insides, coursing around in her rib cage until they found her heart and squeezed.

She'd thought she could buy time, that if she cooperated for a few minutes it would give her a chance to formulate a plan. But there was no thinking now.

The despair in the stone was a thousand times stronger than the void she'd felt from Charbon's mask. That had been a secondhand sorrow.

This was her own. A pit that ate itself. A hole in her soul so deep it could never be filled, so all-consuming she was lost—desperate and alone in her own mind. She cried out in loss. Nothing mattered and everything hurt.

Nothing mattered and *everything* hurt.

"I know what you're wondering," Gatwood said to Krona—he had no idea there was *no room* for wondering. "Did I use this on the others? Yes. I killed one woman once, and I'd vowed to never do it again. Better they go by their own hands. And I had intended to gift it to Melanie. But I think"—he turned toward Mademoiselle Dupont—"I must accomplish this last stretch myself. There is no reason to prolong my little splinter's suffering. I will own this deed as an act of mercy. Swiftness, in the name of the Unknown god."

Melanie began to cry, then to shriek behind her gag.

He addressed De-Lia. "Once your sister begs for death, let her do as her soul commands. Give her the options: needle, tablets, or blade."

His words were distant in Krona's ears, edged with a tin rattle.

Krona's failure today was pure regret.

Her life was regret.

All life was regret.

She could barely sense what was happening beyond the confines of her own body. Barely noticed when Gatwood thanked her and yanked Charbon's mask from where she'd tied it to her belt. Could barely comprehend when Gatwood scooped Melanie into his arms—throwing the healer over his shoulder like a sack of potatoes—and traipsed around Krona.

He was fit, and fast—she'd seen the truth of that when she'd chased him into the torn-out building. He used his age to play on prejudices, feigning frailty, deflecting suspicion.

Though he might have hefted her like produce, vegetables never put up such a fight. Melanie thrashed for all she was worth. Beads ripped free of her dress and veil.

And Krona observed from a distance. She cried out for Melanie, for Gatwood to stop, but only inside herself. She was too far away from it all, too deep in the pit. And though she told herself it was the brooch, that she must resist, the pit swallowed her whole.

Down, down she went. She saw De-Lia slipping away from her in the cellar. She saw Madame Strange, who may have been drug-addled but had certainly not deserved to die. Krona sank past the body of the third bloom, then the second—Hester—who she'd failed to protect. Who was simply trying to look after her own health and a man had killed her for it. Then came the first bloom, drifting by as she fell deeper. If only she'd held on to the mask at the Jubilee, the victim would still be alive. They wouldn't have been nameless, wouldn't have suffered so. And the master archivist, and the dead at the party—

The *varger* at the party. It was her phobia that had caused all this trouble . . .

In a snap, Gatwood was gone out the door. And Krona sank into her despair, finding herself in her most terrible memory, reliving it in excruciating detail, far, far away from the here and the now. Trapped in her own original sin.

It was all her fault.

▷·◁▸·○·◂◁·◃

The farmhouse felt snug. It was warm outside, the sun shining but not blazing. Maman had gone—was it to town?—and Papa had opened all the shutters to let the gentle breeze blow in. He never did like shutters, or glass—they didn't have any glass in the windows because Xyoparian windows didn't have any glass, and they were Xyoparian in heritage, just not in place, he liked to say. Thick oiled cloths were hung over the windows instead of shutters in Xyopar.

Krona toddled around the house—picking up spring leaves and petals that had blown in. They were all kinds—from cherry trees, and apple trees, and redbud trees, and all sorts of trees she didn't know the names of. She wasn't sure what she was going to do with the leaves yet. Maybe sew them together and make a necklace for Lia. Lia had given her a daisy chain bracelet only yesterday, but it broke already. Some things were just fragile that way.

Krona's little mind told her something wasn't quite right. She saw things from an odd perspective, from below, like she wasn't very tall. The chairs in the kitchen were too big, and she could see the underside of the table without bending over. She couldn't possibly reach the wash bin on the counter. But she *was* tall—she was grown. Why was everything so big?

No, that wasn't right. She wasn't grown at all. She was small. A young bean, Papa liked to say.

This . . . this happened. Already.

No, it hasn't. Lia calls that déjà vu.

"Are you in here, De-Krona?" Papa asked, coming in off the front porch.

"Yes, Papa," she said, holding up her collection for him to see.

He had a hefty jaw, hidden in a thick black beard. And his dark, strong

features framed shining eyes that were always smiling whenever he looked
down at his young bean.

Playfully, he plucked a cherry petal from her cupped palms and flicked
it against her nose. The soft, smelly bit of flower tickled, and she giggled.
"Where's De-Lia?" he asked. "I promised your maman I would get feed in your
bellies before she got back."

"She went exploring," Krona said, tossing her find on the table before
climbing into one of the wooden chairs, which groaned and rocked on uneven
feet. "Told me I had to stay here," she explained with a huff. She hated getting
left out of Lia's adventures.

On the table sat Maman's special teapot, next to Papa's armaments. His
needle gun and his special syringe for sucking up vapored varger. It was funny-
looking—round like a bulb, with a nipple instead of a needle on the end. The
teapot and the Borderswatch gear were odd next to each other, two things that
did not belong together, yet lived in harmony.

"You keep your behind planted right there. I've got to finish up my washing,
then I'll see if I can find your sister. She's got to be getting hungry at this hour."

"Yes, Papa," she said obediently.

*No. Tell him no. Scream and cry and pound your fists on the table. Throw
Maman's teapot. Try to play with his quintbarrel. Anything to keep him inside.
Anything to keep him from going into the garden.*

"Good girl," he said, kissing the top of her head and patting her curly hair.

She arranged the petals and leaves in front of her in a half circle, looking
for the most pleasing pattern. Humming a little tune she'd written herself, she
barely noticed as the hinges on the side door, right off the kitchen, squeaked
open.

I don't want to see. I can't. I can't stand it. Don't make me see this again. I can't.

She stopped her song for a moment, dryly sobbing. Confused, she shook
herself, then began to sing again.

Then she heard it for the first time—a deep, resonating growl. An unearthly
sound. It sent a shiver through her little body before her mind even registered
she'd heard it at all.

"Krona!" Papa bellowed.

She turned—both swiftly and slowly to her own mind—to the open door.

Thump, smack!

Her father collapsed under a mound of quill-like fur, half in, half out of the
house. He kicked and punched and the heap on top of him just pressed down,
down, down—

A foul, pungent odor filled the air.

"Krona!" he shrieked again. "The gun! My gun!" His face snapped in her direction as one giant, clawed paw descended on the side of his head. Frantically, he yanked one arm out from under the creature, reaching for her, fingers outstretched, palm open. "My gun!"

The mound of fur turned then, jaws and snout and eyes all focused on her. Sickly green slime dripped from its jaws, onto Papa's temple, and its gaze bored a deep-deep hole into her being.

She went cold. Her body became very distant.

And she *screamed*.

One long, continuous shriek. It seemed to go on forever, coming through her and living outside her, filling the air with pure, unadulterated terror so intense she felt both like her limbs were made of stone and like they were unraveling like twine. She couldn't move, couldn't stop screaming, couldn't do anything.

"Kro—"

Papa's entreaty died as he did. The monster's gaze left her as it delved into her father, massive jaws clamping down on his windpipe and tearing upward, yanking his entire throat away from his spine.

Another scream joined Krona's. De-Lia had come in from the front of the house, just in time to see the grizzled horror. But hers wasn't a wordless call of primal fear like Krona's. Hers was anguished in a different way, filled with sorrow. "Monkeyflooooower!"

De-Lia's hands were on her own temples—squeezing, pressing, just like the padded foot on Papa's skull. Her face contorted into the most pain Krona had ever seen on a face—more so than Papa's now. Papa's face was more surprise than pain.

And then De-Lia saw the quintbarrel.

Krona suddenly gagged, halting her cry. The air smelled of bile and blood.

Determined strides brought the elder Hirvath sister to the kitchen table, and her hand found the gun easily. She leveled it at the monster, barely shaking, with tears streaming down her face. "I'm sorry!" she shouted, pulling the trigger.

►·I·◆·O·◆·I·◄

Krona wanted to die. Swiftly. Like her Papa. But not like her Papa. Not like that at all.

That word: Monkeyflower. She hadn't recalled that was what De-Lia had said that day. Even when Gatwood had said it in the cellar, she simply thought it a control command, a secret word unlikely to be spoken by unwitting company.

But what did that matter? What did anything matter?

"Kill me," she groaned.

She wanted to die. And she would end it if De-Lia wouldn't.

De-Lia didn't move. Krona could only vaguely sense her sister, but she could tell she hadn't moved.

You could use the bottle-barker, she told herself. *Let it fall to the ground. Let the glass shatter. It would be fitting. Papa died because you couldn't give him his gun. Because you were too scared. Die now by varg. It would be ample penance.*

But, De-Lia—

What about De-Lia? Better you both die. Life is suffering, better you end it for the both of you. Then you never have to think about how you killed your father, ever again.

But, Melanie—

Something in her stirred. Something not tragedy and despair. Something not fear and self-loathing.

There were people who needed her. People who would die without her.

Better they—

No!

She squashed the voice.

You can do this. Suppress it. Suppress it like you do an echo. Compartmentalize it. Wall it off. The despair is false. No matter where it comes from, despair always lies.

If she'd been alone, if no one she cared about was in danger, if no one she felt responsible for were in danger, then she might have given in. The despair was thick, and deep, and unyielding. Part of it told her they would be better off without her. But she knew better. She *knew.* They couldn't be, because they needed saving. Her emotions couldn't lie to her about that.

The despairstone could tell her how to feel, but couldn't erase this certainty.

Why hadn't De-Lia killed her yet? Offered her the trio of death yet?

Krona tried to remember the exact phrasing Gatwood had used before leaving. Maybe De-Lia's directions had to be specific.

"I'm begging," Krona said, latching on to the words. "Begging for death."

There. The captain strode to her side. "Which do you choose?"

Krona blinked at her, struggling through tunneled vision. Something was different about the scene. The pouch on the table was deflated, most of its contents emptied—to where?

She tried to take stock of the room, and then, shuddering, she realized what had changed.

The captain had placed more bottle-barkers around Krona's chair in a parody of a sacred pentagon. Six varger in all—one on her lap and five on the floor, within easy kicking distance.

Bits of them manifested in the bottles, distorted, pressing, trying to get at her. An ethereal claw, a bulging eye. Gnashing teeth. A jawbone only half covered in flesh.

Now fear fought with the despair, her vargerangaphobia demanding she give herself over to it. The numbness the despairstone had flooded her with gave way, if only for a moment, to the hot iron of panic. They were too close—all of them. The varger were closing in, pushing at her seams, ready to slither from the bottles and barrel their way down her throat and up her nose and around her eyeballs, dissolving her insides.

Then the panic shifted, and the fear fed the despair, demanding she ask De-Lia to slit her throat, to take her saber and slice into her before she had to suffer the torment of being eaten from the inside.

Why had she ever thought she could fight this, that Utkin might be able to help? The fear was too big; it swelled inside her like a tumor, consuming all the healthy flesh, the parts of her that were well and strong.

Fight it. Fight it! she raged at herself.

"De-De-Lia," she groaned. "I can't . . . we need . . . to help . . . each other."

Just as Krona was locked inside herself by the despairstone, so too she wondered if De-Lia was locked away, able to observe but from an impossible distance. Was it like in the cellar, where she'd seemed aware of the circumstances once unshackled?

Krona thought it was the combination of circumstance and training that gave her moments of self-awareness while lashed to the stone. Perhaps the same could be said of De-Lia. Perhaps they could each stave off the magics long enough to toss them away.

Another overwhelming surge of void and sorrow enveloped Krona, like a torrent intent on drowning her. Her fingers found their way to the bottle in her lap, the corded muscles in her forearms tense with the alternating desires to smash it to the ground and toss it as far away from her as she could, hoping to escape before the vapors could burgeon and come after her.

Wrestling with herself, she stilled her hands, drawing them away from the glass with effort. Krona had to bring De-Lia around before she no longer had the capacity to avoid her own suicide.

I will not give up on you. I will not give up on us, no matter how insidious this magic.

She knew in the back of her mind that all she needed to do was rip the despairstone from her flesh, but as her hand traveled to it, as she touched the ruby with bare skin, the stone shot new tendrils into her palm, stabbing, rending, slithering along the bones of her fingers and down her forearm, freezing it in place. She gasped, her lungs stuttering. She'd only made it worse.

"De-Lia . . . help."

Her sister snatched the bottle from Krona's lap, body shaking, tension rolling through her in waves, as though pulling her two places at once.

Without answering, De-Lia's grip tightened on the jar, her fingers straining as she shook, suddenly angry. With a feral roar, she catapulted the jar directly into the wood floor, smashing it into hundreds of tiny pieces.

Krona cried out—weakly, breathily.

Apparently De-Lia thought her sister had made her choice: death by bottle-barker.

The monster expanded, happy to be free, ready for its first meal. Swiftly, it took shape, the mist forming into a close approximation of its physical form.

It was over. They were doomed. Might as well give in.

Krona slumped in her chair, all the strength and fight draining away. Swiping her saber from the table, De-Lia turned to go, surely to find Gatwood and help him complete his plan—the murder and mutilation of one Melanie Dupont.

But Krona couldn't let her go without saying something. Anything. *I love you. I hate you. I miss you. It's not your fault. I forgive you.*

When she parted her lips, an *I need you* on her tongue, the image of little De-Lia crying out as she saw their father devoured flashed into her mind. And when she spoke, the strange word she did not understand tumbled from her mouth. "Monkeyflower."

Halting mid-step, De-Lia turned, face blank. Krona wasn't sure what would happen now. In the cellar the captain had gone into a frenzy, fighting everything that wasn't Gatwood. Would she do the same now?

"The stone," Krona pleaded, voice barely a whisper. "Get rid of the despair-stone."

The varg swelled, adjusting itself to freedom, growling, pleased as it realized it could burgeon without coming into contact with painful enchanted glass. It hung like a poison curtain before Krona's chair.

De-Lia's features hardened with determination. She stomped back to her sister, raising the sword.

Krona was sure she'd made a mistake. The last mistake she'd ever make.

The blade came down, the point of it just missing the delicate skin of Krona's collarbone. The flat of it hit her hand where it clutched the stone, knocking it away, forcing Krona to tear the brooch from her chest. The ruby slipped from her fingers, tumbling to the floor, skittering across the boards until it stopped with a *thunk* at the base of the window.

Krona screamed now, as the horrid threads unwound themselves, tearing through her muscles and heart just as painfully on exit as they had on entry.

With the despair gone, the fear flooded back in, sloshing around her gut, making her nauseous. She stumbled out of the chair, tripping over herself and collapsing to the floor as she made an awkward, yet successful attempt not to touch any of the other bottles.

Think of what Master Utkin told you. The shard inside you has to shatter—you have to feel the terror and let it shatter. But she wasn't sure she'd ever believed him.

I can't, I can't, I can't. It's too big. It's too much, she railed.

This was no man in a suit. This was real, and unrestrained. She wanted to collapse, to throw her hands over her head and rock back and forth and simply wish it away.

But she wanted to throttle Gatwood even more.

Because of that, this fear was different. It had sharp edges, where her anxiety usually left her fuzzy. This time she wasn't driven by the urge to run away, but the urge to run *toward* something: Gatwood, Melanie. She had to survive, to get out, not just for herself, and not just for De-Lia.

She would overcome the fear if for no other reason than to see her fingers wrapped around the Prophet's throat.

But she would never make it out alone. She had to act, *now*.

Her hands flew to cover her nose and mouth, knowing the varg could eat her that way—would inevitably try to shove itself down her throat. But her fingers wouldn't be enough. There was no way to weave them tightly enough.

She pulled the purple scarf from her shoulders—the one De-Lia had given her to cover Pat-Soon's mask—and tied it around her face so that she could barely breathe. For a moment she felt like she was suffocating—her heart raced wildly, trying to deliver more oxygen even though she was denying her lungs.

The varg, spoiled for choice in terms of food, looked between the sisters, hackles raised, sizing up its prey. The creature wouldn't make a move until it knew it could tear into one of them.

It swirled instead of paced, watching, waiting for the opportune moment to charge for a face and slip itself down a throat. With a low, breathy rumble, it licked its insubstantial teeth.

Krona scrambled upward, her insides inverting themselves and wriggling like a wet mass of worms.

The varg inched toward her, perceiving her—rightfully, Krona thought—as the weaker of the two.

What to do? How to contain it?

The fear was still there, still heavy, but she would work through it. Too many people were counting on her.

A fear of failure overrode all else.

She thought back to the day she'd just relived—the terrible moment when their papa died. De-Lia had saved her then. Her sister had come to her rescue, despite the varg. De-Lia had gripped the quintbarrel in her little fingers and shot. She'd acted when Krona couldn't.

Now it was Krona's turn. De-Lia had saved her that day so that Krona could save everyone else here and now.

Lifting its snout and tilting its head, the ethereal varg scented the air, eyeballing its target. Realizing Krona wore a mask, it quickly turned from her. De-Lia stared blankly at the monster, face and body lax. She made no attempt to cover her nose.

"We have to do this together, Lia. I need you to hear me. Not just listen, but really help me." *How do I get you back?*

De-Lia made no further move to ward off the monster, and it hovered nearer. The stench of it filled the air—stale, like dried sweat. The odor would become more potent once it had a meal, edging closer to fresh death and open wounds.

"Hey," Krona yelped at it, waving her arms weakly above her head. Her limbs felt like overdone soba noodles. "Me. You know I'm easier prey, come to me."

It rounded its half-formed visage on her once more—the ridges of its skull showing through the vaporous bits of its wraithlike flesh. Saliva dripped from its jaws and vanished before the drops hit the floor, floating away to become part of the whole again. It seemed to sneer at her, enjoying the stalk as much as the meal.

Krona latched on to the one thing she'd seen Gatwood use: a trigger word.

"Monkeyflower," she said again. The word burst from deep in her chest with the force of a needle from a quintbarrel. "Monkeyflower."

Her sister doubled over, clutching at her temples, digging her fingertips into her clean-shaven head. *"Krona,"* she whimpered, the name high and tight in her throat.

It couldn't have been the name, so perhaps it was the despondency with which De-Lia gasped the word—whatever it was, the bottle-barker swirled in on itself. Its face disappeared between its hunched shoulders, turning away from Krona only to reappear facing De-Lia, whose every line and movement was the badge of a weakened animal in distress.

"Yes, it's my voice," Krona said. "Listen to my voice."

"Krona, I didn't mean to. Papa, *I didn't mean to.*" De-Lia's eyes flickered violently behind her lids, occasionally flashing the whites.

The varg advanced, closing the distance between itself and the elder Hirvath with the pinpoint focus of all predators who know they are one leap away from a sure thing.

For a moment, the world stilled.

Krona's mind snapped to attention, clearing aside the sticky vestiges of fear with the rebound.

It can't have her.

This singular thought rerouted her adrenaline, moving it through her muscles and commanding them to *move* instead of *still*.

With blood pumping true, joints turning solidly, arms and legs and hips and chest in actionable alignment, Krona sprinted across the floor. She skidded around the cloud, stumbling in front of it, pressing herself into her sister's space, facing her, grabbing her by the shoulders.

The moment wouldn't last, she knew. Her lungs drew a steady breath one moment, and stuttered the next. Just a few more seconds and the whirlpool of clarity in the lake of terror would twist itself into nonexistence.

The varg growled at her. The reverberation seemed to come from the walls and the floorboards, rather than the monster itself. Clearly, it was tired of waiting.

Tendrils unfurled off its back like creeping vines searching for a handhold. They stretched for Krona, twisting and coiling, running up her spine to curl around her rib cage, her chest and arms, slipping up her throat toward her nose and makeshift mask.

"Monkeyflower," she said again, ignoring the prickling of her skin. A full-body shiver racked De-Lia. "It's me. It's your sister. Listen to me. I know I'm not your master. *No one* is your master. I understand why this word gives him power over you, but you are going to take it *back*. Monkeyflower."

"No," De-Lia said weakly. "Don't. Please."

Had Lia ever sounded so childlike? It turned Krona's stomach. "Monkeyflower. I'm going to keep saying it until you do. Monkeyflower."

The bottle-barker's morphing form molded itself to Krona's back, the weight of it almost nonexistent, but the *smell* of it—Krona fought her gag reflex. She shook her head as one of its tendrils prodded too close to the edge of her mask.

"Shut up," De-Lia pleaded.

"Come on. Tell me," Krona commanded. "Why monkeyflower?"

"Don't say it. *Never say that name again.*" There was only a hint of force behind the demand, but it was there.

"Why? Who is it? What is it?" When De-Lia didn't answer, Krona shook her, gritted her teeth and hissed, "Monkeyflower."

"She ate him," De-Lia screeched, her eyes popping open. She shoved Krona, pushing her into the swirling cloud.

The green mass of varg chittered with glee as it washed over Krona. Only moments earlier she would have screamed, inviting the varg in with a gaping mouth, unable to stop herself. But now she was calm. Her fingers went deliberately to her nose and mouth, pinching both as she held her breath.

She could sense it sliding beneath the fabric of her tunic and the layers of her skirts, searching for an alternate route to her lungs. Everywhere the vapors alighted, her skin itched as though covered in ants.

You can't hold your breath forever. It will find a way.

I don't have to hold it forever. Just long enough for De-Lia to come out of herself.

Say it, she willed. *Say the name. Be your own master, De-Lia. Say the word.*

She could do it. Krona was sure. This would work. De-Lia had never let her down. Never.

Say it.

SAY IT.

De-Lia seethed, her shoulders rising and falling with the animalistic gasps clawing out of her chest.

Gods damn it all.

Krona let go of her mouth. "Fucking *say it!*"

The varg's vaporous jaws closed around Krona's head from behind, snapping in front of her eyes and over her nose. The creature gargled its delight as its tendrils found their way under the mask, wormed between her teeth and oozed across her tongue. Her saliva sizzled as it was consumed, like the first foaming of an acid bath.

Krona didn't think about the sour pain, or what was happening to her. Instead, she zeroed in on one surprise sensation. The misty dregs of the monster tasted so . . . *human.*

"Monkeyflower."

Krona could barely hear De-Lia. Vapor stuffed up her ears and gagged her throat. Already her esophagus was dissolving. Her gullet itched, then burned, then ached, then—

"Arrrrghhaaa!" De-Lia let loose an incomprehensible battle cry as she sliced across the varg with something shiny.

It shrieked—the otherworldly howl of a demon in pain.

The long, ropy lines of its feelers yanked themselves from Krona's mouth, dragging spittle and bits of flesh. Krona fought the urge to vomit, knowing the sear of stomach acid would only make the damage worse.

She'd done it: put herself between a varg and her family and lived.

But the struggle was far from over.

Sweat dripped from De-Lia's temples, splattering on her boots and the floor. The gleaming something in her hand was five somethings—five quintbarrel needles, one of each type. She lashed out again and again, cutting a clean path through the ether each time, but the bits of barker always swamped back together.

It hissed and spit and spiked its hackles. Then it transformed, becoming tendrils, slithering away from De-Lia and her needles. Away—toward the window.

The varg poured its essence into the pane, covering it over, bathing the room in a sickly green hue as it diffused the light. Swiftly, it probed the sill and seams, looking for a way out.

"No!" De-Lia cried. She shoved her hands into the vapors, needles in both fists, scraping the metal along those same seams, warding it away from whatever cracks and gaps it might escape through, if only for a moment.

We need to contain it! Krona thought, coughing, throat raw. There was blood on her tongue. She was sure there was blood on her teeth. She stumbled over to the table, still scattered with healers' implements.

She fumbled for De-Lia's pouch just as the varg decided to take another crack at the captain. It spiraled away from the glass, up, up to the ceiling, before plunging down again, attacking De-Lia from the top, whipping around her in a vicious wind. De-Lia crouched down, covering her nose and mouth with her skirt.

Krona's fingers found exactly what she was hoping for: De-Lia's containment bulb. Not even Gatwood was so far gone that he'd bring bottle-barkers into play without a way of gathering them again.

"What kind is it?" Krona shouted, voice a harsh croak. The metallic nipples that allowed the plunger to pull each type of varg into its barrel were attached to the containment bulb by fine chains.

De-Lia understood. She shifted the quintbarrel ammo, holding one in her slashing fist while keeping the others in reserve. First, she brandished a gold needle, but the varg did not respond. She tried silver, then bronze. It blustered away from the bronze needle, the mist losing its shape and vibrating angrily.

"Mimic," she said.

Krona attached the proper nub, slapping it into place. With a deep, painful breath, she advanced. The fear burgeoned the closer she got, her steps becoming more difficult. But she pushed herself onward. She'd already faced this varg once and lived. She could do it again.

De-Lia crouched down, getting as low as she could while the varg raged like a storm, howling like a manic wind.

With her own howl, Krona plunged into the swirling vapors, arms covered over up to the elbows. The bottle-barker burst outward, covering both Hirvaths, asserting its dominance, giving them a taste of its greatness and its wrath.

One hand firmly on the bulb, and the other on the plunger, Krona pulled. Capturing a vapored varg was no easy task. It was tough work, like pulling on a pillar instead of a plunger. Krona felt as though she was trying to separate two halves of a solid stone with her bare hands.

The varg struggled, clawing at her, manifesting talons to scrape at her face and arms. It did not want to go back. It wanted to eat, to be free, to slip out the window and the door and roam through the wedding party.

Krona would not let that happen. No matter how terrified she was, how her muscles shook and her bones ached, she would not let this varg consume one single person.

Its claws caught her under the jaw and at the nape of her neck, trying to dig deep as she pulled it into the containment bulb. Little by little the vapors diminished, swirling inside the enchanted glass where they belonged. And still it held fast for as long as it could, lashing itself at Krona as she yanked at it with the plunger.

One more roar and she was done, the vapors were contained.

Vibrating with adrenaline and fear, she tossed the containment bulb to the other side of the room. The enchanted glass did not fail or break.

Krona threw her arms around De-Lia, whose own body was racked with shudders. De-Lia looked up at her sister, her face solemn.

"Monkeyflower was . . . was its name. I didn't mean to, I was so young and so stupid and—"

Krona knew what she was saying, what she was admitting to. Somehow, Lia had brought the varg that killed their papa into their home. "I forgive you," she said quickly, her voice a rough grumble.

"But, I—"

There was no time to discuss it, no time for De-Lia to explain herself or divulge the entire story. So Krona skipped to the end. *"I forgive you."* Even if the creature had come to them by De-Lia's overactive hands, it had torn through their family because of Krona's indolent ones. "I should have—"

"No. No. It was never your fault, Krona. I should have been braver. I should have told you what happened years ago, I shouldn't have let you waste one minute thinking it was your fault. I've never forgiven you because there's nothing for me to forgive. Forgive yourself."

"Only if you'll do the same."

De-Lia's lips thinned and her eyes watered. She looked up at the ceiling before lassoing an arm around Krona's neck and pulling her in to kiss her forehead. She nuzzled into her little sister's hair, allowing herself a moment to cry.

"We need to go," Krona said softly, stumbling over to snatch Melanie's fallen circlet. She gripped it tightly, fists straining around the metal, before securing it to her belt. "The cavalry should arrive any minute. We'll block the room off and send someone up to gather the bottle-barkers once we've taken care of Gatwood."

"Agreed," De-Lia said. Krona helped her stand, then the captain quickly gathered her pouch and supplies.

Krona wanted to ask her about the mind control. How had Gatwood found her? How had he dragged Monkeyflower's name from her to use it as a trigger? What had she written in that book with the blood pen?

But right now, Melanie and an estate full of wedding guests needed saving. There would be plenty of time to work the hows and the whys out later.

43

MELANIE

The nightmare day that was her wedding

Melanie had never been one for cursing, out loud or to herself. But one thought kept cycling through her skull as she bounced along in Gatwood's arms.

I'm going to kill the son of a bitch.

It was an odd thought, despite her circumstances, because the joystones in her dress sleeves were still attempting to do their work. Her chest swelled and her limbs felt light, but because of the underlying anger it all seemed disgustingly sweet, like a candy one has eaten too much of.

"Almost there, Little Splinter, don't you worry."

She'd shouted for the Regulators upstairs to help her and they'd been useless. Now, as Gatwood swooped down the staircase to the main floor, she screamed her lungs out. But the glove in her mouth kept her muffled, and most of the guests were already in the yard, observing the blessings. She wondered where Clarissa had gone—if one of Gatwood's "people" had gotten rid of her—and if her mother was all right.

Surely by now Dawn-Lyn would have started to wonder why Melanie hadn't twirled her joyous self into the garden.

And Sebastian—he'd be alone in the tent. She imagined the plushness of the fabrics and throw pillows, many woven through with iridescent blue-green silk from the wild silkworms in Asgar-Skan. Sebastian would be sprawled across them, his long body relaxed and waiting.

When she failed to slip in beside him, what would he do?

He wouldn't think she'd fled without him. They'd already exchanged their private declarations the night before. In their minds, they were already married. The wedding was a sparkly formality, a way to make a pretty memory, nothing more.

It wouldn't take long for him to realize something was wrong. He had to know nothing but a tragedy could keep her from him.

She stared down at the heels of Gatwood's boots, his shoulder digging into her abdomen below her ribs. When they hit the foyer, she saw a cape edge out of the corner of her eye.

Thank the gods.

More squirming, more shouting. She expected the squeak of soles against the polished marble as someone ran to her aid—but no. Lifting her head, she watched a man she did not recognize casually approach.

"All clear, Jaxon?"

"The indoor servants were posted where you said. They've all been dealt with."

"Good, good. That should leave myself and Mistress Dupont undisturbed for a while. Post men on the veranda, make sure no one comes inside. They can make up whatever excuse seems reasonable."

"Yes, Prophet. Where will you be?" Jaxon asked.

"The kitchen," he said frankly. "I don't want to make a mess of the master's home."

Melanie did her best *not* to dwell on what he meant.

Through a few narrow halls, past the sitting room and the reading room and the second receiving room, and all the way to the left-most wing of the main building lay the stairs that descended to the galley, the less refined of the estate's two kitchens. The staircase was short, to the point. No one wanted unnecessary twists and turns when they were carrying large trays of hot food. It dumped them into the large room within a few bouncing strides.

Lining the white plaster wall on three sides was a long counter. A knife block stood near a farmhouse sink opposite the main door. Melanie, having been down here for many a meal, instinctually looked for it. Perhaps she could get away, get hold of a blade. She'd butchered enough chickens and deer to know how to use one effectively. But she'd never had to . . . she'd never cut a person with anything other than healer's scalpels. Her gaze turned to the outside door, used for serving the family meals alfresco. It was shut, the drapes that framed its small window pulled tight.

A broad butcher-block island occupied the center of the kitchen, scratched and stained from years of use. Unpeeled potatoes and carrot tops littered it in piles. Gatwood shrugged her off his shoulder, throwing her half onto the block, knocking the wind from her lungs. Remnants of whatever the staff had prepared for the wedding dotted the surface, and the wood smelled of fruit and butter. When she rolled away, bits of flour and crumbs clung to her. Something sticky smeared across her upper arms, while grease slicked her wrist.

Fighting the joystones, she did her best to contain her elation. The rope was slippery now—with lard or butter or moistened soap. It gave her a chance.

Pushing her down with one hand, Gatwood used the other to sweep the block clean. The potatoes and pieces of carrot thumped to the floor.

Melanie's own fists dug into the base of her spine, making her back bow and her shoulders ache. Breath held tight, she wriggled on the wood, sliding herself away from him. The joystones on her sleeves scraped against the stone, a few breaking free, stealing little bits of her false emotion.

Gatwood still held her veil around him like a shawl, using it to fight off his true feelings.

"Ah-ah," he tittered, looping his arms around her waist, slamming her firmly onto the center of the block. Her bound hands punched into the small of her back as she gazed up at the ceiling.

"Let me go," she said through her gag, knowing the words were garbled and would most likely fall on hardened ears even if she was articulate and true. "I can help you."

As he yanked the mask from his belt loop, she tried to roll away, but he caught her with a firm hand. His eyes found the same knife block she'd noted earlier and he hurried to it, selecting a long ham knife. He inspected its edge, his white eyebrows rising appreciatively. "Chef does an excellent job caring for her tools," he said.

Kicking out, Melanie scrabbled backward along the wood as he strode toward her. "No. Gatwood. Gatwood, *no!*"

His fist came up and the blade came down.

The knife held her fast, stopped her slide, but did not sever flesh.

He'd embedded the point deep in the block, pinning her by her skirt, right at the side of her hip.

Hurriedly—wise enough to realize he couldn't keep the upper hand forever—he tied the horned mask to his face. With a strained cry, like he was lifting some giant stone, his spine bowed. The tension in his body only held for a moment before he stood straight again, fully himself.

White wooden teeth sneered at her above a dark gape of a mouth, black tongue coiled within. Brows more sinister than Gatwood's slanted down at her over narrow eyelets. Garish zigzags covered the nose and cheeks, snaking their way up the mismatched horns.

Now Melanie needed the joystones. She relied on them for her sanity.

What in Time's name does he need a mask for?

"As I said, I'm sorry it had to come to this, Little Splinter. But you are a gift from the Unknown, and I'm not about to let you slip away because of a weak constitution. I've seen enough death now, I'm sure I'm ready."

His white-gloved hands tore at her sleeves, ripping away her remaining life-lines. He knew the difference between glass beads and enchanted stones, and plucked the important bits with ease.

Each tiny jangle on the floor was like a needle in the base of Melanie's skull. The joy slowly ripped free, and where she expected to be overwhelmed with fear or anger, instead there was only sorrow fueled by failure.

She'd failed Sebastian. She'd wanted to give him a kind of safety and security in their new family that he'd never known growing up. But instead, she'd only brought him more worry and torment.

She'd failed herself. She'd sought to stand on her own feet, to have a life that was directed by her choices and not others', and now it would bleed away.

She'd failed their baby. It may have come into her belly unplanned, but it was loved deeply. They could have given it a good life. Now it would have no life at all.

"You've never known how important you are," Gatwood cooed, voice hollow behind the mask. "You will be well remembered. You will be the reason the people know of pneuma and its magic. They will build statues in your honor. Everyone will marvel and be grateful for your sacrifice."

He bent over her, and she lifted her head. One of LeMar's scalpels glinted in his right hand.

A protest settled on her lips, but she never got to spit it at him.

The was a rush of color—a form sliding into view behind Gatwood for the briefest instant before the valet violently jerked sideways, out of her line of sight. She yelped, more from surprise than anything else.

Something—someone—had hit Gatwood, taking him to the floor without warning.

Melanie tugged at her skirt and wrestled with the rope around her wrists. This was her opportunity, and she wasn't going to waste it.

Grunting came from the floor—Gatwood and another man.

Faster. Faster. Faster. She didn't know how much time she had. She didn't know who was on the floor with Gatwood. She didn't know if they'd come to save her—as she hoped—or if . . .

She stopped her mind-chatter. She had to focus on getting free.

Despite the slickness, the ropes chafed her skin. Her forearms and hands pulsed with a rawness, the quick blips of her heartbeat punctuating the pain.

As she pulled at her bindings, so she tugged at her skirt. Though the fabric was finely woven, with its heavy embroidery and high thread count, it tore cleanly against the knife's edge when Melanie threw herself from the block, tumbling over the side.

Her cheek smacked the cold floor, and her spine and shoulders gave sickening pops. Buzzing slung itself from one side of her head to the other, and when she tried to stand, gravity insisted she sit down again.

On the other side of the block, savage grunts still emanated. There came the *plathack* of a low cupboard being kicked open, and the subsequent metallic clang of mixing bowls strewn about by a wayward boot.

Bunching her fingers on one hand, wriggling despite her dizziness, she wrenched them through the ropes. The coarse fibers slid across her inflamed skin like egg whites cut through with sharp shells.

The outside entrance to the kitchen now hung open, door thwapping lightly in the subtle breeze.

Escape was within reach.

Whipping the sodden rope to the floor, she gathered her ruined skirts and staggered upright. Her calves burned as she prepared to sprint for daylight.

"Mel?"

No.

Sebastian.

Every bit of Melanie's insides turned to dust and settled into heavy drifts in her feet. Sebastian's strangled entreaty staked her to the floor as surely as the knife had held her to the butcher block.

She closed her eyes. Perhaps this was all a bad dream and she could wake. If she wished for it hard enough, maybe she wouldn't have to look over her shoulder. Or maybe Time would grant her a reprieve—make the hours flow in reverse so Melanie could make different choices and avoid this ugly horror of a wedding day.

But she wasn't asleep, and wishes were for children, and Time insisted on her favors only running forward.

With a heavy sigh teetering on the verge of a sob, Melanie glanced over the top of the block.

Sebastian sat in the V of Gatwood's legs, the ghastly grin of the mask pressed tightly against his right ear as the ex-*Teleoteur* watched her. Gatwood caged her fiancé in, with one arm across his chest and the other pressing the length of the scalpel against his neck.

"You know what happens if I cut here," Gatwood sneered. "You know how quickly this artery will pump all of his blood to the floor if opened. His own heartbeat will kill him—unless you do as I command."

In all her years of working near Horace, he'd never shown a lick of interest in true healing arts, notwithstanding his foray into pseudochemistry with mercury injections. The man could barely tell his brain from his backside when it came to anatomy. How did he know where the carotid artery was?

Gatwood's hand twitched and Sebastian flinched. A single drop of blood oozed onto the scalpel.

"Wait! Wait." Melanie held out both hands to stay him. "What would you have me do?"

"Get back on the block."

Sebastian's eyes trailed her as she inched across the floor. His throat bobbed with every gulp, bouncing against the blade's edge.

She had no intention of dying today. But, if she denied him, he would kill Sebastian.

If she tried to reason with him . . .

He was beyond reasoning, she knew.

And if she attempted to stall, she wouldn't have long.

What could she do?

"Little Splinter . . ." he warned when she did not immediately comply.

He thought her weak. He thought her a thing. He thought her easy to own and easy to command and easy to kill and butcher. She'd done nothing when he'd overstepped his bounds and stalked her to the Iyendars'. She'd done nothing when he'd dropped snide comments—when he called her that wretched nickname.

He thought she would keep on doing nothing.

And that was his mistake.

"Fine," she said, throwing pure defeat into her tone.

She would not let him take her, and he couldn't have Sebastian. They'd defeated Belladino, and now they would defeat his mask-maker.

She'd asked herself years ago what she was willing to do, how far she was willing to go to protect the people she cared about.

Now, she was about to find out.

Slowly, she reached the block and made to haul herself atop it. She lifted a knee, her torn skirt tangling, and she grabbed hold of the pinned knife, as though looking for leverage. Instead she yanked it from its place.

Melanie pitched herself off the block, flying toward Gatwood, knife leading, her entire weight pushing behind it.

During her "compliance" he'd loosened his grip on Sebastian, giving the groom space to scramble away now. Melanie came down hard in his place, thrusting the knife deep. She'd meant to hit his chest—truly she'd meant to kill him. But her awkward launch had foiled her aim.

The knife slid into his shoulder, tearing though muscle, hitting the joint—perhaps even separating it.

A dual howl erupted from his sternum. There were two voices intertwined. Melanie wasn't sure if echoes could feel pain or be afraid, but Gatwood clawed at the wood, sending long fingernail gashes through the paint despite his glove. He fell into the cabinets, thrashing among the upturned bowls, spine bowing and contracting, hips twisting.

Maybe she'd simply created space for the echo to gain control. To take hold of him just as Belladino had taken hold of her.

Before she could do anything more, Sebastian had his arms under hers, ushering her to the open door, thrusting her out and into the garden. "Come on, he won't stay down for long!"

Indeed, Gatwood was already scrambling to his feet, using the cabinets for leverage.

"How—how did you find—?"

Sebastian held her close, eyeing a pair of gruff-looking men headed their way from across the veranda. "Your mother sent me to retrieve the bridal tarts."

Bless her. Gods bless Dawn-Lyn.

And damn everything else in Arkensyre.

44

KRONA

I'm not asking for absolution. I know that's only something I can give myself. I want you to know the truth of what happened. It was my fault for trusting in something everyone told me was dangerous. Now this sin is being used against me. I can't be certain how . . . but I found time vials under the floorboards in my room—vials that shouldn't be there—and an empty varg jar.

And there are clipped voices in my head sometimes. They're hollow, like a memory. But I don't think they're from the past. It's like there's an echo in my mind, wanting to use my body, but I don't know how it got there or how to get it out. And that's not right, either. Whatever's in my head is alive, not some remnant of the deceased. I think . . .

I don't know what to think.

<hr />

Both Hirvaths dreaded what they might find at the bottom of the stairs. Would there be a massacre of guests? A long smear of blood across the white marble, where Melanie's body had been dragged?

It was difficult to tell how much time had passed while they'd confronted the varg. It seemed both like seconds and hours.

But all was calm as they entered the foyer. It smelled of canapés and fruit cocktails, but the scent had a phantom quality. The servant who'd greeted Krona was nowhere in sight. No wedding guests milled about. Perhaps they'd made their way to the garden to await the ceremony.

Krona noted the display of funeral masks in a nook off the entryway. One a plain wooden butterfly, one a poor approximation of a feminine face, and one a crow's visage cleaved in half. Traditionally, the masks of relatives that had passed were given a place of honor near the wedding tent, and it was strange to see them set so far away.

Her stomach lurched as she remembered she was no longer in possession of Charbon's.

Damn it all. Why hadn't she sent it to the den with Thibaut when she had the chance?

Large windows lined the back of the chateau. Waving at De-Lia to hold, Krona crouched behind overstuffed furniture and stone pillars, trying to assess the situation beyond without being seen.

She'd worried about chaos—and there it was.

The insulation in the Iyendar residence was excellent; it dampened out the screams.

The Regulators had clearly just arrived—thank the gods for small favors, and for Theodore de Rex. But they weren't the only armed people streaming into the garden.

Outside, a struggle raged on the veranda. The groom—whose fine doe-skin breeches and white silk blouse were streaked with smudges and torn at various seams—wrestled with two men. Jaxon and Kes. A dash of aqua raced across the lawn toward the billowing marriage tent a hundred yards away, followed by a pained-looking Horace Gatwood wearing Charbon's mask. Melanie, looking even worse for wear than her fiancé, waved her arms above her head, shouting something at her mother, who stood near the gaggle of priests with an ebony-skinned woman who must have been one of the groom's family members.

Guests shot up from where they'd been resting lazily in white folding chairs, sending the rows of garden furniture toppling into one another like ivory dominos. The Chief Magistrate whirled in place, his wife clutching at him, unsure of what to do. Upward of a dozen people scattered every which way—cockroaches revealed in the light. Where a moment before they'd been caterers or ushers, now they were revealed as Gatwood's goons. They attacked the guests where they stood, keeping them back, preventing them from running to the aid of the apprentice healer or her husband-to-be.

One of the cult members on the veranda—Kes—latched on to the groom, clinging to his waist from behind, attempting to tug him to the ground. In response, Sebastian ducked his shoulder and barreled into the second assailant. The three of them toppled down the gray brick steps, kicking and clawing in a heap of limbs.

"Weapon!" Krona shouted, her throat throbbing. De-Lia tossed her the saber, and she caught it neatly. "I'm estimating two dozen hostile cult members in addition to Gatwood." She looked back at her sister as the *click click click* of quintbarrel ammo gliding into its chamber tinkled in her ears.

"Flintlock in one hand, quintbarrel in the other," De-Lia said, flicking the quintbarrel's tumbler into place. She pulled the second gun from the waistband of her skirt. Needless to say, it wasn't standard issue.

"Gatwood give that to you?"

"Yes."

"Then we have to assume they're all armed in like." Krona flattened the pommel of her saber to her chest, taking a deep breath. "Ready?"

De-Lia nodded.

Just to be certain, Krona added, "You still your own?"

With a sly smirk, De-Lia clicked her tongue against her teeth before saying, "Monkeyflower."

Their boots flew across the expensive flooring, leaving scuff marks Krona was sure the Chief Magistrate would forgive. She threw open the glass doors, barreling through with De-Lia on her heels.

The three men still tore at one another, teeth gnashing and coming down on skin. It might as well have been a dogfight. Krona rushed to Sebastian's side, slashing his attackers across whatever vulnerable points she could reach: inside of the knee on one, lower back on the other. They both rolled away with garbled yelps.

The one with the bleeding knee—Jaxon—turned onto his back at the bottom of the veranda, hoisting a pistol. Krona wasn't but a few feet away; an easy target for a steady hand.

Thwap. Trigger finger flinching, he shrieked. A golden needle pierced the back of his hand, embedded through to his palm. He dropped his gun and wrung his wrist.

"Krona!"

Shielding her eyes from the sun, she turned toward her sister's call. De-Lia held her quintbarrel at the ready, tracking another cult member as he ran across the lawn. Vapors curled out of the gun's steam chambers. Finding her target, she fired. There was a flash as the chemicals that hyper-boiled the water charge ignited. Before the man hit the ground, she'd moved on with her sights. *"Melanie,"* she called, once she knew she had Krona's attention.

Both Sebastian's and Krona's heads swiveled toward the tent.

Two of the priests—those representing Knowledge and Nature—had revealed themselves as bad-faith actors. They held Dawn-Lyn, the remaining priests, and the other woman at gunpoint, while Gatwood shouted at Melanie.

No sooner had he laid eyes on his bride than Sebastian was off. Krona tried to stop him, to tell him to stay on the terrace with De-Lia, but he did not heed her.

Son of a—

Krona sprinted after, not far behind.

The grass was hewn low, but still maintained some of its early-morning dew. Bits of it fluttered up above the ankles of her boots, sticking to her shins.

The garden smelled fresh, clean—perfect for a wedding, inappropriate for a massacre.

The two fake priests raged at them while they ran, swiveling the mouths of their guns toward Krona, demanding she and Sebastian halt. When both failed to comply, they fired.

There were more cultists than Krona had anticipated—even with over a dozen Regulators pouring into the backyard, she wondered if they would be able to contain them all. How a valet had managed to gather such a brute force, Krona wasn't sure she'd ever find out. But Gatwood's men were untrained. They approached fighting as if it were a street brawl, and relied purely on their brawn. Clearly, they did not know their flintlocks only had a fair shot under twenty yards. Krona and Sebastian were still a good seventy-five away. The bullets petered out at fifty, striking the dirt ineffectually.

If she was lucky, they wouldn't discover their error until they'd exhausted their ammunition.

. . . Luck always did enjoy biting Krona in the rear.

Realizing they had no hope, Nature's priest pulled a short sword from the grass, tossing Knowledge's priest his firearm so that fey had two to keep trained on the prone captives. Hoisting the sword above his head, the false priest charged.

Moments later, distance covered, Krona met the cultist blade for blade, arms straining as the two swaths of metal collided with a *thwang*. She gritted her teeth and pushed back, using the slight incline of the land to her advantage.

Sebastian had already slid past. Krona didn't see where he ended up.

The cultist bared yellow teeth, his light tan skin cracking around the edge of his mouth. He had an over-wash of cologne—just like Jaxon—which stuck to her tongue, and she fought the urge to spit. His nose was so close to hers over the junction of their blades that she could see the pockmarks in his skin.

Krona parried right, pulling back to deflect his next thrust. She countered with a strike across his abdomen. He leapt away. Sneering, he swept in an arc around her, trying to find what minimal higher ground the lawn could offer.

She pirouetted with him, keeping him at her fore. Glancing up, she saw De-Lia leap from the veranda to shorten the range between herself and her targets.

The cultist caught Krona's momentary lapse. He thrust again, aiming for her soft underarm. At the last second Krona knocked the blow aside.

Focus.

A woman screamed near the tent. She ignored it.

A downward thrust sailed toward her throat, but she blocked it with a drag.

Her saber's length gave her time and distance. He had no hope with his rusted, bulky blade.

Another scream, this one curdled, and Krona's stomach leapt. She had no time for sparring. She needed to put the man down.

His arms flew over his head, muscles rippling as he stored energy for a chop.

He left his belly exposed. Despite his muscle, his flanks were well padded, just like hers.

The days-old wound in her side throbbed as she jabbed for his corresponding hip. The saber slid through his love handle like butter. Yanking the blade sideways, she slashed out his side. He did not scream, but he collapsed. His short sword toppled end over end. His hands both went to the blood gushing from the wound.

Gaze widening in shock, he looked at Krona as though she'd betrayed him. As though he never really thought she'd land a blow.

"You'll live," she spat, before spinning toward the tent.

Gatwood had Melanie on her knees, gripping her tightly by the hair, yanking her side to side. She clawed at his wrists, leaving bloodred lines. Sebastian stood before them with his hands outstretched, pleading. Dawn-Lyn lay facedown in the dirt with the true priests and Sebastian's relative. Knowledge's false-priest waved feir two guns over the group, threatening to put a bullet in any one of their heads.

Melanie's ruddy mark stood out boldly on her forehead.

"Let them go!" Krona demanded, still advancing.

Sebastian spared her a glance, and the fake priest opened feir mouth to speak. But a series of shouts and a rapid round of gunfire drowned out the reply.

Everyone's eyes turned on the house. Krona was the last to look.

Those in black uniforms were clearly gaining the upper hand. Krona identified Tray, Tabitha, Sasha, and a handful of her colleagues by the way they moved. A few of the cultists lay bloodied in the grass, but many more were kneeling, cuffed, ready to be taken to the den, and then, to trial.

This was almost over.

As Krona started to turn back toward the tent, pain tore through her right shoulder. She cried out. Her arm dropped to her side, sword slipping from numb fingers. The only flicker of sensation from her biceps down was the warm trickle of her own blood.

Scraping at her shoulder, knowing what she'd find, her palm fell across a ragged wound. As she pressed, pieces of bone ground against one another. She hissed—more from the reverberation of crushed bone-on-bone through her neck and chest than the pain itself. The joint had shattered. Quickly, her fingertips delved inside, searching out the lead ball embedded within.

Tremors stole her fine motor skills, making the search all the more difficult.

When she sensed a hard, round object popping free—like a bit of resin from a mold—she gasped in disgust.

Spinning, rage turning her vision red, she caught the person who'd shot her in the crosshairs of her attention: Knowledge's false priest. Fey had stopped aiming at Dawn-Lyn and the real priests and had instead *shot Krona*. Seething, unable to lift her right arm to strangle fer as she wished, she pulled back and tossed the bloody round with a shout.

It missed the cultist by a mile, but fey were stunned by her response—eyes wide like a young farmhand who'd realized it had been a mistake to taunt a bull.

Krona *felt* like a bull. She wanted to gouge the false priest's insides out. She'd taken another injury, just as the previous ones had started to knit. She'd been hit again. And again. And she was tired of everyone using her as a pincushion.

Red lines danced across her eyes. Her lip curled. She scooped up her saber with her working arm, raising the pommel as she plummeted forward, ready to backhand fer with it across the chin, though fey were still fifteen yards away.

Another round loosed, this time from feir second gun, missing her face by the width of a water droplet, severing several of her tightly woven braids.

All of these cultists would pay. Every last manipulative, arrogant, harmful bastard making their sickening stand in the Iyendars' yard was going to find themselves on a court bench, facing the gallows.

Quivering, the priest retreated, stumbling over Dawn-Lyn's ankles as fey tossed the second gun aside and produced a third from feir robes. Fey righted ferself quickly—pausing for half a second to consider the woman's feet and if she'd tripped fer on purpose. Deciding it didn't matter, fey pulled the trigger once more.

The shot brutalized a dirt clod inches from Krona's left foot. She paid it no mind, her advance steady.

Losing feir nerve, with no time to reload the single-shot weapons, the cultist whirled, darting down the hill and—unexpectedly—into Royu.

Krona did not slow, still approaching Gatwood, calling out to him to let Melanie go. Krona's right arm was broken, but she couldn't tell if it was dead. It would not listen to her commands. Would not lift or squeeze as she desired.

What good was a sword arm that couldn't clutch a sword?

"Stay back, Regulator!" Gatwood shouted. Wearing Charbon's mask, the valet once again looked like the horror she'd encountered in the cellar. With a hand still in Melanie's hair, he put a foot in the middle of Dawn-Lyn's back. The real priests and Sebastian's relative held still beside her.

"Look around you, Gatwood! Your time as prophet is over. You miscalculated. You are no match for the state."

Sebastian stood before Gatwood and Melanie, pleading for his fiancée's safety. "Master Gatwood, please. *Please.*"

What had these two done to deserve such a day? She would not for a moment believe that any god had condoned this, let alone demanded it.

Why would anyone do this, truly?

Gatwood's explanation for his hold over De-Lia returned to her unbidden: the guilty and the sullen are easy to manipulate.

So, what was *Gatwood*'s original sin? What type of guilt had spawned all of this?

"It's not over until I've found it!" he shrieked, raising a hand toward Melanie's throat. A scalpel glinted in the sunlight. Blood, from a wound in his shoulder that mirrored Krona's, soaked the arm of his jacket and the white of his glove.

Krona did not hesitate. She dropped her sword and ran at him with all her might, knocking both him and his victim to the ground. Krona's well hand found the blade, covered over it—she took it willingly into her palm, letting it find a home there instead of Melanie's throat.

He had to know that this was the end. He was exposed, defeated, there was nothing left for him at the Iyendars'. Why would he keep after his prey? The thrill of the kill couldn't be that heady. The possibility of new magic couldn't be that intoxicating.

His face came close, the artificial sneer of Charbon's mask bearing upward as though it meant to open up and swallow her whole.

The sawdust-and-paint smell of the mask pressed into her nose. She breathed in Charbon, the dregs of his existence. It was a good smell, fortifying. One she hoped to suck in when she personally laid him to rest in his compartment on Vault Hill.

Though she'd put herself between his blade and the bride, Gatwood would not let go of Melanie's hair. So Krona fought dirty. She reached up with her bloodied palm and gouged at his shoulder, dipping her fingers into the wound. The new shock of pain forced him to yield.

Melanie scrambled away, and those on the ground took the opening, rising to their feet.

Krona tussled with Gatwood. Perhaps it was whatever he'd been injecting himself with, perhaps it was his righteous indignation, or the sheer adrenaline of the struggle—no matter what it was, Krona did not feel like she was struggling with a man in his later years.

He turned her trick back around, finding her gunshot wound and digging deep. He used the moment to slither away from her grasp, to raise his scalpel once more. He stood tall, back to the Iyendars' mansion. His elbow jerked high. He prepared to slice Krona across the face, intent on mutilating *her*, on cutting *her* down.

Krona didn't cringe, didn't shy away. She'd faced worse than him today. The pain he could inflict on her was nothing.

Thwack. A slight puff of breath and a minor dip forward was the only indication something had struck him between the shoulder blades.

He turned, aghast, to face whoever had shot him.

Protruding from Gatwood's spine was a silver needle, stuck so surely that no blood escaped. Krona knew it could only have come from her sister's quintbarrel.

"You," Gatwood shrieked, plodding forward one shaky step.

De-Lia, only a few yards afield, did not hesitate. She shot again. The barrel of the gun clacked into place, the steam chamber exploded, and a golden needle whistled across the distance. It penetrated Gatwood's sternum with an unnervingly gentle hiss, like a fingernail drawn over linen.

"I will finish this," he growled. "It's Fiona's work, my wife's work, and I will finish it in her name." He maintained his advance, boiling humors egging him on. "*I should have put you down last night.* Useless. The Thalo can't make true soldiers. You can't force it. It takes *loyalty.*"

"Damn right," De-Lia spat, stance strong, brow furrowed. Her skirts fluttered around her ankles in a soft contrast to the steel of her frame and the steadiness of her quintbarrel. She fired.

In the next instant he sported an iron pin from the inside of his elbow.

That one stung. He tried to bend the joint, but that only pulled the needle deeper.

Krona crawled over to where Sebastian and Dawn-Lyn knelt in the grass, Melanie between them. Krona pulled herself to standing, saber once again in her grasp, but in the wrong hand. She was prepared for any other cultists to dare come near while her sister brought the Prophet to his knees.

Gatwood would pay. For what he'd done to Hester, and the still-unnamed corpses, to Madame Strange, to the master archivist, to Melanie, and to De-Lia.

It was done. And there was no better person to end it than the captain.

Gatwood surged, then staggered. The torrent of humors and potions and chemicals driving him could only push so far, sustain him for so long. Eventually his body had to acknowledge it was beaten, even if it took his brain a long while to follow.

De-Lia closed the distance, and while Gatwood stood, would not stop firing. A nickel needle pierced him above his right knee so that his leg buckled. A bronze needle flew through the air moments later, thunking to a halt in the opposite kneecap.

He toppled to the ground, rolling first to his back and then rebounding to his side with a shriek; the silver needle still stood proudly from his spine. De-Lia retrieved a set of manacles and holstered her quintbarrel, ready to show the puppet master what it was like to be entangled in strings of his own making.

"Monkeyflower," he spit at her. "Monkeyflower. *Monkeyflower*. Kill them. *Kill them all.*"

She bent, reaching for his wrists as he flailed. "Your power is gone," she said.

With a soft sigh, Melanie looked up at Krona, gratitude in her gaze. She clung to Sebastian, her cheek resting heavily against his fluctuating chest, eyes blinking rapidly—though if it was due to sunlight or unshed tears, Krona could not say.

And that wound on her forehead, how had it been made? Now that she was close enough, Krona scrutinized it. The damage had a geriatric quality to it—around the red marking, the skin was rife with fine wrinkles. This was a scar, not a fresh pain.

An enchanter's mark, unmistakably, yes, but also—

Falling to her knees, Krona brushed Melanie's hair up from her forehead, things falling together in her mind.

It looked like . . . It looked exactly like . . .

The missing enchanter's mark from Belladino's mask.

But *how*?

Dropping her gaze to Melanie's eyes, Krona found no explanation, only shock. Blood drained from the bride's cheeks, leaving her face pallid and her skin clammy.

"How did you—?"

"Look out!" Sebastian called to De-Lia.

At first, Krona thought Gatwood had pulled a syringe from his pocket and plunged it into De-Lia's neck. But as his hand fell away and De-Lia crumpled backward, it was easy to make out the dark barrel of a pen, its sharp-edged nib embedded in her shoulder and not—thank the gods—her throat.

And it wasn't just any pen, but the blood pen Thibaut's true name had been writ with naught but hours ago.

Forgetting the captain, still fighting despite the odds, Gatwood took his chance, yanking the needles from his knees and sprinting away up the hill, toward the house.

Krona was back on her feet in an instant.

She chased him for yards—the nerves in her shoulder fluctuating between absolutely numb and purely on fire—before diving for his legs, felling him like a tree. When he hit the ground, she flipped herself and kicked at his face, catching Gatwood under the chin. Charbon's mask came away, flipping end over end to land who knows where.

The guilty and the sullen are easy to manipulate. Gatwood might be insane, but Krona had never heard truer words. She'd been a slave to fear and guilt most of her life. Though she couldn't recall Charbon's exact memories, similar flavors had underpinned his self-loathing. And Gatwood—he'd made the statement bitterly.

Why was he so desperate to throw his life away to reveal this "protomagic"? *What did you do? If this is Fiona's work, why isn't she here to finish it?*

But the answer was present in the question. The ugly truth inherent in the task he believed he had to fulfill.

Gatwood groaned and Krona lost her mind. Forgetting herself, her training, her deadened arm, she fell on him. Yanking hard on his collar, she dragged his face close to hers. Now she could see the whites of his eyes, the depth of the soul beyond. "Is this what you did to your wife? Did you kill her? Tear her open? Drain her blood?"

"Fiona—" he gritted out. "I thought she was crazy. She has to forgive me. I thought she was crazy."

Letting Gatwood fall back, she held her saber in a threatening line across his chest.

"What did you do?"

"I killed her," he sobbed. "Because of the baby. Because after, after Charbon, she killed our baby." Gatwood went limp against the dirt, and he let out the most craven moan she'd ever heard.

Homicide begetting infanticide begetting further homicide. This all had something to do with Gatwood re-creating whatever had led Fiona to murder their child. She'd been criminally unwell, and that unwellness had crept into him once he'd stopped her.

It was all one twisted daisy chain of grief. An infection of the soul. A corruption of will.

"You will die for this," she told him, the words pouring from her chest. The pommel was cold in her hand, heavy. It would take little force to slice down and away, to take from him what he'd tortured out of others. But instead of ending it, she tossed the sword aside.

A Regulator she did not recognize approached the pair, and she nodded to them, pulling herself off Gatwood as though suddenly repelled. "Cuff him, and make sure we put at least three Regulators on him at all times. He will go to court and he *will* face the gallows." Her voice was garbled and raw.

Several feet away, Charbon's mask stared up at the sky, as though admiring the gentle clouds rolling across the sun. She fought the urge to lie down next to it, tired as she was. No matter what was said about Louis Charbon from this day on, she would know that his echo had helped her. For all the evil he had done, something in him had wanted to make it right.

He was *not* redeemed, though. Would never be. What he'd done was irredeemable.

She was sure, somehow, that he'd known that.

She lifted the mask gently from the grass, winding the still-tied loop of ribbon securely around her wrist. She had the Mayhem Mask. The despairstone—it was locked in that room, protected by varger. Her job was nearly done.

But, as she turned back to the valet, she didn't see the Regulator securing him for transport. Instead, they held Krona's saber poised over the center of Gatwood's belly.

Krona had time for one strangled syllable of denial before the blade plunged down, skewering the Prophet, sticking him to the ground as surely as a tent pole. The Regulator put their entire weight on the hilt of the sword, pushing past the point of necessity, eager to have the life drain out of the valet.

"*What are you doing?*" Krona demanded, leaping on the Regulator, thrusting them away.

She slid to Gatwood's side, ready to yank the saber out. But she hesitated. It would be no use. He'd only bleed out faster.

His gloved hand fumbled around the meeting of blade and flesh, the fabric quickly turning from a dirty white to berry red. Gatwood's eyes were wide, but devoid of surprise. Perhaps he'd counted on dying today. "Tell Melanie—my Little Splinter—I'm sorry," he gurgled, dark blood bubbling from paling lips.

Krona set her jaw. "No."

She owed him nothing. Melanie owed him nothing.

He would burden his victims no more.

Gatwood nodded once, as though he knew she could give no other answer. "So this," he said, softly, distantly, "is the Unknown's penalty."

When he'd been still for a long moment, she stood again, pulling her saber free. She whirled on the unknown Regulator, every curse she knew riding on her tongue, vying to be the first to escape her lips.

The Regulator bowed their head, as though the helm were a great burden. With quick hands, they popped the clasp and yanked the helmet free.

When it came off, Krona reeled back and raised her sword. Beneath wasn't some novice she'd only met once or twice. Nor was it a cultist in disguise, turning on his master. Beneath was a face as blue as the sky, with parallel lines of purple design cutting across cheeks and nose and brow. White hair fell over the black shoulders of the uniform. Deep crow's-feet flanked dark eyes—eyes that pierced Krona through and held sure like a hook.

A Thalo puppet.

A woman.

Unmistakable. Clear as day.

"Are you . . . my mist?" she gasped.

"You'll soon understand, when I find you again," she said, gaze stern and solid as the Valley rim. She pulled off one glove and reached out with a bare, blue hand. "But for a moment, see."

Krona thought to strike. She raised the sword. Gatwood's blood shimmered from iron to wine on the blade as it sliced through sunbeams on its way to decapitating a myth.

But she stopped as the woman's hand found her cheek.

"You are not immune to all our tricks," the puppet said, then waved out across the lawn.

Krona blinked several times, unable to truly comprehend what she was seeing. At least half a dozen blue-tinged beings were spread about the garden. They touched a face here, took the fight out of someone there, whispered intently in a man's ear yet elsewhere.

Not *one* mist. Not even close. Just fully realized flesh and blood.

And then, in a flash, the vision and the Thalo woman were gone.

All that remained was a sense of vapor—that shimmer that seemed to be following her. It flitted around her, brushing her cheek. Instead of threat, the touch exuded comfort. Protection.

Had she been guarded by the Thalo this entire time?

No. Gatwood—he'd thought the Thalo his ally.

"What do you want?" Krona shouted. "What are you after?"

"Shh," said a gentle whisper in her ear. "Don't let on that I've allowed you to see. The others must not know I aided you. Change is on the horizon."

"Aided me? You killed—"

But the mist flitted away.

A hand on her dead shoulder yanked Krona's attention to the right. It was Sasha, her faceplate missing, eyes sad.

Had she seen? Had she seen the impossible kill Gatwood?

Before Krona could ask, Sasha spoke, her voice soft and choked. "Go to the captain."

Krona froze. The world narrowed. "She's—"

She looked in her sister's direction, to where she'd fallen. She expected to see De-Lia standing—either cuffing a ruffian or comforting a victim. But she was still down.

No, De-Lia.

Shoving Charbon's mask into Sasha's hands, caring as much about it now—and the Thalo and Gatwood—as she did a piece of trash in the gutter, she tripped to her sister's side.

Melanie cradled the captain in her lap, hand over the spurting wound in her shoulder, while Sebastian struggled to rip his fine shirt into bandages, and Tray pulled at the still-imbedded pen.

Nothing but the breeze moved in Krona's mind. She looked at De-Lia with Tray and Melanie and Sebastian gathered round as though they were all part of a still tableau on a coterie wall.

"No. No—how?"

"I don't know," Melanie said, voice soft but frantic. "It missed the artery by a long shot, it shouldn't be bleeding this badly. And the pen, we can't—it won't come free. It's like it's draining her. I can't stop it."

It was always dangerous, this job. People in the constabulary didn't last long. But she'd never envisioned this. De-Lia was invincible. Her elder sister could never be hurt by something as commonplace as the tip of a fountain pen.

Blood. Everywhere. It pounded in Krona's ears and behind her eyes, and as she knelt—reached out—it stained her palms.

"You—you have salvation sand," Krona said quickly, pulling her blood-slicked hands from atop Melanie's to dig in De-Lia's pouch.

But both the captain and the healer shook their heads.

"Don't," Melanie insisted. "It'll kill her. Our only chance is to save her *now*. The sand would make it so much worse. You have to get the pen free."

"It's like trying to pull apart a piece of solid stone," Tray grunted, his slick hand slipping on the barrel. "Help me!"

Krona wound her arms around Tray's middle, tugging as he tugged. The apprentice did her best to hold De-Lia in place. Still, the magic held the pen fast.

"Once more," Sebastian said, lining up behind his fiancée, holding her as Krona held Tray, and together they pulled from all sides.

De-Lia cried out in pain, but there was a slick sound, and Krona could sense the thread of magic sliding out. It was like the threads that accompanied the emotion stones, only much worse. Thicker, deeper, more physical.

Everyone fell backward respectively as the pen came free—but the blood still flowed. More blood than the wound itself warranted. Melanie took the soiled strips of silk she'd already been using and tried to fill the cut—not staunch the wound, but plug it. But the fluids would not stop.

The top of De-Lia's arm and the side of her neck throbbed a sickly dark purple, her veins straining beneath her skin, solid and thick.

Helpless now, at a loss for anything else to do, Krona sat back, letting Melanie do her job.

De-Lia blinked rapidly, and her lips twitched as the blood drained from them. One of her hands flew to her head, then her face, an edge of panic straining her jaw. Krona caught the fluttering hand, pulling it to her chest, where De-Lia could feel her sister's heartbeat. It was steady; Krona willed it to be slow and even, a rhythmic touchstone.

Sebastian finished shredding his tunic, and Melanie did not skip a beat, thrusting the clean fabric into the puncture, adding more pressure, waiting for some sign that anything they'd done had stayed death's hand.

But the furrow of her brow was not comforting. Krona realized the apprentice knew how to counter injury and sickness, but not magic. And especially not magic that shouldn't exist.

De-Lia was the strongest person Krona knew. Stronger than her, stronger than Papa. "You can't leave yet," she said to her sister, tipping her face toward her, locking her eyes with De-Lia's weakening gaze. "We're going to the enchantment district," she reminded her. Every syllable was difficult to get out. Her throat was hot, swollen. "To find a mask."

Another few strips of cloth were deposited in Melanie's capable hands. She made quick work of bandaging up De-Lia's arm, over her shoulder, around her throat. It mimicked an expensive high collar when she was done, the smooth fabric shimmering with an opalescence. The blood that soaked through took on the form of a flower, moving, blooming. It might have looked like a painted design if not for its constant burgeoning, growing—consuming.

De-Lia's breaths rasped, and her words were edged with a liquid hiss. Though everyone insisted she lie quietly, the captain would not be still. She squeezed at the breast of Krona's blouse, latching tight, keeping her knuckles firmly against the heartbeat beneath. "I—I'm proud of you," she managed, blood and spit dribbling over her chin with every syllable. What had this pen done to her insides? "I'm so proud—"

"And I you," Krona said quickly. Opposing sides of her mind shouted each other down. One side insisted De-Lia would be fine. That this would be a hurdle, but not the finish line. *Do not say your good-byes,* it insisted harshly. As though saying the words would make it come true. As though *not* saying them could prevent the inevitable.

But that was the childish half of her mind. The part that once in a while still dreamed about Papa coming home, walking through the apartment door like he'd been on an extended assignment for the Borderswatch.

The other half of her mind knew. It saw the world for what it was, and could not pretend otherwise.

Hurried steps brought a new set of feet near. Dawn-Lyn, who Krona had lost track of in the fray, stood patiently at the edge of an invisible ring—one that enclosed the sisters and the healer. Tray moved to her side, taking a gossamer swath of fabric from her hands. It tinkled as he knelt next to De-Lia.

"The joystones will make the passing easier," Dawn-Lyn whispered.

Tray arranged the veil over De-Lia's exposed arms, latching on to one stone for himself. Krona did the same.

Krona knew De-Lia—if she were fully herself—would want to die as she was—without stones, without masks, without external influences of any kind. No magic, no medicine. Just her and the ground and the wind and the sky.

But Krona couldn't bring herself to throw the veil aside. She didn't want De-Lia to be in pain, no matter the dignity of it.

When Tray rose, turning away to rub both hands over his face, De-Lia blinked slowly at her sister. Tears rolled out of her eyes indiscriminately, and she smiled—wide. The biggest smile Krona had seen from her in a long time. The joystones were doing their work.

"You—" De-Lia tried, her words barely audible. "You should—" She smiled, preparing herself, building up the last of her energy to get the words out. "Krona, you should play an instrument. The cello, you said—you said—"

I'll never listen to a note of music again, if it will keep you here. "I—"

De-Lia's eyes unfocused. Her fingers uncurled. The heaviness at Krona's chest that had moments before been strained and purposeful went limp and stonelike.

She was there and then she was gone. Life to death.

Melanie moved away, gently settling De-Lia's scarf-shrouded head against the ground. She covered the captain's eyes, closing them.

With an emptiness inside her heart—the muscle beating smoke through her veins, driving the life out—Krona composed De-Lia's limbs, affording her some semblance of wholeness. Krona pulled the purple scarf from around her shoulders—where it had settled into place after she'd used it as a mask against the vapored varg—and arranged it over De-Lia's head, low around her brow, as though to warm her ears. That was when Krona realized which scarf it was, why the llamas were familiar. It wasn't one Maman had sewn, nor one De-Lia had bought, but the purple-and-yellow length of finery loaned to Krona by the tangerine vendor. It had carried treats to their home, and now it would carry her sister away.

Away, away into nothingness. The goddess had tipped over De-Lia's hourglass, letting the grains of her life spill out.

>–•◦–•◦–•◦–•◦–•◦–<

Krona's hands shook as De-Lia's body was carted away. Her hands *shook* and her teeth *rattled* and she could see her own pulse thumping behind her eyes.

Melanie and Sebastian stood beside her, waiting.

All three of them knew what was supposed to come next.

She was supposed to take them back to the den. She should interrogate them. She should call in the state enchanters to look at that blasted mark on Melanie and figure out how in the gods' names it had gotten there.

But she knew. Krona knew. She'd seen so much impossible magic, and Gatwood had said . . .

"How long had he known about whatever magic gave you that?" she said suddenly, waving at Melanie. She didn't look at them. Couldn't make her eyes focus on anything, really.

"From nearly the beginning," Melanie admitted. "It was his mark, after all."

Gatwood had enchanted—?

Krona lowered her face into her hands, covered her eyes, hid from the new knowledge.

She didn't want it. Didn't want to know about any of it.

She pulled Melanie's ferronnière from her belt and held it out for the apprentice to take.

Melanie curled her fingers around the metal, but Krona did not relinquish her hold right away. She looked the young woman in the eye, held her gaze, tried to convey the importance of what she was about to say with the weight and intensity of her stare.

"You need to go," she said darkly. "I don't care where. I don't want to *know* where. For your own good, I never want to see you again. Not a gods damned lawperson from here to the border better lay eyes on you. Do you understand me? You tried . . . you tried to save De-Lia. And I promised I would help you. This is all I can offer. Go, far, *far* away, and I will never tell a soul."

45

KRONA

De-Lia's will made provisions for a mask. Acel and Krona went together to the enchantment district, both wrapped in mourning shawls the bright red of fresh apples, Krona's injured arm in an equally red sling. Utkin said it would heal, eventually. That her full mobility would return.

Unlike her sister.

Hand in hand, they entered the foyer of the lab, which looked very much like an average mask shop. But the masks lining the walls, staring down at them, were all empty. They had no skills to offer, no echoes swimming inside like goldfish. These were vessels waiting to be filled.

The scent of sawdust and organic finishes filled the air. *Teleoteurs*, especially, were also artisans—expert carvers and painters. The enchanter De-Lia had specified in her will had also made Leroux's mask.

A woman in a thick smock and heavy apron, her hands swathed in leather, emerged from the back when she heard the foyer's bell ring. "For Captain Hirvath?" she asked. As they nodded, she gestured for them to come behind the counter. "This way. Monsieur Amador has already arrived with her."

In the laboratory, De-Lia lay on a raised white table, covered in an equally white sheet. The normal deep, deep brown of her skin appeared unnaturally light—whether because of the blood loss or the overall stark white of the room, it was hard to tell—and her features were drawn, like so much more than breath and blood had been stolen from her body. In death, she hardly looked herself.

Tray stood by the body, holding one hand as though to comfort her. He bit nervously at the thumbnail on his free hand—a diversion to help him keep his composure.

"This is the mask she purchased," the enchanter said, presenting a large, well-crafted visage of balsa wood. It depicted a spotted jaguar, its mouth open to let the wearer see through its gaping maw. Framing the cat's face were jungle leaves and a few brightly colored birds. "And I have been working to preserve her ability to wield a quintbarrel gun."

The three of them nodded. Words would come to no one.

From a prep station, the *Teleoteur* retrieved a specialty syringe—similar to the ones used to take the time tax in infancy—with a nickel needle. Inside was a small lead bead, plated with iron, more nickel, and encasing a droplet of mercury which itself encased a droplet of De-Lia's blood.

Enchantments were typically not a one-time process. In order to create a mask, one had to undergo a series of steps prior to death. Fail to complete those steps, and a mask could not be made. Many master-level skills had been lost simply because *I'll get to it later* had been someone's attitude toward their magical legacy.

But not De-Lia. Everything she attempted, she finished. The fact that, at such a young age, she had a will that could be executed to completion was a testament to her dedication in all things.

De-Lia had swallowed and retrieved many similar beads over a period—training the magical metals to find the information locked within herself. From those, the *Teleoteur* had created this perfect bead, which could pull forth De-Lia's knowledge like a lodestone drew iron filings.

The enchanter swabbed the top of De-Lia's head, making sure it was free of grit and excess dander. Carefully, she pushed the needle into her skull. The magic made the needle strong, and it slid through bone as easily as it would butter. As she pulled back on the plunger, Krona was surprised to see nothing in the syringe—no sign of magic, no fluids or other bodily bits. The only sign that anything had happened was the steady, upward roll of the bead to the top of the barrel.

Withdrawing the needle, the enchanter held her gloved palm beneath its tip, as though worried the invisible substance might drip. Quickly, she flipped over the jaguar mask and injected the underside. Where the needle penetrated the wood, her mark blossomed.

For a moment, De-Lia's face appeared. It was nothing more than an airy impression, a pinkish-hued mirage. It was calm, her eyes closed, face serene as though in gentle sleep. And then it faded, sinking into the wood like wisps of smoke.

"What would you like the inside lined with?" the enchantress asked.

"Leave it bare," Acel said.

"And the ties?"

"Black leather." Acel pulled a piece of fabric out of her pocket. "From her Regulator uniform."

Afterward, the enchanter packed De-Lia's death mask in a fancy paper box, and they took her body to their coterie. All Lutador's dead underwent the funeral rituals of the city's patron god. But Krona found little comfort in the reading of Time's verses, or in the review of De-Lia's first year of life. "Time cannot reverse her path," the priest said while her twin sister, who served Nature, stood quietly behind her. "She is ever steady, ever unwavering. And so we shall commit De-Lia Hirvath's body to sand, to the measure of Time's great movement."

Krona and her mother didn't have enough money for an individual hourglass to be stored in the catacombs—that was a noble-born burial. But luckily, the Chief Magistrate had intervened. "It's the least I can do for your family," he'd said. Once De-Lia was cremated, her ashes would go into a beautiful, clear hourglass framed in black-stained wood. If not for the Iyendars' generosity, De-Lia's remains would have been given over to the "sandpit," where nearly all of Lutador's dead mingled. She would have been thrown in with the criminals and vagabonds and enchanters and bakers, who were indistinguishable in death.

Now, De-Lia lay on an altar before the guests, hands crossed firmly at her neck, mask staring blankly at the ceiling. As a member of the constabulary, she was afforded a formal burial uniform. It was the same as she usually wore, save in color. This Regulator garb was snow white. Her cape flowed over the beveled stone slab to graze the top of the stark white helm that sat nestled amongst sprigs of palm leaves.

So still. Not at peace, just . . . still. Empty. The body was hollow and De-Lia had seeped away.

She was in white, but the pews were filled with reds: blood, berry, wine. Flecks of gold and bronze accents glittered here and there, drawing attention to those quivering with grief.

This ordeal had begun in a crowd of neutrals, interrupted by the glare of red grief. Now it ended in a mirror. Time and Nature did like their symmetry.

Though she sat in a river of crimson, Krona thought of blue, of the Thalo woman she'd seen.

Why would a force who could make someone forget they'd murdered, forget that they'd ever seen a Thalo puppet, reveal themselves?

And why did it intend to see her again?

Krona recognized these thoughts for the distraction they were. If she focused on the Thalo—or on the Chief Magistrate awarding her a commendation, and her promotion to captain—she could stop feeling the yank toward the funeral pyre. Soon even her sister's body would be gone. She'd never feel the tug of her hand again, or the stubble of her head . . . or the hidden warmth of her heart.

After the rites, everyone said their final good-byes. A long queue wound its way through the cloister, coming to a head at De-Lia's feet. When Krona reached the body, the urge to tear the mask away made her stumble. Bracing herself on the edge of the altar, she gripped it tight, occupying her hands.

There were so many things she wanted to say, still. Had De-Lia understood how much Krona loved her? Did she believe her sister's forgiveness earnest? Had she even had time to process what their fight against the bottle-barker had meant? Did she know how free Krona felt? Had she been freed herself?

Krona made the sign of Arkensyre Valley, cupping her hands before moving them jointly to her lips for a kiss. When they dropped from her mouth, she spread her fingers toward De-Lia, as though spilling liquid affection from their pads.

Behind her, Acel sniffed wetly. She'd cried nonstop for days.

Krona's tears had not yet come. They were there, welling beneath the surface. She could feel them sloshing behind her eyes now, pressing, but they would not spill.

Instead of tears, her body ached. She longed for De-Lia by her side, more than she'd pined for anything else in her life. And she knew her yearning for De-Lia could not be quelled, not by work, not by pleasure, not by the gods themselves.

Outside of the cloister, Sasha approached Krona. "The blood pen," she began, "has been secured on Vault Hill. Others have been sent to see if the cellar you were in still houses the killer's other contraband."

"Good. That's good."

"But, I think you should know . . . We didn't even clean the pen, Krona. The Magistrate, he wouldn't let us, wouldn't give us a second more with it."

Krona understood, but her soul was tired, so she said nothing. De-Lia's blood would stain the pen for as long as the vaults stood.

Sasha handed her a package. "And we found this in the valet's quarters. De-Lia's name is written on the bookplate, but the pages are blank."

She unwrapped the brown paper to find the bark-bound journal Gatwood had forced De-Lia to write in. He'd said it was a combination of the blood pen and the journal that had enabled her conditioning. But the book was just a book, the pages blank as Sasha said.

Many people were in attendance, and Acel and Krona spent long hours thanking everyone for coming. The entire den was there, and distant relatives, as well as many guests from the Dupont-Leiwood wedding, including the Chief Magistrate and his young granddaughter, Stellina. The girl looked sallow, but smiled brightly. It seemed like everyone connected to De-Lia and this last concern had come, save the bride and groom, who had wisely heeded Krona's directions.

Even Thibaut was there, though he didn't enter the cloister. He stood in the doorway, nodded to Krona when he caught her eye, then disappeared. She'd secretly wanted him to hold her, to pat her hair and tell her everything would be all right. While it was fine in fantasy, somehow she knew, if he'd done such a thing, it would only make her grief that much more stark. She'd feel that much more alone.

After, when the cloister was empty and the coterie was quiet, Krona sent Acel home with the funeral mask and the journal. Before she could join her maman, she had an errand to run.

Krona's grieving gown was a style she cared nothing for: puff sleeves, a skirt that must have been designed for a tail instead of legs because there was no separating them more than an inch, and a low neckline. Acel had bought it from a neighbor for negligible time, so Krona hadn't protested.

But there was no way to ride Allium in such a frock. Outside the coterie, she pulled the ribbon that held bodice to skirt free and yanked the bottom away, revealing black riding pants. She balled the excess into Allium's saddle bag, exchanging it for the purple-and-yellow scarf De-Lia had died in. That she slung low over her hips, securing it with a tight knot.

The usually proud mare blinked at Krona solemnly, sensing she would never bear her true rider again. Krona caught her under the chin, stroking her long nose before resting her forehead against the animal's neck. Allium smelled of hay, of brush bristles and sugar cubes.

"I'm sorry. All you have is me now."

It was difficult mounting the horse with her arm in a sling, but as always, Krona managed.

Yellow and red birds sang as she rode. Though she preferred them to the harsh caws of carrion scavengers, they could not lift her spirits, which sank further the more cobbles Allium put behind them. They made for the Hall of Records—where, Krona was now sure, files had gone missing because of interference by the Thalo. But those were not her concern this grave day.

By the time she arrived at the fruit vendor's stand, utter despair had taken her over, body and spirit. There was no going back. No undoing the fact that De-Lia was gone. Gone.

Her touchstone, her constant. Gone.

She dismounted less than gracefully, stumbling over the crisscrossed gravel walkways to catch herself heavily against a splintering corner of the woman's stall. The fruit was all honey sweet—if the fluttering bees were anything to go by—and were scented in kind.

Despite her blurring vision, Krona looked for swaths of orange, needing to lay eyes on the small globes that De-Lia had so adored.

The vendor approached her slowly, reaching out to cover Krona's hand with her own. When their eyes met, the elderly woman shook her head. "No tangerines today."

She said it with the gravity the statement deserved.

As Krona pulled the scarf from her middle, passing it to the woman with shaking fingers, she started to cry. The dam broke and it all came free. The mask hadn't been too much, the funeral hadn't been too much, but this—the end to a simple pleasure shared by two—was too much.

Sobbing, she sank to her knees. Her fist found the ground, not in anger, but in misery, seeking out the soft powder between the sharp chips of stone.

The vendor said no more, but stretched the scarf taut and draped it over Krona's back, letting it billow down around her. There were no emotion stones in the weave, no falseness to its comfort. The woman knew Krona hurt, and gave all she could: her kindness.

Krona cried for a long time. She had to let it all out, expel her grief in water and gasps like they were poisons her body could not abide. Hours passed and the fruit stand had noticeably little business—something Krona promised herself she would make up for later.

When her eyes were desert dry and just as hot, Krona forced herself to her feet. Her brown hands were covered in gray powder and bits of mud where her tears had mingled with the dust. She tried to return the scarf, but the woman insisted she keep it. "When people die," she said, "all we have are tokens. All they leave are echoes."

Krona thanked her, feeling the words work deep in her bones, giving her hope.

All they leave are echoes. And De-Lia's was waiting for her.

But echoes weren't people. They had no life of their own . . . or did they?

What had Charbon's mask been, really?

When Krona returned home, the apartment felt empty, despite Acel stationed at the kitchen table.

De-Lia's mask stared at Acel, and Acel stared back. But she didn't move, didn't blink, when Krona unceremoniously swiped it away and dropped a brief kiss on the top of her head.

Krona took the mask into her cubby and set it at the head of the bed. It was beautiful, and sturdy, and proud, just like her sister.

You and I were supposed to be here together. The mask you were going to get me wasn't supposed to be your own.

Of all the things Krona wished for—for De-Lia to be alive, for her family to be whole, for the ability to shove the damn sands of time back up the throat of Time's hourglass—what she wanted most was understanding. She wished she'd understood her sister better, that she'd known more of what was in her heart.

They'd wanted to protect each other so much, sometimes they'd forgotten what they were protecting.

The journal was already on her bed, open to the first page. She flipped through it what felt like a hundred times, looking again and again for words, but to no avail. If it was enchanted, she knew it belonged in the vaults. But if it was just paper, she supposed she could keep it. Or burn it. Drop it down the nearest well.

With a sigh she placed De-Lia's mask atop it, and was surprised to see red scrawls bloom out around the wood's edges.

Slipping the mask nearly off the page, she gasped.

Krona knew the handwriting immediately.

Dear De-Krona,

There are many things I don't know how to tell you. Secrets. Terrible secrets. Words have never fit me so well as a quintbarrel. So perhaps a journal is best. Though, reading it, you might wish I'd been strong enough to tell you myself. I've never been that strong, Krona. I may look it, I may act it, but truly . . . And I fear to tell you the things I must. Worst of all, I am afraid. Even with the bracers on, their red garnets and yellow topaz blazing with stolen emotion, I am afraid. Perhaps the gemstones do not help because this is a special fear: fear of disappointing. Fear of known failure. I could go to an Emotioteur *and have them extract the fear permanently. But I can't shake my suspicion of the needles—that the prick can take more than the enchanters claim.*

Krona read the words as slowly as she could, letting De-Lia's confession—her tale of Monkeyflower and sleepwalking, of doubting her dreams, of wondering if she was being manipulated—unfurl.

De-Lia had always been a leader, a discoverer. Even when she was young and had found an anomalous, un-monstrous monster, she'd tried to change the world around her instead of letting the world tell her what she should do and how she should feel.

How she should feel.

Where Krona feared inaction, De-Lia feared an emotional move.

They'd both carried the burden of their papa's death with them for years. But now, Krona could see, it was no one's fault. They'd been children, not heroes. Krona wasn't expected to fire a gun any more than De-Lia had been expected to harden her compassion. It was an accident, a mistake, not a guilt they had to carry for all eternity.

If their papa only knew what a crack shot De-Lia had become, how devoted she'd been to taking down varger, he would be proud, too. And forgiving. Papa had always been forgiving.

Krona cleared her throat and mouthed along as she read the last few sentences, hoisting the book into her lap. "'Good-bye, De-Krona. I'm sorry I couldn't say this to you in person. If you're reading this, I'm gone. I think something is wrong with me, as I said. I'm a danger to you and Maman. I have to leave. I always hated the idea of farming, but perhaps I shall. It's a solid, safe endeavor.

"'Promise me you won't live in fear. The next time a varg, or something else, attacks someone you love, I won't be there to pick up a quintbarrel. If you do one thing in my memory, let it be this: defeat your fear. Rule your emotions, don't let them rule you.

"'May the Twins protect you. Your sister, De-Lia.'"

Krona laid the book on the bedspread and sat next to it. For a long moment she simply stared at the blood ink, trying to comprehend her life, her sister's life, and the myriad of instances that had led up to this moment.

De-Lia had meant to run away? She'd been so close to discovering her own manipulation, and now . . .

Krona felt resolve creep into her. Felt it take hold of her spine. Tighten her jaw, clear her mind.

"We wear many faces," she said, stroking the side of the jaguar's countenance. Gently, she lifted the mask, turning it over once, twice, as though looking for signs of the echo glistening across the painted surface. "Let me wear yours for a time."

With that, she pressed the mask to her face, and let the remnants of De-Lia's life flow into hers.

ACKNOWLEDGMENTS

Big thanks to everyone who helped make *The Helm of Midnight* a reality, including but not limited to, my agent, DongWon Song; my editor, Will Hinton; Devi Pillai (who acquired the manuscript for Tor), Oliver Dougherty; Christina MacDonald; artist Sam Weber; as well as everyone in the design, production, audio, marketing, and publicity departments. And those at Writers of the Future who first published my short story, "Master Belladino's Mask."

I'd also like to thank the members of my writing group, my family, and my husband, Alex, for supporting me with kind words, big hugs, and honest critiques. And Amber Run, for their song "I Found," which I listened to on a never-ending loop while drafting.

And an extra thank-you to everyone who picked up this book, especially the readers who are struggling—whether it be through external battles or internal ones. As Krona pointed out, despair always lies, and no one should be expected to work through depression, anxiety, or a catastrophe alone.

Here are some resources that might be helpful (as of this 2021 printing) if you are facing a time of crisis:

In the United States, the National Suicide Prevention Lifeline can be found at suicidepreventionlifeline.org.

Texting HOME to 741741 in the US or Canada will put you in touch with a crisis counselor from www.crisistextline.org. If you are in the UK, text 85258, and in Ireland text 50808 for the same service.

For specialized support if you are part of the queer community, please visit www.thetrevorproject.org.

For additional mental health resources, including those for people concerned about finding culturally competent care, you can go to www.nami.org.

Thank you all, and I hope you'll be back for book two!

ABOUT THE AUTHOR

MARINA LOSTETTER's original short fiction has appeared in venues such as *Lightspeed* and *Uncanny*. Her debut sci-fi series, Noumenon, is an epic space adventure starring an empathetic AI, alien mega structures, and generations upon generations of clones. *The Helm of Midnight* is her first foray into epic fantasy. Originally from Oregon, she now lives in Arkansas with her husband, Alex, and two zany house cats. Marina tweets as @MarinaLostetter and her website can be found at www.lostetter.wordpress.com.